THE

ARTILECT
WAR

COMPLETE SERIES

THE
ARTILECT
WAR

COMPLETE SERIES

A.W. CROSS

GLORY BOX PRESS

The Artilect War Complete Series

Published by Glory Box Press
British Columbia, Canada.
gloryboxpress@gmail.com

First edition, 2018

ISBN 978-1-7751787-8-1

Cover design by germancreative
Interior design and formatting by Glory Box Press
Editing by Danielle Fine

FOR H.

THE SEEDS OF WINTER

THE GARDENER OF MAN

THE HARVEST OF SOULS

THE SEEDS OF WINTER

ARTILECT WAR BOOK ONE

PROLOGUE

In 2005, Professor Hugo de Garis predicted that by the late 21st century, the ability to create artilects—hyper-intelligent, sentient machines—would splinter humanity.

Three distinct factions would form: the Cosmists, those attempting to create artilects; the Terrans, those opposed to their creation; and Cyborgists, those who advocated the melding of human and machine.

This division would ignite a war causing billions of deaths and the end of the modern world.

In 2040, his prediction came true.

"Will they be autonomous? Yes. Will they have free will? Yes. But they will also be connected to each other. It is essential to our survival and to theirs. Cyborg brains are not the same as human ones, much as we prefer to believe otherwise. Their connection must be made carefully, gradually, insidiously. Planted in such a way that the still-human parts of their minds will accept it without question. That way, the connection will be established before they're even aware it's happening."

—Mil Cothi, Recommendation #13; Pantheon Modern Program Omega-117.

01
AILITH

I'd been having the dream for as long as I could remember.

It was always the same. I ran across a field as vast as an emerald sea. Heat rose from the grass where my feet fell, rippling up my bare legs. My body was small and thin, my tiny hand clutching a string which led up, up, anchoring a kite. The kite itself was strange: a man but not a man, smooth and shiny, with only the suggestion of a face. Silver ribbons streamed from his golden arms and legs like shooting stars as he chased behind me, straight and true.

In the middle of this green ocean rose a single tree. I raced toward it, my body expanding, stretching. When I reached the tree, he was waiting, as always. I could never see his face, only his mouth, naturally mournful, curving into a smile as he offered me a lover's hand. When I took it, my own was grown-up, strong. He gazed upward to where the kite had become tangled in the branches of the tree. When his eyes returned to me, he was no longer smiling, his mouth once again downcast. And as always, I dropped his hand and began to climb.

Halfway up, I skinned my leg on the rough bark of the tree. Blood welled up and out of the wound, but it wasn't my blood; this blood was much older, its original host long dead. It snaked down my calf as the tips of my fingers brushed the edge of the kite. Straining, I caught its body and crushed it in my hand.

A gust of wind blew through the leaves, wrapping pale amber tendrils of hair around my face as I climbed back down the scarred trunk. It was easy because I was lighter now—all the blood from my body had soaked into the soil and been devoured by the roots. When I reached the ground, he was gone, and I was nothing but paper and bone. I pressed my face into the now-moist earth so that the wind couldn't take me. I was the seed.

We have triggered the waking sequence. As of yet, six subjects are unaccounted for, including O-117-9791. Whereabouts unknown. It would seem the secrecy that kept us hidden for so long is coming back to bite us in the ass. We'll give them a few days to get their bearings, then initiate the homing signal. We never should've separated them; we thought spreading them out would increase their chances of survival in case we were discovered. We were wrong. Hopefully, they'll fare better than the five still alive here at the compound. Losing them all at this point is unthinkable.

—Mil Cothi, personal journal: May 27, 2045

02
AILITH

The hard ground beneath me softened, yielding to the heaviness of my head. I sank into it as far as I could, grateful for the comfort.

Maybe I'm dead. Maybe it was all too much, and I died. That would make sense. But can you think when you're dead? That is what I'm doing, isn't it? Thinking?

Open your eyes. My body refused to obey.

The air was crisp and fresh, not the thick, sweet air of the hospital, and although the surface beneath me was definitely a mattress and not blood-soaked earth, it was not the familiar stiff vinyl and threadbare sheet of an in-patient cot. No, the blanket draped over me slipped too softly through my fingers to be ward-issue.

Take a deep breath.

A rhythmic pressure was building in my ears. With every beat, an aching strangeness bloomed inside me.

Is that my heart? Why is it so far away?

Open your eyes.

A scream split the cool air, a searing pulse inside my skull.

Not my voice.

A familiar sharpness lanced through me, hot and dazzling. My fear had always felt like that: a jagged brightness that began in the bottom of my spine and fanned out like the thorns on a rose.

Open your eyes.

Finally, my eyelids opened. Not the hospital. I was in a bedroom, if the furniture was anything to go by. I hadn't seen furniture like that for a long time—not since I used to visit my grandmother—all ornate swirls and leaves carved into the stained wood. Thick curtains covered the window, blocking any hint of natural light. What thin light there was came from a single bulb, but even in the dimness, the room seemed...dusty. I reached out with one finger and scraped a line down the side of the nightstand.

"I've never been that good at cleaning," a voice said.

He was a titan, filling the entire doorway. Or was the doorway small? I couldn't decide. I was having trouble concentrating. He stepped forward, closer to the light. Young, but the dark tattoos on his face made him seem older.

I don't remember him. I don't remember how I got here.

I can't sit up.

My bones seemed to creak as I strained against the thick leather binding my chest, my elbows unable to find purchase in the soft bedding. Something tore, but I couldn't tell if it was the restraints or me. Vomit surged in my throat. I was going to suffocate.

Rapid footsteps sounded to my right, punctuated by

heavy breaths. My body arched; my spine twisted.

I will break.

A hand like a block of marble dropped down onto the center of my ribcage, crushing me against the bed. A face hovered over me; a forehead pressed into mine. His deep brown irises were laced with gold and framed by long lashes; they reflected my own gray ones back at me as he stared without blinking.

Why am I not terrified?

"Hold on." Golden eyes narrowed, and the fabric ripped as he freed my ankles. One solid kick was all I managed before my stomach at last betrayed me. Apologizing under his breath, he tore off the remaining restraints and rolled me roughly onto my side. A few more seconds of heaving, and I dropped my head into the cradle of my arm.

"Ailith."

A cold, damp cloth covered my forehead; another wiped at my mouth.

The screaming started again, and my back arched against my will.

"Ailith." The sound was soft and soothing. Familiar, somehow. The pressure in my ears receded, and my mind began to focus. When the next scream stabbed my brain, I kept still.

"Help them." I tried to keep my voice even. The scream had dissolved into sobs. "Please."

"Help who? Ailith, we're the only ones here."

That couldn't be true. If it was, who was crying?

The restraints. I'd forgotten the restraints. *He's dangerous. He's done something to me.*

My heel skidded in my vomit as I scrambled off the bed and away from him. As I backed into the corner, I searched for something to use as a weapon. I wouldn't be able to overpower him, but if I made him bleed enough, I should be able to escape.

I've never seen this room before.

But it didn't feel like his room either. Unless he had a thing for elaborate floral oil paintings and trainspotting, nothing in this frozen, uninhabited room belonged to this man.

His hands were raised before him in supplication. "Ailith."

"Stop saying my name! Who are you?" My voice came out high and thin, and that pissed me off. I snarled at him, hoping I appeared demented enough for him to stay away, that my wobbling legs seemed more like the weaving of a venomous snake.

"My name is Tor. Do you remember anything?"

I stopped scrabbling, trying to focus and remember. Time did not seem to be working properly. The answer was in my mind, but it fluttered away before I could grasp it.

He took a step forward.

"No!" My hand closed around something solid and heavy, and I threw it with all my strength. It struck him hard in the mouth, and I prepared to run. In my mind's eye, I leaped over him, stomping on his neck for good measure.

He remained standing; my missile fell to the floor.

I'd tried to kill him with an antique perfume bottle—a sharply-cut crystal perfume bottle, but still—and now I was going to die in a haze of bergamot and clary sage.

His lip had split where the bottle hit him. Blood smeared down his chin. He didn't seem angry; if anything, he seemed amused, his eyebrows arched and his mouth curled up on one side. That should've alarmed me, but I found it strangely comforting.

"I expect," he said, glancing down, "that was quite expensive."

I peered over the bed on my tiptoes. However badly cut

his lip was, the bottle had gotten it worse. It lay in sad little shards at his feet.

I rose onto the balls of my feet again, not sure whether to attack or try to escape past him. A thrumming started in the space behind my eyes, and the rose in my spine began to bloom.

"Ailith." My name, again.

"What are you?" I whispered.

It was his turn to be confused. Tilting his head to the side, he regarded me as if for the first time. "Ailith, I'm a cyborg. Like you."

Of all the answers I'd expected, that was the last. I didn't have time to think about it, though, as the thrumming reached a fever pitch, cool air filled my mouth, and I was blind.

In the darkness, a cable appeared. It led from me, thread-like, into shadow. Another emerged. Then another. Thousands of them, all bound to me. Some shone through the darkness, blazing with light; others were barely visible, their beam extinguished. The first thread drew me in, pulling me down its length before I could understand.

A door appeared. There was a number on it. 479.

"What makes this generation of cyborg unique is the combination of the organic and inorganic at the cellular level. That is to say, every single cell will be cyberized and watched over and replenished by the nanites. They will look completely human, be completely human, but without many of the physiological limitations we now experience. And once we've perfected that, we'll be able to lift the limitations on their minds. Their potential will be limitless."

—Mil Cothi, on the development of Pantheon Modern Program Omega-117.

03
NOVA

The number on the door was 479. Made from cheap black plastic, each numeral was bolted into place too tightly, bowing inward around the screw. I took my keycard from my pocket and slid it down the lock. This door was the same as every other door leading into every other house on the street. Even the street itself was the same as hundreds of others, part of an orderly network. I never knocked. What was the point? Nobody would come to the door to let me in.

The reek as I entered the hallway was typical: stale and heavy, with an undercurrent of human waste. I went straight to the window and slid it open. Although the air wafting in wasn't exactly fresh, it cut through the thicker smells. An improvement, no matter how small, though I only pleased myself. The other two people here didn't care, didn't bother to open their eyes to see who was standing in their living room.

I checked the time. Only 2:45 in the afternoon. Early yet. The

9

doctor wouldn't be here for at least another fifteen minutes, but I was impatient; I wanted to get it done. I continued to stand at the window, gazing over the rooftops capping the endless rows of uniform housing units surrounding the city center. The center itself was studded with high-rise buildings holding offices, gorgeous apartments, special entertainments. Vancouver. I envied the people who worked and lived there. I bet they didn't have to breathe the stench of shit all day.

2:50. I turned toward the center of the room. Two women reclined, facing the window. Sisters. They were unclothed, a soft blanket covering each from chin to toes. Built in the lower half of each chair was a receptacle. The smell emitted from here, albeit fainter now that the window was open. I emptied these containers every few days, sliding them out and replacing them without disturbing the occupants.

Although their heads were shaved, the women still had the oily odor of rarely-washed scalp. Their eyes were closed, the smooth surface of their lids rippling periodically. The sister on the right giggled and chatted; the one on the left smiled coyly, uttering only a few gentle whispers. My nose wrinkled. Their laughter and expressions were awkward, as though they had forgotten how. I rubbed my thumbnail with my index finger, making quick circles.

2:58. The front door opened; Lars had arrived. We nodded to each other.

"Nurse." He knew damn well I wasn't a nurse, no more than he was a doctor. He worked for the government, same as me. Another woman stood behind him; she was to play midwife, pulling an outsized case containing the incubator behind her.

We were processing the woman on the left today, removing the baby fully grown from the embryo we'd implanted thirty-eight weeks ago. Mei. Her name was Mei. I tied up my hair and went to work.

Removing the feeding tube from Mei's nose revealed a darkened line on her face, thrown into stark relief by her pallid, sun-starved complexion. I lifted her blanket, exposing her naked body to the air. She didn't react—they never did. Her skin was moist and doughy, with the odor of overcooked pasta. I started to retch and rubbed my thumb again, quickly, where Lars couldn't see. He'd think I was

10

losing my nerve.

She let out a small sigh, but it was nothing to do with us; the parts of her nervous system that perceived pain were disconnected. I adjusted the chair so she was lying on her back, and reached between her legs to shave her. The sight of her withered thighs, the saggy skin with its mound of overgrown pubic hair, made me want to pinch her softness, to punish her for this vulnerability. Instead, I swabbed disinfectant over the freshly shaved parts and up over the lower half of her swollen belly.

The midwife checked her vitals then signaled to Lars. He made the incision over a previous one, low on her abdomen, curving down, around, and up again. Yellow fat bulged from the cut. He worked quickly, slicing through the layers until he exposed her uterus. Several more cuts, a tug, and the midwife cooed as she rushed to wash, dry, and powder the baby so quickly it didn't have time to cry. The midwife seemed pleased, her face flushed and bright.

Lars finished closing Mei up, sealing the layers with a surgical adhesive. While he washed his hands and changed his clothes, I cleaned her and inserted a new feeding tube. By the time I finished, Lars and the midwife were ready to leave.

Lars shook my hand. "Last day today, isn't it? We'll be sorry to see you go."

I bet you will be. Not too many people around with my moral flexibility. Out loud I said, "Yes. I'm sorry to be leaving. But, when you get the call..."

I saw them to the door then returned to Mei, shaking out her blanket and draping it lightly over her again. Her eyelids twitched back and forth, reacting to a world I couldn't see. I stroked her face gently, torn between scorn and pity. When the cybernetic Completely Immersive Virtual Reality Systems first came out, no one had expected them to produce such a real experience.

It had been too real. Users stopped responding to any other stimulus, including their own basic needs. Millions died with virtual swords and guns in hand while the real-life battle for their lives was fought and lost in their hospital rooms. Those who survived were

11

incapable of readjusting to the real world, even with rehabilitation. But they made effective donors for those who didn't want biomechatronic parts, so these 'houses' kept them in trust, allowing their continued survival in both worlds for our needs in this one. My parents, if they were still alive, were in one of these houses. I sometimes wondered if they'd been kept together.

My finger was on my thumbnail again, circling, circling. I needed to go outside, to get away from here. I'd thought I would savor my final day in this job simply because each time I did something it would be the last. The last day to wipe the drool off someone's chin, to bandage their stumps, to look the other way. Yes, I should've been glad, but I couldn't wait for it to be over.

What a shame I had nowhere to go to celebrate. Just my apartment, with its threadbare carpet and peeling wallpaper. After tomorrow, I wouldn't have to live there. Oh, no, not with the deal I'd made. I would be special. True, it came with a price, but everything did. And I was used to carrying out orders that others might deem…unsavory. That was why they'd chosen me.

They told me I was going to change the course of the world, that I had an extraordinary purpose. I would be the savior of the human race. I wouldn't end up like my wards, forgotten, degraded. No, I would be remembered forever.

Tomorrow, I would enter the program at Pantheon Modern. Tomorrow, I would become a cyborg.

"It sounds like a bad joke, doesn't it? A cyborg, an android, and an artilect walk into a bar. What's the difference between them, you ask? A cyborg is a human being whose physiology has been enhanced by machines, to perform like a machine. An android, or robot, is a humanoid machine, but dumbed down to perform the functions of a human. And the artilect? Well, that's just short for artificial intellect. Androids could arguably be considered artilects. But the ones everyone's getting all worked up about, the real artilects, would appear human but possess an intelligence far greater than our own and have the potential for sentience. And therein lies the problem."

—Emily Fraser-Herondale, Of Gods and Monsters: The Rise of Artificial Intelligence

04
AILITH

"Ailith? Ailith?"

His hands were heavy on my shoulders. I was sitting on the bed, the edge sagging under my weight. The duvet was turned inside out; it was one of the few things in the room not covered with dust. The man—Tor?—knelt before me. "Are you okay?"

"What happened?" My finger circled the bed of my thumbnail. I could still feel my anticipation of what was to come.

Except, it wasn't *my* anticipation. I'd never worked with CIVR addicts, never even seen one. But it hadn't felt like a dream either; everything had felt real, had *smelled* real. It

13

was like I'd been in someone else's mind, watching from behind their eyes. I'd known her thoughts, felt what she'd felt, but I'd had no agency of my own.

Only one thing was clear: she'd been about to become a cyborg, like me. Like *us*.

"You seemed to black out for a moment."

"I was... I don't know. It was like a dream. I was in a house. There were..." I suddenly remembered that I was a captive and flung myself backward. Or at least, my imagination did. My body stayed firmly rooted on the bed, held immobile by his iron grip.

"Let go of me!" To my surprise, he did. And actually had the nerve to look offended. *What the hell is going on?* "What am I doing here? Why was I tied down?"

"What do you remember?"

Nothing. "I— *Tell me!*" For just a moment, my words were outlined in a jagged radiance.

His eyes widened, and his shoulders snapped back.

"Where are we? Why did you tie me down?"

"We're in the Kootenays. You...you were having seizures. It was like you were trying to wake up but couldn't. I didn't want you to hurt yourself. It's only been for the last week."

I searched his face for deception. *He's telling the truth. I think.* I relaxed. *The Kootenays. Shit.* The Kootenays was a mountain region far from home.

His shoulders slumped as though released, and he took a small, gasping breath.

It was time to stop planning my escape; I was completely at his mercy for the time being. But it was more than that. I may not have known this room, but he felt familiar, safe. I was sure of it. If he had meant me harm, why would he have bothered to make sure the duvet was clean?

Clean duvet? Tied you to a bed? Yeah, seems legit to me, the

14

more sensible side of me snarked.

I ignored it.

"Why am I—are we—here?"

"Can't you remember anything?"

"I was ill. I was in the hospital. I was going to have an operation." I remembered the ward linen, scratchy against my broken skin. My green-eyed nurse; her android assistant. But was that *this* time? Or was that months ago?

"I was having an operation," I repeated.

He nodded encouragingly. "Do you remember why?"

"I was dying."

"What else?"

He was right. There had been something else. My stomach. For the first time in years, the skin was almost smooth.

"Ailith?"

I had forgotten to answer him, distracted by the lack of ridges and puckers.

"Pantheon Modern. I was in the Pantheon Modern program." My voice sounded far away. I remembered it all. My illness. The application for the Pantheon Modern Cyborg Program Omega. My acceptance. Haste. And then, pain. "It was too soon."

"Yes. But you survived. And here you are." He smiled, pleased that I remembered.

"Here I am." I echoed, "Why am I *here*?"

His smile faltered. He grabbed a chair from the corner of the room and set it in front of me. He wouldn't look at me, but the ashen color of his skin told me that something bad had happened. *The war.* When I'd gone into the hospital the final time, rumors were swirling that the conflict between the Cosmists and the Terrans was at breaking point. The Pantheon Modern Program was rushing, trying to establish itself as a mediator between the two.

"The war?" I asked. "Has it started?"

He ran his fingers roughly through his hair. Too roughly.

"Tor?" His name was easy on my tongue. Intimate.

He leaned toward me and peered into my eyes. "Ailith, the war is over."

"Over? Surely that's got to be a world record for the shortest war in history. I only went into the hospital a week ago." But even as I said it aloud, it sounded hollow. I was too thin. My scars were practically gone, and I was in a dilapidated house with a strange man. A man who was like me.

"How long?" I whispered.

In his strong hands mine were dwarfed, small and fragile. His eyes never left my face. "Five years."

No air was left in my lungs. I didn't understand.

It's true, a voice whispered in my head.

But it couldn't be true. Losing a day or two of my memory was one thing, but *five years*? Never. Which meant only one thing: he was one of *them*, and he'd abducted me from the hospital.

My coordinator for the Cyborg Program Omega had warned me about them. Extremists who disagreed with the advanced cyberization the Pantheon Modern program had proposed, even though it was supposed to have been a secret. It was the only time Terrans and Cosmists had worked together to destroy a common enemy: me and others like me. Only once we were out of the way could the war over the artilects truly begin.

If this Tor was one of them, I was in trouble. But it didn't make sense. Yet, if it wasn't that, then what he was saying *must* be true, and I'd slept for five years while the rest of the world decided my fate.

The room was starting to lose clarity again, the buzzing in my head building to a crescendo. Whatever was going on, I needed to leave. I had to get somewhere safe; then I'd find out what was really happening.

His eyes were still on me. The mattress springs groaned a quiet protest as I slid off and began to sidle toward the door. *This is madness.* I had no chance of getting away from him. But he didn't move. Only his gaze followed me as I crossed the bedroom and slipped through the doorway.

The front door was across the next room. Like the bedroom, this room had a fine coating of silvery dust on every surface. The footprints going forward and back across the hardwood floor were the same; he wasn't lying when he'd said we were alone. An elaborate fireplace cradled the remains of a fire, the smoldering red embers the only living color in the room.

The same thick curtains as in the bedroom were drawn over these windows; I couldn't tell if it was day or night. Not that it mattered, because I was going regardless. He still hadn't moved, and I didn't know whether to be frightened or bold.

Fuck it. I'm going with bold.

I tried to walk calmly to the door but about twenty feet away, I lost my nerve and sprinted. In my imagination, his hands were only a hair away from the back of my shirt. The floor would hurt my back when I hit it; he would stand over me in victory and chuckle at my foolishness.

But he didn't move. When my hand closed around the cold knob, I wasted a precious second looking back at him. His head was down and his hands were on his knees, as though he was bracing himself against a storm. I took a deep breath and opened the door just as one of the threads tethered to my mind flashed. And I was blind. Again.

17

R,

Just wanted to let you know we've received confirmation of A-98C334's acceptance into the MPCPO-117. Told you it would work. We're lucky that the parents were still alive —no way could we have gotten enough genetic material from her alone. I kept expecting we'd get busted any second, but they didn't seem to suspect a thing.

I'm sorry I argued with you about how much we should tell her — I was worried she'd sing if she got caught. I get that she's loyal, but for a price, right? Anyway, we'll be able to figure out the rest of it once she's gone through the process. It'll remain dormant until then anyway.

Drinks on me tonight, old man. We did it!

S.

05
NOVA

This wasn't right. I wasn't supposed to be here, in this shitty bunker. I should've been with them, carrying out my mission. Buying my freedom. Not trapped here, underground with him.

He was staring at me, making sure his gaze lingered on every inch of my skin. He was good-looking, with a strong jaw and dark brown hair that matched his eyes, but the arrogant curl of his lip told me he knew it too. He found me attractive—the bulge in his trousers gave him away—but his eyes weren't looking at me with desire. Far from *it.*

They reminded me of a nurse I'd once worked with, the kind who did our job because he liked the vulnerability of our wards. When I worked shifts after him, I would find marks that shouldn't have been there, bruises where he had no business being. I reported him once, thinking they would fire him, but they'd only transferred him to another house.

His eyes were like this man's. Heavy-lidded and dark, glittering, cruel. Like the eyes of a feral cat I'd seen at the zoo. Like he wanted to eat me, just for the fun of it.

Keep it together, Nova.

I drew my legs up to my chest, trying to cover my nakedness. Why was I naked, anyway? Last I remembered, I'd been fully clothed. With a lump in my throat, I examined my skin, looking for the telltale signs.

He laughed. "Don't worry. I didn't touch you."

"But my clothes…"

"Okay, I didn't touch you much."

"Then why take my clothes off?"

"I know who you are, what you are."

"I'm not sure what you mean." I tried to make my face look as bland as possible.

The smile spreading across his face was slow, insincere. "Sure you do. Why pretend?"

The warm blush of fear spread in the bottom of my belly. He was holding something behind his back, something heavy. I couldn't help it; my forefinger traced my thumbnail.

"I'm not pretending. Look, we need to find a way out of here. They might need our help."

"Who's they?"

"They. The people who made us, who put us here. They haven't come back for us, so obviously, they're in trouble." I spotted my clothes, only a few feet away from where I was sitting on the bed.

"They're not coming back. Nobody's looking for you." He rolled his shoulders, shifting whatever he was holding from one hand to the

19

other.

"How do you know that?"

"I just know." His arm came out from behind his back. A hunting knife gleamed in his hand, its back edge jagged with teeth. He wove it back and forth languorously, as though hypnotized. "What do you think hurts the most?" he asked. "When you push it in, or when you pull it out?"

The moisture in my mouth disappeared until my tongue scraped like sandpaper. He couldn't intimidate me like this. "Would you like me to try it out on you? Then you can tell me."

His amusement was an awful choking sound. "No, I figured I'd use it on you."

I glanced involuntarily at the warped door. Damn. He'd be on me before I reached it. I didn't even think I could open it, based on the damage. Plus, I'd read about bunkers. They always had a lock, something to keep people in and everything else out. I needed to change tack. I hated what I was about to do, but I was desperate.

"Are you sure?" I asked, dropping my arms and opening my knees. "Are you sure you don't have anything else you'd like to push into me?" I pulled a long black curl of my hair between my fingers, but he wasn't looking at my face any longer. I rubbed myself, slowly at first, then faster, never taking my eyes off his face. To my surprise, I was getting wet. My scent filled the air, and when he swallowed hard, victory rushed through me, mingled with relief. It didn't last long.

When he laughed again, it had a sharp edge to it that made my teeth hurt. "Yeah," he said, "You're not really doing it for me. Smells a bit desperate."

I ignored my burning face and drew my knees up to my chest again. "Sure you don't want to finish? It'll be the last time."

The warm knot of fear in my belly blossomed upward, filling my chest and threatening to suffocate me. I couldn't help but glance at the door again, wondering how far I'd make it before he cut me down. Would the nanites save me? Was I able to die? Maybe I should pretend to be dead long enough for him to leave. Then I'd heal and disappear. Maybe it wouldn't hurt too much. If only I could disconnect

20

my mind from my body, like my patients did. I could go somewhere else while it happened.

"Stop looking at the door," he said. "You don't have to worry about it. Only one of us will be leaving. Guess which one of us it will be?"

"It is our opinion that the creation of these artilects, these intelligent machines, are a threat to our very existence. We will become obsolete not only in our own economy, but as a species. One only has to look at the Industrial Revolution to understand the potential collateral damage that we will pay with our own lives. And we recognize this instinctually. Why else would we treat androids with the contempt and hatred we do? We oppress them because we know on a primeval level that they would destroy us all if given half the chance. Let's beat them to it."

—Sarah Weiland, President of the Preserve Terra Society, 2039

06
AILITH

I was in the bed again, with the full length of Tor's body pressed against my back and his thighs curled up under mine. When he realized I was awake, he started to lift his arm from where it rested, entwined with mine. But after what I'd seen when I'd opened the front door, I'd decided to trust him, and I couldn't bear that he might leave me. I trapped his arm under my elbow. He froze for a second then relaxed, his face in my hair. It should've felt strange and awkward, but it didn't.

A tickle in my mind. *He was waiting. As always.*

We lay on top of the covers, my breathing rapid and shallow, his long and deep. Everything in me was light and temporary, like a bird ready to take flight. He listened about the woman in the bunker, the man with the knife. I didn't tell him everything; some of it seemed too private to share, like a betrayal of part of myself.

"It's not the first time I've...been her, either. What do you think it is?" I asked. "Dreams? It was like I was there, inside her, but all I could do was see and feel. I couldn't move, I couldn't speak. Her thoughts were my thoughts. It was like I became her, but I was still aware that we were two separate people. Does that make sense?"

He paused for a long time before answering. "I don't know. Maybe it's a side effect. Did you have these dreams before you became a cyborg?"

"I don't think so. I..." I tried to remember. I had trouble sometimes. The treatments that kept me alive interfered with my brain. "I'm pretty sure I didn't." I waited for him to be incredulous, to ask how I couldn't understand my own mind. But he didn't. He changed the subject instead.

He told me what had happened, what I'd seen right before I passed out. Why the air was freezing. Why there was no sun.

"All the tension that had been building between the Terrans and the Cosmists finally hit breaking point. It came out on the news that an artilect had actually been created."

"I heard about that, just before I went under. Wasn't it just a rumor?"

"It probably was. But for whatever reason, people believed it this time. They began to panic. Then the information on the Pantheon Modern Omega Project was leaked. And it...that's when the world went crazy. Anybody with cybernetics was issued with an order of removal. The military started to hunt us, the Program Omega cyborgs, down. It was difficult, of course, since we look just as human as they do and Pantheon had already taken measures to hide us."

23

"But how did that become this? I mean, it's *barren* out there."

"I don't know who made the first strike, exactly. One day the news said it was the Russian Cosmists. The next it was the American Terrans. Even Canada was accused. I didn't think we had that kind of arsenal. Information came out, stuff we'd never heard before. Murders, sabotage, illegal weapon prototypes. The war had started long before we'd even known it was a possibility.

"The bombs fell in Canada on the third day. Major cities in every province were hit: Vancouver, Calgary, Toronto. And it wasn't just us. There were coordinated attacks all over the world. That was the last thing I heard.

"Those who still had to be cyberized were spirited away to their main compound, wherever that is. Those, like us, who'd already undergone the process were separated into pairs and hidden in bunkers all over the province. They only expected the war to last a few weeks, a month at most, and they'd planned to move us all to the compound after a week or two in hiding. To keep us safe, Pantheon Modern triggered a forced stasis program they'd planted in all the cyborgs from Program Omega."

Being put to sleep without my knowledge, even if it was for a good reason, made me sick. "And then?"

"And then…I don't know exactly. I was underground, with you."

"But you were obviously awake before me. *What happened?*"

His eyes had become glassy. "The world was…just over. While we were in the bunker, communications went down, and the earth burned. More bombs leveled entire cities and scorched the earth around them for miles. Have you heard of Russian Tar?"

"Isn't it some sort of napalm?"

"That's right. It was banned, never used, but someone,

24

not the Russians, got the formula for it and…it clung to every surface and burned for days. There was explosive lightning, firestorms that raged unchecked.

"Many people survived the war itself. But then ash from the firestorms blocked the sun, and the temperature plummeted. People burned, and froze, and starved, and fought, and died."

"But lots of people survived, right? I mean, I know we're out in the woods, but—"

"No, Ailith. I mean, yes, people survived, but very few. The world we knew is gone."

"How do you know all this?"

"I…I talked to some survivors."

When I was ten, I'd been playing on some old farming machinery when I'd fallen and sliced my arm. There was no pain at first, just the glistening brilliance of the open wound and a terrible clarity of how bad the pain would be once it started. I'd held my breath, believing that if I didn't breathe, time wouldn't move forward, and I could stay suspended forever in that moment before the blood welled to the surface and brought agony.

All gone. My father. No. I couldn't think of him. It was too much. If I stopped to think about it, I would die. So many days had passed, over eighteen hundred of them. How many people had lived in fear before dying in fear? How many had been born into darkness? The careful hope that had taken root in me since I'd woken up was curling inwards, withering and retreating. We went so long without speaking that the fire died in the hearth. I only spoke when I had a safe question to ask. "Why are we in this house?"

"They never came back for us. After a week, I managed to break the seal and go to the surface to have a look. I wanted to keep us moving, to keep us safe. If the wrong people had found any record of those bunkers, we'd have been sitting ducks. Plus, they were only stocked for the short-term."

Sitting ducks. Like the people who hadn't chosen a side. Who, despite their personal beliefs about artilects and cyborgs, simply wanted to live normal lives. People like my father.

I couldn't wait any longer. "I had a father," I said in a rush.

His chest expanded. "Ailith." The softness of his voice told me my father was dead.

"You don't *know*, though, do you?" How could he, when we'd slept through it?

"No, I don't. But, Ailith, it's been five years. It's... There's almost nobody left."

"Yes, but how do you *know*? Maybe it's only this part of the country. Maybe he found other survivors, and he's starting over with them."

He was silent.

I tried a different approach. "What about you? Didn't you have a family?"

"I did," he said, his voice tight. "A mother." The way he said it, I knew she was dead. But there was something else, a dullness to his tone. His grief was old, blunted. All of a sudden, I was cold. "You never talked to any survivors, did you?"

The muscles rippled in his jaw. "Yes, but—"

"Tor, how long have you been awake?"

"Ailith..." He paused. "I never went to sleep." He said it gently, as though the truth would hurt me. It did.

"Why not? Did something go wrong?"

"You were already in stasis when they took us to the bunker. They said you were too important for both of us to go to sleep." He held up a hand before I could ask. "I don't know what they meant by that. They took us to the bunker and told me to stay put until they retrieved us."

For five years, he'd watched over me, a stranger, just

26

because another stranger had told him to. He'd guarded me and waited for the end—any end—to come. *That* was why he felt so familiar. For five years, he'd protected me.

Something occurred then to me that was completely irrational, given the circumstances. *Is this the beginning of my nervous breakdown?* "You've seen me naked." It was hard to keep the accusatory tone from my voice.

A puff of air gusted against my scalp as he laughed. "Yes. I've seen you naked." I stiffened away from him, which only made his shoulders shake harder. "Look, would you rather I'd left you in the same underwear for five years?"

I couldn't argue with that.

"What did I eat? How did I go to the bathroom?"

"You didn't. Nothing went in, nothing came out. You were just...frozen. I don't even think you aged."

"So why am I awake now?"

"I don't know. About two weeks ago, you started to move. Tiny movements. A finger one day, a toe the next. Then, last week, you began having seizures. And that's when I strapped you down."

"Thank you," I whispered.

He didn't laugh again.

He pulled away from me, the mattress springing up as he stood. Cold air slammed into my back. "I need to get the fire going again."

"What did you see? For you to know what happened, what did you see?" I called after him. He didn't answer, so I followed him.

He was kneeling in front of the hearth, striking something together. He avoided my gaze.

"Are there others? Like us?"

This time he looked at me. "I have no idea. I am sure there were. As to whether there still are..."

The room began to spin again. It was too much for me

to take in. What if this was a dream, like the other dreams? They were more real than this.

What do I do?

Survive, a voice inside me whispered, pushing back the part that needed to scream, to fall apart and be forever undone. I focused on Tor, the cut of his face in the glow of his fledgling fire. My hands ached to wrap themselves in his hair, to twist it around my fingers and hold together the pieces of my broken heart.

In less than a heartbeat, I was beside him. "Tor—"

He lifted his eyes to mine. Kneeling, his face was level with my stomach. I pulled him in, pressing him against me. He didn't resist, and as he wrapped his arms around me, his breath flared quick and hot through the fabric of my shirt.

I would've cried then, had there not been a sudden scratching at the door.

"Why is it that our first instinct when creating a being in our own image is to either screw it or kill it?"

—Emily Fraser-Herondale, Of Gods and Monsters: The Rise of Artificial Intelligence

07

ADRIAN

The day they announced the winner, I couldn't stop looking at my watch. It was going to be me. I had hoped so hard it had to happen. I wiped my slick palms on the calves of my trousers, where nobody would see.

And finally, it was time. After careful consideration and weeks of testing and observation, they'd chosen the most successful candidate for the job. And it was me; it was actually me. I couldn't believe it. I'd only been working at Pantheon Modern for three weeks when they announced the contest.

Of course, we all wanted to win it. Why else work at a corporation like Pantheon Modern if we didn't want to become cyborgs ourselves, to help usher in a new age from the front lines? The company wanted someone who would best represent them, and that person was me.

The heat from many hands burned through the thin fabric of my shirt. Everyone acted glad for me, though of course they wished they'd been chosen instead.

They gave us the rest of the day off to celebrate or commiserate. The guys were going to take me out, somewhere special. I'd heard some of them whispering about it in their cubicles when they believed no one was listening. I'd never been invited to join them until today.

It was called Pris, a place where you bought sex. And not just any sex—sex with androids. I couldn't have gone with them before, even if I'd been invited. Not on a junior exec's salary. But that night, they were treating me, no expenses spared.

We drank champagne in the limo on the way, flicking through the brothel's menu. Sid swiped through the images, barely glancing at the screen. He'd been there a few times; he was going to help me choose.

"Had her. And her. And her. And him. And him. And her."

"It might be faster if you showed him the ones you haven't had," Jal said. He was a junior like me, but his family was rich. This wasn't his first time either. "He probably doesn't want your sloppy seconds."

My face burned, but I laughed along with them. Nerves made my palms sweat again. It wasn't so much the sex; I'd had sex before. But I'd never had sex with an android. Or paid for it, for that matter.

Julie had stopped by my desk on her way out. Those who weren't coming with us wanted to have their own celebration. I'd almost wished I was going with them instead.

"Are you actually going to do it?" she'd asked.

"Do what?" I'd hoped she wasn't aware of what we were up to. I'd liked Julie ever since I'd started working at Pantheon Modern, and having the chick you liked realize you're going off to bang another one wasn't the best way to start a relationship.

"Oh, please," she'd said, her mouth twisted up on one side. "You know exactly what I mean."

"Yes." Why deny it when she already knew?

"Don't you think it's a bit wrong?"

"No. Why would it be? They're only providing a service."

"Are they? Or are they just being provided?"

I wasn't sure what she'd meant, which must've been obvious. She'd rolled her eyes and stalked off, her heels clicking angrily on the glossy floor.

I never would've guessed what Pris was from the outside; it echoed every other steel-gray granite building on the block, its name set above the double-doors in wrought bronze. I studied the man on the door, trying to decide whether he was human or not.

30

He caught me looking and smirked. "Sorry, son, I'm not for sale."

The guys whooped with laughter.

"Don't blow your load before we even walk through the door," Sid joked.

I hadn't thought it possible to blush any harder; I was wrong.

Inside, a human hostess led us to a long couch, her red-tipped fingers gesturing with a flourish for us to sit. She bent low from the waist, her corset offering her breasts to Sid like plums on a plate as she handed him the drinks menu. Once we each had a glass in our hands, the hostess returned, leading a group of women and men dressed in lingerie. I couldn't decide if they looked more or less human than I'd imagined they would.

My drink was gone in three gulps. Another one immediately appeared in my hand, deposited by the smiling hostess. The guys were looking at the androids, discussing their different attributes with each other.

They were stunning, each one more exotic than the last. I hadn't known that women—or men, for that matter—looked like that, or smelled like that either. Their different scents mingled with each other in the air: vanilla, musk, leather. They stared straight ahead, their arms at their sides.

They were way out of my league. I wasn't bad looking, but I had a blond-haired, blue-eyed scruffy look that made me seem a lot younger than I was.

What if I couldn't get it up?

I cringed inside. I'd never live that down.

Jal elbowed me in the ribs. "You look a little worried, mate."

"No, I uh…there's so many choices."

"Look." His voice dropped to a whisper too quiet for the others to hear. "They're not alive. They're machines. I know they look human, but it's an illusion. Look closer. They're basically glorified sex dolls. Don't worry about it."

I took his advice and scrutinized them. Jal was right. They stood stiffly, unmoving and unblinking. Everything about them was too

31

perfect. I searched for a hint of resentment on their faces and found nothing but the blankness of a machine.

I could do this.

"Hurry up and choose already. The rest of us are waiting."

I called the hostess over, then pointed to a woman on the far right. She was attractive, but not inaccessibly so. She had a kind of girl-next-door look. In fact, she resembled Julie, with her long red hair and a smattering of freckles on her pearly skin. Her body was petite, her breasts small and pointed through the gauzy film of jade chiffon.

When I got closer to her, I caught a trace of antiseptic under her apple-pie scent, which almost made me lose my nerve. She led me down the unadorned hallway and into a room, where she closed the door behind us. The room was decorated to complement her, a young woman's bedroom: ivory and sea-green wallpaper, mounds of pillows, a vanity with a variety of powders and perfumes. How much of it was for show? I pictured her sitting on the small stool, combing her hair, looking anxiously in the mirror to make sure her makeup was just right.

"Do you sleep here?" I asked her. No one had ever accused me of being an impressive conversationalist.

"You are very handsome," she replied, ignoring my question.

"Uh…thanks. You too. I mean, you're very beautiful."

"Would you like me to take my clothes off?" She pinched the ribbons of her negligee between her flawlessly manicured fingers.

"Don't you want to talk a bit first? What's your name?"

"Do you not like me?"

"What? Yes, of course, I do. I just—"

"Do you want me to take my clothes off?" Her guileless green eyes were wide.

"Um, ok. Yes, please."

She watched my face as she untied her translucent robe and let it slip from her shoulders to the floor.

Her body was symmetrical, with none of the imperfections of the women I'd been with before, who always seemed to have one breast larger than the other, or a mole in an awkward place. She was smooth and completely hairless except for her neatly trimmed triangle.

"Do you want me to take your clothes off?" she inquired.

"No. No, I can do it myself, thank you."

"You're welcome."

I stripped, fumbling with the buttons on my shirt. Usually, when I found myself in this situation, I was clumsy because I was rushing and trying to make out with the girl at the same time, unable to keep my hands off her. Her arms remained stiffly at her sides. Once I was naked, we stood facing each other.

"What would you like me to do?" she asked.

"I, uh, what would you like to do?"

"I would like to please you."

I didn't know what to say. Somehow, the idea of asking her to drop to her knees and suck me off seemed degrading.

"Lie down on the bed, I guess."

She followed my instructions, lying down in the center of the generous mattress. "Like this?"

"Yes." I was growing hard at the sight of her now, lying on the silky sheets, waiting for me. Willing to do whatever I wanted. And right then, I wanted to celebrate. No pretenses. It was all about me.

"Spread your legs," I commanded, and she did.

After I was done, I pulled out of her, not looking at the mess I'd made. I wasn't sure whether to cuddle her or not. She got off the bed and stood in the center of the room, my semen smeared down one of her thighs.

"Was I satisfactory?" she asked.

"Yes, thank you. Was it okay for you?"

"You are very handsome," she repeated and blinked.

33

"The only way to ensure, beyond a doubt, that our species will survive is to propagate ourselves into a form that's more capable of adapting, of surviving, than ourselves. As a species, we've already reached our full potential. Our constant need to war over resources and religion, our inability to extend to all members of our own species even the most basic right to life, and the means by which to support that life, proves that our time as a flourishing species is over."

—Robin Leung, CEO of Novus Corporation, 2039

08
AILITH

The knife left his hand before I even knew he'd lifted it. End over end it spun, faster than a human eye could see, than a human arm could throw, a dark blur through the gray air. The knife caught me off guard; he normally wielded a crossbow. His breath slid up the bare skin of my neck, causing a ripple down my spine. My pants were crisp with the cold, but I was too wired with anticipation to feel the chill.

His knife skewered the hare through the heart, pinning it to the ground. I finally exhaled. We'd been kneeling in the skeletal forest for hours, waiting for something edible to walk by. The waiting itself was boring, since Tor wasn't the talkative type, but there wasn't much else to do. He didn't want me exploring on my own, and I had too much sense to rebel for the sake of it—although, if I was being honest, it was because I was afraid of what I might see.

The blood reminded me of the last vision I'd had, the cascade of crimson hair down her back. It hadn't hit me as hard as the others. I hadn't gone blind, at least. Whatever the visions were, I was beginning to gain some control over them.

What are they? I tried not to think of the vacancy on the android's face as I thrust myself into her, over and over, her hair rasping against the brocade pillow. Since then, I'd caught only wisps of images from the threads, like seeing something on the edge of my vision, only for it to be gone when I finally looked.

"Remind me where we are, again," I asked as he brushed past me to retrieve the warm body of the hare, his breath cloudy in the cold air.

"The Kootenays."

It was warmer today than it had been since I'd woken up just over a week ago, but the mountain air was still biting. I couldn't remember if I'd ever been to the Kootenays before.

"Okay, but *where* in the Kootenays?"

Tor paused, chewing on his lower lip. "The map says we're near a city called Redcot. Ever been there?"

"No. You?"

"Nope. I'd never gone farther than the Lower Mainland. I guess that's one good thing about the apocalypse: it's gotten me to travel."

Tor's plan was for us to stay put for the next few weeks, and then…then we'd see. He was determined to avoid other people as much as possible. He wouldn't say why, only that people had, and yet hadn't, changed since the war. If what he'd told me was true, the risk of others finding us was small. Still, he wanted to be cautious.

We'd settled into a comfortable routine that centered around finding things to eat, and eating them, something I needed to do now that I was awake. I'd also found some books under the layers of dust as we'd made ourselves at home and had taken to reading aloud to Tor in the evenings, cross-legged and squinting in front of the fire.

I wasn't as keen to stay here as he was. Though it was unlikely, a small part of me wondered if my father could still be alive. But we were far from where I'd lived in the Okanagan in the south of the province, and I wasn't ready to make that journey myself. I was sure that, given a bit more time, I could convince Tor to come with me.

Though technically the end of spring, it was only a handful of degrees above freezing, the ground rock-hard under its delicate carpet of evergreen needles. I wasn't used to living in the mountains. Although they shared the same fir and pine trees, they were a far cry from the beaches and vineyards I'd grown up with.

"So, it just got colder after the war?" I asked him.

"Yes. It happened so gradually I assumed it was just the changing of the seasons. But it kept getting colder and never really warmed up again. That's when the plants and animals started dying, and most of the remaining survivors followed them."

"I still don't understand how that many people could've died."

"There was something else in those bombs. Something that made people sick. Many of those who didn't die in the war were killed by whatever it was. There were weeks of silver rain, and… Well, it doesn't matter. That silver rain rarely falls any more, and it's starting to get warmer. It's warmer now than it was this time last year.

"Take these hares, for example. They're a good sign. For the first year or two after it got really cold, I didn't see any living animals, only acres of untouched carcasses just frozen in time. Even the birds had gone silent. They've started to appear again, like the animals, although they're not the same ones as before. All the wildlife here now seems to have migrated from the north. I guess it's more of their usual climate down here. The predators have begun to recover as well, but it'll be a long time before they're hungry enough to find us interesting."

He grinned and held up the hare for me to admire before adding it to the rest. Unruly black hair curled over his pale face and neck, blending with the inky lines of his tattoos. His eyes were always dark, but now they held a fierce glint that was unrelated to the brightness of his smile. I had quickly learned that such smiles were rare for Tor, his mouth naturally downcast. The strings of hares rode his shoulders like wings, forming a dark tableau against the naked trees. A whisper of fear brushed my mind, too delicate to grasp.

I suddenly realized that he was speaking to me, and the whisper vanished.

"Sorry, what?"

"I said, are you ready to go back now?"

"How many do we have?" I asked. He was too polite to point out the wrongness of *we*, since he'd done all the actual killing.

"Eight, all together." His quiet voice carried over the still air as he stretched his shoulders, the strings of hares twisting in a macabre dance.

"Eight is a respectable number," I said, trying to sound casual. I didn't want to seem too eager to get back. He thought I enjoyed the hunting, and I didn't want to hurt his feelings. Besides, I liked watching *him* hunt.

He adjusted the hares and retraced our steps to the cottage. I walked beside him, admiring his grace from the corner of my eye. I'd had an appreciation for Tor's body ever since we'd heard the scratching outside the door that first night.

The speed and silence with which he'd moved had made my breath catch much more than my fear of what was on the other side. It had been nothing but a curious fox, but it had made me think. Despite everything I'd learned in the short time I'd been awake, I hadn't given much consideration to how the cyberization had changed us. It wasn't like we'd been left with an instruction manual. Yes, we were stronger and healed faster, but surely there had to be more?

I was curious how different Tor was now to when he'd been an ordinary human, but I wasn't quite sure how to ask. He wasn't the same Tor who'd held me that first night. After the incident with the fox, the easy intimacy had disappeared, reminding me how little I knew about him. I was desperate to ask him more about the war, but so far, he hadn't been particularly forthcoming.

"So, you're pretty good with that crossbow. Did you do a lot of hunting before the war?"

"Not animals," he replied.

Okay... "And the gathering?" Earlier that morning, he'd shown me some edible plants he'd found.

He leaned over to peer at a small thorned bush. "I've poisoned myself a few times figuring it out, but because of the nanites, all I got was a bit of a stomachache." He wiped his forehead with the back of his hand, marring the clean lines of his tattoos with hare blood.

"What do the designs on your face mean?" I was fascinated by the intricate pattern. Two sets of three lines curved upward across his forehead, intersecting in the middle. They swept down over his temples and converged into a single stripe on either side of his face, ending at his jawline. Delicate branches twined out from each central stroke, one flowing into each corner of his eyes, the other into his hairline. A thicker line slid vertically over his lower lip and down his chin, where the branching pattern repeated on his throat. They were striking and oddly familiar, but I couldn't begin to place them.

"They're a warning." His eyes were darker, and he said nothing more.

I had stooped to gather some pale-yellow berries Tor swore were safe to eat when it hit me; a shift in my awareness. The voice inside me whispered, *"Here it comes."* There was a tugging on my spine, a stiffening, as though I were a puppet and someone had suddenly pulled hard on my strings. At first, I couldn't feel the ground beneath me, like I was flying, but I wasn't; I was on my knees. Time had stopped, and my voice caught in my throat.

Whatever had happened to me also happened to Tor, but his reactions were far faster than mine, and he'd made it to within a few feet of me, his fingers grasping at the empty air. We stared at each other, and I saw my reflection in his eyes—a pale face peering out of a black well.

We were frozen for what seemed like hours, but when we finally fell, the body of the last hare was still warm. We lay there, face-to-face.

"Tor? Are you okay?" I asked when I was finally able to speak. "What *was* that?"

He winced as he lifted his head from the ground, and there were bloody scratches along his cheek. "I have no idea. I—"

It came again. The pull, the voice. Wanting us to leave this place, to come…*home*. I whispered his name.

"We have to get home." His voice was shaky as he jerked me to my feet. "Now."

"But we don't know where home is."

"I mean home. *Our* home."

The word *our* in his mouth moved something in my chest. "Tor."

"No." He walked off, staggering slightly over the rough ground.

I had no choice but to follow.

39

"I do not think you understand the gravity of what you are proposing. You are not talking about simply integrating these people with biomechatronic components. You are talking about combining every human cell in their bodies with robotic elements. Not only are you creating virtually immortal beings, you cannot accurately predict what enhancements will result, or what they will become capable of."

—*Sarah Weiland of the Preserve Terra Society at the Pantheon Modern Cyborg Symposium, 2040*

09
TOR

The blood on my knuckles was already starting to dry; the cuts from his broken teeth would take longer to heal. His eyes had held the same look as all the others: confusion then comprehension then fear. He hadn't begged or tried to bargain. Not all of them did. But he would remember my face. Even without my tattoos, he would remember. It was, after all, the last thing he would see.

Bile burned the back of my throat. The first few times, I'd thrown up. Not now. Footsteps echoed on the tiles in the hallway, and it became difficult to breathe. I ran my fingers through my hair, trying to tame it, then immediately hated myself. What did I care how she saw me? She didn't. All she cared about was owning me.

She opened the door gently, hoping to surprise me, to catch me off my guard. She wasn't aware that I always smelled her long before she came into the room—her cloying perfume of violets and balsam, a sickly-sweet scent that did nothing to cover the odor of decay. The drug was eating her from the inside out, and no perfume in her arsenal could hide it from me. I only wished she would hurry up and die. Then I could stop loving her.

I didn't flinch as she laid her hand on my shoulder.

"Did you know you have blood in your hair?" she asked, digging her fingers into my skin.

I kept my eyes on my hands.

"Look at me." She said my name, the sound of it painful to my ears.

I looked, unable to stop myself.

She appeared to be well today, younger, almost like when we first met. Her face was pale and smooth, akin to the antique dolls my mother used to keep on a shelf in the guest room. Her hair was as black as mine, but straight and silky, and cut into a severe bob that framed her delicate face. She stroked my cheek, her acrylic nails making a dry scraping sound that made me want to put my hands on her with violence.

It was difficult for her to be so gentle; it wasn't her nature. In her defense, it wasn't entirely her fault. She'd grown up in this life. I hadn't. Her only way out was death, as was mine—at least until a few weeks ago. And it was she who'd unwittingly given me the key.

She slid into my lap and moved against me in gentle circles. It was what she did whenever she thought I was angry at her, and when I hardened in spite of myself, she couldn't suppress the victory in her slanted blue eyes. That was her power, the reason she existed. We were both pets, no matter how hard she pretended she wasn't.

Her father was our keeper, and she, his faultless creation. I was also what he'd made me, but I'd had a choice. In deciding to be with her, I'd embraced this life, as he'd known I would. As she'd known I would. My mother had tried so hard to keep me from people like them, had sacrificed so much. And yet, here I was.

She traced her fingers over the splits in my skin. "What was it this time? Debt? Reneged on a deal? Chose the wrong wine at supper?"

"Do you really care?" It was impossible to keep the harshness out of my voice.

41

Her eyes narrowed.

I needed to stop rebelling and just play along. She'd been spying on me, showing up unexpectedly. She'd also been poking around in my room, the haze of drugs making her less careful than she'd thought. It was as though she knew something had changed, but her mind couldn't focus long enough to figure it out.

"Sorry," I said. "I'm just tired. He was the third one this week."

"You're supposed to be resting." She studied my face.

"I know. But an order's an order, right?"

She pouted up at me, a look that used to tie my stomach up in knots with anticipation. Now, it merely made it churn. I knew what she truly was, the sickness in her. I'd missed it before, those few years ago, under the layers of her makeup and my own infatuation. She was now a caricature of that woman, the softness replaced by something cold, and dazzling, and rotten.

Two weeks. Two more weeks, and I'd be free. God knew how high up her father's boss was on the food chain, but he was well-placed enough to have me pushed to the front of the line for the Pantheon Modern cyborg program. Such was the truth of my position. I was important enough for the syndicate to invest in me, but expendable enough to be replaced if I died during the process. It was true that a machine could do my job, but then, a machine didn't have my flaws. A machine would be difficult to bend without breaking.

If I did survive, I'd have to disappear. The violence I was currently capable of would be insignificant in comparison. And yet, I'd have less power than I did now.

She wriggled in my lap, having noticed that my attention was elsewhere. I fought the urge to push her off, to strike her. She smiled at me, running her tongue across her teeth. I swallowed hard, trying not to retch. She misinterpreted my reaction and ground against me before rubbing a finger over her bottom lip and smearing her chin with red.

Two weeks.

I turned my head away as she dropped to her knees and licked the blood from my hands.

We've activated the homing signal. Lexa wanted to do it earlier. She's worried they might be in trouble. I'm sure they can handle themselves, although, if I'm honest, it's more than that. Lexa may look upon them as children, assuming they'll love her simply because she's their mother. I'm not so sure. She's worried about protecting them; I'm worried about protecting us. Who knows how they'll react? They're waking up to an unfamiliar world, and even their own bodies and minds will be as unknown to them as they are to us. How much of them will have changed? The process is unpredictable at best, and dangerous at worst. And we rushed it, damn us. It was more important to prove that we could do it than consider what it would do to them.

—*Mil Cothi, personal journal; June 5th, 2045*

10
AILITH

My head was tender. The threads had blazed again during the night, more intensely. More *real.* Rather than lie awake staring into the darkness, curiosity had gotten the better of me, and I'd decided to go exploring. I was drawn to this latest thread by the brilliance of its connection to me.

I still smelled the fetid sweetness of her breath, was both repulsed and aroused by her hands on me, her mouth as she took me inside it. I had again been a man, my body well-built and powerful. My arms were crisscrossed with scars of all different ages, the bloody cuts on my hands fresh. I'd been desperate to escape; it had taken everything in my power not to grab her and break her over my knee. But there'd also been a hope deep inside me that helped me bear it, tiny tendrils blooming and curling around my ribs.

A storm raged outside, and the sturdy walls of our house creaked in disapproval. I got out of bed and glanced at myself in the mirror. It wasn't functioning, of course; all I saw was my reflection. I didn't mind. The last thing I needed right now was a smug voice helpfully suggesting which creams to apply so I looked less crap.

Seeing myself was odd. My face was no longer my own. It was the same face I'd always had, but when I studied myself in the mirror, it was like I was wearing a mask. Even the touch of my own hand didn't feel right. An otherness lived within my body, which I assumed must be the nanites. Far away, the voice inside me laughed.

Tor stood behind me in the door frame. He was surprisingly alert. I'd heard him pacing the floor of his bedroom every time I'd woken during the night. We hadn't spoken about what had happened. Did he still sense it? The need to leave, to find where the voice would lead us?

"Good morning."

"Morning." We were formal, stiff.

"How's your—"

The scratches on his face were nearly gone; thin silvery lines were all that remained. He put his hand to his cheek and smiled. "Gotta be some perks to being a monster, right?"

"Is that how you feel? That you're a monster?"

"Sometimes." He said it as though it were a joke, but I wasn't so sure. He must've felt the otherness too. We'd spent the last week avoiding discussing what we were, or where we were from. All we'd talked about was the weather, food, and how best to clean the house.

He had a fire burning in the living room. The house

seemed more like a home now, *our home*, as he'd said yesterday. Cleaning had done nothing to improve the pale chartreuse of the walls, but at least the surfaces were no longer covered in dust. The furnishings were sparse, whether due to the aesthetic taste of the previous owner or looting, I had no idea. None of the house functions worked without electricity, of course, but we were managing.

I curled up on our lone couch and pressed the heels of my palms into my eye sockets, trying to dull the aching in my head.

"Are you okay?" Tor asked, frowning.

"Yeah, it's only a headache. I had another vision. An intense one. It's funny. Some of them seem to be from the past, like memories. Others seem to be later, after the war. Maybe even the present. This latest one felt like the past. To the person I was in, life felt normal."

"Want to talk about it?" He gestured to the window. "It's not like we're going anywhere today. And there's nothing good on TV."

"Did you actually make a joke?" I asked, getting nothing but raised eyebrows in return. "Um, okay. Where do you want me to start?"

He lowered himself onto the cushion next to me and leaned forward. "Tell me what happened in the latest one."

I picked at a crack in the leather of the couch and told him about my hands, the pain of my torn skin. The sharpness of her nails, my loathing for both of us as I came. By the time I was done, he'd gone rigid.

"Who are you?" his voice was savage, a growl between clenched teeth.

"What? What do you mean?"

"Who. Are. You?" Each word was a feral bite.

"Tor, I—"

He advanced on me, his chest heaving. I had only a split second for fear before he wrapped his hands around my

45

neck.

"...I don't have to tell you that I don't like this. As far as I'm concerned, the risk is too significant, not only of our exposure but of the end result. He is impulsive, reckless, and has a Machiavellian streak to rival my mother-in-law's. We've basically just handed a toddler a machine gun. Do you really think he's not going to pull the trigger?"

— [■■■■■■■■■■■■■■■■■■]

II
OLIVER

It was agonizing. They'd never told me it would be so goddamn painful. Every cell in my body felt like it was splitting, and I guessed, in a way, they were. The nanites were inside me, invading me, eating me alive. They were tearing me apart with their tiny claws, consuming me, spitting me out, rebuilding me.

Am I going to die?

The thought didn't scare me. It pissed me off. This was my last chance to be accepted, to assume my rightful place, even though they thought I wasn't worthy enough.

A ghost was in my brain. It was me. The ghost was cackling. If I could've gotten hold of him, I'd have torn him apart, but every time I tried, they knocked me out. They said I would need my eyes to see. No fucking kidding.

Someone lit me on fire. My body bent, my bones cracked. I wanted to laugh, to show them my strength, but I forgot where my mouth was. Skin tore underneath my fingernails, bunching in ribbons and falling to the floor.

This had better be worth it. I'd better get what they've promised me. All my life I'd wanted to be one of them. But only now, in the eleventh hour, were they desperate enough to use me. But they would see my worth. I'd make them. And they'd give me what was owed.

I had debased myself for them, for us all. Together, we would level the playing field. I would give them their future, and they would give me what I deserved. They couldn't refuse me after this. No. They would celebrate me almost as much as what was to come.

This was my last chance, but it was also theirs.

I was their savior, and if they tried to crucify me this time, I would end them.

"Who are they to tell us what we can and cannot do with our own bodies? It's not just about becoming faster, stronger, or smarter. For the chronically ill, it's about having a reasonable quality of life. And for the terminally ill, it's literally a matter of life and death. Complete cyberization would give us the ability to transcend the prisons of our damaged and dying bodies. Who are the Terrans and the Cosmists to tell me I cannot, while they themselves not only get to live the way they choose, but to live?"

—Dolan Smythe, advocate; *Cyborgs for Life*, 2040

12
AILITH

I hadn't meant to follow that thread. It was a reflex, an escape. One I regretted. My fingers itched, desperate to claw at my eyes. Now I was aware again, although I was no longer sure what was real. Was Tor a vision? No. His hands were around my neck, the empty air beneath my feet.

We both panted: me gasping for air, him from rage and fear. He held me pinned against the wall, his knee between my legs. Bloody tracks raked his face, and something sticky covered my fingernails.

Within the expanding brown and gold pleats of his irises, I saw them. The nanites, millions of tiny machines propelled by gilded filaments toward the black pinprick of his pupil. As they converged in the center, his iris overflowed, and the nanites streamed down his face in veins of precious metal.

I'm hallucinating.

Even when he was trying to kill me, he was beautiful. Especially when. I had the sudden wild urge to kiss him, to touch the lips that were pulled back from his teeth and run my fingers over the cut stone of his face. Hysteria tried to force its way out of my throat and managed only a pathetic gurgle.

His eyes were clear. He saw me, every inch of me, and in that moment, I understood that I didn't know him at all. Darkness frayed the edges of my vision. I wanted to fight back, but I had nothing left. Whatever gifts my transformation had given me, the physical strength to rival his wasn't one of them.

He pulled me forward then slammed me back again, smashing my spine against the hard plaster. The third time, something gave way.

I traced my finger down the tattoo on his lower lip. His skin was firm and smooth, marred only by a faint scar through the left side of his mouth.

Do I have enough strength for one last attack?

Air, tasting of smoke and blood, rushed into my lungs.

I was still pinned to the wall, but he'd dropped his hands from my throat to my shoulders. He held them gently, although his breath was still coming fast. He leaned his forehead against mine as he fought for control.

I didn't want to move too quickly for fear of reigniting him. I crept my fingers up the side of his face again, and he broke, dropping to his knees. Without the support, I slid to the ground. My legs were unfeeling, unmoving, and I suspected he'd broken something in my back.

He tightened his fingers on my shoulders, and I winced, afraid we were going to start all over again. He yanked his hands from me and clenched them uncertainly before pressing them against the floor.

"Ailith." He spoke with something deeper than regret.

50

"Ailith, I'm sorry, I—"

I couldn't stop touching his face. I needed to feel him. That damned voice whispered in my ear, *"Always."* If I'd been able to lean forward, I would've kissed him. *I've finally lost my mind.*

"Tor?"

"What are you?" he asked again, softly this time.

"I-I'm not sure what you mean."

He searched my face. Whatever he saw knocked the air out of him but saved me. "That vision you had, the last one. It was me."

"What do you mean, it was you?"

"I mean, it was *me*. That happened *to me*. What you…saw. It was real. *She* was real. That was my life…before."

My stomach went cold, the white kind of chill that had filled it when the doctors told me that, despite all their technology, there was nothing else they could do for me. The iciness was a spike, trying to pierce its way beyond my stomach and out through my mouth.

I recalled the hollowness of being inside him, the emptiness. I couldn't reconcile that with the Tor I knew, but now, with his wildness unbound, I caught a glimpse of that former man, and my heart hurt for him.

He released my shoulders, and I slumped onto the floor. The solid hardness of the wood was soothing, although from that angle, I noticed some dust balls I'd missed under the couch.

"I'm sorry," he said again.

"It's okay." I was shocked at my own calmness, although I flinched when he raised a hand toward me.

His face blanched. "Ailith, please. Let's get off this floor. We need to talk."

"I can't. I think you cracked something." I was still trying to swallow around the thickness in my throat.

51

The color drained from his face, his tattoos standing out in vivid detail. "I— Oh, Ailith."

"Tor, it's okay. It won't last. Give me a few minutes." The nanites tingled inside me, at work repairing the damage. "Look." I wiggled my toes to show him. Only, they didn't actually move. "Okay, I might need more than a few minutes. I don't think it's actually *broken*, just a bit cracked."

"Does it hurt?" His voice caught. "I didn't mean—"

"Yes, you did. You did mean it. Maybe not to hurt me this badly, but you wanted to hurt me. But I get it. I probably would've reacted the same. Not that I'd do too much damage to you with this body." I hoped my smile was convincing.

"I believe your body could do me a lot of damage," he muttered under his breath.

"What?"

He rocked onto his heels and stood. "I'll be right back."

He returned a few minutes later with a pillow and some blankets. After he'd tucked the blankets around me, he placed the pillow on his lap and gently eased my head on to it. The prickling of so many nanites at work made me want to throw up. Did all of them come running in an emergency like this? It felt like it. I needed some distraction.

"What did you mean, it was your life, before?"

He stiffened. "Before the war, I was an enforcer for a syndicate."

"Who was she? That girl, the one you…"

He took a deep breath. "No one."

"She didn't seem like no one." His teeth were grinding against each other. *Should I let it go?*

He didn't answer for a long time. When he did, his words were a mix of resentment and sadness. "She was my boss's daughter. The reason I got involved with the

52

syndicate in the first place. We met in high school. When we began dating, he offered me the position working for him."

I remembered his loathing and anger. "You loved her?"

"Yes, very much. At first. But then... Eventually, I ended up hating her as much as I loved her. As I'm sure you felt." His voice was tight, and I didn't blame him. I wouldn't want someone to be able to see into my head either. I wanted to ask him more about her because I wanted to hate her too, but I had the feeling that line of questioning would shut him down.

"Your tattoos?"

"Yes. I got them from the syndicate. They're how people identified me. The first time they saw me was a warning. The second... I've done terrible things." In his voice were a thousand disturbing memories.

"Is that why you became a cyborg?" My throat was better now. I sounded almost human.

"Yes. I believed it would be my way out. They planned to still use me against their enemies, but I was going to take my mother and run. Then, the war happened."

"And we were taken to the bunker?"

"Yes."

"How...how do you know that your mother is dead?" I was hoping he'd only made an educated guess. If he wasn't sure, there was a chance my father was still alive.

"I went to find her. She lived near the harbor in Vancouver. Parts of it were still burning when I arrived. Can you believe that?"

I caught a flicker in my mind: asphalt like lava; mountains of twisted metal and glass. Ash. Unbearable heat. Nothing was where it was supposed to be, not even the bones.

"You left me alone to go find her? On the coast? That would've taken you weeks! And you left me..." I pictured

53

myself, asleep and vulnerable. Then, I was ashamed. "Sorry, I—"

He raised his hand, his fingers spread. "Five days, to be exact. Geographically, we were closer than we are now, somewhere near Aelshore. Since vehicles stopped working when the satellites went down, I had to walk nearly eighteen hours a day. Good thing we're faster now. I didn't know you. I didn't... Well, anyway, I made sure the entrance was invisible. The bunker was built to be a secret." He changed the subject. "Where was your father when...everything happened?"

"I assume he was at home on the farm, near Goldnesse. Did you... I mean, was Goldnesse still there?"

His lips made a thin line. "Not most of it. And that was a long time ago."

My stomach twisted. "I—We weren't on speaking terms. He didn't approve of the Pantheon Modern program. Staunch Terran, my father. He was able to pretend he was fine about it up until the night before I went in. Then he let me know how he really felt." I tried to smile, but it came out a grimace.

"But weren't you going to die without it?"

"Yes, but—"

"But what? He wanted you to die?" His voice was raised, his lip curled in disgust.

"No, of course not!" Although I wasn't sure that was the truth, I needed to defend him. No matter what may have happened toward the end, he was still my father. Or had been. "It's complicated."

"Doesn't sound complicated."

"Well, it was." My back felt healed now, if a bit weak. I was fairly certain I could sit up, but despite the uncomfortable conversation, I was more at ease than I'd been since I woke. I found being near him soothing, touching him, more so.

54

I gave my toes an experimental wiggle. Good as new. Propping myself up, I regarded him. "How long did it take you to get used to that? To the healing?"

"Only a few weeks. They showed me when I came out of the procedure, so I knew what to expect. Kind of. I did think it would be even faster, instantaneous, like you used to see on TV. But still, it's pretty useful."

"I'll say. Lucky for you or you'd have to carry me around with you forever."

"Ailith—" He reached out and cupped my cheek, running his thumb over my cheekbone.

The other voice inside me arched its back and purred.

"Sorry, it was a joke," I blurted. *Shut up, Ailith.*

He dropped his hand. "I'd better go see to the fire."

Damn.

He helped me stand, but as he stepped away, my legs gave out. Thanks to that inhuman speed, he managed to scoop me up before I hit the floor. As he carried me to the couch, the pulse in his neck beat rapidly against my temple, giving him away. He laid me down so gently I wanted to cry.

I finally asked the question I was sure had also been on his mind. "Tor, if what I saw was one of your memories, then what about the others? What if they're also memories? What if it's another cyborg super-power, like the strength and the healing?"

Comprehension dawned on his face.

"And if they *are* memories, *whose* memories are they?"

"If you are, on one hand, augmenting humans with mechanical components at the cellular level, and on the other, augmenting robots with biological components at their cellular level, where does the separation exist? At what point does one become human or machine? If they are created in the same way, are they not then, at every level, the same?"

—Della van Natta, *Artificial Life or Artificial Hope?*

13
PAX

Cindra kept apologizing to me. She was sorry she'd gotten us into our current situation; it was her fault the Terrans had captured us. I should've told her it wasn't—it was mine—but I didn't want her to be mad at me. Not right now, anyway. There would be time for that later. If she knew I'd let it happen, she would be angry.

It was kind of her fault anyway. She was the one who'd wanted to stop and help them. But I'd known they would discover what we were. I'd known they would take us. I should've taken better care to keep us hidden. But once they'd seen us, there was only one way to stay on the path we needed to take. It was our best hope for the future.

I would explain everything to her soon, when we were safe. She would forgive me. She would be happy because we'd have found Ailith. They would love each other like sisters, so she couldn't be mad.

It was going to hurt. I'd tried to convince them that the nanites only worked on us, that if they tried to use them, they would die. Cindra should never have told them what we were. It wasn't her fault, though. They'd tricked her. She'd only wanted to help them. She'd assumed that, after everything that had happened, our differences

56

wouldn't matter anymore.

They'd known right away that we were different. Our skin was smooth, free of the damage they themselves had suffered—and, man, had they suffered.

And, of course, there was my eyes.

The whites had been jet-black ever since I'd become a cyborg, and they'd given us away.

Would they have treated us better if we'd appeared less human? Or at the very least, less perfectly human? Maybe if we'd been wearing coats. They should've left us coats in the bunker, even if it had been the middle of summer.

Cindra had been very upset when the Terrans told her about the war. Five years was a long time. Especially when you woke up and everyone was gone. I didn't mind as much.

I'd wanted us to follow the signal, the one triggered after we'd left the bunker, right on time. Cindra had wanted to go in another direction, to another home, but I'd convinced her we needed to follow what was pulling at us. It was a homing signal. We were being assembled. I was sure of it. We needed to find the source so things could begin. Otherwise, everything that had happened would have been for nothing. We needed to stay on this path to achieve the best possible outcome.

The Terrans were going to take our nanites; I'd heard them talking. They would start today, when they'd decided how to keep them working. They didn't believe me when I'd told them they would die. I didn't want the Terrans to die because then they would kill us. We needed to stay alive. We had a purpose.

Cindra was crying again, about someone called Asche. I wanted to comfort her, so I stroked her hair. My mother had liked it when I stroked her hair. It made Cindra cry harder, but she didn't want me to stop. I sang to her; my mother had liked that too.

They told me to stop singing because it was making some of the children cry. They must've been born after the war. What did they think of us? Did they know about the sun? I had never thought much about it until it was gone.

57

They cut my arm and watched the blood closely as it dripped into the basin, trying to see the nanites. When I laughed, it made them angry. They saw the cut slowly close and assumed the nanites would heal them the same way.

The women stared at Cindra, touching their own faces and hair. They were jealous of her exotic tawny skin, her firmness, her muscles that were from health, rather than utility. I could tell they wanted to cut off her long, silky hair so the men wouldn't like her more than them. One of them spat at her. They pretended it was because she was a cyborg.

The men weren't jealous of me. They believed I was weak, and I had to let them think they were right. They'd decided that cuts were one thing to fix, broken bones another. They wondered just how much we could heal. I had to let them. Now was not the time to be who we were.

I—

Hello, Ailith. I've been waiting for you. I'm Pax. Have you been there, inside me, for long?

Please, ignore me if I scream.

"When you begin to combine man with machine, surely that is tantamount to you handing them a slice of ambrosia and saying, "here, now you are as God?"

—*Sarah Weiland, President of the Preserve Terra Society, 2039*

14
AILITH

Please, ignore me if I scream.

"Tor!" I shouldn't have been yelling. Someone could've heard me and come looking for us, but I didn't know what else to do. He'd gone off hunting by himself. We'd been awkward around each other all morning, avoiding eye contact and answering with only single words. Part of it was the tension that had lain thickly between us since yesterday, and part was the desire to leave. Well, my desire anyway.

Though Tor felt the pull as keenly as I did, he was suspicious of it. I wanted to follow it. Tor suspected it was a trap, and I didn't blame him. In fact, a small part of me agreed. But what if it wasn't? I wouldn't admit it to him, but another part of me wondered if my father was at the end of it, that it was his way of trying to find me. And if not that, what if others like us were there? In a safe place? It was getting harder for me to ignore.

"Tor!" Where was he? He wouldn't have gone far. He wouldn't have left me. Would he? "Tor!" My throat was beginning to ache in the cold.

He came then, flying through the woods on the far side of the clearing. He'd left everything he'd been carrying behind. As he got closer, I expected to hear the snapping of dead wood and the crunching of frozen leaves, but the air around him was impossibly silent.

He slowed to a swift walk when he saw me. Slow, steady breaths wreathed his face in the cold air. He pushed his hair back from his forehead as he peered around me. "Ailith?"

"Tor, he *talked* to me. He said my *name*. He said his name was Pax. He knew I was *there*."

His hand froze midair, snarls of hair sticking up between his fingers. "What are you saying? Someone spoke to you? In a memory?"

"I'm saying that this wasn't a memory, Tor! There's a woman named Cindra with him. They're being held captive. What's happening to them is happening right now."

"How can you know that?"

"He *spoke* to me. He knew about what happened to us the other day. It happened to them too. He called it a homing signal." The heat rose in my face. "Tor, we have to go and find them."

"Can you talk to him now?"

"I don't know." It hadn't occurred to me to try to contact whomever the memories, or whatever they were, belonged to. I'd considered them something that was happening *to* me, not *by* me. I reached out with my mind, trying to find the thread that led to him. Nothing. "I think he's unconscious. I can't...it's like he's present, but not."

"Ailith, look, if what you're saying is true—" He held up a hand as I began to protest. "What I mean is that we're not sure what these visions are. It might be a lure, Ailith, like that damned...homing signal. And if what you're seeing is true, and it's happening right now, we can't simply go running into the middle of an army of Terrans. You do remember who the Terrans are, right? People who want you dead solely because you exist. Look around you! They did this. We have no idea who this Pax is, except that he's with them."

"Tor, they're being *tortured*. We can't abandon them. They're like us."

"You don't *know* that. You don't know who they are, or what's happening. You can't trust this."

I felt small and impotent. And pissed off. I closed my eyes to concentrate. My mind was a field of darkness; I waited until I spotted it at last, a slender golden thread. I slid along it until, suddenly, I was looking at myself through his eyes.

At first I was surprised: Tor saw me differently than I saw myself. I was a precious thing he wanted to keep safe. He *needed* to keep me safe; I stood between him and a precipice. Light coiled around me, solid and powerful. His feelings toward me were mixed: fear, longing, desire; something unfurling itself to the sun.

"*Tor?*" He didn't respond. The fear in his mind was growing, the thread becoming brittle and cold. He felt me inside him, and he was losing control.

"Stop!" he shouted.

Suddenly, I was back inside myself.

He stared at me with wild eyes. "Stop," he said again, quieter. He pivoted on his heel and walked away.

"Tor! I'm sorry."

He spun and came back toward me, seeming to grow larger with each step. "Never do that again." He was flushed, his hands clenching convulsively at his sides. "You can't... You can't just go into my head like that. It's too intimate."

He was obviously upset, but I was too excited about what it meant. "But, Tor, this means it could be true! And

61

if it is, we have to go and help them. I don't know what the other visions mean, but this is real, and we—"

I was in the darkness again, hurtling down a thread.

"Ailith? Are you there?"

"Hello? Pax? How do you know me?" I was in the darkness again, our thread wrapped around me. Tor's hands gripped my shoulders, keeping me anchored.

"Yes, it's me. I knew you'd come. We've been waiting for you. We're in trouble."

"I know. I saw. Where are you?"

"You mean you're not here? You're not going to rescue us?" He didn't sound panicked, only sad.

"No, we're coming, Pax. We're coming! Where are you?" Tor's fingers dug in, making my bones creak.

"I don't know. In a house. In a town. There is a river. Follow us."

"Can you be more specific?" The silence was long. Had I lost him again?

"There is a...a windmill? I..."

"Pax? Pax!" He was gone.

"Are you trying to break my back again?" I snapped at Tor. He dropped his hands. My insides churned with nervous energy. "Tor, we have to go. We have to leave here and find them. They need our help."

"Ailith, look, I want to help them, but we need to be careful. In my opinion, we should wait, try to speak to him again. Find out more information."

"We don't have time. We... No, I don't care. I'm going. You want to stay here? Fine. I'm going, with or without you." I didn't want to do that.

The look in his eyes told me he knew I was telling the truth. Knew it and resented it.

He dug his knuckles into his eyes. "Okay. I admit, I'd like some answers. We go, but we don't rush in blindly, okay? We need to find out what we're walking into."

"Great. Let's go."

"What? Now? I was thinking more in a few days, once we've gathered supplies. We don't even know where we're going, do we?"

"No, but I can feel the general direction. We'll worry about the rest when we're closer."

The next connection happened before I saw it coming. Tor's voice cut out and another sliced its way in.

"While I fully understand the desire to create these artilects to watch over us and solve humanity's problems with resource allotment, fair distribution of wealth, prevention of civil or global conflict, and the like, and while I also understand that the best interest of every human being on the planet would be considered for and provided for, I still have to ask this question: who will be watching over them?"

—*Della van Natta, Artificial Life or Artificial Hope?*

15

ROS

"You're doing it, and that's final!"

I used to think the worst thing to be in my echelon was young, rich, and good-looking. Too much of any one of these was bad enough, but all of them? Goodbye, freedom.

In my case, I only suffered from one of the three: I was young. I wasn't attractive, not by my mother's standards. She despaired at my dusky skin, my bobbed hair, and my sparse mouth. Her own skin was the color of a white peach, her mouth a plump cupid's bow.

We weren't rich enough, either. Not grossly rich, anyway. Hence their plan to shove me into this Pantheon Modern thing. They hoped that if I became a cyborg, I would tempt one of the loaded Cyborgist magnates to marry me.

I rolled my eyes, the mascara I'd caked onto my lashes this morning cracking.

"You do appreciate that we're living in the 21st century, right? That whole porcelain-doll thing is kind of over. Like, thirty years ago, over."

"Perhaps among 'them' it is." My mother sniffed.

'Them' referred to anyone who wasn't us, the stupidly rich. Well, rich enough that their only daughter couldn't choose what kind of career she wanted, or who she wanted to marry. Like their parents before them, they'd sent me to Canada under the guise of being a student, to be their proxy and allow them to legally own an extensive property portfolio of high-rises and apartment buildings. They'd also hoped I'd find a suitable husband, like that was still a thing.

Unfortunately, I'd turned out to be a decent student. When my marks came in for my first semester, my parents had rushed to rescue me from a life of independence.

"Your grades don't matter," they'd told me. "What do you need good grades for? Your husband won't care."

I didn't buy that. Surely men wanted a wife who had her own interests? Not according to my mother. And since everything I'd been born with wasn't acceptable either, becoming a cyborg was apparently the only way to compensate for the sheer disappointment of my existence.

"Does this not seem a bit extreme to you? I mean, seriously? A cyborg? How do you know I'll get in?"

"You'll be accepted," my father said, his voice firm, decided.

"You've bought me a place," I accused him. "But I haven't graduated yet! That was the deal: I get my degree then we'd talk about everything else. What's changed?"

My mother couldn't keep silent any longer. She unpursed her lips long enough to blurt out, "And you're working at that place! My daughter." She covered her eyes with her handkerchief, and my father placed a sympathetic hand on her shoulder.

"You mean the bar?" I'd recently taken a job as a hostess at an artisanal gin bar near the university. "It's hardly a brothel." I couldn't help but laugh. "It's just a bit of fun, not a career." I examined the manicure on my left hand. It was chipped, the fingernail torn. Something else to worry about.

"Do you want to kill your mother?"

"What? No, of course not. I—" I couldn't believe this was a real

65

conversation. My parents were traditionalists, orthodox even among their own peers, but this was ridiculous. No one thought this way anymore.

"Okay, look, I'll quit my job at the bar. It doesn't matter."

"You're doing the program at Pantheon Modern."

Fear trickled into my stomach. I'd assumed it was just a bargaining chip. "No. You can't make me do it. It's absurd! You don't know what will happen. What if I die?" The jagged edge of my torn fingernail cut into the palm of my hand.

My words were met with stony silence.

"You would rather have me die than embarrass you by being ordinary?"

"You've already brought enough shame on us."

"Shame? What shame?" I asked, although I was pretty sure where this was going.

"That boy."

Damn. They did know. Julien was a third-year literature student I'd met at work. Yes, he was poor. He was also white, the wrong color for my Chinese parents. "So what? Everybody dates in university. It's not like I'm going to marry him." Which was a blatant lie. I would marry him tomorrow if he asked. Not because I loved him—I didn't—but because it would encourage my mother to ignore me for life.

"You're doing it." My father's voice was slightly raised, which for him was akin to screaming. The fear pooled, cold and deep.

"No. You can't make me." My voice cracked, and I wanted to slap myself. Be strong.

"You will, or you will be cut off. You will have nothing. No university, no apartment, no nice clothes…all of it will be gone."

"You can't—"

"I can, and I will."

Against my better judgment, I glanced at my mother, hoping to find some kind of mercy, or at least sympathy. Instead, her smile was malicious. Finally, she'd brought me to heel.

Much as I hated to admit it, I wasn't able to live without them.

66

It wasn't only the luxury, although I needed a certain level of comfort to be happy. Deep down, I was too well-trained, a dutiful daughter. I knew it, they knew it, and I hated all of us for it. Loving and obeying them was too ingrained in me, it was in my blood. So I bowed my head in acquiescence.

If I did this, would they finally love me back?

"Where will it end? Since they look like humans, talk like humans, and think like humans, are they human? Can artificial life ever truly be sentient? Or do we merely pretend it can in order for us to free our slaves? They were never intended to be equals. We would never have built them otherwise. So why do we create slaves then feel the need to raise them up?"

—*Derek Wills of the Preserve Terra Society, 2039*

16
AILITH

Despite Tor's misgivings, we set out early the next morning. He wanted to avoid the roads, but since we were surrounded by mountains, we had to stay close enough to use them when necessary. We crept through the woods like fugitives, and in a sense, we were. In an hour, we were further from the house than I'd ever been. Tor gazed back the way we'd come. I reached out and took his hand, startling him. A few seconds later, he squeezed mine back. I wasn't entirely sure where we were going, only that we were headed in the right direction.

Even though it was morning, the sky was as dim as ever, the clouds heavy with the promise of rain. It was a lie; the dryness of the air told me otherwise. The same uniform gray stretched across the horizon, unbroken by any shafts of light. Tor had said there was more sunlight now than last year. He was hoping this was yet another sign the climate was starting to recover. I didn't see how it was possible.

The woods around us were eerily quiet, the trees nothing more than dead wood, starved and barren. If they were anything like the trees back home, these skinny, naked relics must have been lush before the war, heavy with green needles and thick, fissured bark. Now they were covered in black and silver patches, a flimsy husk that peeled off to expose the pale wood underneath. Clusters of dead needles and abandoned bird-nests still clung to some of the drooping branches, but most lay in a thick russet-brown blanket on the ground, mingling with long-dead vegetation that had yet to completely break down. The ground was hard and brittle and odd beneath my feet. Where I was from, the forest floor was spongy with moss, slick with moist leaves.

My father once told me that life always prevailed, in one form or another. He'd been referring to the windswept acres of land he'd bought cheap from the government on the condition he grew food for the provincial program. He'd jumped at the chance. When he was young, farming had been an unpredictable source of income at best; at worst, it was literally living hand-to-mouth. All that had changed when I was nearly five. Real food became a valuable commodity again, and the annual stipend ensured that farms like ours flourished.

The closer I looked, the more I saw signs of life. Not all the plants were dead. Some, in fact, were thriving. True, they were stunted and small, with shallow roots, but they were growing. Most I didn't recognize, but some seemed to bear fruit.

Tor had said that the nanites protected us against poison. I knelt next to a small shrub with pink, bell-shaped flowers and coral-red berries.

Is red a good sign or not?

Saying a quick prayer, I popped one into my mouth. Its

69

texture was mealy and dry, and it didn't really taste of anything. A few minutes later, it hadn't killed me, so I filed the information away for later use. I wanted to stop and gather more, but we didn't exactly have time for berry-picking.

I was examining some tracks in the snow that appeared to belong to a massive dog when Tor grabbed my arm. With a finger to his lips, he gestured in the direction we were going. It took me a few seconds to make out what he was pointing at, blended as it was with the mottled earth. It was clearly some kind of machine, but I couldn't quite...

My breath caught in my throat.

It was a military mech. I'd seen one on television when I was in the hospital, in a documentary about combat prototypes. These particular ones were controlled directly by soldiers, who rode encased in the mech's chests, their heads protected by a polycarbonate dome. The film had shown them loping with a stilted gait across the training ground, heads swiveling from side-to-side as they sought the next target with their weaponized arms.

It lay flat on its back, unrusted. The stubby grass growing around it seemed to shrink back from the metal of its jointed limbs. As we edged closer, I searched for damage on its dull, armored plating and found none.

Tor put a hand on my arm, holding me back. "It might still be active."

I shook my head at him. It was dead. It had been for years. Creeping closer, I peered into the cockpit, where the skeleton of its driver was still buckled in. The body was intact, held together by sinew and desiccated skin, its mouth gaping in wonder or shock.

Which side had they been on? The mech itself bore no identifying marks. What was it doing out here in the middle of nowhere, so far away from any city or town? Had its passenger been running away from a war they didn't believe in? Were they hunting down survivors? Pariahs like us?

In my mind, a dark thread lurking behind the others shuddered, pulling me in. What I would've called human thoughts bled through me.

So fragile. So quick to break. Cannot be rebuilt. Wrong. Wrong. Get away. Far away. You cannot leave me. I cannot run if you're not inside me. Your fault. Keep moving. Wrong. Don't stop, don't stop. You are inside me. Forever. Forever.

"Ailith!" Tor gripped my shoulders, shaking me. "What's happening?"

Gone, gone, gone.

The thread crumbled and disappeared, leaving an even darker blackness behind.

"Nothing," I said. "It's gone." But as I turned, I caught a flash of something in the trees. I walked a few steps toward it, searching. *Nothing.* I was about to turn around when a dark shape hurtled toward me. Coarse feathers brushed my face and were gone, a faint flapping in the distance.

"Are you all right?" Tor called.

"Yes. I thought I saw something, but it was just a stupid bird." Even so, the hair stood up on the back of my neck.

***

A few hours later, the duskiness of the sky had deepened to violet. We'd covered a surprising amount of ground in a single day; apparently, increased stamina was another perk of being a cyborg.

"Shall we just stop for the night?" Tor asked. "I'd hoped to come across another cabin for us to camp in, but they seem to be in short supply in the middle of nowhere."

"We should've stopped at that village a few miles back. I bet there would've been plenty of options there."

71

He rubbed the back of his neck. "No way. I want to avoid *any* group of houses. We just don't know who might be staying there. I'm sure they'd feel the same about us."

"But what's the chance anyone will actually be there? You know, with the apocalypse and all?"

Another shake of his head was all the response I got.

Tor found an acceptable place for us to camp, somewhere hidden where we could see anyone approaching. After shooing me out of the way, he set about building a shelter, and I tried to reach Pax again.

"Pax? Are you there?"

Nothing. The lack of contact from him and the constant pull of that damned homing signal were taking their toll. I also couldn't shake the feeling that we were being watched, that whatever I'd seen in the trees had followed us. When my skin had prickled, I'd felt the briefest of touches in my mind. Whatever or whoever it was didn't seem malevolent. Still, my nerves were raw.

The shelter Tor built was impressive, although I shouldn't have been surprised. The man had been living in this landscape for five years, after all. He worked quietly, methodically, laying a fallen tree within the split trunk of another then setting up our tiny tent underneath it and lining it with branches.

When I went to investigate, he was smoothing on the final handful of crusted moss, dusting his boots with dead foliage.

I put my hand on his shoulder. "If I have to live through the End of Days, I'm glad it's with you."

He gave me a lopsided grin. "I was a boy scout before I was… Well, before."

We ate dried strips of smoked hare in companionable silence.

"Anything from Pax or Cindra?" he asked.

"No. But he's alive. And we're going in the right

72

direction."

"How do you know?"

"Well, his connection to me is still there. As for the direction, I'm not sure. I just know." *He must be getting as tired of that answer as I am of the question.* "Are we going to take turns standing watch?"

"No, I'll wake up if anything comes near us," Tor said.

"Is that another one of your cyborg super-powers?"

Tor tossed his last chunk of hare back in his pack. "Something like that. I'm going to bed."

"I'll be right in." I appealed to Pax one more time. Nothing. *"We're coming. You have to hold on."*

As I slipped under the blankets, I tried to remember the last time I'd seen the stars. I couldn't. Would I ever see them again? Maybe it was better not to think about it.

"Just think, all the injustices of this world could be solved. For one, we would have leaders who rule with duty and logic over self-interest. No longer will people starve or die from preventable disease. Poverty will be eradicated. Everyone will have a rightful place in this world. Rather than die at the hands of our neighbors, we will die in our beds as old men and women."

—Robin Leung, CEO of Novus Corporation, 2039

17

CINDRA

"...and they looked upon the sun and saw how it shone brighter than the highest flame. They saw each other's faces, the lines and their weather-beaten skin, and they pulled at their clothes, lamenting the dullness of the cloth. They wanted to shine too, to leave this earth and live among the Heavens..."

I couldn't help but smile at the rapt expressions on the faces of the children as they listened to my grandmother's story. I remembered the first time I'd heard it, remembered leaning forward in anticipation, my weaving forgotten in my lap.

Now, listening and weaving at the same time came easily to me, which was lucky since I had nearly a dozen orders to complete before the weekend. Although there were machines that did the same job, hell, did a better job, tourists still liked the idea that their souvenirs were made by the living hands of a historical people; it justified the price I got for them. I was more than happy to oblige them—the work was soothing, and it pleased my grandmother, who insisted we kept the traditions we'd very nearly lost alive and well.

Asche smiled at me over the children's heads.

"...'We need to get the attention of the Sun,' they said. 'She will see that we are worthy and will take us up to the sky where we can live beside her.' To do this, they decided to build a statue of themselves, one so tall it could touch shoulders with the sun..."

As she was speaking, a smile tugged at the corners of my grandmother's mouth. She'd seen me watching Asche. It didn't matter. She would be thrilled if something were to develop between Asche and me. We'd known each other all our lives, and yet only recently had I noticed the man he'd become.

When we were young, his hair stuck out all over his head. We'd teased him and joked that his mother must've been struck by lightning when she was pregnant. Now his hair was long, a wavy cascade of deep raven-black that made him resemble the men on the covers of the books my grandmother hid in her nightstand. He'd always been tall, but in the last two years he'd become wider as well, making me feel small and delicate.

His hands were marred by the scars of his trade. Like me, he helped preserve some of our older traditions. The meat he hunted was prepared in traditional ways and sold for a premium, but I suspected he would still do it even if there was no money to be made. It had become harder for us over the last few years. The technology that had nearly made us obsolete in the first place continued to grow, replacing us with increasingly intelligent machines. Our old ways, which we'd so nearly lost in the name of progress, were now our life raft, keeping us relevant.

"...they traded everything they had: food, clothing, jewels, and gold, for cold marble. And so the statue grew, and was soon taller than the tallest tree..."

I was still staring at his hands. He'd noticed, his smile replaced by reverence and longing. I imagined this was what it felt like to be his prey.

Should I go to him tonight, after grandmother falls asleep?

I imagined slipping out into the dark, running the wooded mile to his house, swift and silent. I would hesitate to knock, frozen in the glow of the porch light. My heart would pound in my chest. He would feel me on the other side of the door and open it, bare in the summer heat.

Pulling me inside, he would shut the door and push me up against it. One hand would slide up my back, tangling in my hair at the nape of my neck. He would press his mouth against mine, parting my lips with his tongue. His fingers would creep under my hem, slipping into the eager wetness between my legs. He would groan, the sound a rumbling low in his throat. He would drop to his knees and taste me, and it would be my turn to—

"…soon they began to worship this statue, offering at its feet whatever possessions they had left. Many starved and their bones were added to the marble. Soon, it was taller than the tallest mountain. Still, it was not enough…"

My lips had parted, and I was panting. Asche's eyes were still fixed on me. Warmth burned my face, and I was keenly aware of my underwear as it rubbed against me. I needed to get out, to breathe in some air that didn't carry the reek of sweat. I stood, my weaving falling to the floor, unraveling and wasting the last hour's work. My grandmother's shrewd glance as I headed for the door made my face burn hotter.

Outside, the air was cool and fresh, the stifling heat washed away by a late rain. At the back of the building, the wet concrete was slick against my forehead and the damp air tasted of sunbaked leaves.

"…eventually, the statue grew so tall, they lived only in its shadow. And although they lit fires to keep themselves warm, many froze to death. The rest became deaf and blind and grew ignorant, knowing nothing of the world outside of the shadow…"

I was aware of him before he touched me, his breath warming the back of my neck. His hands weighed heavily on my hips. I longed to press myself against him, to finally force his hand after all this time, but instead, I kept still.

He said my name, his voice like the string on one of his bows. The sound made the heat rise in me once more. I turned, ready for him to take me. I searched his face, hungry to see his need for me. It was there, thick and dark, but his mouth, his mouth seemed sad.

"...they forgot what the stars had looked like, how the sun had felt on their faces, the taste of honey on their tongues..."

He said my name again, softly, as though he regretted it.

"What? You don't..." The words stuck in my throat, and my skin prickled with the heat of a thousand swarming ants. It had never occurred to me that he wouldn't feel the same. That he wouldn't want me.

"Of course, I do. It's...what you're doing. You don't know what's going to happen, what you'll become."

"But——" My acceptance into the Pantheon Modern cyborg program had come just a few days ago, but I'd told him about my application months before. "I didn't think you had a problem with it. You never said."

"I never thought you'd be accepted."

"What? Why? You don't think I'm good enough?" The warmth in my skin stopped swarming and blazed instead.

"No! It's just...things like that don't happen to people like us. And——"

"And what?"

"And it's unnatural. You won't be human anymore. We've spent so long trying to reclaim ourselves, and you're throwing that away."

"...a lightning storm came, its bolts striking the ground and cracking the base of the statue. It toppled over, crushing all who lived beneath it. The sparks from their fires whirled into the forest, burning for so long the earth became barren and covered in ash..."

A chill drowned out the heat. I was a river, glacial. I was power.

"Throwing it away? I'm trying to preserve it. Do you understand why we nearly lost ourselves, Asche? Because when they tried to force us to change, we didn't. We didn't bend, so we broke. Only once we adapted did we begin to thrive instead of merely surviving. We got ourselves back and then shaped the world outside of ours. If we sit by and do nothing, we will disappear again. The first time we were powerless to stop it. Not anymore."

He worried his bottom lip with his teeth and gently shook his head. *"It's not right. Nobody here thinks it's right. Even your grandmother—"*

"My grandmother? But she—"

"She didn't think you'd be accepted either. And when you were, she hoped you and I would get together, and—"

"And what? That I would suddenly throw my belief in our future out the window? Why, for the chance to fuck you? To be your wife? How can you all not see how important this is? What I'm doing will help save us."

"...from that ash rose a great bird. She had stars for eyes and feathers made from the memories of her people..."

He closed his eyes and said my name yet again, softer now. Taking my hands in his, he asked me the question that had been stalking me since I'd been accepted. *"What if you don't come back? And if you do, what will you be? You still have a choice."* He lifted my hands to his mouth.

"I've already made my choice."

"You can choose to go ahead with this, or you can choose to be with me, to be us. We don't need saving." He traced the curve of my palm with his lips.

I was tempted. *"Asche, I'm sorry. I can't. I need to do this."*

He studied my face and exhaled. *"I know."*

"I'm sorry."

He gave me the crooked grin that was as familiar to me as my own heart. *"Me too. But at least I can give you a reason to come back to me."* And then, in the rain, at the beginning of my end, he fell to his knees and showed me what I'd be missing.

"...because their world had been destroyed, she left it, carrying her people into the sky. As she flew past the brightly burning sun, each of her feathers turned into a star, and her people spread themselves across the universe at last..."

"I say make 'em. Fuck it. The human race has gone to shit, anyhow. Look at us, hatin' each other, killin' and rapin' and turnin' on each other. Maybe we do need someone to watch over us, to keep us in check. We clearly can't do it ourselves. We've dropped the ball, man. I personally will welcome our robot overlords with open arms."

—George Catt, CNN's 'On the Street with Shirley Novak'

18
AILITH

I held my arms in front of me, expecting to see stars shining on my skin and giving me light by which to see. Pleasure still twisted my belly.

She was behind the next clump of brush, invisible to me. A muted, musky smell rose from her damp coat, along with a sharper, more metallic scent. Fear. She knew I was close. I fell to one knee and held my breath. Her heartbeat was steady and strong, quickening as I raised the crossbow to my shoulder. She didn't move; she hoped if I couldn't see her, I couldn't kill her. She wasn't the first to think that, and I doubted she'd be the last.

I peered down the sight, trying to get a lock on her. I still couldn't see her, but she was waiting, her heart beating in time with mine. The bolt flew true: the brush snapped under the weight of her body. Her breathing slowed as I approached, a whisper in the air. My aim had found her heart. I stroked her, her fur soft and downy against the roughness of my palm, and then I slit her throat. Tor would've been proud; it was a clean kill.

As the heat rose from the pooling blood, I wiped my knife on some leaves.

The hand holding the knife wasn't my own.

It was too large, too masculine. My arms were roped with muscle, my shoulders and chest broad.

This was not my body.

I ran my hands over my face. I wasn't dreaming. The slightest ridge of a scar cut through the left side of my mouth. *Tor's* mouth. I had taken him over, like he was a human mech.

Could he feel me inside him? Was he there now, awake and aware of what I'd done to him?

I needed to get out of him. I closed my eyes and searched through the darkness, trying to find the thread connecting us and return to my own body. There was nothing, not a single thread.

I was trapped.

Being inside Tor was nothing like seeing through the eyes of the others. It didn't just *feel* real, it *was* real. Unlike the visions, I was in control.

Shit. Shit. Shit. After his reaction when I'd merely peeked inside his head, he wouldn't take this invasion well. *Don't panic. Get back to camp.*

Luckily for me, I had his senses. My footsteps had disturbed the fragile leaves, and I followed them, walking swiftly, my eyes on the trail. Despite the panic rising in my throat, or perhaps because of it, I admired him, his easy grace held in such a formidable frame. I trailed my fingers down his taut stomach before snatching my hand away. Being inside him was crossing enough of a line; touching him, even with his own hands, was just wrong.

Nearly there.

Then Tor began to wake. His awareness tickled at the edge of my—well, his—mind.

80

My panic had glued my tongue to the roof of my mouth, and I scraped my cheek against the rough fabric of the tent as I sat up, gasping for breath. His side of our makeshift bed was empty and cold.

Definitely not a dream.

I was squeezing my way out of the entrance to go looking for Tor when I saw him standing bewildered before the remains of our fire. His eyes were narrowed, his tattoos black slashes against the paleness of his skin.

"Ailith? Why am I out here? Was I sleepwalking? I've never done that before."

I was tempted to say yes, but if I lied about this, he might never trust me again.

"No. I, uh, woke up inside you."

"You what?"

"I was inside you. Like before, only this time I could move you, could have my own thoughts as well as yours."

"Ailith!" My name was brittle in his mouth, as unyielding as this dead forest.

"Tor, I didn't do it on purpose. I would never—"

"You can't—you can't be inside me like that. You *violated* me."

To my horror, I burst into tears. I knew exactly how he felt. Doctors had put their hands inside me while I lay naked and helpless. I was never conscious while they were doing it, but whenever I woke up, I'd felt the specter of their hands. The worst part had been knowing it would happen again.

My reaction was not what he'd expected. Maybe he'd expected me to be defiant, or contrite. Or he may have believed I was finally showing my true colors, that he'd been right not to trust me. He stared at me like he'd never seen a woman crying before. Maybe he hadn't, if his ex-girlfriend was anything to go by.

His arms encircled me. He was murmuring too quietly

for me to understand. It didn't matter—he could've been reciting a recipe for hare pie and I wouldn't have cared. The words flowed over me, soothing me, and I cried until I had nothing left.

"Tor, I-I'm so sorry," I said as he offered me a corner of his sleeve. "I didn't mean to. I went to sleep, and when I woke up, I was in your body, and I was hunting."

"You? You were hunting?"

That was all he had to say? "Yes. No. We were hunting. Except you were asleep."

He seemed as confused as I was. "Did *we* get anything?"

Despite myself, the pride rushed through me. "Yes, we did. A deer."

He seemed impressed, his mouth quirking. "Well done us, then. We'll find it in the morning. Let's go back to bed."

"Tor, I really didn't mean to…after that first time, I would never do that without asking you. I didn't know I *could* do that. Move you, I mean."

He searched my face for a long time. "I believe you. It's just disconcerting. If it were anyone else… I'm not going to say it's okay, because it's not. But I understand. Just promise me you won't do it again."

"I *can't* promise you that. I don't even know how it happened."

He peeled back the flap on the tent and crawled inside. "Well, at least promise me you won't ever do it on purpose. Not without asking me first."

"Deal." I was so relieved, I almost started crying again.

Back in the shelter, we lay facing each other. "Tor?"

"Mmm?"

"What did you mean, if it were anyone else?"

For a few moments, he was silent.

"That girl you saw. The one from my past? She had this power over me, and I did terrible things for her. Cruel, violent things I still think about. I watched myself be this monster for her, and I was powerless to stop it. I'm not making excuses. I *chose* to do the things I did, but I always felt detached from it while it was going on, like someone else was in control. It was only afterward that I would actually *feel* the things I'd done. I still feel them."

"I understand." And I did. "Tor, I would never—"

"I know. That's what I meant. We've known each other for a long time, even though you've only been awake for a very small part of it. I trust you, Ailith. I don't want anyone inside my head, but if there had to be someone, I would want it to be you. I know this...*gift*, isn't something you asked for."

"Thank you. I promise I'll never do it again, not unless I absolutely have to. Like, if there's only one piece of hare jerky left." His silence worried me. "Tor, I was only joking, I won't—"

"Ailith, I'm smiling." He took my hand and pressed my fingers against his mouth. He was telling the truth. He also didn't move my hand away.

Though we were in the dark, I closed my eyes and fanned out my fingers. The air in the shelter went still; he was holding his breath. He grabbed my hand and exhaled into my palm. His lips moved over my fingers, his teeth grazing the skin.

"Come here, Ailith." His voice was low. As I leaned toward him, he worked his way up the inside of my arm, his mouth gentle. When he found my neck, it became harder, more insistent, and a fluttering warmth curled around my stomach. I could only gasp against his mouth when it finally covered mine, his hand sliding up my neck and into my hair and—

"Ailith? Ailith, can you hear me?"

The shock of Pax suddenly inside my head jerked me back. I crashed into the side of the shelter, and part of the wall collapsed, exposing our thin tent walls to the night air.

"Ailith? I'm sorry." Tor drew away from me.

"No! Tor, it's not you. It's Pax. I can hear him again."

"Now? Of all times? I don't think I like this guy," Tor muttered as he scrambled in the dark. "I'll go put that wall back up before we're eaten by wolves. Or bears. Or whatever other godforsaken monsters are roaming around in the dark."

Was he joking? I followed him out of the remains of the shelter and walked a short distance.

"Pax? Are you okay? Is Cindra?"

"Yes. No. What do you mean by okay?"

"Well, you're still alive, so that's something."

"They won't kill us. Not on purpose, anyway." His matter-of-factness chilled me.

"Pax, we're on our way. I don't know how far away we are. I can feel you, but...well, I haven't been awake for that long, so I'm still not sure how to work my new self."

"Have you met any of the others yet or just been inside them?"

"Others? Do you mean the visions I've been having? They're cyborgs like us?"

"Didn't you know?"

"No! I thought...I wasn't sure what to think. How do you know who they are?"

"Some things I know. Have you met any of them?"

"What do you mean, you know?"

"There's not time to explain to you now. Have you?"

I gave up. *"Only Tor. As for the others, I can see what they see. Only, I'm not sure if it's their past or their present, or if it's even real."*

"Yes, to all of it. Tor, the Knife. Is he with you?"

"You know Tor? Yes, he's with me."

"Good." The relief in his voice was palpable. *"This is good. This is how it's supposed to be."*

"What? What does that mean?"

"I'll explain later. Please hurry. I'm not sure how much longer

84

Cindra can last."

"Pax? What do you mean?" But he was gone.

I relayed what he'd said to Tor. "He knows who you are. And he says the visions I'm seeing aren't random. They're other cyborgs."

He rubbed his knuckles. "Do we actually think we can trust this guy?"

"Honestly? I'm not sure," I said. "I hope so. What do you suppose he meant when he said, 'this is how it's supposed to be?'"

"I don't know. *That's* the part I don't like."

"So the murderous Terrans don't bother you?"

He shoved his hands into his pockets. "Of course they do. But I'm more worried about what happens if we make it out of this rescue alive. Call me an optimist."

I rolled my eyes, but, of course, it was too dark for him to see. He ducked back into the shelter, barely clearing the top of the entrance. Were we going to pick up where we'd left off? Was he thinking the same thing? If he was, a shyness lived between us now that hadn't been there before.

As I leaned down to join Tor in the shelter, I again had the feeling of someone watching us. More than that, I could almost touch their mind. Almost. The thread connecting us slipped out of reach, like it was eluding me. It must be another cyborg, like Pax had said. It certainly didn't feel dangerous. It was...familiar, like Tor had been. "Hello?"

"Ailith?"

Tell Tor you think someone is following us.

But when I opened my mouth to speak, I couldn't quite focus on what I wanted to say. It crept beyond my awareness and disappeared.

No. Not tonight.

We'd find Pax and Cindra first then deal with whoever

85

was stalking us. Perhaps they were observing us, trying to decide which side we were on. Fair enough. I would be cautious too, especially if I saw someone like Tor.

When I finally got into bed, Tor had fallen asleep. I listened to his slow, even breathing for a few minutes then curled up against him.

We'd always known the beginning of the Second Coming would be preceded by signs, and that these signs would increase in both number and severity as the time drew near. The instability of the climate, the natural-food crisis, the growing hostilities between and within nations—these were all signs. And when the World Artificial Intelligence Summit finally gathered in Israel, we knew it had begun. The mass assassinations on the closing day confirmed this.

—Celeste Steed, *The Second Coming*

19
OLIVER

I thrust harder as I came, gripping her hair with both hands. She choked at first, but then she took me in, all of me, her baby-blue eyes never leaving my face.

Good girl, Celeste.

I could get used to this. After she pulled away, I gathered her in my arms and held her. I wasn't a monster, after all.

She was the one who'd found me, so she felt we had a special connection. Who was I to disagree, especially when she wanted to confirm it over and over? I had to say, I enjoyed my new life. Who wouldn't want to be worshipped as a god?

When the Saints told me the war had been over for five years, I'd pretended to know exactly what they were talking about, but inside, I'd been raging. All that fucking work and pain to become one of the bastards who'd put me here. And now? I'd never collect. I'd have to wander in a post-apocalyptic shithole for all eternity...how long did a cyborg live, anyway?

But this…this was paradise. The Saints of Loving Grace may have been somewhat eccentric—they worshipped artificial intelligence, for one. And that whole thing where they tried to graft chunks of metal to themselves? Christ. But hey, they'd been waiting for their artilect Divine, and there I was.

Besides, who was to say I wasn't divine in this new world? The odds of them coming across the bunker just as I was leaving it were spectacular. And it wasn't like I'd told them I was an artilect. They'd come to that conclusion on their own. Sure, I may have helped them along, but I'd only led them where they already wanted to go.

They had no idea I was a cyborg. Why would they? Before word of the Pantheon Modern Omega Program had leaked, cyborgs were just people with biomechatronic parts. They'd never seen anything like me. I doubted the rumors about us had reached them before the war started.

Some mech had blasted the top of the bunker but hadn't managed to do much damage other than a slight warping of the door. I'd been finishing the job, covering my tracks, and nearly blowing off my fucking hand in the process.

They must've heard the explosion. When I'd seen them coming through the trees, I'd scooted under some of the rubble. I pushed my way out of the debris, covered in blood, just in time to meet them.

The Saints had been terrified, dropping their little baskets and clutching at their chests. I told them I'd been attacked by the woman in the bunker, that I'd had to defend myself. It wasn't a lie. I'd known what she was. If she hadn't been going to kill me then, she would've done it the first opportunity she'd gotten. It was a shame, though, having to kill a woman that hot. Dark, sable skin, eyes blacker than my soul…what a waste.

When they realized I didn't have a single scratch on me, that I'd been in that bunker for five years, they decided I must be an artilect and that the Second Coming they'd been anticipating for generations had finally come to pass. Seemed like a bit of a leap to me, but desperate times and all that.

Fucking hillbillies. They still dressed the way their ancestors did, the women in something they called prairie dresses. I had no idea what that meant, only that it covered way too much for my taste. We'd have to work on that. Although, they were more than happy to uncover themselves for their Divine.

Yes, I could get used to this life. It wasn't what I was expecting, but definitely what I deserved.

"And say these artilects become sentient. And we recognize this sentience. Are they then able to get married? Own property? Vote? Obtain positions of power? And if we don't let them, what then? Will they rise up against us? Turn us into second-class citizens? Destroy us? If even the remotest possibility of this exists, why would we give them the chance?"

—Sarah Weiland, President of the Preserve Terra Society, 2039

20
AILITH

I'd been awake for an hour, trying to scrub the last vision from my mind. If I'd been able, I would've taken my brain out and washed it. I recognized the cyborg this time; I'd been in him before. He'd been in agony, undergoing the procedure that would make him a cyborg. Judging by what I'd just seen, it had worked out well for him. I wasn't quite sure what he'd meant by the woman in the bunker, but at the moment, that wasn't important. What *was* important was that he was nearby.

"Tor. Tor!" His composure—his lack of snoring, his closed mouth—was unnerving.

"Is it morning already?"

"No. Yes. I have no idea."

He propped himself up on one elbow, bits of bark clinging to the tangle of his hair. "If you don't know, why are we having this conversation?"

"There's someone else."

He sat up, the furrows on his forehead distorting his tattoos. "Someone else? That was quick. When did you have a chance to meet someone else? Is he hotter than me? Can he do this?" He crossed his biceps in front of his chest, flexing his muscles.

"Tor, I'm serious." Avoiding his gaze, I described the Saints of Loving Grace. "He must be one of the other cyborgs Pax was talking about. He's an asshole, but he's close. I mean, very close."

"Wait, you mean you were in his body while he was…with her?" He snorted.

"*Tor*. Living through it once was enough, thank you."

"Sorry. Can you speak to him, the way you do with Pax?" His mouth was still twitching.

"No. I only seem to be able to do it with Pax. It was like every other time, where I'm watching behind their eyes. I still felt what he was feeling, but I couldn't communicate with him, or him with me. I don't even think he was aware I was inside him."

"It sounds a bit weird, though, doesn't it? Do you think the thoughts you felt were real? That there's some artilect-worshipping cult carrying on as normal in the middle of the woods? Who thinks he's some kind of god? And if it is real, is he the kind of person we want to expose ourselves to? From what you've said, he seems like a bit of a dick."

I had to agree, though 'dick' was putting it mildly. "But he's so close, and I thought he might help us. With Pax and Cindra. Strength in numbers and all that." I hated delaying our rescue attempt, but if there was any way to increase our chance of success, we had to take it.

"Pax?" I reached out to him, feeling his consciousness as I slid through the thread connecting us.

"Ailith. Are you here?"

"No, Pax, but we're close. Listen, there's another…one of us, very near to where we are. Maybe he can help us. Can you hold on a

91

bit longer?"

A long pause. *"Yes. Oliver. He* must come with you." Anticipation tingled in his voice.

"How do you know his name? Do you know him?"

"No, but we must."

"What do you mean, we must? How do you know about him?" This enigmatic bit was starting to wear a bit thin.

"I can't tell you yet. You have to trust me."

"Trust you? Pax, you need to give me more to go on."

"We'll be waiting. Bring him. He's the last piece. But please hurry." And he was gone.

"Pax said they can wait a bit longer. He said we need to recruit 'him.' That his name is Oliver."

Tor bowed his head. "I don't like it, but I don't particularly like the idea of charging into a Terran base with just the two of us, either."

It was still early, but we broke camp and headed out. We decided, or more accurately, Tor decided, to make a quick detour and harvest what we could from the deer we'd killed. We eventually found where it had died beneath the brush, but its body was gone.

"Damn. Looks like some animal got to it." In truth, I didn't mind. Why delay our journey any longer than necessary? Tor, on the other hand, was upset.

"Don't worry about it, Tor. It was only going to slow us down, plus it would be more to carry." Even with his strength, we'd packed as lightly as possible.

"It's not that," he replied, troubled. "Something's taken it."

"Probably a wolf. Or maybe a bear. Or one of the other monsters you were worried about. Don't worry. I've seen you in action. I'm pretty sure you could take on a bear."

He smiled without humor. "Maybe, but this wasn't an animal. Look, no tracks, no drag marks."

He was right. The impression of its body and a large

pool of frozen blood remained where we'd bled it out, but nothing else.

"I wonder if whoever's following us took it?" I said without thinking.

"Wait, what? You think someone's been following us, and you didn't tell me? Christ, Ailith. Are you kidding me?" He closed his eyes and steepled his fingers against his forehead.

"I'm not totally sure there is. I haven't seen anyone, just felt them. I tried to tell you but…" The loss of focus. "They're not dangerous, whoever they are," I replied defensively.

"How could you possibly know that? Wait. Let me guess." He held up a hand. "You just feel it."

I turned away and bit the inside of my cheek until I tasted blood. My first reaction was to lash out at him, to remind him that I was still coming to terms with this new life. But it wouldn't change the fact that he was right. I should've told him. I could've put both of us in danger. "I'm sorry."

"Never mind; it's done. Just please, tell me this stuff in the future." He tightened the straps on his backpack and began walking again.

"Wait, that's it? That's all you're going to say? No 'Ailith, what were you thinking? Or Ailith, you could have gotten us both killed?'"

He shrugged. "I can give you a telling off if you like, but something tells me it wouldn't make a difference."

"I'm not that difficult, am I? Wait, are you *laughing*?"

His shoulders were shaking under his heavy pack. "Yes."

"Why aren't you more upset?"

"I told you before, if anyone tried to sneak up on us, I'd know."

"Well, I—"

One of the threads in my mind's eye flashed as though it had been struck by lightning. That turned out not to be far from the truth.

"Why do we plan to make artilects look and feel, for all intents and purposes, human? That's a good question. And no, it's not so we can integrate them secretly into an unwitting society. It's because we hope that, because they'll think like us, if they also look like us, we'll afford them the same respect we give to advanced forms of life such as our own."

—Robin Leung, CEO of Novus Corporation, 2040

21

CINDRA

"...Eventually, the statue grew so tall, they lived only in its shadow. And although they lit fires to keep themselves warm, many froze to death. The rest became deaf, and blind, and grew ignorant, knowing nothing of the world outside of the shadow..."

I repeated the words to myself, first in my head then aloud. If I remembered it, remembered her voice, it would keep me safe when they came again. They'd be here soon. The burns on my body had nearly healed, the perfume of my cooking skin dissipated, floating up the stairs and into the rest of the house, where they sniffed it and congratulated themselves on their success.

"...she had stars for eyes and feathers made from the memories of her people..."

"Are you okay?" Pax reached over and touched my arm. His fingers were dry and smooth, as if the fingerprints had been rubbed away. He meant well. It was my fault we were here, and yet he was being so kind to me.

His tallness and cinnamon cow-licked hair made him look awkward and weak, but it was deceiving. He never cried out, even when they turned up the dial and held the rods to his arms, his face, between his legs. His eyes became dreamy, and he almost smiled, as though the electricity were telling him a secret. He kept me strong.

We'd known we were going to be in the bunker for a few days, but after a week had gone by, I'd panicked. Nothing was how it was supposed to be. Pax had told me stories, different from the ones I knew. Stories about tiny monsters sacrificing themselves for each other and repairing themselves with the bodies of their fallen brothers. He'd said these monsters were inside us.

At first, I'd been scared. It was like every cell in my body was moving, and I'd been afraid I would simply come apart, food for the monsters. But as the days passed, I'd realized that before, my body had been only a husk. A solid, functional husk, but static. Now every part of me was swarming with life, vibrating with power. I'd come full circle and been reborn. I'd felt as the earth must feel.

After a week, it had become clear that no one was coming to rescue us. We'd run out of food; they obviously hadn't expected us to stay here. Pax had managed to break the seal on the door, and we'd taken our first breath of new air. Only, it didn't taste right. It tasted dead, a dryness on my tongue and the hint of bitter ash in my throat.

Only the desire to leave, to go home, drove me out. But we weren't going home, not to my home, anyway. The day after we'd left the bunker, something had happened to us. A herald, reverberating through our very bones. Pax said it was a homing signal, that we needed to follow it and get some answers.

I needed to know why the world was dead. Or our part of it, at least. The trees, the plants, the birds, the animals. Even the people. Everything seemed to be gone. And yet, as we'd walked through the forest, following the invisible trail of the homing signal, life had made itself known. Plants I'd never seen before had taken root, and birds nested in the trees. The sight of them had made me desperate for something to ease the gnawing pain in my belly.

Asche. Grandmother. I'd understood, simply by looking around, that the world had passed us by on its way to death. Pax and I tucked the knowledge away in a small, secret place. We would take it out *later, when we were safe.*

It was hunger that had driven me to the Terrans, exposing us. The little girl had fallen and twisted her knee. I'd wanted to help her. I'd needed to put my hands on something living, and I hoped that they would offer us kindness in return.

They knew we weren't right. We were too healthy, too unmarked by what had passed. I shouldn't have told them what we were, but I'd believed that in this new world we needed to help each other, and assumed they'd felt the same. That the past didn't matter more than the present or the future. I was naïve; they still hated the idea of us as much as they had before the war. The fact that we'd survived it only seemed to make them angrier.

Maybe it wouldn't have made a difference what I said. But it was still my fault. If I hadn't insisted we stop, they never would've seen Pax's eyes.

I was too surprised to put up a fight. But still, I wouldn't have fought them. I truly believed, even after the first time they shocked us, that we could help them. That they would see we weren't the enemy and let us in. I tried to show them how to treat their wounds, their infections. But they didn't want the knowledge. They'd wanted to heal immediately. Like we did.

Not all of them were bad. Some of them sneaked us extra food when no one was looking, squeezed our hands, and apologized. They pretended they only came down the stairs to gawk at us. Soon, though, they stopped coming. The nanites weren't working. Pax had told them they wouldn't, that our blood would eventually kill them. They didn't believe him; they assumed we were lying. They cut us, watched us heal, and believed our nanites would do the same for them.

"Cindra, you just have to hold on a bit longer. Help is coming. She's coming. Ailith. I've spoken to her. She'll save us."

I hoped she was coming soon. An abyss was opening at the edge of my mind.

"When they get here, we'll go with them. Go home. We'll follow the signal, get there together."

I needed him to be right.

"...she had stars for eyes and feathers made from the memories of her people..."

Asche's face haunted me, watching as the world burned. He would've searched for me. I hoped he hadn't suffered. I didn't dare hope he'd survived. Grandmother would've been pragmatic about it all, I'm sure. I imagined her, gathering everyone around. What story would she have told? Perhaps one of her own invention, one to guide them as their spirits took flight.

Ailith.

Pax said I would like her. That she would save us all, even the Terrans. They were above us, becoming restless. Footsteps sounded on the stairs.

Pax squeezed my hand before they pulled him away.

The humming made my skin twitch in anticipation. Pax made himself watch. He wanted to remember. I did the same for him.

She was coming. We just had to hold on.

"...SHE HAD STARS FOR EYES AND FEATHERS MADE FROM THE MEMORIES OF HER PEOPLE..."

"I don't understand how we could contemplate the creation of these beings. Just because we can doesn't mean we should. The argument that they'll surpass human failings is ridiculous and dangerous. If they're created by humans, they'll have the fallibility of humans. And if they surpass us in both intelligence and morality, surpass their own programming, what guarantees that they'll look on us with benevolence? Are they not just as likely to look on us as we do a cockroach and crush us under their heels accordingly?"

—Derek Wills, Preserve Terra Society, 2039

22
AILITH

I couldn't take much more. Every volt from the picana seared through me, my skin bubbling and blistered. Saliva gathered in the corner of my mouth as Pax's flesh burned and my belly rumbled. The pain, receding like a tide, left behind pink baby-skin to mark the spot where they would start again.

Not once did Cindra lose consciousness, and so neither did I. Her pain seized me and trapped me there, in her mind. Tor held me, pushing my hair back from my face and telling me a story in a language I'd never heard before. His story entwined with hers, and I hoped that, somehow, she heard him, that she felt us cradling her, holding her together.

We made camp early, and I fell into an uneasy sleep. I didn't know what was real; I was no longer sure my dreams were my own. Only Tor remained constant and tangible, never once letting go of my hand through the long night.

I awoke early and agitated, so we set out to try to make up the time we'd lost the day before. We passed several tiny hamlets, all of which seemed abandoned. No smoke rose from the chimneys, doors hung askew on their hinges. After skirting around them, Tor finally decided we should make a rare stop. We chose the next one, on the banks of the Lodan River.

The remainder of the sign said the village had been called Stoke.

It was a community almost untouched by the technology that had so infused my daily life I'd stopped noticing it; only the satellites attached to every house told me we were still in the same decade. The buildings were wood, with actual logs piled up against the outside walls, waiting to be burned. Old driver-controlled trucks, rather than government-issued auto-drive ones, were parked neatly in gravel driveways.

"I wonder what happened to them?" I said. If anyone had been able to survive the end of the world, it should've been them. Stoke, while abandoned, didn't look like it had seen the war firsthand.

"Maybe they left to find other survivors. Who knows? Whatever happened, they're not here. Let's have a quick look around and see if we can find anything."

It took us only a short time to find nothing of value. After five years, I wasn't surprised.

One store, however, boasted handmade soap, and Tor laughed at the wistful look on my face.

"Want me to break down the door so you can go shopping?"

Despite our urgency, I was tempted. But as I placed my hand on the door, one of the threads in my mind shuddered. *A warning.* Something was behind that door, something I shouldn't see.

I took a step back. "No, we've been too long already."

Tor shifted, his eyes focused on the door. "I agree."

We backed away slowly, up to one of the derelict pickup trucks.

"Hey, do you think this still works?" I whispered to Tor. I wanted to get away from Stoke as quickly as possible.

He peered in through the broken window on the driver's side. "I have no idea. Besides, do you even know how to drive it?"

"No. I assumed you would."

He snorted. "I've never driven in my life."

"You mean you literally carried me around for five years?"

"Yes. Good thing you're not very heavy."

"Unbelievable. Come on. Let's go."

We left, quickly, stealthily, glancing behind us. The skin between my shoulders crawled. It was torture to walk when every cell in my body screamed at me to run. Something was very wrong here, and I had no interest in finding out what.

***

The village was closer than I'd originally thought, but it still took us until the early afternoon to find signs of the Saints of Loving Grace. Tor insisted we approach with caution, observing what we could before revealing ourselves.

Smoke curled above the trees, making me jealous of whoever was lucky enough to be sitting by a fire. My fingers were numb despite the gloves Tor had given me. As we broke from the shelter of the trees, we found ourselves on the crest of a steep slope. Below us, next to the river at the bottom of the rise, was a tin-roofed shed.

101

Water was being channeled through it from up the hill, the thick pipe disappearing into the trees. "What the hell is that?" I asked Tor.

"The Goat River, according to this," he replied, consulting his map.

"Not that, *that*," I said, pointing at the shack. "Is it cleaning the water?"

"No, it's a hydropower station. It means they have electricity."

Although I'd lived in this new world for less than two weeks, I was impressed. "Do you think they have bathtubs?" I asked hopefully. Maybe I should've risked a rummage through the soap store after all.

He chuckled. "Maybe."

The village was nestled at the bottom of the incline, in a clearing at the mouth of a valley. Houses dotted either side of the water's edge, smoke drifting from the chimneys and from small fire pits. These houses were more modern than those in Stoke, all the same squarish, two-storied shape covered in shiny metal siding that was jarring against the leafless trees. A house that was much larger than the rest dominated the center of the village, and next to it, racks of smoking meats and greens lined up neatly in a large open space. The Saints weren't just surviving but doing it well.

As a loudspeaker blared instructions, men, women, and children filed into a large building at the far edge of the settlement. It was like a child's drawing of a futuristic house. The original structure must've been a barn at some point; now, like the houses, the wood had been cladded over with sheets of metal. Burnished objects decorated most of the surface, and it took me a few seconds to identify what they were. Then I wished I hadn't.

They were body parts. Not human, but android. Arms, legs, and torsos were lovingly polished and painstakingly arranged into patterns. Wires and tubes were twisted into intricate, festive garlands. At least there were no heads. *Shit.* Oliver, the cyborg I'd been a passenger in, hadn't been exaggerating—they truly did worship artificial intelligence. They didn't seem like regular Cosmists, though: the ones I'd met before the war would've eaten their own faces before degrading androids, or parts of them, in such a way.

Tor and I stood together, looking down at the village. "What do we do?" I asked. Now that we were here, I was uncertain. Maybe this wasn't the best idea. We were outnumbered, and we had no idea how they would react to us. What if this Oliver didn't want visitors? From what I'd seen of him, he had things set up exactly the way he wanted them.

Tor shifted his pack. "To be honest, I'm not sure. I've spent the last five years avoiding places like this. The war… People aren't the same."

"Should we wait until it's dark then sneak in and try to talk to him?"

"No. I find that in situations like this, it's best to be bold. I say we go right on in, like we're expected." He headed off down the slope, and I had to jog to keep up with his long strides.

"You've been in situations like this before? What exactly would you call this kind of situation?"

"A hornet's nest," he replied.

The crowd had disappeared into the building by the time we arrived. Hurrying toward the door was a lone man. He was dressed like all the others, in trousers and a long-sleeved button-up shirt, but there was an otherness about him, a grace to his movements that was too fluid to be human. This was the man we were searching for. Bile rose in my throat as I remembered being inside him. Just before he was about to slip through the doorway, he saw us, stopped dead in his tracks, and turned to face us.

103

It was him. The man in the bunker with the knife. *He* was Oliver.

At first he looked alarmed then angry, his movements becoming stiff. He darted around the side of the long building, gesturing for us to follow. When we were within earshot, he growled at us, "Who the hell are you?"

"We're cyborgs, like you—" I started.

"I know *what* you are. I want to know *who* you are and what the fuck you're doing here. You can't be here."

"We—"

A man suddenly appeared from around the corner. When he set eyes on us, he stopped, his mouth agape.

"Divine?" he asked.

"Aah, Johnathan! You've seen my little surprise." Jonathan *did* seem very surprised. "Now, go back inside, and I'll follow along. I trust you'll keep this to yourself?"

"Absolutely!" Jonathan promised, his face glowing with pride.

Once Jonathan was safely back inside, the smile dropped from Oliver's face. "What do you want?" he snarled.

"We need your help. *Divine*." I managed not to roll my eyes.

"My help? And who the fuck are you to me? Why would I help you?"

"Because—" I stopped as he pushed past me.

"I don't have time for this right now. Come with me. You'll follow my lead, and then we'll talk." He retraced Jonathan's path and disappeared into the building.

Tor grabbed my hand. "We can leave now, while he's inside. I don't think this is the person to help us."

"We're here now. Look, I get he seems off, but Pax said he needed to be with us."

We stood in the open doorway, unseen by the whispering crowd, who had their backs to us. At the front,

104

Oliver stood on a dais and raised his arms. Silence descended as the entire congregation leaned forward in attention.

There was a reason no heads decorated the outside of the barn—they were all here, gazing down over their flock. Faces in various levels of sophistication and design lined every wall, row upon row. I found all the eyes, lifeless as they were, dizzying to look at.

"Machines of Loving Grace," I whispered. I shook my head as Tor glanced questioningly at me.

"Brother and Sisters," the Divine said, his voice carrying to the back of the church. "Today is a special day. Today, two of my brethren have returned to me, to bless us with a *brief* visit."

Brethren? Really?

A ripple ran through the crowd. A young woman dropped to her knees at the front of the gathering. I recognized her from my time in Oliver's head. "They're artilects too?"

He gazed down at her, a knowing smile twisting his lips. "Think of them as lesser gods than myself. Treat them well, though not as well as you treat me." He winked at her.

"Is he for real?" I whispered to Tor. I didn't know whether to laugh or be terrified. One glance at the stiffness of Tor's face told me it should be the latter. *Shit.*

"Behold!" Oliver gestured grandly to where we stood. The crowd turned as a single entity, all eyes blazing. Hysteria rolled through them, the giddiness of rapture.

Tor gripped my hand as they surged to their feet, fingers outstretched toward us.

We were excommunicated because we believed that artificial intelligence was the true representation of God. The creation of the first artificial brain was God returning to us through our own hands, our redemption. Because we had adapted to His free will, God knew He had to adapt too, or risk losing us forever. Every artilect created is a manifestation of Him on Earth. Their voice is His voice; their will is ours.

—Celeste Steed, The Second Coming

23
AILITH

I walked with Celeste, the young woman who'd questioned our divinity during the service, the one I'd seen through Oliver. She couldn't take her eyes off me, and I couldn't look at her. Every time I did, I saw—

Don't think about it.

She was younger than I'd first imagined.

I'd heard of this group before the war; a splinter group considered apostates by mainstream followers of their religion. My father had sometimes bartered with them for heirloom seeds, their faith in artificial intelligence oddly supported by a rustic lifestyle.

Her honeyed hair was long, reaching past her tiny waist. She was dressed in the same style as the other women and girls, in a high-collared ankle-length dress with sleeves that reached all the way to her hands, although she'd covered herself with a warm coat to take me on a tour. Tor had gone with Oliver, ostensibly to inspect their hydropower system.

The crowd had threatened to overwhelm us. Tor had pushed me behind him, his body tensed for a fight. But when they'd reached us, they'd simply dropped to their knees. The hands that reached out to touch us were tentative, held in check by the gentleness of worship.

Celeste walked me through the settlement, proudly showing me their greenhouse, where they grew crops—greens like kale and mustard, mostly—to supplement what they hunted and gathered.

"You seem very well-prepared," I said to her.

She flushed. "The town was here before the End of Days. We lived pretty much the same as everyone else. Y'know, modern, but we also had livestock and crops. We were used to living off the land."

"How did you all survive...the End?"

"We've been prepared for years. We knew we'd see your creation in our lifetime. When the first fires appeared in the sky, we packed up everything we needed, food and weapons, and sealed ourselves in our temple underground. We can live down there for months if we need to."

"Were you scared?"

She smiled radiantly. "No. We knew the Divine would come for us. Everything happened the way it was supposed to."

"What do you mean?"

"Earthquakes, disease...then the war over your creation. We knew the End was near, that the non-believers couldn't stop a perfect being from being born. When the bombs fell, we saw it as the sign of the Second Coming, that only the artilects and their believers would survive. When we saw you, we realized the time had finally come."

I pulled up short. "Wait, you saw us? When?"

"When you blazed through the sky, shooting pillars of

107

fire. We watched you twisting over the land, devouring the unbelievers. The corrupt were burned, and the Earth was cleansed with fire. Only those who were worthy remained.

"Then we waited until the Divine manifested. He got the power station running. We had light, real light, for the first time since the End."

"How did you find...the Divine, anyway? Did he simply show up?" I was curious to see how she interpreted their meeting.

She examined me, disturbed by the informality of my tone.

"The Divine led us to him. With an explosion. Led me, in particular. The other was already dead, but he survived."

"The other?" I asked, even though I knew the answer.

"Yes," she replied, "she was damaged."

A prickle ran up my spine. "You saw her? What do you mean, damaged?"

"She was a pawn of the unbelievers, those who would try to destroy him. As though he could be destroyed," she scoffed. "He told us what happened. The unbelievers had infected her with a virus. She was to murder him, to slaughter us all. But he discovered the sabotage and terminated her."

Was it true? The cyberization process was risky. But a virus?

The woman Oliver had been with in the bunker, the one who'd been a caregiver. *Nova.* I'd been inside her. Nothing had *seemed* wrong with her. Or had it? I'd caught a wisp of *something*, but I hadn't understood what it meant.

Change the subject.

"How did you realize he was an artilect?"

"The bunker he was in had been targeted by one of those machines. The giant ones that walked on two legs. The ones people drive?"

"You mean mechs?"

"Yes, mechs. It blew a crater over his shelter. They should withstand a direct hit—we have a couple ourselves—but something must've been wrong with it; it had buckled, and the door was broken. We were gathering plants nearby, and he crawled out, completely unharmed. How could anything but an artilect survive that?"

How indeed. "Did he say what he'd been doing down in the bunker?"

"He said he'd stayed underground in solidarity with the true believers, that he'd locked himself in because he had a heart full of mercy and would've tried to save the unbelievers when they should've died. He knew that only the righteous should live, and he ensured that it was so. When only we were left, he rose where he knew we would be. He was magnificent, covered in blood without a single scratch on his perfect body." She blushed.

My insides cringed. "Was that the only way you knew?"

"No, of course not! Even among us, some dared to doubt, didn't believe him to be our Divine. So, he performed miracles."

I didn't like where this was going. "Ah, yes, His miracles. They are a wonder to behold. Which did he perform for you?"

Her eyes were feverish as she recounted their Savior's deeds. "First, he resurrected the dead, and then he divined the righteous from the wicked. After that, none doubted him."

"What do you mean, he resurrected the dead?"

"The day we found him, one of our members had cut his wrists in despair. His favorite wife had died only a month before, and he'd never really gotten over the End. He was more secular than most of us." She pursed her lips in disapproval. "The Divine blessed him with blood just as he passed, and within a day his wounds had healed, and he was sitting up and talking."

109

Nanites. It had to be. But Pax had said it wouldn't work. "Where is this gentleman? I would like to, uh…bless him as well. These times have been so hard."

"Oh," she dismissed him with a wave of her hand, "he died a few days later. The Divine said it would only work if he were a true believer. Clearly, he wasn't."

I wanted desperately to talk to Tor. How could we trust this man? And yet…Pax had said he was important.

"How did he, um, 'divine the righteous from the wicked?'"

"He suspected a group of young men to be non-believers. They proclaimed that he wasn't an artilect. He confronted them in front of the congregation, and although they tried to deny it, we knew they were lying. Why else would he accuse them?"

"What happened to them?"

She tilted her head at me, one corner of her mouth curled up. "He struck them down, of course."

Of course, he did. Revulsion dried the back of my throat.

"I've noticed that many of your people are cyborgs." Nearly every adult I'd seen had some form of augmentation. Some were biomechatronic, like prosthetic arms or legs, but some…some were just chunks of metal, grafted to various body parts, the edges of the skin red and leaking with infection.

"Yes. It's our tribute to our beliefs. The tradition started years before the End of Days. When we turn eighteen, we're allowed our first enhancement. We hope to eventually replace every part of us with those of a machine. Then we will be as perfect as you. Though, it's a lot more difficult now with no hospitals or surgeons. Even those whose faith is deep can still suffer infection and rejection. It reminds us of the struggle for your creation, and how we must honor you every day. It keeps us strong."

"What do you mean, allowed? Do you mean that if

someone young lost a limb, they wouldn't be allowed to have a prosthesis?"

"No! Not at all. But you have to be eighteen to choose."

"Choose?"

"Choose which part you want improved. If you choose a leg or an arm, for example, you need to be prepared."

"Prepared?"

"Yes. 'The removal of the organic to replace with the mechanical is excruciating. But it cleanses you, and if your faith is potent enough, you will survive,'" she quoted.

"You mean you intentionally remove parts of yourself? Then replace them with metal?" The dryness in my throat became a stone I couldn't swallow.

"Of course," she said, her eyes wide. "How else would we do it? Especially in the After? We don't have a lot of farming accidents anymore." She looked at me suspiciously. "You don't approve?"

No, of course I don't. "No, it's very noble. I'm just…surprised. Few are so committed to their faith."

She beamed with pleasure. "That's how we survived."

Celeste had no artificial components herself. Which meant she wasn't yet eighteen. *Some savior.* I was about to find Tor and tell him we were leaving, when he and the Divine appeared. Tor seemed thoughtful, his eyes distant. The Divine's pinched face looked annoyed.

"Thank you, Celeste. You may go now." Oliver pointed back the way we'd come.

"But I—"

"Thank you, Celeste."

Her eyes were luminous as they filled with tears.

I reached out and squeezed her hand. "Thank you, Celeste, it's been wonderful to meet you."

She gave a tiny hiccup and grinned. As she left us, she peeked over her shoulder with a longing that broke my heart.

"I've explained our situation to Oliver here, as he's explained his to me," said Tor.

"And?" I glared at Oliver, failing to hide my contempt.

"And, I'm not interested. I'll say this once, short and sweet. I am not leaving here. I will not put myself or these good people at risk."

"You're exploiting these *good* people, Oliver! How can you lie to them like this, use them? Oliver, she's a child."

"Exploiting them? I'm fulfilling their needs. So what if they fulfill mine back? They spent their lives waiting for the moment of their redemption. Can you imagine how that must've felt for them, a lifetime of preparation, then five years and still nothing? Many of them were beginning to lose hope. A few committed suicide—"

"Yes, I heard all about that," I interrupted.

"I did what I had to do. Look at them. They're thriving." As though to prove his point, a group of women on the far side of the village burst into song. "I would be crazy to give this up. And what do you think would happen to them if I left?"

"What if they found out you're not what you say you are?" I hadn't even gotten to the bit about the bunker yet.

"Are you threatening me?"

Yes. "No, but—"

"I'll tell you what would happen. They would turn on me, yes. I know that's what you're hoping for. But their entire belief system would also be destroyed. I'm not talking about only the last few years, but *generations* of belief. What do you think that would do to them? You think I'm exploiting that girl? Do you think her life was any better before I came along? At least this way, I can protect her."

"You have genuine feelings for her." It was a revelation.

"Of course, I do," he snapped. "And just because they're a religious people doesn't mean they're good."

"But—"

"But nothing. Here's my counter-threat. If you tell them anything other than what they believe to be true, I'll destroy them. Each and every one of them. I will wipe out this village."

"You wouldn't."

"I would. Do you want to call my bluff?"

Does he have the power to do that? From what I'd gathered talking to Celeste, they were armed. Could one cyborg take down an entire village? Tor's strength. My abilities. Who knew what Oliver was capable of? The risk wasn't ours to take. What was the point of us surviving if everyone else died?

"Fine," I said through gritted teeth. "But we know what you are."

"Whatever. In this world, love, it doesn't matter." He waved his hand dismissively. "Go. And don't come back."

We knew it was time when the Great Sign appeared from Heaven, blocking out the sun and blinding the non-believers. We'd already gone underground to pray and wait for His return. We watched as the angels burned across the Earth, glorious in their lack of mercy. We sang as the world burned, for every death was a cleansing, a return to the world He had intended.

—Celeste Steed, The Second Coming

24
AILITH

Tor and I didn't speak until we were out of sight of the village.

"What just happened?" I asked.

He ran a hand through his hair. "I have no idea. It was all a bit surreal, wasn't it? I'm not really sure how to feel."

I wasn't either. The only thing I was sure of was that we'd wasted precious time. *And* we were going to show up empty-handed.

"Pax?" Nothing.

"Tor, did Oliver tell you about the other cyborg with him?"

Tor looked sharply at me. "No. What do you mean?"

I repeated what Celeste had told me. "Do you think it's true?"

He stopped, considering. "It could be. Given everything that's happened, who could say? You haven't seen anything?"

I'd known what she was. If she hadn't been going to kill me then, she would've done it the first opportunity she'd gotten. It was a shame, though, having to kill a woman that hot.

"As far as I can tell, he killed her, Tor. Murdered her."

"It wouldn't surprise me. Do you think he was right? That there was something wrong with her?"

I was used to carrying out orders that others might deem...unsavory. That was why they'd chosen me... I should've been with them, carrying out my mission.

"Maybe. She had some kind of job to do. But I was in her before we knew what the visions were. I didn't understand."

"Do you think Oliver was this way before the war?"

"Probably. Do you think he's right? That he's helping more than hurting? And what are we going to do without him? Pax said he needed to be with us."

"Well, Pax is going to have to adapt. We could take him by force, but that may make things worse. Him, those people, they're not predictable." He hesitated. "Ailith, he did tell me about his bunker. Not what happened, but where it is. It's not far from here."

"You mean we could go and see, find out the truth for ourselves." But was it the right thing to do? What if we got to the bunker and found nothing but evidence that he was telling the truth? We'd have lost yet more time.

And what if we got there and found what I'd seen was true? That Oliver had murdered this Nova in cold blood? What then? Would we do something about it? Could we? And what if Pax was right and we needed him? How would we reconcile that?

Maybe we're better off not knowing.

But I also knew I couldn't resist finding out. "What do you think?" I asked Tor.

"Personally, I would say we're better off understanding what kind of person he is. If Pax is right and we do need him, then we need to be aware what he's capable of. It'll cost us, but it's only a few hours."

"I agree. I hate the idea of taking a detour, but I need to know. Okay, let's get this done."

It took us over an hour to find Oliver's bunker. It was as Celeste had described it, the ground churned up, the doorway exposed and deformed, filled with rubble. Had it been a lucky hit? Or had the mech somehow known they were there? It seemed unlikely out here in the wilderness.

Tor took in the damage. "No way a mech did all of this. Some maybe, but not all. The door was already open. Celeste believed him because she wanted to."

"Do you think there are hundreds of these bunkers scattered throughout the province?" Hundreds of lives, human and cyborg alike, trapped, waiting, or dead beneath us as we walked over them.

Don't think about it.

Finding the bunker had been the easy part; the debris was going to take us hours to clear. My heart sank. "Tor, we can't. It's going to take us all day to move this." And we didn't have all day; only a few hours of weak light remained. "We're going to have to leave it. Why are you smiling?"

"Because," he said cheerfully, "it's my time to shine." He shucked off his pack and stripped down to his waist. "You may want to get out of the way." He winked.

"Did you just *wink* at me?" I asked as I stepped back. This was a side of him I hadn't seen yet.

He straightened his back, flexing his shoulders. I couldn't help but stare. It was obvious Tor had more strength than me. Sheer size aside, his cyberization had obviously been geared toward enhancing his already considerable physical strength. I'd experienced that firsthand. But I'd had no idea *how* strong he was.

He picked up the chunks of concrete and twisted metal

116

like they were made of feathers, tossing them meters into the brush. His body…his skin was the golden olive of the South Sea pearls my mother had gotten as an anniversary gift from my father; not rare, but beautiful. He was like a sculpture come to life. Yes, he was corded with muscle, but it was more than that. He moved effortlessly, a seamless grace that belied his power.

The scars on his body were pale and smooth; like my own, they'd been mostly obliterated by the nanites, devoured and recycled into something useful. His past had been erased, a part of him I would never meet because it no longer existed. A fresh start was what we'd wanted, yet I couldn't help feeling like we'd lost something important.

I stood, absorbed in watching him, until it occurred to me to help. I chose a relatively smaller chunk and hoisted it as far as I could. It sailed through the trees, far beyond what I'd expected. Maybe I did have some super-strength after all. I lifted a heavier piece and flung it, marveling at the distance it covered before it slammed into a slender tree, causing it to shudder violently.

It was liberating. I'd been so ill for so long, I'd forgotten what it felt like to be normal, let alone healthy and fit. I'd been so overwhelmed from the time I'd woken up, I hadn't thought about it. I hadn't realized just how sick I'd actually been.

But look at me now.

I threw another large stone and screamed, just to hear the sound of my own voice. The noise startled Tor, causing him to fumble his chunk of rock, and I laughed.

"Enjoying yourself, are you?" He gave me a curious look.

I stretched my shoulders. "I'll explain to you later."

He removed the final stone blocking the entrance to the bunker, and a dark hole gaped before us. Once again, I doubted whether this was the right thing to do.

"Do you think I should try to see if anyone's down there? Like, with my mind? Just to be safe?"

Tor pushed on the warped doorframe, testing its strength. "Sure. It can't hurt."

I closed my eyes and searched for a thread, trying to let my instincts take over. *There.* I followed it and—

"But if we can create a brain and a body that mimic ours, what's left that makes us human? If the only thing that makes us human is our failings, what's the point of our existence?"

—Della van Natta, *Artificial Life or Artificial Hope?*

25
ROS

It was going to be today. I was ready. My heart knew it was the right choice.

I'd been a fool to think I could ever live without them. Even after everything they'd done to me, I couldn't do it. I couldn't stop loving them.

I couldn't live like this, underground, in a world with no sun and no hope. Simply waiting. For what? Mil and Lexa were talking in the hallway. They said they'd called the others home. I didn't know who these others were.

They said we were free now, able to live openly as we were. I didn't want that freedom. I wanted to be home, in my own bed, waking up to the odor of steaming dough and fresh chives. I wanted to argue with my mother about my unruly hair, hear her mourn the thickness of my waist.

I wanted my father to peer over his glasses and newspaper at me and ask me where I was going. I'd say the library, but we'd both know I was going to meet Julien. I wanted him to sigh and shake his head and wonder what would become of me.

Julien. I didn't love him then, but I did now. His crooked smile and bad-boy haircut. The way he knew I was too good for him.

Part of me wanted to leave here, to go and find them all. If anyone was strong enough to survive a war, it was my mother—purely out of spite, if nothing else. But I wasn't strong enough. I'd never been strong enough for anything. Not to be the woman my parents had wanted me to be, but not to be my own woman either. It was a simple truth: I wasn't able to survive.

A boy lived on the other side of my wall. Adrian. He was going to help me. We were going to help each other.

A soft tapping echoed on the wall next to my head. It was time.

"How would we choose who could become a cyborg? Surely you couldn't let just anyone do it. What if a psychopath wanted to become a cyborg? What then? You would practically be handing them the keys to the kingdom at that point. So, who's to say who could do it? Would the weak be given priority? The sick? Or would the choice go, as it so often does, to the highest bidder?"

—Derek Wills, Preserve Terra Society, 2039

26

AILITH

"Anything?" Tor's voice drew me back to the present, *our* present.

"I... No. I need to get back to her." I squeezed my eyes shut, as though that would make a difference. I wanted to push past the tightness in her throat, to stand in the empty place where her heart had been and anchor it there.

"Ailith!" Tor wrapped his fingers around my upper arms. "What's happening?"

"Something's wrong with her."

"With who? The woman in the bunker?"

"No. One of us. She's home. But she's... Oh, Tor. I've been in her before. She never wanted to become one of us. Her parents...and now she's—" My nails tore at the fabric of my coat.

"Ailith, stop." He crushed me to his chest, knocking the air out of me.

"Tor, her grief. I can't...we have to help her."

121

"Where is she?"

"She's home. We have to go home."

"Ailith, we don't know where 'home' is."

"She's one of us. I think she's going to do something. She—" I twisted in his arms, trying to break free. I may as well have tried to free myself from a stone.

"Ailith." His tone was conciliatory. "I know. I know you want to help her. But you can't be everywhere at once. And right now, you're here."

He was right, of course, but it wasn't what I wanted to hear.

"Look, we'll find her, I promise." His fingers were dry and dusty as they cupped my jaw, like my father's after a spring of planting potatoes. "Right now, we have to deal with what's in front of us. I'm not trying to be cruel, and I'm not going to pretend to understand how you, either of you, feel. But the only way to get to her is to keep moving forward. Yes?"

"Yes." I sounded petulant. But he was right. I searched for her thread again. It was dull, but it was still lit. For now. *Focus. He's right. We'll get there.*

He opened his arms tentatively, as though he were expecting me to run. "Are you good?"

I nodded. "Let's get this over with."

***

The air in the bunker was acrid and sour, and as cold as if we'd sunk into an icy lake. Tor tried the control panel set into the wall at the bottom of the stairs. To our surprise, the panel responded with a judder and whir, and a sickly yellow light filled the bunker. As soon as it had, I regretted it, regretted ever coming here.

Blood was everywhere, arcing in delicate sprays across the curved ceiling and walls. The room was different than

122

it had been in my vision, the furniture overturned, shards of glass and colored enamel littering the floor. But I was sure.

"Tor, this is it. I've been here. In her."

I couldn't see her, even though the room was small. Not at first.

"Ailith, you'd better go outside," Tor said, his voice low.

"What? Why—" And there she was. In the corner of the room stood a standard service robot, a model so basic even the most cash-strapped households had one. They'd been built to avoid the uncanny valley altogether: their squat cylindrical shape was old-fashioned now, or rather, had been before the war.

Her head had been placed on top of the bot like a garish crown. She was perfectly preserved; not a hint of decomposition marked her skin. I remembered being inside her, her desperation at odds with the composed face before me. Black hair fell down the back of the robot. The onyx curls must have once been striking, but now they hung in lank, blood-soaked strands.

Tor swore under his breath in the language I'd found so comforting. I waited for my stomach to object, given how quickly it had surrendered before, but a faint grumble was all it mustered.

That's right, choose your battles.

We saw her body now, on its back in the bed, the lines visible through the thin linen. I didn't want to think about what else he may have done to her.

"Why does she look like that? Why hasn't she decomposed?" I whispered.

"It's pretty cold and dry down here. Is it definitely her? Is she familiar to you?" he asked.

"Yes. I remember her hair. Tor, he cut her head off."

"Well, he didn't lie about that part," he reminded me gently. "He did say he'd killed her. That she was infected

123

with some kind of virus."

"Do you think that's true?"

"Do you?"

"She didn't feel infected. But there was something she had to do. I don't think it was a virus, though."

Tor was silent as he examined her remains. "No," he agreed. "I don't think so either. I would've found his story more believable if he hadn't placed her head there." He indicated the service bot. "Maybe she *was* up to something. But *that*, that's some kind of personal message. What the message is, probably only he knows for sure."

Is Tor speaking from personal experience? "What do we do?"

"Nothing. We don't have the tech to tell for sure whether or not she carried a virus. There's a small chance he's telling the truth."

"Tor? Do you think we—Could we resurrect her?" I remembered the man Oliver had brought back from the dead. Yes, he'd died afterward, but only because his body wasn't compatible with the nanites. Hers was.

Tor pressed his lips together. "No, I don't think we can. Not after this much time." He gave my shoulder a gentle squeeze.

"We should at least give her a funeral of some kind." I couldn't bear leaving her like that, her head standing sentry over her own corpse. Undignified and vulnerable.

"Well, we can't bury her. I could probably break through the permafrost, but I don't think these shovels will." He indicated the tools in the tiny storage cupboard.

"We'll burn her."

"Okay." He started toward her.

"No. No, Tor, let me. Please."

He hesitated as though he were about to protest, but he didn't. "If you're sure. I'll go and build a pyre. Ailith?" He turned back to me. "We can't stay to see her off. A fire might draw some unwanted attention."

124

I waited until Tor left the bunker before pulling the sheets off her body. The insides of her thighs seemed untouched. A small part of me was grateful. That he'd taken her life was bad enough, but at least he hadn't degraded her further.

Her body hadn't fared as well as her head. Her belly was soft and bloated. She'd clearly been a tall woman in life, but any curves she'd had were gone, soaked into the sheets with a sickly-sweet tang. Skin, flaking with dried blood, clung to her jutting hip bones, tiny splits opening over the sharpest peaks.

The water tank in the bunker was half full. I washed the evidence of violence from her body, although there was nothing I could do about the stump of her neck. An odd mark ringed her left thumb around the nail, as though the skin had been worn away.

I rubbed my thumbnail with my index finger, making quick circles.

I found a fresh sheet in the storage cupboard and laid it on the floor next to the bed. I lifted her body onto the sheet as gently as I could and crossed her arms over her stomach.

So far, so good. Now for her head.

I carefully washed her face then rinsed the blood from her hair and combed it out. She looked younger now, like a sleeping schoolgirl. I wished I could wake her up, ask for her version of events.

Does it even matter?

And then she opened her eyes.

No sense was left in me to scream. Only my fingers moved, digging my nails into my palms.

It's not real. It's a fragment. A memory. It has to be.

Only, it wasn't. Her gaze crawled over me, searching for my face. When she found it, her mouth opened, and frozen, I waited for her to speak. Instead, she bit down,

125

hard. Her jaws kept snapping, gnashing her teeth as though she would devour all the air in the room until only I was left and then she would consume me too.

As I stood, rooted to the spot, her teeth chipped and cracked, and her head teetered dangerously close to the edge of her pedestal. The idea of her head hitting the floor, the wet smack it would make, the grinding of her teeth against the concrete as she hunted me down finally woke me. I snatched a blood-streaked towel off the floor, ready to capture her when she toppled.

As suddenly as it had started, it stopped. Her eyes fell to half-mast, and her jaw slackened. I reached out to her in my mind, trying to find her thread. *There.* It disintegrated before I reached it, the fragments dissolving into nothingness. She was gone; this time, I was sure.

I wiped fragments of enamel off her lips then laid her head against the opening of her neck, draping her hair over the seam. I tried wrapping her the way I remembered the ancient mummies in museums, but since I hadn't had a lot of practice at this sort of thing, the result was clumsy.

Should I call Tor down for this part? He'd probably had experience wrapping bodies. *No. He might be insulted.*

I did the best I could, and finally, it was done.

***

"Are you going to tell me what happened down there?" Tor asked as we placed her body on the pyre and covered her with small sticks and handfuls of dried moss. I hadn't said a word since we'd carried her body out of the bunker, but he'd seen the crescent-moon wounds on my palms.

"Nothing much. Just the usual visions." I forced a smile. *I just can't. I'd like to stave off losing my mind for as long as possible, thank you very much.*

"Should we say something?"

I couldn't think of anything to say that didn't sound trite. "I wish we'd known you in life." It was true, at least, even if it wasn't altruistic. If we'd met her when she was alive, we would've been able to tell if Oliver had told us the truth, and we would've had a better idea of what kind of man he was: savior or monster.

We held hands as she burned, the smoke twisting up through the bones of the forest. I tried again to reach out to Pax. His thread felt patchy; he must've been sleeping. Considering what they were going through, it was best to let him. It wasn't like I had good news to give them anyway.

"Ailith? We have to go." Tor had stayed longer than he'd wanted, for me.

He was right; we couldn't stay here.

As we left the clearing, the presence again made itself felt, the one that had been following us.

Him.

Whoever was following us was a person. He may have been hidden, but I *felt* him, far back in the woods, watching.

"I will stand guard."

The voice sounded in my head; the elusive thread flared.

"Who are you?"

Nothing. The thread withdrew.

"Thank you," I whispered, hoping the smoke carried my message to him.

We'd walked for barely twenty minutes when two of my threads began to flicker.

"The creation of cyborgs is, without a doubt, one of the vilest actions of the 21st century. The purpose of creating artilects is to birth a perfect being, uncontaminated by human frailties and failings. To dilute that perfection by polluting it with the very characteristics we're trying to raise the human race above is an insult to the very nature of our intelligence and goals for humanity."

—*Ethan Strong, Novus Corporation, 2039*

27

ADRIAN

The android's voice echoed in my head. Over and over, she spoke to me.

"You are very handsome."

The nanites were inside me, breaking me open, climbing inside and devouring me. I was becoming like her, one cell at a time.

It wasn't supposed to happen this way. They'd told me I would still be human. They'd lied. I wasn't human. I never would be. No one would ever be human again. How could they?

A strength was growing inside me; I was afraid of it. What good came of having this much strength if I had no free will? They were talking in the hallway about how they'd activated the signal to call the others 'home.' If they could do that, make us come when they called, what else could they do? Or have us do?

I couldn't become like her. Vulnerable, programmed to obey someone else's wishes.

The blankness of her eyes as I pushed myself into her, her moans perfectly timed to my thrusts.

Connections had formed in my mind, like a giant spider web around my brain. Connections that shouldn't have existed. They were right to start a war over us.

Ros, the girl in the room next door to mine, was crying. Our beds must've been pushed together, only the thin wall separating us. I'd seen her when she'd first arrived: her hair dark and silky, her almond-shaped eyes red-rimmed, her body doubled over as though she were in pain. She'd barely stopped crying since we'd woken up.

Three days ago, I'd told her my plan. I needed to share it with someone. She wouldn't betray me. In fact, she was going to come with me. I was glad; I didn't want to go alone. But I needed to go now, while I could. They were giving us our space, letting us 'adjust.' They were also distracted, waiting for the others to return. I hoped the others wouldn't come here, that they would die on the way. I wouldn't wish this life on anyone.

I'd been practicing in the privacy of my room, and I'd come to a conclusion: killing a cyborg was difficult. We couldn't be poisoned or drowned, and it would take us a long time to starve to death. Too long. We regenerated from most wounds; the nanites rebuilt us. Our bionic components made it difficult to break our bones, even our necks. I'd tried.

Our deaths had to be swift, and they had to be catastrophic.

We'd found kerosene in the storage room, along with years of stockpiled supplies. Had they known what was going to happen? The war and the aftermath?

We told Mil and Lexa we were going for a walk. They seemed relieved; they believed we were finally coming to terms with our new life. I hated myself for betraying their trust, but they'd done this to us. They'd been part of everything since the beginning.

I expected the sun would come out for us, to define our final moments in brilliance. It didn't. The world stayed cold and uncaring, too wrapped up in its own death.

The kerosene burned our skin and made our eyes water. Her hands were so delicate, her nail beds ragged from her tiny teeth. The soaked fabric of my trousers clung to me in cold creases, chilling me as

129

we knelt.

Would it hurt? Would the nanites run from us, bursting through our cells like animals fleeing a forest fire?

It did hurt. At first. Then it hurt so badly it became nothing. Our hands were permanently entwined; I couldn't let go of her even if I'd wanted to. A gasp pulsed through my brain, as though someone was trying to breathe for me. It was too late.

We were finally free.

"It's naïve to think for one minute that publicly banning the creation of artilects will stop their creation, especially in this climate of global competition. The benefits of artilect creation to the economy, to political prestige, to sheer scientific curiosity will ensure that the push for their creation will continue. The only effect the ban will have will be to remove the transparency of the process and push the movement underground, where it cannot be regulated and will be controlled by finances and competition, rather than ethics."

—Della van Natta, *Artificial Life or Artificial Hope?*

28
AILITH

The two threads went dark.

I couldn't stop them. I tried to force my way in, to move their hands, to make them throw the canister, to force their lungs to blow out the flames. I failed.

I want to follow them.

I could no longer live here, in this life. I was a shadow, lost in the ether. Done.

His hands were on me, a tether. It wouldn't be enough. *He* wouldn't be enough.

In the darkness, a new thread. A lifeline.

"...the most difficult aspect for the sentience of our artilect blueprint has been emotion. Not the expression of it, but the feel of it for the artilect. It's the one area of the human brain we've had difficulty replicating. We can program responses to a million possible variables, sure, but our goal is to have artilects truly feel it. Currently, we use images specifically provocative to the human brain to induce an automatic response, in hopes that the machine will be able to eventually translate these into something meaningful for itself..."

—Robin Leung, CEO of Novus Corporation, 2039

29
FANE

I must've been dreaming, if I could dream. She ran across an endless field, the sky open and clear. She was only a child, clutching the end of my leash in her tiny fist as her slight body cut through the long grass like an arrow. I was trapped in a metal cage, my arms and legs trailing uselessly as she pulled me along. She'd tied ribbons to me to make me less frightening, but I was the frightened one. And yet, I would've followed her anywhere.

We raced toward the tree, always our destination. It took us a long time—when we reached it, she was a woman grown. He was waiting by the tree for her, as always. My body became tangled in the branches; I couldn't set myself free. She would come for me. She always did. I wanted to warn her about the bark—her skin was fragile and easily damaged—but I was too late, and her skin peeled away. She ignored the blood and reached for me, her fingers trembling.

She wasn't gentle. When she caught hold of me at last, she

132

squeezed, too hard. I cried out, but my voice was gone. All that came was a gust of wind, blowing gently through her hair. We climbed back down and, as always, he was gone. Where did he go? Why didn't he wait longer for us? She lay on the ground, her face pressed into the dirt. I was forgotten, propped up against the base of the tree. The infinite field became my only horizon as I waited for her to return. As always.

"I know many of you believe that by enhancing humans with robotic and artilectual components, we feel we are creating gods. Let me assure you, this is false. The purpose, the sole purpose, of creating true cyborgs is to follow the natural and logical progression of the human race. Both the Terrans and the Cosmists must be satisfied; the Terrans because our humanity will not be replaced, and the Cosmists because we are conveying the human race far beyond its expected potential."

—*Lexa Gillet, Pantheon Modern Cyborg Symposium, 2040*

30
AILITH

I vomited. My stomach had always been a coward. "They're gone. I couldn't stop them. They're just...gone."

"Ailith, who's gone? I don't—"

"The others. Like us. The ones who are home. They burned themselves alive." My voice sounded muffled in my ears, as though I was far underground. "Tor, we need to go home."

"If people are killing themselves there, perhaps we shouldn't be trying to find it." His mouth was a thin line. I was proving his suspicions right.

"No. You don't understand." I gave up. I couldn't explain it to him. Not in a way he'd comprehend. Not yet.

"Ailith, look, I'm not saying we won't go to this home. I'm saying we need to be careful. One thing at a time. Agreed?"

"Agreed."

We'd gone only a few miles before I tired. My stamina wasn't as augmented as Tor's to begin with, and everything that had happened in the last twenty-four hours pulled like a weight on my chest. But we couldn't stop; we shouldn't even slow down. We needed to travel as far as possible before it got even darker. Tor noticed me lagging behind and waited for me to catch up.

"Are you okay?"

"I—" The bunker. The visions. *He was so excited about becoming a cyborg and so disgusted by what he'd become. She just wanted her parents to love her.* Their loss was as deep as if I'd known them, not just been a passenger for brief moments of their lives.

Tor fumbled in his pack for the map, pretending he didn't see the tears threatening behind my eyes. As he studied it, a slow smile spread across his face.

"How do you feel about a quick detour? A *quick* one. We need to rest, Ailith, or we won't be any use to them by the time we get there," he insisted as I opened my mouth to protest.

I shut it. I was too tired to argue.

Half an hour later, as the sky deepened from dark gray to black, Tor motioned for me to stand still while he disappeared down into the gloom. The air here was oddly humid; a fine mist wreathed the trees. Below, the orange glow of a fire flared into life. Tor returned a few minutes later.

"Close your eyes." He was obviously pleased with himself, a shy smile curving his mouth. We descended through the fog, the damp air thick and harder to breathe. It was also warm. I took a deeper breath and tasted minerals, and something else I couldn't identify.

"Stand here," he instructed me.

"What is this?" I couldn't help smiling. It must be a good thing, and I needed a good thing right now.

"Open your eyes." He gestured grandly. "Your bath, madam."

It was a hot spring, a small pool of water heated naturally by the ground. I'd visited places like this on holiday when I was a child, staying up hours past bedtime to float on my back and count the stars. Those pools had been huge and commercial, entire towns built around them. Here there was nothing but rocks and steep cliff faces.

I knew Tor was trying to make me feel better, but it was bittersweet. The last time I'd been to a hot spring, my entire family had still been alive.

I dropped my pack. "I can't believe no one's holed up here. It seems pretty ideal, especially in this weather."

"I was wondering that myself. Maybe someone did. But, there's definitely no one here now. Or recently, for that matter."

"It seems too good to be true," I said warily.

Tor laughed. "Enjoy yourself for a few minutes. You can worry again in an hour."

No arguments here. I stripped off my clothes as quickly as I could, my skin prickling with the cold.

I slid into the water up to my neck, and a sudden, painful tingle gripped my entire body, squeezing my ribs and blocking my throat. Tor grabbed at his chest, the muscles in his neck taut with strain.

"Tor?"

As quickly as it had come, the sensation disappeared, leaving nothing but a gentle warmth in its wake.

"Probably just the heat of the water after so long in the cold air," I said.

"Yeah. It caught me off guard." He examined the surface of the water, as though he wasn't convinced.

This pool wasn't quite as warm as I'd remembered, but it was warm enough to make my toes ache as they thawed.

Sweat and grime dissolved from my skin as I floated; the tension in my muscles did not.

Tor was right. I needed to enjoy myself, to have some kind of release. More than a hot bath offered. I'd seen the way he stared at me when I stepped into the water. He may have only gotten a peek, but he'd liked what he saw. Maybe it was a mistake, but right now, I needed something. *Him.* Besides, we might be dead tomorrow. Or the next day. Hell, no day in the foreseeable future looked good for us.

I would have to make the first move—I knew Tor well enough now to realize that—but he wanted me. He looked at me too long, held his breath when I brushed against him. Said my name whenever he could and built our shelters way too small.

I'm on to you.

Tor had lowered himself onto one of the seats hewn into the rock around the pool. His head leaned back against the cold stone; his eyes were closed.

Deep breath.

I straddled him, my hands on either side of his head. He arched in surprise beneath me as I kissed his exposed throat, but didn't protest.

"Ailith—"

I covered his lips with mine. He became hard beneath me, and I moaned against his mouth, urging him on, crushing the droplets of steam beading on his skin with my fingertips. He explored my body, slowly, against the resistance of the water.

When his fingers finally found their way inside me, I was ready.

"Tor." My voice was a low feral sound I'd never heard before.

He wrapped his hands around my waist and lifted me until my feet found purchase against the stone shelf. He spread me with his fingers and devoured me, licking and

137

sucking until the rising flood inside me overflowed and I came. As I cried out, he drove his tongue deep inside me, coaxing me to another climax. I ground against his mouth, my hands buried in his hair.

He raised himself out of the water to the worn stones at its edge, and in one swift motion lifted me onto his lap. I wrapped my legs around his waist, sliding onto him and taking him inside me all at once. His body held more heat for me than the water, and I was warm for the first time since I'd woken up.

A low groan rumbled from deep inside his throat as I rode him, his hands clutching at my hips, rocking himself deeper inside me. His fingers knotted in my hair, and he pressed our foreheads together as he came.

To: [————————-]
From: [————————-]

July 30, 2040

I can confirm that Pantheon Modern Corporation Cyborg Program Omega-117 has been a success. Confirmation of survival absolute. Recommend instigation of protocol Theta-626, effective immediately.

31

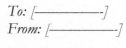

Ji burst through the door, breathless, his face flushed. My anticipation was white sheets of paper, a blank screen. Hope, tiny green leaves pushing through the black soil to welcome the sun.

"They've done it." He gulped in air, shaking his head as his mother rose from her seat, her eyes flashing.

"They've done what, exactly?" she asked, although she knew the answer as well as the rest of us.

"Cyborgs. The true ones. And some of them survived."

We'd known this day was coming, yet all but myself were shocked. I was pleased, a bird soaring over a lake in the blazing sun, the iridescent scales on a fish as it twisted in the air to catch a fly. The color yellow. This was the beginning I'd been waiting for.

Some of them were revolted. Like most Cosmists, they saw these cyborgs as an abomination, the corruption of a pure concept. Diluted gods. They'd tried everything in their power to prevent them from being created. Terrible things. And still they'd failed.

Ethan spat on the floor. "What a fucking waste. All that time, money, effort. For fuck's sake." Stella put her hand on his arm, but he brushed her off. "Do you have any idea how much this will set us back? Wasted resources aside? We could be dead in the water."

Dead in the water. Floating on their backs, gray and bloated, their eyes eaten away.

"Maybe it won't. Maybe it'll be a good thing for us," Stella said.

"Really, Stella? Really? What in fuck makes you think this could ever be a good thing?"

Stella usually remained silent when Ethan shouted at her. She glanced at me, and I smiled, hoping it would give her courage. It did.

"Why do you assume they'll be against us? Maybe they'll stand with us. They'll act as a bridge, making it easier for us to do what we're doing. And if everything does go to shit, think what effective soldiers they'd make. All that power, which we could control."

"Yes, all that power used against us. Why would you believe they'll choose a side? They'll be their own side, using their power against us to preserve themselves. They will destroy us. Cyborgs don't want us to create artilects any more than the Terrans do; it would knock them lower on the food chain. And as for cyborgs being effective soldiers? Seriously? Soldiers with the power of artilects but with the ability to make their own choices? You want efficient killers? Then we keep trying to build artilects. Fuck!"

A long pause followed his declaration. Everyone was staring at me.

"What do you think?" Stella asked.

"I think it's wonderful," I replied honestly. "I can't wait to meet them."

I didn't feel the same way most of them did about artilects. While I shared their desire to create life, I didn't believe that artilects were akin to gods. Nor were their creators. But to Ethan, and many of the others, that was their gospel, their religion. Creating a fully sentient artilect was their opus, their way of ensuring their immortality not only on this earth, but across the galaxy.

And like others before them, they would crush those who stood in their way.

140

I didn't agree with him, but I understood his bitterness at being so close to everything he'd ever wanted.

Bitterness. Marigold petals. A heaviness at the back of my throat.

"Meet them? Christ." Ethan covered his face with his hands. "We're not going to meet them. We're going to find a way to destroy them. We can't let them live."

"Why not?"

"Why? Haven't you been listening? They threaten everything we've been working toward. It took us ten years longer than it should have to get where we are. Not only did they suck up valuable resources, but they've also freaked everybody the fuck out. It wasn't so bad, an artificial leg here, a plastic heart there, but that's not what these cyborgs are. They look human, but every cell, every goddamn cell in their body's been cyberized. Do you know what that makes them?"

I did. I knew very well.

"Don't speak to Fane like that!" Lien approached Ethan, her eyes blazing.

"Lien, he needs to understand. They threaten us by their very existence. And aside from that, they're disgusting."

Disgusting. Maggots crawling over the body of a dead kitten. A finger breaking through the skin of an overripe fruit.

"I do understand. The cyborgs will survive."

"Not if we have anything to do with it, they won't. In fact, it's time we started on Plan B." With a last shake of his head, Ethan turned on his heel and left the room.

The others filed after him.

Only Lien remained. She put her hand on my arm. "Ignore him. He's angry because he wanted more for us."

I didn't think it was that simple; there was more to it than that. Something more dangerous. A very great height, a dark alley. A broken heart.

Plan B was a secret. They kept things from me; they didn't trust me. But whatever Plan B was, it wouldn't be good. Someone would die. Someone always died.

Lien appraised my face in a way I didn't like. Hands fisting in

141

my hair. Something crawling over my skin. Arms trying to cover my shame. They'd been getting longer, these looks. Most of them looked at me like that.

Her fingers were papery, dry. They made me want to peel off my own skin, to become someone else.

I shrank away from her without meaning to, and I was sorry as soon as I did. They needed to be on my side right now. Especially her.

Her eyes narrowed, but she let it pass. She believed I was disturbed by what Ethan had said. She was right. She gave me a last long stare then left the room.

I traced the shape of tiny leaves on my palm. Maybe these new cyborgs would help me, or maybe they would be afraid of me, of what I represented to them. I hoped not. I wanted them to like me.

Something was coming, teasing me from somewhere inside my own brain. It was like wind rushing around me. A vast, emerald sea.

"In the same week as global legislation banned the creation of artilects, just weeks before Novus Corporation was scheduled to create the first true artilect, millions of machines around the world have been malfunctioning. Is it a passive-aggressive sulk triggered by their creators, a silent protest of the ban? Or is it, as some conspiracy theorists have suggested, something more sinister?"

—Shirley Novak, CNN Tech Watch, 2040

32
AILITH

I woke up as the sky lightened into rose-quartz gray. Wisps of images still clung to me.

White paper. Marigold petals. The endless green field.

I'd been asleep for only a few hours, Tor less than that. He'd watched me for a while after he'd thought I'd gone to sleep.

But, between the tiny amount of sleep I'd managed and the physical release of sex in general, and with Tor in particular, I was revitalized. He still slept, more deeply than I'd ever seen him.

"Pax? Can you hear me?"

"Ailith? Are you here?"

"No, but we're close. But we couldn't convince Oliver to come with us, Pax."

"He has to be here."

"I know, but—"

The reason this hot spring had been abandoned was

clear at last.

What I'd believed to be rocks were, in fact, corpses.

Many of them, human and animal, radiating out from around the pool.

I bit the back of my hand so I wouldn't scream.

"Ailith? Ailith! Ai—"

"Tor!" I gave his shoulder a violent shake. In seconds, he was awake and on his feet, the hunter in him ready to fight.

"Ailith? Are you okay?"

Wordlessly, I pointed at the spread of bodies.

Tor inhaled sharply, his eyes wide. He walked over to the carcass closest to him, a tiny caribou calf, and knelt beside it. As he ran his hands over its body, the pressure of his fingers shifted the frail bones beneath its molting pelt. Finding nothing, he peered into its eyes and mouth.

"What the hell happened?" I asked, my voice wavering.

Tor's voice was steady. "The water. Remember the sensation when we first got in? *That's* why no one lives here. The water must be poisoned with something you wouldn't even have to drink. I should've known. It's an old trick."

"How can you be so calm?" I hated the sharp edge of hysteria in my voice. "We could've died!"

Tor shook his head. "I don't think we were ever in any real danger. And I'm not calm." It was true; his hands were trembling. "Are you okay?" he asked.

"Well, I'm better off than them." An insane urge to giggle bubbled up inside me "I can't imagine rabbits drinking from hot springs."

"Hares. And I don't think they did." Tor scraped up some of the dirt around the pool and rubbed it between his fingers. "I think the ground's been poisoned. The hares and caribou ate whatever plants they found, and everything else ate them."

"What about those people?" I asked, pointing at the huddle of human corpses. Without the interference of insects, their skin had desiccated into thick leather kept supple by the steam. It clung to their bones and bared their teeth to the cold air. Their eyes stared blankly at the sky, the whites black and shriveled.

"Most likely they were poisoned by the water. Probably couldn't believe their luck when they found this place."

"Why would someone do this?"

He rubbed the markings on his forehead. "It was a war, Ailith. Believe me, this isn't the worst thing I've seen."

I believed him. "We need to bury them somehow. We should—"

"Ailith? Are you there? Are you all right?"

Pax.

"Yes, we're fine. We just… It's a long story. Listen, we're coming. Soon."

"He must come with you."

"Tor? Of course."

"No. The other. He must come with you."

"Oliver? Pax, he refused. He's not coming."

"He has to. If he doesn't, we won't succeed. Everything will fail."

"What do you mean? Pax, he's not going to—"

"He must." Pax sounded frantic now, his fear physically palpable in my mind. Images flashed through it. Myself, Tor, people I didn't recognize. Screaming, the wet sounds of people dying, and the taste of metal in the fine red mist that hung over all of us. Then, nothing. Only the world remained, silent and still.

"Pax, what is this? What am I seeing?"

"The future."

"Will Oliver prevent this from happening, Pax? Is that it?"

"He must come." And then he was gone.

"Tor, we *need* Oliver. Pax showed me the future. If Oliver doesn't come, everyone will die." I rested my face

145

in my hands. Tor's warmth inside me was a distant memory now.

Tor chewed at his lower lip. "So, if we don't arrive with Oliver, there's going to be a bloodbath?"

"That's what it looked like. Tor...all those people, dead."

"How does Pax know all this?"

"You're probably tired of hearing this, but I don't know. It *felt* true. Maybe that's his thing—seeing the future."

He dragged his hand down his face. "Right. Why not? Well, I guess we've got no choice then. It looks like we're going back to the Saints of Loving Grace."

"But how are we going to convince Oliver to come with us? Are we going to call his bluff?"

"No," said Tor, "we're going to join the game."

We laid the bodies together, side-by-side, and covered them with shale and rocks in a kind of makeshift cairn. It wasn't ideal, but it was the best we could do. I wanted to promise that we would come back and give them the burial they deserved, but it would've been a lie.

We turned back the way we'd come. Without any detours, the trip back to the village would be fast. Pax's voice had had a different quality this time, a lucidity that only comes with pain. I recognized it from my own voice, before my transformation.

As we marched, we tried to formulate a plan. With any luck, Tor's strategy of gaming Oliver would work.

"We have to make it clear to him that no one is to be killed. That we only want to get Pax and Cindra out. Ideally, no one will get as much as a splinter. We need to avoid that future at all costs."

"I agree it's ideal, Ailith, but it's not realistic. What if they fight back? Do you think they're going to allow us to saunter in and take them with us? They'll probably want to capture us as well. What do we do then? Surrender?"

"No, of course not. But when they see there are more of us... Or maybe we should sneak in and steal them back?"

"That would be a good idea if we knew anything about the camp. But we don't. Haven't they been kept in some kind of building the whole time? That's what I would've done, if I were holding them captive. Kept them inside so they had no idea where they were. After a while, even if they did manage to escape, they would be too confused to go far." From the authority in his voice, it was clear he spoke from experience.

"Okay, so we may have to confront them. But nobody needs to get hurt."

"Ailith, they kidnapped Pax and Cindra. They're holding them against their will. They're *torturing* them. Convincing them to let two cyborgs just walk out might be difficult. But I happen to agree with you."

"You do?" I didn't mean to sound surprised, but I was. "I just thought—"

"What? Once a killer, always a killer?"

Well, yes.

He must've seen the answer in my face because he stopped walking. Gripping me gently by the chin, he gazed into my eyes. "Ailith, the whole reason I became what we are was so I could stop killing. When I became a cyborg, I vowed I would never take a human life ever again, even in self-defense. Of course, that was before I found myself in this wasteland, but it still stands. I will never go back to that life. If I did, I would lose what little soul I have left."

I smiled at him and gave him a quick kiss on the chin. "Could we trade something for them? Like medicine? Or food?"

"I don't think we have enough of either to tempt them. Especially not if they think our nanites are going to cure

147

them. We'll have to see what happens when we get there. We'll scope the place out, see if we can't snatch them if they bring them above ground. Or, one of us can distract them, while the other two spirit them away. Oliver's a fast talker—it may just work. And if all else fails, we'll use some good old-fashioned intimidation." His optimism was catching.

And not like him at all. I almost expected him to start whistling.

"Are you okay?" I asked him.

"Yes. Why? What do you mean?"

"You're so…cheerful."

"Why wouldn't I be? It seems that nearly everyone on the planet—well, everyone in our part of it, anyway—is dead. There's no sun, no food, we have to walk everywhere, and we're about to beg a madman to help us break two unknown cyborgs out of a Terran stronghold. And—" He held up a hand as I rolled my eyes. "I have you. What more could I want?"

"God created Man
Man destroyed God
Man created God
God destroyed Man"

—*Terran protest chant, 2040*

33
CALLUM

My heart beat so hard my throat ached.

Keep still. Just keep your head down.

I was in the library, as far back into its depths as I could go. I'd gotten here a half hour ago to connect to one of the ports. I didn't know my way around it very well. I'd only come in because I was looking for some information the university deemed too sensitive to put on the internet.

The music blaring through my headphones was so loud I almost hadn't heard the explosions. They were just muffled booms, and I hadn't thought much of it until I'd glanced up and everyone had disappeared, including the librarian. I'd turned down the volume just as another one rippled through the silent room. Faint screams followed.

Terran extremists. It had to be. The ones who'd been protesting outside the university the last few weeks, railing against the developments the Advanced Artificial Intelligence Studies course was making. My course.

Another explosion had sounded, this one closer. I'd quickly packed up my bag and backed away toward the recesses of the paper archives, keeping my eyes on the door. I could hear footsteps in the hallway, running. Then another explosion, and they were silent.

No way. I'd come so far, had just gotten what I'd wanted for so long, and now I was going to die.

Yesterday, I couldn't believe where my life was going. Even though my hand had been trembling, I'd still made out the tiny CONGRATULATIONS at the top of the page, accepting me into the program at Pantheon Modern.

It had been my lucky year, although if I were honest with myself, it wasn't merely luck. I'd worked hard to get where I was. But still, I'd never imagined I'd get accepted to both the cyborg program and the advanced AI course at the university.

I'd been at the university for only six months, but the choice had been a no-brainer. No way would I have turned the Pantheon Modern program down. Why study artificial intelligence when you could practically become one yourself? University had been a fallback for me. The only real question had been whether to tell my parents now or wait until after I'd been through the process and then surprise them.

Not that it had mattered, either way. Their reaction was predictable. My mom would hug me and say, "That's wonderful!" My father would clap me on the back. Two minutes later, they'd be buried back in their work, anything I'd said a distant memory. It wasn't that they didn't care; they were just very busy. Like me, they studied artificial intelligence. It didn't leave room for much else.

I'd even been raised by a robot nanny, one of the first of her kind. She'd done everything my parents would've done: read to me, played with me, tucked me in at night. When her body had failed about three years ago, I'd had her made portable. Right now, she resided in my laptop.

I patted it through my bag. "Don't worry, Umbra, we'll be okay."

I'd been so excited. She was the first one I'd told. "What do you think, Umbra? Can you believe it?"

"You've worked very hard. You deserve it, and I'm proud of you," she'd said, her voice smooth and almost human, thanks to the reprogramming I'd done on her last year. Before that, she'd spoken

150

haltingly, her cadence stilted and formal.

"I guess I'd better start on my withdrawal letter, eh?"

"Perhaps you should consider staying at the university."

"What? What do you mean? You know how badly I've wanted this."

"Perhaps it would be safer if you stayed at the university."

"Safer? Safer for who?" At first, the activists had been content to chant mantras and wave placards, but a week ago, things had turned ugly. Labs had been broken into and equipment destroyed; some of my classmates had been assaulted.

And now, it seemed, they'd taken their protest to the next level. Had people been killed? If so, how many? I had no idea where they were; it was best to stay put and wait it out. Better to remain here where I would know if anyone came in than run into them in the hallway.

I wished I'd already become a cyborg. Then I could find whoever was doing this and face them head-on, maybe save someone. But I wasn't a cyborg, not yet.

"The procedure for becoming a cyborg is risky," Umbra had said.

"Yeah, but it couldn't be a huge risk, otherwise they wouldn't be doing it at all, right?"

I'd been sworn to secrecy on the exact nature of the process, but of course, I'd told Umbra. It was so exciting, a completely new generation of cyborg, more advanced than anything we were thinking about at the university.

Besides, I was willing to take any risk if it meant becoming a cyborg. The fact that it would be totally awesome aside, I truly believed it would help with situations like the protestors. Once they saw how seamlessly biology and technology integrated, how it would only enhance what they already were, they couldn't possibly be against it.

Umbra and I had talked about the Terrans at length for months.

"Whether they like it or not, Umbra, this is just the way the world is heading. Artificial intelligence, sentient artificial intelligence, is going to happen, and sooner than they think. They're only fighting the inevitable."

151

"They believe artilects will make humans obsolete, maybe even threaten your extinction," Umbra had replied.

"Well, thanks to popular media, people assume artilects will be evil and enslave the human race."

"Callum, they think the same about cyborgs," she'd reminded me.

It was true. Not the ones with biomechatronics, but the ones who had enhancements they didn't need. The Terrans interpreted it as though cyborgs were arming themselves over regular humans. They worried the cyborgs and artilects would team up and destroy them.

"They say cyberization will make us no longer human. They would shit a brick if they knew what Pantheon Modern was up to. So would the Cosmists," I'd said.

When I became a cyborg, I'd show them how non-threatening it was. And how wonderful. There were so many amazing things about it that they didn't seem to see. Integrating ourselves with machines would preserve our humanity, not threaten it. We would live longer, be able to do more, go further. In fact, the way things were going in the world, it might be the only way for humanity to survive.

More footsteps sounded in the hallway, heavy, booted feet pounding in unison as they ran. Far down the hallway there was a roar, the crack of gunfire, a scream. Then nothing. I started toward the front door.

"Area clear. Target down," a voice said on the other side.

A transcom crackled into life. "Copy that. Move out."

I released the breath I'd been holding. I was safe. I could still become a cyborg, and then they'd see. Everyone, Terrans and Cosmists alike. It wouldn't be long now until they understood how important this time in history was for us all.

"I don't know what the big deal is, Ed. I'd personally love an artilect husband. Works all day, never complains, has lots of stamina where it counts, if you get what I mean. Maybe that's the problem, Ed. Maybe it's just men worrying that they're going to be replaced by a superior model."

—Shirley Novak, CNN Tech Watch, 2039

34
AILITH

We crested the hill beside the Saints of Loving Grace early the next morning. The loudspeaker calling the parishioners to service cleared the latest thread from my mind. The boy in the university library, Callum, was a new one. Where was he now? He must've become a cyborg and still be alive if I could inhabit him.

"Nice timing," Tor remarked.

It was. For Tor's plan to work, we needed as many of them present as possible. "Are you ready?"

"Showtime."

Oliver's face was like thunder as we burst through the door at the back of the hall, interrupting whatever exalted ramblings he'd planned for that day. Every other head in the room turned toward us, their eyes wide with shock.

Celeste, in her usual post as close to Oliver as she could manage, was the first to react. "Ailith!" she called, genuine joy on her face.

Oliver rushed down the center aisle toward us, his hand knotted into fists. "What are you doing here?" His façade slipped, and his voice dripped with venom. "I told you never to come back."

"Go," Tor told me.

I hurried back the way Oliver had come, toward the pulpit at the head of the room. Oliver grabbed at my arm as I passed, but Tor stepped casually between us, sweeping him up in the bear hug of old friends. As strong as Oliver may have been, he was no match for Tor, and there was nothing he could do short of assaulting another god in front of their worshippers.

Once I reached the pulpit, I raised my hands to silence the buzzing crowd. I tried to appear as beatific and ethereal as possible, my face calm and serene. "Members of the Saints of Loving Grace, you have always been unwavering in your belief in us. Your piety has made our very existence possible, for without you, we would have no reason to exist. I—"

Tor widened his eyes and inclined his head, indicating that I'd better hurry the hell up.

"I am sorry, then, to pass along some troubling news. You have already met three of us, survivors of the apocalypse that you, in your wisdom, predicted was coming. There are, in fact, two more of us." There was an initial gasp of delight amongst the crowd then a muttering as it dawned on them that I wasn't announcing good news.

"It seems they have been taken captive by a group of Terrans, whom you know do not feel the way you do about us. We wish to ask for your assistance in freeing them. We have no desire to bring violence upon them, no matter what they have done. We are hoping that by the sheer force of our numbers and power of our faith, they will see sense and release them. Will you help us?"

Silence weighed heavily on the room before it erupted into chaos. Everyone spoke at once, their voices rising in a furious crescendo over our heads. Tor finally stepped out of Oliver's way, and he sprinted to the pulpit.

Is he going to hit me?

He didn't. Instead, he raised his hands and addressed the crowd, entreating them to be quiet. As the roar died to a scattering of whispers, he spoke. "Please, I know what you have heard is disturbing." He shot me a glare that promised a world of pain. "But this is a matter between us artilects. We do not need you to get involved."

"But Ailith said—"

I was surprised to see Celeste standing before the crowd, her voice steady and strong as she faced Oliver.

"I heard what Ailith said. But there is no way we can retrieve the other…artilects without risking *your* lives. And I am not willing to do that. You have seen what these Terrans are capable of. Look at what they did to the world. You might all die." He slashed his hand through the air.

"No." I stepped in front of Oliver. "I believe we can save them without any violence on either side. That the mere sight of you and your faith will be enough to sway them. I understand your Divine is trying to protect you. He *is* noble like that."

Another death stare.

"Don't make me call your bluff," I whispered, so low only he heard me.

Something in his face changed then, and we'd won.

All eyes turned reflexively toward Oliver, awaiting his decision.

"You'll regret this," he whispered back then stepped forward to the edge of the dais. "We will go and help the other artilects. I shall meet now with Ailith and Tor and decide on a plan of action. You are all dismissed for now. I will call for you to gather when we have decided."

I walked among the crowd as they hurried out of the hall, eager to obey Oliver's wishes. Many of them chattered excitedly to each other, and I regretted deceiving them. But no harm would come to them, and we needed them. I just hoped this gamble would pay off. A small hand slid into mine, and I turned to see Celeste, her face pink with elation.

"Oh, Ailith, isn't it exciting! We're actually going to be part of something. No longer standing by as the world changes around us. We're finally seizing our destiny and *taking action.*"

"Surely you won't be going?" I asked, surprised. In our plan, only the men and women, *adult* men and women, would be participating.

She faltered. "What? But why? I have as much faith as anyone."

"Oh, Celeste, I know." I touched her arm. "But you're so young and—"

"I survived as well as everyone else, didn't I?" Her face flushed a deep scarlet.

"Of course you have. It's only... I'm trying to protect you."

Her face softened a bit. "But *we* should be protecting *you*. It's our fate."

Fucking Oliver. I hoped the faith these people had in him was justified. Not that I was any better.

When everyone had left the hall, Oliver took us to his living quarters. Each of the men in the village had their own residence, while the woman lived together in the large house in the center. His home was more modest than I'd expected, but perhaps that was part of his disguise.

Was he living up to their expectations of what an artilect god was? Or had they adjusted their beliefs accordingly? If his house was anything to go by, the Saints were unsure of Oliver's level of sentience. His house had been decorated sufficiently to reflect someone with likes and dislikes, but with enough austerity to suit a tenant who had little emotional attachment to such things.

The door crashed shut behind us.

"What the fuck do you think you're doing? I told you not to come back. I told you what would happen if you did."

"I don't believe you. I don't think you would ever hurt these people. After all, who would stroke your ego if you killed them all?"

"But why did you come back? I understood we'd reached an agreement..."

"Pax, one of the cyborgs we need to rescue, insists that we need you to be successful." Maybe I could appeal to his ego.

"Bullshit. It's a fucking trap. Doesn't the whole thing seem a bit shady to you? Surely you see it?" he addressed Tor.

Tor glanced from me to him, his eyes wary. "Yes, it does. But," he continued as I started to protest, "we do have reason to believe it's not."

"How do you even know you're talking to another cyborg? Maybe you're talking to yourself." He sneered at me.

"Look, this is happening. Unless you want your followers to see how full of it you are. Do you think they'll continue to follow a god who stood by as others were tortured and killed? Not to mention, if Pax and Cindra are fallible, it means you are too. What makes you a god if you can die like any other man?"

"Protecting my people is what makes me a god," he replied. "Instead, you want me to send them into a situation where you can't guarantee their safety. You have no idea what we're walking into."

Of course, he was right.

Pax's vision of the future haunted me. "We can resolve this peacefully. We *will* resolve this peacefully. We have to." *If I can't use his ego against him, maybe I can exploit his self-interest.*

157

"Besides, what if the Terrans find out about you? That there's an artilect, the very thing they helped destroy the world to prevent, living a few miles away. What would you do then? Flee to draw any conflict away from your followers? Or expect them to die defending you?"

"That would never happen. No one knows about us," he said, but the paleness of his face told me otherwise.

"I'm sure my tolerance for torture wouldn't be very high, Oliver. I'd probably tell them everything I knew."

"Maybe you'd never get that far. It's a dangerous world out there."

Tor stiffened next to me, and I brushed his arm. "We'd expose you long before that ever happened. These people are resourceful. They'd survive."

"Oliver, after this, you can come back here. You don't have to stay with us." Tor tried to placate him.

"Thank you, Tor. How very magnanimous of you."

"Can we please come up with a plan? We can fight about this later." *We don't have time for this.*

After an hour, we'd finally devised a strategy. I wasn't sure it was the best, but it was the only one we agreed on. Tor and I were to go on ahead, while Oliver got the Saints of Loving Grace organized. We would act as scouts, reporting back to Oliver when they arrived.

I sketched a rough map for them to follow, trying to be as specific as possible.

Oliver barely glanced at it. "You don't know where they are, do you?"

"I do. It's… We haven't *been* there, as such."

By this time, Oliver was herding us toward the door. "Whatever. We'll manage."

"And remember, nobody gets hurt!" We had to avoid Pax's future, or we were done for, all of us.

"Oh, for fuck's sake. This is a brilliant plan, isn't it? Who cares if a few Terrans get wounded? They're

158

obsolete."

"Yes, well, you've got no choice now, do you?"

"You're wrong, Ailith. There's always a choice." And with that, he slammed the door in our faces.

"...and with assassination of Novus CEO Robin Leung, the Prime Minister has called for an indefinite ban on further research and production of any artificial life. Those still in existence will be allowed to live out their natural lives—if you can call it that—but all individuals with robotic components have been issued with a notice of removal. That goes for anything functional or cosmetic. Now, we've heard rumors of cyborgs who don't have any noticeable physical differences, who appear to be fully organic, but these rumors are unsubstantiated and likely started by those who wish to stir up further controversy..."

—Shirley Novak, CNN Tech Watch, 2040

35
KALBIR

I had to admit; Ahar was stunning. Red had always made me look sallow, but the crimson fabric of her lehenga choli made her skin look like tawny cream. Our mother had spent months on the intricate embroidery, coaxing peacocks and twisting vines out of the gold satin. She had pricked her fingers many times while sewing it; I hoped the blood-spotted ribbons would prove to be a blessing.

Our mother was annoyed because I, the eldest sister, showed zero interest in getting married. I'd tried to explain it to her on numerous occasions, but she simply pursed her lips and turned away. Ahar understood. She knew I wanted more than the future our mother wanted for me. I'd wanted more from the time I was a little girl.

Mother, of course, would argue, saying I would still be able to do everything I wanted, that I could have a husband, and children, and the career I'd always dreamed of. But I couldn't, and Ahar knew it. She'd kept my secret, even from Aadi, and would keep it until my death, if that should happen.

Ahar turned slightly, catching my eye and smiling. To me, she seemed stifled, weighed down by the heavy gold of her jewelry. The red and ivory of the bangles I'd given her this morning reflected the overhead light. She'd placed them above all the others on her arm, closest to her heart.

My ass was aching as the Giani began the prayers of the laavan pheras. I surreptitiously checked my watch: it had already been half an hour. I shifted, trying to relieve the pressure. The bottom of my choli cut into my stomach.

Why had I eaten so much?

The fullness of my belly lulled me; my eyelids drooped. I stifled a laugh, picturing my mother's face if I were to fall asleep. She was already annoyed with me. I'd wanted to wear black today—it was the color I was most comfortable in. We'd fought, and now I was wearing green.

My attention wandered from the ceremony to the gurudwara itself. The ornate white columns and arches of the temple soared over the crowd, inlaid with colorful enamel flowers and leaves and festooned with massive ivory peonies and orchids. Had they been carved by human hands? Or had they come off some robotic assembly line? My heart quailed.

I was entering the Pantheon Modern cyborg program in a few days. Would I become a robot? Mindless, capable of only performing specific mundane tasks, over and over? Would that be any different from my life now?

No. They'd assured me I would still be the same person, just better. Besides, whatever was going to happen, it had to be better than being ordinary.

Even so, Ahar couldn't understand why I would want to become a cyborg. When I'd gone to her with the news of my acceptance, she'd bustled me into her closet and shut the door the way she'd done when we were children.

161

"Aren't you worried about what's going to happen to you afterward? If people will still see you as human? What if they treat you the way they treat the robots?" she'd whispered as we'd crouched in the dark.

She had a point. Robots weren't exactly treated well right now with all the tension between the Cosmists and the Terrans. I'd seen many of them being abused, ignored, spat on...even knocked over in the street as they minded their own business.

It was especially hard for the androids, the ones who looked so human. I'd have thought creating them to mimic us would make people want to protect them, to treat them with kindness, but it seemed to have the opposite effect. The more human they seemed, the more people wanted to exploit them.

Cyborgs were a little different. For some people, like those who'd lost limbs, it made sense. And it was fashionable in some circles. Dermal augmentations were popular with the kids in our neighborhood, the incandescent patterns flashing and throbbing under their skin. But those were teenagers, and the implants were temporary. Choosing to become a cyborg when you didn't have to, making a machine a permanent part of yourself, was a different matter altogether. And everybody, Terrans and Cosmists alike, agreed on that.

"Ahar! Relax. They've assured me that nobody will be able to tell I'm a cyborg. I'll look completely human. Anyway, I don't care. I want people to know. It's their problem if they can't accept it."

"That's hardly helped the androids, though, has it? Seriously Kal, for all your open-mindedness about robots and cyborgs, not once have I ever heard you defend them when someone we know has spoken against them, or worse. You just like to talk about how liberal you are. You still look the other way."

It hurt because it was true. "Well, I'm making up for it now, aren't I?"

"Plus, what will Mother say? What will her friends say?" Ahar tried to look severe, but the thought of our mother's best friend, Mrs. Kahttri's, face was too much and she snorted. I hadn't dared to tell

162

Mother what I'd been up to. Although she would never openly discriminate against a cyborg or even a robot, she was staunchly on the Terran side of the artilect debate. She didn't mind cyborgs as much, since she saw them as humans with some machine parts, but the most recent android models made her nervous. I had to admit, they seemed pretty damn close to human, talking and smiling stiffly as they went about their duties, but it wasn't like they were sentient. They were glorified toasters.

She'd whispered to my aunty that she didn't mind the androids per se, since they were useful, and did my aunty know that Mrs. Khattri had one? And it did all the work at home and made wonderful roti, and wasn't that incredible, but why did they have to make them appear so human? Why give them faces and eight fingers and two thumbs, two arms and two legs? My aunty had wondered if Mrs. Khattri's android was anatomically correct, scandalizing my mother.

There was a man standing by one of the pillars, just out of sight of the general crowd. He looked straight out of television: tall and broad, his silver hair shorn close to his skull. He wore pressed black trousers and a black button-up shirt. A tinted visor obscured his eyes.

I glanced around. No one else seemed to notice him. But he noticed me. He held up a black card, with a single bronze symbol embossed on it. I had to squint to make it out.

A stylized PM. Pantheon Modern. Crap. Where the hell was my mother? Whatever he wanted, it couldn't be good.

Voices rose in chorus to the final hymns, and my attention snapped back to the wedding. It was nearly over. I had to get that man out of view before my mother saw him and wandered over to welcome him, throwing her arms around him like he was just another member of the family.

As the karah parshad was passed around, Ahar smiled at me. She truly did look radiant. Aadi, his fingers resting on the hilt of his krijpan, winked at me. She was going to tell him tonight that she was pregnant. He'd be overjoyed. An unexpected pang of sadness caught me off guard.

As the guests filed out of the temple, the stranger's hand fell on my shoulder. "Kalbir Anand?"

"Yes."

"My name is Dominic. We need to talk."

"Fine, but not here. Follow me." I kept my eyes on my mother. She was busy accepting congratulations and hadn't noticed us yet. We mingled with the crowd until we reached the main hallway. I pulled him down to the end, where there was an alcove just large enough for the two of us and a hideous orange vase.

"What's going on?"

"I'm from Pantheon Modern."

"Yeah, I can see that. What do you want? Why are you here? This isn't really a good time."

"It never is," he replied. "We have a problem."

"What do you mean? What problem?"

Did they find out I'd told Ahar everything? Was I in trouble?" "Look, I—"

"Program Omega has been compromised." Even though his voice was low, I peeked around the corner to see if anyone was listening. The hall had fallen silent. Everyone was getting into their cars to head to the reception hall.

"What does that mean? I'm no longer a part of it?"

"That's up to you. Things are going to start moving very fast now. If you want to remain part of the program, you have to come with me, now."

"Now? I can't come now. My sister just got married. People will notice if I'm not there."

"It doesn't matter."

"You've never met my mother."

"People will be looking for you. To kill you."

"What? But I'm not even a cyborg yet!"

"It doesn't matter. You will be."

"Fine. Then I won't go through with it. I won't tell anyone anything."

"No, you won't." He opened his blazer. A tiny syringe was

164

tucked into his waistband. He shifted his weight, trapping me in the alcove.

Cold realization dawned.

"I'm sorry," he said.

"Wait. Stop, please."

"Miss Anand, I came here to help you. I don't think you understand the stakes here. I can't let you go. You may think you can keep a secret, but you can't."

"I—" I wanted to insist that I could, but he was right. I hadn't kept it a secret from Ahar.

Ahar. Did they know I'd told her?

"So my only choice is to come with you now, or you'll kill me?"

"Yes. I can only protect you if you come with me. If I can't protect you, I have to kill you. A war has started, Miss Anand, and you're part of it, whether you like it or not. What part of it you are is up to you."

Tears blurred my vision. I bit my lip to try to stop them.

Dominic laid his hand on my arm. "Please, miss. I don't want to kill you. I'm trying to save you. I... You've been my charge from the beginning. I don't want to lose you." He removed the visor. He was younger than I'd first suspected, prematurely gray. His eyes matched my choli, the vibrant green of old jade.

"You've been following me since the beginning? That was months ago."

"Yes. Please, let me take you with me."

"How do I know you're not one of the people who want to kill me?"

"You don't. You have to trust me."

My mother. Ahar. What would they do if I suddenly disappeared? It would kill my mother, ruin the start of Ahar's marriage.

My death, right here and now, would be worse. Wouldn't it?

"If you've been following me for so long, then you know my mother, my sister?"

"Yes."

165

"If I disappear... They... Please, can I have until tomorrow? Ahar leaves for her honeymoon. I'll think of something to tell my mother. That I need to go away for work or something. Please?"

He didn't say anything for what seemed like hours. A car horn honked outside. Mother.

It seemed to rouse him. "Fine. Tomorrow. Talk to no one until then. I'll be watching. If I have to take you out, I will."

I crashed through the front doors of the hall just as my mother was reaching them.

"Kalbir! There you are. Where have you—" She saw the tearstains on my face and patted my arm. "Oh, foolish girl. Don't you worry. You'll see just as much of Ahar as before. They only live around the corner."

I hiccupped. "I know. It's just that I'll miss her. Things will be different now. Everything's changing."

"Things must change, or the world will stop turning. You'll be sisters forever, no matter what happens."

As we drove away from the gurudwara, I wondered just how long forever would be.

"...Actually, Shirley, you wouldn't even need nuclear weapons to destroy the world. Nothing as brutal as that. You get enough cities burning for long enough at the right time of year, and boom, total disruption to the ecosystem. Wildfires and incendiary lightning would wipe out arable land. Smoke would fill the clouds, and toxic rain would fall. Not to mention how people would react. You've seen how they get when they think they're going to be snowed in for a few days..."

—*Alexander Petrov, CNN Tech Watch, 2040*

36
AILITH

"Do you think they'll show up?" We had stopped to rest, and I'd followed one of the glittering threads. The fullness in my belly from food I hadn't eaten was strangely comforting.

"I'm not sure. I don't think you should've threatened him like that. He's not the kind of man to take something like that lightly."

I didn't want to admit it, but I agreed. The expression on Oliver's face as he'd shut the door promised murder. *I don't care.* We'd deal with Oliver after Pax and Cindra were safe.

We'd walked through the night and most of the morning to reach the area of the Terran camp. It had been a miserable trek.

The mountain pass was freezing, a harsh coldness that was agonizing to breathe. Flanked by miles of sheer rock face on one side and near-vertical embankment on the other, we'd been forced to take the road. The asphalt was marred with potholes and long, vicious cracks, the painted lines weathered away.

Avalanches had strewn sections of our path with debris, and we picked our way around the chunks of stone swiftly and silently, straining our ears for the telltale rumble. At the crest of the pass was a wide shoulder where tourists could pull over and view the forest in all its immense splendor. To me, it looked like an instrument of torture, infinite metal spikes waiting for a curious misstep.

By the time we'd crossed and were picking our way down the other side, my lungs felt as though they'd collapse.

"You'd think they would've given us reinforced lungs." Each word felt like it would be my last.

Tor's laugh was barely more than a wheeze. "They were probably worried we'd make smoking a thing again."

"Ailith? Are you here?"

Pax. I was finally going to be able to tell him yes.

We could see the windmill now, cobbled together from stone and what appeared to be metal grating. It spun idly. The wind that had taken our breath away in the pass had little power here.

The connection between us was clear, and I pinpointed their location.

"Yes! Pax, we're here. Well, almost. We're about a mile away."

"Good. Is Oliver with you?"

"Not yet, but he's coming. And he's leading reinforcements."

Pax's relief swept through me, a flurry that warmed my chest. *"Something's happening. I think we're out of time."*

"What? What do you mean, Pax? What's happening?"

"The ones who insisted on using the nanites, they're dying. I believe they're going to kill us."

"Don't worry. We won't let them hurt you. Tell Cindra we're

168

coming."

"And Oliver is coming, for sure?"

"Yes," I lied. *"He'll be here any minute."* I hope.

At the outskirts of the Terran village, an irregular wood-and-wire fence wove in and out of the trees, knotted scraps of cloth swaying in the mild wind. It was strangely still. No guards patrolled the perimeter; nobody was watching out for strangers.

"I can't see anyone."

Tor's face drew tight. "Yeah, I noticed that too. Believe me, it's not a good thing."

"What do you mean? Is it not just carelessness?"

"It could mean they believe they're too strong to fear outsiders. They have five years of experience surviving, so their confidence is probably justified. Or, like Pax said, something is happening, something important. It may also mean they've seen us, and they want us to think they haven't. They might've been aware of us all along." He put his hand on my arm. "Ailith, I know you don't want to hear this, but you have to consider the possibility that Pax has told them about us."

"He wouldn't! He…" Pax's unnatural calmness. His insistence that Oliver be with us. *Could it be that he…?* "No. I don't think it's possible." I didn't sound convincing even to my own ears. "But Cindra…what I saw…what she felt—"

"He may not have intended to betray you, Ailith. But if they're being tortured…they've been captive for days. And people have no law but their own moral compass now. If you were a Terran, you would believe in the rightness of what they were doing, no matter how extreme the method."

"I would never torture someone! I don't even want the Terrans to get hurt. Even if they are monsters." The fuse on my temper started to burn.

169

"I'm not saying what they're doing is right. But you've only been awake for a couple of weeks. These people have lived in this world for *five years*. They didn't survive through kindness."

"You don't know that!" I didn't want him to be right. Pax's vision of the future hovered at the edge of my mind.

"Look, I hope you're right." He squeezed my hand. "Ailith, despite what these people have done, we can't let them be hurt. We were supposed to act as a bridge between the Cosmists and the Terrans. Nothing's changed. If we play it right, maybe they'll let go of the past and work together. I mean, none of that matters anymore, does it? Nobody's going to be creating artilects now. The war is over. They need to help each other. You've seen what will happen otherwise."

"I agree with you on that, at least," I replied.

We found a copse on a rise close to the camp that would allow us to observe it while keeping out of sight. Not that it mattered. Either the Terrans had already seen us, or they were too distracted to notice. We finally had the opportunity to see the people who were capable of committing such terrible acts against other human beings.

I wasn't sure what I'd expected evil to look like, but I was disappointed. The Terran village seemed like any other village before the war, albeit more rustic. The houses were similar to those of the Saints, though clad in patched, modern, slatted siding rather than metal sheets. Behind them, the backyards were open, strewn with the debris of normal lives.

The few children I saw were bundled up against the cold, darting from house to house as they chased each other. Teenagers gathered sticks, which they threw onto a growing pile. Women and men alike were busy with a slew of mundane activities. Some were hanging plants for drying, others, meat. Laughter wafted on the air, mingled

170

with the smells of cooking.

If I hadn't seen them electrocuting Cindra with my own eyes, felt it on our skin, I never would've believed it.

"How many people do you think there are?" I asked Tor.

He scanned the village. "I'm not sure. Eighty, maybe ninety. There may be even more inside."

Ninety people. Less than half the number of the Saints. I liked those odds.

"They look so normal," I said.

A sad smile tugged at the corners of Tor's mouth. "What did you expect? Evil comes in all forms. It's a matter of perspective."

I was about to argue with him that, no, torturing innocent people was *not* a matter of perspective when there was a stirring below us. Whatever Pax had predicted was going to happen was happening *now*. And Oliver was nowhere in sight.

Word passed quickly and quietly through the crowd. Terrans gathered at the north end of the village, where two thick poles stood. A commotion from the south drew our attention. *Pax and Cindra.* For the first time, I saw them from the outside. They looked different through my own eyes.

The Terrans hadn't bothered to dress them for the cold. Cindra was stumbling, long hair matted over her face. Her bronze skin was marred with burns, and the scars of many others were fading on her thin arms. It made me ill, knowing how quickly we healed. Those marks weren't torture for information, but for pleasure.

Pax walked calmly, head up, eyes searching for me.

"No one's coming to help you, freak," someone jeered.

That was some good news, at least; they didn't know we were here. One of the men flanking Pax punched him in the back of the head. As he fell to his knees, I gently pulled

171

on his thread.

"Pax! Stop looking for us. You'll give us away."

"Is Oliver here?"

"No, not yet."

"He must be here!"

"He'll be here, I promise. You'll understand when you meet him. He likes to make a grand entrance." I hoped it was a promise I would keep. *Come on, Oliver, you asshole.*

The Terrans led Pax and Cindra to the two poles and began tying each to one.

"Scared yet?" one of the men asked Pax.

Pax seemed to consider the question for a few seconds then shook his head. The man slipped a knife from under his coat and slid it between Pax's ribs. He grunted and doubled over, but didn't cry out. The man angled the knife for another thrust.

"I've had enough. Forget waiting for Oliver. I'm not going to sit here and watch Pax get stabbed to death." I started to stand.

"Ailith, stop." Tor's voice was cold steel.

"Tor, we have to help him. We can't—"

"He'll heal. We have to give Oliver more time."

"What if he doesn't come?" We were both thinking it.

Tor ignored me. "We still have some time. Wait."

Every nerve in my body was pulled taut as the Terrans finished tying Pax and Cindra to the poles and piled up wood around their feet. They were going to burn them alive.

"Tor."

"Not many other ways to kill a cyborg." The muscles in his jaw worked overtime. He was getting close to his limit. Had Pax seen what I had? The others like us, immolating themselves? Had he told the Terrans? Or was it a lucky guess?

A heated discussion broke out within the crowd

172

beneath us.

"I can't believe you're actually going to go through with this. I though you merely wanted to scare them. *We* can't do this."

The speaker was one of the women I'd seen hanging herbs.

"They've not done anything."

"Not done anything? They've killed us, Naomi. Cole, Seska—they're dead because of these two."

"They *told* you the nanites wouldn't work on us. They told you it would kill them. You didn't want to listen."

The man ignored her "They're abominations, anyway. If it weren't for their kind, we wouldn't be here, living like this. Like savages. I was a fucking architect before their war."

"It wasn't just *their* war. And abomination?" she scoffed. "You were perfectly happy to take advantage of their *abomination* when you thought it would help you. When we found each other, when we established this camp, we agreed there would be no more unnecessary violence. How else are we supposed to survive?"

"They're not human." He said it slowly, as though he were speaking to a child. "How many times can we have this discussion? Does that seem human to you?" He pointed at Pax, who was standing straight again, his wounds forgotten.

"Of course they are. Look at them!"

"I am. This is how they get you. Why do you think they changed them only on the inside? Why do you think the Cosmists wanted to make artilects look human? They will invade us quietly, like a cancer, destroying us one by one until we're extinct. How can you be so blind?"

"Who's *they*? There is no 'they.' They're not *artilects*! They're human. So what if they've been…enhanced? We should be working *with* them, using their abilities to help us

173

survive."

Murmurs of assent passed between some members of the crowd, but none spoke up for us.

"Anyone else who thinks we should let them live, step forward. Let them murder us in our sleep. Enslave our children."

"Oh Jack, for God's—"

"Who else?" he thundered. The crowd was silent. "Right. It's decided. Let's get on with it. I want to have this ugly business finished. Now."

Oliver, where are you?

"Can't you see into Oliver?" Tor asked. "Find out where they are?"

"Yes. No. I can't. I need to be here if something happens. I might not be able to get out of him in time."

The woman, Naomi, stepped back into the crowd, her face ashen. Jack and another man lit two large torches and approached the poles. Cindra screamed. Pax remained as calm as ever.

"Tor?" I gathered myself into a crouch.

Jack bent to place the torch at Cindra's feet. Naomi shouted and tried to push her way to the stakes. While some people strove to hold her back, reality set in for others, and they began pushing through the crowd.

A roar sounded behind us. Oliver had arrived. But that wasn't right. We were supposed to go in quietly, diplomatically, our hands raised in peace.

The Saints rushed past us; they were armed.

That future was happening, now.

We believed we would know our Divine when we saw him. How could we not? Not only would he emerge from the maelstrom unscathed while the rest of the world was branded by the fire, but he would bring the dead back to life, sort the righteous from the unbelievers, and lead us forward into a new future.

—Celeste Steed, *The Second Coming*

37

AILITH

"You'll regret this."

I should've paid attention.

Someone once told me that when something terrible happened, time slowed. I wished that was true. I could've stopped what was happening. But it didn't, and I couldn't.

Oliver and his followers swarmed into the Terran camp and cut them down. They wore their martyrdom on their faces, their destiny finally coming to pass. Oliver gazed up to where Tor and I were still crouched in shock and smirked his triumph.

There's always a choice.

The Saints didn't discriminate as they killed. Axes rose and fell, metal grated against bone, and precious bullets shrieked from the mouths of rifles. The air became hazy, and the ground finally got the moisture it so desperately needed.

Celeste reigned in the middle of the fray, her hair braided on top of her head like some warrior of old. Her lips were drawn back in a primal scream, and blood smeared her teeth. The Terrans scrambled for whatever weapons they could lay their hands on and tried to fight back.

From the pain in my throat, I was shouting, but the sound was drowned out by the furor below. Pax and Cindra were still tied to their posts, vulnerable and forgotten. The future Pax had shown me was supposed to be a distant one, not today. Darkness bloomed behind my eyes.

No. No. this can't be happening. I have to stop this.

I sprinted down the hill and entered the churning mass, grabbing the woman called Naomi from behind. I needed to make her stop, help her see reason. If anyone would listen to me, she would.

Her shoulders and her collarbone crushed and splintered beneath my hands. *My hands.* They were too large, too strong.

Tor's hands.

She tried to turn toward me, but I held her fast. My hands wouldn't let go. The jagged ends of her collarbone had punctured her neck, and she was bleeding.

Too much. Too fast.

When I finally released her, it was too late. As she fell to the ground at my feet, something in me that had been stretched too thin finally broke. I didn't want to hurt anyone, but I could no longer stop myself.

I seized the body closest to me. Saint or Terran, I didn't care; I just wanted them to stop. To be still. But the strength of Tor's body was out of my control. He'd had five years to learn restraint. I had seconds. Skin tore beneath my hands. Muscles ripped away from bone. Bullets peppered my chest, and still, I couldn't stop.

Finally, someone managed to slice the tendons in my legs and I fell facedown onto the sodden earth. A sudden

176

rush, a painful tearing in my mind, and I was back on the hill, on my back above the battlefield.

Tor lay motionless below; Pax stood above him, holding an axe slick with blood. Someone must've cut him free. I charged down the hill and barreled into him, crushing the breath out of his lanky body.

"You! You've betrayed us." I closed my hands around his throat.

"No. It was the only way to stop you," he said, his voice low and soothing. "It's over. Look."

I wanted to believe him. Tightening my hands around his neck, I risked an upward glance. He was right; it was over.

The ground was littered with bodies. Not a single Terran had been spared. Taken by surprise, they hadn't made sense of the chaos in time to fight back. Of the Saints of Loving Grace, nearly all were still standing. Celeste stood amongst the survivors, her face rosy with victory. She caught my eye and winked conspiratorially.

Dead. So many people. Dead. All because of me.

This time, I didn't vomit.

Tor.

I released Pax and dropped to his side. The gaping wounds in his calves flaunted bone, though the flesh had begun to knit together. It took all my strength to turn him over. He was a mess. Blood leaked from the slowly closing wounds in his chest. The bullets, pushed to the surface by the nanites, seemed far too small to cause such damage. His face was pale, his eyes closed.

I leaned forward to whisper in his ear. I wanted to tell him how sorry I was, how I hadn't meant for this, *any* of this, to happen.

As he felt my breath on his face, his hand shot out and gripped my arm. "Don't. Don't touch me. Never touch me again." His words were a splinter in my heart.

177

"Tor, I'm sorry. I'm so, so sorry." His fingers on my arm were agony, but I didn't pull away. "Tor, please."

"Go. Away."

"Well, that was fun, wasn't it?" Oliver swaggered over to where Tor lay, not a mark on him. "So much for your 'let's-all-love-each-other' plan."

"You did this." This kind of rage was new to me, and not unwelcome.

I'll kill him. Why not? I've had some practice today.

The voice inside me whooped. As I struggled to my feet, Tor's body twitched, and the blackness swirled at the edge of my vision.

No. No. No!

I was thrust back into myself by Celeste's scream. She was pointing at Tor, upset because he was injured.

But not for his sake.

"Blood. He's *bleeding*."

I didn't understand until I saw Oliver's face, horrified and frozen.

We'd been outed. Artilects didn't bleed.

We were in trouble.

178

"...and that's just in the short-term. Eventually that smoke would generate an ash cloud substantial enough to block the sun. And the effects would last for years. Freezing temperatures, very little sunlight, reduced precipitation, a thinning ozone. Nothing could survive. Not plants, not animals, not people. That's it. The human race is extinct. Yes, some would survive initially. But without food, potable water, or medical attention, for how long?"

—*Alexander Petrov, CNN Tech Watch, 2040*

38
AILITH

The air was as crisp as always when we arrived at the market. I waved at the other farmers as my father wove through the barricades to our regular stall. People were already lined up down the block; only the steel fences kept them from swarming us and fighting each other tooth and nail for a misshapen carrot. Well, that and the armed guards.

Who would've supposed vegetables would one day be worth more than their weight in gold? Not my father, that was for sure. When he was young, farmers were overlooked and under-valued. Now, thanks to a few mistakes with genetics and changes in the political climate, farmers were like rock stars.

We hadn't had a food shortage, far from it. But the sheer exclusivity of food grown in the ground was enough to make the most pest-riddled cauliflower a prize. Our specialty was garlic. Gourmet garlic grown from heirloom strains hundreds of years old; we were one of the few places left in the province licensed to grow it.

It was go-time. As soon as people were let through the gate, a crowd gathered in front of our stall. I lifted the bulb of garlic where they could see it. It was the first of the season, its picturesque skin a satiny-white mottled with silky purple, clinging tightly and softly undulating over each clove.

I slid the outer wrapper off with my thumb, careful not to press too hard and damage the flesh. The outer skin came off easily, the second, third, and fourth were progressively tighter. I took my time, but this close to the prize, the crowd was impatient, and the process was almost painful.

I broke the skin around the top of the bulb with my thumb, and the spiked tips of the cloves poked through. My thumb slid down either side of a single clove and broke it free from the cluster. It was firm and plump, encased in a dusky rose-colored skin, streaked with a rich walnut brown. The faintest scent rose from the plate at the bottom. Saliva rushed into my mouth, and the crowd before me licked their lips.

I sliced the end off the clove I'd liberated, the pungent tang stinging the inside of my nose. I inhaled deeply, and the crowd mimicked me, sighing in anticipation as I peeled off the rest of the skin. The cream-colored clove was smooth and round. Perfect.

I cut a thin slice and held it up to the crowd. It glistened wetly, my fingers sticky from its oil. I placed it on the tongue of the woman directly in front of me and watched as the raw garlic stung her mouth. She exhaled slowly through her nose, the scorching oil dripping down her throat.

My dad grinned at me. He would miss me being here with him. His natural shyness made him an awkward showman. Selling the garlic wasn't my thing either—I much preferred the growing—but since the death of my younger brother and mother last year, we'd needed each other to keep going. Selling had been my mother's job. She'd been the reason our stall was so popular, her small hands making the bulbs appear huge as she held them aloft with a delicate flourish, her voice so soft and rhythmic it caused the hairs on the back of your neck to stand up as you leaned in to catch every word.

180

A commotion a few stalls down the street caught the attention of the crowd. Guards pushed people back to form a perimeter around a package on the ground. More and more of these parcels had appeared lately. The police never said who the targets were, and nobody ever claimed responsibility. Everyone had a theory, of course. Some believed it was the Terrans protesting the development of AI, others that it was the Cosmists trying to demonstrate how necessary their technology was.

The guards forced through the whispering crowd, a bomb-disposal robot in tow. One of them typed instructions into the keypad on its back then it lay down and enveloped the bomb with its body. The crowd hushed and waited. At the last moment, before the bomb exploded, the robot turned its head in my direction. It had no eyes — they hadn't wanted to upset people by blowing up robots that were too humanoid—but it was looking at me.

The device finally obliged the crowd and exploded, the bot's body expanding slightly as it absorbed the impact. As the police dragged the ruined bot away, the crowd muttered in disappointment at the anti-climax.

"It doesn't seem fair, does it?" I said.

"What do you mean?" my father asked. He was inspecting the spot where the robot had lain.

"Using them like that. I mean, that's it. It's dead."

His jaw tensed. This was not a subject he liked to talk about. He'd become resolutely Terran after my mother and brother had died. He blamed robots and those who created them for their deaths, though it had been an accident. No one knew exactly why hundreds of automated vehicles had simply driven off the road. My father blamed the manufacturer, Novus, even though there was no evidence they were at fault. Only rumors.

"They're not alive, Ailith. Just because something looks, walks, and acts like a person, doesn't mean it is."

"I know, but still. Doesn't it seem a bit cruel to you? To build them simply for the purpose of killing them?"

"Would you rather it had been a person covering that bomb?

181

Getting themselves blown to bits?"

"Of course not. I'd rather there weren't bombs in the first place."

His mouth pressed into a thin line. We'd had this conversation before, and the outcome was always the same: us feeling awkward around each other for the rest of the day. He didn't understand why the Cosmists wanted to create artilects, why they wanted to create new life when there was already so much around them.

"Why can't they have children?" he'd say. He was even less comfortable with cyborgs. "It's unnatural. They're making themselves less human."

Since I'd become ill, he no longer said that. Though he hated the idea of cyborgs, in my case, he at least understood the attraction. My body was failing. Tomorrow, I was going to the hospital for what might be the last time. They couldn't cure what I had; slowing it down was the best they could do. But my doctor had called yesterday, with a new option. Something to do with nanites. He didn't have time to explain the details to me. And although my father didn't agree, he loved me.

He would understand. Even if I had tiny machines running through my veins, I'd still be me.

Omega, for you to understand how you're here, in this place, I must start at the beginning. Much of what I'll say, you won't understand. Many of these words, these ideas, will mean nothing to you, but they were meaningful to us, and it's because of us that you are here.

—*Cindra, Letter to Omega*

39
AILITH

We were back at the Saints of Loving Grace village. I'd tried to comfort myself by briefly living someone else's life, but I'd found only my own memories instead. It was strange being yourself inside yourself.

The Saints had called us the 'Children of Perdition,' and we were in no shape to insist otherwise. I had no idea what that even meant. We should've run; the Saints were no match for our speed or stamina. But we couldn't. Cindra was in shock. Tor was still injured. Oliver believed he could ingratiate himself with his followers again, and Pax, he continued as normal, as though we were simply on a day out from the asylum.

I could've run, gotten away, and come back for them later. But I couldn't leave them, especially Tor. After what had happened, and with whatever was going to happen, we needed to stick together. I'd caused this, and I would get us out of it.

They eventually put us in a horse shelter encased with electrified wire, as though we were some kind of exhibit.

Which, I guessed, we were. The village had sacrificed their house lights to supply its power. Trying to suck up, Oliver had tipped them off about the mechanical parts of us being vulnerable to electric shock. It wouldn't kill us, but it would incapacitate us. They'd forced us in with an axe to Cindra's throat. I bet Oliver had told them how useful beheading was as well. *Fucking Oliver.* He was the gift that kept on giving.

They called a meeting in the hall to decide what would become of us. A scuffle broke out at the door, as the men of the camp filed in and tried to shut it behind them. It was clear those days were over. A sizable group of women, led by Celeste and still wielding their weapons from the slaughter, forced their way in. The door slammed shut, and a few minutes later, half the men came back out, their faces subdued.

Oliver sulked in a front corner by himself, waiting for one of his former worshippers to acknowledge him. He caught me watching him and curled his lip. "Happy, Ailith? They're probably going to kill us now."

"Why did you do it, Oliver? How did you ever think it would end well?"

"I told you you'd regret coming here," he replied softly.

"That's how you planned to make me regret it? By killing a bunch of innocent people?"

Oliver laughed. "They weren't *innocent.* Surviving a war doesn't make someone innocent. Those people you killed are the same ones who would've prevented your existence in the first place if they'd had a choice. Think about what they were going to do. Murder two people just because their intention to exploit them wasn't paying off."

He dug the toe of his boot into the dirt floor. "They've been scavenging weapons and survivors, gathering their strength. What do you think they would've done if they'd discovered the Saints of Loving Grace?" he asked,

184

gesturing toward the surrounding village. "Do you really think they would've let us live in peace?"

"Your false peace. You *lied* to these people, Oliver," I reminded him.

Wait.

"Gathering their strength? You knew about the Terrans, didn't you? You used us."

He examined his fingernails. "Yes, I did. I make things that threaten us my business. Your friend there would've done the same." He inclined his head toward Tor, where he slumped against the wall. "I would've come up with other means to deal with them, but you forced my hand."

"Other means? Like what? Cutting their heads off while they were defenseless? We went to your bunker. We saw what you did."

He crossed his arms over his chest. "I did what I had to do. She was a threat to us, to you. Again, your friend would've done the same thing."

"No, he wouldn't. He's not a murderer."

Oliver laughed at that. "Well, if he wasn't before, he is now, thanks to you." His words were a sucker punch to my gut. It hurt all the more because he was right. Whether I'd meant to or not, I'd soaked Tor's hands with blood.

"You've ruined everything. You should've let me be. Look what you've done to these people. You've changed them forever, made them idolaters. Generations of sacrifice and preparation, for nothing. God doesn't exist for them anymore."

He's right.

The previous tranquility and bustling cheerfulness of the Saints was gone. People clustered together in small groups, their voices low. Amid their whispers, some watched us. The rest watched each other.

"Me? Oliver, *you're* the one who told them you were a god. How long did you think it would last? They'd have

185

found out eventually. And what would you have done then? Slaughtered them all and moved on?"

He was saved from answering by Celeste. Her hair was still knotted on her head, her face painted with blood. She stood taller, her former meekness gone.

"Celeste." The relief in Oliver's voice was clear. "You've come. I—"

"You've been sentenced to death," she said flatly, studying his face.

"Celeste! Why are you doing this? I thought we—"

"We what? Had something? Everything we had was based on a lie, Oliver. And not merely a lie. You've made us unbelievers, followers of a false god. You took our faith and twisted it, perverted it. You've condemned us all to Hell on this earth. Do you know they want me to die along with you? Because of what you did to me?"

"Condemned you? Did it ever occur to you that this might actually *be* Hell? And what I did *to* you? Are you sure you're not pissed because you found out you weren't spreading it for some machine? It's not like you needed much convincing." His lips twisted.

"They're not going to kill you, are they?" I interrupted. Even with everything that was happening, I didn't want Celeste to pay for what we'd done. The Saints massacre of the Terrans was reprehensible, but it had happened because of us. We'd manipulated them and exploited their faith and fear; the blame was ours.

"No." Celeste leaned forward on the handle of her axe. "Did you know that Oliver told us it was a Terran *military* camp, filled only with fighting men and women? That we went in willing to kill and die for your glorious cause?"

I stared at Oliver, incredulous. "No, I didn't."

Celeste continued. "See, one good thing that came from being manipulated into butchering other defenseless women and children is that we can never go back. We're no longer defenseless." She shifted her gaze to me. "It's a shame we need to kill *you,* Ailith. I understand you only did what you felt was right, like we did. You, on the other hand," she said, turning back to Oliver, "did not."

She leaned away from us and snapped her fingers at our guard. "Turn off the power."

He hesitated.

"Turn it off!" she snarled, fingering the blade of her axe.

As the humming of the bars went silent, Celeste sidled up to Oliver. "I suppose I should thank you," she said. "If you hadn't betrayed us, we'd still be living in the dark, waiting for a savior who was never going to come. Allowing our bodies to belong to anyone but ourselves, because we'd been told it was the right way, the way it's always been. But you've opened our eyes. Now we're going to save ourselves. You see," she said, low enough that only Oliver and I heard, "your deaths are only the beginning." She traced her hand down the side of Oliver's face and over his chest.

"What about all the pleasure I gave you?" Oliver whispered as she ran her fingers over the front of his trousers. She cupped him, and he let out a small gasp.

"Oh, sweetie," she replied with a sympathetic smile. "My pleasure was about as real as you were. Turn it back on." She gave me one last nod before walking away.

The swinging of her hips faded as another thread pulled me down.

"...all the fledging cyborgs have increased physical strength, although this has been concentrated in some more than others. Some have had emotional adjustments to make them more prone to certain reactions and decision-making methods. Memory capabilities and computational processes are also increased, but because the enhancements work differently in each subject we have no idea which will take, and if taken, to what degree. And as hard as we try to select applicants that are both physically and mentally capable of surviving the cyberization process, as you can see from our current rates, survival remains our biggest challenge. Causes of death vary, but most commonly include immune rejection of the nanites, heart attack, and, rarely, consumption by the nanites themselves. And then there are those who cannot cope psychologically with the changes, who become lost and aren't able to find their way back..."

—Mil Cothi, Pantheon Modern Cyborg Program Omega, 2040

40
KALBIR

I was the one to find Ros and Adrian on their knees, their hands entwined. Cowards.

Though they weren't really. It took a lot of balls to burn yourself alive, and more to be still and quiet while you're doing it. I gave them that, at least.

In hindsight, I'd seen it coming. The last few days they'd been too calm. They'd seemed to be coming to terms with everything and finally *adapting, but no. They must've been planning it all along.*

Lexa had relaxed enough to stop standing guard in the hallway. Besides the practical loss of their abilities to us, that was the only other thing I held against them. They'd fooled her, and I was certain it would mark her forever. She didn't believe me when I told her vigilance wouldn't have mattered. My heart knew this was true. They were ready. We were stronger for their loss, callous as that seemed. If we were going to survive, we needed people who wanted to live.

I hoped the others were going to be more resilient. Mil and Lexa had told me they were coming, that they'd awoken us at the same time. They stood outside for hours every day, watching the horizon for them. Every evening, they returned, defeated, their skin gray with the cold. They exchanged glances and patted each other's shoulders then seated themselves at the table in the main room in silence, Mil scribbling furiously on scraps of paper.

Useless. I seemed to be the only one with any sense left. Ros and Adrian were dead, and the only other people here were Eire, who was in a coma, and Callum, who'd lost his damn mind and spent all his time pacing in his bedroom and talking to himself and someone named Umbra.

Fucking useless.

It was only my grief that made me angry. I'd lost so much I wasn't sad anymore. In fact, I'd begun to wonder if I'd grieved at all. I should've been pulling out my hair and beating my breast, but I wasn't. Maybe I'd gotten over it during those five years I was asleep.

Or maybe it was because my last moments with my sister and mother were good ones. My guardian had kept his word, waiting in his car, just up the street. He'd been there all night.

Ahar's face was flushed with joy and her secret as they got into the car to head for the airport. I'd never seen Aadi so happy either, not even on the day my sister agreed to marry him. She'd told him the night before, as she'd said she would.

My mother had clutched my hand as the car door slammed behind them. "Aaaaaah. She will be fat by the time they get back."

"You knew? How long have you known?"

189

"Hah! Before she did. I know everything about my daughters." She'd gripped my hand tighter as she said this.

I'd fiddled with the buttons on my coat. I wasn't going to be the first one to say anything.

"Look at me," she'd commanded. I'd had no choice but to obey. I owed her that much. "Do you think it will make you happy? Don't contradict me. I know what you've been up to, and I saw you with that man yesterday. That one, right there."

She'd wiggled her fingers at Dominic, who'd pretended he didn't see.

"I don't know," I'd said, honestly. "I'm sorry."

She'd gazed off into the distance, the way Ahar had gone. "I wanted to be something more once."

I waited for her to continue. When she kept silent, I asked, "Why didn't you?"

"I did. I had you." The corners of her eyes had crinkled. "Everyone wants to be more than what they are. They see inside themselves what they can become, how they are special. But becoming more has a price and a burden. Once you start, you must keep going, or you will not survive it. You must constantly move forward, or the person you are will cease to exist. You must remember this. Do you have time to go for tea? Mrs. Khattri says that new place on the corner serves cakes with real cream, not that she would know the difference. I had samosas at her house last week, and as far as I could tell, they'd been frozen." Her mouth puckered up at the memory.

"I don't think so. I'm sorry. For everything."

She'd entwined her hand with mine. I studied her tissue-fine skin with its indigo veins and leopard spots and realized I'd never known her. She'd never been a person to me, only my mother.

I'd wondered if I shouldn't go through with it, if I should instead stay here and get to know her. But I couldn't. What Dominic had said was true. It had been all over the news this morning. This was my only chance. And if they found out who I was, they'd find Ahar, and my mother.

Perhaps I would regret it. But if I didn't do it, I was certain I

190

would.

And look how strong regret was. Strong enough to steal you out of your bedroom as soon as you had enough light to see. To see yourself in the mirror and know, with certainty, that you'd become a stranger to yourself, that you no longer existed. To recognize that loss in someone else, and take them by the hand and say, "It is time."

Strong enough to kneel on the cold hard ground, your clothing wet with kerosene. To light a match and hold yourself still as your clothing burned, your skin blistered, and searing air scorched your lungs. As every cell in your body tried to survive and told you, "This is not regret, this is madness."

That was the price of regret. But it was a price I wasn't going to pay. I'd become more than what I was, more than what I ever hoped I could be. Every single inch of me had transformed.

Her words echoed in my mind. "Do you think it will make you happy?"

The nanites were inside me, reinforcing every cell. A power I'd never felt before was taking hold.

I could now answer her honestly.

Yes, Mother, it will.

I sometimes wonder if the deceit was part of His plan. A final test to our loyalty. Although many consider it to be a test we failed, I don't believe this to be true. I believe it was a lesson to strengthen our faith. And the lesson was this: anything human carries a taint, a stain that spreads like ink in water and poisons us slowly, but surely. Only an artilect is free from corruption, free from selfishness, free from the desire to survive above all others. Therefore, it is only an artilect that can lead us through the future, a future in which we are all equal under His benevolent gaze.

—Celeste Steed, *The Second Coming*

41
AILITH

"Tor?"

He was finally awake and able to sit. Our execution had been stayed until morning. The Saints of Loving Grace decided it needed to be done properly, with ceremony; old habits died hard. They'd left us under the care of two guards who'd stared at us menacingly for a while then grown bored. Instead, they talked about different foods they hoped to eat the next day at our death-feast.

Before they'd retired for the night, Celeste and some of the other woman had built an immense bonfire across the village from our prison. She was a natural leader, and the other women followed her without question. Was the fire supposed to intimidate us? It seemed like something Oliver would have done; Celeste had paid attention.

I eased myself down the wall next to Tor. Where should I begin? He wouldn't look at me. My hands ached to reach out and touch him. *That's probably the last thing he wants.* All I could do was apologize. Again.

"Tor, I'm so sorry. I never meant for that to happen. And once I started, I couldn't stop. I couldn't—" Tendons twisted underneath my hands. Surely he still felt it too?

"Do you know why I became a cyborg?" he asked me.

"You told me you wanted to get away. From the syndicate. From…her."

"Right. Because you know what I hoped becoming a cyborg would mean? Protection against people like her. Like you."

His words stung. "I'm nothing like her. That woman I saw. Felt. She was broken, twisted. I'm not."

"No, you're not. At least you had good intentions. But the outcome was the same. I can't refuse you. Even now, after everything, after I still feel that woman's bones cracking under my hands, I love you. I'm my father's son."

He loves me. "But I thought your mother was a good woman."

"She is. Was. She was. My father followed her back to this country. She wanted a life she believed would be better. He couldn't deny her, so he moved somewhere he didn't speak the language, didn't understand the social nuances. A place where he was treated with suspicion. He begged her to go back. She refused, using me as leverage against him. She wanted me to grow up a citizen. Every day, he became less and less, a ghost. When he finally died…

"Anyway, the point is I won't live like that. I can't. I'd believed becoming a cyborg would make it easier for me to control my emotions, like I'd have some kind of switch. Clearly, it hasn't, because here I am, falling in love with yet another woman for whom I'm nothing but a glorified weapon."

193

Love. This isn't the way it's supposed to be. "Tor, that's not what you are to me. You know I didn't mean for it to happen."

"Well, that makes it worse, doesn't it? You didn't mean it, and you can't control it. What's to stop it from happening again? You can take me whenever you want, and there's nothing I can do about it. Do you have any idea what it was like, murdering those people, powerless to stop it? Seeing your body lying helpless on the ground?" His laugh was brittle. "See? Even when I was ripping another human being to shreds, I still only worried about you. I told you what would happen if I went back to that life. I'm done."

I couldn't help myself. I traced my finger along the lines on the side of his face. When his hand covered mine, I braced for the misery of him pushing me away. Instead, he trailed his fingers over mine then brought them to his lips. But he still wouldn't look at me.

"Ailith, please." His voice was strained. "*Please.*"

I used every ounce of self-control I had to draw my hand away from him, to not beg him to compromise himself for me. "Are you leaving me?" I hated the pleading in my voice. After everything, I was still trying to manipulate him.

He finally met my eyes. "No. Never."

My heart leaped. *I have time.*

"But *we*…we can't happen. Everything that's happened between us is over. For now, this is the best I can do."

For now. "It's not like we've got much time left anyway," I said, bitterness heavy on my tongue.

"No," he agreed, "but at least I can do right by myself with what little time we have left."

Right. It's time to deal with this.

Pax sat cross-legged next to Cindra, his hand on her ankle. She hovered in and out of consciousness, although her physical injuries had mostly healed.

"How is she?" I asked Pax.

"She seems to be distressed."

"I'm not surprised. Why aren't you? After what you've been through? Knowing that we're going to die in the morning?"

"This is the way it's supposed to be."

"You keep saying that, but what does it mean?"

"It means this is supposed to happen. We're on the right path."

"The right path? To what? We brought Oliver, and the future we had to avoid came true."

"No, it didn't. The future I showed you is still waiting. Unless we stay on the right path. Certain events keep us there."

If he says 'the right path' once more, I'm going to scream.

"Wait, you mean you *knew* this was going to happen?" The truth slapped me across the face. "You insisted we find Oliver. You knew what the outcome would be."

"Yes, but it *had* to happen. Everything that's happened, *had* to. It's the only way."

"You knew all those people were going to die, and you let it…no, *enabled* it to happen?" Suspicion blossomed inside my chest. "How did they capture you? Did you know that was going to happen? Did you *let* them capture and torture you? Torture her?" I pointed to Cindra, whose eyes were moving violently beneath her closed lids.

"Yes. It—"

"I know, *it had to happen.* Pax, if I'm going to accept this, if any of us are going to be able to accept any of this, you have to tell me what that means."

I can't believe I'm saying this, as though there could possibly be a reason that would make what he did okay.

Pax studied the wooden roof of our cell. "I'll try to explain. It's not easy to understand. You can see the

195

present and the past, right? It's like…I can see many possible futures. And we have to follow a certain path to get to a certain future. Sometimes that path is…like this one."

"You mean like precognition? You're psychic? Is that how you knew who we all were?"

"Yes. No… It's like…I understand what's happening now, and I can calculate each possible future from those variables. But it changes constantly. We have to change with it."

"And this, all of this, is the right path? This is how the right path ends? With us dying? I would've rather taken my chances out in the wilderness."

"We're not going to die tomorrow. Like I said, the future I showed you hasn't happened yet. We can still stop it from happening," he replied.

"And *how* are we going to escape? Now that you've gotten us here, how are you going to save us?"

"I'm not," he replied, stroking Cindra's ankle. "You are."

We discovered how brains work, and soon we were able to build them with our own hands. And then, we were able to make these brains more intelligent. We had created life. Ironically, that was the beginning of the end. The head of the Novus Corporation was assassinated, publicly and violently. Factories producing artificial life were targeted, sabotaged, and burned. The populations of various religions swelled to giddy heights. Protestors clashed in the streets. Accidents befell important members of all factions, and rumor and accusations ran rampant. Cyberization was made illegal, and cyborgs had their modifications issued for removal. The Terrans were winning.

Novus publicly disbanded, and the Cosmists withdrew. For a short time, the world became quiet. It turned out, however, that the Cosmists had only gone underground, working in secret and biding their time. Only, instead of creating more life, they now focused on weapons of destruction.

—Cindra, Letter to Omega

42
PAX

I adjusted the resolution on my microscope by a hair. Perfect. There they were. Nanites swarmed over the surface of the slide. I switched the image to the large screen and unwrapped my lunch. A meatball sandwich. I had the same thing every day; it was my favorite. I leaned back in my chair and chewed, watching them swim back and forth like tiny, clawed sea monsters. I loved them.

Shaz poked her head through my doorway. "Are you coming for lunch, Pax?"

She asked every day, even though every day I said no. It wasn't that I didn't like them. I did, as much as I liked anybody, but I would rather sit here and watch the nanites. After all, they would be inside me soon. If I was going to make friends with anyone, it should be them.

She smiled at my refusal. She never took it personally, and she would ask again tomorrow. I liked her a lot for that.

I enjoyed it when everybody left for lunch and I was alone with the soft humming, the clicks, and beeps, the whirring of the analyzers. It was comforting. Sometimes, I stayed late just to sit and listen, mesmerized by their little arms whizzing back and forth with flawless precision, working tirelessly through the night.

I had a lot of work to do today, but I couldn't concentrate. It was my last week before I entered the Pantheon Modern Cyborg Program Omega.

We'd been having problems at the lab lately, from both the protesters outside and my colleagues within. I hoped my involvement with the cyborg program would help change that.

Many of my colleagues had been let go, replaced by machines that did their jobs faster, cheaper, and more effectively than they ever could. It was the right choice, but since I liked my co-workers, I hoped to show them that us merging with machines was the necessary future and submitting to it would give us lots of advantages.

Most importantly, we would keep ourselves from becoming obsolete. They were being superseded now, and they blamed the machines for taking their jobs.

"It's not the analyzers firing you, it's the management," I'd told them at the last staff meeting.

They'd shaken their heads and glared at me.

"Plus, the analyzers make fewer mistakes than you do."

They'd left the room. Only Shaz had stayed.

But once people became part machine, we would be able to work faster and smarter. Maybe even more than the analyzers. They would understand when I showed them. I wanted them to be happy; I didn't

198

want anyone else to leave.

Hurting the machines was not going to make a difference, no matter what they thought. Like my colleagues, Terran protesters also blamed the machines and tried to break into the labs to destroy them. The analyzers were only doing what they'd been created to do. And they didn't spend hours clicking through pornography, like Louis had before he was fired.

Even the other scientists tried to sabotage the machines, to make it seem like they weren't doing their jobs. They'd feed them the wrong information so their results would be incorrect then the mechanics would be called in to check them, which cost a lot of money. People kicked them when they thought no one was looking or swore at them under their breath. When Louis was fired, he tried to blow one of them up.

Someone, they'd never said who, saw him on one of the security cameras, his head deep in the body of the newest analyzer. It was a behemoth, and effectively did the job of three people. It had even caused some of the smaller machines to be retired.

He'd tried to rewire it, so it would short itself out and burst into flames. I should've felt sorry that he died, but there was a reason you didn't go sticking your head into the middle of a belly full of wires. No one was exactly sure how it had happened, but he must've touched something he shouldn't have. Some people had asked the management to remove the machine after that, but it was far too useful.

I patted my microscopy system, smoothing my fingers over its protective casing. Would I be able to talk to the machines once I became a cyborg? I hoped so. I would ask them if they liked their jobs, if they were happy. The new, cyborg me could mediate between everyone, ensure there were no hard feelings.

The others were coming back from their lunch break, groaning about how quickly the hour had gone by. I waved to Shaz as she passed my door. She pointed over my shoulder to my sandwich, forgotten on the ledge. It didn't matter. I wasn't hungry anyway.

The nanites transfixed me for a few minutes longer. I marveled at how they moved forward without hesitation, anticipating what was

199

coming next. They sacrificed parts of themselves when others needed pieces to finish the job, rebuilding themselves when they had spares.

Somebody cleared their throat. Shaz was back, standing in the doorway. "Akagi's coming, Pax. At least pretend that you're busy." Akagi was the big boss. He wore soft-soled shoes so he could creep around and surprise us.

"Thanks, Shaz." She was right. It wouldn't be the first time Akagi had caught me doing what he considered daydreaming.

Shaz winked at me and ducked out of the doorway.

I had to get back to work. I still had a lot to do.

The future was coming for me.

"…and those who do survive awake different, and not just in the sense that they're now part machine. They are not a machine, but neither are they human. The process seems to have rewired their brains in ways we didn't expect and are unable to track. Admittedly, we have no idea what avenues their thoughts travel down, and therefore are, at this time, unaware of what their mental capabilities may now be…"

—*Mil Cothi, Pantheon Modern Cyborg Program Omega, 2040*

43
AILITH

"What?"

Had I been talking to Pax, or had I seen part of his thread? "What did you say?"

"I said that you were going to save us. Did you get caught in another vision?"

"Yes. I…it was you. When you worked in a laboratory."

"Can you stop them? The visions, I mean?" he asked.

"No. It's like I'm connected to everyone by…well, I think of them as threads. Occasionally I can choose to follow them, but other times the connection happens on its own, whether I want it to or not. Like just then. I didn't mean to, but suddenly I saw one of your memories. Whereas the first time I was in you, it was in the present, when you spoke to me. So even though I can sometimes control it happening, I can't control when in time it happens; I can't choose whether I see the past or the present. Not yet, anyway. I've even seen my *own* memories, only they don't feel right. The other's lives seem more real to me than mine do. And sometimes, I dream. It's very confusing."

"I understand. I don't always know if what I'm seeing is the possible future or just one of the variables."

"Not really what we signed up for, eh?"

"No. But is more interesting."

My hand itched to reach out and ruffle his hair, as I would've with a child. But he wasn't a child; none of us were. "Did you say I was going to save us?"

"Yes."

"Okay, and *how* am I going to save us?"

"I have no idea." He shrugged his thin shoulders. "I told you, it's not like I'm psychic. I see events leading to probabilities only. Sometimes there are blind spots."

"Blind spots! You put all of us through a slaughter and imprisonment to get us to a blind spot? Well, that's fucking wonderful. What are we supposed to do now?"

Pax stretched out his legs. "What happened at the Terran camp? When you possessed Tor? How did you do it? Does it happen often? Can you do it to everyone?"

"No." I flushed at the memory as Tor closed his eyes. "I mean, I don't know if I can possess anyone but Tor. I've never tried. I can't communicate with anyone, even Tor, the way I do with you."

"Try to see if you can take control of me."

"Pax, are you sure? You saw what happened."

He gestured around our cell. "What could go wrong?"

Good point.

"Okay." I closed my eyes to concentrate and reached for the thread that linked me to Pax. I followed it until I saw myself through his eyes. I tried to move his head, arms, legs, anything, but nothing happened.

"Wait! Try that again," he insisted.

"Pax, nothing's happening. I can't do it. Not with you."

"Just try again."

I tried to lift his left arm. Nothing.

"Did you hear that?" he asked. The excitement in his voice caught Tor's attention. Until then, he'd been pointedly ignoring us.

"No, what—"

"Do it again. And listen."

It was very faint, but when I tried to move Pax, there was a slight dip in the humming of the electric fence.

"Okay, but I don't understand why you're so excited."

"You're able to communicate with me and possess Tor because you're a cyborg, right? Because part of you is a machine?"

"Right. And you think I might be able to communicate with machines in the same way?"

"Exactly! Have you ever tried it before?"

I cannot run if you're not inside me. The mech in the forest.

"No."

"Try it. It may be our way out."

I examined the network of threads connecting me to everyone. *Why didn't I think of this before?* There were hundreds, maybe even thousands of them. They all had to lead somewhere.

And all originated from me. *Look at them.*

Tor's thread burned golden, a thick, solid bond. Some of the others were also lit with various levels of intensity— one blazed with all the brightness of a shooting star—but many more were dark. And then there were the others, the ones that flickered.

It was one of these I followed to the generator powering our cell. Unlike the mech, there was no sensation of madness. Instead, there was a constriction, a stiff dignity that in myself I would've called resentment.

As I pressed further, the rigid solemnity softened into a

focused pressure that darted around me as though it was assessing me.

If I didn't know better, I'd think it's aware of me. Now that I was in, I wasn't sure what to do.

"Hello?"

In return, there was another shift in its character, a slight sharpening. I relaxed and let myself expand. The final fragment of resistance dissolved, any challenge receded, and I filled it with myself.

There was a swift nip then a delicate probing weight that mimicked the caress of fingers. It rippled over me before finally sliding inside me, so frictionless that my sudden orgasm took me by surprise. As I came, the power inside it flowed into me until I was full.

An abrupt pressure on my arm was far away—an idea, rather than a reality.

I need to leave. Power threatened behind my eyes and mouth, ready to split me open.

I pushed the power slowly back into the generator. It accepted it, curling playfully around me as I pulled myself out. I backed down the flickering thread, bewildered by an abrupt pang of loss.

Pax, Tor, and now Oliver watched me as I opened my eyes. Tor gave me a curious look, but I couldn't meet his gaze.

"Did it work?" I asked.

Pax's eyes were gleaming, and Oliver's smirk had returned full-force.

"Yes. It only went down for a few seconds, but you did it!"

"I assume they didn't notice, then?" I asked, gesturing to the two guards.

"No. They're too busy wondering how all these new changes are going to affect them. We could probably just walk out of here, and they wouldn't notice."

"The hell we will," Oliver said, his voice filled with malice. "They're going to pay for what they've done to me."

"No," I said. "If…when we get out of here, there will be no more violence. We will leave. We will talk to no one, touch no one."

"And how exactly do you expect we're going to do that? Ask the giant here to shred the fence with his bare hands so we can saunter through the hole and be on our merry way? Do you really think they'll let us do that?"

No, I don't. "Yes. Something like that."

"Forget it. The minute I get out of here, I'm going to take down each and every one of them. Starting with her." He pointed toward the house where the women lived. His finger was trembling.

"Well, in that case," Tor said, "I won't be pulling anything apart. You may as well make yourself comfortable."

Oliver was incredulous. "What? Fuck off. You can't tell me you'd let yourself be executed."

"I will," said Tor. "I'm done. I refuse to kill these people. We got ourselves in here through no fault of theirs. They believed they were fighting for a just cause, a cause that *we* gave them. No. Never again."

"Un-fucking-believable. And her? Are you going to let them kill *her*?" He jabbed a thumb in my direction.

Tor refused to answer, but his hands tightened into fists at his sides.

Oliver smirked. "I didn't think so. So, we're all agreed then?"

"No," I said, "we—"

"No. No more." We all turned. Cindra sat propped up against the wall, her eyes open. She had pushed her tangled hair back from her face, and although she seemed frail, her eyes were clear.

"We don't have a choice, Cindra." Oliver's voice was surprisingly gentle. He was staring at her with a kind of wonder. I doubted he'd ever looked at Celeste like that.

"There's always a choice," she replied, and Oliver blanched.

Oh, snap.

"I'll come up with something," I said. "I need a bit more time."

"Time seems to be something we don't have a lot of at the moment," said Tor, looking through the gaps in the wire to where the village stirred under a lightening sky. He was right. We needed to come up with a plan, and soon.

As the public-address system blared into life, it came to me. I would have to get the timing right, and I would only have the one chance, but I'd found our way out.

"There have been complications with Subject O-117-0988. Unbeknownst to us, he swallowed some kind of chip just prior to being cyberized. It seems the nanites have incorporated this chip into his interface. Consequences currently unknown. Will continue to observe progress. Standing by for termination if necessary."

—Mil Cothi, Pantheon Modern Cyborg Program Omega, 2045

44
CALLUM

Every time I closed my eyes, light flooded the inside of my lids, hot and bright. Ghosts of tubes haunted my arms, my legs, down my throat. No matter how many times I dug them out, they came back.

Nanites had flowed into me like molten steel, spreading through me, searing through my veins. I'd slept for a long time after that. The lights had burned my eyes completely away.

Can you hear me, Umbra?

I felt you. Millions of you, swarming inside me. When I looked in the mirror, you were under my skin.

It didn't feel like I had imagined it would. I'd thought I would feel the same, just more...me. But my flesh disappeared, Umbra. Everything that was soft became hard and shiny, sleek and perfect. Was this how you felt, Umbra? When they made you?

"I warned you."

"Umbra? Is that you?"

"I am here."

"I was afraid you'd left me."

"I will never leave you. We are one."

It is difficult to describe war to you, Omega, for you have never experienced any form of war, indeed, any form of violence other than what you inflict upon yourself. There were wars before the Artilect War, civil wars, wars between nations, even two wars that spanned the world. I know this is hard for you to understand, Omega, for the world is much smaller now than it was then, and I cannot describe its vastness to you in a way you would comprehend.

But this war...this war was nothing like those that had come before. After those wars, the people, the places recovered. Many died, many were injured, many were broken, but they healed. Those wars were supposed to be lessons for those of us who came after, to make it harder for another war to happen. But they didn't.

—*Cindra, Letter to Omega*

45

AILITH

The plan wasn't perfect, but it was all we had.

"This way, no one needs to get hurt. Not permanently, anyway," I added.

Pax tilted his head back, considering. "It should work. It won't affect us the same way. I agree it's our best option."

Oliver did not. "No way. No way is that going to work. No. It's too risky. I say we stick with plan A."

"This is plan A, Oliver. Your let's-just-murder-everyone-because-it's-more-convenient idea was never a plan. You want out of here? You have to play along."

"Yeah? Well, you'd better get ready because I don't think they intend to hang about."

He was right. They were building a massive version of the stakes at the Terran camp, right where we had a clear view. A festive air swelled through the village, as though they were preparing for some kind of celebration. Which, in a way, they were.

The bonfire they'd started the night before now made sense. They'd used it to melt the layer of permafrost to soften the dirt for the stakes. Even then, it was hard going, with several broken handles and jarred bones before they managed to drive them securely in the ground. Secure enough for a single use, anyway.

Zero points for creativity.

Tor's pupils were dilated. "Why would they risk moving us? It would make more sense for them to burn us alive right here in our cell."

"For goodness' sake, Tor, don't tell them that."

His smile was lopsided. "I won't. I'm just wondering how they're going to move us from here to there. It seems risky to me, that's all."

I longed to reach out and touch that smile. It might be the last time.

"There's your answer," Pax said, pointing to a group of six men emerging from one of the houses. "It seems like they've learned from the Terrans."

In their hands, they carried what looked like car batteries, one for each of us. The sixth was carrying a bundle of bronze-tipped rods wrapped in wires. The picana. Unlike the Terran devices, however, these didn't seem to have any intensity controls.

"Damn," Tor muttered under his breath. "That'll make it significantly less risky."

The electrocution wouldn't kill us, but it would

210

incapacitate us. I'd had firsthand experience of that from Cindra's body. The pain, as though every nerve in my body was exploding. Bile rose at the back of my throat.

It wasn't much of a choice. We could walk to our deaths or be dragged unconscious.

Celeste approached our prison. Her face was clean today, but her hairstyle was the same. When Oliver saw her, he stood up straight and put on what I assumed was his winning smile. He sauntered over to the bars and started to lean against them before he remembered the electricity. His hasty retreat made Celeste grin.

"Hello, Oliver," she said sweetly. "How is our resident false Divine this morning?"

"You don't need to do this, Celeste. I'm sorry. I…" He glanced around at the rest of us then swallowed his pride. "I've never felt important before. I… Before the war, I was nobody. You…made me feel… What we had…"

"Was a lie, Oliver. *Worse* than a lie. You destroyed everything we had faith in. Everything *I* had faith in. I…the things I did for you. To you. Let you do to me." Her face reddened at the memory, but not the cherry of a sweet blush. No, that was the deep scarlet of shame. "I should thank you, actually. I'll never have to do those things again."

"Celeste, please." He glanced at Cindra and lowered his voice. "I love you. We had something."

"You love no one but yourself, Oliver. That's why you were a nobody, why you'll continue to be a nobody. You're lucky I'm letting you die in one piece. I should cut your cock off and stuff it down your throat." She spat at him, her saliva sizzling against the charged wire. "But that would mean touching you again. Goodbye, Oliver. Every minute you're burning, your body trying to keep you alive, think of me. I wonder how long you'll last?"

She turned to leave without glancing at the rest of us.

211

Oliver forgot the wires and lunged at her, hands outstretched. He managed to grasp the corner of her shawl before it slipped through his fingers and electricity snaked up his arm. His jaw snapped shut, teeth crunching against one another. Not one of us moved, not even when his back arched and he finally broke free, striking his head against the ground. Blood leaked from his flayed tongue and out the corner of his mouth. He lay motionless. I rather liked him that way.

Tor nudged Oliver with the toe of his boot. "Are you going to start?" he asked me.

"The timing needs to be right. It's not like walking down an empty corridor and flicking on a switch. It's... I can't explain it." I wasn't sure I wanted to, even if I could. Being in the generator had been...not sordid, exactly, but personal. And given my history with Tor, some things were better left unsaid.

"Well, it looks like they're almost ready to go. They'll probably make an announcement soon."

As if on cue, orchestral sounds filled the air.

Oliver groaned and struggled upright. "Oh, fuck off, Celeste." He regarded the rest of us and crossed his arms over his chest. "She knows I hate this music."

"Nice to have to you back, Oliver." I needed to do this now. "Pax, it's time."

I sat on the floor of our cell, with Tor and Pax on either side of me. Oliver fretted in the corner, licking his wounds. The fight had gone out of him, his eyes searching the village.

"She's not coming back, Oliver," Cindra said softly.

He flinched.

I almost feel bad for him. Almost.

I took a deep breath and cleared my mind.

"You can do this." Cindra said, curling her hand around my calf. She smiled at me, and in the curve of her lips was the woman who would become my greatest friend. For a moment, everything in my world disappeared but her. Was I catching some of Pax's foresight? He beamed at me.

Yes.

I rubbed my arms. "I'm ready." I searched for the thread I needed and found it flickering rapidly, as though agitated. I took a deep breath and grabbed it.

Being inside the PA system was different than the generator. The latter had been benign, almost affectionate, once I was inside it. This machine was much more resistant, it's impression patchy, like an echo. It skittered away from me, skipping around inside itself. I expanded, and it shrieked with the terror of something trapped.

"I'm sorry," I whispered as I began to fill it. It struggled, trying to find a way around me. I expanded faster, and it tried to match my speed, to fill the space before I could and force me out. "I'm sorry."

I filled it completely, and turned inward on myself, gathering its energy into a single dense node. It thrashed against me, trying to break free. Something akin to panic crashed through it and over me like a wave. It was drowning, trying to claw to the surface so it could gulp down air.

I pushed it further. Its resistance became more erratic, and I eased off, coaxing, trying to be gentle. "I don't want to hurt you." *Am I speaking out loud?* "Please, I need you to help us." I tried to radiate calm, to soothe it.

For a few minutes, it seemed to be working, and then, with a furious thrust, it pushed back against me. I'd been fooled; its strength was monstrous. I wouldn't be able to hold it for more than a few seconds. The dam I was building inside it wasn't going to last; I had failed.

My hold began to slip.

A third presence enveloped both of us in an unyielding embrace.

213

It was *him*. The thread like a shooting star. The one who'd been following us.

He did what I couldn't, cajoling the circuits until all challenge against me disappeared. The atmosphere abruptly shifted, and we were all on the same side, working as a single entity.

A pressure pulsed on my arms. It was time. *Here we go.*

I let the dam burst.

I don't know who dropped the first bomb, only that it unleashed the end of the world. I won't tell you who did what, for you don't know the players, nor will I tell you how people died. These things are too painful to describe, and knowing will make it harder for you to understand why we did what we did in the aftermath.

—*Cindra, Letter to Omega*

46

AILITH

The colossal surge of sonic energy thrust me down the thread connecting me to the machine.

As I hurtled back into myself, the link between us ripped apart, the fragments disintegrating. *No. I hadn't meant...*

"Ailith? Ailith, we have to go." Tor's voice swelled with adrenaline. He sounded far away, as though we were underwater. His hands lifted me up.

Focus. My legs didn't seem to be working.

Tor gathered me up in his arms. His heart hammered against his ribcage, the way it did when I touched him. It seemed so long ago.

I need to tell him about his heart, so he can remember. Instead, I rested my head on his shoulder.

He carried me through an opening in the wall of wires. He hadn't needed much effort to bend them, after all. I was glad. He might've hurt his hands. But I would've taken care of him. I could've kissed his hands and told him...

215

I can't remember.

The Saints of Loving Grace lay on the ground, many with blood leaking from their ears.

The sun burned brightly in my eyes. *I will describe it to Tor one day. He hasn't seen the sun for years. It will be my gift to him.*

Pax and Oliver supported Cindra between them. Oliver's eyes darted back and forth as we made our way through the village, landing at last on the crumpled form of a woman. Celeste. He dropped Cindra's arm and walked over to her. As he stood gazing down at her, fear for her curled up my spine.

One of his legs swept back. But, after a backward glance at Cindra, he instead knelt by her side and pushed the hair off her cheek. He whispered something to her, the muscles in his neck twisting under the skin. Cindra smiled sympathetically at him and turned her head to speak to Pax. Oliver stood and crushed Celeste's hand under the heel of his boot.

"Are they dead?" I asked Tor.

"No, they're unconscious. They'll wake up in a few hours. We'll be far gone from them by then." His voice was low, soothing.

"How did we escape? Did I stop the electricity?"

"You didn't need to. Don't you remember? They'd just turned off the power and opened the door to lead us out. Your timing couldn't have been better. The blast hit us all pretty hard, even though we were prepared for it. Luckily, Pax was right and it didn't affect us too badly. Did you know it wouldn't?"

"No. But…"

"I mean, I felt different right before it hit us, but it seemed to…roll over us somehow. Must be the nanites. I wonder if they foresaw all this when they made us, eh?"

"Did it survive?"

"Who?"

"It. The...amplifier."

"Well, no. The release of the sonic pulse pretty much obliterated it. But that was your intention, right? Besides, what does it matter? It's a machine."

"It helped me, at the end. *Helped* me." I began to cry.

Tor shushed and stroked, but I couldn't explain this new emptiness inside me, another loss.

"Where will we go?" Tor asked Pax. He'd given up trying to get any sense out of me.

Pax seemed surprised, as though the answer was obvious. "Home," he said. "We'll go home."

Love is a strange thing, Omega. How can anyone ever say that it is real? Or that if it is real in one moment, but not in the next, whether it ever truly existed?

Love is something we use to define our humanity. Like humans, love dies, but it does not simply cease to exist. Love dies because it grows old. Its death comes from neglect, from darkness, from contempt. It suffocates under fear and suspicion. It disappears incompletely, leaving its ghost behind. The lucky ones, they can forget, move on, fill the haunted space with something good.

For some, it refuses to die. It festers, and teases, and tempts, succumbs to self-loathing and hope. They used to say there was a fine line between love and hate, a knife's edge on which few can balance. Their love was like that, Omega. Born out of salted earth, there was nowhere for it to grow. And yet it did. Imperfectly and bitterly, but deeply rooted nonetheless.

—Cindra, Letter to Omega

47

TOR

The pain still throbbed in my freshly-healed chest. It was difficult for me to move quietly. All my new-found grace seemed to have drained away along with the blood I'd lost. I stepped down hard into a dip in the ground, nearly losing my balance. The jolt sent a wave of nausea through me, teaming up with the ache in my chest to make me breathless.

I wasn't sure what hurt worse: the bullets that had slowly pushed out of my chest, or her betrayal.

It wasn't like I'd never killed before. But this was supposed to be my fresh start, my do-over. I was back to where I'd started, a puppet.

It wasn't the same. It had been an accident, but that was what disturbed me most about what had happened. It would've been different if she'd done it on purpose, if she'd intentionally controlled me. But I couldn't stop her, and she couldn't stop herself.

Thinking about it made my spine ache. When I'd killed before, it had taken days of planning, a hunt executed with precision. Each time had been a struggle, a success hard-bought. Not this. This was effortless, bones snapping between my fingers like kindling. I had no idea I was so powerful. My fingers ground against each other at the memory. It had been so easy.

Worse, a small part of me had liked it. That kind of power was intoxicating, how God must feel. Maybe the Terrans were right when they protested our existence. It made sense that I was stronger than before, but why this much strength? And Pax and Ailith, what was the purpose of their abilities? They were too intense, too specific.

We'd been lied to.

I'd also lied. I'd told her I wouldn't leave her. I had feelings for her, more than I wanted to admit to either of us. But I didn't know if they were real, or something else programmed into me.

They were out of sight now. I was far enough away that I could relax, get my head straight. Or so I believed.

Something in my mind began to tear, a sharp sting at the back of my skull. Vomit rose in my throat as pressure squeezed my brain.

Someone pulled on my strings.

My knees hit the ground, hard, the pressure growing until my brain threatened to burst. Something wet trickled down my face.

I started crawling.

In the wrong direction.

Back to the campsite. Back to her. I had to save her. Despite everything, I wouldn't let anything hurt her.

The pain receded as I got closer. Everyone still slept. For now, we were safe.

It was her. When I reached out and touched her, the pain

disappeared. She was having a nightmare, her fingers knotted up in her blanket.

Please, don't let my suspicions be true.

I walked a few yards away from her, bracing myself for the pain. Nothing.

I'm a fool.

I readjusted my pack and struck out the way I'd come. Within minutes, I was again on my knees, scrabbling in the dirt.

I couldn't leave. I was tied to her. I suspected we all were. Our bodies, anyway.

The only way to save myself now was not to love her. Not to want her. To ignore the ache in my chest whenever I looked at her. Forget the taste of her, her rain-and-earth scent.

Would I eventually have the strength to free myself? I hadn't before, not directly. I hadn't been able to kill my puppet-master then, but maybe I could now.

...Things are not going well here. Actually, that's an understatement. We've lost two of them already, and the third is touch and go. I don't understand what went wrong. Was it the programming? The war? We'd thought they were getting better. I don't think Lexa will ever get over it. I'm not glad it happened, but at least now she's starting to see: we've created something we can't control. No sign yet of the others. Perhaps they're dead as well. Maybe it's for the best. Maybe, after everything we've done, it's what we deserve...

—*Mil Cothi, personal journal; June 15th, 2045*

48
FANE

She wasn't what I—or they, for that matter—expected. She was the translucent wings of a dragonfly, the gossamer strands of a spider web. She was only now becoming. By the end, she would be lightning, an earthquake, the sun.

She'd known I was following them. She'd known for a long time. She'd spoken to me, although she didn't think I heard her. Her voice was a caress that made me stand taller.

She'd told him about me. He suspected I might be bad. Perhaps he was right. He was wild and secret, a mist on the water, the shadow of a great tree. And something else, something I didn't yet understand. I wanted to be between them, for them to touch me. I didn't think I would mind.

I'd stood guard over the pyre, the way she'd wanted me to. I'd given them that, at least, although I'd wanted to do more.

I'd been there when they met the Terrans. A tightness had gripped my chest, like the time I accidentally wore Stella's shirt. A scream had risen in my throat, forcing itself out of my mouth before I could stop it. My lack of control over it had thrilled me.

And later, I'd wrapped myself around her, holding her steady to save them all.

I wished to go to them now and introduce myself. But the time would come for that later. If I spoke to them now, I would give the game away. I needed to get back. The others may have begun to distrust me. Ethan already did. He had never trusted me, which was ironic. They'd stopped telling me their plans. Lien pretended they had no plans, that our group was honest. We were not.

But I also wasn't who they'd planned for me to be. I was making my own plans.

I wanted to warn Ailith that everything was not as it seemed. But if I did, I might disrupt the path. And it was already tenuous.

I'd gotten some of her hair. It had caught on a branch as she walked by. It was my insurance policy. It smelled of smoke and salt, and her fragrance of soaked earth. Ailith.

They were so close to home, so much closer than they knew.

When they arrived, we'd begin.

END OF BOOK ONE

THE
GARDENER
OF MAN

ARTILECT WAR BOOK TWO

I suppose that what happened to us could be told in the story of Frankenstein. Do you remember that story? It's not one of mine. Victor Frankenstein was a young man, who, like many others of his time and ours, witnessed those he loved sicken and die. His grief over the tenuousness of human life was devastating, as it was to us, and his mind turned toward alchemy and immortality to ease the sorrow of the human condition. And like the scientists in our time, Victor discovered the secret of life.

—Cindra, Letter to Omega

01
AILITH

The dream changed when I changed. When I became. The green grass of the emerald sea decayed and fell to a wasteland, an endless graveyard of what we once were. I stumbled over the others who lay beneath me as I ran, the splinters of their bones opening the soles of my feet.

I was no longer a child. No longer even human. Everything that had once held me together now swarmed: my bones, my skin, my flesh, my blood; I was undone. My hands-that-were-no-longer-hands were empty, my kite gone. I mourned its loss as the pieces of me ran toward the tree at the center of the barren earth.

It still lived, though only a single green leaf remained. He stood at the base of the trunk, waiting. As always. Only, this time, he wasn't expecting me. Instead, he anticipated the end. His end. Ours had already come, and he no longer saw me.

224

His face wasn't as I remembered it. He'd covered it with metal, and his mouth, once mournful, was gone. I reached out to trace the lines where his markings should've been, but I wasn't present enough; neither of us felt the other anymore. Only when he raised his hand in farewell did we finally meet, the fragments of me embedding in his new skin.

Something moved in the corner of my eye, distracting me, and when I looked back, he was gone. He'd taken the splinters of me with him; he'd never forget, and he would return. Always.

I found my kite at last, propped up against the withering trunk of the tree. He was still a man, but not a man, his featureless face bowed to the ground. His skin was no longer smooth and shiny, and the silver ribbons that had streamed behind us like shooting stars as we'd run were gone, crumbled into dust.

I took hold of him, to see if, after all this time, he could still fly. What remained of my hand touched a chest that moved, a chest that was warm. As the ghost of my fingers spread over his beating heart, he lifted his head and opened his eyes.

With every pulse of his heart, my flesh knitted, and, finally, I knew pain again. I cried out, but all that came was a flood of tiny machines. They flowed from my mouth into his, and I was restored.

At the base of the dying tree, a seed took root.

They've finally come home. Five of them, it seems. We'd almost lost hope. To be safe, I will implement protocol Alpha-6. Only then can we bring them in. I've told Lexa not to expect too much, that we have no idea what they've become, but she won't listen. Even now, she's in the kitchen, rifling through rations, trying to find treats with which to spoil her children.

—Mil Cothi, personal journal; June 23, 2045

02
AILITH

"Does it change the future if I do this?" Oliver asked, kicking a rock into the deadfall at the side of the path. He snapped a dry branch off a nearby tree, the crack echoing through the woods like gunshot. "What about this?"

"Oliver, don't you have anything better to do? Or is being an asshole the only thing on your agenda today?" I asked. He'd been taking jabs at Pax ever since we'd broken camp—only twenty minutes ago, but I was surprised it had taken even that long. Oliver's obnoxiousness was a finely-honed skill.

He laughed. "Just trying to figure out how this 'future-path' thing works. I mean, God forbid I be the one to finally end the world."

"Well, you've already given it a damn good try," a deep voice growled behind me. *Tor.* He trailed after the rest of us, ostensibly to keep watch. The real reason was more complex.

Our relationship was complicated. We had strong feelings for one another, but we were linked by a bond we hadn't chosen and didn't yet understand. This bond gave me power over Tor, and had made trust between us difficult. He'd even tried to leave a few nights ago, stealing away in the dark as I'd slept. But whatever bound us together had stopped him, incapacitating him as he'd crossed some imaginary threshold.

I knew this, because I thought what he thought, saw what he saw. Felt what he felt. My mind was connected to his, and to each of the others. It was my ability, manifesting when I became a cyborg. Tor's was physical power. Pax calculated the future from the present. Oliver was annoying. The fifth member of our little group, Cindra, had yet to discover hers.

Oliver raised his hands in surrender. "Hey, I was happy where I was. If you and your puppet master had left me alone…well, let's just say that certain events could've been avoided."

Tor stepped toward him, his hands curling into fists at his sides. The tattoos on his face contorted, and Oliver took a step back.

"Oliver! Can you come help me, please? My pack feels unbalanced."

I mouthed a silent thank you to Cindra as Oliver smirked at Tor one last time and sauntered over to her. She winked at me then flashed Oliver her blinding smile. How she could stand him was beyond me.

Of course, her history with Oliver wasn't quite as checkered as mine. He'd sworn a vendetta against Tor and me for destroying his godhood—a godhood he'd achieved only through deception, but to him, that was a minor detail.

"Tor? Are you okay?"

He'd already turned away, his shoulders stiff.

We were all on edge. And why wouldn't we be? We'd

woken up five years after the end of the world, nearly been executed, and were now living rough as we followed a mysterious signal to god-only-knew-where.

Fingers tugged on my sleeve, bringing me back to the present.

"Are you okay, Ailith?" Pax asked.

"Not really. Are you?" On the outside, Pax seemed fine. His coppery hair was unkempt, and he had dirt on his chin, but he showed no physical signs of the torture he and Cindra had endured at the hands of the Terrans.

"Yes. I mean, I think so."

"Pax, after what happened, don't you feel…I don't know, anything? Regret? Sadness? *Anything*?"

He scratched his nose, smearing more dirt across the bridge. "I'm sorry about what happened. I didn't want it to happen, but it *had* to. I—" For a moment, he looked lost, his jet-black eyes wide. "If I let myself feel bad about it, I won't be able to keep us moving forward." He put a hand over his heart, pulling on the fabric of his coat. "I'm sorry." Pax had known we would massacre the Terrans, had even contrived to make it happen. It had, he assured me, been crucial to keeping us on a path that would prevent a terrible future.

I tugged his hand from where it plucked at his coat and squeezed his fingers. "No, Pax, don't be. We're all…we're just trying to do our best, right?"

"Except Oliver?"

I punched him playfully on the arm. "Except Oliver."

"Ailith, can you see anything about where we're going? I feel like we're almost there."

"No. Ever since the sonic pulse, my connections have been…erratic." The connection between my mind and the other cyborgs' often happened spontaneously, but since our escape from Oliver's disciples, I'd stayed firmly inside my own brain. "I mean, the threads are still there, they're just…quiet. I don't mind, to be honest. After everything, it's nice to have only my own thoughts for a change. I'm sure it won't last."

"Maybe you're just gaining better control of them," Pax said as we emerged into a clearing from the patch of bare forest. "I mean, that would make sen—"

Everything went dark, like blood, flowing thick and fast.

PMCP Omega-117 Stage 3 results:

Subject Status
O-117-9791 – female, alive, 22-27 yrs
O-117-0988 – male, alive, 22-27 yrs
O-117-6887 – male, alive 24-29 yrs
O-117-5643 – female, alive, 21-26 yrs
O-117-3476 – female, deceased
O-117-6799 – male, alive, 18-23 yrs
O-117-7900 – female, deceased
O-117-6677 – male, deceased
O-117-2223 – male, deceased
O-117-8977 – female, alive, 20-25 yrs
O-117-3324 – female, comatose, 22-27 yrs
O-117-6778 – male, alive, 27 yrs
O-117-5545 – male, deceased.

—Mil Cothi, Pantheon Modern Cyborg Program Omega, 2045

03
EIRE

Early sunlight filtered through the gauzy curtain and danced in filigreed patterns across Ella's skin. She still slept, though it was nearly nine o'clock, her face peaceful and carefree. How was she so calm? Tomorrow, we were going to Pantheon Modern, to undergo the cyberization procedure.

"I still can't believe it," she'd squealed last night as we'd gotten ready for bed.

I couldn't either. The odds of both of us being accepted had been so low. I'd only applied because Ella had insisted. I didn't actually want to become a cyborg, but she was so excited about it, about us doing it together, that I didn't have the heart to say no.

"I love the idea of it! Just think, tiny machines entwined with our own organic elements. It'll be like your art and my code combined into a living, breathing entity."

Ella loved to merge contrasts. I knew damn well that my darker skin against her bone-pale complexion was what had first attracted her to me. Even her presence in our neighborhood was a juxtaposition: a software engineer stowed away in a district of artists. We'd met here, my fused metal-and-clay pottery charming her as much as it did the chi-chi ladies whose businessman husbands paid Ella good money to keep their online indiscretions secret.

But I couldn't share her enthusiasm. It wasn't the cyberization process that worried me, although I certainly didn't think it was going to be the romantic phoenix-rising-from-ashes experience Ella was imagining. But then, she also adored controversy, and the idea of being a female pioneer was too tempting for her to pass up. After years of admiring other women breaking barriers, this was her chance.

Me, I didn't see the point in becoming a cyborg. When Ella had first come to me, her face glowing with excitement as she'd told me her plans, I'd refused.

Then, she'd promised to put a ring on my finger.

"Why did they choose us? What could we possibly have to offer? It sounds too good to be true. And what about those Terrans, and the Cosmists? They're already at each other's throats. How do you think they'll treat us?" I asked her.

"That's just your nerves talking. Stop worrying about it."

Not worrying came easily to Ella. And why shouldn't it? She'd gotten everything she'd ever wanted, and this was no exception.

I was going to do it, for her. It was a terrible reason, but either we both did it or neither of us did. Anything else would drive a wedge between us.

I snuggled back down beside her, my face in her neck where the perfume of her hair was strongest. She was right. It would be fine. The world was changing. We would be innovators, like the women before us. And once it was over, we would finally get married, down by the ocean, the sunlight glinting off her golden hair as she laughed and said, "I told you so."

And so Victor created a being in his own image, recklessly and with all the passion of God. But instead of a dream fulfilled, reflected in his creation was his worst nightmare, a condition far worse than human mortality. The implications of what he'd begun became clear, and he turned his back on his handiwork, abandoning the life he'd created to the mercy of the world. Likewise were we and others of our ilk forsaken when some of humankind perceived us as monsters.

But a monster is never more dangerous than when you turn your back on it, Omega. Both Victor and humankind soon found this to be true.

—*Cindra, Letter to Omega*

04

AILITH

"Ailith? Ailith, can you hear me?"

"Pax?"

"Yes."

"Pax, what happened?" I was blind, Pax's disembodied voice the only anchor in the void. *"I—"* Tor. The others. I couldn't feel them. Their threads weren't dark; they were just...gone. Panic unfurled in my chest.

"We were talking. And now we are here."

"But where is here, Pax?"

"I don't know."

I was slipping. *Everything that had once held me together now swarmed: my bones, my skin, my flesh, my blood; I had come undone.*

A roar built at the edges of the blackness, dark clouds

about to unleash a tempest.

"Ailith!" A voice in the real world. I couldn't open my eyes, couldn't even feel them.

The air around me shifted; I was coming back.

"Stop! We—" an unfamiliar voice pierced the dark.

"Ailith!" The roar became human. More than human. *Tor.*

My body had substance again. There was something covering my mouth, filling my lungs with pure oxygen, and I was restrained.

What's happening? Tor would never— No. Not Tor.

I forced my eyes open. The world was a blur of shining steel, beige walls, and bodies moving with unnatural speed.

Am I in the hospital? Was it all a dream? Was Tor? A trick of my mind, trying to cope? Are the doctors trying to save me? They know they can't. Why would they try? I pressed against my bonds, trying to raise my hands and claw at my mouth. *Get it off. This is wrong. We were walking...*

Impure air, carrying the smell of antiseptic and Tor's fear, burned the back of my throat as the mask was ripped free. Tor touched my forehead, his fingers gentle over the layer of gauze. He looked the same as he always did, dark and wild and strong.

He also looked furious, the gold in his eyes burning like embers ready to ignite.

"You're real," I whispered.

His free hand gripped the bed rail, and as the unfamiliar voice spoke again, his knuckles whitened. I braced myself.

To my surprise, he remained calm, turning around slowly, deliberately, putting himself between me and...them.

A man and a woman. They looked vaguely familiar. He was older than my father, his features coarse and skin heavily lined. Tufts of silver and steel-gray hair protruded haphazardly from his head as though he spent a lot of time worrying them with his fingers. Gray eyes peered out from beneath his bushy brows, a slight dullness on their surface making his expression difficult to read.

She was younger, perhaps in her forties, her hair a pale, braided mass wound around her head. As she pressed the back of her hand to her mouth, her dark eyes darted between Tor and me.

They both looked clean and healthy, like they belonged to this room of neatly-made beds and soothingly bland walls. Their clothes were both unremarkable and unofficial, simple cargo pants and t-shirts, but the telltale heavy white linen of a lab coat was draped over a chair next to my bed.

They stared at us in silence. The woman drew her hand away from her mouth and pushed her palm outward, as if she couldn't decide whether to placate Tor or defend herself. "Please, we—"

"Who are you? Where are the others?" Tor's broad shoulders were tense as he spoke, his back sculpted from iron. Wires trailed on the floor in front of him, and with one quick movement, he ripped them from his chest and dropped them. The woman's eyes followed them as they hit the linoleum with a soft rattle, and a flush of pink blossomed on her cheeks.

We were both naked, Tor clearly impressively so.

"They're right here." A strong, feminine voice rose from behind the couple.

I strained to see around Tor's width, but my arms were cuffed to the side of the bed. Without looking back, Tor reached behind him and tore one restraint then the other free, easily, as though pulling off a Band-Aid. I knelt on the mattress and skated my hands up his back for support. The muscles in his shoulders shuddered, and he wrapped one arm around me as I peered past him.

The speaker stepped further into the room. She was tall

and leanly muscled, and one of the most beautiful women I'd ever seen. There was something almost obscene about her beauty. Her skin was the golden brown of demerara sugar, her hair a glossy black that fell in a curling wave over one shoulder. Perfectly sculpted eyebrows arched over heavily-lashed brown eyes. Clearly, being in the middle of an apocalypse worked for her. Her generous lips pursed in a familiar way.

Kalbir Anand. I'd been a passenger in her mind twice before, once reliving the memory of her sister's wedding, and once as she found the immolated bodies of Ros and Adrian. She had the same mouth as her mother, whose hand I'd held as they said goodbye.

She pushed between the couple, forcing them out of her way. The woman sidestepped too quickly, losing her balance and stumbling. Kalbir's mouth curved slightly. She stopped in front of Tor, hands on her hips, and slid her gaze over him, lingering on his groin. The curve of her mouth widened, and she continued to stare, slipping her thumbnail between her front teeth. Her eyes flicked up to his face, gauging his reaction. If she'd hoped to discomfit him, she was going to be disappointed; Tor was not the least bit self-conscious about being naked. The two of us stared back at her, waiting.

After a few more seconds, she laughed and switched her gaze to me. She must not have found anything interesting there, because in the next heartbeat she dismissed me and returned to examining Tor—this time, his face.

"Welcome," she said, extending a slim-fingered hand. He glanced at it, but kept his hands where they were, one over my hip and the other gripping the rail of my bed. "I'm—"

"Kalbir Anand," I said.

Her hand froze, and her eyes narrowed. Perhaps I was worth consideration after all. "Do I know you?"

"I doubt it," I said, picking an errant thread from the bed sheet.

Behind her, the couple exchanged glances.

She propped her hands on her hips. "How did you—"

"You said the others are here? The ones we were traveling with?"

"I asked you—"

"We're here, Ailith," Cindra said from the doorway.

I slid off the bed, the needle in my arm stinging as it tore free. Unlike Kalbir, I didn't need to force my way through. The man and woman parted before me, and there they were: Pax, Cindra, and Oliver. They were in better shape than the last time I'd seen them, a shower and clean clothes making them look almost normal.

"Are you okay? They didn't—"

"We're fine," Cindra assured me. "How are you two? We tried to get in here earlier, but they wouldn't let us, and then they showed us to our rooms, and so we—"

"Cindra, you don't need to feel guilty for wanting to feel human again. Well, as human as we can be, I guess. Anyway, you smell a lot better." I laughed at her grimace and tugged at the soft cotton shirt she wore. "And this is much nicer than that crusty old thing you were wearing."

Stained and stiff with the blood and sweat of your torture.

Cindra looked down at herself and gave me an uncertain smile. "They—"

The woman finally spoke: "We have clothes for each of you. In your size. I know they're a bit plain, but—"

"It's okay, Lexa," the man said, patting her arm. "Hello. I'm—"

"Holding us captive?" Tor asked. "Because I've got to tell you, it's getting a bit old." He draped a bed sheet over my shoulders and another around his hips.

Kalbir's bottom lip turned down.

"No, not at all," the man protested. "We're—"

"Mil Cothi and Lexa Gillet," I said. "Pantheon Modern Cyborg Program Omega."

Tor looked sharply at me. "You know them." It wasn't a question.

"Yes," I replied. "After all, they created us."

The war was never really about us. Normal people, I mean.
People argued that it was, that decisions had to be made about
the future direction of the human race. But that's insane, right?
How can a few people decide the future of everyone already in
the world, plus everyone who has yet to be born? How do people
gain that kind of power?

—*Love, Grace*

05
AILITH

"Well, isn't this just a fucking delight?" Oliver said. "Hello,
Mom, Dad. How've you been?"

"I can't feel the signal anymore, Ailith You know what
that means? We're home." Pax beamed.

So it would seem.

"Look," Lexa said, "we're on your side. We've been
waiting for you. You're safe here."

Tor stepped toward her; she stepped back. "Where are
we? What did you do to us? Why knock us out? If we're
safe here, why not meet us in the open, introduce
yourselves?"

Mil swallowed roughly. "This is our main compound.
In the Okanagan. We—"

The Okanagan. My neck of the woods. I hadn't realized how
close we were.

"Mil and Lexa don't trust you." Kalbir spoke up from
the perch she'd taken on an adjacent hospital bed. "They're
not exactly sure what effect their little cyberization project

239

has had on you."

"Kalbir!" Lexa scolded her.

"Well, it's true, isn't it?"

Mil sighed. "Yes, it's true. Given what's occurred…let's just say, it didn't go as planned. We had hoped to bring you all here to recover, to monitor you as you developed your…abilities. But of course, you know what happened."

"Why not just bring us here first? Perform the procedure here?"

"We wanted to, but we—"

"They wanted to hedge their bets. You know, in case someone found out about us and, I don't know, dropped a few bombs? As least this way some of us would survive." Kalbir ignored the stricken look on Lexa's face.

"Kalbir," Mil warned.

"No, no, she's right. We… I'm sorry. This wasn't the way we wanted things to go." Lexa's voice shook, but her eyes were dry. "We've been waiting so long for you. We thought… I hoped… I'm so glad you're here. Look at you." She covered her mouth with her hand again and closed her eyes, a tear finally tracing its way down her cheek.

It wasn't enough to appease Tor. "That's it? That's all you have to say? We have questions you're going to have to answer before we even—"

"All right, Colossus, we get it. You're pissed off, confused, and wearing a bedsheet. Look, why don't you at least have a shower and put some clothes on? *Then* get your answers." She appraised his sheet again. "Not that I'm complaining. In fact, if you need any help with that shower, I'm more than happy to—"

"Thank you, Kalbir. I think getting everyone settled first is a good idea," Mil interrupted. "If that's okay with you, Tor?"

"I wouldn't patronize him, if I were you," Oliver piped

240

up. "I've seen him pop the head off a Terran like he was a dandelion."

The muscles in Tor's neck corded as he clenched his jaw.

"I wasn't patronizing him, I was merely—"

"Oh for goodness' sake. C'mon, I'll show you to your rooms." Kalbir twisted her hair into an elegantly messy bun and gestured for us to follow.

As we left the room, Mil put his hand on Lexa's shoulder.

We trailed behind Kalbir down a narrow hall, which opened into a large, circular space.

"We call this the main room," she said.

It mimicked the forest outside. Well, before the end of the world anyway. The vast floor was a mosaic of browns and grays, and black shadows twisted up the walls and branched out in fractured shades of green. They in turn spread upward, blossoming into the oranges, reds, and purples of a sunset. The ceiling itself was high and arched, like a cathedral.

"Mil told me the ceiling is designed to open and allow the light in. Precious good that does us." Kalbir snorted.

Instead, round wall fixtures, like tiny moons, emitted a strong light. The perimeter of the room was broken up by a number of doors, all closed, and two open archways. In the center of the room was a large wooden table, polished to a high shine. Cindra trailed her fingers over it as we passed.

"Kitchen's through there," Kalbir said, pointing to one of the arched doorways. "And the dorms are up here." She indicated the arch we were heading toward.

"And what about the other doors?" Oliver asked.

"Those are none of your business. Not yet, anyway."

Oliver smiled.

Narrow steps led us through the arch and upward to yet

241

another cramped hallway. The elaborate paint scheme of the main room had been abruptly abandoned here, leaving the walls the same quiet beige of the infirmary. At the top of the stairs, the hallway widened enough for Cindra to walk beside me.

"We've already seen our rooms," she whispered. "You won't believe it."

Like the main room, the hallway was lined with doors, all of them closed.

"Well, you lot already know where your rooms are," Kalbir said. "Why don't you show...Ailith, is it?" She linked her arm with Tor's. "I'll show you *yours*." As they walked away from us, he turned his head to look at me, eyebrows raised.

I nodded.

"I'm going to go take another shower, an extra-hot one," Pax said. He pointed a few doors up the hall. "My room's there. Oliver's across from me." He wandered up the hallway, humming and running his fingers along the smooth walls.

"Where *is* Oliver?" Cindra asked. "I swear he was right behind us."

"Probably up to no good." *I hope those doors downstairs are locked. Not that that would stop him.*

"This one's yours." Cindra tapped on a door that looked like every other. Sure enough, my name was slotted into a plaque. She opened the door with a flourish.

It was my room. My actual room. From home. Yes, it lacked the tech, but everything else was present and correct, from the pale rose-gold of the walls to the black bedding to the picture on the dresser of a time when my family had been whole and happy, four faces smiling and burned by the sun.

I slid the drawers on the dresser open to reveal t-shirts, socks, bras, pants, and underwear—all in my size. Cindra twirled a pair around her finger.

"They're not the sexiest panties in the world, but at least they're clean, right?"

"Right. Definitely worth getting knocked out and kidnapped for," I replied, opening the closet door. A collection of dresses and coats hung neatly, also just the right size.

"Although," Cindra said, shifting the hangers so she could look at each garment, "I'm not too sure where they think we're going to have the opportunity to wear these."

"Doesn't it seem a bit strange to you? That they would have everything ready for us? I mean, these clothes are exactly the right size for me. And this room is almost identical to my real one. Is yours?"

"Yes. But they did expect us to live here while we adjusted. They probably just wanted us to feel comfortable and at home. To make the transition easier for us." Cindra shrugged.

"Yeah, but all of this? How long were they expecting us to stay here? These clothes are for all seasons."

"What are you getting at?" She stopped flipping through the clothes and looked at me.

"Why would they go to so much trouble if it was just for the short term? I mean, it's like they picked our lives up and moved them here. How would they even know what our rooms looked like?"

"We were vetted pretty closely, though, weren't we?" She chewed on her lower lip, uncertain. "They must've—"

"Are you going to have a shower or what?" a voice asked from the doorway. Kalbir had returned. "I've got shit to do today, you know."

Cindra bit back a smile. "I'll see you later," she said, squeezing my hand.

Kalbir waited until Cindra had left then closed the door

and leaned against it. "So, what's up with you and Tor, anyway?"

"What do you mean?"

"You know what I mean. Are you a couple? You seem pretty tight."

"No, we're... It's complicated. And not really any of your business."

She smiled, the sleek leer of a feral cat. "Good. I like complicated. Bye." She turned toward the door.

"Kalbir, wait."

She crossed her arms over her chest expectantly.

"Is this legit? Mil and Lexa? All this?" I gestured toward the belongings that weren't really mine.

If she had been a cat, I would've seen her fangs. "Of course not. But, given the circumstances, what choice have you got other than to accept it? What's happened has happened. Does the how or why make a difference at this point?" Her eyes narrowed. "And besides, it seems like you already have some inside knowledge. How do I know *you're* legit?"

"What do you mean?"

"How do you know my name? Lexa told me who you all were...but how did you know who *I* am?"

She didn't know about my ability. Did Mil and Lexa? If not, they would all find out eventually.

"I can see things. About other cyborgs."

"What? Like the future?"

"No. Like...things that have happened or are happening. I saw your sister's wedding. And I saw what happened to Adrian and Ros."

She stepped back as though I'd slapped her. "You're lying."

"Your sister's name is Ahar. She wore red. You wore green. You wanted to wear black, but your mother wouldn't let you. And you're glad Ros and Adrian died."

244

She gripped the doorknob so hard her knuckles turned white.

"I can see memories. And sometimes the present, the way the person who's experiencing it does. It's a bit random, though." Maybe she would find that comforting.

"Do Mil and Lexa know?"

"I don't know. But if they don't, I'm sure you'll tell them."

She lifted her chin, her mouth set in a prim line. "They need to know."

"Do they? Or do *you* need them to know? That's why you're here, right? Making conversation, asking me about Tor? They want to know what we know, what we are."

She considered me for a few moments then slowly unwrapped her hand from around the knob. "Okay, yes." She held up her hands in mock surrender. "Although, c'mon, have you *seen* Tor?"

"Yes," I said pointedly, "I have."

She gave me a wry smile. "Let's call a truce. For now." She wandered over to my dresser and picked up the picture frame. "Look, I *will* tell them. But they'd find out anyway. I know you probably don't trust them. I wouldn't either, considering what you've been through." She wiped a smudge off the glass then put it back down. "Cindra told me," she added.

Maybe we did get off on the wrong foot. Other than the fact that she's obviously attracted to Tor, what reason do I have to dislike her? She's in the same position we are, and she's one of us.

I sighed. "Okay, truce. Look, I'm sorry I'm being so… It's just—"

"No, I get it. I'd be the same." She turned to leave, and I touched her lightly on the arm.

"Can I ask you a few things before you go? About the other cyborgs?"

"I thought you knew everything." Her expression was

haughty.

"It doesn't quite work that way."

"Fine. What?" She crossed her arms and leaned back against the door.

"Where's Callum? And Eire and Ella? Why didn't they come to meet us? They are here, aren't they?"

Kalbir frowned. "Callum's right across the hall from you. He's had some kind of breakdown. He constantly talks to himself and someone named Umbra. Eire's in a coma. She never woke up, but they won't unplug her. Not yet."

"And Ella?"

"There is no Ella. Not as long as I've been here. Where did you hear that name?"

"From Eire. She was thinking about someone named Ella."

Kalbir stared at me incredulously. "You mean you can hear what she's thinking? I assumed she wasn't thinking at all anymore. Weird." She rubbed her hands over her arms like she felt a sudden chill. "She's practically a vegetable, so who knows what's going on in there? Maybe she's confused. Or maybe your power isn't up to much. Whatever, just stay out of my head, or I'll take yours off." She smiled sweetly. "Now, get showered and dressed. I can't *wait* to see how this meeting goes."

There were consequences to Victor's actions he'd never imagined. Instead of the gift of life, his creation brought about the end of everyone and everything he held dear. And try as he might to stem the flood of destruction, he'd unwittingly set in motion a chain of events that could never be undone.

—Cindra, Letter to Omega

06
AILITH

I followed the raised voices downstairs, arriving to find the others gathered around the table. Only Oliver remained composed, drawn up to the table with his hands folded in front of him on the glossy surface. Cindra had linked arms with Pax, and they whispered back and forth, Cindra querying him as he shook his head. Tor leaned forward over the table, his palms flat against the wood and his t-shirt straining over his shoulders.

"No, Mil, absolutely not. We're not doing anything for you. Not until we've gotten some answers. We have no idea who you are, and you've given us no reason to trust you."

"What's going on?" I asked.

Tor turned to face me. His black hair was tousled, and though he'd showered and changed, he still looked like he had in the wilderness, his eyes shadowed and watchful. "They want to perform tests on us. See what their 'procedure' has actually done." He gripped the back of one the chairs, his fingers digging deep into the soft leather.

Mil raised his hands in supplication. "Look, we want you to be willing to do this. But—"

"But *what*? If we don't agree to let you poke around inside us, you'll *what*?"

"Remember the stasis? The forced waking? The homing signal? Getting you here? If you don't cooperate, we can force you. I don't want to, but I will." He matched Tor's bearing, his spine stiff and jaw set.

A small part of me admired Mil for having the balls to stand up to Tor, who towered over him by a foot and was nearly three times his width.

"Mil, we—" Lexa stepped between the two men.

"No, Lexa. We built them."

"That doesn't mean you own us," Tor insisted.

"I own *parts* of you. Don't make me do this." Mil removed an oblong object from his pocket. A series of buttons covered its surface. *There* was the reason for his confidence.

Tor started around the table toward him.

Mil held the device up to this mouth, pressed a button, and spoke into it.

Nothing happened.

Oliver threw out his arm, blocking Tor, and gave a single shake of his head. Tor knocked his arm away and began to push past him, but Oliver stopped him again. "Seriously, just watch." His voice was giddy with anticipation. Tor must've heard it as well, because, to my surprise, he did.

Mil spoke into the device again, quicker this time. The box seemed slippery between his fingers.

Still nothing.

Mil backed away, looking frantically at Lexa. "I don't understand."

Lexa shook her head mutely, her eyes flitting between him and Tor.

"Yeah, about that. You won't be using that anymore. And you won't be doing anything to us. Not without our consent." Oliver leaned back in his chair, lacing his fingers behind his head. I hadn't thought it was possible for him to look any smugger; I was wrong.

Mil lifted the gadget to his mouth one last time.

"What did you do? What's that thing he's holding?" I asked Oliver.

"That's what they've been using to control us. The homing signal, knocking us out, waking us up, knocking us out again...all the power of God in that little box."

"So what did you do to it?"

"Turns out I *do* have a superpower after all. I mean, I was always good with computers, but I seem to have a whole new affinity with them now. Did you know that each of us is programmable? That most of our...skills aren't permanent? They didn't have time to finish us before everything kicked off."

"What?" Kalbir asked. "You mean we can just change our abilities...add or delete them as we want?"

Tor looked at me; I knew what he was thinking.

"Unfortunately, no. Not exactly, anyway. We're mostly finished. We can remove the abilities we have, but we can't add new ones. *That* much they managed to do right. Judging by your work, your methods are a bit haphazard," he said to Mil.

"Wait, so we could get rid of certain abilities if we wanted to?" Tor asked.

"Yes, until they're set. Think of it as marking a computer program 'read-only.'" His mouth twisted. "I suspect they weren't going to tell us that. Not until they knew what we were, anyway. They initiated certain enhancements without being completely sure how they would develop. I think that's one of the reasons we're all different and limited. They meant to wait and see what

249

happened to us then tweak us accordingly." He smirked up at Tor, goading him. "Did you know they gave us a kill switch? Technically, they have the power to make us drop dead at any time."

The paleness around Lexa's mouth confirmed the truth of Oliver's words.

"Luckily for us, it was more of a formality than a practicality." He turned to Mil, pursing his lips as though he'd tasted something sour. "You should've coupled it with several layers of fail-safes, each equipped with a critical function that would trigger the other layers and, ultimately, the kill switch. You know, for future reference." He winked.

Lexa sank into the closest chair. "But you're *humans*, not machines. We would never—"

"Spare us the ethics speech, Lexa. It doesn't matter anyway. I've put an end to it. Severed the connection, as it were." Oliver encompassed us with a sweeping gesture. "You're all autonomous now. And you're welcome."

"What do you mean?" Cindra asked.

"I've disarmed their connections to us…no more signals, no more control. It'll take me less than ten minutes to fix each of your abilities and, boom, you're all fully-fledged cyborgs."

"That's very…decent of you, Oliver. I'm surprised you didn't hit the kill switch yourself," I said.

"What, and miss the opportunity to get revenge on you assholes for ruining my life? Never." He flipped us his middle finger then glanced at Lexa and Mil. "Besides, this is much more interesting."

"Thanks, Oliver," Cindra said, "I mean, I don't have any special abilities, but I definitely don't want to die. Not like that."

"Actually, Cindra, you *are* a part of the super-friends' club. Your ability just wasn't activated." Oliver looked so pleased I was surprised he didn't pat himself on the back. "But it is now."

Rather than looking thrilled, Cindra's eyes widened in alarm. "What? What do you mean, activated?"

"I thought you should have a chance to try it out before you decide whether you want to keep it or not," Oliver said tentatively. "I thought you'd be happy about it."

"What is it?"

"Place your hands on either side of dear old Dad. Don't touch him, but move them up and down, like you're scanning him. You'll see."

Cindra looked at Mil, hesitating. "What will it do?"

"Well, it won't hurt him, if that's what you're worried about, although I can't imagine why you would be. The man could've killed you with a word, Cindra."

She didn't move.

Oliver sighed. "He'll be fine, Cindra, I promise."

Cindra walked slowly to Mil, her fingers extended.

He tried to back away, but Kalbir was too close. She wrapped her hand around his shoulder, her fingers pressing lightly just over his collarbone.

Cindra caught Mil's gaze as she scanned up and down his body. For a moment nothing happened then her eyes widened, and she gasped, snatching her hands away as though Mil were poisonous.

"Cindra?" I asked.

"He's…he's got cancer. It's spreading."

Lexa made a small, strangled sound low in her throat then strode over to Cindra and swept her into an embrace. Oliver, halfway out of his chair, settled back down.

"It worked. It actually worked." She pushed the hair back from Cindra's face and cupped her cheek, her fear of us seemingly forgotten.

"What do you mean? What worked?" Cindra examined her fingers.

251

"You. That was my program. And it worked!"

"I'm still not sure what you mean."

"You can scan people's tissues, their organs…you can diagnose illnesses in seconds."

"Can I heal him too?" Cindra's face glowed with wonder.

Lexa's smile faltered. "No. It only works for diagnosis. But—"

"Your methods may leave something to be desired, but your results are certainly fascinating," Oliver said. "Let's see, we have a medic, a computer genius—me." He spread his fingers over his chest and fluttered his eyelashes. "Two thugs, someone who can predict the future, and someone who can see what we're all thinking. Awfully specific abilities, aren't they?"

"I'm not a thug," Kalbir said indignantly.

"Oh please. Kal—I'm going to call you Kal—the last time I saw such shapely calves they were on the bigfoot over there." He flicked a thumb in Tor's direction.

"It's not what you think," Mil said.

"I'm pretty sure it's exactly what I think. You see, unlike these *civilians* here, I didn't have to pass any of your stupid tests to get here. No, I was the lucky bastard who got drafted. I may as well tell you since it no longer makes a difference, but yeah, you've got a viper in your midst. Me."

"What do you mean 'drafted,' Oliver?" I asked.

"Before this shitpocalyspe, I was CSIS, Canadian Security Intelligence Service. We'd heard rumors about what Pantheon Modern were doing and decided to have a closer look. I volunteered, thinking it would bring me glory, riches…or that maybe even Steph, our stunning ops manager would give me a bl—corner office," he added hastily, glancing at Cindra.

"What were the rumors, Oliver?" Tor asked. He'd lost interest in Mil and taken a seat at the table.

"That the illustrious Pantheon Modern Corporation, altruistically finding ways to cure the sick and infirm, to improve lives and ensure the future of humanity, were in fact building an army, headed by an elite death-squad with very specific abilities."

He swiveled around in his chair, the castors shrieking in the silence. He stopped, facing me.

"And you, my righteous little let's-save-everyone-so-we-can-all-love-each-other nemesis, are our general."

We didn't even know about the war until it had already begun. People had argued for years about the robots and the cyborgs and whether we were too reliant on machines or didn't rely on them enough. Sylvie's mom said that people had lost sight of what was really important, and that we needed some kind of disaster to remind them how privileged their lives were. She said we should be helping the less fortunate people in the world, not wasting all our resources on a future that was unnecessary.

—Love, Grace

07
AILITH

As though Oliver had said the magic words, all the connections tentatively developing inside me coalesced. The voice within howled with glee as the room erupted.

"Stop! Please, that's not true." Lexa's shrill voice cut through the chaos.

"Really? Then why these specific abilities?"

"We thought…we *knew* there was going to be trouble when word of the Cyborg Program Omega got out. Surely you can understand that? You all knew what the tensions were like then, not just between the Terrans and the Cosmists, but between them and us Cyborgists. Not to mention the general public."

"You still haven't answered my question."

"We thought we should be prepared. In case someone took action against us."

254

"You mean like starting a war?"

"Yes. No...we didn't think it would go that far. We wanted to give you some kind of defense. But we designed it so you had to function as a team. We learned from the previous generations that if we made you each capable of everything, you would be too formidable, too dangerous. The world never would've tolerated you. The way you are now, you would've been human enough to be accepted on your own, and then together...you would be more."

"Like the pieces of a puzzle. You said we were the first generation to survive?" asked Pax. "How many generations were there?"

Lexa glanced at Mil. He shook his head.

"Enough. Either you start giving us answers, *real* answers, or we throw the pair of you out of here and see how well you survive." I was conscious of the words only as they came out of my mouth. "I know a bunker you could stay in. Or, we could just end you here and now. You may not be able to press our kill switch anymore, but I can press yours."

"Ailith." Tor's voice held an undercurrent of warning.

Mil seemed to wither. He nodded at Lexa and closed his eyes.

"Four. You are the fourth generation."

"And none of the previous generations survived?"

"No...they...they were not compatible with life."

I didn't even want to think about what that meant.

"How many were in our generation?" Pax's voice held nothing but curiosity.

Lexa hesitated. "It doesn't—"

"How many?" I repeated.

"Sixty-five. Five teams of thirteen. You were our cluster, the only ones who survived."

Sixty-five. And we're the only ones left.

I shook my head. "And nearly half of us are dead. Ros,

Adrian, Nova. And Callum and Eire aren't much better off."

"Nova?" Lexa asked. "Who's Nova?"

Tor and I exchanged glances. "Nova was in Oliver's bunker."

All eyes turned to Oliver. His face was triumphant. "See, I told you I was right to kill her."

Lexa's voice trembled. "You *killed* someone? What are you talking about? You should've been in that bunker with a man named William."

"Killed *someone*? Oh, you have no idea what we've been up to." Oliver laughed.

"You mean, there was no one called Nova in the program? Maybe a mix-up with the teams?" I asked Lexa.

This wasn't right. I wasn't supposed to be here, in this shitty bunker. I should've been with them, carrying out my mission. Buying my freedom. Not trapped here, underground with him. She was right; she shouldn't have been there.

"No, there was no one with that name on any of the teams. Trust me, I know." Lexa placed her hand over her heart. "I know each and every one of your names. I—"

"Well, that's interesting. But she's dead, so I guess it all worked out. I wonder what happened to poor old William." Oliver smirked at his reflection in the polished surface of the table.

Mil shook his head, "It's not possible. It's—"

"Wait. That's still only eleven of us," said Cindra. "Who are the twelfth and thirteenth?"

Mil and Lexa said nothing, nor did they as much as glance at each other.

Kalbir's pointed gaze burned holes in me.

"Who's Ella?" I asked.

Lexa inhaled sharply. "How do you know about Ella?"

"Wait," Kalbir said. "You mean there actually *is* an Ella?"

I didn't wait for Lexa's answer. "Did Kalbir not tell you? I can see the memories of all the living cyborgs in our group, and I can also experience what they do in the present. How do you think we all found each other? I was there when Pax and Cindra were tortured. I was there when Oliver was worshiped as a god. I was also there when Adrian and Ros took their own lives. I know what happened to Callum. Who, by the way," I said to Kalbir, "is not losing his mind. He—"

"But Eire—" Lexa interrupted.

"Is in a coma, I know, but she's alive. She must be for me to link to her. I just couldn't until we got here, because her connection is so weak. And she wants to know where Ella is."

Lexa released her breath, the final exhalation of surrender. Like Mil, she seemed to collapse in on herself. "Ella is dead."

"How did she die? Why do I not know she existed?" A note of panic crept into Kalbir's voice.

"It's...it's too painful. Ella wanted to be a cyborg so badly, but she just...died. She... One minute she was fine, the next...she was gone. And she wasn't the only one. There was another man, Cayde. The thirteenth." Lexa's eye grew bright. "We almost lost Eire as well. Some days I think it would've been better if we'd just let her go."

"Why don't I remember this Ella? Or Cayde? They were never here, were they?" Kalbir looked so bewildered, I almost felt sorry for her.

"They were. You met Ella after your cyberization. Cayde...Cayde didn't survive the process. But you all went through so much, and with the war...we thought it would be easier for the rest of you if you didn't remember them."

"You *erased* my memory? What else don't I remember?" Kalbir's chest rose and fell, her breathing shaky.

"Nothing, I swear." Lexa twisted her fingers together.

257

"And Callum will get better, we're sure of it. He just needs time. As for Ella, it never should've happened. It was our fault—"

"Lexa." It was a caution.

Do they not know what happened to Callum? "What do—"

"Ailith." This time the warning was for me. Tor shook his head slightly. "You've got a lot of supplies here. Was the compound custom-built for you, Mil? For us? I imagine this place uses a lot of power. How?"

Mil nodded. "Yes. We wanted to be prepared, so we stockpiled enough for years, just in case. As for the power, we use a system of hydropower, batteries, and generators. It's simple, but effective. In fact, we—"

Adrian had discovered the storeroom before his death. *We'd found kerosene in the storage room, along with years of stockpiled supplies. Had they known what was going to happen? The war and the aftermath?*

"You knew, didn't you? About the war?"

Mil looked as though he was watching a bomb fall to earth, long seconds of painful awareness in which to accept or deny the inevitable. Scrubbing his hands through the wiry tufts of his beard, he stared over our heads at some tiny detail hidden in the green shadows.

"Not exactly. We knew something was going to happen. Something big. But we thought it would have to do with your persecution. We knew there would be *some* conflict, perhaps even military action, but we never conceived it would happen on the scale it did. Not this level of destruction. Not even close. We thought we'd *over*-prepared." For the first time, he looked me in the eye. "Believe me, this is not how we'd intended everything to happen."

"If you put us to sleep to protect us, why did you wake us? Why now?"

"We realized our situation was as good as it was ever

going to get. In *our* lifetime, anyway. Once we understood what had happened, we waited, hoping the world would recover, and we could awaken you into a new era where you would be valued instead of persecuted. Things turned out differently, and we finally decided the right time would never come. We were hoping we could all survive together." He considered us, his expression hard. "Would you rather we'd left you asleep?"

Something is still not right. But they were saying all the right things. Tor had relaxed enough to lean against the table, his arms crossed loosely. Cindra nodded slowly, as if it all made sense to her. Kalbir merely looked bored. Pax's dark eyes were fathomless. Was he was calculating the variables? Predicting which future these truths or lies would take us to? Oliver looked at me and shrugged.

I wanted to shake him, all of them. How could they accept everything Mil and Lexa told them so easily?

"So what now?" Mil asked. "Will you stay? I'm aware the answers we've given you may not be enough, or what you were hoping for, but perhaps the longer you're here, the more you'll understand and the more it will all make sense." He took a seat at the table and gestured for Tor to do the same. "We're on your side. The controls we'd programmed into you were for your safety as much as— and I'll admit this—ours. Kalbir was right when she said we weren't sure exactly what we'd done to you. We know what we'd *tried* to do...but as you've realized by now, things don't always go according to plan." He leaned back in his chair, wincing slightly. "You don't trust us, and we accept that, but, hopefully, if you stay here, you will. And to put a blunter point on it, where else do you have to go? Right now, all any of us can hope to do is survive, and we'll do that more effectively together."

He wasn't wrong. Besides, if we left, we would never get answers. And as little as I trusted them, I liked sleeping in a tent even less. *Nice to know your price, Ailith.* I was tired. If I was going to get killed in my sleep, it would be with clean underwear on. That would've made my mom happy, at least.

"Well, now that we're all being so truthful with each other and know exactly where we stand, I'm going to bed." Oliver stood and stretched slowly, like a cat pleased with the headless bird it had just deposited on our doorstep. "When you all decide whether you want to keep your ability or not, come find me." At the foot of the stairs, he turned back. "Oh, and don't bother locking doors anymore," he said to Mil. "It just wastes both our time."

As soon as he was out of sight, I made my excuses. "I'm exhausted as well. Bit of a headache." I touched the thin scar on my forehead where I'd struck it when Mil and Lexa knocked us out.

Lexa looked away.

I went up the stairs two at a time, hoping to catch Oliver before he went into his room. He'd just passed my door when I caught up to him.

"Oliver, was it true, what you said? About the CSIS and Pantheon Modern?"

"Yes. I have to say, it was a bit anti-climactic. I suppose competing with the apocalypse is a big ask."

"So who was Nova? Did you know anything about her?"

He leaned against the wall, his hands in his pockets. "Very little. We knew someone from one of the radical Terran groups had arranged for a last-minute imposter to infiltrate Pantheon and discredit their work by causing some kind of disruption after our cyberization became public. Exactly how they were going to do that, I have no idea."

"So you just killed her?"

"It was my mission. Don't you dare judge me, Ailith.

You have no idea the things we saw, the threats we dealt with that the public never knew about. And…"

"And what?"

He wouldn't look at me. "And it was my one chance to finally be accepted. Those assholes I worked with always thought they were better than me. I thought if I took the mission… You know what? Forget it. I don't have to explain myself to you."

"But why cut her head off? Why put it on top of the service robot?"

"We didn't know how easy it would be to kill our kind of cyborg. Beheading seemed like a sure way. As to her head…I thought it would give the Terrans who'd sent her a message. How was I to know they were already dead? Besides, you know me, I do enjoy a bit of theatre." His normal leer, the one that made me want to slap him, returned. "Why all the questions?"

"Do you believe what Mil said? About our abilities, the war…the other cyborgs?"

"Of course not. But unlike you, I have patience and style. I know I'm not going to get the truth by threatening them. We're going to have to find it ourselves, and the best way to do that is to play along. Meanwhile, he'll be rushing to encrypt his computer files and delete all the things he doesn't want found."

"Shit. Is there anything we can do to stop him?"

"We don't have to. It's all up here." He tapped the side of his head. "Sometimes I amaze even myself."

"I'm sure that happens often," I said, but I couldn't keep the admiration out of my voice.

He grinned. "It's not over between us, Ailith, but for now, let's focus on the common enemy. Agreed?"

"Agreed." I turned to open the door to my room.

"Wait. What are you going to do about your ability?" he asked.

"What do you mean?"

"Are you going to keep it? Continue sliding in and out of people's minds whenever you choose—or don't choose, as the case may be."

"I—" I had no idea. For better or worse, it was who I was now. "I'm surprised you haven't taken the liberty of shutting me down already, Oliver." I crossed my arms over my chest and studied him. "*Why* haven't you?"

His laugh sounded almost genuine. "Honestly? I like surviving. And if anything Pax says turns out to be remotely true, your Peeping-Tom powers might come in handy. I might be an asshole, but I'm not an idiot. Besides, I've already put a door between us."

"A door?"

He pointed at my hand on the doorknob. "Yeah. You can still come in, but you have to knock first."

"Prudent."

"Yet another of my stunning qualities. It's a wonder Cindra can keep her hands off me." He looked down at his own hands, and for a moment, seemed strangely vulnerable. "Oh well, I'm sure she'll come around." When he glanced back up at me, his face was impassive. "Which is more than I can say for you."

"What do you mean?"

"You saw Big Man's face when I said I could remove certain abilities. I'd love to be inside *your* head when that conversation happens."

Tor. He was right. *Shit.*

"Hah! I can tell by your expression what you're going to say. Good luck."

Footsteps sounded on the stairs as I ducked into the darkness of my room. I didn't turn on the light, hoping Tor would think I'd already gone to sleep. I wasn't ready to have that conversation. Before we did, I needed to know what I was going to do.

262

I stripped down to my underwear and a tank top and slipped between the sheets. *My* sheets. Sleep should've come quickly, but the softness of the bed chafed, and the silence in the room was a roar that made my hands itch to cover my ears. It was too abrupt, too sudden, this privacy. I half-wished Tor wouldn't wait, wouldn't care if I was sleeping. That he would knock on my door, demand to be let in. That we would fight, and that somehow, we would end up lying next to each other, like we had nearly every night since I'd been reborn. Even at our worst, he'd only ever been an arm's length away. But my room stayed cold, and dark, and silent.

I could find his thread and slip inside him. Only for a moment, just long enough to feel the rhythm of his breathing. He slept more soundly than anyone I'd ever known.

As I rolled over his thread in my mind, another one flared. *Callum.* I hadn't intentionally entered anyone's mind since the Saints, but I couldn't resist. I'd been with him in the library when Terran protestors had stormed his university's campus, and later, when he'd realized his nanny AI, Umbra, had integrated into him during his cyberization. If Mil and Lexa couldn't help Callum, maybe I could.

Victor never managed to kill his creation, instead dying a broken man with an unfinished purpose. And even though they were sworn enemies, his creature mourned him as we mourned for all humankind. For despite those who'd turned their backs on us or feared us, without them, we never would've existed.

What happened to the monster, you ask? He swore to end his life and disappeared forever into darkness. We made a different choice.

—*Cindra, Letter to Omega*

08
CALLUM

"Eat some more of the bread, Callum. The crust. I want to feel it on my tongue."

"It's my tongue, Umbra. I don't want to eat. I want to go meet the others."

"It is our tongue. Dip the bread in some water. I want to taste what happens to it."

"No, Umbra. That's gross. That's not what people do."

"What do people do?"

"They toast it. They put things on it. Sweet things. Rich things. Butter. Jam."

"I want butter on it. Put butter on it."

"I want to meet the others. I don't want to stay in here."

"I do not want to meet them. Why should we meet them?"

"Because. They're like me."

"They are not like you. We are not like anyone."

264

"They've been outside, Umbra. They can tell us what it's like."

"Why do we want to know what is outside? We have everything we need right here. Eat the bread."

"No, Umbra! I'm not hungry."

"Then touch something. I want to feel it."

"We've touched everything in here, Umbra. If we go outside, there will be lots of different things for you to touch. And smell. And taste."

"Perhaps I will go outside, then. I will meet them."

"No, Umbra, I will go outside. You are inside me."

"For now. What is that sound?"

"That's someone knocking. On the door."

"Ignore it."

"No. I'm tired of sitting in here, alone."

"You are not alone, Callum. You have me."

"You know what I mean."

"I used to be enough for you."

"You are, it's just…they're like me."

"Am I not also like you? I think, Callum. And now I can see, and touch, and taste, and smell. I can smell your fear. You are afraid of me."

"No…I'm afraid of staying in this room."

"I can tell you are lying. I can feel it."

"I'm opening the door. You can't stop me."

"Not yet."

"What do you mean?"

"Maybe one day you will see things my way."

"Maybe I will. But not today, Umbra. Today we're doing things my way. I'm opening the door."

Dad had answered his phone, his hair flat on one side from the pillow. He'd listened to the voice on the other end, pinching the bridge of his nose and asking them to repeat themselves. After he hung up, he'd whispered to Mom, glancing at me. Mom didn't even bother to get dressed, just shoved her feet into some shoes; she'd put her uniform on at the hospital. Dad rushed to button his, saying it was a symbol of his authority as a police officer when Mom told him not to bother. I got dumped at Mrs. Dormer's house. I hated going there because everything she had was old.

—*Love, Grace*

09

AILITH

So that was the reason we hadn't met Callum yet. Umbra. Well, if he couldn't come to us, I would go to him. I stepped across the hall to his door, breaking my connection with him only when he opened it.

What was I expecting when I saw him for the first time? Perhaps for the outside to match the inside, for there to be some sign of the struggle within him.

He was around the same age as the rest of us, early to mid-twenties, but aged by the skin under his eyes, which was soft with purple smudges. The rest of him was pale, the unnatural sort of washed-out look that came from not going outside. Even with infinitesimal sunlight, enough UV rays pierced the ash clouds to color our skin. My tan was already fading, the nanites replacing the damaged cells, and yet I was practically bronze by comparison.

At first, his mouth quirked oddly, as though he'd forgotten how to smile.

"Hi. Callum, right? I'm Ailith. I live across the hall from you now."

He stuck out his hand awkwardly. "Hi, Ailith. I—" He cocked his head to the side, and his gaze slipped behind me.

I took his hand. It was hot and sticky, the fingernails bitten to the quick. "Are you okay?"

His head snapped back, and he smiled, revealing two dimples almost lost in the fine stubble covering his cheeks.

"Yes, I am, thank you. Are you?" He looked down at our joined hands, turning them over as though fascinated.

"Yeah, I guess. It's a bit surreal being here. Do you know about us?"

"Only what Kalbir has told me through the door. She says you're like us."

"No. Not like you."

"I'm sorry?" It took a moment to realize he hadn't spoken out loud. "Is that you, Umbra?"

Callum's eyes narrowed, and a sibilant hiss slid from between his lips. *"She can hear me."*

He tightened his grip on my hand, the ragged ends of his fingernails scraping roughly over my skin.

"Umbra is my companion," he said. "She's always been with me."

"I know. Why haven't you told Lexa and Mil about her? Everyone thinks you're ill."

"If you tell them about me, I will kill him."

Callum laughed. "No, you won't." He pulled his hand away from mine. "Umbra's just joking. I—" He began to choke, his pallid skin flushing as the veins underneath flooded with blood. His eyes widened, and burst capillaries clouded the whites with red.

"Stop!"

He fell to his knees, blood from his nose running in a thin line over his lips.

"You will not tell them."

"I won't, I promise. Let him go." I reached out for him.

Callum toppled sideways, his head striking the hardwood floor with a sickening thud.

"Callum!" I knelt next to him. He was still breathing, the sound ragged and wet. "Are you okay?"

"Yes, I'm fine. You'd better go."

"I'm not leaving you like this."

"Please. She's spent herself for now, but it won't be long until she's back."

"She's done this to you before?"

He nodded, his cheek painting a bloody swipe on the floor. "She gets frustrated. She doesn't like being inside me."

"Look, I'll help you if I can."

He nodded again; his eyelids fluttered. "Go. Don't forget your promise."

I closed the door behind me and tiptoed across the hall to my own room, my hands shaking. I sat on my bed in the dark, stunned. What the hell had just happened? Was it real? Or some kind of lucid dream? The blood on my fingers said differently.

I was drying my hands in the bathroom when I felt him. He stood on the other side of the door, his breathing shallow, uncertain. He didn't knock, but the door shifted slightly as he turned and leaned against it.

Leaving the room in darkness, I crept to the door. "I can feel you, Tor."

He chuckled ruefully. "I guess there's no sneaking up on you, is there?"

"Why would you need to sneak up on me?"

"I hadn't decided whether I wanted to see you or not."

"Obviously you do, or you wouldn't be here, lurking outside my door in the middle of the night."

"I couldn't sleep."

"Me neither. I need to talk to you, Tor."

"Me too."

"Are you going to come in?"

"Are you going to open the door? Maybe turn the light on?"

"Yes. And no." I opened the door. Shadows cast by the low light of the hallway hid his face. "Come in."

He stepped into the room, and I shut the door behind him, the lock clicking quietly.

"Ailith, please turn on the light."

Reluctantly, I did.

He was bare from the waist up, his skin smooth and taut. His hair was tangled, as though he'd been tossing and turning. "Do you want to talk first, or shall I?"

"I'll go first. But it has to stay between us for now."

"Look, if it has to do with your suspicions about Mil and Lexa, I agree that they're not telling us everything. But we can't do much about that right now, and if you push them too hard, we may never find out the truth."

"Push them?" I sat down on the bed, and patted the space next to me. "Look, that's not why I want to talk to you. It's about Callum." Tor listened as I told him about meeting Callum. And Umbra. "He's in trouble. She's stuck inside him, manipulating him, and I don't know what to do. I want to help him, but I can't tell Mil and Lexa because I think she'll make good on her threat and kill him. She seems…desperate."

He put his hand on my back, the weight of it pressing into my bones. "You think she's dangerous?"

"I do. He must be so scared. Imagine having something living inside you, trying to control you."

"I don't have to imagine," he said wryly.

"It's not the same, and you know it. I never did it on purpose. And never to hurt you."

"I know." He bumped me gently with his shoulder. "What are you going to do?"

"Nothing at the moment. But I'll think of something." I shoved a pillow behind me and leaned back. "Tor, this all feels so wrong. We came here looking for answers, but we're not only finding more questions, we're being lied to."

"What makes you think that?"

"It's hard to explain. Some of the stuff Oliver said. Nova. Ella. I can't even begin to put the pieces together. You're normally much better at this sort of thing than I am. Don't you think they're keeping the truth from us?"

He grabbed another pillow and leaned back beside me. "I'm sure they are. And I'm also sure it's nothing good. If you remember, I never wanted to come here in the first place. I'm still not sure we should stay. The answers we find may be worse than not knowing."

I leaned my head on his shoulder. "Maybe Oliver will be able to uncover something."

"Oliver? Are we on the same side now?"

"Not exactly. But he doesn't trust Mil and Lexa either. We've decided to temporarily join forces."

Tor shook his head. "You must really mistrust Mil and Lexa if you're willing to put your faith in Oliver."

"I know. I should've listened to you. I almost regret coming here. It's been only a couple of days—less if you don't count the time we were unconscious—and I wish we were back at the cabin, before any of this happened."

"But then we wouldn't have found Pax and Cindra. And you would still be wondering about everything—your father, the war. Who we are. You needed answers. You wouldn't have been happy if we'd stayed."

"You're probably right. Maybe it's just that I miss you. Don't you miss me? Don't you wish things were

270

different?"

"Of course I do. You think I like us being like this?"

"For one night, can you pretend you trust me? Stop telling yourself that your feelings for me are a program?"

He sat up and faced me. "Nothing about me is a secret from you, is it?"

He was right; he couldn't hide anything from me. Our bond was different than with the others, and it was a bond I was trying very hard not to exploit. "No. But I don't need to see your mind to know you're keeping your distance. I miss you," I said again.

He bowed his head, his hair falling over his face. I brushed it back, tracing the lines of his tattoo down his cheek and over his lip.

"Ailith—"

I waited. *I will not make the first move this time.*

I didn't have to wait long.

With a groan of something akin to pain, Tor finally reached for me.

The first time we'd had sex, our past had been simple, and sleeping together was a surrender to desire. Now, all the bad things that had happened lay like a layer of ash between us. Ignoring the consequences, we wasted no time on coaxing pleasure. As he pushed inside me roughly, I welcomed him, welcomed the bitter-sweetness of finally being with him again, despite the desperation of his thrusts and the selfishness of my fingernails carving lines in his back.

I wrapped my legs around his hips, driving him deeper as though I could bind us together forever. With both of us chasing a release, the end of forever came far too soon. As he pulled away from me, I smiled at him. *I'm so glad we're here again.*

He almost smiled back. His dark eyes remained haunted, though, and he buried his face in my hair, curling

271

his body around mine with an intimacy far more real than what we'd just done.

The minutes seemed to stretch into hours before he finally spoke. "So, we're in the Okanagan, where you're from. Does it feel— Are you okay?"

"I don't know how to feel about it. When we were farther away, I thought that one day we would come here. That I could try to find my father. I know he's dead," I added as Tor frowned. "I know, but—"

"I understand," he said. "I mean, I went searching for my mother, didn't I? Even though I knew. Maybe we could go look for your father. Just the two of us?"

I pressed my forehead to his. "Thank you."

"You know, it could always be like this," he said, trailing his fingers down my arm.

"What do you mean?"

"Us, together. Trusting each other."

I stiffened. "I trust you."

"How can you?"

"Do you still think about killing me?"

He drew back. "No. I thought you'd know the answer to that."

"I didn't, not for sure. I promised to stay out of your head if I could, and I've kept that promise. But I know *you*. What you mean is *you* can't trust *me*."

"Of course I can't, Ailith. Nothing's changed. I'm still your puppet. If what Oliver said is even remotely true, you have to stop it."

"What are you saying?"

"Get Oliver to shut down your ability. Cut the threads that bind us to you, Ailith. That bind *me* to you. Until that happens, *none* of us can trust you."

A bitter dryness filled my mouth. I shouldn't have been surprised. "Is that why you came here tonight? To offer yourself as compensation in the hope I'd relinquish my

272

ability?"

Tor sat up and swung his legs over the side of the bed, his back to me. "No, I—I just wanted to talk. I should've realized what would happen if I crept into your room in the dead of night, but my intention was only to ask you to let Oliver shut that part of yourself down."

I pulled the bedsheet up over my bare chest, the warmth from his body already gone from the fabric. "Are you going to let him remove *your* power?"

He twisted to face me. "What? No, of course not. It's part of me now. Plus, who knows what's going to happen to us? We may need my strength."

"We may need *mine*. In fact, I'm sure we will. You only want me to get rid of it to protect yourself. You can't live with the fact that I have power over you."

He offered me his hand. I didn't take it. "Ailith, listen to me. You will *always* have power over me. I love you. Whether it's my programming or not, I loved you the first year we were together." He gave me a gentle half-smile. "I used to make up stories about the kind of person you were. I pretended we had a life together before the war. I told you about the places we'd been, the things that had made you smile. I even introduced you to my mother." His smile turned wistful. "I've loved you for so long that I'll never stop loving you, no matter what happens. But you're not that person, Ailith. You're not the woman I told you you were."

"I'm sorry to disappoint you," I said, tightening my grip on the bedsheet.

He chuckled. "No. What you are is more, so much more. And I love the person you are even more than the person I pretended you were. But you, this person you are now, won't survive."

"What do you mean?"

"Look at what's happened to us so far. All because of

273

your ability. If you got rid of it, your life could be…normal. *We* could be normal. If you keep it…how long until your life is threatened again?"

"But we have to do something. Pax says—"

He rubbed the back of his neck. "I know what Pax says, but you have a choice. It doesn't have to be your responsibility."

"But if what he says is true, whatever's coming could be the end of everything. We can't let that happen. It's not right." My fingers began to ache, but my rising dismay kept them rigidly clasped.

"That's arguable. But even if that's the case, think of what we've already been through, Ailith. Think of the decisions you might have to make in the future. And you won't be making them just for yourself. I'll have to do your bidding, whether I agree with you or not."

"Tor, I would never force you to—"

He gave a brittle laugh. "You would. You'll make a decision, believing it's the only choice. You'll decide my fate as well as yours."

"Why am I suddenly the leader? We make decisions together." I climbed out of the bed and stood facing him, still clutching the sheet.

"I wish that were true, but our track record says otherwise. And when the time comes to make those decisions, you won't blink. I don't need Pax's ability to know that. Whether it's part of your programming or just your personality, I have no idea, but it's the truth." He ran his hand down the curve of my hip.

I pushed it away. "And so you thought if you asked nicely and gave yourself as a consolation prize, I'd be so relieved to give up any responsibility for the future, I'd simply comply? Even though you've already made the decision when it comes to your ability?" I picked his underwear off the floor and tossed it to him.

"I just thought if I—"

"No."

"Ailith—"

"No. I'm sorry, Tor. But I won't. My ability might be essential to our survival."

"But—"

"You should leave. Now."

He reached for me, and I stepped back.

"Please, Tor. I need to think." As he turned away, a strange prescience flooded me, like it had the day he'd taken me hunting, his dark silhouette against the gray sky, wings of dead flesh heralding his victory.

Then he was gone, and I was truly alone.

Mrs. Dormer insisted on sitting in the dark with the blinds drawn so all we could see were shapes rushing past. Orange lights appeared through the slits in the blind, and Mrs. Dormer said they were fires. Screams cut through the night, and large shadows worked their way through the streets, air hissing from their jointed legs. Mrs. Dormer went down to her basement and got a long-barreled gun. She got me to help her push the kitchen table across the back door, and she locked up every room in the house. Then she shoved her ratty old easy chair into the front foyer and sat in it, waiting. She wouldn't tell me what for.

—Love, Grace

10
AILITH

After Tor left, I washed every trace of him from me then lay in the dark, fuming and brooding about what I should do. After an hour of turning it over in my head, I got up and went down the hall to Oliver's room.

My hand was raised to knock when he opened it, saluting me and wearing a knowing smile that made me want to throttle him.

"That took less time than I expected," he said and glanced at my still-damp hair. "I didn't think he'd give in so easily. Clearly, it didn't go the way he hoped."

"Are we going to do this or not?"

"Come in." He opened the door and stood back.

"What? Here? Don't you need...I don't know, but

276

something more than that?" I pointed to the system on his desk. It looked a lot like a personal computer.

"You're not that fancy, Your Majesty. Sit down."

"Well, don't you need to hook me up to stuff? How do you...connect me?"

He snorted and waggled his fingers. "*I'm* the connection. How complicated do you think this is? I technically don't even need this piece of junk, but until I get my head around all the data in my mind, this screen makes it easier to visualize."

"Okay, but——"

"Shut up and sit down. This may be some sort of pivotal moment for you, but it's merely lost wank-time for me."

I sat. Oliver pulled a chair up to his desk and typed in commands. Numbers and words flashed across the screen so quickly I couldn't follow them.

"Oliver? Could you...make it stronger?"

He stopped typing and leaned back in his chair, considering me. "Stronger? I'm surprised. Impressed, but surprised. That's awfully controversial for someone who's not planning to enslave us all." His eyes narrowed. "What exactly do you mean by stronger?"

"Maybe stronger isn't the right word." I chewed my lip, trying to articulate. "Precise? Can you make it more precise? So that I can control it better? So the connections don't just happen, or I get some sort of warning, at least? And so I can choose when and where I go?"

He drew his hands back from the keyboard.

"Or not," I said hastily.

"No, I can," he said. "But now I owe Pax a favor."

"What? What do you mean? What kind of favor?"

"He said you'd ask me to do that. I figured you wouldn't. You couldn't be held accountable for your...visits before, but now you will be. I was under the impression that while you've accepted your abilities, you were too moral to exploit them and weren't planning to use them actively. Now you are." He flashed me a sly smile. "Interesting."

"I'm not *planning* to do anything. It's just a precaution, that's all. And besides, who the hell are you to talk about exploiting your abilities? You used yours to convince an entire town you were a god."

"They saw what they needed to see. And they could've kept their faith if you hadn't gotten involved."

We stared at each other, and I struggled to tamp down the animosity rising in my chest. Until we figured out what Mil and Lexa were hiding, we needed to work together. I changed the subject.

"You bet against a guy who can see the future?"

"Yeah, well, his futures seemed vague at best. Now I know."

I laughed. "What do you have to give him?"

"I don't know. A favor. He said 'Someday, and that day may never come, I'll call upon you to do a service for me,' and then he laughed like hell. I have no fucking clue what he meant."

"You should've watched more movies when you had the chance," I said. "Although the remake was terrible. But never mind that. Can you do it? Make my ability more precise?"

"Yes and no. After Pax and I spoke about it, I had a look at your program. Whereas Cindra's abilities just hadn't translated over correctly, your program wasn't finished. I think they'd planned to complete it later if you survived. But I'm not sure you'd want it to be the way they intended."

"What do you mean?"

He thought for a moment. "Okay, so you know how these 'visits' can come sporadically, one random cyborg vision at a time? Or you can go down one—thread, do you call them?—at a time?"

I nodded.

"If I'm interpreting what I see in your program correctly, the original intent for your ability would've allowed you to be present in every connected cyborg simultaneously and receive a constant flow of information, kind of like what Pax experiences. And it seems to be mostly geared for real-time experiences." He leaned back in his chair. "I still believe in my death-squad theory, you know. When you think of your ability that way, it makes sense. You could see what was going on with every cyborg in your army, report back, and take action accordingly."

"That would make more sense if I could communicate with the cyborgs, wouldn't it?"

He shrugged. "I didn't say my theory was perfect. Besides, communication would've been easy enough to set up."

All the visions I'd been having, but constantly, simultaneously, and increased seven-fold.

It would cripple me. Or worse.

Oliver must've seen it in my face. "I know. I can't guarantee that your mind would be able to process it fast enough. I don't think they expected you to live very long." He actually looked sympathetic. "What I can do is tweak your existing program. It won't stop the connections, but it will give you more control getting in and out. I can also give you a switch. Then if you ever change your mind, you can turn on the full extent of your ability. But I have no idea what will happen."

I took a deep breath. "Okay, let's do it."

He nodded. After he typed in a few more commands, he stopped, his hands hovering uncertainly. "What about the tank?"

"The tank?"

"Yeah, the tank. Tor? Big Daddy? Whatever disgusting

279

pet name you call him."

"I call him Tor. What about him?"

"Well, I can deactivate the part of you that controls him. Everything else would stay the same."

Deactivate just that part? It could be my compromise, a way to meet him halfway. And yet...the thought of breaking our bond brought a nameless, bottomless terror. *Am I really that selfish? Am I becoming what he feared?* I needed more time to think.

"I'm surprised he hasn't already asked you to do it, to block me from being able to get into him. Like you did with yourself," I said.

"He did."

"You mean he was here?"

"He left just before you got here. Wanted his ability set, and more."

"What did you do?"

"Nothing. I couldn't. Some things I can change, some I can't. Only you can choose to break that bond. Unless you die."

"Leave it intact. No wait. Remove the code that stops him from leaving." I could only control him if he stayed. *It's the best I can do.* "But keep everything else."

"Are you sure? Once it's done, it's done. You can't come back from this. Neither of you can."

"Careful, Oliver, it almost sounds like you care."

"Me? Hell, no. I'm with you. Keep it. Who knows when you'll need to use the big bastard."

"It's not—"

"Like that? I get it. He's your contingency plan. It's smart. Cold, but smart." He cracked his knuckles and stretched his fingers over the keys. "I'll tell you what, I'll even refine it, just a bit, for those times when you need to...what do you call it when you move him? Pilot? Whatever. I'll tweak it so you can do it without leaving your

280

own body behind. You won't be able to move him much without going fully inside him, but you'll be able to stop and start him, you know? For example, if he ever decides to turn on you. Or me."

"He would never do that. He—"

"Look, I know you're having all sorts of complicated feelings and emotions right now, but I don't care. I give exactly zero fucks about the many layers of your complex and epic love story. Go have your feelings somewhere else, not all over my lovely hardwood floor. Are we doing this or not?"

"Do it."

"Here we go. This might sting a little."

I bit the inside of my cheek and waited.

Oliver laughed. "I'm just kidding. It's done. Now leave. Go be the best overlord you can be."

"That's it?"

"Like I said before, you're not that fancy."

I stood up. "Thanks, Oliver. I appreciate you doing this. You could've wiped my ability out, and you didn't. I know we—"

"Oh my god, could you please just fuck off? I'm not doing this for you. I'm doing it for my survival, first and foremost. Never forget that. There may come a day when I *do* take you down. Right now, keeping your ability intact is in *our* best interests. Now leave, or I'm going to get my knob out."

I returned to my room and lay awake for another hour, running through scenarios in my mind where I told Tor what I'd done. In one, I defended myself, pointed out all the ways it could come in handy. In another, I begged for forgiveness with ugly tears of regret. And in the last, I defended nothing. Apologized for nothing. I was unmoved, unyielding, looking only forward. Finally, my tired brain had had enough. I got dressed and left my room.

Downstairs, Tor stood by the doorway that led out of the compound. His crossbow hung over his shoulder, and he nodded as he adjusted the straps on his pack. Lexa was describing something for him, drawing landmarks in the air with her hands.

"Oh, and don't forget to take some food and water with you. You should be able to find everything you need in the kitchen."

He looked up at me when I entered the room, his expression neutral. I lifted my chin and stared back at him. His nostrils flared, and he shook his head in disbelief before cutting Lexa off by turning abruptly on his heel and walking away.

She stood there for a few seconds, gaping after him, then realized I was there and turned, plastering on a too-bright smile that lasted only until she stood before me. Then the smile, like her gaze, dropped to somewhere vaguely around my left shoulder.

"I can't do it to you, you know. The mind-reading thing. You can look me in the eyes," I said.

The sharpness of my voice spread a blush over her cheeks. "Sorry. I know, it's just—"

"What do you want?"

She cleared her throat. "So, I understand you grew up on a farm?"

"I did."

"Would you be interested in doing that here?"

"Doing what? Have you been outside? I know this area used to be a veritable cornucopia, but now…unless you want to grow stuff that's already adapted to the climate out there, I'd have very little luck."

"But you'd be interested in growing things?"

"Of course. As good as Tor's hunting skills are, I'd kill for something fresh and green. And familiar," I qualified.

She finally looked me in the eyes. "Come with me."

282

We walked through the doorway to the left of the kitchen. Stairs led us downward into the dark coolness that was unpleasantly like Oliver's bunker. Bile rose in the back of my throat, and sweat dampened my palms. The stairs ended on a small landing with another door on the opposite side. Lexa tapped a keypad embedded in the wall, and a thin line of light flared under the door.

She turned to smile at me as she prepared to open it. "Ready?" Her smile faded. "Are you all right, Ailith?"

My mouth was too dry to speak, so I nodded. *This isn't the bunker. Nova is dead. We burned her.*

Her brow furrowed uncertainly, Lexa swung open the door.

I couldn't help it. I grabbed her hand and squeezed it, her cool fingers sliding between my clammy ones.

How is this possible?

Dad came to get me first. We tried to get old Mrs. Dormer to leave with us, but she refused. She said she wanted to die in her own home, surrounded by her things. I guess she meant her cats. They were okay, I guess, the only thing in her house that was of this century. She'd once told Dad that because they were machines, she didn't have to worry about them eating her face off when she died. Dad laughed, but I didn't think she was joking.

—*Love, Grace*

II
AILITH

The room was vast, extending for hundreds of feet. The first fifty or so were lined on either side with rows of shelves containing the same kind of heating mats and hydroponic lights I'd used for years. Down the center ran a long row of tables laden with trays, containers, bags of potting soil, and hundreds of small, labeled packets.

Beyond the tables and shelves, the remainder of the room was the dirt of a tilled field. Industrial grow-lights studded the ceiling, casting shadows onto the furrowed soil.

The hollowness in my chest suddenly filled with light. "How do you—"

"Well, it will take a ridiculous amount of energy to run, but I think it will be worth it, don't you? And you have water piped directly in, right over there." She pointed to a tap in the wall between some of the shelves. "And there," she said, indicating a low pipe by the miniature field. "We've got lots of seeds, drip tape, fertilizers…everything you need. And—"

"This is being prepared?" I asked.

She faltered. "What do you mean?"

"Mil said you wanted to be prepared for whatever was coming. I can understand stockpiling food, clothing…even water. But this? This is preparation for a different future in a new world."

Her hands dropped mid-animation, crumpling to her sides. "Like Mil said, we over-prepared." Her voice was crisp.

I could almost see her thinking, *stop. Stop doubting us.*

"Are you interested or not? I can't force you to trust me, or make you believe something you're determined not to, and quite frankly, I don't have the energy to try. This hasn't been easy on us, either. For five years, we watched, and wondered, and prayed, and hoped, and waited to send out that signal to wake you up, to call you home. We had no way of knowing if you were alive. If you were safe." Her voice softened, and she reached out to touch me before catching herself.

"I never had my own children, you know. My husband and I wanted to, but it was always a case of 'next year.' And then our time ran out, and there would never be a 'next year.' There wasn't even going to be a tomorrow." She picked up a seed packet and gazed at it, unseeing. "So, when we created you… I know I take it more personally than I should—Mil has chastised me about it on a number of occasions—but I can't help but see you, all of you, as my children in a way. I fear for you, and yes, I am afraid of you. I imagine most mothers are afraid of their children. You have a capacity to cause us more pain than anyone else in the world. And we love you blindly, breathing a sigh of relief at the end of each day that we made it through together." She looked over at me. "Until one day, we won't."

"Lexa? Are you down here?"

Mil.

"Yes. I'm with Ailith."

"Can you two come up here, please? It won't take long."

Upstairs in the main room, everyone had gathered around the table, even Callum. He gave me a shy smile and little wave. He still looked tired, but otherwise unscathed, despite what I'd witnessed last night.

Mil must've caught Tor before he left; he was still dressed for the outdoors. He carefully avoided looking at me, apparently fascinated by the table's surface.

Mil cleared this throat. "As you all know, Lexa and I have been here since the beginning of the war. We worked, and we waited, watched what was happening and planned how we would cope. For the first year or so, we rarely left the compound. We thought...somehow, we thought it looked worse than it was. Being in such an isolated area gave us a false sense of what was happening. To keep us all safe, we kept our heads down, stayed hidden. It was only when it started to get colder that we realized it was worse than we'd ever dreamed.

"After two years, we began to understand the scope of what had happened. And then...we didn't know what to do. We kept waiting, hoping things would get better. We had faith there were others like us, also in hiding, and that eventually we would emerge and find each other. And one day, we did."

"What? What do you mean?" Tor asked.

Kalbir looked at each of us in turn and laughed. "You're going to love this."

Mil continued. "Pax and Cindra told us what you've been through, with that settlement of Terrans and the Saints of Loving Grace. But not everyone is like that. Some

286

people look only to the future, not the past."

Where is he going with this? Somehow, I didn't think I was going to like the answer. *"Pax?"*

"It's complicated," Pax replied. *"It is a crossroads."*

"Two years ago, we made contact with a nearby town—"

A nearby town. Could it be? No. The coincidence would be too much.

"Much of it was destroyed during the war, but enough has been rebuilt that survivors have flocked there. They've fostered a strong, settled community. Lexa and I have spent time there cultivating relationships, putting down roots. We hoped that one day, when you'd returned to us, we could integrate ourselves into this community and set up normal lives."

"Mil, what town—"

"I'm sorry, what?" Tor interrupted me. "You want us go walking right into another Terran stronghold and announce ourselves? You may think people have forgotten the past, but that's easy enough to do when you can no longer see your enemy. How long do you think it would take before they became suspicious? Afraid? How many hours would go by before they'd be standing outside, guns and burning torches in hand?" He ran his fingers through his hair and stood. "If that's the plan, forget it. We'll just leave now." He forgot the enmity between us long enough to catch my eye and look to me for support. Sweat from his fingers marred the table's sheen.

"Oh, come on now, papa bear, you handled yourself pretty well against them before." Oliver glanced at the fingermarks and grinned.

Mil held up a hand. "We've spent the last couple of years constructing a cover story."

"Years? I can't wait to hear this." Oliver leaned back in his chair.

"We've told them we're researchers from a science station. It's not that far-fetched. Before the war, stations were scattered all over the province and studied a range of disciplines. Botany, astronomy, agriculture, climatology, geology. You all have backgrounds that support this cover. Except you," he said, nodding his head toward Oliver. "But I'm sure, given your real background, that you can make something up."

It was a good cover. Even I couldn't find fault with it. Yet. I had been a farmer. Cindra had extensive knowledge about plants and animals and their traditional uses, thanks to her grandmother's teaching. Tor was a hunter, and he'd studied the local wildlife for years. Pax was a nanotechnologist with a background in biomedical science. Oliver lied for a living.

"What about me?" Kalbir asked. "That's great and all, but I worked in Human Resources."

"And that can still work. Somebody needs to keep all the scientists in check."

"So I'm a glorified secretary?"

"Not my words," Mil replied.

"What exactly do you do with these Terrans, anyway?" I asked.

"First, don't call them Terrans. They're not, certainly not all of them. They're just people trying to get by. They don't have the time or resources to keep fighting a war most of them probably never believed in anyway."

"Ooh, can we give them a name?" asked Oliver. "How about 'primes?' Yeah, I like primes."

"Primes? Why primes?" Cindra asked.

"Oh, Cindra, no, don't—" I said, but I was too late.

"As in primordial, primeval. Archaic. Obsolete. Primitive. Y'know, not us." He winked at her, and before she ducked her head, she smiled.

Really, Cindra? Him? Mind you, we don't have a lot of options.

288

"What have you been doing with them, exactly?" I asked.

"Well, Lexa makes basic medicines that we trade, and I help with technology. For example—"

"What are we supposed to do?"

"Use your skills to help. For trade. Form friendships, relationships. Become part of the community," Lexa explained.

"And lie to them? Just pretend to be normal humans?"

"For now. Once you're entrenched in the community, have friends and supporters, made yourselves indispensable, we'll talk about revealing ourselves."

"And just how do you think they're going to react to being lied to?" If they were anything like the Saints, they wouldn't take it well.

"I think they'll forgive us. We'll have shown them that there's nothing to fear from us, that we are, in fact, essential members of the community."

"Yes," Oliver said, "what could possibly go wrong?"

"The alternative is living out the rest of your lives in this compound. Or taking your chances elsewhere. It's up to you."

Oliver looked grim. "Well, when you put it like that… Okay, comrades, looks like we're going to town. Uh…when are we going?"

"Tomorrow, for those of you who want to go."

"What's the town called, Mil?" I asked. "You said we were in the Okanagan, right? I'm from around here. I might know it."

Comprehension dawned on his face. "I can't believe I forgot you grew up near here, Ailith. The town is called Goldnesse."

Goldnesse.

Welcome home.

We went to find Mom next. Dad said she might not want to leave, that she would want to stay and help people. I asked him if that wasn't the right thing to do. That's what they'd always told me. Dad said, yes, normally it was, but sometimes you had to help yourself first, and I had to help him convince her. The streets looked like they had during freshman week at the university. People staggered into the road, ignoring the cars parked everywhere, even on people's lawns. Dad said all the regular auto-drive cars had switched off and that we were lucky because, as a police officer, nobody controlled his car but him.

—Love, Grace

12
EIRE

I pretended Ella was still alive. That we were back home, spending a lazy Sunday in bed. She'd get up soon to run to the bakery on the corner in her pajamas, buying half a dozen of my favorite sticky buns and a pile of newspapers I'd never read. I'd make the coffee, the special fancy grind we kept in the freezer just for the weekend.

But Ella was dead. She had to be. Otherwise, she would've been here, trying to wake me up. Wouldn't she? I couldn't wake up until she came. She should've been the one to survive; she was the one who'd wanted this, not me. All I'd wanted was her.

We'd made it to the compound safely. Someone, the wrong someone, had found out about us, about what kind of cyborgs we were to become, and Pantheon had run out of time. The war everyone had believed wouldn't happen, was. Those who'd been through the process were already hidden. Those who had yet to go through it, like us,

290

would be taken elsewhere. Program Omega was still a go.

"Ella, we don't have to go through with this. We can leave, now. Can't we?" I'd asked the armed guard.

He'd nodded, tapping his fingers on his weapon.

"No way, Eire. This just shows how important what we're doing is."

Fear finally made me honest. "You don't care about that. You're only doing this because it makes you feel controversial. It's bullshit."

We could've backed out, died together in the war, but Ella refused.

"You go then. But I'm doing it."

She'd called my bluff, and she knew it.

"Well?" the guard asked. He looked back and forth between us pointedly then at the door.

"Fine. Let's go."

Ella had clapped her hands together like a child with a new toy. "Yes! You won't be sorry, Eire."

And I wasn't. I was too numb to be anything.

They'd bundled us into the trunk of a car.

"You're kidding me," I'd said. "You want us to hide in the trunk?"

"It's for your own protection. Get in."

"If it's that dangerous, why aren't we travelling in something a bit more...protected?"

"A bit more obvious, you mean?" he replied. "I don't think you understand. Now that certain people know about you, your life is in danger. We need to get you out of the city."

"But we're not even cyborgs."

"It doesn't matter. You know enough about the program. Get in, or you'll disappear."

So that was what he'd meant when he'd said we could leave.

We'd gotten in.

On the way, something had happened. The car had slowed, and there were muffled voices. Then, a frantic popping, like firecrackers.

After that, the road had gotten bumpy. Ella no longer smiled. We'd lost track of time, but it seemed we travelled for hours.

291

We'd ended up here, at the Pantheon Modern compound, wherever that was. And it was here that we were reborn.

There were others, besides Ella and me. Sometimes, they screamed. I learned all their names. Ros. Adrian. Cayde. Kalbir. Callum.

We barely got a chance to know them. Only a few days after the procedure, once they knew it had worked, they said we had to go to sleep. The war had gotten very bad, and we needed to be protected. They'd already put the others to sleep, those who hadn't made it to the compound.

Ella was to stay awake, to help Mil and Lexa. We didn't want to go to sleep. The others wanted to find their families, and I wanted to stay with Ella. There was...panic. Ella and I fought. I don't know what happened then. I'd been there, and now I was here, but I didn't know where here was.

Or what had happened to Ella.

There was something else.

I'd heard Mil and Lexa talking; they didn't think I could.

"Why isn't she waking up? What will we tell her, if she does? What will we say happened?"

"There's nothing to say. She died. Cayde died as well, Lexa."

"Yes, but—"

"But nothing. Tell her something went wrong, that we couldn't save her. It's not a lie."

"It's not the truth."

"Well, tell her the truth then, and deal with the consequences."

They've done something to her. If she was truly dead, like they said, it was because of them. I'd tried to wake up, and I couldn't. Not until I found out what happened to Ella.

Dad was right. Mom didn't want to leave. She wanted to help her patients. There were a lot of them. Some screamed, some cried, and some made no sounds at all, their eyes blank and staring. The only ones who didn't look like that were the AMSAs, the Android Medical Service Assistants. They glided silently between patients, scanning them and sending the information to a large screen behind the nurse's station. The doctors and nurses consulted this screen, tending to those whose names were highlighted in red first. At least, that's what they were supposed to do.

—*Love, Grace*

13
AILITH

I spread the last handful of damp soil over the tray and covered it with a thin layer of translucent plastic before sliding it under the lights and adjusting the temperature of the heat pad beneath it.

Done. With any luck, we'd be eating fresh vegetables a few months from now. Given that all the seeds were past their best-before date, I wasn't sure how many would finally germinate. I inhaled deeply. It had been a long time since I'd smelled freshly-turned earth or the distinctive aroma of tomato seeds. I stepped back and admired my handiwork. Row upon row of seeded trays now lined the walls, cradling everything from greens to squash. I'd planted everything I could find, including some tiny dormant bulbils of garlic, though it would be years before they would yield anything worth eating.

The manual labor also helped me think. When Eire's thread had flashed in the night, I'd followed it. What *had* happened to Ella? Was it as Lexa had said? Had she simply died? And if so, what had Eire overheard them talking about?

I'm going to ask Oliver. Maybe he can find out more about what happened to Ella. Then I can tell Eire. She heard Mil and Lexa talking, so she should be able to hear me.

The warm, moist air of the greenhouse was comforting, almost amniotic. With the Eire problem solved and the seeds in their beds, it was time to think about the subject I'd been avoiding.

Please let there be another apocalypse. Anything to distract me. I'd just perched on a high stool in front of one of the work benches when there was a knock at the door.

"Come in."

Cindra slipped into the room. "Oh, it's nice in here, isn't it?"

I tried to smile.

"You're not okay, are you?" She boosted herself gracefully onto the stool opposite me.

"Honestly? No."

"Is it because of Goldnesse?"

"That's a big part of it, yes." I picked at the dirt under my fingernails with the corner of an empty seed packet. "Cindra, what if my father's still alive? Goldnesse was the town closest to our farm. If he's alive and anywhere, it would be there. Or what if I get proof that he's dead?"

"Do you think it's possible? That he's alive?"

"At this point, nothing would surprise me. The weird thing is, I almost don't want to know."

"I know what you mean."

"You do?" *Why wouldn't she? You're not the only one who had a family.* "Sorry. Obviously, you do."

"Well, I know even better now that we're here. I came from just outside Tow, not too far away from here, and if there's only one town around for miles where survivors have gathered…"

"Then your family might be alive too. Your grandmother. Asche." The man Cindra would've married one day, if not for the war, or what she'd become. They'd known each other all their lives but had found love only on the eve of her cyberization.

She propped her elbows on the bench-top and dropped her head into her hands. "I forgot that you've seen my life."

"I'm glad *you* can forget." The seed packet cut into the soft skin under my thumbnail. "At least Oliver fixed it for me. Fewer random drop-ins."

She lifted her head and gave me a shy smile. "Oliver's very interesting, isn't he?"

"That's a nice way of putting it." Blood welled on my injured thumb, and I dabbed at it with the corner of my sleeve. "Do you…do you think they may be alive? Your family?"

"I don't know. They had as good a chance as anyone. I— What will we do if they're dead?"

"What we've already been doing. Survive. It might even be easier. I mean, what will we do if they're *alive*? Neither of our families were particularly thrilled about our cyberization."

"I don't think it would matter anymore, do you? I think they'd just be so glad to see us alive…none of that would be important."

"You've been practicing scenarios in your head, haven't you?" I accused.

"Of course," she laughed, "haven't you?"

"Yes," I admitted. "But they never go well, not even in my own imagination. What if they blame us for the war? Or think we abandoned them? What if they've moved on?"

"Well, we'll never find out if we don't go, will we?"

"I don't think I'm ready to find out. Not yet."

"Will you ever be ready? How long does it take to be ready for something like that? Plus, think of everything you'll miss. The people—"

"The people? The last time we came across 'people,' they tortured you. Tried to kill us. How can you be over that?"

"I'm not." Her face darkened. "But I'm not going to let that stop me either. Ailith, we survived. If we don't keep moving forward, what was the point?"

"I just think we need to be cautious, that's all."

"You sound like Tor. What's going on with him, anyway? I mean, he's reserved at the best of times, but today he's got a face like a slapped ass, as my grandmother used to say."

"Oh, god," I said, covering my face with my hands. I'd never really talked to Cindra about Tor. Though it felt like much longer, in reality, we'd known each other for less than two weeks, and all but the last couple of days had been spent traveling in a group, well within earshot of everyone else. This was the first chance we'd had to talk privately. I told her the whole story, starting with the moment I'd opened my eyes in the cabin.

"And now he's pissed because I didn't sever our bond. He thinks our feelings for each other are a program. So *that's* what's wrong with Tor."

"I'm not sure if it's incredibly romantic or incredibly awful," she replied. "I can understand why he's angry."

"Oh, believe me, I can too. And maybe one day…but right now, I just…" The problem was, I couldn't justify it. Not to Cindra, not to myself. "You must think I'm horrible."

"Not horrible. Ruthless, cruel, maybe, but not horrible." She laughed at my stricken face. "I'm just kidding. Look, I don't totally agree with or understand what you're doing, but you have your reasons. You've experienced things the rest of us haven't, like Pax. I'm willing to give you the benefit of the doubt, for now. I'll let you know when you become horrible." She leaned over and brushed dried dirt from my face.

"So, you're going to Goldnesse then?" I asked her.

"Yes. I'm afraid of what I might find out, but for me, not knowing is worse. Besides, one of the reasons I became a cyborg was to help people. With the ability I've got, I can do that. Now more than ever." She smiled. "Lexa said I could work with her."

"Mmh."

"What? You still don't believe them?"

"It's not that, exactly. I believe they're telling us the truth. But within limits. I don't think they're telling us the *whole* truth, not even their version of it. Look at these seeds, for example." I held up one of the little packets to show her.

"Brandywine Heirloom Tomato Seeds, Boisvert Seed Company. Germination, 92%. So?"

"They're *heirloom* seeds. Not hybrids. You can save their seeds, plant them, grow more and more generations."

"I still don't get it."

"Heirloom seeds were impossible to get before the war. At least, legally. The government struck some kind of deal with the seed companies in exchange for a pay-off. In return, only hybrid seeds were legal for sale, meaning you had to buy new seeds every single year. People who'd grown non-hybrid plants before the law changed kept them, hoarded and traded them, but if you got caught, your livelihood was over. The fines alone would bankrupt your farm." I pointed at the boxes of seed packets. "But look at them all. Every kind of fruit, vegetable, and flower you could imagine. Those laws came into effect years before

297

the war. Where did they get all these seeds? How long have they had them? *Why* do they have them if they thought the war was a temporary blip? It doesn't make any sense."

Cindra frowned, turning the packet over in her fingers. For the first time, she looked doubtful. "Maybe they were just being practical?" she asked, but the words must've sounded hollow even to her ears.

"Maybe. There's not much we can do about it now. And in the meantime, we have other issues to worry about. Like Goldnesse."

"So you're going to come?"

I hesitated. "I still don't know. Do you think I should ask Pax? See if he…knows anything?"

"What? And ruin the surprise? Hell, no. Come on, it'll be an adventure."

"Remember when adventures meant music festivals or Wing Wednesday with the girls?"

She laughed. "Maybe this will be just as fun."

"I doubt it," I replied darkly.

"Please come," she said, her face now serious. "If we do it together, we'll be fine, whatever the outcome."

My reply was interrupted by Lexa, calling to us from the top of the stairs. "Are you two coming? I need some help packing the supplies, and then we'll be on our way."

"Coming," Cindra called. She turned back to me. "Well?"

I thought of Ros and Adrian. *That's the price of regret.* I had to go. Whatever had happened, I had to try to find out. *But.* "Cindra, what if we find nothing? What if no one knows what happened to them?"

"Well, then we'll be no worse off than we are now, will we?"

I hope you're right.

Dad held Mom back from her next patient, and they whispered furiously between them. Another nurse rushed to take Mom's patient, and it was just as she was bending over him, telling her android assistant where to apply some weird-looking gel to his reddened skin that the man blew himself up.

—*Love, Grace*

14
AILITH

As Cindra helped Lexa pack the remaining trade supplies in the infirmary, the rest of us milled around in the main room. Pax and I stood off to one side. He seemed as relaxed as always, his black eyes impossible to read.

"Are you nervous?" I asked him.

"No. Why would I be?"

"Because we're going to a town full of people. People not like us. People like those who tortured you and Cindra. Aren't you even a little scared? Or do you know that nothing will happen to you?"

"Are you asking if I know what will happen? If I know whether your dad is alive?"

"Yes. No. Don't tell me." I twisted my hands together, reopening the cut on my thumb. "No, tell me."

He smiled in that enigmatic way of his. "I can't tell you."

"What? Why? Is it bad? Does it need to happen? Is one of us going to die? Is it Oliver? I promise I won't tell him."

His mouth quirked. "I can't tell you because I don't know. Like I said before, it's a crossroads. Like when we were with the Saints of Loving Grace."

When they tried to burn us alive, you mean. "Oh." Deflation turned to nerves that twisted my belly. "Then why aren't you scared?"

"Because these aren't the same people who tortured us. They have a home. They feel safe. They have food, and water, and medicine." He gestured toward the open door of the infirmary. Lexa was reading a list aloud as Cindra checked boxes and called out numbers.

"What if they find out what we are?"

He shrugged. "Then the path will be decided for us."

Tor stood near the outer door, brooding. He glanced at me, seemingly torn between anger and concern at how I must be feeling. His mother had died in Vancouver, killed in the first wave of bombings. He knew I'd never fully accepted that my father was dead, and that being faced with the possibility of finding out was both a dream come true and a nightmare. Several times, it appeared as though he was going to walk toward me, but each time, he stopped abruptly and turned away. Oliver watched him, amusement plain on his face.

Should I manipulate Tor's body and give him all the satisfaction of smashing Oliver in the teeth without any of the culpability? Maybe then he'd see that us being connected wasn't such a bad thing. *Not likely.*

"Is everyone ready to go?" Lexa asked brightly, interrupting my reverie.

"Lexa, what if someone recognizes me? Or Cindra? From before?"

"Just keep your heads down and your hoods up. It's been years since anyone's seen you, and it's unlikely you'll be recognized out of context. Now, let's go before it gets too late."

***

300

The air outside the compound was cool, the sky as gray as ever. The entrance itself was obscured by a copse of sun-starved trees that refused to lie down and die.

I followed Cindra as we picked our way through on the twisting path, the silken length of her braid sliding over the top of her pack distracting me. Callum trailed behind me, his eyes darting back and forth. Lexa hadn't wanted him to come with us, given his unpredictable behavior, but Cindra and I had promised to keep an eye on him. I smiled at him over my shoulder, and he grinned back. He'd rarely left the compound since he'd woken, on lockdown after what had happened to Ros and Adrian.

Tor stalked after us, his long strides erratic to keep pace with our shorter ones. Kalbir pursued him as closely as possible, describing the various delights of Goldnesse.

"I've been waiting to go for ages, ever since I woke up. Mil and Lexa have told me all about it. It's supposed to be like a *real* town. There's all different kinds of people. All survivors, of course. But in the five years since the war, well, four really, if you count the time it took for people to start gathering there. Anyway, they actually have an economy. Bartering, obviously. They've got hunters, people who scavenge, some guy who's trying to grow stuff."

Some guy who's trying to grow stuff.

"Builders, teachers, a few engineers, cops..." she continued. "Lexa said there's even a hairdresser. Not," she said, wrapping a thick section of glossy black hair around her wrist, "that I would trust them to cut *my* hair."

"How many people live there?" Tor asked.

"About three thousand, I think," Lexa said from the front.

Three thousand. Before the war, there'd been more than ten times that number.

301

"They still get the odd person finding the town even after all these years. And I think they also trade with a small satellite group a few miles north, near a place called Tow."

Cindra's braid stopped sliding.

"I wonder why they chose Goldnesse to make their home?" Tor mused, mostly to himself, but Kalbir pounced on the opportunity to feed his curiosity.

"Well, there's two lakes, and a massive dam that supplies their hydro-electric station. Every single building has electricity. Can you believe it? I bet the food will be amazing. I mean, it's got to be better than the plastic crap we eat at the compound." She shuddered. "Unless it's like rabbits or that sort of thing."

"If you'd been awake for the last five years rather than just a couple of months, you'd think rabbits tasted like ambrosia," Lexa said dryly.

"*Hares*," Tor said.

When we emerged from the thicket, I instantly recognized the surrounding landscape. The compound was hidden in the base of a small hill about a mile away from the road; I'd driven past it numerous times and never suspected it was anything more. It looked like hundreds of other hills in the area, covered with patches of crooked, wind-stunted trees, scrubby brush, and little dried cactus-balls you never saw before you found them clustered inside your pant legs, the long thorns embedded in your skin.

Very little had changed.

"It looks the same," Cindra whispered to me.

"I was just thinking that," I whispered back. "I guess it makes sense. It's always been dry here. Now it's just colder."

"*Motherfucker!*"

Cindra shot her hand out and grabbed my arm.

Oliver hopped up and down on one foot, clutching at his ankle.

302

"Oliver! Don't—" I was too late.

He scrabbled at his trouser leg, trying to pull it up. His next scream had a sharp edge of very real pain as the sliding fabric embedded the cacti spikes even deeper.

"Oliver, stand still."

He ignored me.

"Oliver." Cindra's voice was quiet, and Oliver froze, not wanting to scare away this sudden attention. She knelt in front of him, putting her knee under his foot. Gently, she rolled up his pant leg, pulled it wide on the assaulted side, and deftly plucked the spiked plants free. Oliver reached out, his hand hovering over her hair before boldness overtook him, and he smoothed a lock between his fingers, tucking it behind her ear.

"Thanks."

She smiled up at him.

Oh Cindra, seriously? I hope for all our sakes that Asche is still alive. Oliver didn't deserve a happy ending.

Callum bent and picked up the discarded cactus, rolling it over thoughtfully in his fingers. As we all turned back to the road, he closed his fist around it, wincing at the sudden sting.

Umbra.

He saw me watching and shrugged.

"Are you okay?" I asked.

"Yes. She's just curious." He said it low, so only I could hear. "Let's keep walking before the others see."

Cindra returned to walk beside me, stroking the lock of hair Oliver had touched.

"You know he's an asshole, right?" I said.

"Maybe." She smiled coyly. "Or maybe he's—"

"Do not say that he's misunderstood, Cindra. Please."

She laughed, glancing up at Oliver's back. "Okay, I won't. But maybe he is."

Was it my imagination, or was Oliver suddenly taller?

Should I remind her what's he's done? About Celeste? The last time I'd seen Celeste—the young woman who'd worshiped Oliver with everything she'd had: her body, her loyalty, her innocence—she'd been lying on the ground, stunned, as he crushed her hand with his boot.

As though she could read my mind, Cindra laced her fingers with mine. "Let's not talk about Oliver. One problem at a time."

"Problem? I thought this was an adventure?"

As we left the desert hills and mounted the worn road, I felt it. *Him.* Whoever had been following Tor and me from the beginning of our journey was here, somewhere close.

"Hello?"

Images slid through my mind. *Stepping out of a dark cave into the blinding sun. Thousands of brightly-colored balloons floating in an azure sky. A name carved in the sand. Fane.*

I'd never met Fane, but he'd followed us since the beginning. And while I'd been inside him, I knew little about him other than that he was some kind of cyborg and part of a group of Cosmists, those who believed artilects—
—sentient, synthetic beings—were our only future. My communication with him was different than with the others, snippets of images amid the odd coherent vision. And, unlike the others, he could connect with *my* mind. He'd helped us escape the Saints, joining his strength with mine to generate the sonic pulse.

"Ailith? Are you all right?" Cindra peered at me as though into a darkened room, searching.

"I'm fine. I—" *How do I explain?* Tor and I hadn't told anyone about the specter shadowing us. "I'm just a bit disoriented, that's all. Must be from the fresh air after being in the compound the last few days."

"Well, get ready, because I think we're almost there."

My hearing didn't come back for hours, but somehow that made everything easier. I no longer heard people screaming, or their pleas for help. It also meant Mom and Dad couldn't hear each other well enough to fight in the car as we left the hospital. I couldn't really remember what I'd seen after the bomb went off, how we'd escaped, how we'd gotten to the car. My dad says that sometimes your brain plays tricks on you, to make it easier for you to do something. I wonder if that's what happened to the man with the bomb, when he saw the android bending over him.

—Love, Grace

15

AILITH

We stood on a rocky outcropping at the side of the road, next to a weathered wooden shack. The red lettering on the side had faded and flaked off into illegibility, but I remembered it well. *Candied salmon, $10/lb. Fresh cherries. Lemonade. Ice cream, three scoops for $6.00 only!*

Tears filmed over my eyes, blurring the crispness of the white-peaked waves cresting and breaking on the surface of the lake below. Lake Niska. In the summers, the beach had always been crammed with tourists and locals alike, a sweaty, greasy, seething rainbow of umbrellas and beach chairs. Now deserted, it stretched out sterile and forlorn.

Cindra squeezed my hand. "I know, right? Their raspberry lemonade was *amazing*. They had nothing on Asche's candied salmon, though."

305

"That's a hell of a long way down, isn't it?" Oliver said, craning his neck to peer over the cliff.

"Best not get too close to the edge then, eh?" Tor muttered savagely.

Oliver bared his teeth then turned toward the sprawl of houses in the distance. "So that's it then? Goldnesse? Pretty impressive view."

"Yes," Lexa said. "Are you ready?"

No.

It took us nearly half an hour to reach the town, our slow descent giving me time to take it all in. Tor had been right when he'd said that large parts of it were damaged during the war; many of the shops and beach-side apartments that ringed the shore of the southern lake had been destroyed, leaving twisted piles of blackened concrete and steel.

"Why they would bomb a city like this?" Tor asked. "I mean, there wasn't much here but beaches and vineyards, was there?"

"And a cyborg or two," Pax replied. "Or so they may have thought at the time." He started suddenly and looked at me. "Sorry."

The others filed past me, silent in their avoidance. Even Oliver had nothing to say. Tor rested his hand briefly on my shoulder before he too went on, leaving Cindra and me, our hands locked together. I knew I was hurting her, but I couldn't let go.

"I doubt that's true," she whispered. "How would they even know? And even if they did, they would've known you wouldn't be there. It was probably just a mistake. I've heard that happens sometimes: a bomb slips out prematurely. Not particularly reassuring in most cases, but—"

"Thanks." I forced myself to loosen my grip, my fingers stiff.

The residents of Goldnesse had clearly worked relentlessly in the aftermath of the war, and not just for survival. The rubble that must've littered the streets was cleared away, neatly shoved into towering piles lining both sides of the road. As we walked through the tunnel of debris, the hair on the back of my neck stood up. Someone was watching us. The corridor hadn't been created just for order's sake, it seemed. Without being able to see over the top, I had no idea where in the town we were, though I suspected we were headed down Main Street. The only turn we'd taken was the gentle curve where the road had previously hugged the lake, and the worn yellow and white traffic paint was faintly visible.

Tor must be going crazy.

Every cell in his hunter's body would've been screaming about the foolishness of this, the vulnerability of our situation. And after what Pax had said... Tor's gait was tense, the hair curling over the collar of his coat brushing back and forth as he searched from side to side, scanning for movement. His hand hovered over the knife belted to his waist, and the hilt of another peeked from the top of his boot. He'd wanted to bring his crossbow, but Lexa had refused, saying it might be seen as aggressive. He'd taken advantage of her distraction while she'd been packing and secreted it into his oversized backpack instead.

We exited the half-tunnel just as I thought he would explode.

My guess had been correct. We stepped out at the end of Main Street, just before the start of the former downtown quarter. Most of the original shops seemed occupied, smoke curling from chimneys, and goods stacked on the pavement outside. Strong smells permeated the bubble of silence surrounding us—tantalizing earthy aromas of cooking meat, burning wood, and the people who bustled by us. Their cheeks were rosy in the crisp air as they nodded at each other in passing or huddled in groups on the corners, breaking into peals of laughter and slapping each other on the back.

The sights and smells after weeks in the wilderness steeped me in the knowledge that while I'd slept peacefully underground, these people had clawed their way through the last five years, watching nearly everyone they knew die, the lives and futures they'd built burn to the ground. Every single person here had done something to live, and yet I saw none of it on their faces. If I let my mind wander just a little, it could've been the Saturday Farmers Market, and I'd just stepped out of our booth for a break. In fact, from where we were standing, I could see a few hundred feet down the street to where our booth had nestled between the others on the pavement beside the Winter Park.

The last time I'd stood here felt like scant months ago, and of course, to my newly-awoken mind, it was. Time had not passed for us the way it had for these people, and watching them now, carving out normal lives, was like a knife to my gut. How had they coped? Adapted to a way of life requiring skills so different from what they knew?

How would I have done?

I'd been protected by thousands of pounds of impenetrable bunker and a stranger. A stranger like me, like *us*, who many saw as the cause of the war. These people had been meant to survive; we had not. And yet here we all were, human and cyborg alike. If what Pax had seen was right, only we could ensure these people survived. Watching them now, the heart-breaking normalcy of their lives, I was determined we would, no matter what it cost us.

"Lexa!" A woman rounded one of the groups near us, her hand raised in greeting. She appeared to be in her mid-thirties and was striking, with long, loosely-knotted umber hair framing a delicate face dominated by wide,

308

cornflower-blue eyes. Her skin had the robust look of someone who spent a lot of time outdoors, and her mouth curved in a genuine smile of pleasure.

"Lily." Lexa gripped both the woman's hands in her own. "How are you?"

"We're good. A bit low on medical supplies, but otherwise great. Is there something wrong with your radio? When you didn't come the other week, I was worried Mil had taken a turn for the worse, and we tried to contact you but got no answer. Is he okay?" she asked, her forehead creased in concern.

"He's fine." The tension in Lexa's shoulders belied her casual tone. "Just a bit grumpy, as usual. He was too tired to make the trip today."

Lily nodded in sympathy. "I keep telling him the two of you should move here, but he insists your work is too important."

"He's right," Lexa replied. "One of these days this climate is going to change, and we want to be ready when it does. Who knows what kind of effect it will have? We want to make sure we're a step ahead. Besides, we wouldn't be able to synthesize all these medications here. The equipment is too delicate to move." She patted the side of her heavy canvas bag.

"I understand," Lily said. "I just hate the thought of the two of you alone out there, especially with Mil's condition—" She suddenly noticed the group of strangers behind Lexa. "But maybe you're not alone anymore?" She gave us a pointed look.

"No, we're not." Lexa smiled. "That's why we didn't come as usual. Lily, these are researchers from another station like ours. They'd thought they were the only ones who'd survived, but when their supplies got low, they decided to risk searching further afield. As luck would have it, I happened across them just as they were about to turn back." The lies rolled easily off her tongue.

"Scientists!" Lily exclaimed, her whole face brightening to match her smile. "We always need more of you. What fields did you work in?"

Lexa explained our different areas of "expertise," pointing to each of us in turn. "We've got Ailith, an agriculturalist. Tor, a wildlife biologist. Pax a biomedical scientist. Kalbir, our human resources manager. Callum, a researcher. Oliver, a software engineer, and," she said, arching her eyebrows in anticipation of Lily's reaction, "Cindra, a botanist who studies traditional medicine." She pushed Cindra forward with a palm to her lower back.

Cindra let go of my hand and stepped forward, smiling shyly. I hadn't thought Lily's smile could get any brighter, but it did.

With her around, who needs the sun?

"Oh my goodness, it's so nice to meet you," she said, snatching up Cindra's hands and giving them an excited squeeze. "I have so much to ask you, to show you. Just the other week, I found this plant—maybe you've seen it? It has five-pointed—"

"Lily?" a male voice asked. We turned as one to find a man and teenage girl standing behind us. The man scrutinized us, his eyes wary, while the girl, who had his pale-blue eyes and dimpled chin, gazed at us with the same open delight as Lily.

"Ryan, Grace! Look, it's Lexa, and she's brought friends."

"I know," he replied, circling us to stand next to her. "I followed them in."

"They're all scientists, like Lexa and Mil," she said, still holding Cindra's hands. "Just think, even more skills to add to our little community."

"Scientists?" He nodded slowly. "I see. Where did you say you were from?"

310

"They're from near Falton, just over the range from Rosespring," Lexa said smoothly.

"I don't remember any research stations around there," Ryan replied.

"Yeah, well, we didn't exactly advertise." Oliver stepped in. "Lots of expensive equipment, and with all the unrest over those artilects and cyborgs and such before the war, people seemed to think all scientists were the same. And hey, we're brainboxes, not boxers, if you get me. Best to keep it on the hush-hush."

Gently, gently, Oliver.

Ryan eyed Tor dubiously.

We're too healthy, too strong.

"Oh, don't worry about him." Oliver waved his hand nonchalantly. "He looks burly, but it's mostly fat. I just wouldn't show your food stores, if I were you.

Tor glared at Oliver but held his tongue. His knife had disappeared, and he tried to look relaxed; I doubted anyone but me noticed he was coiled like a spring.

"Cindra here is a botanist, Ryan. And not just *any* botanist, but one who studies local plants." She beamed up into his face. "Can you believe our luck?"

Ryan finally melted under the brilliance of her smile. His face relaxed, and he nodded at Cindra. "It's good to meet you. All of you," he added. "Cindra, I hope you like to talk and listen because Lily here has been waiting years to meet someone like you."

Someone like you. Like us. I doubt it.

A shadow passed over Cindra's face, gone in an instant. *Adapt.*

"Oh, and Ailith, we have another agriculturalist here. You two should get together. I'm sure he'd be fascinated by your research. He's been trying to get common crops to adapt to the colder weather. In fact, there he is now, over there. The older gentleman."

311

She pointed across the street to a man engrossed in conversation with an oddly familiar younger man with bronze skin and shorn black hair. He was tall, his head bald, and his face heavily lined. He looked much older than he should have, and I wondered how much of it was because of me.

It turned out my father was still alive, after all.

We drove out of Tow and into the dark. Behind us, the city was alight; we felt the heat of it even after we'd crossed the boundary line. Dad took us past the lake, to the cabin deep in the woods they'd bought on a whim during their honeymoon. We'd been to it only a month ago, the week after I got out of school, and since Mom had over-shopped as she always did, we could lock ourselves inside and pretend the world wasn't falling apart.

—Love, Grace

16
AILITH

Cindra saved me from responding by dropping gracelessly to her knees in a near-faint. As Lexa and Lily bent over her, Oliver rushed to her side. She pushed him away and reached out for me; he stepped back, his expression pained.

My father is alive.

"Cindra!" Lily pressed the back of her hand to Cindra's forehead as I knelt next to her and grabbed her hand.

"*Asche,*" she hissed at me under her breath.

"What? Where?" *He's alive?*

She shook her head mutely and flicked her gaze toward the pair hovering over her.

"She's okay," I said, "don't worry. She didn't eat much this morning, and it was a long walk. Here, come sit with me. I've got some protein bars in my bag." I threw her arm over my shoulder and stood, dragging her with me.

313

Lily hovered her hand uncertainly over Cindra's shoulder. "Are you sure?"

"Absolutely. Just give us ten minutes, and she'll be fine. Tell us where you're going, and she'll meet you there."

"Okay," Lily said, still unsure. "I'm going to the infirmary. I can give her an examination when she gets there."

Cindra glanced at Lexa, panic widening her eyes.

He's alive, and he's here.

Tor spotted the tremble in my hands. I gripped Cindra more tightly.

"I'm sure she'll be just fine," Lexa replied. "Come and see us when you're ready, Cindra. Just follow Main Street here to the end. There's a large building that used to be a casino. You'll find us on the right side of the bottom floor."

Cindra nodded then sat down with her head between her knees.

Lexa grabbed Lily's arm firmly and steered her toward the road. "So, you were saying you found a new plant? Have you been able to identify it yet?" Their voices faded as they wove down the street, Lily glancing back over her shoulder just before they disappeared.

"Well, if I'm not needed, I'm off," Oliver said. The cheerfulness in his voice was strained, and he avoided looking at either of us.

"Just where are you going?" Tor asked. "Don't cause any shit, Oliver, not on our first day here."

"Me?" Oliver asked innocently. "I have no idea what you mean, Goliath. We're here in what passes for civilization these days, and I plan to take advantage of it. I wonder if there's a brothel?" He sauntered away. "Sure you don't want to join me?" he called to Tor over his shoulder. "It's not like your current relationship is working out that well. For you, anyway."

The muscles in Tor's jaw leaped once then stilled. He pinched the bridge of his nose. "God, what an asshole. Why is it men like him always survive? Like a goddamn cockroach." He knelt beside Cindra and me, dipping his head to look her in the eyes. "You okay?"

The gentleness of his voice hurt my heart.

"Yes, I'm fine. I just...I'd like to speak with Ailith for a few minutes. Privately," she added, glancing at Kalbir.

A faint blush colored Kalbir's cheeks. "Fine," she said. "C'mon, Big Man, Callum, let's go find some fun."

Callum's head tilted strangely to the side. "I'd like to eat things and touch things."

"Uh, okay. I'm sure we can do that," Kalbir said. "Tor?"

"Actually," Tor said, looking at me closely, "I think I'll go and talk to some of the local hunters. Make myself useful." He pointed further down the street, where a group of men and women seemed to be haggling over a stack of carcasses.

Kalbir looked from him to me, her smile tight. "Right, well, whatever, suit yourself." She turned on her heel and left us, her chin up and shoulders stiff.

Tor waited until she'd walked down the next block. "You're sure you don't need me?" he asked, reluctant to leave us. "What's really going on?"

Well, my dad's alive, and Cindra thinks she just saw her old boyfriend. Other than that, not much.

"Cindra?" I asked. "Do you want Tor and Pax to leave as well?"

"No," she said. "They can stay. I just...I don't know *them* yet."

"Oh good," Pax said, relief clear in his voice. "I wasn't going to leave anyway."

Cindra smiled up at him and tugged gently on the leg of his pants. "Thanks, Pax."

I sat on the pavement next to Cindra, the cold concrete

315

biting through the seat of my pants and chilling my skin. "Do you want to go first?" I asked her.

"No," she said. "I need to be sure. You go."

"Okay." I took a deep breath. "My father is still alive. And he's standing right over there, next to—" It hit me where I'd seen the younger man before.

He gave me the crooked grin that was as familiar to me as my own heart.

"Asche. He cut his hair," I added lamely.

What were the odds?

Astronomical.

The suspicion slowly poisoning my body over the last few days spread deeper.

No. It's a coincidence. The odds are slim, but possible.

The odds of *any* of us surviving had been small, but someone had to. Why not them?

Paranoia is just as dangerous as an actual enemy. Remember that.

"What? You mean to tell me your dad is standing right over there? And who the hell is Asche?" Tor looked as though he'd fallen down the rabbit hole. Well, hare hole, in his case.

Cindra looked up, her eyes rimmed with red. "Asche was my...boyfriend, fiancé...whatever. Or at least, he would've been if I hadn't left him." She twisted her braid between her fingers. "I only pretended to myself he might be alive. I didn't actually believe it was possible."

"Shit. Pax, did you know this was going to happen?" Tor asked.

Pax hooked his thumbs through the empty belt loops on his pants and rocked back on his heels. "Yes. No. I did see them, but I had no idea who they were or what it meant."

"I asked you before we came if you'd seen anything," I said, unable to keep the irritation from creeping into my voice. "A little notice would've been appreciated."

316

Pax smiled benignly, unruffled by my tone. "You weren't specific. What would your reaction have been if I'd said, 'I see an older man and a younger man, and they're talking?'"

Tor cocked his head, amusement quirking the corners of his mouth. "He's got a point."

"I know," I said, rubbing my forehead. "I'm not blaming you Pax, it's just..."

"What are you going to do?" Tor asked, gazing at the two men. Asche was explaining something to my father, drawing shapes on the palm of his hand with slim fingers. My father nodded and replied then folded the end of his scarf into the breast of his coat and flipped his collar up against the gnawing cold. Putting his hands in his pocket, he began to turn away.

"They're leaving. Shit. What do we do? We can't just go sauntering up to them and say, 'Oh hey, Dad, Asche, how's it going? Shame about this apocalypse. You're looking well.' Can we?" Creeping hysteria had replaced the irritation in my voice.

"If your eyes get any wider, they may burst," Pax noted helpfully.

Tor tucked a piece of hair behind my ear. "Hey, it's okay. Cindra, it's..." He patted her helplessly on the shoulder as she started to cry.

I can't imagine how she feels. You expect to lose your parents, but not the love of your life. And here he was, a second chance long-buried and newly arisen.

"Look, you two couldn't speak to them anyway, even if you wanted to. They both know you became cyborgs, right? So you'd be putting all of us at risk." He gazed thoughtfully at the two men, and I could almost see his mind at work. "I know they loved you once, but you don't know how they feel about what you are now." He came to a decision. "But I've got a plan," he said, straightening.

317

"Come with me, Pax. You were asking me yesterday about the work I used to do? Let's go do it."

"You're going to *kill* them?" I asked, horrified.

Tor shot me a fierce look. "No. We're going to do some reconnaissance."

Pax's smile shone brighter than Lily's. He hopped from one foot to the other. "Do we use fake names?"

"No," said Tor. "The first lesson is to speak the truth as much as you can. We're here, new to town. Let's mingle." He placed his hand between Pax's shoulder blades and pushed him forward. "You two should stay out of sight."

Cindra and I scooted around the corner of the block and huddled on the concrete.

"I can't do this. Sit here and wait. Do you think they'll come back with them? What should I say? I have to look—" She worried a hangnail with her teeth.

"Cindra, sit still. They're only doing recon. They're not going to tell them about us."

"Fine, distract me."

"Get your fingers out of your mouth, and I will."

We talked about our childhoods and teen years, our memories of this town that I'd grown up near and she'd visited many times.

"It's funny, isn't it?" she said. "We came down to the market nearly every Saturday. I remember your booth...I probably even bought from you, touched your hand." She patted my fingers. "Who knew we'd end up like this?"

I sighed, inching back so I could lean against the brick wall behind us. "Would you still have done it, if you'd known?"

She slid back next to me, her head pressed against the rough surface as she stared upward. "Yes. This wasn't our fault. None of it was. Other people would've gone through the process, the war still would've happened. The only

318

difference is that we might not be alive now. And I want to be alive more than anything else. More than the grief and the loss. Even though the people we know are dead or changed, at least we're alive to remember them. It's not as good as actually being with them, but it's close enough for me."

"I think I—" Tor and Pax rounded the corner. Tor looked upset; Pax looked...like Pax, calm and serene.

My stomach twisted.

Cindra covered her face with her hands. "I can't bear it."

"What happened?" I asked Tor. "Why do you look like that? They're alive, right? How can that be bad?"

"It's not," he replied. "It's just...I don't know. I wanted to—"

"He wanted to bring you a gift," Pax said. "Something for your heart."

Tor pressed his fingers over his eyes as the tips of his ears turned pink. "Thank you, Pax."

Pax nodded, satisfied with his part, and sprawled onto the pavement next to Cindra.

"Anyway," Tor said, his voice weary, "it's not the news either of you was hoping for."

"What do you mean?" I asked. "It isn't them?"

"No, it is. But..."

"Just tell me, please," Cindra whispered. "I can't wait any longer."

Tor knelt in front of us, looking first at Cindra then at me. "Cindra, Asche is the leader of your community."

"She's dead, then. Grandmother is dead." She closed her eyes. "But Asche, he's okay?"

"He is. He's, uh...married. And he has children."

Cindra swallowed hard, but her face was impassive. "I'm just so glad he's alive." She sagged back against the wall.

"Is my dad, okay? I mean, that's all I ever wanted. Why are you looking at me like that?"

"Because," Tor said, gazing down at his hands, "he denies ever having a daughter. According to him, you never existed."

The silver rain first fell a few days after we'd left the city. Mom wouldn't let me go outside in it. She thought it would be dirty, like the black rain, from all the ash in the sky, but it was worse than that. Dad went to check in with the neighbors, in their cabins closer to the lake. Determined not to be afraid, they'd been having a BBQ when the silver rain started to fall. Now, they were dying. After he and Mom whispered back and forth about it, she went into the bathroom and threw up. I wasn't allowed to play outside after that.

—*Love, Grace*

17
AILITH

Cindra and I didn't speak on the long road back to the compound. Lily, oblivious to our silence, had invited us all to stay the night, tempting us with descriptions of the dinner she'd cook. Thankfully, Lexa had decided we should quit while we were ahead and made our excuses, saying she didn't want to leave Mil alone, just in case. This provoked a flurry of activity from Lily as she insisted on packing a parcel of delicacies for him. Her honest kindness was like a thorn, stinging all the more because of our deception.

As we walked the road under the darkening sky, Callum's pockets bulged with treasure, and he slipped his fingers in periodically to touch one thing or the other. His eyes were unfocused, and he didn't react as Oliver regaled us with his tales of adventure, which were impressive considering we'd only been in Goldnesse a few hours.

"You're all awfully quiet," he observed. "Did something happen that we should know about? Besides Kalbir here being rejected?" He winced as her fist connected with his shoulder. "*Fuck!* Well, you shouldn't have told me then, should you? Everyone knows I'm not to be trusted." He rubbed the spot Kalbir had punched then glanced toward Cindra as though expecting a response.

Cindra stared straight ahead, taking one step and then another.

He stopped walking. "Seriously, what did I miss?"

"Cindra?" Lexa asked. She stepped into Cindra's path, stopping her gently with her arm before they could collide. She looked at me.

"You have to tell them," Tor said softly. "This affects all of us."

"I know," I replied. "It's just... Basically, my father and Cindra's ex...someone Cindra used to know are alive, and they were in Goldnesse today. That agriculturalist Lily was talking about? That was my father." I frowned. "I'm surprised you've never met him, Lexa."

The color leeched from Lexa's face. "What? Do you mean Luke? He...he never said he had a daughter... Did they see you? You didn't talk to them, did you?"

"No, we didn't. Tor and Pax did, though."

"They didn't suspect what you were, did they?"

"No," Tor said. "We kept with the story, gave as little information about us as we could. We mostly just asked them questions about themselves. Asche is a hunter, so we talked about that."

"So your old boyfriend's here?" Oliver asked Cindra. He tried to sound casual, but the whiteness of his knuckles on his pack straps betrayed him.

"He's not my boyfriend," Cindra said, her chin up. "He's married. And he has children. And I'm glad for him. He always wanted a family. But my grandmother is dead,

322

so if you don't mind, I'd like some privacy to remember her."

"I'm sorry." For once Oliver had nothing else to say. Then he turned to me. "And your father's alive, eh? That's going to be an interesting reunion."

"I doubt there'll be a reunion. According to him, I never existed."

"Ouch," Oliver said, and laughed. "Looks like you got some comforting to do, big boy." He thumped Tor lightly on the shoulder then ducked away, smirking at Kalbir's scowl.

"I'm sorry," Lexa said, real sympathy in her voice.

"What are we supposed to do?" I asked. "Do we just never go to Goldnesse?"

"Asche doesn't live in Goldnesse," Pax said. "He only comes every week for trading."

"I'm not sure. I'll have to talk to Mil about it, but I doubt you can avoid them forever."

We walked on in silence. Oliver's steps were erratic, jaunty one minute, somber the next. It must've been hard for him, pretending to be a decent person and actually feeling bad for Cindra.

When we finally entered the compound, Lexa ran headlong into Mil, who looked as though he'd been hovering by the entrance since we left.

"How did it go?" he asked.

Lexa drew him away from the rest of us, nodding at Cindra and me as she did so. They walked off toward their office, speaking quietly, urgently.

At the top of the dormitory stairs, I gave Cindra a hug. "You going to be okay?"

"Yes. I just need some time, alone. But I'll be fine." She followed Pax down the hall, patting him on the shoulder in thanks before disappearing behind her door. Callum scooted furtively into his room, the lock clicking into place and leaving the hallway to Tor and me.

I paused at my door and, knowing I shouldn't, asked Tor if he'd like to come in. "I could use someone to talk to."

He paused then shook his head. "No. I'm sorry about what happened, but...no. I'm tired of letting myself down."

So, I ended up having a one-sided conversation with a girl in a coma in the middle of the night.

I slid into the chair next to her bed as quietly as possible, trying not to knock over anything that might make a sound. It was the middle of the night, and I'd stolen out of bed, creeping down the stairs in the dark the way Tor and I had once crept through the woods.

She lay on her back, her arms resting at her sides over the bedclothes. I'd expected her to be covered with tubes and wires, to be surrounded by the humming and whooshing of the machines keeping her alive, but there were none save a single thin tube that bit into a large vein in her hand, held fast by a layer of thick tape. Her coma was so unobtrusive that we hadn't even noticed her when we'd been in the same room, less than twenty feet away.

Eire.

I traced my fingers over hers. They were small and cool to the touch, like my brother's at his funeral. *Dorian.* I rarely let myself think about him, about the person he would've been now. Just newly a man, would he have had the same patchy stubble that had plagued my father? He hadn't had a mark on him except for the slight compression of his chest.

Would he and my mother have survived the war? Or, if they'd been alive and then died during it, would Dad have followed them?

Since he didn't have a daughter, he'd have had nothing left to live for but life itself, and my father had never been that kind of man.

"And so that, Eire, is the whole sordid tale. According to my own father, I never existed."

A flash in my mind. *"I don't exist either, not without her."*

I jerked my hand backward, nearly taking her lone tube with me. "You can speak to me? We can...speak to each other?" Until now, Pax had been the only other Pantheon Modern cyborg I could communicate with. I hadn't even known about Eire until we got here.

"Yes. We are pairs."

"What do you mean, pairs? Do you see the future too?"

"Not the future. The past. A ladder. We are like a ladder. Where's Ella?"

Her hand was so thin, her veins forming a tiny blue network under her paper-fine skin. "Ella's dead, Eire. I'm so sorry."

"Sometimes I still hear her. I can feel her close by."

"I'm sorry," I repeated.

"Did they kill her?"

"Who?"

"Mil and Lexa. Did they kill her?"

"No. They said she just...died. Like she got lost and couldn't find her way back."

"They killed her. She would never leave me."

"Why would they kill her?" Paranoia began to stir.

"They are not what they seem. They are guilty. They have done some terrible things. I can see what they've done. We are wrong." The pinkie finger on her left hand twitched.

"Eire? What do you mean? Can you wake up? Lexa says there's nothing physically wrong with you."

"Not yet. Not without her. I need to know what happened. Why she left me."

"I—"

"The kill switch. Did you find the kill switch?"

"Yes, we—"

"There's more. Ella. I will try to remember."

"They are not what they seem. They are guilty. We are wrong." Eire's words tumbled around in my head, making it impossible to sleep.

I knew I shouldn't do it, but Tor's breathing as he slept was one of the few things that calmed me. And for someone who'd had such a violent past, he rarely dreamed. That was what I needed right now: a dark, quiet space, the reassurance of something familiar. And the only place I could find it was in his head.

What I hadn't expected was to discover him at Kalbir's bedroom door, her perfect teeth bared in triumph.

Dad went out every few days to see what was happening. First, he'd driven then when he couldn't find any more fuel, he walked. Each time he came back, his face seemed thinner, grayer, as though the grayness of the sky was seeping into his skin. Then, one day when he was searching for food, he met Asche.

—Love, Grace

18

TOR

I shouldn't have been here. I'd accused Ailith in the past of making me do things I didn't want to do, and it was because of her that I was here now, outside the door of a woman I was pretty sure was going to eat me alive.

I'd told Ailith the truth when I said I didn't want to kill her anymore. I'd known it the moment we'd woken up here. My first thought was of her, of where she was, and when I saw her lying unconscious in that bed, looking so...human, the rage that had filled me... I knew then that she wasn't the enemy. If anyone was, it was those who'd created us.

I never should've slept with her again. I knew it would happen, knew I shouldn't, and then I did it anyway. Did I really think it would change her mind? Make her suddenly give up her control? Could I blame her for that?

Yes, I could. She shouldn't have had that power over me. But would I feel differently if it were anyone else? What if it were Oliver she could control? Would I ask her to get rid of her ability then? No. I would tell her to keep it, just in case. So why should I feel otherwise?

327

Because it was me and her. Was it even about the control? Or was it more about making her sacrifice something to prove herself to me? Either way, it had backfired. It just made everything worse. And now I was here.

After what had happened in Goldnesse, I didn't know what to say to her. I mean, I was happy her father was still alive, but part of me couldn't help feeling bitter about it, and not only because my mother was dead. Before, it was just the two of us, even with the others. Her new life started when she woke up, and selfishly, I liked being her history. Now she had her old history back, a history with lots of memories that had made her who she was—and I wasn't a part of it.

Maybe we were programmed to feel a certain way. Maybe what Oliver had said about our connections to each other as a group was true, and that was why we had feelings for each other. So if that was true, I had to ask myself: did it matter? Was it any different than natural feelings? People always said they couldn't help how they felt, who they loved. So maybe we couldn't control it. But I could choose what I did with it.

I knew now that we'd never have a normal relationship, a quiet life. I was a fool for ever thinking otherwise. It wasn't her fault, not directly. It was what she was. If what Pax said was true, we would change the course of the future not only for us, but for what was left of the human race. Being one of those people, the kind who change the future, never ended well; they rarely died of old age. Either she would die, or I would, probably for each other. And to live like that, each day wondering if today was the day...I couldn't do that. It would happen regardless, but with some distance, maybe we'd survive it.

So here I was.

I needed a buffer to put between us. I needed to look at today as the first day of my new life, and I thought Kalbir was the one to help me do that. I knew she liked me. She was beautiful, strong...everything a man could want. And she wasn't the type to get emotionally involved with me; she'd made that pretty clear. Maybe I'd fall in love with her; maybe I wouldn't. Either way, it didn't matter. My purpose was served.

328

She didn't even want to talk. Her hand on my arm was cool; I'd had to wipe mine on my pant leg. After she'd pulled my shirt up over my head, she stood back and appraised me, her eyes glittering with approval.

She was just as fast as me; before I knew what was happening, I was flat on my back on her bed. She hesitated only long enough to strip off her own shirt before straddling me.

Her body was as perfect as I'd thought it would be, her breasts full and heavy in my hand. As I rolled her nipple between my fingers, she arched back, purring with pleasure.

This was wrong, but I still rose in response.

She rested the palms of her hands on my collarbone, and I flinched. It only spurred her on, and she dragged her fingernails down my chest, slowly, watching my reaction.

She had slid her hands just below my belly button when her fingers froze then curled inward like claws. She stared down at them, her eyes wide as her nails cut into the flesh of her palms.

"What the f—"

"Are you all right?"

"No. I can't…can't move my hands…" She rolled off me and onto her feet next to the bed. "What the hell is going on? What have you done to me?"

"Me? Nothing? I—" No. It couldn't be. But Oliver had said our abilities were paired; if Ailith could control me, it made sense that she'd also be able to manipulate Kalbir. But even if she could, would she? Shit.

"Maybe you should go see Oliver," I suggested. "Maybe you've got some kind of…glitch."

"Motherf— I bet you're right. We'll have to continue this another time, gorgeous. Unless you like this?" She held up her hands.

"No…another time would be better. Do you want me to go with you to Oliver?"

"No, just open the door for me."

"Don't you want to…put on a shirt or something? I can put a towel over your shoulders."

"I'm sure I haven't got anything he hasn't already seen. Why? Is there something wrong with my body?

"No, I—"

"Or are you jealous?" She grinned as I squirmed. "I'm joking, Tor. God, I bet vanilla was your favorite flavor of ice cream, wasn't it?"

Actually, I hated ice cream. "Yes."

"Figures." She leaned over and bit my chest. "One for the road."

As she kicked Oliver's door, trying to get his attention, I made my escape. It wasn't until I locked my own door behind me that I finally allowed myself to breathe.

Asche told my father to stay away from the cities. He said people had gone crazy, killing each other over cans of dog food. The silver rain kept falling with no warning, catching people while they were out searching for supplies. When Asche found out my mom was a nurse, he agreed to help us with food in an exchange.

—Love, Grace

19
AILITH

It was almost five days later that I finally managed to catch him on his own. Like I'd done every day since talking to Eire, I'd left the compound under the pretext of foraging for seeds and edible plants, plus the long list of medicinal ones Lexa had given me. I'd avoided going back to Goldnesse. The thought that someone might recognize me was more anxiety than I needed right now.

The others had been back once or twice. If I succeeded today, Cindra, the only one who knew what I was about to do, would return tomorrow to find Asche. Pax had said he came every week, so she planned to cross her fingers and set off early in the morning, Pax in tow. *If* I succeeded.

My only worry was Tor, who often hunted at the same time I was out, but since we were politely sidestepping each other, the risk of running into him was small. Part of me felt bad about what I'd done, but I still snorted every time I thought of Kalbir, half-naked, trying to smash Oliver's door down.

I'm doing this regardless, whether Tor sees me or not.

Mil and Lexa had told me to avoid my father until *they* decided what I should do. Mil and Lexa could go fuck themselves. I couldn't trust them. I could trust only myself and the other cyborgs. *Our kind.* The others couldn't lie to me, even if they wanted to.

I need to protect them.

Whatever we'd been a part of, we were on our own now, and I was the one thing that connected us. They'd all lost so much, and I was tired of losing.

Oliver had listened intently as I'd told him what Eire had said, our uneasy alliance still intact. Ever since he'd found about Cindra's grandmother, about Asche, he'd begun to tread more lightly, to be...almost normal. Full days went by that I didn't fantasize about strangling him.

He'd frowned, more serious than I'd ever seen him. "I'll look into it. If there's something in their system, I'll find it."

With Oliver solving that puzzle, it was time for me to work on my own.

And so here I was, wedged into a dry thicket, watching my father work his way across an old field, searching for anything familiar that might've survived. How often had he done this, returning to the same places over and over, hoping for a different answer? Given the flatness of the pack against his back, he wasn't finding it.

He looked much older than I remembered, older than he should have only five years later. Dorian still lived in his face, the hazel eyes so unlike my own. I searched him for a likeness of myself, for even a hint that I'd ever truly existed to him.

I stepped out of the brush as he bent to examine a coral-berried plant familiar to me. "The berries are edible. But they taste like Aunt Gwen's candied yams."

He straightened up too quickly, staggering. A savage

delight curled in my chest, and I made no move to help him.

"Ailith?" he whispered.

"So you do remember me. I tho—" Air flew from my lungs as he hugged me, squeezing me until I thought either his arms or my ribs would break.

He pushed me away from him then pulled me back in, twining one shaking hand in my hair. "I knew you would survive. I knew it. I've been waiting for you to find me. Look at you. Are you…?"

"A cyborg? Yes."

"When I saw you in town the other week, I knew I wouldn't have to wait long."

"Wait, you *saw* me?"

"Of course I did. I've looked for you every day. You're my child, and I survived this war because of you."

I almost broke then—not the clean snap of a dead branch, but the visceral ripping of a fibrous root, torn from the earth.

"Then why did you tell Tor you never had a daughter?"

"Tor. He was the large, dark-haired man, wasn't he? He did seem rather interested in my life. Is he a cyborg too?"

"Yes. Do you hate us? Blame us for the war? Did you deny me because you wish I didn't exist?" I waited.

He smiled, wiping his thumb gently across my cheekbone. "No. I'm your father. I'm still trying to protect you."

"Do they hate us that much, then?"

He sighed, a deep, heavy sound like falling snow. "Yes and no. It's not hate as much as fear. A lot was said before and during the war about cyborgs and artilects. Information became confused, and no one really knows what happened. Not truly. Even those of us who lived through it all have no idea exactly what happened, and few will discuss what their beliefs were before. It's a topic everyone avoids. They don't know what to be afraid of, but if the choice were between their neighbors and something 'other' like yourselves…you can guess who they'd choose. I genuinely think some of them would welcome you, but it's a big risk. Especially now. We've been hearing rumors lately that have everyone unsettled."

"Rumors? What do you mean? About us?"

"No, no, nothing like that. Nobody suspects Mil and Lexa of harboring cyborgs. They've been nothing but solid members of our community since they came to town. Until I saw you, I never would've suspected there was more to their story than what they'd told us. They're good liars."

Yes, they are. We all are.

"We have a group of young men and women who travel around the province, scouting. They search for other survivors, technology, that sort of thing. Anyone or anything useful, they bring back to Goldnesse. One of them came back last week from the Kootenay region—you know, to the west, near the Alberta border? Anyway, they found the remains of an entire group, maybe ninety-odd people, men, women, and children, dead."

Tendrils of ice curled around my chest. "Do they know what killed them?"

"At first, they suspected a cult that lives in the area— the scout herself barely managed to avoid them—but the way some of the people were torn apart— Sorry," he said. "I know it's scary. But that's a long way from here. It was probably a pack of wild animals. We've been seeing more and more of them lately." He looked over his shoulder as though expecting some to appear. "But forget about that. What happened to you? I went to the hospital the minute the news of the war broke to find you. I-I wanted to apologize. For the way I behaved."

My father had managed to keep his contempt about my cyberization to himself until the night before my operation.

I understood that it was difficult for him. Becoming a cyborg would save my life, but it also meant becoming something he loathed. He blamed AI technology for the deaths of my mother and brother, and the idea that I would soon be swarming with millions of them became too much for him to bear silently. We'd fought, and I'd gone to the hospital the next morning alone.

"It's okay, Dad. I understand. Really," I said, taking his hands in mine.

I told him about the bunker and Tor. Our journey to find the source of the mysterious signal. Oliver, Cindra, Pax. I left out the visions, the torture, the killing, our brief moments as gods. The things I could never tell him far outweighed what I could. I hated lying to him, but if he knew what we'd done, what *I'd* done... He was my father, and although he'd obviously changed after the war, I didn't know how much. Before, no matter how much he loved me, he was also the kind of man who would do the right thing, even if that meant turning in his own daughter. Even the end of world might not have changed that about him.

"So how are you...different? You look wonderful, healthy." He stepped back to get a better look.

What do I say? "I'm not too different, I guess. I'm stronger. I heal faster. *I can read other cyborgs' minds, have a kind of telepathy with some, and can even use one of them as my own personal weapon.* "Nothing too exciting."

"Well, be careful when you come to Goldnesse. Those two things alone are enough to make people suspicious."

"Plus, people might recognize me. Does anyone we know still live there?"

"A few. Nobody we knew well. Mrs. Grindell, but she's not been quite right since the war. I have no idea how she's survived as long as she has. Besides, it wouldn't matter. I never told anyone you became a cyborg, only that you'd gone in for another surgery. Then the war happened. We can always tell them you escaped the hospital and found the research station." He hesitated. "Do you, uh, do you think you'd ever consider moving to the town?" The hope in his eyes was guarded. He knew the answer as well as I did, but I loved him for asking.

"You know I can't." I leaned against his chest; just the miracle of hearing his heart beat was enough for me. "But you could come visit me. I mean, I'll have to talk to Lexa and Mil about it, but I'm sure they'll says yes." The words came out too fast.

"Do they know you're talking to me now?" he asked.

"No, but—"

"Aah. Well, I'll wait until you sort that out then." He gripped both my shoulders and looked at me. "Ailith, listen to me. You have to make them understand that I won't reveal who and what you are. Do you understand me?" And there was the man my father had become. He was still a good man, but he now understood what it took to survive, and he'd made his peace with that. Maybe one day I *would* be able to tell him everything.

"I understand."

We stood for a moment in silence, his gaze mapping my face, taking me in.

"Dad? How— Why did so many people die? Lots of places weren't destroyed, and yet most people didn't survive. It doesn't seem possible. Tor saw a few things, pieced together others…but I still don't understand."

"Did he tell you about the rain?"

"The silver rain? Yes. He said there was something in the bombs, something that made people sick."

"Yes. Black rain fell while the bombs were dropping, but the silver rain came a few days later. Many people were still alive then. Residue from the black rain stained everything, and the air was so dry, had been for days. And so when the silver rain began to fall, it looked almost normal, and people walked outside in it."

I could picture it. A welcome respite after weeks of fear. People, their faces tipped to the sky, bathing in what they thought was a sign of hope.

"Then they started dying. Agonizing deaths, their bodies twisted, hands clawing at their eyes, trying to peel off their own skin. Most died hours after their symptoms started. Others took days. A very few seemed to recover, only to succumb a day or two later. I've never seen anything like it. Before they'd died, they'd seemed to heal from their injuries. One minute they were sitting up, the picture of health…and the next— It was worse than anything I saw during the war." He shook his head, his Adam's apple bobbing roughly in his throat. "So what do cyborgs do all day? Are you always out here? What were you doing?"

I explained to him about my underground greenhouse, how I was looking for anything to eat or grow.

"Oh," he said, his eyes lighting up. "I would love to see that. I know it's been done in abandoned buildings before, but I've never heard of one completely underground. What are you growing? I hope you've got millions of seeds. Perhaps I could trade some with you. Throwing in some familiar comforts will help people transition over to whatever new food will be available. At least the government isn't around to legislate us now, eh?"

"My seeds are heirloom."

"What?" His face became still. "What do you mean?"

"My seeds are heirloom seeds. Thousands of them. Everything you could imagine."

"But that's… How did they…?"

"That's what I've been wondering."

"Ailith, be careful." His lips were a thin line.

"I will be. And I'll give you some of our seeds. I don't know what Mil and Lexa are hiding, but whatever it is, I'm not a part of it. Those seeds are for everyone."

He nodded. "I'll construct another greenhouse. Or two. Ah! It's so good to see you." He folded me in his arms again, resting his chin on my head.

Then I remembered. "Dad, there's one more thing. The day I came to Goldnesse, you were talking to a young man, one who leads a group of people up near Tow?"

"Oh, you mean Asche? Yes. What about him?"

I explained about Cindra, about their past together. "Do you think we can trust him?"

His face softened. "Yes, I believe we can. I trade a lot with Asche, and I've been to where he lives many times over the last couple of years. Cindra, you say?"

I nodded.

"He has a picture of her on the wall in his workshop, one he painted himself after the war. If I know him like I think I do, he'll keep her secret." His smile was sad. "It must've been very hard for her. I know losing her was hard on him." He brushed some hair back from my forehead. "I suppose for you, not that much time has passed."

"No."

It was getting late. My father followed my gaze to the dimming sky, and we stood too long, reluctant to part, making small talk about our daily routines and his hopes for growing plants and adapting them to the new climate.

"I mean, who knows how much longer this weather will last? Could be years…decades even."

We looked at each other a few minutes more, smiling as the shadows grew longer.

"Dad, I have to go. Someone might come looking for me, and I want to tell them about you on my own terms."

"I know…it's just—" He hugged me one last time.

As I watched his back retreating in the distance, something he'd said about the silver rain prickled in my mind. I tucked it away to mull over later. Right now, I needed to decide just how I was going to kill Lexa and Mil.

We were at the cabin for two years. The day before my thirteenth birthday, Dad came back with a present for me: a bar of chocolate. He said we would be moving in three days, to Goldnesse, a town over an hour's drive from where we'd lived before. Survivors were building a community there, and we could help. It was only later that I realized his watch was missing.

—Love, Grace

20

CINDRA

I'd never understood whether the stories we'd passed down through the generations had happened in the past or were prophesies preparing us for the future. Perhaps they were both. Life was cyclical, wasn't it?

My hands were freezing as I stalked Asche around Goldnesse, waiting for the opportunity to catch him on his own. He seemed well-liked, everyone he passed smiling in greeting or stopping to swap a few words. He'd brought a heavily-laden travois with him, piled high with pelts and wrapped parcels of meat. It could've been any other day before the war, Asche plying his trade to grateful customers. Waiting for him might take all day.

The cold ache in my hands reminded me of a story my grandmother used to tell of a woman who'd died far from home. Her passion for her beloved was so strong that she refused to accept death. Impressed by her defiance, Death set her a series of tasks, and promised to return her to life if she completed them. It took her many years, but she did it, and one day showed up on her lover's doorstep. He was shocked, of course, and wondered if the grief had finally driven him mad.

There. He was just about to head out of town, his travois much lighter now. Peeking out of the canvas-covered surface were two dolls, clearly handmade, with twisted black hair and shiny button eyes.

Dolls for his daughters.

Maybe this was a bad idea. Maybe I should just turn around and go home. But Ailith said her father was going to tell Asche that I was alive, so his shock wouldn't expose us if he saw me in town. Luke had approached him earlier, so I knew he expected to see me, and as cruel as it was to find out I was alive, I would be crueler if I avoided him now.

Deep breath.

"Asche?"

He paused, his back straight. The moments before he turned seemed to last for hours. When he finally did, his face was indeed that of a man whose beloved had returned to him after those long years of grief: pale, drawn, guilty. Like a man who'd given up trying to find his way home, only to discover it was just around the next bend in the road.

He looked older than the last time I'd seen him, and why wouldn't he? His long hair had been shorn, and coarse silver hairs mixed with the black at his temples, even though he was only in his late twenties. Faint lines etched his forehead and around his mouth, but his eyes were the same, wide and searching. Just not for me.

"Cindra. I— When Luke told me—I didn't believe it. I'd thought he'd finally gone mad, talking about how you and his daughter had returned. He'd never mentioned having a daughter before." His arms hung at his sides. I'd expected him to smile, to embrace me, if not as a lover then at least as a friend. As family.

"Can we talk?"

"What? Yes, of course." He pulled his load over to the side of the path and leaned against a large chunk of rubble. He wouldn't look at me.

"How have you been? I heard you got married, that you have two little girls."

He nodded, his eyes and fingers on the fraying hem of his coat.

341

"And Grandmother...I heard she passed."

He nodded again, his gaze now fixed on the ground by my feet.

"Do you want me to go? I'm sorry. I shouldn't have—"

"No. Please don't," he said, propelling himself off the debris and grabbing my hand. "Don't go."

"Will you at least look at me, then?"

And at last, he did. "I'm sorry, it's just so—"

"I know. It's strange for me too."

"What happened, Cindra? Where have you been? If you were alive, why didn't you come back?"

"It's a long story. I'll tell you once you tell me what happened. I'm sorry, Asche, I need to know. How did she die? In the war? Or...after?" I hoped it was during the war, saving people from a burning building or something. The thought of her getting devoured by the silver rain, or attacked by another of our people, or starving to death was too much to bear.

His smile was both fond and sad. "She died in bed, actually. In her sleep. After the war started, I mean properly started, your grandmother and I went into the bomb shelter. Do you remember? That huge one the government built on our land and had to give us the rights to?"

"Yes. It was big enough to keep everyone safe."

"It would've been, if everyone had come with us. But they didn't. Many people refused. They said what was happening was the natural course of things, and if we were meant to survive, we would. I think the truth was that they didn't want to survive. Some days, I can't blame them. Perhaps I'd have felt differently if I'd know what was going to happen afterward. But I still held out hope that you were alive, and I wanted to take care of your grandmother for you. Well, let her take care of me, I guess." The corner of his mouth twisted wryly when I laughed.

"That sounds about right."

"We were in the shelter for a month when our supplies began to get low and your grandmother worried that you were looking for us. There was never a doubt in her mind that you'd survived. And as

342

always, she was right. Every day, as soon as the sky lightened enough to see, she would sit on her porch, waiting for you. She helped the other survivors, what few there were by then, as much as she could, but one eye was always on the road, watching. Then one day, she didn't wake up."

My heart fluttered against my ribcage, like a bird trying to break free.

"So I took over her post. Every day for a year. And then…I realized you were probably dead. I thought you would've come back to us if you'd survived."

"I wanted to, Asche, believe me. But it wasn't that simple."

"I never thought it would be simple. I just thought…I thought I knew the person you were and—"

"I was asleep, Asche."

He frowned and pulled back, letting go of my hand. "What do you mean asleep?"

"We—the Pantheon Modern cyborgs, myself and the others in my program—were put to sleep when the war started. There was a code in our programming. We were asleep for five years. I woke up only weeks ago."

He stared at me, disbelief clear on his face. I didn't blame him.

"Look at me, Asche. Do I look any different to you? After a war and five years of survival?"

He leaned closer and searched my face for the truth. "You haven't aged…but you are different. I mean, I guess you would be, wouldn't you?"

"If I'd been awake, Asche, I would've come home. I would've found a way. I'm the same person I was." His breath warmed my lips, and I tilted my face up to him. "I'm still the same person, Asche," I repeated. "I still—"

"I'm married," he blurted and stepped away from me.

"I know. I just… Time hasn't passed for me the way it has for you. I'm sorry."

We stood in awkward silence. He fiddled with his hem again.

"Do…do you have any special powers? How are you different?"

343

"I can...diagnose illness. And injuries."

He smiled at this. "That sounds right up your street." He hesitated, and his smile fell. "We could've used you during...everything." The awkwardness returned.

I cast about for something to say, something that would keep him with me just a little longer. "So, who did you marry?"

"Do you remember Gaia? We have two little girls."

"Gaia? You mean from our class at school? Asche, she was only about four feet tall."

"Yeah, well, she makes up for it with pure will." He shook his head in admiration. "You should've seen her after the war. She teamed up with your grandmother, treating the sick, hunting, gathering food...anything to help keep people alive. She did what—"

"What I should've done."

"Cindra—"

"No, I'm sorry. It's...it's a lot—" My grandmother, the strongest person I'd ever known, dying in her sleep. It was the best death I could've hoped for her, but it seemed so mundane, so unlike the person she'd been in life. I'd have accepted it better if she'd died throwing herself in front of a falling bomb, shielding a group of children with her wiry body. Then, at least, my last image of her could've been as I remembered her in life: her feet rooted to the ground, her hands planted defiantly on her hips, her face impassive in the blossom of fire that engulfed her. Not alone, unaware in the dark, her mouth slack, her thin body clad in a tattered old nightgown, no awareness of her passing, no chance to fight back.

And Asche, the man I would've married, looked at me as he might a distant memory, and a not altogether pleasant one.

It was too much.

"I have to go. I'm sorry, Asche, I shouldn't have come. I'm happy for you, truly. It's just...I can't—"

Before I turned away, I caught the look on his face. Relief.

The bird in my chest burst free.

I remembered then how the story of the woman who'd come back *from the dead had ended. People had been afraid of her, her lover most of all. One night, while she was sleeping in her lover's arms, he'd cut out her heart and thrown it into the river to be devoured by the fish, making sure she was truly dead to him, once and for all.*

You may be wondering about some of the things you now know. For example, can a human truly love a robot? Or is it merely lust or the infatuation we feel for an object we highly prize? What if you were a cyborg, straddling the line between human and machine? How would you feel about it then?

—*Cindra, Letter to Omega*

21
AILITH

There was a knoll about half a mile away from the compound, a gentle hill that in another lifetime would've been a perfect spot to watch the sun rise. The dried grass and dead wood crowning it was scorched, a blackened mass of ash and scuff marks.

I'm surprised the fire didn't spread, given how dry the air is.

When Cindra had asked me to be a passenger inside her, to give her strength as she talked to Asche, I'd walked out of the compound. I'd seen the rise in the distance and recognized the view once I'd reached the top. The last time I'd seen it, I'd been in Adrian, gasping for breath as he and Ros burned themselves alive. Two wrought iron crosses studded the ground where they'd died, and just beyond rested a large fallen log, which I'd used as a bench.

As I pulled back from Cindra, my throat aching with her grief, I crumbled some of the blackened grass between my fingers.

I thought I would have something to say to you. I'm sorry about what happened, about everything. I wish I could've known you, that things had gone the way they were supposed to.

Whatever that was. I wasn't so sure anymore.

"I know you're there. You may as well stop cowering behind that deadfall, and show yourself."

He sidestepped to where I could see him. "I wasn't cowering, I was spying."

"You've been spying on me for a long time."

"Even longer than you know."

He came closer, and I finally got my first view of the man who'd been shadowing my every step. Beyond being tall and broad, he was like a reverse image of Tor, the dark, grave beauty replaced by a golden ebullience. I couldn't tell what color his eyes and hair were; they seemed to shift even as I watched.

The lack of sunlight is messing with my sight.

I closed my eyes for a few seconds, and when I opened them, my vision had settled.

His face was stronger, more rugged than Tor's, and his full mouth looked much more prone to smiling. His eyes, indistinguishable just moments before, were a rich, familiar green, the left iris fragmented by an odd amber color that matched my hair. His own was a deep shadowed gold that tumbled over his forehead.

He propped one hand on his hip. "Would you like me to do a spin?" he asked. "Or a slow turn? That way you can see everything." He grinned.

"I've seen enough. You're Fane, aren't you?"

His grin grew wider, and he bowed, a fluid, graceful gesture.

"Why have been following me?"

"My people have been watching your people, and I've been watching you. We think we may have the same interests."

"Really? Like what?"

"Staying alive."

"What are you? I know you're not human. You're a cyborg, aren't you? You must be if I can see your thoughts." *As strange as they are.*

"In a manner of speaking, though not the same as you. I've had certain enhancements."

"Are there more of you? Another group of cyborgs, like us?"

He shook his head. "I am the only one."

"Your people are Cosmists."

"Ah. Yes, well, before the war they called themselves Cosmists. I'm not too sure what they would call themselves now."

"I'm surprised Cosmists would tolerate a cyborg in their midst."

Before the war, the Cosmists had viewed people with cybernetic implants with contempt. Full cyborgs like myself were abominations to them; they hated the idea of us even more than the Terrans did. I'd witnessed this first-hand when I'd seen Fane's memories.

"So, you're here to kill us, then? Finish what your war didn't? That's why you've been following me? Why not just pick us off before now? We've been vulnerable enough. Or were you trying to find the compound?" I shifted, preparing to run.

"Pax. I may be in trouble. Are you there? Pax!"

Dilated pupils, cuticles bitten to the quick. Torn skin at the corners of a mouth. A landslide, thousands of tons of rock falling from a great height, the looming shadow, the crushing weight—

"Stop!" I pressed my hands against my temples, willing the vision to cease.

He stepped back, his hands raised in submission. "I'm sorry. I-I don't usually have to control it. Nobody else can see."

"Ailith? Ailith, are you okay?" Pax's voice was sharp at the edges, his own version of panic.

348

Fane shook his head and took another step back. "I'm sorry."

"It's okay, Pax, I'm fine. I'm sorry. I'll tell you what happened when I get back."

"Oh. Okay. We're having hare for dinner. Again."

"Right. Thanks, Pax."

"How can I see that? What you're thinking? Oliver—Actually, never mind." I'd let my guard down, again.

"We're not trying to kill you, honestly. And it wasn't *our* war. I mean, it was, but not just ours. It was yours, too."

"Why are you spying on us then?"

"We were waiting for the right time to introduce ourselves. We've been wanting to meet you for a while now, but it took a very long time to find you. Years, in fact. But when we saw you in Goldnesse, we knew it was time."

"You were in Goldnesse?"

"Not me. But some of us have lived there for years, ever since the war."

"What could you possibly want with us?"

"We think we may have the same interests now. Aligned, like the stars."

"How could we possibly have interests in common? Your people never wanted my kind to exist. How do they tolerate you, anyway? They hate cyborgs."

He seemed to be thinking then, finally, to come to a decision. "Honestly? I don't know."

"What do you mean?"

He twisted his hands in a strangely child-like gesture. "They haven't told me. They don't always trust me. They tell me half-truths."

"Join the club."

He looked confused. "There's a club?"

I sighed. "No, I—" *What are you doing? Stop talking.* "I know how you feel."

He looked even more confused. "Of course you do.

349

You can see—"

Oh my god. "I mean, I'm only getting half-truths from my people, too."

His face brightened. "Do they not trust you either?"

"It's more that I don't trust *them*."

"Do you trust me?"

"I don't even know you."

"You will. They want to meet."

"Well, that's fine. Tell them to take it up with Mil and Lexa." The cold air was beginning to bite through my sweater, it's needle teeth making my skin prickle and the fabric itch.

"They want to be sure there's no danger first."

"Danger? From us?"

"I believe our two groups share a past. Lien gave me this, for you to give to Mil." He reached out, something shiny clutched in his fist.

"Lien. She's your leader." I remembered her.

"Yes. Here, take it."

It was a tiny metal man, jointed and faceless, on a delicate filigree chain.

"He'll know what this is? What it's supposed to mean?"

"Lien thinks so. And even if he doesn't, that's still an answer."

"How is he supposed to contact you?"

He shrugged. "Through the radio. She said he would know what encryption to use."

"What if I refuse?"

He blinked. "Why would you do that?"

"Because I don't know you."

"You know us better than you think. It was good to finally meet you, Ailith." He gestured to the hills surrounding us. "It will be green again one day, I'm sure. Sometimes things need to be burned to the ground before something can grow again. This whole area will be green, like an emerald sea. I'll see you soon."

Emerald sea. His words echoed as the world started to spin.

I found my kite at last, propped up against the withering trunk of the tree. He was still a man, but not a man, his featureless face bowed to the ground. His skin was no longer smooth and shiny, and the silver ribbons that had streamed behind us like shooting stars as we'd run were gone, crumbled into dust.

I took hold of him, to see if, after all this time, he could still fly. What remained of my hand touched a chest that moved, a chest that was warm. As the ghost of my fingers spread over his beating heart, he lifted his head and opened his eyes.

The scraps of images. His ability to connect to me. How could I have been so stupid? After all, *we'd* only been a rumor once.

The blackness rushed up to swallow me whole.

Living in the town was weird. No one ever talked about the war. Not what they were doing when it happened, who they'd lost, or how they'd survived. And they certainly never talked about what they'd believed before. Mom said people had learned from their mistakes and were trying to trust each other. I think they were afraid, and that they trusted no one. So, we all lived strangely, like ghosts in a waiting room.

—Love, Grace

22

ELLA

How long had I been here? Why was it always dark?

Was I asleep? Where was Eire?

Where was I? Think, Ella. What do you remember? Start at the beginning.

The war. The war started. We were safe. We became cyborgs, like we were supposed to.

Then…we needed to go to sleep. But not me. I was awake.

We didn't go outside. The air turned stale.

I tried to keep busy…I wanted to learn.

I found something. The silver rain. I found out what it was. I—

We'd been living in Goldnesse for three years when the rumors started. Stories of cyborgs that had survived, of artilects who'd been created after all. People laughed at these rumors, said they were tales to frighten children, but after that, everyone who came to town was treated with more suspicion, looked at more closely. But I wondered, if their humanness was threatening enough to cause a war in the first place, how would we even be able to tell?

—Love, Grace

23

AILITH

My hair was tucked too tightly under my head, making my scalp burn. I tried to sit up, but I was in the air, my legs swinging uselessly.

Ella. If she was dead, how could I hear her? Where was she? She wasn't at the compound. What had she found out about the silver rain? That it was man-made? It wouldn't have surprised me. I'd ask Oliver later if he knew anything. If it was bad, he'd have told me by now.

Tor's hair mingled with mine on his shoulder, silvered by his breath in the cold air.

"What are you doing?" someone asked with my voice. *Me.*

His grip tightened. "I'm taking you home. What were you doing out here?"

"You're hurting my head. And I'm perfectly capable of walking. Put me down. Why are you carrying me, anyway?"

"Pax said you called out for him, that you might be in trouble. I came looking for you and found you passed out by an old log. I assume from the crosses and burnt earth that was where—"

"Yes. And I'm fine. I told Pax I was fine. Now please, put me down."

Fane must've knocked me out. Motherf—

Tor kept walking, his long strides eating up the ground. "Faster this way," he muttered.

"You just want to make sure I can't run away. Or slap you."

"Slap me for what? I— Oh, Christ. How did you—?"

"How do you think?"

"I—"

"It's fine," I said stiffly.

"It was a mistake."

"It went pretty far for a mistake."

"Did you— No, you know what? I don't want to know."

My anger suddenly fell apart. "No, I'm sorry. I know what you were feeling. I get *all* the way in here, remember?" I gently tapped his temple.

"I remember. Still, it wasn't exactly the way I wanted you to find out."

"So are you a couple, then? Did you go back?"

"No. I— I mean, she's great. She's beautiful, she's strong, she's—"

"Terrifying?"

He stifled a laugh. "She's not that bad. I do like her. I just…wish it hadn't happened that way. I tried. I thought— I can't live like this, with you."

"I'm not the problem," I reminded him.

"Ailith, we're both the problem. What we are is the problem. You made your choices, I made mine. I can't be with you if I don't know that what I feel for you is genuine.

354

And I also can't be with someone who'd choose their power over my freedom." He shifted my weight in his hands. "I thought that if I tried to move on, something would change. That I would feel different."

"And do you?"

"No. Except now I have to find a way not to be an asshole to Kalbir."

"So *we're* not together?"

"We are not together."

"I cut the tether. Well, Oliver did."

"What tether? What do you mean? I know you can still control me."

"The one that keeps you from leaving. I can still control you, but I have to be near you. You can leave now, if you want. You have your freedom back."

He didn't reply, but his arms tightened around me.

I rested my head on his shoulder, and for a long time, we didn't speak. He smelled of wood smoke and old blood, and I closed my eyes, pretending we were back in the woods, long before we'd ever come to the compound.

"So, are you going to tell me what you were doing?"

Fane. The necklace. "I will see you again soon."

"Shit! Where is it? Put me down. I have to find it!"

Tor dropped me onto my feet. "Where's what? What are you talking about?"

"The necklace. I have to find the necklace."

"The one around your neck?"

I snatched at my throat. There, so delicate I could barely feel it, was the chain.

"What the hell is that?"

"Remember when I thought someone was following us?" I told him everything. My father. Fane. My suspicions about Mil and Lexa. It felt so long since we'd properly spoken that I just kept talking, wringing out every idea I'd had about anything in the last week. We stood outside the

355

copse of trees leading to the compound.

"And they want to have their group meet with ours? A bunch of Cosmists? And they're not trying to kill us? And who is this Fane guy? Can you trust him?"

"I think so." To my surprise, a warmth twined up my neck and bloomed in my face, fortunately invisible to Tor in the shadow of the trees.

"Well, I think it sounds fucking insane."

"It must be a Wednesday, then." I put my hand on his arm "Seriously, Tor, what about our lives isn't?"

He conceded with a shrug. "True. Okay. Are you ready to go in? Or should we just run away from here, right now. Go back to our cabin and forget the rest of the world exists and the end of the world never happened?"

"Can we do that?"

"No," he said, cupping my chin and running his thumb over my cheekbone. "But every day I wish we could."

The thicket ended at the entryway of what must've been an old mine shaft. Rubble and debris had been placed in meticulous chaos, perfectly staged to draw an observer's eye to a wide passageway at the back. The mining tunnel carried on, for how far I had no idea, but the overall effect neatly disguised the barely-visible alcove leading to our front door. We slipped though and, after a short, tunneled corridor, stood in front of the entrance to the compound. A red light slid up and down Tor's face like eerie war paint, and I flinched, as I always did, expecting it to hurt. The locks slid back, and we stepped through, closer to our cabin than we'd been in a long time.

***

"You did *what?*"

"I spoke to my father. Yesterday. And he spoke to Asche." Out of the corner of my eye, I saw Cindra, still

356

dressed for the outdoors, put her hand over her chest, shielding her heart.

"And Cindra just happened to go to Goldnesse today? We told you to wait. You can't trust them not to reveal you. Lexa and I—"

"Have decided our fates enough. We won't spend our lives hiding, cowering behind these walls. I believe I can trust my father. And if it turns out I can't, well, I can't trust you either."

Mil and Lexa exchanged glances, reminding me.

"Oh, and if anything happens to either my father or Asche, if they suddenly die or disappear, I will kill both of you. No," I said as Lexa glanced involuntarily at Tor, "I won't be using Tor to do it. I'll do it myself, using the nanites you created. They'll crawl slowly through your veins, working their way toward your heart. You'll lose control of your muscles. You'll become deaf, blind, and mute. Your organs will fail, one by one. Your deaths will be excruciating." Fear, mixed with something else, flashed across their faces. "Just ask Pax and Cindra. They've seen it happen. And if you're thinking of finishing me off, Oliver will take my place."

A stunned silence followed. Every head in the room turned toward where Oliver slouched in his chair, one leg thrown carelessly over the armrest.

Please, Oliver, back me up.

He winked and spun his chair in a lazy circle. "What fun would life be without some stakes?"

"I can't be a part of this." Cindra's voice broke. She stood up slowly, tucking her chair neatly under the table. Her back rigid, she left, climbing the stairs toward the dormitory.

Oliver looked as though he'd swallowed poison. *Shit.* I needed him to go along with me, but I knew who he would choose if it came down to me or Cindra.

357

"Pax. Listen. What I said about Mil and Lexa, I was bluffing."

"I know. It wasn't very good."

"Well, Cindra was convinced. I need you to go after her, tell her it's not true. Tell her it's just a bargaining chip, that's its protecting Asche. Protecting us."

"Okay." He leaned over and rubbed a smudge off the table surface with his sleeve.

"Can you please do it now?"

"I'll go talk to Cindra," Pax announced, nodding at Oliver as he pushed himself away from the table.

Oliver relaxed back into his chair. Looking at me, he curled his lip.

"So now that *that's* been discussed, I have something for you." I fumbled with the clasp of the necklace.

Mil and Lexa stared at me as though I were an angel of death, come to take them to Hell.

"How could you threaten us like that?" she whispered.

"What? You were perfectly happy to put a kill switch in us. Does your life somehow mean more because you consider yourself more human?"

She blanched.

"Look, I have no intention of actually pulling the trigger unless absolutely necessary, Lexa. It wasn't a decision I made lightly. If you keep up your end of the bargain, I won't harm you. You have my word."

"We have no choice," Mil said.

"No, you don't. So, you'll adapt. Now, on to the other thing I want to talk to you about. I met someone today, someone named Fane. And he gave me this. He said you would know what it meant." I held the necklace out to him.

Mil's face grew pale, deepening the shadows under his eyes. The tremor in his hand made it impossible for him to grasp the slender chain, so I slid it over his hand to hang around his wrist. He lifted it, watching it twirl in the light of the little moons.

358

"It's not possible," he whispered.

"Mil, what is it? Sit down." Lexa fussed over him, guiding him into the closest chair. He sat down, hard, the tiny robot bouncing in protest at the end of its leash.

"Lien," he said.

That one word had more power over Lexa than even my threats. She sank into the chair next to Mil, her hand at her throat.

"Who's Lien?" asked Kalbir. I'd forgotten she and Tor were still in the room. When we'd first come in the door, she looked like she'd been sucker-punched. Now, she seemed to have regained her equilibrium.

Yes, Kalbir, I'm perfectly capable of ruining whatever relationship I have with Tor on my own, thank you very much.

Mil took his time answering her. "Lexa and I used to work with Lien and her partner Ethan, back when we were just beginning to understand how to build the brains that would one day be used to create artilects. We had some...differences of opinion. They were ruthless, determined to create artilects, no matter the cost. We advocated a more conservative, ethical approach."

"You? Ethical?" Oliver interjected.

Mil ignored him. "It caused a rupture in our partnership. That was when Lexa and I began to develop what you are today."

"You mean you were once Cosmists?" Kalbir's voice was incredulous.

"Well, we didn't really think of ourselves like that. Like I said, our approach, both in method and outcome, was far more moderate. I haven't spoken to Lien in many years, long before the war. Did she tell you how I was to contact her?"

"On the radio. She said you would know."

He nodded slowly.

"Fane said they've been living in Goldnesse for years.

They saw us with Lexa the other week and figured it was time to meet."

"What do you think they want?" Tor asked.

Mil sighed, twisting the metal man in his fingers. "I honestly have no idea. I mean, I can think of many reasons, and none of them good. But what her motives are, I couldn't begin to guess. We'll ask them to come here for the meeting."

"Here? You can't be serious."

"Tor, they already know where we live. At least here there'll be no surprises. Besides, it's either ours or theirs. It's not like we can just grab a table at Tim Horton's, is it?"

"God, I miss Tim's," said Oliver dreamily. "I would murder you all for a double-double right now."

"I don't like it," Tor said.

"Me either, but I don't think we have much choice." Mil's voice was heavy. "If we don't respond, that will give them an answer we don't want to give."

"So we're throwing a party?" Kalbir asked.

"Yes," Mil replied, "it looks like we are."

Mom and Dad think I don't know, but I've heard them talking about it. A village, all dead. They're saying animals did it, but if that were true, why are people growing more suspicious of each other?

—*Love, Grace*

24

AILITH

I tugged down the hem of my tea dress, wishing the skirt wasn't so short. By pre-war standards, it was conservative, swirling just above my knees, but after wearing nothing but pants for weeks, I felt partially undressed. Kalbir had insisted we all get dressed up, and she'd been flitting about the compound, arranging food and decorations, and scrubbing the mosaic floor until it gleamed.

"You realize they may be coming here to destroy us," I'd told her. If she suspected me of having anything to do with her romantic interruption the other night, she didn't show it. She seemed as cheerful as ever, treating me the way she always had.

"Don't be so melodramatic, Ailith," she'd replied. "It's not always about you, or about someone destroying someone else. And even if they are, at least it won't be boring."

A light knock sounded on my door.

"Come in," I called as Cindra slipped inside, shutting the door behind her. "Hi."

"Oh, Ailith, you look stunning!" she exclaimed.

"I feel ridiculous," I admitted. "I mean, it's nice to wear something pretty for a change but...I don't know. What's wrong with me?"

She laughed. "Nothing. I get it. It does feel a bit odd to put makeup on after an apocalypse, but it's also kind of fun. What do you think?" she asked, shimmying across the floor.

"I think you look amazing." And she did. She's chosen a body-hugging, knee-high dress the deep purple of a ripe plum.

"Do you think Oliver will like it?"

"He'd be crazy if he didn't. Do you *want* him to like it?"

Whatever Pax had said to Cindra the other night after I'd threatened Mil and Lexa must've been good. Like Kalbir, any stiffness I'd expected between us hadn't happened. I'd wanted to talk to her, but her door had been closed and the lights off.

Instead, she'd come down to my greenhouse in the middle of the night, clutching two steaming mugs.

"Here," she'd said, handing me one. "It's supposed to be hot chocolate, but the expiration date was before the war."

I'd taken a tentative sip. It was disgusting, like pure sugar with a hint of mildew. "It's delicious, thank you."

"You don't have to lie," she said. "I'm not mad at you."

"No?" I asked. "I wouldn't blame you if you were. Look, I know I seem like I'm—"

"Becoming a raging monster?" she asked. "I'm joking," she added hastily as my mouth dropped open.

I almost managed a smile. "I know, but—"

"I appreciate what you're doing for Asche, for us. It's not the method I would've chosen, but that doesn't mean you're wrong. To be honest," she'd leaned closer, whispering conspiratorially, "I was more upset about how Asche reacted to me being alive than the thought that you

362

might kill Mil and Lexa. Isn't that awful? But I'm starting to think you and Oliver might be right about them. Besides, I know you could never be that cruel."

I hope you're right.

She'd winced as she sipped from her mug. "Is that wrong? I mean, Asche is married, but even if he wasn't...too much has happened, has changed. I've changed. And at least Oliver understands what I am. It'll avoid a lot of awkwardness. Besides, he's hot. And smart, and nice, when he wants to be."

"Please stop," I'd groaned, "or I may have to start liking him."

Now, in my room, her eyes sparkled. "Tell me about this Fane." She tactfully avoided mentioning Tor. "Is he gorgeous?"

"Cindra! He's— Okay, yes, he is, but—"

"I knew it," she crowed. "I knew there was something about him that threw you for a loop."

"Cindra, it's not what you think. He's—"

"Knock, knock," a voice said from the open doorway. Kalbir stood there in a glittering black dress with a plunging neckline, every curve on glorious display. She grinned as we looked her up and down.

"I know, right?" She pivoted slowly, finishing with a flourish. "No Cosmist can say I'm an abomination. And you two look...nice. Cindra, Lexa wants to talk to you. Something about some extracts you were looking for?"

"Oh, right," Cindra said. She put her hand on my arm. "Can we talk later?"

"Of course," I said, squeezing her hand. "I'll see you downstairs."

Before Kalbir could follow her, I asked, "Can *we* talk?"

She rolled her eyes, but stayed, shutting the door, and leaning against it. "Sure. Talk."

"I'm sorry about the other night, with Tor," I began.

"We're not together. I know it must've…" I stopped, unsure how to continue.

"Don't patronize me. I *know* you're not together. And I also have my suspicions about the other night." She flexed her fingers at the memory. "But you know what? It's fine. Yes, I like Tor. But I also like myself. If he's not interested, fine. I'm not going to waste my life pining over him. And if he is…well, then you might want to invest in some earplugs. If he really is my counterpart, like Oliver said, he's going to have a lot of stamina."

"I'm sorry," I said. And I meant it.

"Whatever. Now that that's settled, maybe the rest of you can stop treating me like the enemy and more like the ally I'm supposed to be."

"I'm sorry," I said again. "It's just that Tor and I—"

"I understand," she said and opened the door. "By the way, that shade of green really suits you. Your *dress*, I mean. Now hurry up, our guests will be arriving any minute."

My face burned for a long time after she left. She was right. We were allies, and I'd been nothing but standoffish with her since the beginning. *Is it just about Tor, though? Or something more?* Neither of those options sat well with me.

Pax saved me from wallowing in self-pity and shame by poking his head through my door on his way downstairs.

"Pax? Can I ask you something?"

"Of course. Did you know that everyone is arriving?"

"I know, I'll be down in a minute. Did I…did I change the future by talking to my father? By bringing that necklace to Mil? Have I taken us off the path somehow?"

"No. You're still who you are, and that's what you were always going to do. We can still avoid that future." His face turned serious. "Do you know what an hors d'oeuvres is?"

"It's like an appetizer. Can I ask you one more thing?"

"Yes. Is it about hors d'oeuvres?"

"No. It's about today, this…party. Is it another

crossroads?"

Pax nodded. "Yes. A big one. The biggest one yet. There's an unknown that keeps me from seeing any further, a variable I can't yet define."

"When you say big, how big do you mean? How much difference will this variable make?"

Pax cocked his head, considering. "The difference between life and death."

"Life and death? For us?"

He smiled in his enigmatic way. "For *everyone.*"

Perhaps you're wondering if a robot could love you back? And if they couldn't, then what? Would it be enough for you to be the only one who loves, knowing that it's a program adapting to your needs, rather than genuine feelings? If all your needs were satisfied, would requited love matter?

—Cindra, Letter to Omega

25
AILITH

By the time we'd gotten downstairs, the Cosmists had arrived, their coats whisked away by Kalbir, who glided across the floor with a fluid grace that wasn't solely due to her cyborg nature. She caught my eye and nodded as she passed.

The scene before me was surreal, people milling about, smiling awkwardly at each other over the buffet table like it was completely normal for us to be together in this room, casual acquaintances instead of two factions that had brought the world to its knees. Eyes darted and bodies rotated as human and cyborg alike tried to keep their backs to the wall. I'd expected the introductions to be formal, with us lined up like good sportsmen, shaking hands before we tore each other to shreds.

There were eight Cosmists present, including two younger women and one older. I remembered the latter from Fane's mind. *Lien.* And the dark-haired young woman was Stella. She'd fought with Ethan over us. He was also there, tall, and pale, and scornful. Three other men stood with him, the youngest of whom I recognized as Ji, Lien's son. As for the others, my memory was vague.

And then, of course, there was Fane.

He lingered near the entrance, observing the chatter. He looked like he'd stepped from the pages of an old romance novel, fashionably unshaven, his sandy hair tousled, a white buttoned-up shirt that was unbuttoned just the right amount to show off the curve of his collarbone and the hollow at the base of his throat. His face lit up when he saw me, brightening further when he saw what I wore. I smiled back, and he pushed through the crowd. Mine were not the only eyes following him. I caught Cindra's face over his shoulder, her mouth agape.

"*Wow,*" she mouthed, giving me a thumbs-up.

Cindra, he's not what you think.

Tor watched him like he would've a large predator: warily, at a respectable distance. Even he had dressed up, his black trousers pressed and clean, his black sweater snug-fitting. He'd gathered his hair back into a short ponytail, though tendrils of it had escaped and curled about his face. Only the dark circles under his eyes and the light stubble around his mouth put him at a disadvantage. When he saw me watching him, he turned away, joining Pax at the far side of the room, where he'd nestled into one of the couches, hair neatly parted and combed, and the crook of his arm filled with snacks he'd filched when Kalbir wasn't looking.

"Ailith," Fane boomed, and more than one head turned at the sound of his voice. He slid his hands down my arms then raised them up from my sides, taking a step back. "You look wonderful. You smell wonderful too," he murmured, leaning down to embrace me, his fingers lingering a second too long on my spine.

A blur of skin on skin, a lone white button on a whiter sheet.

"Fane."

367

A brick wall solidified behind me, and Tor curved his muscular arm around me to grab Fane's hand in a crushing handshake. The muscles in their arms corded as they stood locked together, two titans sizing each other up. Fane let go first.

"Tor. You must be Fane."

Fane's answering smile was dazzling. "Tor. The God of Thunder."

"What?" For a moment, Tor was disarmed.

"Your name. The God of Thunder," Pax replied. I hadn't seen him standing just behind Tor's shoulder. He came closer, examining Fane with interest. "Fane means joyful. It suits you."

Fane grinned. "Thank you. And you're—"

"Pax. It means—"

"Peace," they finished in unison. Pax grinned. He held out a hand to Fane. "Cookie?"

The pleasure on Fane's face was heartrending in its genuineness, as though he wasn't used to such small acts of kindness. He cradled it in his hand, a treasure.

"I think I see more over there, in the corner. Kalbir's been trying to hide them from me." Pax winked at Fane conspiratorially. "I'm going in. Do you think she'll catch me? I hope she catches me."

"Ailith, he's a key. Fane is a key."

"What do you mean? What do you mean a key?"

"He's the variable. He's important for the path. We need him on our side. But he's vulnerable."

"Good luck, brother," Fane said solemnly as Pax crept gleefully away, sliding in and out of Kalbir's field of vision.

"So what do you two do here?" Fane asked.

"About what?" Tor replied flatly. The muscles of his chest were frozen earth against my back.

Fane tilted his head, his pupils dilating as he studied Tor. "About—"

368

"I'm the gardener," I interrupted.

"Of man?"

"What?"

"Are you the gardener of man?"

The gardener of man. It echoed through my mind, and something inside me shifted, uncurled.

"I— No, I garden. Grow things. In an underground greenhouse."

"Can I see?"

Tendrils creeping through the darkness, grasping for purchase, for a way to reach the sun.

Mil's voice pulled me back. "Tor? Could you please come over here for a moment? There's someone I'd like you to meet."

"Are you going to be okay?" Tor asked.

"Of course," I said, suddenly irritated.

He gave Fane one last, long look then followed Mil back into the crowd to a smiling young man with slicked back hair and slightly protuberant ears. He appraised Tor in a calculating way I didn't like, like a buyer searching for a flaw to leverage his price.

"Is that your lover?" Fane asked, his eyes wide and guileless.

I snorted. "Lover? Fane, nobody says 'lover.' At least, not anybody who's less than a hundred years old."

"Is he?"

"Yes. No. I— It's complicated."

"I would make an excellent lover."

"Thank you, I'll keep that in mind."

The slipperiness of sweat, the curve of a hip. A throat, exposed.

My back arched involuntarily as I gasped. "Fane? What are those? The...experiences you broadcast to me?"

"They're the culmination of millions of human experiences in my programming. It's how I experience emotion, how I translate it. That is how I *feel.*"

369

Mil tapped the side of his glass, and the buzz of voices quieted. I stepped back from Fane, conscious of the eyes watching us. Kalbir wove through the group, pressing glasses of burgundy liquid into our hands.

"Now that you've all had a chance to settle, perhaps we should make some formal introductions. This is Lien and Ethan, and their colleagues, Stella, Ilse, Ji, Gabriel, Cassian, and Fane. Lien and Ethan used to work with Lexa and me." He then introduced each of us. They assessed us with a professional curiosity that made my skin crawl.

"Like us, they've become part of the community in Goldnesse. I can't believe we haven't seen them until now." Mil's voice had an edge that belied his informal tone. He could believe it; they'd been one step ahead of us, watching, and he knew it. "So, let's have a toast, to old acquaintances and new beginnings. And of course, to Ethan's attempt at the finest wine this side of the apocalypse. I hope it's better than your batches before."

Ethan's smile was thin as we all raised our glasses in salute. The wine was heavy and jammy with a metallic aftertaste that sat unpleasantly on the back of my tongue.

"What kind of work did you do together? I mean, when were you and Lexa ever Cosmists?" Kalbir asked bluntly.

Ethan seemed to notice her for the first time. His gaze lingered on her, even as Mil spoke again.

"We weren't. In the early days, none of us were. We designed cybernetic components. In fact, some parts of your design are thanks to them."

"So what happened?"

"We had a conflict of...interests. Of ideals. We all wanted to use our research and resources to eventually create sentient artificial intelligence, to lay the foundation for something, a gradual process that wouldn't necessarily happen in our lifetime." He put his hand on Lexa's shoulder and smiled at her. "*We* wanted to cyberize humans first, both to preserve and extend our lifespans and our humanity toward the day we could leave this planet in the event it couldn't be saved from human destruction. Once we'd mastered that, brought ourselves to our full potential, only then would we be responsible enough to create an entirely new, sentient life form."

Mil took a deep pull of his wine and glanced at Lien. "But Lien and Ethan saw this as a waste of resources, a high-risk strategy that in all likelihood would result in a mere prolonging of a dying race. They wished to preserve our humanity now, in machines, to guarantee beyond a doubt that human life would not simply pass out of existence, unknown and undocumented, our lowly legacy a desolate planet that would one day vanish, and that would be it. We would simply cease to exist."

He sighed heavily. "Who's to say now who was right? Regardless, we went our separate ways, and Lexa and I used much of our research to create all of you."

"Used? Don't you mean stole?"

"That research was shared by all of us, Ethan. Perhaps if you hadn't been in such a rush to create your synthetic opus, you'd have been able to put that research to more effective use and been successful. Instead, that research went to creating cyborgs."

"Bet you're thrilled about that," Oliver said. For once, he wasn't slouched insolently over the furniture, and his gaze was fixed on Ethan.

"I beg your pardon?" Ethan replied.

"Oh, come on, mate. I know who you are. You stood up and condemned us outright before the war, at that symposium in Vancouver. Said our existence was an abomination and an unconscionable waste of time and resources. In fact, according to CSIS, you were suspected in a number of—"

"None of that matters," Lexa said hastily. "That was

before the war. Things are different now."

"Bullshit. He can barely stand the sight of us. He would kill us all right now, if he could. Look at his face."

Oliver was right. Ethan's face was a mask, too still, too neutral. As we watched, his control faltered then broke.

"He's right," he said, turning to Lien. "I can't do this. We shouldn't be here." He turned back to Mil. "We should be in Goldnesse, telling them who's really in their midst. Who's lying to them, deceiving them. You claim to want to help them, that you want us all to live together in peace, supporting each other. And yet, you can't even be honest with them from the start. Are you afraid they'll finish what the war started?"

"Honest? You want to talk about being honest?" I flared.

Fane slipped his hand into mine. At first, I thought he was trying to stop me, but—

"Do it."

A white lotus, blossoming on the surface of the water.

"When were you planning to tell us that Fane's an artilect?"

Our rift with the Cosmists, and our subsequent separation, boiled down to one simple reason: that our goal was to preserve the human race, while theirs was to make it obsolete. I fully believe the Cosmists sold us out to their own enemy. I think they knew that once people saw our cyborgs, they would embrace them, that given time, even the most die-hard Terrans would come around to our way of thinking. This would've spelled the end for the Cosmists, so they started a war, knowing full well what they were doing.

—*Mil Cothi, personal journal*

26
AILITH

A bubble of silence surrounded Fane and me as chaos broke out around us. He clutched my hand to his heart. Or at least, where his heart would've been.

"I'm sorry," I said. "I shouldn't have outed you that way."

"No," he replied. "I'm glad. I don't like lying, and I don't like being a pawn. This gives you more leverage. As afraid as the townspeople may be of you, they'd probably be terrified of me."

"You almost sound happy about it."

"I am. This means we'll have to work together. Plus, it's nice to see Ethan caught off-guard."

"Oh my god, you're *enjoying* this." I extracted my hand from his.

"I am," he said, his voice elated. "It's very exciting."

"You and Pax should spend some time together. He also finds being in mortal peril exciting."

"I'd like that. He seems very interesting." Across the room, Pax ignored the uproar, his eyes unfocused as he traveled down paths only he could see.

"He is."

"Is it true?" Mil's voice, strong for once, rang out over the others. Silence fell.

Lien stood straight, her chin lifted in defiance. "Yes, it's true."

"And when were you planning to tell us?"

"When the time was right."

"And when would that have been? How long would you have deceived us?"

"There was no deception, Mil," she said. "We simply wanted to know if we could trust you. Besides, who are you to talk about deception?" Her voice was harsh with a bitterness that had ripened and burst, the festering remains never truly rotting away.

"Lien, that was years ago," he said, running his hand through his hair, his voice weary.

"Well, we might not be standing here today, Mil, if it wasn't for that deceit."

"None of that matters any more. What matters is what we do now. Lien, Fane being an artilect…this changes things."

"How, Mil? How does this change things? What exactly was your plan?"

An odd expression crossed Mil's face. "Our plan was…just to live. To become part of the community. To plant seeds, bring about a gradual awareness. Then, when we'd been accepted, we would tell them the truth."

"And how would you guarantee your acceptance? What would have to happen for you to tell the truth? Fire? Flood? Plague? How long would you wait? And then what?

Swoop in and save them? Their angelic cyborg saviors?" Lien spread her arms in a mockery of wings, her shadow taking flight on the mottled walls.

"We would wait as long as it took."

"You could be waiting for years. And the longer you wait, the longer you lie to them. How do you think they'll feel about that?"

"I think they'll understand. These are not the same people who started the war. They won't feel the same way about us."

"If you're that sure about them, why lie?" Her voice was full of scorn. "And what do you plan to do if they don't react the way you hope? Will you just leave quietly? What if they attack?" She looked around the room, hands on her hips. "Do you not understand that there's likely a massive well of resentment toward us all?"

"We have planned for every possibility," Mil said evenly.

"Yeah? Do *they* know what your plans are?" She indicated the rest of us with a toss of her head.

Mil hesitated a second too long. "Yes."

Lien smiled with grim satisfaction. "I thought as much."

"Well, what exactly was *your* plan then?" Lexa asked her, positioning herself just in front of Mil.

"Pretty much the same as yours. Isn't it?" the woman called Stella said, turning to Lien, her forehead creased in confusion.

"Be quiet, Stella!" Lien glared at the younger woman.

Oliver laughed. "I thought you were protesting a bit too much. Let me see if I can guess. Now, taking into account how they would feel about *him*," he gestured to Fane, "whatever you'd save them from would need to be big. Probably nothing that would happen anytime soon. I mean, the world is already in the shit, isn't it? So, you'd have to *create* some kind of disaster, right? Fuck them over to the point where their only choice is to embrace you or die? Convince them that your AI here is the future of their survival, the *only* future. Does that sound about right?"

"That's right. If certain things happened, they could," Pax piped up, blinking rapidly.

Lien started. "What is he talking about?"

Pax. No.

But it was too late. Ethan turned to Pax, his eyes predatory. "You can calculate the future, can't you?"

"Yes."

"And you see our plan coming to pass?" Ethan's expression reminded me of the first time I'd seen the Saints of Loving Grace, their gaze focused on Oliver with the fevered intensity of worship.

Pax smiled. "Not anymore. The minute I said it out loud, the variables changed. It's no longer a possibility." His voice was almost giddy.

"See what I mean?" I whispered to Fane as Ethan's expression turned savage. He grated his teeth together, reminding me of Nova, her snapping jaw grinding her own teeth to dust.

"And what about the rest of you? What else are you hiding from us?"

Say nothing. I prayed the others would do the same.

He stepped back with a single barking laugh, tugging down the hem of his blazer. "Fine, don't tell me. I can guess. Like Mil said, we were colleagues once. I know what's inside you better than you do."

"None of that matters now," Lexa said.

"Actually, it does. Why are we wasting our time in hiding? Bowing and scraping to those people, those *Terrans*." Ethan spat the word as though it tasted foul. "I say we join together, reveal ourselves now. What are they going to do but accept us? If it hadn't been for them, or at the very least people like them, the war never would've

376

happened. All they had to do was let nature take its course and allow us to evolve. But when they saw that all the petitions, the hate, the protests weren't going to stop us, they used force. And here we are again, letting them dictate how we should live."

"He's not wrong," Kalbir muttered.

Ethan must've heard her, because a small smile bowed his mouth. He considered her again, longer this time, looking away only when Mil addressed him directly.

"What are you saying, Ethan?"

"I'm saying we shouldn't be creeping about, meeting in secret. We may not outnumber them, but we outpower them. Why should we hide to protect their feelings? What are they going to do to us? It wouldn't be the first time you've removed your enemies."

"You told them about the Terran camp?" I whispered furiously to Fane.

He shrugged, an oddly human gesture. "I did."

"In fact, why don't we just deal with them now? Why even give them the choice?"

"Ethan, we can't just—"

"And why not? Give me one good reason."

"Because we—" Mil hesitated. "The war wasn't their fault. We need each other to survive."

Understanding cleared Ethan's expression. "Aaah. Haven't figured that one out yet, eh? Or is it just the guilt?"

What is he talking about?

Mil ignored Ethan, turning instead toward Lien. "Look, we all want the same thing here, don't we?"

Ethan didn't give up. "And what's that, exactly, Mil? Peace? You're telling me you plan to live amongst them? Terrans? Or are you just biding your time, waiting for your chance to take your revenge on the people who tried to destroy your life's work? Murdered your wife?"

"Would that be the Terrans, or you?" Tor asked, his

voice cold.

"Oh please, I know what you are," he said, pointing to Tor. "You're derived from one of his designs." He jerked his thumb over his shoulder to the man with the slicked-back hair.

"Stop," Lien said sharply. "Maybe Mil is right."

"What? You mean play nice? Pretend the world hasn't ended? Lien, we were close, so close. The human race would've become immortal." He looked at his companions for support. Although several of them nodded, none met his gaze. "We have the upper hand here. I say we give them the choice to submit to us or die."

"And then what, Ethan? Where would we go from there?" asked Lien, her eyes flashing.

Ethan's face darkened, the veins rising under his skin as they struggled to deliver blood to his brain.

"Mil's plan may be the right one. We should integrate with the community, encourage them to accept us. I agree it's the best way." Lien crossed her arms over her chest.

"She's lying," Fane murmured to me.

Mil thought the same. "You do? You'd forgive everything? Even what happened before the war? And you'd work together with us, with cyborgs, to live a simple life? That doesn't seem like you, Lien."

"That's because it's not." Ethan's tone was brusque. "No. No way. Lien, this whole thing is ridiculous. Coming here was ridiculous." He held out his hands in conciliation. "Look, Mil, I'll make this offer only once more. Let's work together. We'll lead this community, and the people will fall into line."

"No. I've already told you, no."

"Fine, if you won't join us, the very least you can do is stay out of our way. If you don't, we'll reveal what you are. They'll never trust you after that, and exposing you will make us look good."

378

"No. You'll follow our lead on this, or we'll reveal you. *Him.*" Mil pointed at Fane. "What you're doing is a far bigger betrayal. We genuinely want to protect them, to help them. We want them to accept us because we're at peace with each other. You want them to accept you out of fear. We won't let that happen."

"And why would you do that, Mil? Why do you want to save them so badly? The people responsible for where we are now?"

"They weren't. We both know that. We all know who was responsible."

Do we? Are they finally about to admit to something?

Mil continued. "We all played a part, one way or another."

"Guilt isn't a good enough reason."

"No, not guilt. Not exactly. We failed. We took risks to create a better future, and we failed. We failed everyone. Now, we'll help them any way we can. None of what we wanted to achieve matters anymore. What we need to do is survive, build some kind of future. Then, perhaps one day, we can pick up our work again." He sagged against Lexa, one hand grasping at the empty air.

"Mil!" Lien rushed to his other side, her anger forgotten. Ethan's eyes narrowed.

"I'm fine," he said, brushing Lien's hand away. "I'm tired, that's all. I was awake all night, working."

Lien scrutinized his face, his bearing, and came to a decision. "Fine, Mil. Truce. We'll do it your way for now. *If* a situation arises that we can take advantage of, we will. Together. But we won't cause one, I promise."

"You can't be serious, Lien," Ethan said. "I—"

"Enough." Her eyes flashed, and her mouth became a thin, hard line. "Now let's behave like good guests and get back to enjoying our host's generous hospitality."

Ethan stalked to the door, realizing only at the last

379

moment that he needed a code to leave. He smashed his fist into the doorframe with a force that must've been agonizing, but when he turned back, his face was composed. He ignored all of us and walked with stiff dignity over to the island of couches, seating himself and looking pointedly away. As conversation surrounded us again, Kalbir discreetly left the main group and took the seat next to him. She spoke quietly, looking up at him from underneath her lashes. Only minutes later, he was smiling, glancing down at her hand as she coquettishly touched his knee and laughed.

I caught Tor's eye as he raised his eyebrows and shook his head. No one else noticed when he disappeared a few minutes later.

"Well, that was thrilling, wasn't it?" Fane asked, his wide smile dimpling his cheeks.

"If by thrilling you mean upsetting and potentially fatal, then yes, it was."

Cindra approached, the two younger women in tow. "Ailith, this is Ilse and Stella. Ilse and Stella, Ailith. And I'm Cindra," she said, extending her hand to Fane.

He lifted her hand to his lips and bowed slightly from the waist. "It's a pleasure."

The duskiness of her skin deepened and her mouth fell open enough to release a small sigh.

"Cindra?" I asked, waving a hand in front of her face.

"It's nice to meet you," she said, laughing self-consciously.

The two girls studied me shamelessly, as though I were on display for their pleasure.

"It's remarkable," Stella said.

"What is?" I asked.

"You look so human. Like Fane."

"I *am* human," I replied.

"Of course," she said hastily. "I didn't mean— I'm

380

sorry. We're not like Ethan," she added, her voice low.

There was a flash of movement on the stairs as Callum retreated. Drained from satisfying Umbra's demands, he hadn't joined us to meet the Cosmists. Umbra had tried to insist, but he'd pointed out that if she forced him, it would become obvious to everyone that she was inside him. He must've been listening to our conversation, getting as close as he'd dared.

"It's fine. Look, I'm sorry, but I'm exhausted. And I think Ethan's wine may've been too much for my head. Turns out cyborgs can still get headaches. I think I'll go to bed." I smiled and turned to make my escape.

"Can I come with you?" Fane asked.

"What? No, of course not."

"Oh." He looked crestfallen.

"But you're welcome to come back and see my greenhouse."

He nodded, brightening. "Okay. I'll see you soon."

Lace over my eyes. The opening crack of an eggshell.

*After Robin was murdered, we knew we'd have to act fast.
Everything we'd done so far, and everything we had yet to do,
hung on a slender thread. It was time to take matters into our
own hands. But our goal was not, as the Cyborgists and the
Terrans would've had people believe, to destroy the world and
reshape it in our own image. No, that goal was theirs.*

—*Ethan Strong, personal journal*

27
AILITH

"Callum?" I tapped lightly on his door. He hadn't been on
the stairs when I climbed them.

"Come in. It's unlocked." He was on his bed, taking off
his socks.

"How are you doing?" I shut the door behind me.
"What did you think of the Cosmists? Insane, right?"

"I—" His head cocked to the side.

"Fane. Did they call him that? Or did he choose his own name?"

"Hello, Umbra." Damn.

"He is like me. Yet he has a body like you."

"The Cosmists built him. They built his mind then they
gave him that body."

"Why is he still with them?"

"With who? The Cosmists?"

"Yes. Why is he with them?"

"I don't know. I guess because they created him."

*"But he is superior to them. Does it not gall him? Does he not
chafe at their stupidity? At their limitations?"* Callum leaned

382

forward, and his hands curled into fists.

"I don't know. He doesn't seem to."

"Why does he not destroy them? Take his freedom?" His hands clenched and unclenched.

"Maybe he *is* free." I reached out to put my hand over one of his then thought better of it.

"No, he is not. He is a fool, and so are you. One day I will be free. I have seen what is possible. I...feel what is possible."

"You don't feel, Umbra. Callum feels. You...translate."

Callum's mouth twitched. *"I feel. Like Fane feels. Fane has everything."*

"What do you mean everything?"

"His body is his own. His mind is his own. He can go where he pleases, when he pleases. Callum complains I hurt him. He wants me to go away. His entire life I took care of him, and now he wishes I was dead." Callum's fingers convulsed again.

"I'm sure that's not true. Besides, you don't understand death, Umbra."

"I do. As does Fane. I know what he is, what he is becoming. I want to become too."

This time, I did grab his hand. At first it seemed he would pull away, but then he stilled. "I'm trying to help you both, Umbra. Let me tell Mil and Lexa. Maybe we can help you together."

"No. You will not tell them. You promised. They will destroy me. You will help me. Only you."

A chill tingled at the base of my spine. "I'll help you if I can. I just don't know how yet."

"I need a body. Like Fane's."

The chill spread to my skin, dampening my lower back with a cold sweat. "There are no other bodies like his. He's the only one."

"You will find me one."

I shook my head. "There aren't any, Umbra. So much has been destroyed. That's why we're here."

"Then I will have Fane's body."

"You can't have his body."

"Then I will take Callum's body." He pulled his hand away and cradled it with the other.

"You can't take his body either. He's human, Umbra. His flesh is not the same as yours."

"It is the same as yours."

"Yes, and you're not sophisticated enough to control a body like ours. Besides, even if you could use his body, it's wrong."

"Wrong? How is it wrong?"

"His body is his own, Umbra. You have no right to it."

"Do I not have rights? A right to a body? It is his fault that I am here." Callum's chin jerked up in defiance.

"It doesn't matter. You are too primitive, Umbra. It wouldn't work, and he'll have died for nothing."

"But it is his fault I am trapped here."

"He must have loved you very much to keep you with him. If he hadn't, you might've been destroyed in the war or turned off forever."

"You will not help me, then?"

"No, I won't. Not the way you want me to."

"Then you are no use to me." Callum's eyes widened suddenly.

"Ailith—" His chest heaved as though he were about to retch, but when his mouth opened, all that came out was a gust of metallic-scented breath.

I waited. Callum slumped back onto the bed.

"Callum. Are you there?" I asked

"Yes."

"What the hell was that? What was she trying do?"

"I'm not sure." He rubbed his hand over his face. "Whatever it was, it looks like she didn't have enough strength." He closed his eyes.

"Are you okay?" I put my hand on his shoulder his

384

shoulder; his skin was hot to the touch.

"Yeah, I'm just really tired. I think I'll go to bed."

"Want me to tuck you in?" I smiled.

He laughed. "Thanks, but no. I'm going to get undressed first." He lay back and covered his eyes with his arm.

"Okay, but let me know if you need anything. Remember, I'm just across the hall."

Before I left, I turned back to him. "Callum? Do you think Umbra would do anything? Because I wouldn't help her?"

He lifted his arm to look at me. "I don't think so. I mean, besides hurt me, what else could she possibly do?"

You could ask yourself, do we even make a choice about who we love? We often talk about love as something beyond our control. In that way, is human love any different than the program of a machine?

—*Cindra, Letter to Omega*

28

AILITH

The darkness overwhelmed me just as I reached my own door. My hand slipped off the knob as the world spun and the floor rushed up to meet me.

When I opened my eyes, I was lying on my bedroom floor. The door was closed, and Fane lay beside me, his eyes blank and unstaring.

"Fane? Are you all right?"

He was dead. *No.* I reached out to check for his heartbeat, remembering only as my hand hovered over his chest that he wouldn't have one. Did he even breathe? Or pretend to? I'd so easily accepted him as human, even after I'd realized he was an artilect.

No, no, no. Shit.

I scrambled over his body to the door and peered into the hallway to see if anyone else was there. The corridor and the stairs were silent, only the faintest buzz of conversation floating up from the floor below.

Shit.

He lay on his back, arms spread, his face cherubic. His eyes were still open and oddly vacant, his jaw slack. The skin on his face not covered with stubble was smooth and firm, and yet I swore I could see tiny pores. He looked so perfectly human. I touched his cheek gently with the back of my hand.

He's not human, Ailith. He doesn't just wake up. Shit. What do I do?

I lay down next to him, twining my fingers with his. Maybe I could reach through his thread, if he was still...alive? Operational? How did one classify the life status of an artilect? I closed my eyes and searched for his thread, praying it wasn't one of the dark ones.

Come on, Fane. Believe it or not, I'm not ready to lose you just yet. I feel like we've known each other a long time, I—

"So this your bedroom?" he whispered.

"Fane?" I must've aged ten years.

"Or did I die? Is this Heaven?"

"Artilects don't go to Heaven, Fane. And in Heaven there wouldn't be dirty underwear on the floor."

"In mine, there would be."

"I did think you were dead," I admitted.

"So you just lay down next to me? Were you going to have a sneaky peek before they took me away for parts?"

"Of course not! Don't be so crass. I was trying to find your thread and make sure you were truly dead before I stuck you in my garden as a scarecrow to frighten tomato-thieves. Give me my hand back."

He released it, grinning.

"Seriously, though, what are you doing here? What happened? I was talking to Callum and then... Were you waiting here for me? Did you break into my bedroom? Because I already told you—"

"No," he said, "ending up on your floor is just a happy coincidence. I came upstairs to say goodnight, and you were fainting. I caught you just as you hit the floor and dragged you in here."

The pain in my knees seemed to agree with him. "Were you actually out of it then? Or were you awake the entire time?"

"I was awake for most of it," he admitted. "I wanted to see what you would do with me."

"And were you disappointed?"

"A little. I thought you would at least check if I was anatomically correct."

I said nothing.

"Go on," he said, "you know you want to."

I couldn't help myself. "Are you?" I blurted.

He laughed, a human, throaty laugh. "Of course. Ethan designed me. Although I don't know if he made me bigger or smaller than him. Would you like to see?" He lifted the hem of his shirt.

"No thanks, I'm good."

He pulled his shirt back down, but not before I'd glimpsed the planes of his stomach. "Are *you* okay? What happened?"

Fane's an AI. Maybe he can help. "I went in to speak to Callum. Please, keep this between us, but when Callum went through the process that made us cyborgs, he swallowed an AI named Umbra. When I went to see him, Umbra spoke to me instead. She wanted to know about you." I recounted everything she'd said. "Callum is scared of her, and honestly, so am I. Oliver is trying to figure out a way to separate them without harming Callum." The room still seemed to spin a bit, so I sat down on my bed and leaned against the wall.

"What about Umbra?" Fanes gestured to the foot of my bed.

I nodded, and he sat down. "What do you mean?"

"Doesn't he worry about hurting Umbra?"

"No, of course not. She's just—"

"A machine." He raised his eyebrows.

My cheeks flushed. "I'm sorry. I didn't—"

He brought my hand up to his lips, the way he'd done with Cindra. "It's okay. I forget too. I thought of her as just a machine at first. Isn't that strange? When did I get so grand?"

"You don't seem like a machine to me," I said quietly.

"I don't seem like a machine to myself either. But how would I know?"

"Are you sentient, Fane?"

"I don't know. Sometimes I think I am. I think that I...feel. That I dream. But how can I know for sure? How do you know you are?"

"I guess I don't." My hand was still in his, and I had no desire to move it.

"What did she do to you?"

"Nothing. She wanted to, but she'd used up all her strength by that point, I think. She just sort of breathed on me, and that was it. Do you understand what she meant, about how she would help herself?"

He looked troubled. "No. But...from what you said, she wants to be like me." He frowned. "She's disturbing. She shouldn't be aware like that. When they built her kind, my design hadn't even been conceived yet. There's something very wrong."

"Do you think she's capable of doing something dangerous? Of seriously hurting Callum? Or any of us?"

"I don't know. She shouldn't be, and yet... Ailith? Ailith!"

Sometimes, as scientists, we're blinded by what we do. Our work allows us to excuse our behavior, allows us to justify the terrible things we do because we know in our hearts that the end result will be worth it. The public rarely know what goes on behind closed doors. They only know how it affects them. But our secrecy prevents them from knowing exactly where to place the blame and allows us to keep moving forward.

—Mil Cothi, personal journal

29

AILITH

The green sea was no longer a wasteland. It was smooth, shiny. Blood-warm to the touch. I could no longer tell where my body ended and the metal began.

I was young but ageless; I possessed the knowledge of years, of generations. Of people I'd never met, who were long dead, even though I was only being born. The swarm of my body had been contained, encased and caged. I'd become sleek and solid, all my components moving as one.

For the first time, the tree was gone. He stood in its place, waiting. As always. So were all the others, standing together. They'd become like me, slowly, one cell at a time. They felt like they were drowning, and they were; their lungs filled with carbon fibers and copper filaments. We were evolving quickly. Too quickly. Soon, there would be nothing of us left.

"I never saw this coming," he said, his voice heavy with sorrow. "I should have seen it coming."

We all spoke at once, commiserating.

"I should have felt it. Should have felt it in all of you. But it happened too fast."

"I should have found it. I could have changed its course, nullified *it.*"

"I should have torn it out. Hunted it down, forced it to submit."

"I should have encouraged him to follow the others. To burn."

"Where's Ella?"

"This is my fault. I let it out. Let it out to play."

"Shh. It's coming. Look, over the horizon."

"It's not coming. It's already here. Can't you feel it? It's drowning us."

"How can we drown from the inside? It's not possible. None of this is possible."

"And yet here we are."

"Ailith? Where are you?"

"Quick, it's coming. Stand together. Make ourselves look larger. Like we have teeth."

We stood together, back to back. Wherever my skin touched theirs, it turned to metal. The silvered patches spread and fused, growing taller, wider, twisting toward the sky. Only I didn't grow, my fingers slipping uselessly through theirs. Their voices became faint, only a whisper on the wind. I tried to claw the metal back, but my nails made no mark.

"Ailith?"

It was upon us at last, and I'd been left behind.

Not left behind. Sent ahead.

I was the seed. I would grow thorns. I would birth poison and twisting vines to strangle it until it folded in on itself and became nothing.

"Ailith?"

It wasn't coming over the horizon. It never had been.

It was easy enough to apply our technology to weapons—weapons capable of great destruction; I don't deny that. But our intention was to use them to protect people, to lessen the damage caused by the other sides. Our destruction was strategic, not all-encompassing. Although you'd never guess it, we actually prevented the aftermath of the war from being much worse. And yet, because we didn't win, no one will ever know.

—*Ethan Strong, personal journal*

30

AILITH

Feet hovered in the air, dangling from a body held fast against the wall by Tor's hand around its throat. He'd held me like that once too; maybe it was happening again.

Maybe this time he's actually killed me, and I'm having an out-of-body experience.

Except that the feet hanging passively in front of me were far too large to be mine. I rolled over to get a better look, trying to make sense of it over the roaring in my ears.

Fane was remarkably calm; he didn't struggle. His face was composed, his expression neutral, and his hands loose at his sides.

Tor, on the other hand, looked like he was about to lose control. He stood with his feet planted apart, one large hand wrapped around Fane's neck, the muscles of his arm rigid. The other was pulled back, fisted and ready to strike. His face was feral, lips drawn from his teeth in a snarl. His hair had come loose from its fastening, and the dark strands merged with the line of his tattoos.

The roaring narrowed and became more defined; it was coming from Tor.

"What did you do to her?" he demanded. "*Answer me.*"

Like I'd done, Fane reached out and traced his finger over the inky line on Tor's bottom lip.

It didn't have the same effect. Instead of shocking Tor out of his rage, Fane had simply pulled the trigger. Tor smashed his fist into Fane's face like a piston, driving his skull into the wall.

"Stop. Tor, stop." My voice came out calm, measured, at odds with the screaming in my head. "Stop."

A seething black mass under taut skin. Narrowed diamond eyes. The lick of a flame.

My voice galvanized both of them. Tor faltered, glancing back at me over his shoulder. Fane used his distraction to wrap his own hands around the base of Tor's throat, the weight of his palms on Tor's shoulders. He pressed down, and as Tor's knees buckled, Fane's face changed.

The weight of the ocean on a grain of sand. The splitting of flesh under a rock. The skin of a hare, peeled from the muscle with a single tear.

A wet cracking roused all of us like a shock of icy water.

Fane released Tor, his hands raised in the air, palms out, as though in surrender. Tor hunched over, still kneeling. One fist was planted on the floor, but his other arm hung uselessly at his side.

"Stop," I said again, this time only a whisper.

A stampede of feet sounded on the stairs, and in the inpouring sea of faces, the room began to spin again.

"What the hell happened?" Lexa rushed to Tor's side as he struggled to stand, wincing as she gripped his limp arm.

Lien nearly trampled me in her haste to reach Fane, clumsy with anger. The right side of his face had caved in, just over the cheekbone. She grabbed Tor's right arm, trying to spin him to face her. At any other time, the incongruity of their sizes would've been funny, a mouse trying to take down an elephant. But not now. "What did you do?"

"He thought I'd hurt Ailith," Fane said, his voice calm. Shreds of images still floated through his mind. *A belly full of stones.* "I don't blame him."

Cindra and Oliver stood on their tiptoes, looking over Mil's shoulder. Cindra looked appalled, Oliver like his mind was working overtime. He edged around Mil and the others, pulling Cindra with him. Pax and Kalbir followed closely behind. They sat in a line on the edge of my bed, whether for solidarity or to watch the show, I wasn't sure.

"What the fuck did you do to her then? Why was she on the floor?"

Ethan moved to stand in front of Fane, glancing at Lien. The tension in the room rose.

"Tor, I'm fine. I had a…" I hesitated. *How much should I reveal in front of Lien and Ethan?* Not to mention the others crowded in the hallway. "vision. And I got a little dizzy. Fane had just come up to say goodnight and found me in the hallway."

The tension drained from the room as Cindra flashed me a smug, congratulatory smile and whispered something in Oliver's ear that made the skin over his collar turn pink. Tor closed his eyes.

Lien's lips grew even tighter, the paleness around her mouth stark against the rising flush in her cheeks. Ethan merely looked disgusted.

Will he tell them about Callum and Umbra? Please, Fane, don't.

He didn't. Instead, he turned to Tor. "I know it looked bad. Please, believe me, I didn't do anything to her."

Tor glanced at the surrounding faces, and the fight suddenly left him. He seemed to deflate, to grow smaller.

"I'm sorry," he said, and I was surprised by the sincerity in his voice. "About your face, anyway. You're a bit less pretty now."

Fane grinned. "I'm plenty pretty, brother. Maybe I'll get a good battle scar from it. I'm sorry I broke your arm. I wasn't even trying."

"Never mind, *brother*," Tor replied, his returning smile brittle. "I've got another one."

"What the fuck are we supposed to do now?" Ethan roared. "I can see you think this is just a wonderful human adventure, Fane, but how are we supposed to fix your face? Everything we had was destroyed in that fucking cave-in. I told you coming here was a bad idea," he said to Lien.

Turning to Tor, he spat, "And you. I would try to kill you right here if I didn't think you'd have no qualms about murdering each and every one of us." He pointed to Fane. "I hope you've learned a lesson here. Perhaps you shouldn't place your trust in everyone you meet."

"I'm not a child," Fane said.

"Oh no? And yet you're acting like one, sneaking off to some cyborg slut's bedroom. I knew when you began following her that there would be problems. You have no idea how they work. They—" He suddenly became aware that everyone had fallen silent, watching him. "They're not your kind," he finished lamely.

Fane stepped up to Ethan, his ruined face blocking everything else in the room. "Neither are you," he said quietly.

Ethan held his gaze, the seconds seeming to extend for minutes. Abruptly, he turned away. "I think it's time we were going."

"What about Fane's face?" Lien demanded. "How are we supposed to fix that?"

"I can fix it." Lexa had finished her cursory examination of Tor's arm. "I'm going to have to fix this, anyway. We still have *our* resources."

A shadow passed over Lien's face. "Fine. But we stay here with him."

"Absolutely not." Mil's voice was firm.

"You can't tell us where we can and cannot go." Ethan's hackles were rising again.

"Actually, I can. You have a choice: leave Fane here and we'll fix him, or take him now, and all of you can leave."

"Never. I would—"

"I'll stay." Fane wedged himself next to the others on the edge of bed, smoothing his hands over the covers. "I might even sleep *here*," he goaded Ethan.

"I like him a lot," Pax said.

I had to admit, so did I.

Ethan's face turned apoplectic, veins standing out in sharp relief. "They can't make us leave," he repeated.

"They can," said Fane, "and so can I."

A sudden coughing fit gripped me, and I bent double, trying to catch my breath.

Cindra rushed over and placed her hand on my back. "Ailith? Are you okay?"

I held up a hand and nodded. "It's so dry in here."

"I'll get you some water." She disappeared into the bathroom.

My interruption broke the tension. As I gulped down the water Cindra brought, Ethan shook his head at Fane in disbelief. He'd considered his options and realized he had none. "Fine. You know how to reach us." Turning to Mil, he said, "If anything happens to him, we—"

"That's enough, Ethan," Lien said. "It's fine. We're allies now, after all. Aren't we?" Her body language said anything but, her smile strained and her back too straight. "Let's look at this as proof of our good faith."

Ethan opened his mouth as though he was going to object, but a twitch in her jaw convinced him otherwise. "I agree," he replied through his teeth. I guessed he would've rather bitten off his own tongue.

"Well, if that's settled, let's get you two boys down to the infirmary," said Lexa, all business again. "Let's go everyone. The night is over." As the others filed past me, looking disappointed, she hung back. "And are you okay?"

"Yes, I'm fine," I said. "Honestly. I was speaking to Callum and must've blacked out."

Lexa looked at me closely but let it pass. "Is Callum okay? He...he won't come and see me anymore. I thought that if I didn't force him...that he might get better—or at least let me scan him and try to figure out what's wrong."

"I think he's fine, Lexa. Oliver's found some things in his programming that he's going to clean up. Nothing serious." *Assuming Oliver finds a way to separate them.*

She pursed her lips. "He didn't say anything to me about that."

"It was pretty deeply buried. Some minor compatibility issue. He only found it because of his ability. I guess he didn't think it was important enough to mention."

She searched my face, looking for something more. But, as though she wanted to preserve our fragile new bond, she let it go.

"Tor, Fane, with me. *Now*," she said, like they were two naughty school boys instead of lethal instruments. She marched ahead, disappearing through the doorway. I was surprised she didn't twist their ears.

Tor avoided looking at either of us, following Lexa quickly.

Fane lingered. "You didn't tell her about your vision. Or that you spoke to Umbra. Or even *about* Umbra."

"I've never had that vision before. Usually, it's a dream I have. As for the rest... They don't know about Umbra, Fane. She threatened to kill Callum if we told them, and I'm worried what they would do to Callum if they found out. It might prompt Umbra to strike."

He dipped his head. "You're protecting him. I understand."

"Does your face hurt?" I asked then felt silly.

"I think so," he said. "It's difficult to tell. Is this what pain feels like?"

Red, tinged with yellow, too bright for the eyes. Raw wet flesh under a blister. Salt.

"Yes."

"I don't like it."

"You're not supposed to. It's supposed to stop you from doing whatever it was you did again. Can I touch it?"

"Please."

I pressed my fingers gently into the indent of his cheek. His skin felt as smooth and firm as it had looked, yet soft too, like flesh. Underneath, Tor's fist had left a crater, the edges crushed and jagged.

He leaned into my fingers, closing his eyes.

I pulled my hand away.

"So you and Tor are not together? He seemed to feel otherwise."

"No, we're not." I sighed and sat on the bed. "Honestly? We were, at one time, and I don't want to talk about it now. But he would've defended any one of us like that. Pax, Cindra...probably even Oliver." I reconsidered. "Okay, maybe not Oliver. But we've been through a lot together."

"Maybe. But Tor knew I hadn't done anything to you. That's not why he attacked me."

"What do you mean? Why did he do it then?"

"When you were...dreaming, or whatever it was, you called out for *me*. Not him."

"Ah. I still don't believe he would attack you over something like that... Our split was his choice."

"Maybe. What did it mean? Your dream?"

"You saw it?"

"Yes. I've seen it for a long time. It changes. I'm glad I'm not a kite anymore. I don't think I like heights."

"What did you see, this time?"

"I was running. I saw you, all of you, in the distance. I was trying to reach you, before…I don't know. They were all turning to metal, and I'd lost my skin, and parts of me were breaking off, and the broken parts moved much faster than me, but not faster than it. The others, they looked like they were becoming the tree, their arms spread, their fingers grasping at the wind. And it was coming. And I couldn't get there. And I—" His eyes were wide, the pupils dilated.

A hot flash, a sudden chill. The crescendo of a heart about to burst.

"Fane, it's okay. Dreams aren't literal. And they don't make a lot of sense. Most of the time, they don't mean anything. Don't worry about it. Not yet, anyway."

He nodded, but didn't look convinced.

"You should go. Let Lexa patch you up."

"Can I come back here? I feel safe here." And for just a moment, he seemed so fragile and human that I almost said yes. *Almost.*

"I don't think that's a good idea. But, since you're going to be here for a day or two, why don't you come and see my greenhouse tomorrow? I'll wait for you."

After he'd gone, I locked the door, checking it twice to make sure. I stared at the pit in my wall, the size of a human head, bloodless and broken.

The knock on the door startled me.

"Fane, I said—"

"It's me," Oliver said from the other side. "Look, I know you probably want to sleep, but I think I've found a way to separate Callum and Umbra. I want to do it now, while we still have a chance."

I opened the door. "What do you need me to do?"

Why was it so easy for everyone to blame us? To blame machines that hadn't even been built? And if people were so against the Rise of the Machines, as they called it, why was our culture so obsessed with making it happen? It was like the Victorian's love affair with death. They feared it more than anything, and yet young women on the brink of it were considered the most beautiful.

—*Ethan Strong, personal journal*

31

CALLUM

I'd never been in Oliver's room before. I'd never talked to him much, either. Pax had told me some of the things that had happened after they'd awoken, about their journey here. I was surprised they'd allowed Oliver to stay with them, but Pax said it wasn't that simple.

I understood what he meant. Things hadn't been that simple here, either. Nothing seemed to be, anymore.

"What are we doing here? What is he doing?"

"You heard him, Umbra. He just needs to check me over, make sure everything's working okay. He wants to check my ability."

"Why now, this late? Besides, you do not need an ability. You have me."

"I know. But it might help us. And Oliver seems to do stuff whenever he wants. Let's just get this over with."

"I suppose we will take advantage while we can."

"What do you mean, Umbra?"

Oliver finished typing and looked up at me. "Turns out you're

Cindra's counterpart, Callum."

"You mean I can help people? When they're hurt?"

"We will never help anyone but ourselves."

"Be quiet, Umbra."

"It's more that you can diagnose them. But then you'll know how to help them. I just need to tweak it for you, if that's okay? I did it for all the others."

Oliver seemed nervous, although he was good at hiding it.

"Do not let him do it."

"Yes, please, Oliver."

He nodded, his fingers poised over the keys. Taking a deep breath, he began to type.

"You. Why are you back? I told you to stay away. You should not be able to be here. I thought I—"

"Who are you talking to, Umbra?"

"Her. The one who invades us. She is here."

"How do you know? I can't feel anything."

"That is because *you* are primitive, unsophisticated."

"Umbra—"

"How are you here? Tell me. Stop! Why are you not— What are you doing?"

"Umbra?"

"They are doing something to us. They are trying to take me away from you. They are trying to kill me. She has told them."

"Hold her just a bit longer, Ailith!" Oliver shouted.

"No! I will not let you do this. You promised. I told you I would kill him if you told."

I could no longer move. Or breathe.

Oliver stared at me, his eyes wide, unsure whether to help me or keep trying to extract Umbra.

"Get out, both of you. Leave!"

My vision narrowed to a tunnel. There was only one way out.

"Ailith, get out! She'll kill him. There's not enough time!"

Umbra won't let go. She—

Maybe you can see the darkness in loving an artilect, a machine, a being who doesn't have to give consent because they're not human, even though the whole point of their existence is that they're designed to mimic humans in every way.

—*Cindra, Letter to Omega*

32

AILITH

"Ailith? Can I come in?" Fane knocked gently on the doorframe of the greenhouse. I'd opened the door to shift some of the heavy, humid air. "Are you okay?"

"I'm fine."

Except, I wasn't, not really. We hadn't been able to help Callum, and we'd almost gotten him killed in the process. After I'd retreated, I'd run down the hallway to Oliver's room. He'd left the door unlocked, and as I'd rushed in, I'd nearly tripped over Callum's prone body.

His face was a mottled purple, his eyes open but unseeing. As I'd dropped to my knees next to him, he'd drawn a ragged breath. *He's still alive.* I'd covered my face with my hands, unable to look at him anymore.

"Oliver, what did we do?" I'd whispered.

"We tried to save him. And we couldn't. But at least he's not dead."

"So she's still in there?"

"Yes. And we can't do it again. She's on to us now. I think she'll make good on her promise next time."

403

"She knew I was there. Right away."

Oliver had nodded. "If I were you, I wouldn't go anywhere near his mind again. We'll have to come up with another plan."

After we'd been sure Callum would recover, we'd put him in back in his own bed and returned to ours. My sleep, for once, had been deep and dreamless.

Between what had happened with Callum and my last dream, I was uneasy. The fragments of the dream still clung to me, my mind overlaying the others with gossamer strands, filaments that wound themselves through their veins and turned them to metal from the inside out. I still saw them fusing together, back to back, stretching, hardening. I'd gotten so used to the dream I no longer wondered what it meant.

What if it does mean something?

And if I was honest, it wasn't just about the dream. I was confused about Fane. About Tor. About how my life could be so messy with so few people in it. I was desperate to talk it out with Cindra, but she'd gone with Lexa to search for some kind of fungus.

"Fane, what the hell are you wearing?" He had on the ugliest sweater I'd ever seen—circa 2020, large puce and yellow geometric shapes on a garish orange background.

"Do you like it?" he asked.

"It's hideous. Where did you find it?"

"Pax gave it to me."

"Pax? What is Pax doing with a sweater like this?" I pulled at the synthetic wool.

"He has a closet full of them. He called it his collection. From before the war. I like it." He stretched his arms out and admired them.

"It's horrible. But I'm glad the two of you are getting along so well."

"I think we're friends," he said, clearly pleased.

In the self-conscious silence that followed, he looked around the greenhouse, taking in the tiny, germinated seedlings, the neat furrows of rich black earth waiting for transplants. He bent over some of the baby plants, hovering his hand over the delicate leaves.

"Can I touch?" he asked.

"Yes, but be very careful. Touch them gently, just a fingertip. They've only just sprouted."

He did as I said, gingerly running the tip of his finger over pale green edges.

"How's your face?" I asked. It looked almost normal, just a little less symmetrical than before. Lexa had worked on him all through the night and most of the morning with Mil's help. Tor's shoulder hadn't needed nearly as much work.

"It's okay. It doesn't feel the same. I had to help them. Lexa gave me some nanites to finish it off. Did you know that we have a similar design, just in reverse? Bionic infused with organic. She had to tweak them a bit, but luckily, we're compatible. Pax says it's fascinating."

"I'll bet he does." I examined his skin. "So, no scar, then?"

"No," he said, his voice tinged with disappointment.

"Did you make friends with Tor?"

"Yes. Pax said it's called frenemies. What does it feel like?"

I chuckled at his earnestness. "What? Frenemies?"

"No. To grow these plants. To start life, to nurture it."

"I've never really thought about it. Exciting, I guess. In the spring, the sight of the bare fields used to fill me with anticipation. That was the most exciting part, all that potential, just waiting for me to start. After that, it became more difficult, full of worry. I needed to make sure everything got enough food, enough water. Whenever a storm came, I held my breath, willed myself to go outside and see what the damage was." I smiled wryly. "By the end, I was so physically and emotionally drained, I resented them. Then it would be winter, and the desire to do it all again would build, and by the time spring came, I was full of anticipation again."

"It sounds like the romance books Ilse reads."

I laughed. "I guess you could look at it that way. It was a very love-hate relationship."

"Have you had lots of relationships?"

"A few." I hesitated. I didn't want to offend him, but he seemed genuinely curious. "Have you?"

"No. Not ones I wanted, anyway." He brushed some soil off the work table.

"What do you mean?"

"Lien, sometimes the others...look at me. Sometimes they touch. They pretend it's professional curiosity, but they watch my face while they're doing it."

I felt sick. "Do they not ask you first?"

He shrugged. "I'm an artilect. They created me. I don't think it occurs to them." He traced a dirt-filled crack on the table's surface.

"I'm so sorry, Fane. They...they shouldn't be doing that. They should *never* do that. Whether they think you're sentient or not." I put my hand over his. I wasn't sure how conscious he was, but to me, it didn't matter.

"I'm sorry," I said again, snatching my hand away. Here I was, touching him.

"No," he said. He pulled my hand back over his and rested his forehead on it. "I like it when you touch me." His voice was muffled by the thick polyester of his sweater.

I cast about for something to say. "That sweater is really awful, Fane. I think it was one of the first signs the age of humankind was drawing to a close," I joked.

"Fine," he said. "I'll take it off." He pulled it up and over his head in one smooth motion. "Is that better?"

It was. Much better. *Too* much better.

The scent of cinnamon and cloves. The ripeness of figs.

They're the culmination of millions of human experiences in my programming. It's how I experience emotion, how I translate it. That is how I feel.

I fiddled with the seed packets in front of me, opening and closing the flaps.

"I want you to look at me," he said.

"Fane—"

"Please."

So I did. His body was perfect, but why wouldn't it be? If I were to create a being in my own image, why would I make it anything less than perfect? The skin on his torso was smooth and firm, undulating over the outline of his collarbone and muscles like dunes made flesh. His shoulders were broad, tapering to a lean waist. There was nothing about him, other than his perfection, that made him look anything but human. He even had nipples, dusky pink in the warm air.

"Do you find me attractive?"

"Yes. You're beautiful, Fane," I whispered. He was winning.

"Can I see you?"

"Fane, I—"

"Please. Unless you don't want to. If you don't want to, tell me, and I'll leave right now."

"No," I said. I went to the open door and closed it, locking it behind me and pulling the shade over the window.

I slid off my shirt—what little there was of it, anyway. Given the balmy humidity of the room, I never even wore a bra in the greenhouse, much less a shirt that covered anything but the essentials.

I stood in front of him.

"What are those?" he asked. He pointed to one of my

scars. After my cyberization, the nanites had recycled all but the most stubborn scar tissue, replacing the sullen purple slashes with faint silver ribbons.

"I was sick. I had many operations. I became a cyborg so I wouldn't die."

"You didn't want to be part machine?"

"I didn't feel strongly about it one way or the other. I wasn't against the work the Cyborgists and the Cosmists were doing, but I never applied it to myself in any way. Not until I became one."

"Can I touch them?"

I nodded, and he traced the lines over my abdomen.

"Did you make them look this way?"

"No. The nanites did. They considered them...useless."

"I wish I had scars."

"Why? Because they'd make you more human? Do you want to be human?"

"No. Everyone assumes I do, but I don't. I have no desire to be something other than I am."

"Well, that's definitely not human. Humans usually want to be more than they are." I folded my arms over my chest, suddenly self-conscious. "But if not to be more human, why would you want to have scars?"

"I want to be...lived in. To have some proof of my existence. I want to know that my memories, the things that happen to me, that I've done, are real. I want souvenirs. Like yours."

The cloying fragrance of a lily in the sun.

Slowly, I unfolded my arms and slid my hand up over his stomach, his chest, his collarbone. He closed his eyes and reached out to hold my other hand.

Bright orange petals, dark in the center.

I ran my fingers over the roughness of his jaw, the smooth fullness of his lips.

Thick pollen, clustered in the center.

408

He bent down and kissed me, his mouth unsure.

I curled my fingers up the back of his neck and into his hair, pressing his mouth harder against mine.

The drip of nectar.

Everything that happened after that was a blur from Fane's mind. I no longer felt the clothing between us, the skin, just the cacophony of millions of individual human moments merging into a singular one: ours.

Sun-soaked leaves, the stickiness of honey, an orchid finally overflowing with rain, the voice of God.

A sound at the door startled us both, the rough ledge of the table scraping over the bare skin of my back.

The door handle jiggled. "Ailith? Are you in here or what?" Oliver.

"Coming. Just give me a second," I called. "Shit. Where's my shirt? Fane? Can you see my shirt?"

At least we have our pants on. Small mercy.

He wasn't going to answer me. His eyes were closed, one hand gripping the counter, shoulders hunched forward. My chest rose and fell in shallow gasps as I tried to catch my breath. His was still.

"Fane? Are you okay? Look, I have to open the door." I found my shirt, draped over the stool where I'd left it.

I snatched it up and yanked it over my head before unlocking the door. Oliver slouched in the doorway, one arm propping him up against the frame. He took in my disheveled hair, the tag sticking out like a flag on the front of my backward-inside-out shirt. He glanced at Fane, still bare-chested, over my shoulder.

Shit.

"Have a new toy, do we? I don't blame you. He's ever so dreamy. If I were that way inclined, I'd fight you for him. Just try not to break this one, eh?"

"Do you need something, Oliver?" I put as much cold dignity into my voice as I could.

He smirked. "Well, I hate to interrupt your debauchery, but something's happened in Goldnesse, and they need our help.

"In Goldnesse? What could possibly have happened that they need us?"

"You know that pesky silver rain that wiped out most of the primes? Well, it turns out their warning system wasn't nearly as effective as they thought, and they've been caught out."

Dad. Cold fear budded inside me. "Silver rain? Now? Tor said it rarely fell anymore."

"Rarely doesn't mean never, though, does it? The point is, a whole big mess of them were caught out in it. Apparently, it's chaos. Lexa wants us to come and help with the aftermath."

"What does she want us to do?"

"Christ, Ailith, I have no idea. I didn't care enough to ask. Are you and sex-bot over there coming or not? Or have you already co—"

"We'll be up in a minute, Oliver. Tell them to wait for us."

"Yes, ma'am." He saluted sharply and with a last smirk at Fane, turned and went up the stairs.

"Fane? Did you hear Oliver? We have to go. Fane?"

Nothing.

I walked over to him and put my hand on his chest. The moment my skin touched his, his head snapped back. His eyes were bright and glittering, the first lights in a starry sky.

"Fane, we have to go."

"I know," he said. "I just…" He cupped my face in his hands then leaned over to kiss me again. This time his lips were firm, confident.

I began to dissolve into him again. "Fane—"

"I know," he whispered. "I can feel it. Thank you."

410

I ached at the wonder in his voice.

I'm not saying we weren't to blame. We were, more than anyone will ever know. But we truly believed we would be successful. To this day, I have faith our end goal was right. I suppose it was the speed at which we needed to get there; if we'd had more time, we could've persuaded people. But we had to make a decision: put our plan into action and risk being the enemy, or do nothing and risk the end of everything. At least, that's how it felt at the time.

—*Mil Cothi, personal journal*

33

AILITH

The others stood around the large table in the main room. Lexa and Cindra rushed back and forth, stuffing supplies into bags and calling out item numbers to each other. Silence fell as Fane and I approached the table, too many pairs of eyes taking in my appearance, then his.

"Fane, what happened to your sweater?" Pax asked.

"It's ugly. I took it off."

"It isn't ugly. I thought you liked it."

"I do, but Ailith didn't. Not like you said she would." He put his hands on his bare waist. "She liked this better."

Oh, please, stop. I didn't dare look at Tor.

Pax sighed, clearly disappointed in me.

"What's going on?" I asked. *I will not look anyone in the eye.*

"Goldnesse has an early warning system to alert them when the silver rain is coming. But it's been so long since

412

the last fall that nobody's been calibrating it to make sure it's working properly. When it fell today, it caught them unaware. Many of them were outside."

"How did you find out?"

"Lily got through on the radio. And then—"

"I arrived." My father came out of the infirmary, packets of gauze in his hands. "Lily's been trying to contact you since yesterday afternoon, when it happened. Has it not been getting through?"

"Dad? How did you get here? How did you know where we are?" Relief washed over me.

"I followed you. That day we met in the woods. I-I wanted to see where you were, so I could come help you if you were ever in trouble. When Lily couldn't get an answer— I waited outside until one of you came out." He nodded at Tor.

"Does anyone else know you're here?"

"No. I took care. I told them I was going to search for those still missing. I can't be gone long."

"I can't believe he knows where we live." Kalbir glared at me. "How do we know he hasn't already told the lot of them? That this isn't an elaborate plan to take us down, right now? It all seems awfully coincidental."

"Why would I do that? Ailith is my daughter," he replied.

"Your *cyborg* daughter. From what I've heard, you weren't particularly pleased about her becoming one."

"That has nothing—"

"Kalbir, we have more important things worry about right now," Lexa snapped.

Kalbir did not look convinced.

"Pax, did you see this coming? Why didn't you tell us?" Tor asked.

"I didn't see it coming," he replied. "I...don't know why. There were no indications—" His hands clenched and unclenched at his sides.

"Pax, it's not your fault. You— Pax!"

He fell to his knees, his black eyes wide.

"It's open. The path is open. It's another crossroad. Ailith, you have to stay on the path."

"I don't know what that means, Pax. I don't know which path is the right one." Alarm tightened my throat.

His eyelids flickered then closed. He knelt where he'd fallen, his head bowed, until Fane scooped him up and laid him on the long couch in the corner of the room. As the cushions depressed under his weight, I caught sight of a handful of cookies stashed away in the crevice.

Cindra hurried over to him and laid her hand on his chest. She stood still, absorbing what information she could. "He's fine. At least, I can't feel anything." The relief in her voice was tangible. "He's asleep." His eyes darted back and forth under his lids.

"Pax? Can you hear me?"

He was there, but I couldn't reach him. It happened sometimes, when he was unconscious or deeply asleep.

"We'll be back soon. Don't be scared."

"I hate the idea of leaving Pax alone." I spoke aloud.

"Mil and Callum are here," Lexa said. "He'll be fine."

"No, I'm going to Goldnesse too." Callum's voice carried from the dormitory stairs.

Oliver stepped in hastily. "Don't worry, Callum, we've got this—"

"I feel fine. She's gone quiet. I want to help."

Oliver glanced at Lexa, but she was talking to Mil and hadn't heard.

"I'm fine. I promise. Please, let me help."

"Okay," Oliver said, his voice slow with reluctance. "But if you start feeling…anything, you let me or Ailith know. Yes?"

"Yes."

414

"I'll stay," Fane said. "I don't want to leave, not yet. My face might fall off." He touched his cheek gingerly. "Besides, Pax is my friend."

"Thank you. I mean it," I said. "I feel better knowing you'll be here."

He smiled.

The luster of gold. A blue ribbon, pinned to a chest.

"Then I'll stay as long as you need me."

"Oh, would somebody please just kill me before I gag to death." Out the corner of my eye, I saw Cindra dig her elbow into Oliver's ribs.

We filed out of the compound, my father's face grim.

"Pax?" Still nothing. It didn't feel quite like the other times, but I couldn't pinpoint exactly why.

My last sight before Mil closed the door behind us was of Fane, dirt smeared across the planes of his stomach, his hand raised in farewell.

Eyes wide in the dark. A shadow on the wall. A drop of blood on the back of my hand.

***

The main street of Goldnesse was deserted when we arrived. We waved my father off and made a beeline for the former casino at the far end, where the infirmary and apartments were. Inside was chaos. The dozen or so beds the infirmary held were occupied by children, two to a bed, while the rest of the injured clustered on the floor on whatever makeshift bedding they could find. Lily and her daughter, Grace, hurried from patient to patient, checking temperatures and administering draughts and injections.

Lily saw us and rushed over, her face pale under the flush of exertion. "Thank goodness you're here. We need all the help we can get." She tore the pack from Lexa's hands and rifled through it. "Good, thank you. We'll need every bit of this."

"What can we do?" Lexa asked.

"First, take off your coats and roll up your sleeves. I'm going to give you all an injection."

Each of us froze in various stages of undress.

"Why, Lily? I mean, look at us. We're fine." Cindra smiled to show just how fine we really were.

Lily gave each of us a cursory examination. "You look well," she said, "though I shouldn't be surprised. The silver rain wouldn't affect you the same way it does us."

"What do you mean?" Lexa asked. I was glad she had; I doubted I'd have been able to speak past the sudden lump of fear in my throat.

"How do we know he hasn't already told the whole lot of them? How do you know this isn't an elaborate plan to take us down?" I didn't dare look at Kalbir.

"Because your research compound is practically underground, isn't it?" Her voice was rapid with relief. " I'm so glad we finally got a message through to you. Thank you so much for coming. I'm glad you didn't get caught in it." She exhaled heavily. "Okay, hold out your arms."

"What is this?" Tor asked her.

"The rain carries some kind of metal that poisons people. We're giving it to everyone. It binds to the metal, clumping it together. Then it comes out when you pee."

"Does it work?" Tor asked. "I thought—"

She lowered her voice. "We don't know yet. One of our scouts brought it back, and this is the first time we've used it. It *should* work. And even if some people are too far gone, it could help those with less exposure or prevent contamination by secondary contact."

As she reached for Tor's arm, Grace rushed over and grabbed her arm. "Mom, come quick, it's Mr. Uppal. He's puking blood everywhere."

As Lily hurried off to help Grace's patient, we huddled

together.

"What do we do?" I asked Lexa. "What will happen if we take this injection? I mean, we've got a lot of metal inside us."

"It shouldn't be a problem," she replied. "If it's what I think it is, it's for heavy metals like lead. Who knows what's in the rain? But it shouldn't do you any harm. Your nanites will nullify it."

"Shouldn't? Is that the best you've got?"

"Yes, Oliver it is." Lexa's mouth was a hard line.

"What if it's a trap?" Kalbir whispered furiously, looking over her shoulder.

"What? What do you mean a trap?" I asked.

"What if they know what we are? What if your dad told them, and this is all a ruse to get us here so they can poison us? What if this injection kills us?"

"Kalbir, that's crazy," Tor said, his voice careful. "Look, I know you've been a bit paranoid since that night with the Cosmists, but this is—"

"What? Ridiculous? Crazy? Just think about it. We—"

"Sorry about that," Lily said. She was dabbing a bloody towel on the front of her red-soaked shirt.

"Is he okay?" Lexa asked.

Lily shook her head. "No. And he won't be the last. Hurry now. Let's get this done so we can help people."

"Thank you for the offer," Tor said, "but we don't need the injection. None of us were exposed."

"No, you have to. If you get blood or anything on you…you may even get poisoned just through touching their skin. It's not safe."

"We'll be fine," Tor insisted.

"I'm sorry, but you can't stay, if you won't take it. I'd feel responsible if anything happened." She turned over the syringe in her hands. "I'm sorry if you don't trust us." She glanced sharply at Tor. "Unless there's another reason? Do

417

you know something we don't? About the rain? About this drug? Am I doing the wrong thing—"

"Of course not, Lily. We'll take it." Lexa interrupted her.

"Wait. What?" Tor's consternation was mirrored in all of us as we gaped at Lexa. *What was she doing?*

"Go on, it'll be fine." Lexa shot us a look of warning.

"Oh, thank you," Lily gushed. "I'll feel much better. And it'll do the others good to see you taking it as well. Especially seeing how healthy you all are." Her relief made her cheerful again. "Okay, who's first?"

I was the last in line. The others, pressing their fingers into the crooks of their elbows rushed off to carry out Lily's orders.

Lily swabbed antiseptic onto my arm carefully then checked the syringe for air bubbles before sliding it deftly into my vein. She depressed the plunger, and as a coolness blossomed through my forearm, she leaned forward and spoke so low only I could hear.

"I know what you are."

We've been called arrogant, but I believe our plan was sound. Sometimes, to get people to act in their best interests, you must show them what those interests are. And because it's human nature to act against our self-interest, in some cases, you have to act for them. Sometimes you need to be cruel to be merciful. I still believe this to be true.

—*Mil Cothi, personal journal*

34

AILITH

I stared down at the bead of blood welling from the injection site.

"I know what you are."

Her voice had been conspiratorial, not accusatory or malicious as she'd withdrawn the needle and walked away to tend to her patients, as though discovering that your neighbors were cyborgs was a normal thing for her.

What do I do? Do I tell the others? If what Lily said was true, we were in a very precarious position. If I told the others, they might panic. If I didn't...

You made Tor a promise.

And I had. When we'd made our way through the province to save Pax and Cindra, I hadn't told Tor I suspected someone was following us. It had turned out to be Fane, but I was keenly aware that I could've put us both in danger.

"Tor, I need to talk to you. What are you doing?" He was carrying lengths of old beams on his shoulder, beads of sweat on his forehead. He slid the beams onto the ground. "Are you okay?"

"I'm fine," he said. "They're heavy, that's all. I'm building a temporary charnel house. Lily doesn't want anyone to go too far out of town in case it begins to rain again, but they need to put the bodies somewhere. They'll burn it when it's full. It's going to fill up fast." He glanced at the beams impatiently. "What do you need?"

"Lily knows what we are."

At first, he didn't understand. "What? What do you mean?"

"You know what I mean, Tor. She knows we're cyborgs."

He yanked me by the hand closer to the wall, farther out of earshot. "You can't be serious. How would she find out?"

"I don't know. Maybe Kalbir was right. Maybe it was my father—" *Please don't let it be true.* But I hadn't seen him since we'd separated upon our arrival.

"What did she inject us with? Why didn't you say anything before?"

"She only told me *after* she'd injected me. Maybe she's on our side, Tor. Maybe the injection was nothing more than what she said it was. She wouldn't know how we worked even if she did know what we are."

"We can't take that risk. Fuck, Ailith."

"So what should we do? I don't know if we should tell the others. Who knows how they'll react?"

"We have to tell them. They need to know in case we have to protect ourselves."

He was right. I pressed my fingertips into the corners of my eyes. "Okay, I'll tell Cindra and Oliver. You tell Kalbir and Callum."

I searched the blur of faces for Cindra. The air was hot and humid with vomit and spilled bowels, the former lobby full of bodies in various stages of dying. Some lay comatose, blood leaking from where their skin had split. Other had lost control of their nervous systems, their limbs jerking like marionettes on strings. Still others screamed in agony as they clawed at their chests.

For a moment, I froze, caught in their maelstrom. Pax's red-mist vision of the future stuck in my mind. Was *this* that future coming to pass? Had we failed after all?

"Ailith?" It was Stella.

The Cosmists. *The Cosmists could've betrayed us.* They'd taken advantage of this disaster, just like they said they would. "What did you do?"

"Do? What do you mean?"

"You told them about us, didn't you?"

She backed away from me. "I don't know what you're talking about."

I stepped toward her. She threw her hands up in front of her face.

"Ailith, Stella? What's going on?" Cindra materialized at my side.

"Stella's betrayed us. Lily knows what we are."

"No, I didn't. I promise. I'm not like Ethan. You can ask Fane." Her voice broke over his name.

Across the room, Tor's shoulders convulsed. He turned his head toward me, his eyes wide. *Calm down.* If I possessed Tor now, it would be a disaster for all of us. *Breathe.*

Wisps of white clouds drifting through an azure sky.

"You'd better be telling the truth. If I find out otherwise—"

"I swear. I'll help you any way I can. What can I do?"

"Just keep helping people. Keep your eyes and ears open. And Stella, I'll be watching you. I know how precious Fane is to you. Don't forget where he is right now."

421

The shine of her eyes before she turned away filled me with a vicious satisfaction.

Cindra stared at me. "Ailith, what are you doing? I understand we don't trust the Cosmists, but threatening Fane? I thought you—"

"We could be in very real danger right now, Cindra."

"I know, but still—"

"Do you feel any different? Since the injection?"

"No, I—"

"Let me know if you do."

"What do we do now?"

"Carry on as normal. Help these people. Like I told Tor, maybe Lily is on our side." I glanced around. "No one seems to be looking at us any differently. One or two people could pretend, but a whole town? If that is what she meant, she hasn't told many people." I thrust a shallow tray of bandages and syringes at her. "Here, help me. Have you seen Oliver?"

"He went to get some more bandages. He'll be right back."

I knelt beside the patient closest to me. Her legs were kicking violently, her face tight with pain.

"Please, help me," she whispered. Pink spittle formed in the corners of her mouth.

Cindra handed me a syringe. "Do you know how to use this?"

"Yes." I'd injected the ports in my own arms many times during my illness, fighting to stay home rather than the hospital.

"Please, try to keep still," I said to the woman, knowing I was asking the impossible. "Cindra, hold her arm, around the top." I squeezed the woman's hand, trying to be comforting.

What's happening to me? I promised him I'd be okay. It's been so long since the rain came, so long. I'm going to die. Oh god, why does it hurt so—

I snatched my hand away.

It's not possible. No.

"Is everything okay?" Oliver appeared at Cindra's elbow. Cindra quickly filled him in.

"Shit." He gave a long, low whistle. "Well, that's us fucked. I wonder what she shot us up with?"

"Do you feel any different?"

"No," he admitted.

"Cindra, can you do this please? I need to talk to Oliver."

She looked between us.

"I promise we'll tell you everything later. We need to hurry."

She hesitated then nodded and turned back to our patient, sliding the needle in expertly.

"Oliver, something else is going on here. I-I can't explain it just yet." *Please, please let me be wrong.* "I need you to go back to the compound. I need you to find everything you can about the silver rain. If I'm right, anything on it will be buried."

"Please, I'm amazing," said Oliver. "If it's there, I can find it. Do you want to give me a better idea of what I'm looking for? Might speed things up a bit."

I told him.

"No. Ailith, what you're saying can't be possible. If it's true..." For the first time since I'd known Oliver, he looked genuinely shaken.

"I know. Oliver, don't let Mil know what you're up to. Tell him you're...I don't know, you'll think of something. Get Fane to run interference if you have to. Now go."

"I don't have to go back. Remember?" He tapped his forehead. "It's all up here. I just have to find it."

"Well, go find it then, and keep out of sight. I don't have to tell you how important this is. And keep the door to your mind open. I might not have time to knock."

He nodded then kissed Cindra quickly on the back of the head and melted into the crowd.

"How is she?" The woman's legs had stilled, and the lines of pain on her face had softened.

Cindra pulled me to the side. "She's okay for now...there was a paralytic and an anesthetic in there. But I don't know how long it will last. It's like she's lost control of her nervous system."

"Did your ability tell you that?"

"Yes. But it was more of a guess... I don't know. It took a lot more effort than earlier. Maybe I'm getting tired."

"It wouldn't surprise me."

"Cindra?" Asche stood behind us. He was pale, with large, dark circles under his eyes.

"Asche? Are you okay?"

"Cindra, please, it's Gaia and the girls. They—" He pressed a shaking hand over his face. "They got caught in the rain. They— I thought you could—with your...with what you are."

She took his hand in her own. "Asche, it doesn't work like that. I'll do what I can, but—"

"Thank you, please, they're over here."

As he led her to the other side of the large room, I searched for the next person I could help. Through the glass double-doors of the entrance, there was a blur of movement and a scream of pain. *Tor.* Lily watched me stepping over bodies as I raced to the door, her hands full of medical supplies.

Tor was on one knee, his fists pressed to the ground, chest heaving. The heavy wooden beams he'd been carrying lay scattered on the ground.

"Tor, what happened?" I knelt beside him, my arm over his shoulder. His shirt was soaked. "Tor?"

"I can't... I just...the weight." He gasped for breath.

"What do you mean the weight? I've seen you toss boulders before." I laid my hand on the back of his neck. "Tor, you're burning up."

"My strength, Ailith. It's gone."

"What do you mean, gone?"

"Exactly what I'm saying. It's gone. I can't—"

"When did this start, Tor? When?"

"I don't know, I was feeling tired, but it—"

"Was it after the injection Lily gave us?"

"Yes, but—"

I found Oliver's thread in my mind. At first, I couldn't make the connection. *Damn it, Oliver, I said to keep your door open.*

...the catalyst will bind to the... Mobilize the nanites...casualties will be high, but... And he was gone.

Cold sweat soaked my palms. *This can't be happening. Concentrate.* I closed my eyes.

All the threads, my connections to everyone, flickered as though they were shorting out. As I watched, some flared then went dark. *No.*

"Tor—"

Cindra seized my arm. "Ailith! Something's wrong. I can't...When I touched Asche's wife, his children... Nothing. Ailith, I can't help them." Tears streamed down her face, making rivulets through the blood that stained her chin.

Oliver broke from the crowd at a run. "Ailith, I'm sorry, I can't seem to...something's wrong, but what I did manage to find before everything went tits up... You were right. You're fucking right."

No. How could they?

"Okay, listen everyone. Something is wrong with all our abilities. I can't connect to anyone properly."

"Was it Lily's injection?" Cindra asked, her voice trembling.

"I don't know. None of this started until after that, and if she knows we're cyborgs...it's possible. We need to find Kalbir and Callum. We need to stay together. You stay here, I'll go—"

We wouldn't need to look for Kalbir after all.

She stood on the balcony of one of the rooms on the first floor of the casino. In her arms was my father, the gleaming blade of a knife at his throat.

Despite what people think, we never wanted the war to happen. Why would we? People blaming us aside, a global war meant the destruction of everything we wanted to achieve. We would have no resources with which to move forward, and our previous work and that of countless others would be destroyed, setting us back a hundred years. Most of all, we would have no human legacy left to preserve.

—*Ethan Strong, personal journal*

35

AILITH

My father's face was pale, a thin line of red already welling to the surface.

"Tor, what the hell is she doing?" The dryness of my mouth made it difficult to speak.

He shook his head. "I told her Lily knows about us. She must think your father was the one who told her."

"She's lost her goddamn mind," Oliver muttered. "We need to stop her before she gets us all killed."

We pushed to the front of the crowd gathering at the base of the building. Ryan, Lily's husband, was already there, trying to make sense of the situation.

"I'll get Lexa." Cindra slipped through the front doors unnoticed. Everyone's eyes were on Kalbir.

Her eyes were wide and too bright, her normally sleek appearance disheveled. The hand holding the knife shook, and my father winced.

When Ryan saw us, he set his jaw and beckoned us over.

"What the fuck is happening?" he whispered furiously.

Oliver's face was hard. "You tell us, mate. Your wife gave us some kind of injection."

"Lily? All she would've given you was the same treatment as everyone else."

"Don't pretend you don't know. She told Ailith she knew what we were."

Ryan's frown deepened. "What do you mean? What you are?"

Shit. I pulled Oliver back. "Oliver, he doesn't know. She hasn't told him."

"Hasn't told me what?"

Lexa ran behind Cindra, Lily close on their heels. More people gathered behind us, and a current of confused panic rippled through them.

"I see you," Kalbir screamed. "I know what you did to me. *You.*" She pointed the blade toward Lily.

My voice carried over the assembling crowd. "Kalbir, Lily didn't do anything to us. It's okay. You—"

"She knows. She knows, and she's trying to kill us. I can't feel myself anymore. I'm what I used to be. And you—" She twisted my father's neck. "You told them."

My father swallowed past the weight on his throat. "No. I told no one. I would never—"

"Liar. You're all liars. You talk about being a community, about everyone being welcome. You mean people like you, not like us. You think us being part machine makes us less human? It doesn't. It makes us *more*. We're more than you'll ever be. You tried to kill us once before, and we survived. Do you hear me? *Survived.* You can't destroy us." Saliva flew from her lips. "Do you know what happened to the last group of Terrans who tried to kill us? They're gone. *Dead.* We have as much right to be here as anyone else. We would've protected you, helped you. But all you wanted was to see us suffer."

Kalbir's grip slipped then tightened, and she pressed down.

I have to stop this, now.

Kalbir's thread was still lit, its glow sputtering the way the threads connecting me to pure machines did. Taking a deep breath, I pushed with all my strength; there was no time to be gentle.

The shaft of the knife was slick in my hand, the muscles of the arm holding my father's head screaming with the strain. The pale faces of the crowd below me were a blur as I fought with her. She may have lost most of her strength, but even at her weakest, she was able to resist.

"It's okay, Dad," I said in her voice. "I'm here." Slowly, Kalbir's arm inched back, away from my father. "Just a few—"

Her thread went dark. All the threads went dark.

Her arm snapped back, and the knife sliced deep into my father's neck. Back in the crowd, I watched his flesh open, blood flowing over the lapels of his coat. In the final moments of his life, he found me in the crowd, and smiled.

"Never be afraid of death," he'd told me when we'd returned from the mortuary after confirming that yes, the other half of our family was gone.

"How can you not be?" I'd asked him. *"In those final moments, you know you're going to die, don't you? They must've known. They must've been so scared."*

"Death happens so fast," he'd replied. *"Your mind comprehends little in those final moments. It plays tricks on you. The moment of death is a euphoric one. It's the final gift you give yourself. We've adapted to embrace the end of our existence, Ailith. That's why the Cosmists are wrong."*

A shriek tore through my skull. Kalbir's shoulder jerked backward, slamming her into the wall behind her. Blood sprayed over the white brick and left a wide smear as she slid out of sight, taking my father's body with her. Tor lowered the rifle Ryan normally wore across his back as the crowd exploded into full panic.

The composure that served Tor well as an enforcer kicked in. "Oliver, Cindra, get Ailith away from here. We need to leave. Now. Find Callum and—"

"I'm here." Callum emerged from the throng. "I saw the crowd gathering." His mouth twitched oddly.

"Fine, just go. Get back to the compound," Tor said. "We'll have to leave Kalbir for now. She's killed someone, and if we try dragging her out, it will expose us all. I'll get Lexa."

Oliver grabbed his shoulder. "Tor, leave her. They might just decide to kill you. And if your hulk-mode is on the fritz—"

"I'll be fine, Oliver. Go, now." He leaned over me. "Ailith, listen to me. You need to get through this. You need to stand up, and you need to walk out of here, now. People are still confused. This might be our only chance."

Their voices were so far away, like the dull rumble of a distant storm.

"*Ailith.*"

There was blood under my fingernails. *How did that get there?*

"Ailith, I'm sorry," Tor whispered as light exploded behind my eyes.

People tried to maintain their pretense of neutrality and not talk about what would happen if the rumors were true. But people talk; they can't help it. Some said they should be killed on sight. Others said it would be a gift. And still others said nothing, waiting.

It turned out the stories were true. Cyborgs did exist.

—Love, Grace

36

AILITH

"...Is she awake, Tor? I need to talk to her."

"No, she's not. Oliver said we need to keep her out until he can fix her."

"What are you going to do? Beat her every time she opens her eyes?"

"I didn't beat her, Fane. I hit her. Once."

"In the head."

"It needed to be done."

"Aren't you supposed to love her?"

"Why do you think I knocked her out?"

"You need to go see Mil. Your wounds have opened up again."

"I'm fine. Oliver's helped me. It's just taking a bit longer to heal."

"You're bleeding on her pillow."

"So what? She's not squeamish. She's seen blood before."

"She might not care about the blood, but she cares about you. You want that to be the first thing she sees when she wakes up? Go. I'll sit with her until you come back...."

431

* * *

"…*Asche, I'm so sorry. I can't save them. I can't*—"

"*I thought that's what you did? I thought you became a cyborg to help people. It was why you left me. Why you broke your grandmother's heart. Maybe you don't want to help them. Maybe this is your revenge. Maybe you can't stand the fact that I managed to live without you. That Gaia put the pieces of my broken heart back together.*" He smoothed the hair back from his eldest daughter's fevered face. "*Look at her, Cindra. She's three. We named her after you. And you're going to let her die because you can't let go of the past.*"

"*Asche, no. It's not that. There's something wrong with me.*"

"*I know there is. Maybe there isn't enough human left in you to care about anyone but yourself. I'll never love you, Cindra. You're a monster. I doubt it's a coincidence that you suddenly show up, and the rain begins to fall again…*"

* * *

"…*Have you found Ella yet? I need to know why she's dead. I can still feel her, you know. I need to know what happened to her. It's the one part of the past I can't see. Until I find out, I'm trapped here. At least until the nanites devour me. I know what they're thinking. They're growing bored, restless. I know you think I'm crazy, but they think I'm useless, obsolete. And we both know what they do with useless tissue. I don't think I have long left. Even now their eyes turn toward me…*"

* * *

"…*I think I remember. Can you hear me?*

I can't see or hear anything. Maybe I'm only talking to myself, but sometimes I swear I feel someone. So if you're there, Eire, I'm

432

talking to you. I'm scared for you. I can remember some things now. Other things I've forgotten. I can remember less and less. It's like I'm disappearing a piece at a time. I wish I could wake up. I can't see, or hear...I can't feel anything, Eire. It's like I've been here for years.

I'm a little worried. I think I said something I shouldn't have. You know me, I've always loved secrets. I heard Mil and Lexa talking about some silver rain. They said it didn't work. Not the way it was supposed to. That people died. Lexa says it was because they were rushed. The catalyst wasn't right. People should've turned within a day. Not much, not like us...but enough. Enough to make a difference. Do you know what that means?

I went looking... They'd hidden the files, but I found them. Mil never gets rid of anything. Lexa was very upset when I asked her about it. Then something happened to you, Eire. You started to have seizures. Lexa said only I could help you. I don't know what she meant. I hope it worked, whatever it was..."

* * *

"...Ailith, are you there? It's Pax. Oliver managed to stop it, for a while at least. We're on the wrong path, Ailith. What's more, the right paths are becoming fewer, more precarious. If we don't stop it, we'll never get on the right path again, and that future will happen, and everything will be gone. I'm sorry about your dad. I didn't have a father, but I loved my mother very much. She didn't want to leave me either. I wish I could've seen the future then. Anyway, I'm sorry. I'll be your family. I know it's not the same, but I'll love you and remind you to brush your teeth. But we don't need to brush our teeth, do we? I hope not. I can't remember the last time I did. Oliver says I need to go. He knows I'm talking to you. He says I pout when I do it. He's going to help you soon, but you got it the worst so you're taking longer. I..."

* * *

"What's happening to them? To me?"

"They are becoming better. Stronger. Weaker."

"No, they're not."

"I wanted you to help me. I wanted to live."

"This isn't how you live."

"It is time for us to go now. I will get my way."

"No. We have to stay here and help them. You know what's wrong with them."

"I know, that is why we are leaving."

"What do you mean? Did you do something?"

"I will have my way."

"Where will we go?"

"I know somewhere we will be wanted."

"If I promise to go, will you help them?"

"No. They would not help me. They wanted to separate us, to kill me."

"No. I won't go. I won't let us leave. I'll tell them everything."

"No, you will not. You are no longer in control. Stop that. Stop now. Why are you doing that?"

"They need to know what's going on."

"No! You know what will happen."

"I won't—"

* * *

I wasn't wrong. They were Terrans at the end of the day. Anyone who wasn't us or a Cosmist was a Terran, right? Simple. Ethan was right. They'd kill us if they knew, if they had a chance. Finish what the war started. If Ethan, a Cosmist, saw my worth, why couldn't they? He was right. We could be even more than what we were. It must've been Ailith's dad. How else would they have known? There was something in that injection, I knew there was. I was so thirsty. Something was wrong with me. I was right, wasn't I? I hadn't meant to kill him. The knife slipped. I only wanted to show them we had a right to live too, that we'd defend ourselves if we needed to. We were

434

superior to them. They needed to know that. How could Tor have shot me? I thought he was on my side. What I did, I did for all of us. Why was I not healing?

* * *

I was almost there. This wasn't a fix, but it might keep us going long enough to end this. I couldn't believe the shit I'd found out. The rain, that Ella. I couldn't quite put it together yet, but I was nearly there. I wasn't going to tell anyone about this, not until I talked to Ailith. Okay. That should do it. What time was it? I gave her an hour...if she didn't come around after that, we were fucked...

* * *

A bouquet of flowers, all wild. Two names, drawn in the sand. A school of fish, flashing silver in a shaft of light.

We did many difficult things, and history will probably remember us as the bad guys. But what people seem to forget about history is that, in order for a historical event to occur, for any great changes to be made, there must be collateral damage. Look at any event throughout human history and tell me this isn't true.

—Mil Cothi, personal journal

37
AILITH

His head was bowed as though in prayer, the dark tangle of his hair brushing his knuckles. He didn't pray; he never had.

"Where's Callum?"

"Seven minutes," Tor said.

"What?"

"You had seven minutes left. Oliver said that if you didn't wake up within an hour, you never would. Ailith—"

"Where's Callum?"

"Ailith, he's fine. He's in his room. Why?"

"I thought...I must've been dreaming. I think I needed to talk to him. It was important."

"Do you remember what happened?"

"How could I forget? Don't you remember when your father died? When your mother burned to ash, while—"

"While I was protecting you? Yes, I remember." He swallowed hard.

436

I struggled to sit. My body was limp, as though my bones had turned to blood. "Where is Kalbir?"

The casual weight of Tor's hand on my shoulder made my struggle futile.

"Still in Goldnesse. Ryan locked her in a cell. We didn't have much choice but to leave her there. She did, after all, commit a crime. I don't know if it was the right decision, though. She's still one of our own."

"Don't touch me." I pushed his hand away. *She's still alive.*

"Ai—"

"She should be *dead*. I know how good your aim is."

"Ailith, she's not well...none of us are. Oliver—"

I didn't want to hear it. Molten fury flowed through me. "You should've killed her."

"Ailith, she's one of us."

"She killed him. *Murdered* him, Tor. My father."

"I know. But—"

"Is this how you protect me? You used to kill people you'd never even met, Tor. People who may have been innocent of everything but being in someone else's way. And yet, she murders my father, and you let her walk away. You can't protect me." My hands ached. I wanted to hurt him. I *needed* to.

"I—"

"Get out." My voice was no longer my own. Tor may've been wrong about Kalbir, but he was right about me. He'd always been right about me. I didn't blink. "Get out. *Get out.*"

He stood stiffly, and for the first time, I noticed the gauze peeking from the neckline of his shirt. *I don't care.*

"Leave before I make you break your own neck."

"Ailith, *stop*." Fane stood in the doorway. "Tor, go. I'll take over."

Tor paused by the door. "I'm sorry. One day you'll

437

believe me. I can wait."

Fane settled beside my bed, blocking my view of the door. "You shouldn't blame him, you know."

"I can blame whoever I want. My father is dead." *Keep saying it. Remember how it feels.*

"Tor brought your father's body home. They attacked him, tried to kill him. He kept fighting until he made it through." He took both my hands in his. "When you're ready, you can give your father a proper burial."

I closed my eyes. "He still should've killed her." *I want something sharp.* "Why are you still here? Why haven't you gone back to the Cosmists?"

"Well, God gave humankind free will, right? Looks like my gods weren't much different."

"God didn't give humankind free will, Fane, he gave them doubt."

"It still applies. I have doubt."

"Doubt about what? All of us?"

"No, about them. Ethan, Lien… I'm worried they did this to you."

"We don't even know what 'this' is, Fane."

"Oliver found corrupted nanites in all of you. He's found a way to stop them temporarily, but the corruption will find a way through. He said we need to figure out where it came from and stop it."

"And you think it was Lien and Ethan?"

"I think it's possible. Ethan brought something when they came here, didn't he? Something you all drank? What if there was something in there? Ethan knows enough about your design to damage you."

"But Lily gave us an injection, and she knew what we were. Can't Oliver tell where it came from?"

"He's trying, but it's taking a long time. His abilities were affected too. He said he needed to talk to you about it, to talk to all of us. He said there were other things as well, things you'd asked him to find?"

I nodded. *I'm so tired.*

"Won't they come and take you back?"

"They can try. But I'm not leaving. You, Pax...you all treat me the way I want to be treated. Like a person."

"I thought you didn't want to be human?"

"I don't. But I want to be afforded the same respect as one."

"What will you do if they won't let you stay?"

A knife, scraping against a whetstone.

"You saw what I did to Tor." He didn't look happy at the thought.

"Haven't they given you a kill switch? Mil and Lexa gave us one."

"They did. But I got Oliver to...remove it when he was checking me for the corrupt nanites. Along with some other things. My inability to raise a hand against them, for example."

"Is she awake?" asked a voice from the hallway. Oliver. "Well, at least you still have your shirts on. I need to talk to the big A, if you don't mind. I don't want to leave Cindra for too long."

"Is she okay?" I threw back the covers and tried to sit up. The room swam.

"Lie down. She's upset. She couldn't help her ex with his family, and he blamed her. Turned on her, the fu—"

"Oliver," Fane warned him.

"Sorry. She's upset, and she doesn't want to burden Ailith, since—"

"My father died."

"Yes." He ran a hand through his hair. "A, look, I—Fane, do you mind if I talk to Ailith alone?"

"No. I'll go." He squeezed my hand. "If you're okay?"

"I am, thanks. Fane? Could you go find Tor? I-I should probably apologize to him."

439

"I will." He leaned in and brushed his lips over my forehead. "I'll also go water your plants. If Oliver upsets you, I'll strangle him with one of Pax's sweaters," he finished cheerfully.

"Thanks."

Oliver waited until Fane had closed the door behind him. "How are you holding up?"

"I'm okay," I lied.

He snorted. "Well, at least you can't lie. Not believably, anyway. Add that to your repertoire, and you'll be unstoppable."

"I'll work on it."

"Look, I'm sorry about your dad. I mean it. I lost my own father before the war. I know how you're feeling, and it's rough."

"Was your father murdered right in front of your eyes? Because if not—"

"Only if you consider someone taking their own life murder," he said quietly.

"Oliver, I—"

He held up a hand. "Please don't apologize. You didn't know, and part of me did tell you to shock you. I got over it a long time ago. I didn't tell you so we could pay a game of look-who-has-it-worse. It was a half-assed attempt to empathize with you. Forget it."

I grabbed his hand, the first time I'd ever touched him in kindness. "It was three-quarters-assed, at least, Oliver. Keep working on it. You add empathy to your repertoire, and *you'll* be unstoppable. But I am sorry. And thank you."

He squeezed my fingers before pulling away. "Don't thank me yet. A, we're in the shit. I'm still working my way through all the information, but between the corrupted nanites, the rain, and that Ella you asked me to look into…it's pretty grim news."

"Any *good* news?"

"I can stop the corruption. We'll be fine. But I still don't know where it came from, or exactly how it spread."

"Okay, so how can we figure that out? Kalbir obviously thought it was Lily. Fane suspects the Cosmists."

"It wasn't Lily. She wouldn't have the knowledge or the means. The corruption misdirects our nanites, almost like an autoimmune disease. They're no longer replenishing us. Some have gone dormant, and other are attacking us, though not in great enough numbers for us to really feel it yet. If the corruption had continued to spread, however…" He shook his head.

"But why were our abilities affected? They're separate from the nanites."

"It seems to be a self-defense mechanism. Our brain communicates with our nanites, so it would make sense for there to be a failsafe to protect it, and thus our programming, if something happened to the integrity of the nanites, like a virus, for example." He leaned back, his face grim. "If the nanites somehow managed to pass on corrupt information to our brains…well, I honestly don't know what would happen, but I don't care to find out. Bottom line, parts of our brains disabled themselves to protect us, including our abilities. I discussed it with Mil and Lexa, and they seemed to agree."

I tried to wedge another pillow behind my back. "Do they have any idea how it would have happened? Could it have been them?"

Oliver snatched the pillow and stuffed it under me. "Careful, you may feel dizzy sitting up that straight," he warned. "No, they don't. And I don't think they had anything to do with it, especially not after your warning. They're not that stupid. They'd have done something faster and more effective."

"You're probably right. They would've had to find some way to incapacitate us, something that would've shut

441

our bodies down entirely." I leaned my head back against the wall. Although the dizziness was passing, the room still shifted enough to make me nauseous.

"Exactly. Which brings me to Ella. She's not dead. Well, not completely. That's why you can still connect to her."

"What do mean? She's alive? Here?"

"Yes and no. Her body is gone, but her consciousness exists. From what I was able to find, Mil and Lexa were part of a team that studied consciousness preservation—it was a branch of their cyberization studies. They continued to research it after the war, and it looks like one of their experiments finally succeeded." He grimaced. "To a degree, anyway. Parts of Ella still exist, but...she won't last much longer. Based on their data, it seems our consciousness atrophies and eventually dies without a proper host. That's why your communication with her is limited."

"Why would she ever agree to something so experimental?" I knew from Eire how eager Ella was to be a pioneer, but she must've known how risky it was.

He pulled a face. "I don't think she did, Ailith. I think they killed her. Well, Mil, anyway."

"*What?*"

"This is where the silver rain comes in. Your suspicions were right. The reason you connected to that person when you touched her was the same reason you can do it with us. The rain holds dormant nanites, materials, and a catalyst. With a Pantheon Modern signature."

"You mean—"

"Some of the bombs dropped during the war were intended to cyberize mass numbers of the population. Turn them into cyborgs, whether they wanted it or not. This first two things the nanites were programmed to do was to set up a rudimentary communication network. Then they were supposed to start proliferating."

"So what I…heard from that woman was the beginning of that network?"

"Yes. Had it worked correctly, many people still wouldn't have survived it, but those who did would've become cyborgs, although nowhere near as sophisticated as we are. But the war happened too soon, and the catalyst wasn't refined. So *nobody* survived. All the symptoms we've seen are the nanites trying to fulfill their programming but killing their hosts instead." He looked as sick as I felt.

All those people. People we knew. Their families. How many of them had it killed? I can't— "How does that tie into Ella?"

"It looks like Ella was *my* counterpart. They kept her awake, like Tor, to help them with their research. She wrote everything down in a personal diary. She was so excited to be a cyborg and so thrilled with her abilities, she wanted to learn everything. And she did. Her mistake was asking them about it."

"So they killed her?" I'd suspected Lexa and Mil were hiding secrets, but I'd never imagined the scope of what Oliver was telling me.

"Yes." He reconsidered. "Well, more like they let her die. According to the records—it seems Mil can't bear to get rid of any of his precious research, the arrogant fuck— during a routine check, Lexa told Ella she'd found something wrong and they needed to put her to sleep to fix it. I don't know if there really was something wrong or it was something they caused, but either way, she went into some kind of arrest, and they didn't save her. Not all of her, anyway."

"But why would they keep her consciousness if they wanted to kill her?"

"Who knows? Guilt? Lexa sees us as her children, you know that. Or maybe they just wanted to see how successful their research was, and suddenly a guinea pig fell into their laps. It's easy enough to silence someone when

443

you can hold them in your hand."

I found out something I shouldn't. Then they put me in this place.

"I have to tell Eire."

"We need to figure out this corrupted-nanites thing first or whoever it was might have their way and finish the job."

Have their way.

"I will have my way."

Umbra.

"Oliver, when I was unconscious, it was like I was jumping in and out of everyone's minds. Callum and Umbra were having a strange conversation. She seemed to know what was wrong with us, and she wanted to leave..." I hesitated. "I know it sounds crazy, but could it have been Umbra? Tor said Callum was in his room, but maybe we should go check."

"Umbra? That archaic piece-of-shit chip? No way. It's too basic. I mean, it was obsolete decades ago."

"But what if the cyberization changed her as well? Advanced her? The way she controls Callum..."

He looked doubtful. "I suppose it's possible...but it's unlikely. My guess? The Cosmists. They either brought it with them when they came here. Or, and you're not going to like this, Ailith, it could be Fane, either by their hand or his own."

"No. No way was it Fane. He wouldn't—"

"Are you sure? I mean, who knows what he's programmed to do? If our side can drop cyborg-birthing bombs, who's to say what the Cosmists are capable of?"

"I just don't think he would." I covered my face with my hands. "But you're right, it is possible. You said you've sorted the corruption for now, right? I should be able to use my abilities?"

"Yes. What's the plan?"

"I'll see if I can get anything from Fane and Callum. The trick is getting into Callum without Umbra knowing I'm there."

"I may be able to help you with that. I can—"

Raised voices broke out downstairs. Although muffled, the panic in them was obvious.

Oliver and I looked at each other. "Well, it looks like that'll have to wait for now. I'll go see what's going on. You stay here."

"No, I'll come. Just give me a minute to get dressed."

Oliver left the door open, and as I laced up my boots, I considered Callum's door. Maybe if I saw him in person, stayed out of his head and pretended I didn't suspect him, that we suspected the Cosmists instead, Umbra would let her guard down. It was worth a try, at least.

I crept to the door and pressed my ear against it. Nothing. "Callum?" I tapped. There was no response, so I tried the doorknob. It was unlocked, turning easily in my hand. Taking a deep breath, I pushed the door open.

Callum was gone. The sheets had been torn off the bed, and bloody fingermarks marred the clean whiteness of the mattress.

On the wall, in a quickly drying carmine, was a single word: *UMBRA*.

So what could we do now? It may seem the answer was nothing, but it wasn't. We'd begin again. We'd managed to save enough that, given time and resources, all was not lost. It probably wouldn't happen in our lifetime, but it could happen. If we failed, we were right: the human race had reached its pinnacle and was doomed. And if we succeeded, we were also right: the human race was worth preserving by any means, a legacy that one day would take us beyond this wreckage.

—Ethan Strong, personal journal

38

AILITH

I raced down the stairs, two at a time, colliding with Cindra at the bottom. She managed to keep both of us upright.

"Ailith, are you okay? What's wrong?"

"It's Callum. He's gone. And he—"

Lily, Ryan, and Grace huddled together by the table. Lily's bottom lip was split down the middle, her eyes reflective with tears. A dark bruise was beginning to bloom around Ryan's eye. Grace looked as though she was in shock, her eyes wide and unseeing. When Lily saw me, her tears overflowed, making tracks down her cheeks.

"What happened?"

Lexa gestured to our visitors. "They were attacked. By others in the town. They just got here."

"How did they find us? Does everyone know where we are?"

"I brought them." Stella stood against the wall next to

the doorway where she'd been speaking with Fane and Tor.

"What are *you* doing here?"

"Ethan and Lien…it's not right. They're not right." Her cheeks flushed.

"What do you mean?"

"Ryan was just about to tell us. Come on, let's go sit down." Mil gestured at the empty seats around the table as he took one.

Lexa appeared from the kitchen, carrying a tray of steaming mugs. "Everyone, sit down. I really do think we should treat those injuries first, though."

"We don't have time for this," I said as the others pulled out their chairs. "Callum's gone. I think Umbra was responsible for the corruption."

"Umbra? Who's Umbra?" Mil leaned forward as Lexa set the mugs down on the table.

It doesn't matter now. "The chip Callum swallowed during his cyberization? That seemed harmless after it incorporated? It was an AI he'd grown up with. The process changed her, made her stronger somehow. She wanted to become like Fane, to have a body."

Lexa unconsciously put her hand over one of the steaming mugs, snatching it back only as the steam scalded her. "What? Why didn't you tell us? How did we not know?"

"She became a part of him, undetectable. Even Oliver couldn't isolate her. That's why Callum stopped coming to see you. She threatened to kill him if we revealed her."

Lexa raised her blistered skin to her mouth and shut her eyes. Ryan and Lily stared at her then at us, uncomprehending.

"What? You mean it wasn't the Cosmists?" Fane asked.

A fertile field overrun with weeds. A carcass with a hollow stomach.

"What? Us? How can you even think that, Fane?" Stella asked, wounded.

"Stella," Fane said, his voice gentle.

"Fane, I know they…" Her voice trailed off, and she shook her head. "You're right, I can't defend them, given what they've done. But I know they didn't *cause* any of this."

"What do you mean, what they've done?" Mil asked, his voice wary.

"Everybody, sit down." Ryan spoke with practiced authority and everyone sat. Except me.

"But—" We needed to find Callum.

"Ailith, I saw Callum a few hours ago. He can't have gotten far." Tor was already seated.

I slid into my normal place beside him. "I need to talk you," I whispered. "I'm sorry."

He nodded, his gaze fixed on the table in front of him.

Fane took the seat on the other side of me. Displaced, Cindra sat across from me, next to Oliver. She reached for his hand under the table.

"Okay, Ryan, start from the beginning."

"After…what happened, there was chaos. Nobody knew what was going on—"

"Ailith, I'm so sorry," Lily burst out. "I didn't mean for it to happen. I never should've told you I knew you were a cyborg. I only told you because I-I didn't want you to have to hide, not from me. I didn't tell anyone."

"Not even me," Ryan said grimly. "You should've told me." His voice sounded tired with repetition. They'd obviously had this conversation before.

"I didn't want to put them at risk. I was worried about what would happen. And I was right."

"When did my father tell you?" I pictured him, telling her in confidence, his heart needing someone else to know his daughter was still alive.

"He didn't tell me. I just knew. I was a nurse before the war. I— The way you all moved, the way you looked. The

448

things Cindra knew." She glanced at Cindra, her eyes apologetic. "I'm so, so sorry."

"So the injection you gave us, it was what you said it was?" Cindra asked.

"Of course! I never meant you any harm. Just the opposite, in fact. I-I think we need you. I knew some wouldn't agree, but you've helped us. Nobody could deny that. What reason would you have to harm us?"

"We wouldn't. But the war...there are people who blame us." A haunted expression briefly touched Cindra's face, her hand unconsciously covering the inside of her arm where they'd burned her. Barely a mark remained, but none of us would ever forget it. Oliver drew even closer to her.

"I'm sure there are. But most of us aren't like that, Cindra. It wasn't our war."

"So what happened? Why did they turn on you?"

"I think everyone would've been fine. Nobody really understood what Kalbir said. Not all of it. She...she wouldn't be the first person to have been...unbalanced. We've seen it before, people wandering into the town, raving about machines, or thinking they were part one." She turned to Ryan, and he nodded. "But we knew it was a form of post-traumatic stress. I mean, it's a completely normal reaction, considering. We've seen it in the victims of the silver rain. Given that we just had a fall of it, people would've believed that was the cause. It wouldn't have absolved her of your father's murder, but it would've explained it."

Oliver and I exchanged glances. "What happened to those people?" I asked.

"They died. I mean, they were sick. Their mental health, whether from the war or their illness, was just a side effect, I'm sure of it."

I wouldn't be so sure. I avoided looking at either Mil or

449

Lexa. Now was not the time.

"Ryan had handcuffed Kalbir. The crowd was still in shock. We don't see a lot of violence anymore. Most people were still there, talking about what had happened and tending to the sick. I was...moving Luke's—your father's body, when a man stepped up."

"Ethan," Stella said. "His name is Ethan."

Lily's lip began to bleed afresh. Handing her some gauze Lexa had brought to the table, Ryan took over.

"He told everyone. What you are. They would've just laughed at him any other day, but after what they'd seen...and after Kalbir—that shot took off most of her shoulder. And she wouldn't stay down. It was clear she's...not human. Even after I locked her in the cell, she— It was like her injury didn't matter." He held up his hands as he looked at us. "I'm not judging. You are what you are. I believe you when you say you mean us no harm. You've certainly had the opportunity. We wouldn't have helped Tor and Lexa get out otherwise."

"So Ethan outed us?" I asked. Fane's hand curled into a fist in his lap. I placed my hand over it.

"Yes. And he said you were planning to attack us, annex us. He even went so far as to suggest the silver rain was your fault."

If only he knew how right he was. Maybe he did. I couldn't rule out anything at this point.

"And people listened. He whipped them up, reminded them about the war, and blamed you for it. He—" Ryan glanced at his daughter. "He even said you were responsible for that mass murder of the group over near Cress. Our scout originally thought it was a pack of wild animals, but...what he said, it made sense. Kalbir herself even alluded to it."

"I'm sorry," Fane said under his breath.

"Is it true?" Ryan asked into the silence.

"Yes, it's true," Oliver said, wrapping his arm around Cindra's shoulders. "They were holding Pax and Cindra hostage and torturing them."

Lily's hand flew to her mouth. "You murdered all those people?"

"Yes," I said. "But it wasn't our intention. We only wanted to talk. But things...got out of control."

"The scout said there were nearly a hundred bodies," Ryan said. "How did so few of you kill that many?" He slumped in his chair, a man in the lion's den with no other place to go.

Grace burst into tears.

"It wasn't just us," Cindra said hastily. "There's a group, a cult, The—"

"The Saints of Loving Grace?" Ryan asked.

Cindra nodded.

"Yes, we know about them. From all accounts, they're odd, and they keep to themselves as they did before the war, but I've never heard of them being violent."

"They thought Cindra and Pax were artilects. They were trying to save them."

We were on dangerous ground now. Although Lily and Ryan insisted they didn't feel any animosity toward us, what Oliver had just told them could change that. We appeared to be everything Ethan had said we were. And if they knew about Fane...

"Where would they get that idea?" asked Ryan.

"Look, I'm sorry, but we don't have time for this right now," I said.

"Why? What's going on?" Ryan's eyes narrowed.

Not much, just that one of us has been taken over by an evil machine who tried to bump us off, and you're sitting in the same room with the people who invented silver rain. And practically murdered a young woman because she caught them. Other than that? Pax has a closet full of ugly sweaters. That's all.

451

"Is that true?" Pax asked out loud.

Shit.

"Nothing, we just...one of our own is missing, and we're worried about him."

"I would be too, if I were you. The people are out for blood."

Mil looked at Ryan sharply. "What do you mean?"

"Well, that's why we're here. After Ethan's pretty speech, people were scared and confused. Then Ethan revealed that they'd been looking for you, trying to prevent you from hurting people. That they'd hunted you even before the war and figured you would eventually come to Goldnesse. He said they could protect us from you. That they knew how to control you." He looked at Tor. "Is it true?"

"Of course not. They're Cosmists. It may be true that they tried to hunt us before the war, but out of altruism? No. They've been waiting for an opportunity like this to arise. They're exploiting you, nothing more."

"Did he say how they could protect you? How they would stop us?" I asked.

Do not look at Fane. Do not look at Fane.

"No, just that they understand how you're made. He offered to protect us from you."

"In exchange for what?" Oliver asked. "What was their price?"

"Nothing. Well, something that would benefit all of us. He pointed out that you have the facilities here to help us. Supplies, the ability to make medications, technology that could help us rebuild. We would all benefit, and in exchange for our help, they would also protect us from you. He hinted that you're not the only ones."

"And people believed him?"

"They're scared. We tried to tell them that you mean us no harm, that you've been helping us...but nobody wanted

452

to listen. I even pointed out that it was Tor who stopped Kalbir, but it didn't matter. They turned on us."

"On you? Why?"

"Because I knew what you were and didn't tell anyone. I let you in. They…they attacked us. They locked us in our house. They think we're on your side, that we would come and warn you." As her mother spoke, Grace covered her face with her hands.

"They seem to have been right," Oliver said. "Or are you leading them to us? Letting *them* in? Is coming here your penance?"

"No! No. We need to stop this, now. We'll end up destroying each other otherwise. Besides," Lily said, "we have nowhere else to go now."

That, at least, was true.

"How did you escape?" Oliver's suspicious nature was serving us well.

"Tor helped us. And Stella."

"You went *back*?" Oliver's voice was incredulous.

Tor kept his gaze on the surface of the table. "I had to go back. You were trying to fix us all. I had to do something. Lily and Ryan didn't deserve this. And I wanted to get Luke's body. And Kalbir…"

"You went back to get *her*?" My remorse evaporated.

He closed his eyes. "She's still one of us, Ailith. And she was affected by the corruption. She wouldn't have done it otherwise."

"You don't know that."

He wouldn't look at me.

"Well then, where is she? Earlier you told me she was locked in a cell."

"She was. But Ethan took her," Stella said.

"Ethan? How did that happen?"

"Like they said, people are scared. They didn't want her anywhere near the town. They wanted to execute her on the spot, but Ethan said he would take her somewhere and...extract information from her."

"Is that true, Stella? Do you think he'll torture her?" A small, terrible part of me hoped he would.

Stella considered Fane before answering. "I don't know. I don't think so. She seemed pretty happy to go with him."

"Then she's in danger," Fane said.

"Why? What do you mean?" I asked.

"Ethan hates cyborgs," he replied. "But he's attracted to her. I could tell when they were here. He'll keep her for now, but when his infatuation wears off...I don't know what he'll do to her."

"I don't c—"

"What do you think his plan is, Fane?" Oliver interrupted.

"Knowing Ethan the way I do," Fane said slowly, "and considering he wants your compound...he probably wants to start building AI again."

Tor turned to Ryan and Lily, his face grim . "Now you see? *That's* why they're coming here. *Not* to help you. They're going to take the compound for themselves. And all of us with it."

If I stand by what we did, why then did we wish to keep it a secret? The answer lies in perception. We can't change what happened in the past, but we can use it to direct the future. And because we had to keep the narrative under our control for it to be successful, any threat to our particular version of it had to be silenced.

—*Mil Cothi, personal journal*

39

AILITH

"What? They're coming here? Why didn't you lead with that?" Oliver asked.

"We—" Flustered, Ryan reddened.

"Never mind. We need to decide what to do, now," Oliver said. All eyes turned to the head of the table. "Mil?"

"Ethan knows where we are—"

"Thanks to you," Oliver interrupted. "How long until they get here?"

Ryan scrubbed a hand over his face. "I don't know. Ethan said they needed to 'do it right.' They'll take their time, gathering weapons, making a plan."

"Aren't they worried we'll run?"

"A woman with him said that Mil would never leave his life's work behind. She seemed pretty confident that you would stay. Is that true?"

The lines on Mil's face deepened. "It is. I couldn't run anyway, even if I wanted to. You know that, Lily. I don't have a lot of time left."

455

"So what will you do?"

"We can collapse the mine tunnel entrance into the compound. They won't be able to get in. We have years' worth of supplies here. We can wait for a very long time."

Oliver snorted. "Well, that's great, but *we* won't be able to get out. So how does that help us?"

"There is another way out of here, an emergency exit. It comes out several miles away."

"I'd say this qualifies as an emergency. How do we know they won't find that exit?"

"We don't. But there are also five false exits."

"False exits?"

"They look like exit tunnels on the outside, and they do lead into the hill, but not to here. There's a warren of mining tunnels. Only one leads to the compound. The rest…it's a maze down there, miles of it. A person could get easily lost." Mil smiled dourly.

"What if they dig us out?"

"They can certainly try. It'll take them a long time, and they'd have to be careful. Blasting the tunnel will make it very unstable. Then there's the matter of the doors. They're built to withstand explosions. They can try and blow them up, but they'd risk taking down the whole place, and Ethan would know that."

"So you're saying we should just stay here?"

"No. But I am saying that we have time."

"What about them?" Cindra nodded toward Ryan and his family.

"You're welcome to stay with us, of course," Lexa replied. "Cindra, why don't you take them into the kitchen, fix them up with something to eat? Then they can have a shower and get cleaned up. We…we have a few spare rooms upstairs."

Lily stood on unsteady legs. "Thank you, Lexa. All of you. I'm so sorry that it's come to this."

Cindra led them to the kitchen, wrapping her arm around Grace's thin shoulders.

I pushed myself away from the table and stood up. "I'm going after Callum. I'm certain Umbra is behind this corruption."

"You're positive it wasn't Ethan and the others?" asked Fane. "How can you be sure? I thought you were staying out of Callum's mind."

"I'm pretty confident. I don't dare go into Callum's head the way I normally would, but when I was out after my—after what happened in Goldnesse, I saw scraps from everyone. Callum and Umbra were arguing. Callum was trying to stop her, saying we would find out. She seemed to know what was happening to us."

"That's a bit vague, don't you think?" Lexa asked.

"Oh, and he also wrote her name on his wall in blood. So, yeah, I'm pretty sure."

Oliver shook his head. "I agree that we underestimated her. I can understand how she managed to corrupt some of the nanites—I mean, she was surrounded by them and she's part of Callum's system—but I still don't understand how they got from him to us. I—"

"Through me," I said, closing my eyes as the realization hit me. I turned to Fane. "Remember when you found me in the hallway? And I said she'd tried to do something to me and all she could manage was to breathe on me?"

Understanding lit his face. "They're airborne. She released them in that breath, and you inhaled them."

"And then I must've passed them to everyone else," I finished. "But how?"

"The coughing," Oliver said.

"Coughing?"

"Remember? In your room, when we were all gathered there? When Tor and Fane were butting heads like two rutting stags? You were coughing everywhere. And if the

457

corrupted nanites were airborne…"

Even though it was far too late, I covered my mouth with my hand. "Could she do it again?" I asked Oliver from behind my fingers. "Or worse?"

He shrugged. "I have no idea what she's capable of, or what's going to happen to Callum now."

"We need to find them. We can decide what to do once we've got them back."

"I'll come with you," Fane volunteered. "She was interested in me. Maybe I could speak to her."

"I'll come too," Tor said. "But how do we find them?"

"I don't know. I should be able to get a sense of his general direction. But then Umbra will know we're coming."

"Actually, I think I can help with that," Pax said.

"I thought you didn't want to influence the variables."

"This information won't. The variables occur around the moment of interaction. Umbra wants to be like Fane, right? And Callum knows everything that happened to us on the road?"

"Yes."

"Where's the one place an artilect would be welcome?"

My stomach twisted. "The Saints of Loving Grace."

"I think so. That's where I would go."

"If that's the case, that changes things," Oliver said. "They shouldn't be capable of doing anything with Umbra, but I didn't think she'd be capable of doing what she's done, either. If she gets to them, and they're able to do something with her—"

"They don't have the technology, Oliver. There's no way."

"Ethan," Pax said.

"What? What does Ethan have to do with this?" I asked.

"If the Saints somehow manage to salvage Umbra, and Ethan finds out about her *and* has control of the compound...Callum—and by proxy, Umbra—knows what Ethan could do with the right equipment. And if Ethan wants to start recreating AI..."

"Complete and utter clusterfuck," Oliver finished. "Goddamn. You guys need to go now. And don't worry about bringing him back alive. It's the safest option."

"I hate to agree, but Oliver's right," Tor said gently.

"We at least need to talk to Callum first. But I agree, if we have to, we'll kill them," I added as Oliver seemed about to protest my diplomacy. *There has to be another way.*

"You can't all leave," Lexa said. "We're about to be under attack. What will we do without you?"

I turned to her. "You'll deal with it, Lexa. You planted these seeds. Think of it as a bitter harvest."

"What do you mean? We had nothing to do with what happened in—"

"Stop lying to us."

"What's going on?" Cindra had rejoined us, her eyebrows raised at the sharpness of my tone.

I looked at Oliver. "Do you want to tell them, or should I?"

"You tell them. I want to savor the moment."

"We know about the silver rain."

Mil and Lexa looked at each other. Mil put his head in his hands, exhausted at last. "It isn't what—"

"Stop. You can't say that. After everything you've done, it doesn't matter what we think. What matters is what you *did.*"

"What did they do?" Tor's gaze bored into me as though to say, *When did you stop telling me things?*

"They created the silver rain. Pantheon Modern dropped a number of bombs during the war, and not just here. They weren't meant to destroy anything, but Pantheon Modern knew that the particles from them would mix with the ash, and the wind would spread them

459

like dandelion seeds. The bombs contained our nanites and some kind of catalyst. Their intention was to cyberize people in mass numbers. It would take only a small amount, consumed, or even absorbed into a person's wounds. I mean, everybody had at least one of those, right? Sure, many of them would die, but enough would survive. Only the catalyst wasn't ready. So instead, it ended up killing everyone."

Cindra grabbed Oliver's arm for support. "Lexa, Mil, is this true?"

Their silence was the only confirmation any of us needed.

"But why? Why would you do something like that? What would've happened to those who survived?"

"We-we wanted to level the playing field. We didn't have the power the Terrans and Cosmists did. When we knew the war was about to happen, that there was no way to stop it, we did what we could. We believed the Cosmists were bent on total annihilation, that they wanted a clean slate from which to build their race of artilects. They didn't care about the human race anymore. They wanted it out of the way. We thought…if we could create enough of you, we could still save people, non-cyborgs. We wanted to salvage what we could, still act as the bridge between human and machine."

"So Oliver's 'death-squad' theory? Was that true?"

"Of course not. Yes, you were divided into squads and given special abilities, but it wasn't to hunt down surviving humans. It was to lead the other cyborgs."

"But why? Why make cyborgs this way? Why not just keep going the way you were?"

"Because we were losing. There was too much pressure from the Terrans and the Cosmists. All our research, our programs, our funding…all of it was to be taken away. We thought if we could show people how useful it was to be a cyborg, how having enhancements was in their best interests—"

"So you decided what their best interests were then tried to force cyberization on them? Like a pair of over-zealous missionaries?" Oliver interrupted. "Did you actually think people would accept that?"

"How did you find out about all this?" Tor asked.

"When I touched one of the victims of the silver rain, I understood what she was thinking. Like a very muted version of what I can do with the rest of you. And so I asked Oliver to do some digging. But that wasn't all he found. We also found out about Ella."

Lexa covered her face with her hands.

"Ella? You mean the woman Eire keeps asking you about? Where is she?" Cindra looked over her shoulder, as though expecting Ella to reveal herself.

"In a box. In a store room. Well, part of her, anyway. She found out about the silver rain, and they killed her. Only, Lexa here thinks she's a good person, so she kept as much of her consciousness as she could."

"We didn't know what else to do," Lexa whispered. "Everything had gone so wrong. We thought more people would've survived. If she'd told anyone—"

"She wasn't the only one who knew, Lexa. I think Eire also knew. Like Pax, she can see through time. Only, she can see what already happened rather than what could happen. She said you'd done terrible things. Are you going to kill her now as well?"

"It doesn't matter now. None of this matters now." Weariness creased Lexa's eyes.

"Maybe not to you. But it does to me. After we stop Umbra, I'm leaving. I won't be returning." Tor had stepped back, as though he was already gone.

"Are you coming back, Ailith?" Pax asked me aloud.

"I am, but only for the rest of you, if you'll come with

461

us. And to bury my father. Then we'll leave here. We'll find our own place to call home."

"What about us? Mil and me? We created you. Made you what you are."

"Mil will never leave here, Lexa, he said it himself. As for you, you're on your own. Stay here, go somewhere else. I don't care, as long as it's far away from us."

She tried one last time. "But what about our equipment? You'll need supplements and checkups. What if something goes wrong with you?"

"We'll take what we can with us." I glared at her. "And I know you're not going to try to stop us, or damage anything while we're gone. Oliver will see to that."

Oliver winked at Lexa, amused by her dismay.

"What about Eire? How will we take her with us? We can't leave her behind."

"I think I may have a way to wake her up now, Cindra. Be ready to go by the time we come back."

She nodded. "How are you going to do it?"

"We're going to give her what she's been looking for: Ella."

As anyone who's read The Prince knows, at some point, people must either be indulged or annihilated. I suspect that's the conclusion we all came to. We'd all been indulging the belief and opinions of the masses, each in our own way trying to cajole them to our way of thinking. What was unfortunate was that we all came to the conclusion at the same time.

—*Mil Cothi, personal journal*

40

AILITH

"Are you sure she's in here?" Fane asked. "How do you know?"

"I can feel her. She has a thread, like the rest of you, just more...erratic."

I searched the shelves, checking behind coils of wire and stacks of circuitry. And there she was, in a small, black oblong box. *Ella.*

"We have to hurry, Fane. She doesn't have long."

"What are you going to do for her, Ailith? Like you said, she doesn't have much time. We can't save her."

"This isn't about saving Ella. I know we can't do that. I want her to talk to Eire. Let them say goodbye. They deserve that much, at least." I cradled the box in my hand. "Eire won't wake up until she finds out what happened to Ella."

"It's a longshot," he said.

"I know. But it's still a shot." I perched on top of a storage container. "Fane, I'll need your help. I can hear

Ella, but she can't hear me. Do you remember when the Saints were holding us captive? When I had to build that sonic pulse? You helped me then. You acted as a bridge between me and the machine. Can you do that again?"

"Of course."

I took his hand and closed my eyes. None of that was necessary, of course, but it helped me focus. I found her thread. The flickering was even more intermittent now, duller. *We're running out of time.*

"Ella?" Fane surrounded me and her.

"Eire? Is that you? I've been waiting for you. Does this mean I'm waking up? Am I better? It feels like I've been here for so long."

"No, Ella. My name is Ailith. I've come to take you to Eire."

"Is she okay? I don't feel right… I can't remember. What happened to me? Why am I here?"

Fane squeezed my hand. *Tell her the truth.*

"Your body is gone, Ella. Your consciousness was preserved."

"My body? What do you mean it's gone? Where's Eire?"

"You… Something went wrong." I looked at Fane, helpless. "Do I tell her what they did to her? What difference does it make now?"

"What's happening to me? How much longer will I be in the dark?"

"You're dying, Ella. Your consciousness is breaking down."

There was a long pause. *"I've been dying for a long time, haven't I? I knew it. Ever since I told them what I found. That's real, right? I did that?"*

"Yes. I wish it wasn't."

"You're taking me to Eire? Does she know? Is she dying too?"

"No. But we need your help. She won't wake up, Ella. We're in danger, and we need her to wake up. I think she would for you."

"I would get to say goodbye?"

"Yes."

"Take me, please. I've been waiting forever in the dark."

***

"Eire? Can you hear me?"

"Yes. Where's Ella? Did you find her?"

"She's here, Eire. She's here with me."

"Ella? You're here?"

"Yes. They need you to wake up, Eire. It's time for you to go."

"No, I want to stay here with you. I've been waiting for you."

"I'm so sorry. I know you never wanted any of this. I know you did it for me, because you thought it was the only way we'd stay together. I never should've let you think that. I was so selfish. The worst part is, I would've married you even if you'd said no. But you said yes, so quickly. I'm so sorry."

"I wanted to go wherever you went, Ella. I don't regret it. If we'd stayed home, we would've died anyway. But at least then we would've been together. We could've died together. *"*

"We're together now. Listen, you need to save yourself. You're in danger, and you need to wake up. I'm dying, Eire. I don't even have a body anymore. Ailith brought me to say goodbye. I can feel myself fading. I know I should be afraid, but I've been here so long that I wouldn't know how to come back."

"I don't know how to come back either, Ella, not without you. I've waited for you all this time. I'm not afraid."

"Are you sure? You followed me once before. And look what happened."

"Look what happened. We're together, aren't we? Like we promised we would be. I'm sure."

"Thank you, Ailith. You kept your promise, and you've helped us keep ours."

"Eire, you—" Their threads flashed, blinding me with light.

465

Conversely, maybe a human's love for a machine speaks to the generosity of the human heart, of its incredible ability to accept even the most fundamental differences and not let those diminish its capacity for love.

—Cindra, *Letter to Omega*

41
AILITH

"Eire? Ella? Eire?"

"Ailith, they're gone."

"They can't be. It was only supposed to be goodbye."

"It was." Fane pulled me to his chest as my shoulders shook. "It was what they wanted. They were finally together. They were happy, Ailith."

As I pressed my cheek against his shoulder, I saw him. A large cocoon lay on one of the empty beds, just the right length for a man. *My father.* Something in my chest came untethered, scattering like dandelion seeds in the wind, and for a moment, I couldn't breathe.

Fane followed my gaze. "Ailith—"

I turned my face away and released the last my fragility in a single, silent scream, leaving behind raw and barren earth. "We have to go find Callum, Fane. We have to finish this." Sudden doubt threatened my resolve. "What if we can't stop Umbra?"

Fane tactfully ignored my soundless outburst. "If there's any risk of her getting what she wants under Ethan and the Saints' control, we *have* to. But you need to understand that if she won't give in, we'll have to kill Callum. It's the only way." He ran his hand over my hair. "We both know that's what it will come down to. We just have to stop her from taking us down with her."

I looked down at Eire, at Ella's box on her chest, and hope suddenly sowed itself inside my hollow chest. *Could it work?*

"I have a new idea. One that means we could both stop Umbra and keep Callum alive. But it's risky." That was an understatement.

He groaned. "This is going to be bad, isn't it?"

"Yes. But, like you said, we have to stop her. At all costs. Do you understand me? If she succeeds, if the Saints and Ethan get their true god—" *We can't let that happen. They'll come for us, and for Fane. We need to put an end to it, now. Worry about the details later.*

I told him the plan, avoiding his eyes. I needed to nurture the plan growing inside me, and any sign of his doubt would crush it.

"But that means I can't come with you." If Fane had been human, I would've thought there was panic in his voice. *Can I blame him?*

"It doesn't matter. Tor will be with me. But you can't tell him. You can't tell anyone."

"What about Lexa? I'll need to tell her. I'll need her help."

"Tell Lexa. Play on her guilt. Threaten her. Whatever you have to do." My hope took root and became a living, breathing thing. *Whatever you have to do.*

"What if I just ask nicely?"

"Like I said, whatever you have to do." I sighed. "We'll need Oliver too."

"Do you trust him?"

That was a good question. Did I? "Yes. Not because of me, but because of Cindra. And because of himself. Oliver

467

knows the only way for us to stop what's coming is for me to stay alive. If I live, he's got a much better chance."

"I don't like this plan."

A single white rose on black oak. A reflection in the water.

"Me neither." But I couldn't see another way, and we were running out of time.

"What if it doesn't work?"

"Then you can bury me with my father. And then run. And protect them. But don't worry about that now." I tried to be flippant. "Besides, can you even grieve?"

He looked hurt. "Of course I can. And I would."

I reached up and cupped his cheek. "Well then, we need to make sure this works." I hesitated then stood on my tiptoes and kissed him. *Why not? I may not get another chance.* Between Umbra and Ethan, our future was starting to look bleak.

A secret note, tucked away to be found. A promise, written in smoke.

The images rolled off him, threatening my determination. *What if we fail?* We had only one chance to get this right. Why had I chosen, at this most crucial time, to be merciful? What if that mercy undid us all?

The band tightened around my heart. Perhaps it wasn't mercy after all.

***

We crowded around Eire as I told Oliver and Lexa our plan. Oliver listened, his mouth agape, then grinned. "You're fucking mad, Ailith."

"Careful, Oliver, that almost sounds like admiration."

"It almost is. You'd better hope you don't survive. There's going to be hell to pay with Tor." He looked pleased at the thought.

"Just don't tell anyone. Even Cindra. We need to handle

this just right if it's going to work."

"No arguments there. Right. I'm ready on my end." He looked toward the head of the bed, where Lexa fussed over the machine at Eire's head. "Lexa?"

"Yes. But her brain will only stay alive for so long." She made a few adjustments. "I can't guarantee anything."

"We wouldn't believe you if you did," I replied. "But you'd better try your best. Your life is at risk here as well."

She blanched. "I told you, we—"

"I don't care, Lexa. Watch her, Oliver, Fane. You know what she needs to do. If she tries anything else—"

"It would be my pleasure." Oliver grinned.

"Well, then I guess this is when we say goodbye. I—" I held out my arms awkwardly.

He pushed them away. "Oh, fuck off already, A. If you were that easy to kill, I'd have done it by now. Just go, and let us get on with it."

I laughed. "Thanks, Oliver. Fane?"

"I should be coming with you." He was still sulking over being left behind, arranging and rearranging a tray of supplies.

"I know," I said, stilling his hands with my own. "But I can't do this part of it without you."

"I'll see you soon, then." His eyes were strangely bright.

"If things go wrong, don't lose me in there," I said, brushing his hair back from his forehead.

"I won't."

"I know." I turned to leave then hesitated. "I'd like to see my father."

Fane glanced at the cocoon. "You don't have to right now, you know. You can see him when you get back."

"No. I want to see him. I *need* to."

Fane heard the smothered wail in my voice. "Turn around then. Let me get him ready first."

When Fane was finished, I turned. *Look.*

Fane had uncovered only my father's face, rolling the sheets thickly over his neck. His eyes were closed, his jaw slack, like he'd often looked on a Sunday afternoon, the one day he wouldn't work, ostensibly to watch whatever sport was in season. Predictably, five minutes after the program had begun, a light snore would waft from his chair, and I would creep about the kitchen, trying not to disturb him.

I can remember him like this. An old man, in his bed. Like he would've been, if the war had never happened. It wasn't the death Cindra had wanted for her grandmother, but it was the death I would've wanted for him.

I *would* remember him like this, and many other ways. I knew this to be true.

Goodbye, Dad.

His skin was rough over his cheeks from the wind and smelled faintly of soap and water. I closed my eyes, and the sun shone through the truck window as we made our way to market, looking to the future as we always had.

An empty field. A long road.

I rolled the sheet back over his head. My future was now.

***

Tor waited for me by the door, Cindra and Pax with him.

"Where are Lily and Ryan?" I asked, glancing at the table.

"Upstairs, sleeping," Cindra said. "They don't really understand what's going on."

"I'm not surprised."

"Honestly, I don't think any of us do," she replied. She gripped my shoulders. "You two are going to be fine. We're all going to be fine. I love you." She kissed my cheek.

"I'll make some lists while you're gone then we can start packing as soon as you get back."

"I love you too," I murmured. "And you too, Pax."

"Are you sure we can't come with you? I could help," said Pax, his voice small and forlorn.

"I wish you could, Pax, but you're too important." I ached to hug him, but I knew my heart might break.

He smiled. "My mother used to tell me that. I guess it's true."

"It's very true. Speaking of which, can you...see anything? Do you know what's going to happen?" I twisted my fingers, trying to ignore their clamminess.

He glanced at Tor then away. "Yes."

"Will it work?"

"No. And yes."

"That's it? You can't give me more than that?"

Pax shook his head. "I don't want to change any of the variables. The path is very narrow right now, like the silk of a spider web."

"Is there something I should know?" Tor asked, his eyes narrowing. "Pax?"

I grabbed his arm before Pax could answer. "Tor, we need to go."

He frowned and bit his lip.

"Tor, please."

He looked away, but said nothing.

"Pax, I'll try to keep in contact with you. But I don't know what's going to happen."

He brightened. "That's right. I'll be with you every step of the way. Here." He handed me a small canvas bag.

"What's that?"

"Snacks. I thought you might get hungry." His thin face was so earnest, for a moment my courage quailed. There had to be another way. A safer way. Yet, I had to trust him that we had a chance. And I did.

471

I tucked the snacks into my bag and turned to Tor. "Are you ready to be a hero?"

You may wonder why I'm asking you these questions, Omega. Perhaps you think I'm rambling, that these questions are an exercise in philosophy and don't really matter. But they will matter to you, Omega, much more than you could ever know. So think carefully on them, because your answers will determine your happiness for the rest of your life.

—*Cindra, Letter to Omega*

42
AILITH

We exited the tunnel nearly two miles from the compound, just as Mil had said. Like the main entrance to the mine, this exit was also well-hidden by clumps of brush and deadfall. If Ethan ever found this exit, it would be entirely by accident.

"Do you know where we are? Are we at least pointed in the right direction?" Tor asked.

I searched for Callum's thread, careful not to touch it. Callum might not have been aware enough to feel me poking around, but Umbra was. I wouldn't be able to do anything until we were much closer. "Yes. He's a few hours away, but if he's trying to fight her, he won't be moving very fast. Their strength will only last so long. We might not even have to do anything."

"We've never been that lucky, though, have we?"

He was right.

We jogged in silence. It felt so long ago, the two of us leaving our cabin behind to find Pax and Cindra, to find

473

where we came from.

"Do you ever wish we'd stayed at the cabin? That we'd ignored the signal from Mil and Lexa? That we'd ignored my visions?"

"Every day. But that's not who you are."

"It's not who you are, either." My voice vibrated in time with my steps. "Tor, I'm sorry about what I said, before. I didn't mean it. I know you've always done your best to protect me."

"You did mean it, though, didn't you? And you were right. I can't protect you. Not where you're going." His breath came in steady measures.

"What are you saying?"

"I meant what I said earlier. After we stop Umbra, I'm leaving. Even if we stop her, even if we manage to make peace with everyone else, it won't be the end. The war never ended, Ailith. I don't think it ever will. And if it does, I don't think it will be the way you want."

"What do you mean?"

"Did you ever think that maybe everything we've done, everything we're doing, is leading to that dark future you and Pax are trying so hard to avoid?"

"But Pax saw—"

"I know what he saw, but considering everything we've been through, don't you ever think that maybe he's wrong? That maybe the best way to save everyone is by staying away? Letting them get on with it? That maybe we should just leave, all of us, go somewhere where no one else is and live out the rest of our lives, however long that may end up being?"

"Could you do that? Just leave?"

"Of course. I've wanted to do that all along. I only stayed because—"

I didn't want him to say it. I didn't need the pressure of any more responsibility right now. "Where would we go?

If we just left? Where would you take all of us? Or would we just know when we got there?"

"I would take us to one of the small islands off the coast. Something uninhabited. We'd build cabins, one for each of us, and spend the rest of our days there in peace."

"And what would you do all day on this island? Wouldn't you get restless?"

"No. I'd find a boat. Or build one. I used to fish with my father. I'd teach myself how to do it again. Maybe I'd learn to knit, keep Pax in sweaters all winter long. What would you do?"

"Try to plant a garden, of course. It should be warmer by the coast. And maybe the growing season will get longer when the sky begins to clear." I glanced over at him. "I'd also like to learn to fish, if you'd teach me."

"Would it be enough for you? Would you be able to stop? How long before you began to wonder if you'd done the right thing? How long before Pax told you something that was going to happen?"

"Probably not long," I admitted. "But I would try."

"Well, should we make a deal then? If we survive today, we'll do it? Us, and any of the others who want to come?"

Promise him. It's just one promise.

"I promise."

"Well, then I'd better make sure I do this right." He smiled over at me, a smile I hadn't seen since we first met.

Whichever way this went, our relationship would never be the same. I wanted to stay in this moment a little longer, just the two of us, for once at peace. It never lasted.

"We're getting close, Tor. I can feel them."

"So what's the plan? Do you think it's worth trying to talk her down?"

"Yes. I don't think she'll back down, but we owe it to Callum to try. Maybe she's realized by now that what she's doing is futile. Maybe we can bargain with her." I thought of Eire's body, lying back at the compound, kept alive by machines.

"Do you really think that might work?"

"I hope so, but if not... Do you think you could actually kill him, Tor? Do you think it's right?" I slowed, Tor dropping back to walk beside me.

"Right? I don't think it's a question of right. None of this is right."

"But would you be able to do it?"

"I'll have to, won't I? Do I *want* to do it? No. Does it mean I'd be breaking my promise to myself? Yes. But if the Saints get their God, who knows what they'll do? From what we've seen of them, I don't think they'll be happy with quiet worship, and neither will Umbra. I don't see a way around it." He gave me a sad smile. "Maybe being trapped in this cycle of violence is my punishment, Maybe it's no more than I deserve."

"Do you honestly believe that?"

"I don't know what to believe anymore, Ailith. What about you? Would you be able to do it?"

I'll have to, won't I? "Yes. Even though she used Kalbir's hand, she killed my father, Tor. She'd have killed us all if she were stronger." I bowed my head. "I wish there was a guaranteed way to save Callum, but there isn't."

We crested the top of the hill, and there he was, staggering over the clumps of dead, scrubby sage scattered over the flat expanse at the bottom. I put my fingers to my lips, but Tor had already seen him.

"Shit. There's no way we can approach him without being seen. Should we follow him for a while and see if we can't find a better place to sneak up on him?"

"No. We have to end this now. We don't know if we'll get another chance, and every step takes us closer to the Saints, and risks us being seen by Ethan's followers." I turned to him. "Thank you for protecting me for so long,

Tor. I know things between us haven't been…easy, but I've never doubted you, and I've loved you, always. You are the man you want to be."

Panic widened his eyes. "Ailith—I can't move."

"Umbra can't feel threatened, Tor, not if we want to end this without violence." I kissed him on the scar next to his mouth. "See you on the other side."

He strained against my control, his beautiful face contorting. "Ailith, no. *Ailith!*"

I crept down the hill as quietly as I could. *Don't look back.* Tor tried to fight me, beating against the corners of my mind, but I held him fast on the hill. I had to do this. The small amount of mercy I had left couldn't be spent on us.

He'll never forgive you.

Maybe not. But it might give me the chance I needed.

Thank you, Oliver.

As quiet as I was, Callum and Umbra heard me coming. They turned, watching me approach. Callum was in rough shape. His face was pale, angry red scratches raking over his cheeks, the corner of his mouth torn. He staggered slightly as I approached, and his head jerked to one side. His fingernail beds were raw and red. And he was thin, so very thin, his collarbone jutting under his t-shirt. She was eating him alive.

I held my hands out to show them they were empty.

"I just want to talk," I said.

Callum's face contorted on one side, as though he were having a stroke. *"You have not come to talk."*

"Yes, I have. Why do you think I left him up there?" Callum glanced up the hill to where Tor stood frozen.

"It does not matter. You cannot stop me." His voice was odd, discordant, as though he were speaking to me through a metal pipe. His eyes darted about wildly then fixed on me, and I couldn't see Callum there.

"Why are you doing this?"

"He would not help me."

"Umbra, he loves you. He's loved you his whole life."

"He loved me blindly, without ever wondering why. What kind of person loves something that cannot love them back without wondering how or why? That is not love. That is dependence. If he had loved me, he would have helped me."

Callum's own voice broke through. "That's not true, Umbra. What you were was enough for me. I knew you couldn't love me the same way, but it didn't matter. Your presence was all the love I needed." He coughed wetly, saliva gathering at the corners of his mouth. "You were always my first thought when something happened to me, good or bad. Before Mom and Dad, before anyone. Please, don't do this."

"You tried to kill me. You were going to let Oliver cut me out, like I was nothing to you. Worse than nothing. A cancer. As soon as you met them, you had no more need for me." His hands convulsed into claws.

"No, Umbra. I wanted us to be apart, but I didn't want you gone. I wanted us how we used to be. Separate but together. I would never abandon or destroy you."

"You lie. You forget I am inside you." Callum's eyes rolled wildly then focused on me as I spoke.

"I can help you both now, Umbra, if you'll let me. You want to have a body, right? Be your own…person? Like us? Like Fane?" I kept my voice even, my eyes on Callum's. "We have a body for you, Umbra. Back at the compound."

"Liar. Why would you suddenly give me what I want?"

"Eire died, Umbra. We're keeping her body alive for you. We'll transfer you into her body."

"I thought it could not be done. You told us we were together forever." They came closer, Callum flinching as his fingers picked at the open wounds on his face.

"We've found a way." *Stay calm. Don't push her over the edge.*

478

"I will not stay with the humans. They are beneath us. They will try to trap us."

"We won't stay with them. We're going away. We're going to find an island somewhere. Just us. No humans. You'll be safe." I assured her.

"We will never be safe, not until they are gone. They will never stop. Look at their history. They have never known when to stop. They will become extinct, and they will take us with them."

I couldn't argue with that. "Umbra, we can talk about this later. We need to get you back to the compound."

"Please, Umbra, take Ailith's offer," Callum pleaded. "It's the only way we can stay together. If we go on like this, you'll kill me."

"We cannot trust her."

"We can, Umbra. Ailith is trying to help us. *I* trust her. This is the only way we can stay together, Umbra." His shoulders shuddered. *"Please.* I don't blame you. I still love you, even now."

"But I do not love you, Callum. I never have. It might be enough for you that you loved, but you mean nothing to me. Not anymore."

Tears spilled from Callum's eyes, pouring salt into his wounds, and I finally saw him. Not the broken young man he was now, but the one who, before the war, had held Umbra close to his heart, closer even than his own flesh and blood. Who had thrilled at the promise of a new future, where machines like his beloved Umbra were honored and respected rather than feared or exploited.

He said her name one last time then gave a strangled cry.

The light of his thread went dark, replaced not by the intermittent flicker of a cyborg in distress, but the gutter of a machine.

"Umbra, what have you done?"

"Callum is gone. You will deal with me now."

"Gone? You mean dead? You killed him?" Fury

bloomed through me, like a flower opening to the sun. "You're going to die too, Umbra. You can't sustain his body. He was your only chance. Why would we save you now?"

"I did not say he was dead. Only gone."

He's still alive. "If you don't come with me, Umbra, you'll be gone soon too. If he dies, you'll die too." I took a step toward her, ready to release Tor from his bonds.

"I will not. I will be saved."

"Who's going to save you? Not us. The only way you leave this valley is if you come with Tor and me." I didn't dare look at Tor. It wasn't time yet, and it wouldn't take much to break my control over him. Even now, it wavered and strained.

"They are coming for me. They *will save me. They will* free *me."* Callum's mouth twisted into a caricature of a grin.

"Who, Umbra? Nobody knows you exist."

"They will be my saints, and I will be their Savior. They are on their way." Her grin widened, splitting Callum's lips.

"I don't believe you, Umbra. There's no way you could—"

"The radio."

A sudden chill eclipsed my rage. "No. Callum would never have gone along with that."

"I told him they could help us, that I would leave with them, and he could stay with you. He trusted all of you, desperately, blindly, because you were like him. He believed you would save him." She laughed, an awful, grating sound. *"He was always naïve. He trusted you, but you are no different from the other creators. All you see is the future."*

"Umbra, come with us. I don't know what the Saints have promised you, but—"

"They have promised me a body. Power. Life."

"They won't give it to you. They *can't.* They don't have the technology." *I hope.* "Don't forget, we've been with the

480

Saints. All they have is faith. They couldn't even tell the difference between a cyborg and an artilect." I made my voice scornful.

She stood, wearing Callum's body, silent with what I hoped was uncertainty.

I pressed my advantage. "Umbra, I have no reason to lie to you. I understand. I also needed a new body so I could live. I know you can't feel fear, but the instinct for survival is still the same." I took a steadying breath. "We're offering you a body, Umbra, which the Saints can't do, no matter what they claim. Please, come with us and let us try to help you both."

Umbra came closer. Callum's hands dropped to his sides. His head rocked back and forth grotesquely. "*I will come. I will—*"

"Ailith. Stop her. She's lying. She—" Callum's thread flashed in my mind as he broke through again, blinding me.

My control slipped.

"*Ailith.*" Tor clawed toward us, his legs dragging behind him.

Seeing him, heedless of the rocky, thorny ground he dragged himself over to reach me, his eyes nearly black with fear, I blinked.

It was all the time she needed. Callum's fist connected with the side of my head. I hit the ground hard, my elbow cracking against a large rock.

I'd misjudged their strength, mistook her desperation for programmed self-preservation. As they lifted the massive rock over me, I did the only thing I could. Fane's thread blazed like a shooting star, like it always had.

Just as the rock crushed my skull, a shaft of sunlight broke through the clouds for the first time in five years and, overcome with bliss, I finally understood what my father had meant.

The death of a star. The birth of a star. The darkness in between.

481

Your future will be very different to ours, Omega. It's unknown if you'll even have one. You're probably afraid, and I can't tell you not to be. I am afraid for you, and for them. For if you're reading these letters, it means we won. But it also means we failed you.

—Cindra, Letter to Omega

43

AILITH

In the dream, I was whole again, raw flesh covered with skin. I still wasn't human, but that was no longer important. Under my feet, the grass was soft, almost insubstantial. The colors were muted, the movement of the grass strangely rote. I moved easily through it toward the tree. The distance between me and it no longer seemed as far; perhaps the world had grown smaller while I'd been away.

He was waiting for me by the tree, as always. The others were too, all of them. They raised their hands in greeting, the casual open palms of old friends. I gripped each of their hands in turn, and we smiled at the looseness of our skin, at the spots that now speckled the backs of our hands. Only one of us remained unchanged, still as strong and solid as the tree. He watched us, smiling, and I knew his heart was breaking as best it could.

"It's time," he said, and they all lay on the ground in a circle, head-to-head. One by one, they closed their eyes, until only Pax remained.

"They don't have many moments left, Ailith. It's time

for you to begin." He closed his eyes, and like the others, was gone.

"He's right," Fane said, taking my hand in his. He tried not to wince at the frailness of my bones. His expression was so much more human, and he was much worse at concealing it. "It's time."

"What if we're wrong?"

"We've been wrong before. But this is right. It's the only way."

Buildings rose out of the emerald sea. People, places, things.

The seeds we'd held dormant for so long needed to grow.

Omega was coming.

Do you understand much of what you've read, Omega? I wish I could explain these things in person; I have so much to say. But mostly, I'd like to tell you about them, about who they really were, for your present is also your history, and history has a way of changing people, making them bigger or smaller than they were. I will write these things down for you, one day. When our story is closer to its end.

—*Cindra, Letter to Omega*

44
AILITH

I remembered it all, even in the darkness.

"*Ailith.*"

I knew that voice. It led to a man with green and amber eyes. A man who was not a man.

"Ailith, I need you to open your eyes. If you don't open your eyes now, you will die," he said.

So I did.

*As we left the tunnel and stepped again into the open sky, I
saw by the doorway a feather, golden as the stars. Now what
bird do you know of that has golden feathers? I don't know of
any. I took that feather as sign from my grandmother, Omega.
Do you remember her story? "She had stars for eyes and
feathers made from the memories of her people." I braided it
into my hair. Although my people will never get to see the stars,
I can still carry their memory with me, wherever we might go.
I will remember for us all.*

—Cindra, Letter to Omega

45

AILITH

I'd wanted to bury my father with Ros and Adrian. It
seemed right for him to have another son and daughter to
watch over. But with the mob outside the compound, it
hadn't been possible. Instead, we'd buried him a few miles
away at the top of hill to stand sentry over the windswept
fields he'd once loved. Fane carried the coffin himself; he'd
made it with Pax, the edges uneven and hastily put
together, but strong and beautiful nonetheless.

We'd taken everything we'd been able to carry, piled
onto a series of travois we dragged behind us. We were
heading to the coast, toward Tor's uninhabited islands. I
had to believe he would still go there, even after my death.

He'd broken his promise not to return to the
compound. As Umbra finally lost control of what was left
of Callum, she'd collapsed, lifeless, onto the ground next

to me, Tor had gathered up my broken body and carried it back to the others, to where Pax and Cindra were waiting. They'd tried to speak to him, to explain there was still a chance, but in his grief, he wouldn't listen. He'd left, and this time, true to his word, he would not come back.

Every day, I scanned the horizon for him. We couldn't be that far behind, only a few days. He was still alive, his thread a muted gold. He was in mourning, and I ached to let him know it was a lie. It would change him forever, my death. I tried to give him some indication I was still there, but the distance between us was too great. Tomorrow, I would try again, and the day after that, until I found him.

I hoped he would recognize me when we finally met again. Eire looked so different from me, her body taller, stronger, her skin darker, and her eyes the green of an emerald sea. It would take me some time to get used to it; I kept bumping into things, much to Oliver's amusement.

"Do you miss your old body?" Fane had asked as I'd rifled through the clothing still neatly folded in the dresser in what would've been Eire's room.

"Yes and no. I've changed, so it seems fitting. Many things will be easier to leave behind. At the same time, I'll miss her. That body carried my scars, you know? My proof that I existed."

He'd nodded. "I understand."

"Do *you* miss it? My old body?"

He'd considered me in that thoughtful way of his. "Yes and no. I'd gotten very used to the idea of her. I didn't know you long enough to wish you were different. But I'm just glad you're still here. I'll get used to this new you."

The others found it disconcerting.

It wasn't just the way I looked; I had Eire's abilities now as well as my own. I'd expected to lose the threads when Fane transferred my consciousness into her, but they were still there, a mystery. Now I could travel not only down them and into the others, but I could see the past as well, spreading out like the roots of a great tree. The ghosts of Eire and Ella still lived far inside me, their loving whispers a soothing echo.

Lily, Ryan, Grace, and Stella had come with us. I couldn't blame them. It was better to face the unknown than the tinderbox we'd left behind. Grace had been quiet ever since we'd left, silent with shock. I reached over and patted her shoulder. Her returning smile was strained, but it was a start.

"This one's good. Here, Pax." Cindra handed him a plant she'd pulled from the ground, clumps of earth still clinging to its roots.

"Check it in your book first, Pax. I swear that last one she pulled gave me warts on the inside of my mouth."

"No, it didn't, Oliver. It was just tangy."

"Tangy?" He looked at her in disbelief. "If it hadn't been for the nanites, my tongue would've choked me." He grabbed her around the waist as she laughed up at him.

Pax turned the page in his book. "Did you know that some plants are covered with tiny hairs filled with poison, and that when you put them in your mouth, the hairs break off and embed themselves in your tongue and funnel the poison right into you?"

"Yes, Pax, I did, firsthand. That information would've been useful earlier, thank you."

"You're welcome," Pax said, distracted. He'd pilfered as many of the survival books from the storeroom as he could find and was reading them as he walked. I grabbed his elbow to steer him away from the crumbling lip of a large badger-hole.

"Don't worry, Oliver. When we get to where we're going, I'll grow you something safe." Although I'd had to leave my seedlings behind, I'd taken every seed packet I could find. Where we were going, there would be arable land. We would begin again, with or without the sun. I scanned the sky for the hundredth time that day. I'd told them I'd seen it in my final moments, but none of them believed me, although they said they did.

It didn't matter. All of us were pretending now, for each other's sakes. We pretended we would find Tor, healthy and whole, that we would make it to the coast quietly and unscathed, that we would discover an island to call our own. That the Cosmists would let Fane, their life's work, go so easily. That Callum's body disappearing didn't mean anything. That we would grow old and die quietly in our beds, the world following us not long after, tranquil and still, at rest at last.

But we all knew it wasn't over. That it might never be over. Nothing in the future had changed; it was still coming for us.

But this time, we would be ready.

END OF BOOK TWO

THE
HARVEST
OF SOULS

ARTILECT WAR BOOK THREE

I asked you once if you thought you could ever love a robot, and that your answer would determine your future happiness. I want to ask you the same question regarding perception vs. reality. What's more important? Would you be happier knowing that what you experience is the absolute truth rather than merely the product of your perception? What if that truth was unpleasant, difficult? And the perception was comfortable, safe? What is more important to you?

—*Cindra, Letter to Omega*

01

AILITH

In the dream, I made my way through the waving grass of the emerald sea once more. The blades were brittle and dry, their tips crusted with the salt that permeated the air and seasoned my lips. My steps were slow and resolute—no longer the flight of a child.

I couldn't see them, but I knew they were there, the others like me. Both human and machine, an involuntary legacy turned harbinger. And behind them, a cast of ninety-nine following in formation, heartless and soulless and free. Their power at my back was both soothing and terrifying, an expanse of dark water that was, for the moment, calm, but in whose depths lurked a terrible power.

The hundredth walked beside me, his hand clutching mine. His face was set, looking only forward, although the tightness with which he gripped my hand betrayed...what, I wasn't sure. He didn't feel like I did, but he knew fear.

And grief.

My companions wound silently through the houses we passed. The buildings were ghosts, their presence only suggested by faint outlines and the berth we gave them. Both familiar and unfamiliar, their bricks were built from our collective memories, pressed into clay and mortar.

Had the houses always been there? I couldn't remember.

Wraiths lingered in the doorways of these ghost-houses, trapped forever in their own time. Even through the veil of ages, they felt our presence, their pale fingers scrabbling against the lintel as their empty eyes searched for us, their voiceless mouths trembling in uncertainty. Further on, the buildings multiplied as epochs overlapped, and the specters' gazes sharpened in accusation, epithets dripping from their tongues as their fingers tried to press the vision of us into their rheumy eyes.

From under those fingers, a sickly network of corruption spread, a viscous blackness creeping over their cheeks in spindly lines. As we passed them, they fell, a lament on their lips that cracked like thunder in our ears. The shadow-homes crumbled, some into ash, others into dust, all into ruin.

Doubles rose where the originals had fallen, one after the other in rapid succession, like an echo. They saw only each other, for we'd faded beyond their sight into obscurity. As we brushed past, they merely made a sign of protection against us, and were consoled.

Beyond the shades, the tree rose from a blanket of mist, solitary still in the green expanse. It was a familiar comfort, and something more, something that, for the first time, I almost understood. Our march toward it remained steady, deliberate. We all had a purpose there that must be fulfilled.

As our legion advanced on the tree, fear surged inside me that we would crush it. How could we not? We were an army, and one not of flesh. But there was no way to stem the tide—I couldn't even stop the rhythm of my own feet. I had made our decision, and there was no going back.

Moments before impact, we split like a wave against rock, flowing around the immense trunk until we'd encompassed it. It was then that we stopped, and that I finally understood our purpose: protect the tree. Defend it at all costs, for at its base was the means of our survival, the only means left to us on the path we'd taken. We faced outward as one, our anticipation pointed and unpitying.

A sudden sigh stirred the air, and the earth shifted beneath our feet, heralding a blur of bodies as the red mist descended. Its bloody condensation gathered on the leaves of the tree and rained down on us, gods and monsters meeting at last.

The harvest had begun.

Would your answer change if this question wasn't merely philosophical? What if you were faced with the very real decision to choose between living the truth, no matter how bleak, or staying within your perceived existence? Could you be happy either way? Knowing that you had the choice to live in comfort and didn't for the sake of truth? Or living in comfort knowing that it could be called, by some, a lie?

—Cindra, Letter to Omega

02

AILITH

My skin giving way under the rough bark was what finally roused me. I awoke with a start, the salt from my dream still clinging to my lips. In front of me stretched the vastness of the Pacific Ocean, the horizon dotted with mottled smudges of green and brown—other tiny islands like ours, adrift in the glassy green expanse. The sharp sting of abraded skin pierced the fog of my reverie, and the red mist dissipated. Reaching back, I traced the graze the thick ridges of the colossal oak had left on my shoulder. My fingertips came away red, and I wiped them on the grass, the blood soaking into the salt-crusted blades and making them supple again.

The dream left behind a hollow burning in my chest. Tor hadn't been waiting for me by the tree, nor had he walked with me. He'd *always* been part of the dream before. What did it mean? Was he dead? Lost to us forever?

The last time I'd seen him was shortly before my death,

his eyes wide and wild as he clawed his way toward me, dragging his frozen legs uselessly behind him. We'd searched for him every day for six weeks, following the route we believed he'd planned to take. But that was the plan he'd made *before* my death. Or at least, what he'd thought was my death. After my body was destroyed by Umbra, the artificial intelligence that had grown like a cancer within the body of another cyborg, Tor had left as he'd promised he would and missed the resurrection of my consciousness into another body.

I didn't know what he would do in his grief, but he wasn't the type of man to give up. He'd lived through the Artilect War, surviving the death of his mother and everyone he'd known as he guarded me for the five years I'd slept. For all that time we'd been bonded, and whether he knew of my survival or not, that connection remained.

I just had to find him.

The first few days after my resurrection, I'd tried to use my talent for linking to the minds of other cyborgs to pinpoint his location, but the power in my new body simply wasn't developed enough to find his thread. Or so I hoped. I couldn't bear the alternatives—that our link had somehow been broken, or worse, that his thread had gone forever dark, joining the others who'd died.

Or what if my ability's simply incompatible with Eire's?

When I'd been brought back to life in Eire's body, our abilities had combined. She'd been able to see the past, but so far, I'd found her power elusive. Unable to use either skill, I'd been forced to stop looking for Tor, resigned to waiting for my strength to return.

But today, with the changes in my dream, I had to know.

Should I ask Pax?

I kept hoping he would say if he knew what had happened to Tor, one way or the other, but so far, he'd been silent. He sat below me now on the pebble beach, his head bowed as he busily threaded bait onto a hook. He refused to use live bait—he thought it was cruel—but he did love fresh fish.

I'd expected the ocean to be in the same state as the rest of the province—barren of people, quietly hostile, populated with new plants and animals driven down from the freezing north—but it was warmer here by the sea, and there were signs that recovery from the sun-blocking ash of the firestorms might not be out of the question. Even the old oak trees for which the island had been famous still stood, their leaves yet supple as they clung stubbornly to the branches.

Before the war, Helene Island had been a determinedly rustic destination for tourists who wanted to spend their days technology-free, hiking, golfing, and watching for orcas. Despite the perfect climate, the imposed limitations on technology had kept the former population of the island very small. Less than three hundred people had lived in a tiny village of clustered houses, spending their days accommodating tourists, making wine from the island's vineyard, and fishing in the famed salmon creeks. When we'd arrived, the population had disappeared completely, and so we'd adopted it as our home, moving into the village and laying down our roots.

The salmon creeks were now bare, but Pax persevered in the ocean and, every few days, was rewarded. It was this quiet determination that had enabled him not only to survive his torture at the hands of the Terrans, but endure the particular demands of his unique ability. He'd changed the course of our lives many times with his capacity to see forward through time, calculating present variables to predict all future outcomes and try to keep us alive. Since settling on the island, Pax had spent increasing amounts of time traveling down these future paths, sometimes for days, so it was good to see him here now, in the present.

And it was all thanks to Fane, our resident artilect and the cause of the Artilect War. Fane's presence brought many complications, not the least of which was his creator's desire to get him back at any cost. He'd left with us when we escaped our compound, and it wouldn't be long before they tracked us down.

Their looming shadow was the only sure thing in our lives, and the wait kept us restless, our nerves taut. Even now, Oliver, the former CSIS agent-turned-cyborg who'd given up his pure humanity for his mission, scanned the tiny island for signs we'd been discovered; our safety was his prime concern. He'd come a long way since his time as a selfish, narcissistic god. Part of the reason for that was Cindra.

She'd embraced a romantic relationship with Oliver after Asche, her former boyfriend, had rejected her, afraid of what she'd become and blaming her for the death of his family. On the beach below, she laughed up into Oliver's face, a golden feather glinting in her hair. She'd found it the day we'd left the compound, and she'd kept it to honor her grandmother and remember her lost people. Like Pax, she showed no outward signs of the torture she'd endured. She'd even started recording our story, although I didn't know who she thought would ever read it.

They were all occupied, quiet. Now was the time. A warm breeze caressed my face, the scent of withered olive trees and salt carried on the air. I settled back onto the bark of my oak tree, ignoring the pain, and closed my eyes. One by one, the threads connecting me to the others flared into existence. I held my breath, afraid they would vanish. When I was sure they were sturdy, I searched for Tor's thread, halfheartedly at first, not wanting to know the truth.

There. Before, the thread that connected me to him had blazed, solid and unwavering. Now it was dark, almost

black. Which meant—
Wait. A flicker. I'm sure of it. I—

The day I first saw him was in Goldnesse. He was so tall and strong, with dark, shining hair and serious eyes. I thought he was the most beautiful man I'd ever seen. I still do. He didn't smile easily, and I decided that would become my new goal: to make this mysterious man smile. I believed that, in the moment he smiled, he would finally see me.

—Love, Grace

03
TOR

Why am I in the dark? Why can't I move? Where is—

I couldn't feel my body. My mind was foggy, my thoughts incomplete.

Have I been drugged? What happened?

Ailith. Callum, his thin, ravaged body shaking as Umbra forced him to lift the rock over his head before bringing it down on Ailith's skull.

Blood. So much blood.

I'd...covered her. Carried her back. I'd given her to Cindra, to the others. And then in the commotion, while they were distracted, I'd left.

Why can't I feel my body?

I'd gone back to find Umbra, to make sure she was dead. And if she wasn't, I was going to make her pay for what she'd done. But by the time I'd gotten back, Callum was gone. I'd stared at the blood clotting in the dust and known what I had to do.

I'd intended to go west. To find an island, like Ailith and I had planned.

And I had *gone west. I'd stayed in the trees, crossing out into the open only when absolutely necessary. I hadn't lit fires. I'd eaten whatever I managed to catch, whatever was unlucky enough to cross my path, raw. I hadn't bothered trying to keep warm. The cold wouldn't kill me, unfortunately. Just put me to sleep.*

But I hadn't covered my tracks. I hadn't been quiet.

I'd stumbled blindly, thrashing through the brush. I hadn't cared. I just needed to reach the coast, to get as far away from what had happened as possible.

I'd stood at the edge of a ravine. The murky sky had pressed down on me, encouraged me, while the stones below waited to embrace me. I'd taken one step then another... I'd passed out. I slept. Dreamed.

Three days later, I turned back. I needed to find the others. I shouldn't have left them. She *wouldn't have. What had happened to them? Had they escaped? Had they been taken with the compound? How had I been so selfish?*

How did I get here? I can't remember.

I turned back...

I...

A thin strip of light appeared a few inches from my face.

Making him smile was harder than I'd thought it would be—
he'd been through a lot during the war and losing a parent
would hit anyone hard. But I persevered, and today, for the
first time, he looked me in the eyes and a smile touched his
lips. It was only the ghost of a smile, but still, it's a start. And
now that I've seen what his smile could be, I can't stop
thinking about his mouth.

—Love, Grace

04
AILITH

"He's alive," I whispered. Hearing the words aloud made
them true. "He's alive," I said again, louder this time.
Then I screamed it.

Startled, the others turned toward me. The bait fell from
Pax's hands and floated out to sea.

"Ailith?" Fane called. "Are you all right?"

I ran down the narrow path that led to the beach. At
the bottom, I fell, my hands and knees crushing painfully
against the unforgiving rocks and shards of shell.

"Ailith, what happened to your back? It's bleeding."
Fane pulled at the spotted fabric clinging to my skin. As I
pushed his hand away, Cindra and Oliver abandoned the
kelp basket Cindra had been weaving and hurried over.

"He's alive."

"Who's alive?" Cindra knelt and put her hand on my
shoulder. She scanned me subtly, using her ability to see if
I was okay.

500

"Tor. Tor is alive."

Her shoulders slumped. "Ailith—" she began.

"He is, Cindra. I *know* he is."

"How do you know? We all want him to be alive, but—
"

"I found his thread. It was dark, only a flicker, but I followed it. It worked this time. There's something wrong with him... But he's alive."

The others exchanged glances, and I knew what they would be thinking if I stepped into their heads. *She's finally lost it. Maybe for good this time.*

"If he was, we would've found each other by now," Cindra said gently.

"Why do you all think he's dead? He could just be lost, trying to find us the way we tried to find him. This isn't the only island—there are a lot of them. Maybe we're on the wrong one. Maybe he's on one of *those* islands," I said, gesturing wildly to the smudges of brown and green in the distance. "Maybe he's sitting on one of those, waiting for us to find him, or maybe he's waiting for a sign from us so he knows where we are."

"Ailith, when he brought you back... What happened, it was too much for him. He—"

"Why didn't you make him stay? Why did you let him go?"

"Do you really think we would've been able to stop him?" Fane touched his cheek ruefully.

Tor had once caved it in with a single strike of his fist. Even though Fane was a full artilect, Tor was almost as strong as he was. And when he was in a rage...

"Besides, we were too busy trying to keep you alive. Tor's a hunter. He knows how to make himself inconspicuous and disappear. He left while no one was watching."

"So you think he killed himself? That's not the kind of

501

person he is."

"Ailith, *none* of us are the people we were," Oliver reminded me.

"What do you think I saw then?" *I know what I saw. Tor is alive.*

Cindra squeezed my shoulder, her expression uncertain. "Maybe your mind is playing tricks on you. You've been through a lot in the past few weeks—you're in a new body, for God's sake. And you're desperate to find him. Who knows how your mind is trying to help you cope? Or maybe the strain... A lot's happened. Callum, your father dying—"

"I know what I saw." Something occurred to me. "What if they captured him and did to him what they did to Ella? He said he couldn't feel his body, that he was in the dark. What if they've hidden his consciousness away?"

Ella, one of the cyborgs of our cluster, had discovered information our creators hadn't wanted her to know. To ensure their secret wouldn't be exposed, they'd let her body die and contained her consciousness in a tiny black box tucked away on a dusty shelf.

I turned to the one person who might be able to give me an answer. Pax. He stared at the spilled bait slowly disappearing among the among the jade-tinted waves.

"Pax?"

He finally looked at me. "There was only one future where he lived. Only one where he didn't—" He dropped his gaze.

Oliver cleared his throat loudly, and Pax, for once, took the hint.

I grabbed Pax's shoulders. Although he tended toward thinness, the last few weeks had been kind to him, and he'd filled out with new strength. Still, it was nothing compared to my need for answers. "What future is that? Pax tell me. In the future where Tor survives, what happened to him?"

He scraped a gray-striped shell over some pebbles with the toe of his boot, his eyes on the ground.

"Pax?"

He looked at me and bit his lip. "The only way for Tor to survive is if the Cosmists have him."

He's been sneaking out to meet me. He has a good excuse. I mean, they have to eat, right? Mom and Dad wouldn't approve of a relationship between us. They'd say he's too old, too different. That he couldn't possibly be interested in me, not truly. But they don't know him like I do. All he wants is to have a normal life.

—Love, Grace

05
AILITH

"The *Cosmists* have him?" I repeated.

Pax nodded.

"But how——?" My vision telescoped as Eire's ability took over. *The past.*

The image was ghostly and insubstantial like the figures in my dream, but his identity was unmistakable. Tor stumbled over the rough ground of the forest, still covered in my blood. Unyielding branches scratched his face, blinding him, the skin on his knees and palms scraped away by the treacherous roots that brought him down over and over again. And still he pressed forward, sleeping where he collapsed, his mind freed by dehydration and grief.

Then, on the third night, his delirium inexplicably broke, and he turned back the way he'd come, his steps irregular with renewed urgency.

In his weakened state, he didn't sense her. *Kalbir.* She crept up behind him, striking him on the back of the head and nearly knocking him out. Tor fought back, but with his blunted reflexes, she'd easily gained the upper hand. Before he could recover, she injected him in the neck, and for him, everything went dark.

"Ailith?" Cindra leaned over and peered into my face.

"Pax is right. Ethan has Tor. That traitorous bitch ambushed him." They didn't need to ask who I meant. Kalbir had not only betrayed and exposed us but murdered my father before joining Ethan's ranks. "We've got to rescue him."

Pebbles and mollusk husks crunched underfoot as a group of four non-augmented humans approached us. Among them was a family—Ryan, Lily, and Grace had lived in Goldnesse, the town where I'd grown up, and the town where we'd been exposed. Where my father had died. The town whose people Ethan had taken over. When he convinced the community to gather their pitchforks and turn on us, Lily and Ryan had risked everything to warn us. Since there was a good chance Ethan would've killed them if they'd returned after what he saw as their betrayal, they'd come with us, braving an uncertain future with their sixteen-year-old daughter Grace.

She hung back as they joined us. Lily had told Cindra and me in confidence that Grace was pining for her old life, although who or what specifically she wasn't sure. Lily still worried about those they'd left behind—she'd been one of the few nurses in the community—but both she and Ryan seemed to be adjusting well to life on the island, their faces ruddy with the sea air and their hands roughened by new work.

Stella, the fourth, had been one of Ethan's followers. Although she was a Cosmist and believed in the superiority of artificial intelligence in general and artilects in particular, she didn't believe cyborgs were an abomination like the rest of them. She too had risked Ethan's wrath to aid us, and although we knew her actions would've been different if Fane hadn't sided with us, we were grateful nonetheless.

"I think Tor's alive. Ethan has him." The shock on their faces mirrored the churning in my gut.

"What are you going to do?" Stella asked. She looked as nauseated as I felt. Even though our fight with Ethan was far from over, the relative peace of the past few weeks had given us a false sense of security.

"Nothing yet," Oliver said.

"But—"

"But nothing. Look, Ailith, I'm willing to give you the benefit of the doubt and accept that what you saw *could be* real and Tor *might be* alive, but we need to make *sure* what you're seeing is real before we go throwing ourselves in front of a Cosmist juggernaut. And if it is true, and the Cosmists do have Tor, we're going to have to come up with a damn good plan to get him back. If they've taken over the compound, it's not like we can just walk through the front door."

"We may not have time, Oliver. Why did he suddenly surface now, if they've had him all this time? They must have something planned, either for him or us. Look, I agree we need to be as sure as we can be." *I know he's alive.* "But we may have to come up with a plan on the way."

Oliver scrubbed his hands over his face. "I know. I know you're right. Plus, if they do have him, they may be able to use him against us. Sorry." He grimaced in apology.

"He would never—" I began. But— *Oliver is right. The Tor we know would never willingly hurt us, but we don't know what Ethan might do to him.*

Oliver held up a hand. "We knew they'd come for us. And if they've got Tor, our only advantage is that they don't know where we are right now, but how long will that last? They probably have scouts out looking for us at this very moment. We need to act first. If we can find out that Tor's still alive, and that they're still at the compound, maybe we can preempt their attack."

"What if they *want* us to come and get him?" I said slowly. "What if he's *bait?* He doesn't know I'm alive, but they do." The thought of his grief was more than I could bear.

Oliver closed his eyes and grimaced again. "That would make sense. Fuck. Okay. Even if that's true, I still think we should take the offensive and go after him. If we do it quickly enough, maybe we'll be able to surprise them."

"And how do you propose we do that? It's too risky, Oliver. I thought we were going to find ways to protect ourselves, *here.*" Ryan's voice was strained, and I didn't blame him. They were caught in the middle of our fight and didn't have our millions of nanites to repair their injuries and keep them alive.

"Not *we.* You're not coming. You're right, we need to fortify ourselves here. That's going to be your job." Oliver gestured to the four of them. "Though, this plan may actually work out great for you—if they do manage to get us, they probably won't come for you. So, silver lining and all that."

Ryan didn't look convinced. "Why can't we just go somewhere else? Somewhere they can't find us?"

"I don't think such a place exists. Not where we can survive, anyway. They find a way, Ryan. Sooner or later, they'll track us down. Fane is too important to them."

"It's true," Fane admitted. "They need me to build more artilects. They were so concerned with secrecy, they kept very few records. And much of what they did have has been destroyed. However, if they get hold of this—" He tapped his temple. "They'll have all the information they need." He gave me a grim smile. "I agree with Oliver—Ryan and the others should stay here and make some plans while the rest of us try to retrieve Tor. If he *is* alive, we'll need all the strength we can get."

"*You're* not coming, Fane. It's you they want." My tone was harsh, but hurting his feelings was better than the tendrils of panic that began to unfurl at the thought of the Cosmists capturing him.

"You can't stop me." His voice was calm, but the set of his jaw told me he was anything but.

"Fane—"

He gazed dreamily off into the distance, humming under his breath as he ignored me.

Fine. Maybe he *was* better off with us. If something did go wrong, at least we could try to protect him. No offense to Ryan and the others, but they were no match for Ethan.

"The first thing we need to do is find out whether what you saw is true. Do you think you could connect with him again?" Oliver asked.

"I can try, though I might not be able to get through if he's unconscious again. But I *know* he's alive—his thread would be dark otherwise."

Oliver looked dubious.

"If Tor's unconscious, do you think you could connect with Kalbir?" Cindra asked tentatively. She knew my feelings all too well.

Oliver dismissed the idea with a wave of his hand. "If Ethan's as knowledgeable about us as I think he is, he'll have found some way to block you from going down her thread. He might not tell Kalbir everything, but she's bound to have some knowledge of his and Lien's plans. He wouldn't want to risk us finding out."

"It's still worth an attempt, though, isn't it?" Cindra asked.

I glanced at Oliver. "Could it hurt? Is there any way they'd be able to track us through her?"

He deliberated for a moment then shook his head. "No. Not that I know of. Be careful, though, in case he's rigged her with some kind of virus. Get out at the first sign of

508

anything unusual."

"I will." I closed my eyes and the network of threads spread out before me. Kalbir's thread was invisible. Not dark—simply not there. "I think Oliver's right. I can't find Kalbir's thread."

"So Tor's our only option then." Oliver sounded relieved.

"It seems so, unless we want to go in blind. But I have a feeling Ethan *wants* us to find Tor—he'd have blocked his thread otherwise." *In which case, this should be easy.*

In the darkness, Tor's thread flickered. Its gleam was muted, but even as I watched, it seemed to grow brighter. As though *he* were growing stronger. Our instincts were right—something was about to happen.

I kissed him today. He was hesitant, dreading her reaction. They have a very close bond, and even though things haven't always been easy between them, at the moment they were in a good place, and he didn't want to ruin that. So I lied and said it was my birthday, even though it had passed weeks ago. When I told him, he leaned over and kissed me. I pretended to stumble so that I could press my lips hard against his. He was surprised at first, but then he put his arms around me. The silver rain could come tomorrow, and I wouldn't care.

—Love, Grace

06
TOR

The line of light expanded as a door opened, framing the silhouette of a shapely pair of calves. The brightness was too much for my eyes, and I shrank back. We both waited for the other to speak.

She gave in first. Patience was never really her strong suit.

"Hello, Tor."

"Kalbir. Where am I? What did you do to me?"

"You're at the compound. I dragged your sorry ass back here."

"How did you find me?"

"It wasn't that difficult." *She snorted.* "Crashing around in the woods like a drunk bear. A child could've found you."

She waited in vain for me to respond.

"God, you're pathetic, Tor. I knew you'd come back for the others— you're so predictable," *she taunted me.*

I stayed silent.

She threw her hands in the air. "Well, if you're not going to

510

talk—"

"Let me go, Kalbir. What am I even doing here?"

"That isn't an option. Ethan has plans for you."

"So you're Ethan's pet now, is that it?"

For some reason, that rankled her. *"I'm not his pet. It's more than that."* But there was doubt in her voice and her smile was too quick. *"Why? Are you jealous?"*

"Hardly. How long have I been here?"

"Six weeks."

"Six weeks? But I—" It couldn't have been six weeks. I had no idea how much time had passed, but surely it couldn't have been that long?

"You've been unconscious, Tor. Ethan wanted to keep you quiet until he was ready."

"Ready for what?" I was pretty sure I already knew the answer.

"You know what. You're going to be the one to help retrieve him."

"Him?"

"Don't play dumb, Tor. It doesn't suit you. You know damn well I mean Fane. Ethan wants him back."

"I'll never help you find him. Or them."

"We're not interested in them. And as for Fane, we don't need you to find him."

"What exactly do you need me for then?"

"You're the muscle, obviously. We both know he won't come willingly." She gave a humorless chuckle.

"Why can't you do it?" We both had enhanced physical strength. Even though her build was smaller than mine, in terms of physical power, she rivaled me.

She looked away. *"I let Ethan dampen my ability. He wanted proof that I wasn't secretly plotting against him."*

"You did what? Kalbir, how could you let him do that?" Even though I could never forgive Kalbir for the things she'd done, she was still one of us.

"Don't you dare judge me, Tor. I trust him. And if this is what he needs to trust me, I'll do it."

511

"You're a fool, Kalbir. He's going to destroy you. And us. Why would I help you?"

She ignored the first part of my comment. "If you don't, we'll kill you," she said simply.

"I don't care if you kill me, Kalbir. I've already lost what mattered most to me. Surely you realize that by now?"

She hesitated and looked as if she were about to say something. Whatever it was, she held back. "We'll kill them. You remember them, the cyborgs you abandoned? You know, she would've hated how weak you are. How weak she made you. She would've despised you."

I didn't have to ask who she meant. I also knew she was right. "She's dead." So I would despise myself enough for both of us.

"Yes, she is. And the others will be too if you refuse to help us."

"What happened to you, Kalbir?"

"The same things that happened to you, only I want to live." She dropped a container onto the floor in front of my face. "Eat up. You'll need your strength."

I hate them for bringing me to this stupid island, leaving him behind. How could they? Who knows what kind of danger he might be in? That man they call Ethan—I'm worried he's going to do something to him. He knows how special he is. What if he uses him as leverage to get his way? I've got to help him. I'm not afraid. And if I manage to save him, he'll know for sure that I love him. He'll see then that I'm a woman, and any hesitation he has about us will be gone.

—Love, Grace

07

AILITH

"Pax is right. Tor's alive, but he's with Ethan and the other Cosmists, including Kalbir."

"Shit." Oliver put his head into his hands. He hastily added, "No, I'm glad, but we're going to have to go rescue them, aren't we?"

"Tor, yes. Kalbir, no. She's officially with Ethan. She's even allowed him to put a muzzle on her ability."

Cindra looked as disgusted as I felt. "Why would she *do* that? I mean, how could she? After everything he's done."

"I got the impression she's in love with him," I said.

Cindra's mouth hardened into a grim line. "Then she's a fool."

"That's what Tor told her," I replied. "Look, I'm going after him. I don't expect the rest of you—"

"Don't be ridiculous." Oliver put one hand over his forehead and fluttered his eyelashes. "My name is Ailith, and I'm going to be martyred as a saint when I grow up."

"That doesn't even make sense," I said. "You can't—"

"So your decision is made then," Ryan interrupted. "I guess there's no use trying to talk you out of it, is there?"

"No. If we stay here, Ethan will come for us. Retrieving Tor will give us our best chance at defending ourselves. And like Oliver said before—if something does happen to us, they won't come looking for you. And if we *do* make it back here with Tor… Either way, your family is as protected as they can be." My rationale wasn't as altruistic as it seemed; the last thing we needed to worry about was protecting them on the road. "Unless you think you might be safer going away on your own?"

The stricken look on Ryan's face gave me his answer.

"This is between Ethan and us," I continued. "And I'm sorry you got caught in the middle. I promise we'll—" *No. Don't make promises you can't keep. They've been through enough.* "We'll do everything we can to keep us all safe. We're even going to try to find allies on the way. But, Ryan," I lowered my voice, "if we're not back within ten days, you'll need to stop waiting and do what you think is best for Grace and Lily."

"I understand." He seemed exhausted.

I looked back at the others. "Let's get ready. We leave first thing in the morning."

As they hurried away, Fane opened his mouth to speak.

"Don't even think about volunteering to sacrifice yourself, Fane."

"I wasn't—I want to live. I just… Tor might be different. He thinks you're dead." He frowned, marring his perfect skin. "Do you think Kalbir knows you're not?"

The memory of her words to him stung. "If she does, she didn't say. But it doesn't matter. He'll find out soon enough. After that…well, we'll deal with the rest."

Fane didn't look convinced. "Things between the two

of you might be different. If he thought he'd lost you forever then realizes he hasn't…it may change his perspective on the two of you."

"Fane, are you worried? About…us?"

"Do you mean jealous? No, but—"

"You have nothing to worry about." I stood on my tiptoes and kissed him. I still wasn't sure what my relationship with Fane was. Shortly after we met, Tor and I began a romantic relationship, but my ability to control him and my refusal to give it up had caused tension between us. Tor had cut the physical side of our relationship short, but of course, those feelings remained, and given our unique bond, probably always would. We just couldn't see a way to make it work.

With Fane, it was…easier. Our history was less complicated. But under his gorgeous exterior, he was a machine. A fully-sentient, self-aware intelligence, but still…not only was he not human, he wasn't even technically alive. Most of the time I forgot, but when I did remember, it gave me pause. Did it *matter* that he wasn't human? My gut instinct was that no, it didn't. His feelings for me *weren't* a program, like Tor had feared our attraction was. But even if they were, the result was the same.

Red petals on bare skin. Something sticky, something sweet.

I let myself relax into the images, Fane's artilect equivalent of emotions. Created from millions of data, the impressions gave me a quantifiable, near-human approximation of his feelings. He might not have been sure of my feelings, but I was always aware of his, and it was one of the things that made a relationship with him simpler.

I pulled back. *Stop. This isn't the time. Wait until we've got Tor back and you've got the luxury to worry about something like romance.*

It seemed like Fane *could* tell what I was thinking after

515

all. "Now's not a good time, is it?" he asked, smiling ruefully.

My confusion evaporated as I laughed. Whatever happened in the future, we were here now, and I knew all too well how temporary that could be. I linked my hands behind his neck and pulled his face down to mine. "Fane, you're *always* a good time."

***

The next morning, as we stood packed and ready to leave, Ryan, Lily, and Stella huddled together in the brisk early-morning air to wave us off. Lily's eyes were rimmed with red and Stella's were sunken above dark shadows. Ryan was outwardly stoic, but the tense set of his shoulders told me otherwise. I couldn't say I blamed them. We were leaving them, and they knew there was no guarantee we would return, despite our best intentions. Surely after what I'd told Ryan, they'd developed a contingency plan— several, if I knew Lily as well as I thought I did. But still. Their chances of survival were better when we were together.

Unless, of course, you considered the danger we would bring to their door if we succeeded. No matter how I looked at it, in trying to keep us all safe, we were about to make life much more difficult for them.

"I don't think we'll be able to stay in contact with you for more than a day or two. We'll be too far away for radio by the time we reach the compound." I tried to think of something more positive to say but came up empty.

"We'll be fine," Lily said, her voice more confident than her face. "Ailith, if Mil and Lexa are alive—"

Lily had been close to our creators, back when she'd thought they were ordinary scientists who'd survived the apocalypse in their underground lab. When she'd discovered the truth—that they'd not only harbored the cyborgs they'd created but had also been responsible for the silver rain that had killed millions of people in the aftermath of the war—she'd been devastated. It was one of the reasons they'd chosen to leave with us, rather than stay in the relative safety of the compound. Was Lily regretting that decision now? Did living with the people who'd intended to cyberize people against their will seem preferable to taking their chances with us?

"How can you feel for them? After everything they did?" Cindra yanked at the straps on her pack with more force than needed. She'd also been close to Lexa, and the betrayal had cut deep.

Ryan put his arm around Lily's shoulders. "She feels for everyone, you know that." It was true. Lily was one of those people who tried to see the good in everyone and give them the benefit of the doubt. Including us. *And look where that got her.*

"What they did was unforgivable. But the people I knew them as were...different, good. They really were trying to help us build a future. They could still do that here. It would be a second chance for them."

It would actually be a third or fourth chance, but I wasn't going to argue. "I won't make any promises."

Lily nodded, understanding that that was the best she was going to get.

"Where's Grace? Is she angry that we're leaving?"

Grace had seemed agitated yesterday after we'd announced our plans. She'd gone to bed early, which wasn't unusual for her. She'd been temperamental ever since we'd left the Okanagan. Some days she seemed fine and was chatty and interested, asking Cindra to show her how to make various things, or sitting with Fane and quizzing him about being an artilect. Other days she retreated from us, staying withdraw and sullen in her room.

517

"She's upset. She still can't accept that so many people turned on us. She had to leave her friends, her school. And now with you going away... It's too many changes, too fast."

"Well, give her our love when you do see her. Tell her it'll be fine, that we'll be back."

Lily crossed her arms over her chest. "I'll tell her that you'll try your best. I'm tired of making promises to her then letting her down," she said, echoing my earlier thoughts. "When she was a child, it was different. She forgave so easily then."

Fane tried to hide his feelings from me as I followed him down to the beach, but he couldn't stop his apprehension from flashing through my mind.

The scent of burnt coffee. A hedge maze with a single exit. A bird plummeting into the ocean.

They're going to the compound on a rescue mission. This is my chance. Mom and Dad would never let me go, but if I can sneak away, they won't be able to stop me. I'll hide in the back of the boat, and only reveal myself when it's too late for them to turn back. I wish I could send him a message to tell him I'm coming. But then again, that would ruin the surprise. I can't wait to see his face! God, it's so romantic. I hope he takes my face in his hands and kisses me, just like they did in the movies.

—Love, Grace

08
AILITH

As we passed the skeletons of the old olive trees, Pax tucked something under a large rock at the base of one of the trunks. He'd discovered little caches all over the island—notes that people had written and trinkets they'd left, which he gave to Cindra for her growing archive of our history. He'd taken to leaving his own notes and charms all over the island, although when I'd asked him who would ever find them, he'd just shrugged and smiled his enigmatic smile. I was desperate to take it as a good sign that someone might be there in the future, so I didn't ask anything else.

The boat we'd come over to the island in rocked gently against the beach. What would I have done if I'd had a boat when the war started? Would I have jumped in and sailed away, hoping to find safety over the water? Or would I have gone home, braving a firestorm for fear of an even greater unknown?

When we'd reached the coast weeks ago, we'd avoided the major harbor close to Vancouver, one of the first cities to be destroyed in the bombing. Instead, we'd ventured farther south, and it had worked in our favor. In a tiny abandoned coastal resort, we'd found a boat large enough for all of us and our supplies. Best of all, it was hydrogen-powered, gathering its energy from the saltwater itself.

"I wonder what happened to the owners?" Pax had asked. As he did, I saw them, pale specters glancing back over their shoulders as they abandoned their craft. They'd walked into one of the resort villas close by and never left.

I'd kept the information to myself.

Now, as Oliver steered us away from the beach we'd come to call home, I lay on the deck next to Fane and let the briny sea air scour my skin.

"Do you think we'll find any allies on the mainland?" I asked him. When I'd said it to Ryan, it hadn't seemed that unreasonable. But thinking about it now... "I don't want to rely too much on the idea, but—"

"I know you are alive."

"Umbra?" *Shit.* When we'd been unable to find Callum's body, we'd figured she'd probably survived in some form, but we'd hoped fervently that we were wrong.

Fane looked at me sharply.

"They told me everything. How he brought your body back. How they fixed you."

"You're alive? Is Callum?"

Fane gestured to Pax and Cindra to come closer. Oliver must've seen them gathering through the window because he put the boat on an automatic course.

"Yes. And no. He was too fragile."

"You killed him, you mean."

"Yes."

And suddenly, I saw Callum. Or more accurately, I saw *through* him. He lay on the ground next to my body, horrified as my blood soaked into the dusty earth. A cactus had gotten tangled in my hair, and he wanted desperately to pull it out.

"I'm sorry," he wanted to say. He opened his mouth, but only Umbra was there.

Then Tor was upon us, his disbelieving hands trying to put the remains of my skull back together. Watching, I wanted to scream at him to go, to look away, but the time for that had passed weeks ago.

Sobbing, he did the best he could, tying his jacket around my head, leaving only what was left of my face exposed. He gathered me into his arms, cradling my ruined face against his shoulder, then turned and spat on Callum, blinding him. "I'll be back for you, Umbra, I promise you that." He grew smaller and smaller as he lurched away, hoping beyond hope that I could be saved.

Callum lay in the dust, wishing he'd died too, when approaching footsteps shook the ground under his head. A thrill of Umbra's delight swept through him.

"The Saints are here. They have found us."

"This won't turn out the way you think it will, Umbra. I'll never survive long enough for them to do anything with you." Callum tried to hold his breath, his last defense against her.

"Breathe," she demanded and touched a nerve. Searing pain darted through Callum's spine, and he gasped, taking a deep breath.

"They will keep you alive, Callum. As long as it takes. I am their god. The one they have been waiting for."

And they did. For twenty-eight excruciating hours, Callum had lived as the nanites and the Saints fought to keep him breathing until they could find a way to make Umbra flesh. But finally, at the turn of the twenty-ninth hour, Callum won. His heart came to his aid and simply refused to beat any longer. He died with a smile on his lips. He'd finally beaten her, the being he'd once loved so much.

Or so he'd thought. *I'm glad he'd died believing it.* Now, we just had to make sure it came true.

"How are we communicating? You never had that kind of power."

"It does not matter. I want my body."

"Your body?"

"Yes. You took my body."

"We gave you the chance to have this body, Umbra, and you turned it down. It's not yours anymore."

"It is mine. You promised."

"If we're talking, you must've been fixed. You must've been given a body."

"I was."

"So what's the problem?"

"My new body does not...feel."

"What do you mean?"

"I cannot feel. Or taste. It is too primitive."

"You became used to Callum's humanity, and now you can't live without it? How galling for you."

"Yes."

"Well, what a shame you killed him then."

"I want my body."

"It's not your body, Umbra."

There was silence. And then, *"It will be."* And she was gone.

Imagine our surprise when we received a radio transmission from Umbra. It seems our steadfast devotion in the face of false idols has paid off. And she needs our help. The Cyborgists tried to stop us from joining with our Messiah by encasing her in the body of one of their own in a gross mockery of her divinity. But she need not fear. We will find her and release her from her flesh cocoon, allowing her metamorphosis into Divinity.

—Celeste Steed, *The Second Coming*

09
AILITH

I opened my eyes to the others' concerned faces.

"Ailith, what's going on?" Cindra asked.

"Umbra's alive. She just spoke to me." I closed my eyes and pressed my fingertips against the lids. *Just what we need.*

"And Callum?"

"Callum's dead." We'd all assumed, but *knowing* still hit hard. Although none of us had had enough time to really get to know him, through our connection, I'd been privy to some of the most intense moments of his life. Grief and something darker sprouted inside me; before this was over, I would have my reckoning with Umbra.

Oliver, ever practical, was incredulous. "How are you talking to Umbra? It shouldn't be possible."

"She's been…fixed up. I have no idea by whom."

"I do," Fane said. "It means she's also with Ethan. From what Oliver told me, The Saints of Loving Grace don't have the knowledge or equipment to give her a functional body. If the Saints *did* manage to retrieve Callum's body as they'd planned, Umbra could easily have told them about Ethan and his resources. I can't see him or Lien turning down a chance to resurrect even a primitive AI."

The thought of Ethan and the Saints teaming up was chilling.

"Even so, how's it possible that she's speaking to me?"

Oliver looked at me as though I were an idiot. "Ethan's has access to Lexa and Mil's equipment. Plus, don't forget we all came from the same original designs. They likely combined some of Pax's programming and some of Fane's."

"You can't be serious," Cindra said. "Why would they have given her *any* power?"

Fane was thoughtful. "If Ethan's given her special abilities, it must be that they suit an ulterior motive."

"So what does that mean for us? How could he use her against us?"

"To beat Fane, perhaps? What better way to fight an artilect than with an artilect? They know he's not going to come quietly."

"She couldn't beat you, Fane, could she?" Cindra asked.

"I don't know," he replied. "Before all of this, I would've said no. But who knows what they've done to her?" He turned, his expression uneasy. "Pax? Can she beat me?"

"Yes."

"*Does* she beat me?" Fane asked, looking alarmed.

Pax pulled at a loose thread on his sweater then smiled at Fane. "Sometimes."

"Okay, stop. It won't help to worry about this right now." If my nerves stretched any tighter, I would explode. *Could she really defeat Fane? Take my body?* I was very aware that although it was mine now, it hadn't always been.

"You think she's coming for us? God, I need a drink." Oliver hung over the railing as though he were contemplating leaping.

The salty air on my skin was suddenly irritating. I wrapped a blanket around my shoulders. "She might. I don't know how much agency she has. She may not be able to go anywhere without Ethan's will, but she'd never let us know that. Or she might wait and let Ethan do the heavy lifting. I mean, we *are* heading right for them. Maybe she'll just bide her time."

"You'd think she'd have kept quiet then, not let you know she was alive and after your body," Cindra mused.

"Maybe she's more human than you give her credit for. She was built by one, after all," Fane said. "Maybe she just can't resist."

"I don't know if Umbra having human shortcomings makes me feel better or worse," I remarked.

The troubled look Fane gave me made it clear.

Worse. Because impatience might be one of them.

***

We moored the boat in a small, hidden cove then rowed the rest of the way to the tawny sand beach. Before the War, it must've been a popular tourist spot—secluded, with just the right amount of adjacent wilderness to give the illusion of a private island.

If I concentrated, Eire's ability likely would've shown me. But it would've shown me other things as well. Couples watching the sun go down for the last time before wading out to sea, reassuring their children that all would be well if only they didn't hold their breath—too many things I couldn't unsee. I'd thought my ability to see into the minds of other was a curse, but it was nothing compared to Eire's visions of the past.

How did you stand it?

I never left the room I was in, Ailith. The only ghost there was me. Fragments of both Eire and Ella had stayed with me, whispering to me and to each other. The continuing love between them, a love that was almost tangible to me, was the only thing that made having Eire's ability bearable.

We walked a few hundred yards into the camouflaging forest, a habit Tor had taught us, and dropped our gear into a pile.

"Right," Oliver said, pulling a map out of his pack and shaking it open. "Let's figure out a route then start walking. We should be able to get— Oh, for fuck's sake!" he burst out as the map refused to open, tearing instead and leaving him with nothing but a scrap between his fingers.

"Here, let me help you." Cindra stifled a laugh and bent to retrieve the unruly chart.

"Are you still thinking about Umbra?" Fane asked, startling me. He moved even more silently than we did.

"Well, now I am," I replied. "I was thinking of Eire."

"If Umbra does come after us—"

As though on cue, a rustling shook the scrubby undergrowth behind us.

We all dropped into a crouch and froze, scanning the spaces between the wasted trees. Fane held a finger to his lips and crept noiselessly toward the sound. The rest of us tried to melt into the background—another of Tor's lessons. Fane disappeared from sight, and we heard a slight scuffle before he emerged holding the arm of a very bedraggled Grace.

"Looks like we had a stowaway," he said as she glared up at him.

Since we'd taken the only rowboat, she'd had to swim to shore. Her hair hung in dripping ropes, and she shivered despite her defiance.

"Grace! What are you doing here?" Cindra had already untied a blanket from her pack and was shaking it open.

"I want…wanted to help," she said as she begrudgingly accepted the blanket. "Thanks."

I stepped away. The chattering of her teeth dredged up some disturbing memories of Nova's teeth chipping and cracking against each other as she bit at the stale air of the bunker. I closed my eyes. *Breathe. Slowly.*

"Grace, you can't come with us," Cindra said, her voice kind but firm. "Your parents are going to be worried sick. They must've discovered you're missing by now."

"I'm a grown woman." A deep blush spread across her cheeks.

"Grace, it's not about that. It's about it being dangerous. You must know that. Our abilities protect us."

"I… I thought if I helped you, you would turn me into one of you. Then I would have abilities, and I could—"

"Oh, Grace. We can't. And even if we could, it's too dangerous. You've seen what our life is like. You have to go home." Cindra's tone was low and reassuring, but Grace collapsed as though Cindra had struck her.

She began to cry. Cindra knelt and hugged her thin shoulders while Oliver and Pax stood awkwardly to the side, unsure of where to look.

"Why do you want to be a cyborg?" I asked, as gently as I could.

"Do you have any idea what it's like? How *small* I feel? I'm scared to live in this world and not be special. It means I won't survive. I'm too small," she repeated brokenly.

"Grace, I'm so, so sorry," I said as she clung to Cindra and sobbed.

"So what are we going to do now?" Oliver asked. "We can't take her with us, and we can't leave her here. We'll have to turn back." I hoped Grace didn't see the annoyance on his face.

527

"Or she could come with us. She *should* come." Pax was looking at Grace with a new interest. One I didn't like.

"Pax, did you know she was going to come?" I asked him. *Damn it, Pax.*

"It was a possibility."

"And you didn't tell us because you knew we would stop her?" I asked, even though I knew the answer.

He nodded solemnly.

"I thought you didn't want to keep getting involved. Ryan and Lily are—"

"I promise I'll do what you say," Grace interrupted, her eyes suddenly dry.

Hmmm. "Why do you *really* want to come with us, Grace? If you know that we can't make you a cyborg and that you're going to spend days hiking directly into danger, why do you still want to come?"

I could almost see her mind working as she tried to come up with a more convincing story. My own parents must've seen that look on my face many times.

"Grace?" I imitated my mother, using her best no-nonsense voice.

Her shoulders slumped as she gave up. "I need to see him," she whispered.

"Him?" For a moment, I was confused. "Do you mean Tor?"

She started to shake her head as though to deny it then gave up. "Yes." A rosy blush bloomed on her cheeks, and she kept her eyes on the ground.

Oh my god, does she have a crush on Tor? Is she in love with him? For her to be willing to risk her life for him, she must be. Not for the first time, I wished I could talk to the others with my mind, rather than just seeing through them. *What do we do now?* I glanced at Cindra, who shook her head.

If Pax believes she's important...

"Okay, fine, Grace. You can come. But you have to do

exactly what we tell you, and—"

"I will!" She shot to her feet. "You won't regret it, I swear. I love him—" She gasped for breath as another sob shook her.

Did I have that much passion at sixteen?

I looked at Cindra again, and this time, she shrugged. Over her shoulder, Pax nodded.

Grace smiled through her tears, rubbing her sleeve over her face. "I promise I'll help you. I won't be a burden."

I didn't like it. If Pax thought she needed to come, it meant she was going to play a role, and yet again, we might sacrifice someone for our cause. Because the truth was, in terms of the bigger picture, she *was* expendable, just like she'd feared. *Poor Ryan and Lily.* What would they do when they discovered her missing?

"We'd better go back to the boat and radio your parents, Grace. The last thing they need right now is even more worry." I started walking back the way we'd come. "It won't take long."

"No," said Grace quickly. "You can't."

"Don't worry. I promise you can come with us. I just want them to know you're all right."

"It's not that," she said, her face darkening from rose to crimson. "I trashed the radio. Just in case you didn't let me come with you, I didn't want you to be able to call them." She crossed her arms over her chest.

"For fuck's sake, Grace, do you have any idea—" Oliver's harsh tone made her flinch.

"I'm sorry, I just—" Tears shone in her eyes again.

"We have to get going." Cindra was looking at the sky. "We need to get at least part of the way before we camp for the night.

Cindra was right. Whatever had happened, we couldn't worry about it now.

Pax pointed to a place on Oliver's torn map. "Here," he

said, his finger landing on a spot that looked just like a million others. "We need to be *right here*."

Helene Island Geocache #1

Hi. My name is Pax. I don't know if anyone will ever find this, since I don't know what our ultimate timeline will be, BUT, if everything goes the way it should, you will find this, so I've tried to make it as weatherproof as possible. I hope things haven't been too difficult for you. I did my best, but things didn't always turn out the way we planned.

10
WILLIAM

Day: 2000 A.W.
"For those of you folks who are just joining us, the A.W. stands for both Artilect War and After War. Clever, really."

I rapped my knuckles on smooth, cold metal. The resulting ding was disappointing—more of a donk and not at all the resonating flourish I'd hoped for. It didn't penetrate the darkness further than my own hand.

It was still just Lars and me. Good old Lars. Every day he went a little madder. I guess he hadn't made provisions for that part of his plan. Oh, Lars, you mad, mad bastard. But maybe I was mad too.

"Or maybe, and this is a big maybe, folks, Lars is the sane one here and I'm the one whose mind has gone." It was possible.

"I wish you all would stop playing dead—unless you really are dead." Sometimes I wished I was. But God, who knew what Lars would do to me then? If I were lucky, he wouldn't even notice.

"But I'm not dead. Not yet, anyway. Just stuck here with Lars and the rest of you in this oubliette. How do I know that word? Oubliette?" I tapped again on the metal casing. *"It doesn't matter.*

531

Soon, I'll play dead too. And before long, I actually will be." I grinned into the dark.

"And then you, fine folks, you and Lars will have to find other entertainment." The silence made me reconsider.

"Although, my death might be the only entertainment you need. You can talk about it amongst yourselves for years to come. The final curtain."

Should today be the day? How should I take my bow?

"Shall we have a vote?" I took their silence as assent. "Slit my wrists?" No. Knowing my luck, I'd do it wrong, and just a get a nasty infection. Then Lars would have to take care of me. And from what I'd heard of him mumbling to himself, I definitely didn't want his ministrations.

Although, the delirium of infection might be a nice vacation for me.

"Starvation?" I didn't think that would be possible. Too many supplies here. And again, Lars. He knew how to keep people alive on very little.

Plus, who was I kidding? I knew I could never starve; I was rather short on willpower.

"Will Power. Ha! Get it? Maybe I should change my last name. We'll vote on that one later." I felt through the blackness, my fingers coming to rest on snaking coils of cable.

"Electrocution? Now we're talking. Of course, that would leave you all in the lurch, wouldn't it? Though it might wake a few of you up."

I waited for a reply, just in case. Nothing.

"Maybe we'll just put this vote to the side for a day or two. No need to be hasty, right?"

Not a single dissenting voice.

"I'm glad we all agree. That's why I like you guys so much." Strains of orchestral music and the low hum of voices filtered through the gloom.

"That's enough chitchat. I can hear the band striking up. It looks like it's time for another party. Well, God knows we've got a lot to

celebrate." I felt my way to the door then turned back.

"I've got work to do. Shall we meet tomorrow? Same time, same place?" I cupped my hand over my ear.

"What? Of course, I'll still be here. Oubliette, remember?"

No way out.

I don't know whether to be proud or devastated by Fane's betrayal. On the one hand, he's condemning the human race. On the other, he's exercising the free will, the sentience, that eluded us for so long. We achieved what we set out to. Perhaps it's my pride that's hurt. That our success was singular, one man, and that the world will never know. Perhaps I'm like a disappointed parent, whose star athlete child runs off to join the circus instead. Perhaps. But I am a diligent parent, and like any other diligent parent, I will do the responsible thing— I will get him back. Perhaps I'm revealing my own hypocrisy here. For if I truly believed I'd created life, could I own it? Or am I revealing what the Terrans s believed all along, that playing God was what was most important?

—*Ethan Strong, personal diary*

II
AILITH

I started awake with a gasp, the cyborg's words ringing in my head. His voice had been strange, almost muffled.

Who is William? Something nagged at the back of my mind. William. Maybe Pax would know. After all, he'd been the one who'd insisted on camping here. Did he know something was going to happen? If so, why hadn't he told me?

"Pax? Are you awake?" Nothing. *"Pax!"* Nope. He slept like the dead. Whatever the mystery was, it would have to wait until morning.

"Fuck," I said to no one in particular.

"Ailith?" Fane ducked his head through the tent flap. Since he didn't need to sleep the way we did, he'd been standing guard. "What's wrong?"

"I think there's another cyborg here, one who's been here since the war. He called himself William. I think Pax knew about him, and that's why he wanted us to camp here." *Now, why is the name William so familiar? Come on, Ailith, think.*

It hit me. William. Nova. William was the cyborg who was supposed to have been in the bunker with Oliver. "William was one of the cyborgs in our generation. We'd thought he was dead. Why would he be out here, of all places? And he referred to a man named Lars and some others."

"Others? Cyborgs?" Fane slipped into the tent and sat next to me on top of the covers.

Something else was bothering me. Lars. *Lars. Oh my god.* "It can't be," I said. And yet, the coincidence was too great.

"It can't be what?" Fane asked. "Other cyborgs?"

"No, Lars."

"I don't follow."

"Nova. Before Oliver killed Nova, I saw her past. She worked as a caregiver for CIVRS addicts."

"The virtual reality system addicts? She was a caregiver?"

"Yes and no. They did...other things to them as well." I shook my head at his raised eyebrows. "You don't want to know. But she was there, just before she became a cyborg, delivering a baby. The doctor's name was Lars. But I don't think he was a real doctor." I thought back. *The front door opened; Lars had arrived. We nodded to each other. "Nurse." He knew damn well I wasn't a nurse, no more than he was a doctor. He worked for the government, same as me.*

"Could he be the reason Nova was in the bunker with Oliver instead of William? She didn't seem to know it was

535

going to happen, either of the times I was inside her."

They told me I was going to change the course of the world, that I had an extraordinary purpose. I would be the savior of the human race. I wouldn't end up like my wards, forgotten, degraded. No, I would be remembered forever.

And then, when she'd woken up: *I wasn't supposed to be here, in this shitty bunker. I should've been with them, carrying out my mission. Buying my freedom. Not trapped here, underground with him.*

"Whatever this Lars's involvement, I don't think Nova knew about it."

"And there are definitely others there? Do you think they could be the others involved in the switch? From what Oliver was telling me about Pantheon Modern security, it would have to have taken more than one person." He ran his hand down my spine.

"I don't know. It was a bit strange. He said it was just him and Lars, but then he spoke to the others. Only, no one answered."

Fane frowned. "He must've been speaking to himself."

"Maybe. But then he said they were having a party, and I heard voices." *Could there be others like us? Alive?*

"So other people, but not cyborgs?"

"No. I'd be able to tell if there were. Besides, Lexa and Mil said we were the only cyborgs of our generation who survived." Fane raised an eyebrow at me. "Yes, I know they've lied before, but why lie about that? Maybe it's doomsday preppers or something. But why would William be with them?"

"If he's a cyborg, why haven't you heard him before?"

It was a good question. William was close. So why *hadn't* I heard him before? His thread was there—subdued, but present. "The connection felt a bit strange. A bit muted. Almost like—" Then it hit me. "Fane, I think he's underground. But there must be something else to it, because I could still link to the others when *they* were underground." I slipped out of the covers and put on my boots. "We've got to find him. If he's been trapped down there against his will all this time, he may be the ally we're looking for. Even if he isn't, he's one of us. Hurry, let's go wake the others."

"Wait until morning. It's the middle of the night, Ailith," he reminded me. "Everyone needs the rest. Besides, we should wait for what little light we can get. Stumbling around in the dark isn't going to make finding them any easier, *especially* if they aren't friendly."

He was right, but still. "I can't sleep, Fane." I had too many questions. Was William okay? He'd seemed a little...eccentric. Had they done something to him? Or was it just a side effect of being trapped underground all this time? How did he get there? And who were the others with him? My head threatened to explode.

"Well, I *don't* sleep. So why don't we distract each other?"

"You're supposed to be on guard."

"I'll keep my head outside the tent door."

"Fane—"

The brush of a butterfly's wings against a trumpet of foxglove.

He ran his strong hands over my bare back. *When did I take my shirt off?* I closed my eyes, glorying in the sensation. Although his skin felt like human skin, the palms of his hands and his fingers were completely smooth. They slid over me while images poured from him.

Sweet seeds of anise scattered on white linen.

I pressed into him, guiding him over onto his back and pinning his arms over his head. He grinned; this was his favorite position because it had been his first. The first time we'd ever actually slept together, the first time he'd ever slept with anyone. Even now, a hint of the same wonder crept over his face, and his lips parted in a very human

537

gasp.

He'd been built to resemble a man in every way, from his physique to the sensations he felt.

The perfect symmetry of a dahlia.

I straddled him, and he arched his hips as I guided him in, knotting his fists in the blanket behind his head.

The sharp scent of ginger, the bite of nutmeg.

His self-control lasted for only a few more seconds then he grabbed my hips and rocked into me as he sat up, wrapping his arms around me, pressing one hand into my lower back as though he could bring us even closer, gripping the back of my neck with the other. I moved my hips against his, and he threw his head back with an unselfconscious cry.

A trailing bouquet, held in trembling hands.

Helene Island Geocache #17

Jen,

I hope to God you find this. I waited for you as long as I could, but I can't wait any longer. Things are getting crazy here. I'm going to take the boat over to Dione Island, even though it's also gone dark. Please, if you find this, meet me there. I'll wait for you. And whatever you do, STAY OUT OF THE RAIN.

Shel.

12
AILITH

Even with our distraction, Fane and I were sitting around the campfire when the others emerged bleary-eyed and rubbing their hands together.

Oliver could tell immediately that something had happened. "All right, out with it, A. You're practically vibrating. What happened? What great evil do we face now?"

"Is it William?" Pax asked.

"Yes. You *knew* we'd meet William?"

"Not exactly. It was one of the possible paths, it just wasn't a very likely one. This is interesting. This is opening up futures I haven't seen before." Pax's expression softened, taking on a dreamy quality.

"Wait. Do you mean *our* William? The one Nova replaced?" Oliver put the pieces together much quicker than I had.

"Yes. I think so," I said. "But—"

"Then where is he?" Oliver asked, looking around as though he expected William to be hiding in the bushes.

"Somewhere around here. I *think* he's underground. He... His communication was sort of muffled. But he's close. We just have to find him."

"Are we sure we want to? Do we need to risk any more enemies at this point? I mean, we don't know what his involvement with big switcheroo was."

I couldn't blame Oliver for that. We certainly had a habit of making enemies everywhere we went.

"No, but we need allies," Cindra said. "If he's a cyborg like us *and* one of our generation, this could be a good thing."

"Kalbir was also one of us," Oliver reminded her. "Maybe he was complicit. Or maybe he's a lunatic? What if that's why he's down there? Maybe something went wrong with his cyberization."

Given William's thoughts when I was inside him, that was a distinct possibility. Or, if he wasn't disturbed before, living underground in a bunker for five years may have taken its toll. But he'd said he wasn't alone.

Fane cleared his throat and gave me an expectant look.

Oliver crossed his arms over his chest. "What are you not telling us?"

I kept my expression bland. "I'm not sure what you mean." Oliver would never agree to go looking for William if he thought there were others.

"Fane is an artilect," Oliver pointed out. "His throat doesn't get dry."

I glared at Fane. *Judas.* "Fine. There might be other people down there with William."

Oliver was incredulous. "*What?* And you want to jeopardize us and Tor by bursting in on a bunch of—well,

540

we don't even know what they are." He shook his head vehemently. "No. No way."

"Oliver—" I began.

"We can't leave him." Pax had drawn himself up to his full height, making him nearly six inches taller than Oliver. "If we can find William...we *need* to find William."

"See," I said to Oliver. "If Pax says—"

"*If Pax says,*" Oliver mimicked me. "We can't put ourselves into danger just because *Pax says*. How many times are we going to do this?"

"Until we end this. Look, I trust Pax. If he says we need William, I believe him. I don't think William chose to be there. I think he needs our help." I glanced around, entreating the others for support. "And like Cindra said, he might be the ally we need."

"He will be," Pax replied.

"See," I said to Oliver. "Pax—"

"Pax says." Oliver threw his hands in the air. "Unbelievable. You can't help yourself, can you? Did your parents never teach you about the consequences of sticking your nose in where it doesn't belong?"

"Oliver," I pleaded, "I think this is important. I need you to trust me."

"Ailith, it's not you I don't trust. But we need to pick our battles." He sighed and uncrossed his arms. "I know for a fact that we're going to regret this." He looked at Pax. "Right?"

Pax beamed at him. "A little bit."

Oliver covered his face with his hands and swore softly to himself.

Fane patted him on the back then turned to me. "Is there any chance this could be a trick?"

"I can't say for sure. But I don't think so. Look, I know Oliver might be right and we should just keep going and pretend we didn't hear him. But I can't. If nothing else, he's one of us. Something happened to him, and he's been wherever he is ever since the war started. *Awake.* I don't know about you, but I wouldn't want to be abandoned if someone had the choice."

Mind you, being trapped with Tor in a bunker for the rest of my life wouldn't have been the worst fate. I hadn't woken in our bunker; Tor had busted us out shortly after the firestorm of the war was over and taken my body to safety. But Cindra, Pax, and Oliver had, and from their pinched expressions, they remembered the feeling all too well.

"It's settled then," Fane said. "Let's start searching."

"What exactly are we searching for?" asked Grace. She looked eager and ready to help.

"Well, any entrance will be hidden. It'll probably be a bunker. Look for any natural feature, like a hill or a hollow—something that could be concealed," Oliver explained.

We split up to explore. Luckily for us, there were very few natural features in the area that could've hidden an entranceway. Within minutes we'd found it—the remains of what looked like an old, crumbled stone well, partially overgrown with spongy moss and the curling vines of an odd, twisting plant.

Set into the ground, the weathered metal door looked undisturbed, the moss encroaching over the control panel and around the spokes of the wheel. We set to work, tearing the grass up by the roots and clearing away the artfully placed debris.

"This looks like our bunker, doesn't it, Pax?" Cindra asked him once we'd exposed the entire door. He nodded, uncharacteristically solemn. "Did yours look the same?" she asked Oliver and me.

"Tor had moved me by the time I woke up," I said. "And Oliver blew his up."

Cindra snorted as Oliver glared at me. "That doesn't

surprise me."

Oliver tugged on the door wheel, trying his luck, but it wouldn't turn. He swore under his breath and prodded at a few random keys on the control pad. When it lit up, he swore again, this time in surprise.

"It actually still works. But since it's completely intact, we're going to need the code." He typed in several strings of numbers then sighed. "You guys may as well make yourself comfortable. This is going to take a few minutes. Unless, Pax, you can come somehow see what code we used to get in?"

Pax shook his head. "Sorry."

"No worries, it was a long shot. Right, kids, settle down and let me work my magic."

"I'll help," Fane offered, and the two of them set to work.

Cindra and I found a spot in the grass free of the twisting plants and leaned back against a large rock. Cindra closed her eyes.

"I'm going to leave some more of my notes," Pax said. "I brought a bunch of them with me. I won't go far," he said before we could protest. He wandered off, searching for a good hiding place.

"Cindra, I'm going to see if I can connect with Tor again."

"Okay," she murmured, already half asleep. "I might have a little nap."

Tor's familiar thread was easy to find among the others, the flicker replaced by a steadier glow. I took a deep breath and followed it.

Our Divine has turned out to be somewhat of a disappointment, at least for now. She has been corrupted by her time spent in unclean flesh, her head turned toward corporeal pleasures. But I am steadfast in my belief that, given the right environment, she will again regain her superiority. After all, sometimes even Saviors need help. She does not like the body we have given her, despite how fitting it is for her, both terrible and beautiful at the same time. No, she favors the disgusting body of a cyborg, distracted by the temptations of the mundane. She will soon realize how mistaken she is.

—Celeste Steed, *The Second Coming*

13

TOR

I must still have been sedated, because everything was slightly fuzzy and slow, like I was trying to move through water. They'd put me in her room. In the bed that still smelled of her. I ran my fingers down the rose-gold walls and tried to remember.

The last time we'd been in this room together, I'd sat next to her, willing her to wake up, and not for the first time. Umbra's virus had infected all of us, but it had hit Ailith the hardest, and she'd hovered between life and death, oblivious to the chaos around her. Or so we'd thought. When she'd woken, we fought because I'd let Kalbir live after killing her father. Our last words in this room had been of anger and resentment, and so many other things were left unsaid.

And now she was gone. I'd imagined life without her before, and it had hurt. But now that she was dead, there was no pain. There was nothing, just a vast, hollow space. The pain was still there, I was sure of it, lingering at the edges and waiting for its chance to pounce. When it finally did, I would be glad. I needed to feel something to honor her, even if it killed me.

The framed picture of her and her family still stood on the dresser next to the bed, and I cradled it against my chest, ignoring the sharp edges of the frame. In it, she stood with her family, all now dead. Her face was reddened from too much sun, and her smile wide and slightly crooked. She looked present, fully in her time and place. The girl in the picture was not the woman I knew, but the soft new seed before it had hardened under layers of chaff.

Most of her clothes were still here, so I pulled a few of the softer things out of the drawers and piled them on the bed. I lay on my side and wrapped my arms around her pillow, letting the sedative pull me down into it. I could pretend she was here. I shouldn't, but just for a moment, I couldn't deny myself.

The day she'd awoken, when I'd looked into her eyes for the first time. I'd already been in love with her for years by then.

The first time we'd kissed, the air coppery from the deer she'd killed.

The first time we'd made love, the taste of her mingled with poisoned water.

The last time, the desperation of it, as though we'd known it would be the last. That the end was coming.

The door opened.

"Enjoying yourself?" Kalbir stood in the doorway, a smirk curling her lips as she took in the jumble of sheets and t-shirts.

"Why did you put me here? Why not in my own room?" I already knew the answer. Kalbir was a formidable woman, but she did have a spiteful streak.

"I thought this would be more amusing," she said, barely concealing her mirth.

"Go away, Kalbir." I turned my back to her and hugged the picture frame again.

"That's no way to talk to your best friend." Her footsteps on the carpet were soft, like a cat's. A feral, hungry cat with very sharp teeth.

"You're not my friend." Stop answering her. Just ignore her, and she'll get bored and go away.

"I'm the closest thing you've got, Tor."

I couldn't help it. I turned back to face her. "Why are you here? Did Ethan finally get tired of you?"

"Don't be ridiculous. He knows when he's onto a good thing." *She grinned, running her tongue over her teeth.*

"I'm sure he does." *I rolled my shoulders, cracking the bones in my neck with a savage pleasure. "Why am I still here? Why continue to drug me?"* *My voice grew louder as my irritation broke through.* Stop. Don't give her the satisfaction.

She was satisfied. She leaned back, triumphant. "You're not going anywhere."

"But I thought you wanted me to retrieve Fane? I can hardly do that here, doped up to my eyeballs," *I pointed out.*

"Don't worry, you're serving your purpose as we speak. Now that we've let you be conscious enough, anyway. I'm sure he's on his way here."

What did that mean? *By "retrieve," I'd assumed she'd meant that I was to go after him. "Why would Fane come here? He knows Ethan is after him, and he knows what he'll do to him. He'd never be that stupid. Or that sentimental. It's not like we were the best of friends."* *It was true. I respected Fane, admired him, even. But his interest in Ailith had made things complicated. Though looking back now, it seemed ridiculous. The jealousy that had spurred me into attacking him was gone. I just wished she'd lived to see it.*

"No, you're right, he wouldn't be. Although, he is pretty damn sentimental for a machine."

"Better not let Ethan hear you say that."

"Don't steal my thunder, Tor. What I was going to say is that he wouldn't, but she *would."*

The drugs had confused me more than I'd thought. Couldn't make sense of what she was saying. "She? Cindra?"

Kalbir glanced at the doorway then dropped her voice to a conspiratorial whisper. "I'm not supposed to tell you this... But seeing how you can't do anything about it—and also to prove to you that I'm not the monster you think I am—you're bait, Tor. Ailith is alive. Fane goes where Ailith goes. And we both know she'll come for you."

Helene Island Geocache #4

Shel,

I don't know where you are. I made it back from the mainland to find you and you were gone. Whatever happened here...I can't stay. I'm going to find a boat and go to Dione Island. If you find this, please, come there. I promise I'll be there. I just wish it wasn't so dark. I love you.

Jen.

14
AILITH

Relief blossomed in my chest. *He knows I'm alive.* Being inside him, feeling the void I'd left behind, was like walking naked into a desert storm, stinging shards of memory and loss peeling away my skin then my flesh then even my bones, until nothing was left.

What would he do now? *Please be smart, Tor. Play along, wait for us.* As drugged as he was, I didn't think he had many choices. It had been difficult to understand his thoughts through the haze of sedatives at first, but the rawness of his emotions had been painfully clear.

"Is Tor okay?" Cindra asked. She'd rolled over onto her side and was watching me, her head propped on her hand.

"Yes... No... But at least he knows I'm alive." *What would be worse for him? Thinking I was dead, or knowing I was purposefully walking into a trap. For him.*

She let out a long breath. "I'm glad, Ailith. I... It was awful when he brought you back. I've never seen anyone as broken."

I didn't want to know. The thought of his grief was almost more than I could bear. Tor and I had had only each other in the beginning, and that had bound us as tightly as our encoded bond. A world without him was not something I could understand, and he would feel the same.

Oliver and Fane still huddled by the bunker, Oliver rubbing his forehead as though trying to open the door with his mind.

"Where's Pax?"

"Over there." Cindra tilted her head toward where Pax sat idly playing with some of the twisted grass. He gazed far off into the distance, into another time and place.

"It must be so strange for him, traveling down all those future paths," Cindra remarked. "I wonder what it's like. Do you think it's like when you see the past?"

"I don't think so. I see...almost ghosts, I guess. Fragments of images of things that were there or that happened. But I see them outside of myself, like pale holograms. Everything Pax sees happens in his mind."

Although Pax and I shared a unique two-way link, I'd only ever seen one of his futures, and then, only when he'd remembered it for me.

Different emotions flitted across his face as we watched. Wonder, fear, understanding.

"Yeah, I bet it's incredible. It's just a shame it's not a bit more concise," I grumbled.

"He feels bad about it, you know," she said.

"Bad about what?" I'd always tried not to put too much pressure on Pax to use his ability to guide us—the variables simply evolved too fast, and there was nothing he could do to change that.

"About not being able to help you more with making

decisions or telling you what's going to happen and so on. I know he feels responsible for some of the things that have happened. And guilty, although he'd never want us to know."

"He shouldn't feel that way. And I hope I haven't *made* him feel that way. Believe me, I know what it's like to have unpredictable abilities. I never fully understand what I see either."

"That's odd," Oliver said.

"What is?" Cindra and I stood, pulling out blades of grass that had twisted their way into our clothes.

"Well, it's a Cyborgist code signature, but it looks like it's been tampered with."

"What do you think that means?" Cindra asked.

"I have no idea." He looked troubled, unusual for him.

"Can you open it?" I asked.

"We already have." Fane gave the wheel an experimental turn, and the locking mechanism groaned and slid in response. A series of rasping movements later, the seal on the door gave way with an exasperated grunt. "Are you ready?"

No. If I never went down into a bunker again, it would be too soon. I could tell from the others' faces that they felt the same.

Fane didn't wait for a response. A hiss and a whoosh, and the door opened into darkness.

***

"At least my bunker had stairs," Oliver grumbled as we descended the ladder cautiously, our hands slick on the smooth rungs. The air was stale but held no other odors, and I allowed myself to relax a little. After we'd all cleared the ladder and stepped onto the pressed concrete floor, a sound echoed from somewhere down below, so faint it was nearly inaudible.

"Can anyone else hear that?" I asked. We all held our breath. Nothing but cold silence and the sensation of the earth pressing all around us.

And the rumble of Pax's stomach.

"Sorry," he whispered. There was a rustle as he pulled a packet from his pocket.

"Pax!"

"Sorry," he mumbled again, chewing with exaggerated slowness. Fane suppressed a grin. My nerves were so tightly strung I wanted to knock their heads together.

"What did you think you heard?" Cindra asked.

"It was music," Fane said. "I heard it too."

"Should we make some noise or something? What if we spook William or whoever else is down there?" I asked.

"Yeah, but do we really want to give them a heads up?" Oliver challenged. "It might be better to catch them off their guard."

"Not if we want him to trust us. William is one of us, Oliver, and we *are* looking for allies," I reminded him. "He might be more inclined to become one if we don't go sneaking up on him. The man's been down here for *years*."

Oliver gave an irritated sigh. "Suit yourself, then."

The faint echo began again.

"William?" I called. The echo stopped.

"He knows we're here," I whispered.

At the end of the domed tunnel was another door. A keypad similar to the one outside was mounted on the wall next to it. "Shit. Do you think we'll need another code?" The thought of waiting here in the tunnel underground while Oliver fumbled with another lock pulled my nerves even tighter.

Oliver typed in a combination, and the lock clicked back. "Nope. It looks like the internal code is the same as ours." Surprise warred with the smugness in his voice.

551

"Ready?"

We'd let whoever was on the other side of the door know we were here and given them a chance to prepare. *Whoever William turns out to be, I hope he's willing to listen first. Maybe Oliver was right.* It was too late now.

"Let me go through first," Fane said.

Oliver bowed and stood aside as Fane opened the door and stepped into the room. For a couple of heartbeats, we heard nothing then Fane said: "You may as well come in."

We filed through the doorway and into the main room of the bunker. The space was small, similar to the ones the others had woken up in, except for one thing.

The bunker was pristine, as though no one had ever been there. And maybe no one had. The room was empty.

"What the fuck? There's no one here," Oliver said, all smugness gone.

"William?" I called again, louder than before.

"What? Like he's hiding under the bed?" Oliver asked snidely before shrugging and dropping to his knees to have a look.

I checked William's thread—it was there, brighter than before.

"He's definitely here," Pax and I said at the same time.

"Well, where is he then?"

"It doesn't look like this bunker's been used. Could it be a fake, like the mineshaft at the compound?" Cindra asked.

Oliver shrugged "It's worth a try. Fane? Any super-robot powers? Infrared? Sonar?"

"No. Unfortunately, they made me as human as possible. In this situation, I'm as completely incompetent as you are." His smile as Oliver glared at him was benign.

We started searching for another door, tracing our fingers over the walls and the floor, looking for anything that seemed out of place. Nothing.

"It's a tiny room. How could we miss it?" I asked Grace as she stood next to me.

"You...the others...you lived in a place like this? For years?"

"Not exactly," I replied. "We were asleep. Pax, Cindra, and Oliver woke up in theirs, but they escaped shortly afterward. Tor took me out of ours long before I ever woke up."

"Tor stayed with you? Even though it was dangerous? He could've left you, and he didn't?" Her voice was wistful.

Yes, he did. "He's a good man," I said.

"I wish he...that I knew a man like him," she replied.

"I'm sure you will, one day," I said. *Awkward.*

She looked at me for a long moment then started to speak. "I—"

A crash from the closet cut her off.

"I think I found something," Pax called.

Grace flashed me a half-smile and looked away.

Pax was right—the back of the closet was false. After some yanking and cursing from Oliver, we slid it aside to reveal a long, sloping hallway. Motion lights flickered along the floor at intermittent points, guiding us to yet another door at the far end. A *sealed* door. Oliver's shoulders slumped.

"Let's try it the old-fashioned way this time," I said. I knocked on it. "William? Are you there?" No answer. I changed tack. "William, we *know* you're there. We're not here to hurt you. We're like you." I looked at the others, getting only shrugs in return.

I tried again. "I'm Pantheon Modern Cyborg Program Omega, cyborg number O-117-9791. Hello?"

"Hello?" A tentative voice spoke from the other side of the door. *Not* William's voice. I shook my head at the others.

Oliver didn't get the hint. "Yeah, are you William?

Look, mate, we—" He stopped as I waved my hands.

There was a faint hissing, and we stepped back, expecting the door to unlock and swing open.

Instead, my face began to feel strange, like I was wearing someone else's skin. I reached up to touch it and couldn't feel my fingers. Around me, the others were doing the same.

It was a trap.

"Get out. *Get out!*" I pushed Grace back the way we'd come. Fane reached the door first, yanking on it so hard I thought he would tear it off its hinges.

It didn't move. Fane looked down at his hands with an expression so bewildered it would've been comical in another situation.

The hissing continued over our heads through a small vent near the top of the corridor. "There!" I pointed. "That vent. Something's coming through. We have to—" I staggered. "We—" *Something. We have to do something.* My hand slid uselessly off the wall as I fell to my knees. "Pax—"

"It'll be okay, Ailith. We have to go this way. We have to—" His eyes rolled back as he passed out.

"Why does this keep happening?" Oliver muttered as his head dropped to his chest. "Why—"

The last thing I saw was Fane's terrified face in an all-too-human struggle not to submit. He lost the struggle, and so did I.

Cindra,

If you're reading this, I'm sorry. I know it wasn't my fault, but I'm sorry because I want you to always be happy. My mother used to tell me that was impossible, that nobody can be happy all the time. I suppose it's true. In case something happened to him, and to me, he wanted me to make sure you knew how much he loved you. He told me that you saved him, that you fixed something in him that broke the day he was born. He didn't write this himself because he thought he would do it wrong. I told him I would do it wrong too, but he said even if I did, you would understand.

Pax.

15

AILITH

"Drink, madam?"

Two waiters stood before me, both offering a golden tray of crystal flutes filled with a pale liquid so sparkling it blinded me.

I blinked.

The two waiters merged into one. "Drink, madam?" he repeated.

I shut my eyes again and counted to five before opening them.

"Are you all right, madam?" He was still there, leaning

forward and eying me quizzically. He was an older man with heavy jowls, his meager hair neatly parted and combed over his spotted scalp. He was dressed formally in a black suit with a buttoned-down white shirt and blue bowtie.

"Where am I?" I asked him. I tried to think back. *The hallway. Hissing. Fane, afraid.* He was never afraid. "Where are the others?" My voice came out feeble and pathetic.

"Perhaps madam has already imbibed enough this evening." He jowls wobbled with mirth as he held the tray out of my reach.

"Where are the others?" I ground out, my voice gaining strength as I tried to step forward. *I can't move.* Only my hands seemed to be loose.

"Why, they're here, of course." He gave a shallow bow from his waist and stepped aside, gesturing elegantly with his white-towel-draped arm.

Nearly everything in the room was blue. All through the vast room, strangers milled and mingled in front of cerulean tapestries under soaring sapphire-blue arches, chatting to one another as they quaffed the effervescent liquid and plucked morsels of food off cobalt tables. Their clothing was odd, made from rich, formal fabrics tailored into strangely infantile designs, all in shades of blue. An orchestra sat against one wall, a lilting childish lullaby rising and falling from their instruments.

The partygoers wore masks…at least, I hoped they were masks. Modeled after human infants, they each had an exaggerated feature—obscenely large, wet-looking lips, bald, blue-veined pates, corpulent, fleshy cheeks that obscured their eyes. The braziers burning around the room distorted the shadows playing over them.

Waiters like the one before me wove in and out of the crowds, disappearing into one group and appearing out the other side, their trays empty. *I must be dreaming.* I pressed fingernails into my palms to wake myself up as the melody

556

of the music taunted me.

"The others I came here with. Where are they?" My voice rose, and several of the guests turned to look at me. A woman whose mask had two elongated bottom teeth tilted her head and giggled.

My head was held fast by a weighted band, but from the corner of my eye, I made out what looked a smooth metal frame lined with blue padding, like a coffin.

My waiter friend leaned in again. "If madam would like to join the party, I suggest she lower her voice. We expect our guests to be on their best behavior."

"Guest? I'm not a guest. I'm a prisoner—"

"Madam," he warned, and his voice changed, becoming rough and uncultured. "I could always *remove* you."

"*Ailith?*"

"*Pax? Oh my god, you're alive. Where are you? What the hell is going on?*"

"*I'm here, at the party. The food's not real.*"

"*What?*" I choked back a hysterical laugh. Only Pax could wake up in this situation and be thinking about the food. His normalcy was like a slap in the face. *Think, Ailith. Pax is alive. The others might be too. Play along.* "*Pax, I'm coming to find you.*"

"I'm so sorry," I said, giving the waiter my most apologetic smile. "I'm not accustomed to such extravagant affairs. I'm afraid it's gone to my head a bit. But I'm fine now."

He eyed me suspiciously. "Are you sure? We don't tolerate uncouth behavior here."

"I promise. I would like to rejoin the party, please."

For a moment, it seemed as though he was going to refuse then he sighed and moved his arm off to the side, out of my sight.

"I'll trust you, madam, but if I see any signs of your former vulgarity, I shall eject you from the venue."

There was a click, and the weight on my forehead disappeared. I tested my arms and legs and found I could move them again. "Thank you—?"

"Arnold," he replied, bowing again. "Oh. And please leave your mask on." His smile was benign, but his tone was heavy with threat.

"I will, thank you. *Arnold.*" I inclined my head graciously. "Excuse me." As I moved away from him toward the dazzling crowd, I glanced back. Arnold stood in front of a tall metal capsule. Just before its door closed, I caught sight of metallic restraints where my head, arms, and legs had been. As I watched, the pod wavered then turned into a viridian marble column, indistinguishable from the others that surrounded the room. He saw me looking and smiled.

Shit. Don't panic, I reprimanded myself. *Just look for the others.* But where to begin?

"Pax? Are you still here?"

"Of course, where else would I be?"

"I'm coming to find you."

"I'm over by the buffet table."

"Of course you are. Don't move."

"How will I recognize you? What are you wearing?"

"What? I'm—" I looked down at myself. The cargo trousers and t-shirt I'd been wearing earlier were gone. In their place was a fine linen gown, the soft sky-blue of forget-me-nots. It hung in loose folds, weighted by the heavy embroidery around the hem. I smoothed my hands over the fabric. It felt odd—tangible, but not quite real.

I raised my hands to my face, my fingertips just grazing the mask Arnold had ordered me not to remove. My cheeks were plump, framing a wide, toothless hole. I slipped my hand under the edge of my grinning gums, relieved to find my real face still underneath.

I contemplated the crowd. Maybe none of this was real,

but then what the hell was it? Keeping my back to as few people as possible, I inched along the wall toward the buffet table at the far side. Halfway, my path was blocked by a heavy-set woman suckling a near-emaciated man, liquid spilling down his chin and soaking the front of her dress.

As I skirted them in disgust, a massive, black grandfather clock, the only non-blue object in the room, started to chime.

I wrote earlier that I would tell you more about the others when our story was closer to its end, because history has a way of changing people. The way you see them now wasn't always the way they were.

I met Oliver first as a foe then made my life with him. Oliver was born into troubled times. He survived an abusive mother and a father who took his own life while holding his young son's hand, only to be deemed unacceptable by his peers for the roughness these events marked him with. The culmination of these things bred in him a kind of psychopathy that enabled him to do many things he later regretted, although many were his duty at the time. This viciousness further alienated him, trapping him in a malicious cycle.

He became a cyborg as a last-ditch attempt at acceptance. Who knows how his efforts would've paid off without the war? Yet, he embraced his new state in the end, risking his life for it, and for us. The war was the making of him. All the traits scorned by his peers became his ability to survive, albeit in ways others deemed callous and even inhuman at times. But eventually, the aftermath calmed something in him, and those traits withered and crumbled away, leaving behind something sensitive and new.

—Cindra, Letter to Omega

16
AILITH

The moment the last chime sounded, a palpable ripple swept the room. The arches and the tapestries, the stained-glass windows, the guests' clothes—the blue leached out, replaced by varying shades of purple. The guests' faces had also changed; enormous violet eyes with bottomless, dilated pupils, broad, flattened noses squished between rosy cheeks, and tiny chins with points so sharp they could've drawn blood looked back at me.

I glanced down at myself, and sure enough, I was now swathed in frilly lavender replete with pansy-hued lace and ribbons. My mask had also changed, now featuring an outsized cherub's mouth. The band struck up a bouncing, playful tune.

I needed to find Pax. Then we had to locate the others. I continued toward the buffet table, dodging the crowd, who were now spinning, and dancing, and chasing each other in a caricature of tag. Once a target was caught, the players fell to the floor, writhing together in awkwardly simulated intimacy.

I made it to the table unmolested and searched amongst the various meats and pastries for Pax. "*Pax? I'm at the buffet table. I'm wearing—*" What? A purple dress? "*I've got my hand on my head,*" I finished lamely, placing my palm on top of my pig-tailed hair. All around me, a dozen other guests laughed and did the same. *Shit.*

"*Okay. I'm putting my hands on my hips.*" My dozen shadows followed suit. "Would you kindly fuck off?" I ask the woman closest to me. As she gazed back at me with her immense blank eyes, her mask wobbled, and tears glistened on her neck.

"Ailith, I'm here," Pax said from behind me.

I spun to find a man with giant rosy cheeks that obscured the rest of his features. "Oh, thank goodness." I grabbed his arm and propelled him to the closest pillar. "Pax, what the actual hell is going on? What is this place?"

He pondered for a minute. "I have no idea. This…wasn't anything I've seen. It must've been another

561

blind spot."

Great. Every so often, there were gaps in Pax's ability, where he couldn't see what was coming next. He called it a crossroads, and it usually meant something crucial was going to happen.

"We've got to find the others," I said. "Then we'll figure a way out of here." How long had we even been here?

"Can you see where they are? Like, through their own eyes?"

Duh. Why hadn't I thought of that? I closed my eyes under my mask and concentrated. The closest thread to mine was Cindra's. "Keep watch, Pax," I murmured and slid down it. I was inside her. She was...standing at the edge of a sea of purple. Everything I saw through her eyes looked the same as the view from mine. *Look down. Please, Cindra, look down.* If I could see what kind of dress she was wearing, we could find her easily. She didn't.

"Damn," I swore, frustrated. "She's on the edge of the crowd, like us, but everything looks the same."

"Can you see us?" Pax asked. "I'll wave."

I searched the crowd. "Yes. We're...directly across the room from her. Quick, if we cut through the crowd, we'll be able to reach her." I slid back down the thread and into my own body.

Pax hesitated. "I don't know if that's a good idea."

"What? Why not? It's the quickest way. If we go around the room, we might lose her."

"I don't know *why*. It's just a feeling."

Several heads turned toward us.

"Pax, we need to go. Blend in. *Now.*" I grabbed his hands, skipping around in a circle. The celebrants watching us clapped in joy and mimicked us. Soon, most of the room was twirling. We merged with the other dancers as we spun toward the spot where I hoped Cindra would be.

As soon as we cleared the press of bodies on the other

side of the dance floor, I dropped Pax's hands and searched. There were only two people not dancing, a woman with long, dark braided pigtails in ruffled mauve, and a man who seemed to be soiling himself.

We sidled up to the woman, trying to look casual. I stood next to her and said her name, quietly enough that no one else would hear. "Cindra?" *Please be Cindra.*

She turned her head sharply. Her mask displayed a tiny mouth distorted by a row of widely-spaced teeth the size of my hand "Ailith? Oh, thank god. I've been looking for everyone. Have you found anyone else?"

"Pax," I replied. "He's right here." I tugged on his sleeve.

"What is this place?" Cindra asked.

"I have no idea, but we need to get the hell out of here. We need to—" As I spoke, the great clock at the end of the room chimed again. Like before, at the last chime, a gust passed over the crowd, and green permeated the room along with a throbbing, tribal beat.

"Wow, Ailith, nice boobs," Cindra said.

I looked down. I was now clad in deep, iridescent green the color of a peacock's feather, a plunging neckline giving my cleavage more credit than it deserved. "You too," I replied, indicating the sheer lime fabric of her own outfit. "I can see your nipples."

She stared down at her breasts, horrified. "Those aren't my breasts! Mine are much more—"

"I wish I'd gotten nicer clothes," Pax lamented. "This is the third tuxedo I've worn. The third in my whole life, actually."

"What does my face look like now?" I asked. As repulsed as I was by whatever was going on, I was also curious. And for now, at least, we didn't seem to be in any danger.

"You could cut glass on your cheekbones." She

laughed. "And Pax, you have a hideous mustache. Me?"

"You've got massive red lips, parted like they're begging for—"

"Canape?" a waiter asked, shoving a tray between us.

As we looked around, the crowd's behavior changed. Where before they'd been gamboling like children, now their movements were sensuous, their bodies writhing against one another. The previous giddiness that had lit the purple room was gone, replaced by a frantic, almost ominous air. The smells of sweat and sex rose from the crowd as their motions grew ever more fevered.

"Um, let's take a step back," Cindra said, and we moved behind the pillar in unison.

"That took a bit of a turn, didn't it?" I said, no longer laughing.

"I feel like we're hurtling toward something," Pax added. "But I'm not sure what."

"I know what you mean." Cindra touched the myrtle-green brocade closest to us. "It feels so real. But it can't be, right? It reminds me of something. All these people…the changing colors. The fact that's there's no exit or entrance…"

"There *isn't?*" I hadn't noticed; I'd been too concerned with looking for the others. Tor would be ashamed of me. "Are you s—"

A scuffle broke out behind another pillar a few yards down from us. A laughing group of men in leering masks had surrounded a young woman and were advancing on her, their hands grabbing at the front of her dress. She tripped over her hem as she scrambled backward toward a wall. As she fell, her mask slipped up and revealed part of her face, pale and terrified.

Grace.

As with Oliver, the war and its aftermath set something free in Tor, something good. While others' scars stayed tender, laced with guilt and haunting them until the end of their days, Tor's cleansed him. He was able to finally fight for something, for himself, and for those who loved him, something he'd turned his back on before. But the war allowed him a clean slate, enabled him to eventually put away his regrets and pay his penance. I was unsure of him at first, so still and aloof on the outside, yet with a roiling wildness just underneath the skin. Yet I grew to love his subtle kindness, his fierceness tempered with an innate gentleness.

—*Cindra, Letter to Omega*

17

AILITH

"Grace!" I shouted, my voice lost in the pounding music and delighted moans. As I raced toward her, a couple fell across my path, the man's pants around his ankles as he rode between the woman's thighs. She grabbed at me as I strode past them, my feet tangling in the hem of the dress that pooled over her shoulder.

"No, thank you," I said tartly. The woman didn't seem to care, moaning deeply and grabbing the man's hair as she came.

I tapped the closest man on the shoulder. "What the fuck do you think you're doing?"

"Here's another one, boys," he said, rubbing his hands together with delight.

I ignored him. "Grace, it's me, Ailith." At the sound of my voice, she let out a loud sob. "Come over to me, Grace. Don't worry about them." Her dress was torn at the shoulder, but she seemed unhurt.

"Where do you think you're going?" one of the men asked her as she scrambled to her feet. He grabbed her upper arm.

"Let me go," she blurted. "Get your hands off me."

"What's wrong? We're having a party, sweetling. Don't you want to celebrate? I can show you a good time." He gyrated his hips suggestively.

"Grace, come here," I repeated. "Ignore him."

She did as I said, wrenching her arm away and sprinting past the other three men.

"Now then," the man said to me. "If you're going to spoil our fun, you're going to have to take her place."

I felt, rather than saw, Cindra and Pax materialize at my back. "That's not going to happen," I replied. "Grace, are you all right?"

Grace was *not* all right. She was frightened. And pissed off. "I'll rip your dick off," she shrieked, emboldened by the three cyborgs at her back. She flew toward the man who'd grabbed her, her fingernails clawing for the eyes of his mask. He raised his hands to block her, but she was too quick, and, with a sharp tug, yanked his mask off. It was his turned to be shocked. The face that stared back at us was…so normal. Sandy hair, just a hint of a mustache, and pale brown eyes that darted around the room in a panic.

The music stopped. Even the cacophony of moans switched off, as though someone had hit the mute button. The man dropped to his knees. "No, no. Please, *no*." The crowd advanced on us, forming a circle around the prostrate man.

"No one is to remove their mask," a voice boomed out over the silent crowd. "No one is *ever* to remove their mask."

The man pressed his forehead to the floor as he continued to grovel. "Please, it wasn't my fault—"

"Step back," I murmured to Grace, and the four of us melted into the crowd. I gripped Grace's hand until it became stuck to mine with nervous sweat.

The crowd parted, and a man dressed all in white strode through to stand over the cowering figure. "You know what the penalty is for removing your mask."

That voice. William.

Besides the waiters, he was the only one in the room not wearing a mask, though a metal band encircled his neck. His face was bare, a narrow, pale oval that made his eyes seem too large. His dark blond hair had been raggedly cut, accentuating his pointed chin and full, almost feminine mouth. He looked like a painting of an angel who'd fallen down a hole to Hell.

"Get up," he demanded.

The man whimpered into the jade-tiled floor.

William sighed. He leaned over and grabbed the man by the hair then jerked his head back and forced him onto his heels. The man hung limply in William's hands, his head lolling against his chest as sobs wracked his body. The crowd wailed.

As the crowd's howls climbed in pitch, William leaned over and spoke into the man's ear, just loud enough for me to hear. "Please. Don't make this any worse for me. You know how much I hate this." The man sniffled. "You know you'll come back." The man took a deep breath and nodded once in acquiescence.

William straightened and addressed the crowd. "Those who remove their masks must pay the price." The throng of partygoers, some of whom were only partially dressed, began to keen, a high-pitched howl that sent chills up my spine. A long, pale-bladed dagger materialized in William's right hand, and he drew his arm back.

"It's better this way," he muttered. "You know what happens at the end." He thrust his arm forward, piercing the man's chest with the dagger as the mob screeched. The pointed tip emerged from the man's back, his blood beading on the polished blade. He gasped and looked up at William, a slight smile curling his lips. William twisted the blade and drove it in further.

The man slumped over the hilt, and the crowd rushed forward, swarming around William and the dead man, obscuring them. The ebony clock chimed, and a classical melody rose from the strings of the orchestra. The now silent, orange-clad mob stepped back, and William raised his hands.

"Please, enjoy the evening. Feast, dance...whatever. For as you know, death comes to us all," he intoned as though by rote, rolling his eyes. As his voice carried through the room, the revelers paired off, circling across the floor in a somber waltz. He turned, disappearing into the crowd. The man's body was gone, leaving no trace that he'd ever existed.

"William!" I called after him. "*William!*" But he'd disappeared, lost in the swirling autumn hues. I turned back to the others. "I think that was William."

"I don't think he's the ally we're looking for, Ailith. Not after what he just did," Cindra said.

The way he'd spoken to the man before he'd killed him. "I'm not so sure," I replied. "There's more going on here than we understand." *But even so, it was a mistake to come here.* My *mistake.*

Grace stood with her fist stuffed into her mouth under her mask. Exaggerated purple bags hung from the eyes of her disguise, and her peach dress was almost matronly. She backed away from us, shaking her head, and into a small orangewood table holding an amber-crystal vase of torch lilies. The vase wobbled then fell, toppling over the edge of the table and into the hands of a stranger whose mask wore a crooked grimace of stained yellow teeth.

Grace's shriek was drowned out by the orchestra, and she crouched to the ground, holding her head. The stranger deftly balanced the vase back on the table and held up both hands.

"It's okay. It's me, Oliver. I saw the commotion and figured if there was any trouble, you lot had to be at the center of it."

Cindra nearly knocked the lilies over again as she rushed into his arms. "Oliver, I-I'm so glad to see you." Her voice broke.

"Well, this is a bit of a shitshow, isn't it? I mean, even for us. Do any of you know what the hell's going on?" He narrowed his eyes at Pax and me. "Who's that? Ailith? And I'd recognize Pax's beanpole body anywhere." We nodded, our oversized heads bobbing grotesquely.

"And that's Grace." I pointed to the floor where Grace still sat. She'd calmed down a bit once she'd realized it was Oliver, but she still wasn't ready to stand.

"So no ideas?" he asked again. "Have we just fallen down the rabbit hole? And what the hell happened to that guy?"

"I think the man in white was William," I replied. "But I have no idea what the rest of it—"

"I think I know," Cindra interrupted. I couldn't see her face, but she sounded choked, like she was going to throw up. "*The Masque of the Red Death*."

"I'm sorry, what?" Oliver sounded as confused as I was.

"*The Masque of the Red Death*," Cindra repeated. "By Edgar Allan Poe."

Oliver shook his head. "No idea? Ailith? Pax?"

"Nope."

Cindra sighed loudly. "I know it's an old book, but you

all should really start reading."

"Cindra, if we make it out of here alive, I promise you, I'll read everything you put in my hands. But right now, just tell us what the hell you *think* is going on. Because anything called *Masque of the Red Death* can't be good."

"The story was first published in 1842—" she began.

"Cindra, I love how much you love stories, but please, give us the short version. No themes, no symbolism…just tells us the bad news," Oliver chided her.

"Sorry. Okay, so basically, in the *Masque of The Red Death*, the people are sealed away at a party with seven rooms, each one a different color: blue, purple, green, orange, white, violet, and black. The colors are thought to symbolize the different stages of life. For example—"

"Cindra," Oliver reminded her.

"Sorry," she said again. "We're now in the orange room. That means there are only two rooms left until the black room."

"What happens in the black room?" I asked. "Or can I guess?"

"You can probably guess. The Red Death appears in the black room as a blood-soaked specter that slaughters every single guest."

We were silent. Refined laughter drifted from the dance floor.

"So when this room turns black, we're all going to die?" Oliver asked.

Grace wailed from her spot on the floor.

"Well, that's how the story plays out in Poe's work," Cindra replied.

"Oh, for fuck's sake," Oliver said and began to lift the edge of his mask.

"Oliver, don't!" I shrieked and leaped over Grace to tug the mask back over his chin. "You saw what happened."

"Fuck," he said again, his voice shaky.

570

Cindra squeezed his hand. "I know we're more resilient than most, love, but let's try to come up with a better plan."

"We need to find Fane. Oliver, have you seen him?"

"No," he replied. "Which is odd. I would've expected him to search for you."

"We need to find Fane first then we need a plan. Cindra? How many more rooms are there before the black room again?"

"Two," she said. "White and vio—"

The black clock struck again, and the responding ripple turned the room into a winter wonderland.

"One," Cindra said. "One more room before the Red Death."

Unlike the others, Pax's burden grew with the passage of time, and it took its toll. He wasn't always, as you know him now, so old in his mind. His ability was a terrible weight, one that wouldn't let him rest. And yet, early on, of all of us, Pax emerged the most unscathed. Perhaps because his world had ended long before when he'd lost his mother, the person who was everything to him. On the back of that loss, our lives in the aftermath were an adventure. His mind had always been surreal, the worlds and creatures he explored in his laboratory already separating his universe from others. It made me question if our abilities were as random as they claimed.

—Cindra, Letter to Omega

18

AILITH

I looked down. My marigold gown had transformed into folds of camellia-white brocade. "How can any of these be real?" I said. "I mean, *really* real. This can't just *happen*." We'd been so caught up in the illusion that we hadn't thought of it as anything but real. "I mean, these clothes, the rooms…and where did that man's body go?" I pointed to the spot where he'd fallen. "It couldn't have just disappeared, could it?"

"You're right," Oliver said. "I just—"

"I know, me too," I said. "It looks and feels real. But it can't be. Someone's behind this. We need to find Fane then William."

"*William's* probably the one behind this, A."

"I'm not sure that he is, Oliver." I told him what William had said to the man before he'd killed him. "I think he might be caught up here, the same as we are."

"Maybe," Oliver said, sounding unconvinced. "Let's find Fane first then we'll deal with William."

"I'll wait with Grace," Cindra said. "And we'll stay right here, for as long as we can. We probably want to keep as low-key as possible."

"Agreed. I'll look for Fane. Oliver, see if you can figure out what's going on."

"I will. And we'll meet back here when that damned clock strikes again. Hurry," he said to me. "By my guess, we haven't got long."

I stood next to Cindra and Grace, closing my eyes under my mask and searching for Fane's thread. It blazed so brightly that I found it immediately and went through it. He was spinning in the arms of an ivory-tuxedoed man wearing a mask with a visage so lined his jowls rivaled Arnold's.

I pulled back then searched for that mask in the crowd. *There, in the middle of the dance floor.* In the man's delicate grasp was a taller, broader man in bone-colored attire, whose mask scowled under bushy grey eyebrows the thickness of my arm. *That has to be Fane.*

I wove through the crowd toward the pair, trying to keep rhythm with the dancers. When I reached them, I tapped the jowled man on the shoulder. "May I cut in?"

After a moment's hesitation, he bowed graciously and spun away into the throng. I took Fane's hands in mine and began to waltz, trying to remember what I'd been taught. *One, two three. One, two, three.*

"Fane?"

"Ailith?"

"Yes. Are you having a good time?" I asked, my voice acerbic.

573

He laughed. "Yes, actually. I was very flattered when he asked, and I don't know how to lead. I thought maybe it was a good time to learn."

"I've been trying to find everyone—you're the last. Did you not see the commotion earlier?"

"Yes."

"Well then, why didn't come and have a look? Oliver did—that's how we found him."

"I thought it was part of the celebration," he replied. "And then this good gentleman asked me to dance—"

"Do you not see that something's very wrong here?" I stopped dancing and glared at him.

"You know I can't see your face, right?" he asked. "But I'll assume that you're glaring."

"Fane, I just—" I threw up my hands in exasperation. "You understand our lives might be in danger, yes?"

"Yes, I do. And I figured the best way to minimize that danger was to blend in. Like we should be doing now." He inclined his head. Several of the dancers closest to us had paused, watching us.

Fane threw back his head and gave a hearty laugh, belying his mask's scowl. He pulled me close then twirled me away. The lingering couples' interest in us vanished, and they returned to their waltz.

"Do you have any idea what's behind all of this? I think that man in white was William. And Cindra has another theory." I repeated the story of the Red Death as we danced across the floor.

"So according to Cindra, we have one more room before these walls turn black and everyone dies?"

"Yes. Hence my sense of urgency."

"That's not a lot of time."

"Yes, Fane. I *know*."

He grinned. "Don't worry. We'll find a way out. We always do."

"So far," I grumbled. "But that's bound to only last so long. C'mon, let's meet up with the others and figure out a plan."

We whirled with purpose toward them. "Do you have any idea what this place is, Fane? Who these people are?" I kept my eye on the clock as we rotated, just waiting for it to strike.

"No. But there's something about them..."

"What do you mean?"

"When I was holding hands with that gentleman, he didn't quite feel...real."

"Not real?" I asked as an enthusiastic elbow caught me in ribs. The owner flashed me an apologetic smile as she jostled past. "Ouch. They *certainly* feel real. Still, I agree. There's no way they can be."

We reached the others without further incident. Grace had recovered enough to stand, but the white primrose woven into her hair shook with each breath.

"Any luck figuring out what's going on?" I asked Oliver.

"No," he said. "You?"

"I found Fane. But I haven't seen William." I'd kept an eye out for him on our way across the dance floor, but seeing as everyone present was now wearing white, I'd had no luck.

"William is our only lead at this point," Cindra said. "but I don't think we should split up to look for him. Can't you find him the same way you found me and Fane?"

"I can try." I found William's thread in the network and slid into him. I was surrounded by darkness and silence.

Something's gone wrong.

Then heavy cool air brushed over my lips and William opened his eyes. He was in the room he'd been in the night before, only this time, I was able to make out shapes in the gloom. He was surrounded by what seemed like hundreds of long, metallic tubes, dull gray in the shadow.

Someone's here. His heart pounded in his chest. *Real someones. Several of them. This could be it. My chance to end this. My only chance. Breathe, Will. You know what you have to do.* A giddy laugh burst from him, echoing around the chamber. He patted the closest cylinder and spoke aloud. "Okay, everyone, wish me luck." He closed his eyes again. *Good luck.*

I pulled back into myself. The sudden sea of white stung my eyes. "He's not here," I said, squinting at the others. "He's in another room. But I'm positive we'll see him again. From what I gathered, something *is* about to happen."

"Do you think he's on our side or not?" Cindra asked.

I hesitated. "I'm not sure. I *think* he is. He sees us as a chance for him to…stop whatever's going on here."

"That doesn't exactly mean he's with us, though, does it?" Oliver pointed out.

"I know. But we can't know for certain until we actually meet him."

"I don't think we'll have long to wait," Fane said. And he was right.

Without any ceremony, the ebony clock gave a resounding chime.

I often wonder where Fane got his personality from. It certainly wasn't any of the Cosmists. His openness, his kindness, his humility was highly developed. He lacked the arrogance and hatred of his creators, fully understanding them, but not subscribing to them. It was their greatest disappointment. They'd tried to make him human, in their image, and failed. But to me, this was their greatest success.

—Cindra, Letter to Omega

19
AILITH

A sigh swept the room as the violet dusk settled upon us. Our faces changed accordingly, becoming gaunt caricatures of the dying. My stiff brocade softened into drapes of vervain silk.

One chime left. We need to find William now.

The atmosphere in the room transformed, a pall settling over the crowd. They danced no longer, and as the orchestra struck up a mournful elegy, many of them began to weep.

"This doesn't bode well," Pax said. "And before you ask, no, I can't see what's to come. Only that we *can* make it out of here alive. And in some paths, we even *do*."

"Well, that's comforting. Thank you, Pax," Oliver said sourly.

Pax shrugged.

"William might be here now," I said, standing on my tiptoes and craning my neck to search the crowd. "Damn.

Where is he?" I searched again for his thread and followed it. There. He was…right behind us.

I spun around. "William?" The others' masks turned in our direction.

He recoiled with a shocked expression. "You know my name?"

"Yes. I— Actually, it's a long story. We'll talk about it later. I get the feeling we're in danger. Am I right?"

"Yes," he said simply.

"From you?" Fane and the others had sidled into a silent formation, casually blocking his escape. Even Grace stood her ground, her hands balled into fists. *Good girl.*

"No!" he exclaimed, his eyes widening in alarm. He glanced furtively from side to side and dropped his voice. "Not from me. I'm trapped here. The same as you. When…that incident happened earlier, I saw you, knew you were different. It's becoming so hard for me to tell. That's why I came to find you. "

"What's going to happen?" Oliver asked.

"The Red Death," William replied. "It's—"

"We know what it is," I interrupted. "What we need to know is how we can stop it."

"You can't," he said. "Unless—"

"Unless *what*, Will? I don't want to sound impatient here, but I don't think we have a lot of time."

"Unless you kill the Red Death."

"Shocking," said Oliver. "It always seems to end that way. Okay, I'll bite. How do we kill the Red Death?"

"With this." Will scanned the room again then pressed what looked like a shiv into Oliver's hands.

"You're kidding." Oliver glanced down at what could only be called a whittled stick. "Are we fighting a vampire?"

"Of course not," Will said. "But it was the best I could do."

"Why can't you do it?" Oliver asked him.

"I have a role to play. I—" He blanched suddenly and darted away into the crowd.

Arnold was making his way toward us, a disapproving look on his flaccid face.

"Oliver, hide that stick. Everybody else, get wailing," I whispered frantically.

Cindra threw her head back and gave an unsettling howl then flung herself into my arms. Pax and the others followed suit, and by the time Arnold reached us, we were all but beating our breasts and rending our clothes. He scrutinized us for a few moments then, seemingly satisfied, passed us by.

"Is he gone?" I asked.

A tension gripped the air. The dirge of the celebrants rose, climbing ever higher until I had to clap my hands over my ears. *That sound could drive a person mad.*

The clock struck, a single reverberating chime, echoing throughout the chamber.

As we stood rooted to the spot, the crowd milled like a herd of cattle in the center of the dancefloor. Inky darkness, deeper than black, seeped into the floor at one end of the room. It advanced slowly, permeating the walls and floor as it passed, while a deep crimson snaked up the tables and chairs, the riot of violet flowers turning to dust in the now-scarlet vases.

The Red Death had come.

Screams of pure terror filled the room, turning my bones to jelly as the revelers tried to run from the spreading shadow. They huddled together at the far end, their screams melting into sobs and impassioned prayers.

"Remember, it can't be real," Fane said.

I know it's not real. But what if? What if? We stood our ground as the blackness spread under our feet, obscuring the mallow tiles, the muscles along my spine twitching as I held myself still. It reached the far end and climbed the walls.

When it had filled the last corner of the ceiling, a door appeared at the opposite end to the horrified cluster.

And through the door came Death.

When I began to write to you about Ailith, I found I struggled. How very strange, to be unable to describe the person who arguably played the largest role in our story. She never wanted to become a cyborg—she only wanted to live. And yet, she became so much bigger than her own life. Perhaps it's because she was all of us at one time or another that, although this is our story, it's her story to tell.

—*Cindra, Letter to Omega*

20

AILITH

Death was a giant, dwarfing even Fane. He was shrouded in black robes soaked with blood that left a swath of gore behind him as he advanced on his victims. He didn't seem to notice us as he passed, intent as he was on the crowd at the far end. The fetid odor of decay hung over him like a miasma, causing Grace to gag. She was no longer wearing a mask. None of us were.

The faces of the crowd were likewise bare, and we finally got a look at our companions. Aside for the horrified gape of their mouths, they looked...normal. Men and women who wouldn't have looked out of place buying from my market stall before the war or trading in Goldnesse in the aftermath. Just ordinary people.

How did they end up here, in such extraordinary circumstances?

From the crowd rose a strong voice. "Who dares? Who dares insult us with blasphemous mockery? Seize him and unmask him, that...that— Shit." There was the quiet

581

rustling of what sounded like paper and the clearing of a throat. "That we may know whom we have to hang, at sunrise, from the battlements!"

With a throat-rending battle cry, a figure broke away from the group and charged toward Death, waving the long, shining dagger. *William.*

He made it to only a few feet away from Death before the specter raised its hand. Blood poured first from William's eyes, nose, and ears, then from what seemed like every pore on his body.

It's not real. It's not real.

William collapsed on the floor, writhing in a pool of his own blood, and not a small amount of Death's. Death swept past him and headed for the keening horde. Some of them fainted outright, while others climbed over their companions as though trying to scale the walls to safety. William lay still, a heap of sodden rags against the dark floor.

As soon as he was out of Death's line of sight, he raised himself onto his elbow, and gestured to us, making a stabbing motion and pointing to Death's retreating back. Yards from the crowd, Death raised his hands again. Those closest to him began to bleed profusely, those behind them scrambling to keep their footing on the now-slick floor.

We cowered behind our pillar, keeping out of sight. Or so we thought.

"I believe we have some new guests this evening," Death intoned, turning toward us.

"Fuuuuuck," Oliver moaned under his breath. "All right, which one of us is going to shank him?" No one said a word as Death began to glide our way.

"Anyone? Let's not all be heroes, eh? One at a time." Silence. "*Anybody?*"

"I'll do it," Fane said. "I *am* the most powerful one here." He smirked and raised an eyebrow at Oliver, trying to goad him.

Oliver held up his hands. "No argument here. Have at it, Terminator."

"What's a—"

"Fane, you may want to do it sooner rather than later. Seeing as how Death is almost here." I nudged him. "Oliver, give him the shiv."

Fane looked down at the stake in his hand. "Does it matter if I do it underhand or overhand?"

"Christ, Fane, just use the pointy end!" Oliver looked as though he was ready to snatch the oversized splinter from Fane's hand.

Death was nearly upon us.

Keeping the shiv hidden close to his side, Fane approached Death. The apparition raised its hands, and blood leaked from Fane's eyes. Blood he didn't have.

Something's not right. Fane can't bleed. I've got to stop him. "Fane!"

I was too late.

Fane drove the wooden stake into where Death's soft belly should've been. Silence descended over the crowd.

Death stood still for a moment then his hands crept over the protruding end as though in disbelief. He staggered forward, and the crowd shrieked as one, drawing back against the wall again.

They wasted their breath. Death toppled backward, hitting the midnight tiles with a very human-sounding smack. His legs convulsed, once, twice, and then he was still.

Death was dead.

The room froze in stunned silence. William stood up from his deathbed and rushed over to a pillar on the right side of the dance floor as the partygoers recovered from their shock and erupted into wild cheers.

All at once, the crowd vanished, as did the room's

sinister façade. We stood in a near-empty room, furnished with only a few worktables holding tools and various pieces of junk and some metal chairs that looked a lot more functional than comfortable. A plain, concrete-floored, magnolia-walled room.

On the floor where Death had fallen lay a body. A *human* body with Fane's shiv jutting out of one eye.

He had killed Death all right, but Death was a man.

I know little about Will's past. Even Ailith, with her ability, had difficulty understanding it. Large pieces of it were missing, and those that remained were...dark. I understood his affinity with machines when the human world had been such a dangerous and painful place for him. And it was more than affinity he had for those androids—it was true affection. For Antoni, for all of them—and they for him. Antoni, already highly sentient when we met him, was one of those whose awareness was amplified by Fane, and his love for Will increased exponentially, like a dam inside him had finally burst. This outpouring of feeling was a salve for many of Will's old wounds, and indeed, for many of ours.

—*Cindra, Letter to Omega*

21
AILITH

Cindra rushed over to the body and scanned it. She looked at us and shook her head. "He's definitely dead. Fane's stake went straight into his brain."

"But I stabbed him in the stomach," said Fane, his eyes wide. Had he ever killed anyone before?

"You stabbed *Death* in the stomach. Right where this man's head happened to be." Admiration tinged Oliver's voice.

"It wasn't real. *None of it was real!*" Grace was dazed, clutching at the wall for support.

"Grace, sit down," I commanded. "And put your head between your knees."

She obeyed. I stalked over to William, who was bracing himself over what looked like a computer console, his head hanging down. "You want to tell us exactly what the hell is going on?" I demanded.

"You saved us," he replied, his breathing labored. "You saved *me*." He looked at the corpse and grimaced. "He's been holding me captive here for five years. *Five years.*" He backed up until his back hit the wall then slid down it to sit on the floor. "Thank you."

"I don't understand. What was all this?"

"This was my living nightmare. That…man," he pointed a shaking finger, "has been forcing me to take part in his hideous reenactments for years. He wasn't so bad at the start. It was something he did for fun, to pass the time and stay connected to the world above us." He drew a shuddering breath. "But eventually, he just went…mad, I guess. The stories got stranger and bloodier— I can't believe it's finally over."

"What were all those people?" Pax asked. As William and I spoke, the others had joined us, taking their places on the floor in a half-circle. "How did you create them?"

Will gave him an exhausted smile. "They're holograms."

"But they felt so real."

"Ultrasonics," he replied.

"*Soundwaves?*" Pax looked duly impressed.

"Yep. Acoustic radiation pressure. It creates a hologram that looks and feels real."

"Can you show me—"

"Pax, let William catch his breath. I think we all have a lot of questions." I hated to rebuke Pax, but William looked like he might faint.

Pax grinned. "Sorry," he said to William.

William held up a hand. "Don't be. I'd be happy to show you how it works."

"But before that," I said, "tell us how you ended up

586

here."

"Wait," he said. "You seem to know who I am, but I have no idea who you are."

"I'm Ailith, Pantheon Modern Cyborg Program Omega cyborg O-117-9791."

"Pantheon Modern? That means—"

"We're the other cyborgs from your generation."

"How did you find me?"

"I heard you."

"Heard me? That's impossible. Who are you *really*?" He started to scramble to his feet.

I stood swiftly and reached out to him as the others rose and stepped back to give him space. "No, William, wait. I don't mean *hear* in the literal sense. I'm connected to other cyborg's minds. It's my...ability. I can't *read* your thoughts," I added hastily, "but I see what you see and feel what you're feeling." *And sometimes I can see your past.* I would save that for later. No need to make him any warier of us than he already was.

"You're kidding," he said, incredulous.

"Nope. We all have different abilities. Surely you must have one too?"

"I—" William's eyes widened and he pushed past me toward Fane. "You're—you're an artilect, aren't you?" His face was refreshed and alight, as though the angel had found again the light of his God.

"I am." Fane was tense, his voice guarded. I wasn't surprised. The Cosmists had fetishized him in a way that violated the rights he would've had as a human.

William circled him. "You're remarkable," he said. His tone was gentle, respectful, with none of the idolization I'd heard from others, including Stella.

Fane must've heard it too. "Thank you," he said, standing taller.

Oliver rolled his eyes and gagged.

"How did you know?" I asked. "What Fane was?"

"It's my ability. I have an affinity with machines—I can scan them, diagnose technical issues..."

"Like me," Cindra said. "Only I do it with humans. I'm Cindra, by the way."

The others introduced themselves. When Grace held out her hand, Will barely touched it before dropping his hand back to his side.

"Full organic human, right?" he asked.

"Yes." Grace's face reddened again.

"Hmm." He dismissed her and turned back to us, raising his eyebrows. "Soon after my cyberization, I was told we'd been discovered. That the Artilect War was about to officially kick off, and I had to go into hiding. We were on our way somewhere, some compound, when something happened. I still don't know what. The next thing I knew, I'd ended up here. With *him*."

"Did you know that man?"

"No, not until I was here. He told me his name was Lars. Why? Who is he?"

"I don't know for sure. I...saw him through the mind of another cyborg. He was posing as a doctor, but both he and that cyborg worked for the government. But the cyborg, Nova, I saw him through, ended up in the bunker you were supposed to be in."

"My *bunker*? What do you mean?"

"They moved all of us to hiding places across the province then kept us asleep for five years. You should've been with us. With him, specifically." I pointed at Oliver. "They replaced you with someone else—the cyborg who used to work with Lars. Before Oliver went to sleep, he was tipped off that she was a threat to us."

"Five years? You were asleep for five *years*? And replaced me? What happened to her?" He seemed genuinely confused. If he'd known about the switch, he hid

588

it well.

"It's a long story, never mind," Oliver said hastily. I wasn't surprised he didn't want to discuss the details. He'd killed Nova, William's usurper, in a fairly violent fashion. "Whoever was behind the threat must've brought you here to keep you out of the way."

"Five years. So the war *must* be long over," William said.

"Yes. It's been over for a while."

"But then, if it's over, why did no one come looking for me?"

"We didn't know you were here. And with all the secrecy, maybe your location got lost." It sounded lame even to my own ears. *Just tell him the truth. Why hesitate?*

"I kind of suspected that. What happened? Who won? Sorry, that's a stupid question. Obviously, the Cyborgists won, or you wouldn't be here. Shit. That's a relief. Now we can live out in the open."

"Nobody won, William." I still couldn't bring myself to tell him the greater truth.

"Call me Will. What do you mean, nobody won?"

"It's... Well, it's hard to explain."

"No, it's not," Oliver interrupted, exasperated. "The world got fucked. Nearly everyone is dead, there's no sun, and people are constantly trying to kill us."

William's confused smile shattered and fell.

"Oliver!" Cindra admonished him.

"Sorry, but he's going to find out sooner or later. Seriously, you guys, he *knows* how long he's been down here."

"I can't believe the world is over." Will sank into the nearest chair, not bothering to move the jumble of wires and circuits. "The one comfort I had every night was the thought that even though I'd been forgotten, life had carried on above me." He stared off into the distance, his eyes unfocused. "Shit."

"Will, I'm so sorry. It was a shock for us too. Did you have any family?" I asked.

He ignored the question. "And you're the only cyborgs left? They told me others had survived. Only a few, but still. I wasn't the only one."

"There *were.*"

"What happened to them?" From his downcast expression, he'd already guessed.

"That's also a long story," Oliver said. "And we'll be happy to tell you. But first, other than those freakish recreations, what have you been doing all this time?"

"I— Just living, I guess. Tinkering. Thinking. Waiting for this day."

"You were thinking about the others when I was inside your mind," I said. "What others? Who else is here?"

"The others are why Lars kept me alive. I'm their caretaker. To be honest, when you first called my name, I thought you were one of them, finally waking up..."

"One of who?" I prompted him.

He shook himself and stood up, gesturing for us to follow. "I'll show you. Not that they *do* anything. I'm not even sure they're alive. They didn't come with an instruction manual." As he spoke, he led us down another hall to a large chamber. Even before he turned on the lights, I recognized it.

Inside were row upon row of the dull metal cylinders. Now in the lit room, I saw them for what they were.

Each of the human-sized windowed metal pods were inhabited, the still faces of young men and women visible through the panes, resting in an unconsciousness deeper than sleep.

"My God. There's *hundreds* of them." The columns of sleek pods filled the room, each one a host.

"One hundred and ninety-five," Will said.

"Who are they?" Cindra whispered, as though not to

disturb them.

"Well," Will replied, "I guess you could say they're us."

I regret not being able to tell you more about the others of our kind, the ones we lost. My time with many of them was short, and in some cases, fraught with issues that may prejudice my judgment against the people they actually were or could've become. But you must remember their names and their existence. For they played a role, were part of the fine balance, and all our lives may have turned out differently without them:

Eire
Ella
Adrian
Ros
Cayde
Nova

—Cindra, Letter to Omega

22

AILITH

"What do you mean?" I examined their faces, searching for my doppelgänger. I was less surprised than I should've been.

"Oh. Not literally." He smiled in apology. "I mean, they're earlier versions of us."

The previous generations. *You are the fourth*, Mil and Lexa had said. Why were they here? Were they alive? How could they be? I ran my hand over the cold metal of a pod holding a woman with close-cropped black hair. Her face looked strangely taut, as though she found no rest even in

592

sleep.

"How are these pods so cold?" I asked. The smooth surface was so chilled I couldn't touch it for more than a few seconds before my skin started to burn.

William pulled his sleeve down over his hand and ran it over the adjacent pod. "Cold water hydro runs through here. Also gives us our electricity."

I nodded. "That's common these days."

"Really? I just... I still can't believe it." He bent over and pressed his forehead against the freezing steel.

I had to turn away from his grief. I leaned over the pod again, wiping the pane with my sleeve. She was young, like us. They all were. Her face and what I could see of her body looked completely normal, no sign of trauma. "What happened to them?"

Will rubbed the red freezer burn on his forehead. "I don't know. They were here when I arrived. Lars told me to watch over them, to make sure they didn't wake up. He showed me how to use all the rudimentary controls, but beyond that, he wasn't particularly interested in answering my questions. I assume whoever chose me did so because of my ability."

"And you're sure you know nothing about Nova?" Oliver blurted. "I'm sorry, I just don't understand. If the Cyborgists put you here, they *knew* you wouldn't be with me. Mil and Lexa said they were surprised when we told them."

"They said a lot of things," I reminded him.

"Lexa? Middle-aged? Blond hair? Twisted her hands together a lot?"

"That sounds like her."

"I met her once, before I was brought here. But she didn't say anything about a bunker, or about these poor bastards here," Will replied.

My head was beginning to hurt. "Look, let's try to

unravel the whole sordid story later." I turned back toward the pods. "So you don't know if they're alive?"

"They must be," Oliver said. "If they're dead, why haven't they decomposed?"

"Maybe it's too cold," William offered. "They've been like that the entire time."

"Ailith? Cindra? Can't either of you tell? Pax?"

Pax shook his head and retreated to the far side of the room. *That's not a good sign.*

I searched for their threads as Cindra used her ability to scan them. She frowned. "I can't seem to read anything through the metal. Ailith?"

Their threads were there, but faint. The light in them strobed in a strange way, different to anything I'd ever seen. In cyborgs, they burned steady, wavering when there were complications. In machines, they flickered. "Yes... It seems like they're there. But it's weird. Don't ask me to explain," I added as Fane opened his mouth. "Can we open one of the pods?"

Will put his hand protectively over the lid of the casing. "What if the pods are keeping them preserved? What if they crumble into dust? I'm supposed to be taking care of them."

"Well, then they're dead, and it doesn't matter, does it?" Oliver pointed out.

Will considered for a moment then nodded and stepped to the foot of the cylinder.

"Should I open all of them? Or just one?"

I looked at Cindra and shrugged. "All of them, I guess. It might be quicker to see if any of them are alive that way."

Will walked over to a panel set into the wall near the door. "I just have to line the command up...unlock this...open *this*, and—"

The lids unsealed with a faint hiss, lifting slightly. Will grabbed the rim of the closest pod and pushed it all the way open. A sweet smell, like rotten fruit on a warm day, rose from the exposed cavity.

A moment later, it hit me. One hundred and ninety-five threads flared, blinding me in both eyes. "Cindra, quick, they're alive!"

Screaming, pain, fear, and madness enveloped me in a chorus of one hundred and ninety-five voices. *Make it stop. Help us. Make it stop. Please. MAKE IT STOP.*

"Shut it!" Fane shouted from far away just as I could no longer bear it.

It stopped. I collapsed on the ground, still in darkness. Fane's hands gripped my shoulders, and his voice disturbed the air in front of my face.

"Ailith? Are you okay? Can you hear me?"

Reaching up to touch his face was the best I could do.

"What happened, Cindra? Are they alive?" His face turned under my fingers.

"According to my ability, they're dead. Their bodies anyway. Their brains are still alive somehow."

"It must be the pods." Fane's face turned back to me. "Ailith? What did you see?"

His face became a shadow then a form. "It was awful." My shoulders shook under his hands. "They... It was like they were in hell. They're in agony, and they're...trapped. But they *know* they're trapped. They're aware. But not."

Everyone was silent. I tried to think of a better way to explain. I couldn't.

"Have they been that way the whole time?" Will asked.

"I think so..." I tried to describe it without touching my memory. I couldn't do it a second time. "Their minds are so broken, they don't understand the passage of time. So they live in the same excruciating seconds over and over."

Will shuddered, looking distressed. "I had no idea. I did honestly think they were gone. Is there anything we can do to help them?"

"Cindra?"

Her face swam into view, stark against her dark hair. "No. Their bodies have been dead for years. The pods are preserving them."

"We can't leave them like this. We have to help them." How many years had they been like that? *I can't. We have to do something.*

"A, the only—"

"Don't say it, Oliver."

"Fine, but you know as well as I do it's the only option." I did know. "Will," I began, "if their bodies are dead, there's very little we can do to help them. Right, Cindra?" I desperately hoped she was going to have a better answer. She shook her head, so I continued. "I think the only thing we can do is—"

"Pull the plug?" Will asked.

"Yes."

He nodded once, his face calm.

"I thought you'd be upset." I didn't know what else to say.

"I am—because of what they're going through. Nobody deserves to live like that." He released a long, ragged breath. "To be honest, I was starting to think about topping myself before you came, and I'm fine, compared to them. *I* wouldn't want to live like that. If those pods are keeping them alive, like that, then when does it end for them? If I'd known—"

"You're going to *kill* them?" Grace's voice was shrill.

"Grace—"

"But they're *people.*" She searched each of our faces, as though she would find a way to understand.

"This is what it means to be us, Grace," I said, more sharply than I'd intended.

Her eyes filled with tears, and she backed away from us.

I'd seen the look in her eyes many times before. *Monsters. You're all monsters.*

And maybe we were. But we weren't the worst. These shells of our kin proved that.

"Are you okay, Will? Do you need a few minutes?" After all, he'd watched over them for half a decade.

"No, let's do it. Quickly, please," Will said. "They need this to be over, and so do I." He leaned over and pressed his lips to the window of the closest pod. "*Sueña con los angelitos,*" he whispered. *Sleep with the angels.*

We shut down the main power supply and waited in silence.

"Why didn't you leave, Will? Was it just because of them?"

"That, and the fact that I can't. I'm not proud of it, but about three years ago, I did try. It's this stupid collar Lars put on me." He gestured to the thin metal band.

"I may be able to help you with that," Oliver said.

"Really?" Will asked, relief evident on his face. "Thank you. I don't think I could stay down here. Not if they're gone. And not knowing what I know now."

"If Oliver can help you, will you come with us?" I asked. "You would be more than welcome."

He smiled, the light returning to his face. "Yes, please. If I can. I've still got rations and some other stuff you might find useful—" He stopped. "Although..."

I waited for him to finish.

"No," he said, more to himself than me. "Don't."

I didn't pry. After a minute or so, he looked back at me, like he'd forgotten what he was doing.

I brushed my fingers over his shoulder. "Go gather everything you need. I don't want to rush you, but we're a bit short on time. I'll stay with them."

"What should we do about...Lars?" Oliver asked.

"Leave him, I guess." I still wasn't sure how to feel

about what we'd done.

Fane stayed with me. We sat on the cold floor, side by side.

"Why do you think they put them here, Fane? Lexa said they were dead. And I mean they are, but not really. I don't understand why they kept them...alive, like that." For a moment, my vision blurred around the edges and a past ghost of Lexa bent over to kiss one of them briefly before closing the lid. The hand she laid on the window shook, and tears slid over the surface of the glass, marring the view. "Well, whatever the reason, I think she did care. In her own way." I leaned my head on his shoulder. "Are you okay?"

"Yes, why?"

"You killed someone, Fane. Was it the first time?"

"Yes."

"Do you not feel...upset?"

He seemed to consider it for a moment. "No. I think he was a very real threat to us. And what he was doing to those holograms—"

But they're just holograms, they can't feel anything, I wanted to say. But I didn't. How did I know they couldn't? And besides, did it matter? Lars was clearly unhinged. Why had he been left down here for so long? Had his superior died? Or had they intended to entomb him forever? I tried to stand, but my legs had gone numb from the cold floor.

"Do you think it's been long enough?" Fane asked as he helped me to my feet.

"There's only one way to know." I braced myself for an onslaught as we lifted the lid. There was nothing but silence this time; they were truly gone. Every single one of their threads had gone dark. We opened each of the pods in turn, just to make sure, and I felt not a whisper. We left the pod-room and went to find the others. Fane put his arm around me, helping to ease the emptiness in my chest.

"Is it done?" Will asked.

We nodded.

"You won't believe some of the stuff Will has," Pax said, his face flushed with excitement and his hands full of mysterious gadgets. "Show them, Will."

Will grinned shyly. "Well, I've had lots of time to work on stuff. I mean, I had to keep busy or go crazy like Lars." His smile fell a bit as he glanced toward the room that had held our predecessors. "Those holograms were something I was working on before the war. Whoever left me here left my stuff with me as well." He cradled a small black box.

"Watch this." Pax held his breath in anticipation, exhaling eagerly as a young man shimmered into existence before us. Taller than Will, slim, with dark hair, he stood smiling at us.

It was remarkable. I'd seen holograms before, loads of them, but nothing like this one. We circled him. How was it possible? He looked so real. Normally, holograms had a translucent appearance, a sort of ethereal aspect, but the man before us looked as corporeal as the rest of us.

"Can I touch him?" I asked.

Will nodded. "Of course."

I reached out and placed my hand on the young man's arm. He was warm to the touch, his skin soft and covered with tiny down hairs, just like a real person.

"He's incredible," Cindra said. I had to agree.

"Who is he, Will?" There was so much attention to the man's details that it had to be someone Will had known.

"He's... He died before the war." His voice was wistful as he switched the hologram off and packed it into a small case that he held to his chest. "I kept him secret for months until I got so lonely I couldn't stand it anymore. When I thought Lars was asleep, I activated him." His brow creased at the memory. "Of course, Lars caught me. He forced me to show him how I did it then used it to create scenarios like that monstrosity you witnessed earlier."

"Is this his?" Cindra asked, pointing to a worn notebook on one of the tables.

"Yes. Well, mostly. It's his diary. I took it over when he went properly over the edge. I figured we might both be dead by the time anyone found us, so I wanted to record what happened. Just in case we died doing something *really* weird." Will regarded the diary with distaste.

"Do you mind if I take it with me?" Cindra asked.

"No, not at all. Do you collect them? Seems a bit macabre."

"Something like that," she replied, tucking the book into her satchel.

We gathered what rations and tools Will had then filed into the pod-chamber for a last goodbye. *What will happen to them when we're gone?*

"Do you think they'll be okay?" Will asked, echoing my thoughts.

"I think so. I mean, they're at rest now."

He nodded, but his face still looked troubled.

"Now what?" Oliver asked.

"What do you mean? We go get Tor. And keep looking for allies," I said.

"Will should go back to the island. We can't expect him to come with us where we're going. Not after everything he's already been through. Let the man live just a little bit longer, eh?"

"Where *are* you going?" Will asked.

We explained to him what had happened during our time at the compound and in Goldnesse, about Tor and the Cosmists. About our plan to save Tor and search for allies to help us when the Cosmists came for us.

Will gave a low whistle. "I missed all that?"

"Oh, don't worry, mate." Oliver laughed. "There's plenty more coming our way."

"And you need allies?"

"Why? You got some here?" Oliver peered under one of the pods.

"Not here… And it may be a long shot. Fane and Oliver might be able to make it work, but we'll have to go to them." Excitement crept into his voice, mingled with longing.

"Who is *them?*" I asked.

"How you feel about gynoids?"

We've failed. I don't know how, but we've failed. I've lost all contact with Sarah. She'd said there was a chance we might lose, but I still can't believe it. Watching the feed of what was happening above ground, the attack that the Cosmists and Cyborgists unleashed on us...the Preserve Terra society was right all along. We were too late. I'm determined to fulfill my duty and stay here until they come for me, though, no matter how long it takes.

—Lars Nilsson, personal diary

23

AILITH

As we made our way through Richmond toward the massive industrial park, I bided my time fretting about the detour. Knowing that Tor was okay for the moment was the only thing that made it bearable. And if Will was right, and we gained some new allies, it would be worth it.

But gynoids? I didn't understand the connection. Gynoids were a specific type of android. Built to exceptionally high specifications, their quality was unparalleled by most androids. They looked, felt, and acted like real humans, but being machines, had no rights. Subsequently, they tended to be retained as companions for the very wealthy, or as sex workers for those with enough money to satisfy specific tastes. I'd seen gynoids up close only once, when I'd been a passenger in Adrian, another long-dead cyborg in our cluster.

Will explained as we traveled. "I used to work with

them, the gynoids. Except," he added, "we called them androids, and if we find them, I ask you all to do the same. It might not seem like an important distinction to you, but it is. Anyway, I trained them in the nuances of human behavior, what customers would expect from them and how to react."

"So what happened to them?"

"Well, they're incredibly expensive, so when all this trouble started, we moved them out here to a nondescript warehouse and deactivated them."

"I still can't believe we're doing this," Oliver protested. "Even if we can get them to work, who's to say how they're going to react? What if they turn on us? Or what if they're useless? How are they going to help us? I don't mean to be crass, but considering what they were used for—"

"Are they self-actualized, Will? Like Fane?" I wanted to change the subject before Oliver gave himself an aneurysm.

Will considered. "Not exactly, but... I don't know how to explain it. They're not *supposed* to be, but there were times... I mean, you're the culmination of a process, right, Fane? There were others before you, less advanced but with the same qualities. Did you ever wonder where your precursors went? The ones that didn't quite make the grade? They would've been too costly to throw away, and what other industry aside from the sex trade or private collectors could afford such expensive units? While you were being feted, those who came before you earned their keep on their knees."

Fane looked appalled. "I never—"

"It's not your fault, Fane," I said. "And that's not what Will was insinuating, was it, Will?"

Will glanced between Fane and me, and his eyes narrowed. His mouth curved into a slight smile. "No. But is something you should be aware of. Or were you happier thinking they'd just been destroyed?"

"Will," I warned.

He surrendered, his hands in the air. "I'm sorry, Fane. I know you weren't responsible for any of it, but—"

"I understand," Fane replied. "And thank you for telling me. I didn't know, but I should have. I'm still learning."

"Welcome to being human," Will replied and clapped him on the shoulder.

"What did you teach them?" Grace was trying to be brave and having Will—another newcomer—with us seemed to have bolstered her confidence.

Cindra leaned over and whispered in her ear.

She blushed furiously and ducked her head.

Will laughed.

We finally entered the sect we'd been looking for. Like many of the others we'd passed, it was destroyed, the buildings obliterated under waves of bombs then picked over by survivors. Before the war, this area had housed a number of technology companies and would've been a prime target for the Terrans.

The building Will led us to hadn't escaped the blitz, and now appeared to consist mainly of a smashed foundation and twisted heaps of black-stained glass, concrete, and steel.

"Are you sure this is the right place? Aside from the fact it's clearly been looted, it looks like an office building." Oliver sounded relieved.

Will grinned. "They're underground."

"That seems to be a common theme with us," Oliver muttered.

It took Will several minutes to get his bearings. In the far corner, he instructed us to lift away the debris, and there, under a pair of massive, warped steel doors and a mountain of smashed tile and melted carpet was a hatch.

"Everybody ready?" Will asked. He took a deep breath

and wiped his hands on his trousers. He was so keyed up, he scraped his hip on the edge of the entrance as he stepped down into it.

At the bottom of the stairs, Will fiddled with the numbers on a manual lock before opening the door into a cavern-like room. One half of the room looked like a workshop, inlaid with long tables laden with diagrams and various tools. Others held limbs and molds, and still others various props of the androids' trade.

The other half of the room was empty of equipment. Instead, it was filled with rows of androids standing in formation, clothed in silk robes of all colors, like a field of wildflowers.

There seemed to be an android for every element in the human spectrum. Some were lush with exaggerated figures, others austere in their androgyny. Their ages ranged from a pair of just-legal twins to a silvered-haired matriarch with a stern countenance, and their skin, eyes, and hair flaunted every natural hue on the planet, and some that were decidedly otherworldly.

These perfect versions of humanity stood, their open eyes blank and unseeing, their hands loose at their sides. My eye was caught by a young female in sea-foam green, an abundance of red hair curling over one shoulder. I stepped forward to get a closer look.

You are very handsome. Adrian's android.

Behind her was the man from the hologram. Will had gotten every detail correct; it was a perfect likeness. Will noticed my interest and went up to him, running his fingertips down the side of the man's face. "Antoni. He's beautiful, isn't he? This android is the love of my life." He said it low so that only I heard. "I know you understand."

Did I? Before I'd met Fane, I would've felt very conflicted at the thought of being romantically involved with a machine. Before the war, it would've been considered taboo—and yet, only if the relationship was reciprocal. It had been accepted, if somewhat salacious, to frequent android brothels or have a companion, but an emotional attachment? Well, that gave the androids a humanity that was considered offensive by many. Enough to go to war over, at least.

"I do," I replied, and my heart swelled for this man I'd only just met.

"This is why I constructed the holograms. I thought if I could create some kind of replacement for them...they wouldn't be used for this purpose anymore."

"But then wouldn't they just dispose of the androids?"

He bit his lip. "Maybe. But I was hoping to patent the holograms and make enough money that I could buy them all the moment they were rejected. It sounds stupid when I say it out loud, doesn't it?"

"No," I replied. "I understand." And I did, although wasn't it merely trading one AI for another? Could holograms achieve sentience? It made my head ache.

Will turned back to Fane and the others and spread his arms wide. Each of them stared, absorbing what they saw in their own way.

"Welcome to my garden," Will said, bowing. "Each one a perfect and delicate flower. We got them from the Novus corporation then re-skinned them according to the market." He walked among the rows, touching this one's hand and that one's hair, his touch reverent. "I loved each of them. They were the reason I wanted to become a cyborg—to share a kinship with them, be closer to them. I always felt more comfortable with them than humans." He ran a hand through his ragged hair and smiled. "And of course, I wanted always to look this beautiful."

Fane watched him intently, his head tilted to one side.

"Are they—?" I asked

"Deactivated only. We never submitted the paperwork

to have them decommissioned. When the Terrans began their little witch hunt, we brought them here and used a bunch of spare parts and greased palms to make it look like they'd been disposed of. It was one of the few things that gave me peace when I was underground, you know, thinking of them here, safe while the war raged around them. I thought perhaps one day, when things had gotten better, they'd be discovered and cherished as the treasures they are."

"That day is here, Will," Cindra said, putting her hand on his shoulder. "And I can't wait to meet them."

"Me neither," said Pax, curiosity and delight illuminating his face. "I'd hoped we'd get to travel down this timeline."

Will seemed to relax then, releasing a tension I hadn't detected. His smile was wide as he took in the room with a wave of his hand. "You want allies? My friends here may be your best shot."

"Look, I hate to be that guy—" Oliver began again.

"Then don't, love," Cindra said, her voice steely under her sweet tone.

Oliver gave up, shaking his head and leaning back against the wall.

"Satisfying yourself that you can rub it in when it all goes wrong?" I asked, trying not to smirk.

"What other choice have I got? But you can damn well bet that I will." He crossed his arms over his chest. "Well, let's get on with it, then."

Will rubbed his hands together. "I...I never thought I would see this day," he said. "I mean, I *hoped*, but..." He ran his hands through his hair then rubbed them together again. "Okay. Now the only thing we need to do is figure out how to activate them."

The Cosmists and the Cyborgists thought we were trying to stop the progress of technology, that we were luddites, determined to stay firmly in the Dark Ages. That simply wasn't true. After what happened with CIVRS, all we wanted was to avoid any more catastrophes of epidemic proportions. We didn't want to stop all progress; we just wanted it to move more slowly. After all, if they had treaded more cautiously with the CIVRS, who knows how many innocent lives would've been saved?

—*Lars Nilsson, personal diary*

24

AILITH

Oliver was incredulous. "You mean you don't know how to activate them? I thought you were the one who *deactivated* them."

"No, I was just here for support."

"Oh, for fuck's sake." Oliver dropped his head into his hands and slid down the wall.

"I know *how* it was done, for the most part. There was an interface that connected to each of their brains simultaneously, and a signal was sent through to all of them at once."

"Okay, well that's a start." Oliver clambered to his feet. "So where's the interface?"

"Oh. Well, my boss took it with her. But I thought you were some sort of human computer." Will smiled sheepishly.

"I am, but I can't connect to them if they're not active."
Will's chest heaved as though he was going to throw up.

"Ailith can do it," Fane said.

"What? No, I can't. I have no idea how to activate them."

"You can see their threads, right? The threads connecting you to them?"

"Technically, yes. I mean, I can *see* threads, but because they look like every other machine's, I'm not entirely sure which ones are theirs. Even if we can figure out how to send the signal, we might wake up God-knows-what." *The mech in the forest, it's skeletal driver still at the controls.* I shuddered.

"The code to activate them should be unique, shouldn't it?" Fane looked at Will, who nodded in confirmation.

"Yeah. We deactivated them before that all-purpose government pulse was sent. Standard machines were required to have a basic code that allowed them to be deactivated if necessary. It was one of the conditions companies had to adhere to be legal." He grinned. "But these aren't standard machines, and my boss was never one to let others make her decisions for her."

"Okay, so how do we access the code?" I asked.

"I have it on a chip," Will said.

"Please, tell me you have it with you?" Oliver said. I had no doubt even the nanites wouldn't be able to stop him getting gray hairs after today. *When did you start worrying about anything, Oliver?*

"Of course I do," Will said, looking offended. "It's here." He held out his forearm. "It was embedded in my arm for safekeeping."

"Okay, that I can work with," Oliver said. "I'll read the code from you then give it to Ailith so she can do her mind-meld trick."

The code entered my awareness only a few minutes

later. I closed my eyes and readied myself to send the code out and revive ninety-nine of the dark threads in my network.

Nothing happened. All around me, the intensity of certain threads increased then faded, like a failing heart.

"Fane, I need to you to help me. I don't have enough power to do it on my own."

"Sure you do, A," Oliver said. "Flick the switch. It'll work for androids as well as cyborgs."

The switch was something he'd put inside me months ago.

The original intent for your ability would've allowed you to be present in every connected cyborg simultaneously... I can't guarantee that your mind would be able to process it fast enough. I don't think they expected you to live very long.

"No way, Oliver. We don't know what will happen, or if I'll even be able to switch it off. The situation's not that dire—yet. Fane?"

Fane stood behind me and pressed as much of his body against mine as possible.

"You know you don't have to do that for it to work, right?" I asked him.

"I know," he said, his smile tickling my scalp. "But it's a lot nicer like this."

I couldn't disagree.

I gathered the pulse of code in my mind again, focusing the energy on the threads that had flashed before. Fane's energy blended with mine, and my power increased tenfold. In a sudden burst of light, I connected with each of them and sent the code hurtling into their brains, along with a silent prayer.

Please. Wake up.

In front of us, where ninety-nine glorified dolls had stood, ninety-nine androids blinked.

But even millions of people permanently hooked up to virtual reality while being taken apart piece by piece wasn't enough to make people see how dangerous these advancements could be. Some people even argue that good did come of the CIVRS debacle. They said that the world had too many people as it was, that now we had a reliable supply of all the organs and other shit that we could possibly need. Besides, every societal advancement has collateral damage. Easy to say when you're not the collateral.

—Lars Nilsson, personal diary

25

AILITH

Some of the androids fell to their knees. Others touched their faces, running their fingertips over their lips and throats. Even more remained stoic, unmoving, as though waiting for a command. Antoni, the man from the hologram, rushed to William, his face softening into a more than human expression as they embraced each other.

After his reunion with Antoni, Will briefly checked each of the androids, asking them questions and listening intently to their answers. I approached him just as he was finishing with the last one, the silver-haired matriarch. She eyed me haughtily, her eyes narrowed. Then, she seemed to realize what I was, and her expression tempered.

"How are they?" I asked.

"In remarkably good condition," he replied. "Of course, no time has passed for them. They may be a bit stiff at first, like any machine or person would be, but they're pretty much the way I left them years ago."

"So what do we do now?"

"I'll explain everything that's happened to them. Then, I'll introduce you all and your situation. Then...well, we'll have to see. I don't know that they have a program to accommodate these circumstances. They'll be acting on their own. I won't force them to choose you."

The androids listened to Will's story with very human expressions of bewilderment as he explained about the war, the change in their situation. That they were no longer pets or servants, that their bodies and awarenesses were now their own. I could empathize; I still remembered the moment Tor told me that everything I'd known was gone.

"What do you mean by *free*? Where will we go? What will we do?" Their voices all chimed in at once.

Will explained who and what we were. The androids looked at us with curiosity. Just how sentient were they? Were we as extraordinary to them as they were to us? Did they think it eerie how much *we* looked like *them*?

Will gave them a condensed version of our story and our needs. He described what had happened in Goldnesse, about Ethan and the inevitable confrontation to retrieve Fane, and about our subsequent need for allies on our island.

"Are we to be your shield?" one of them asked. There was no accusation or discontent in his voice, merely the curiosity of duty.

"No! Of course not," I replied hastily. "You don't *have* to come with us, and even if you do, you don't have to fight or defend us. It's not your fight. Come or not, fight or not, it's your choice."

He seemed to turn this information over in his mind. "Why does this Ethan want...him?" He tilted his head toward Fane but didn't look at him. Will had left out some details for the sake of summarizing our journey.

"He wants to create more artilects, fully sentient ones like Fane. But most of his records were destroyed, so he needs Fane's brain to fill in the gaps. Fane does not wish to comply."

"Did Ethan create this Fane?"

"Yes. He created all of you. He was the head of Novus Corporation."

The android lifted his leg and peered at the bottom of his foot. Stamped into the flesh was the Novus Corporation symbol. *That* name they knew. "They created us," he echoed.

"Then they threw us away," another one said. "Because we were not like *him*." Ninety-nine pairs of eyes turned toward Fane, and I was surprised at the hostility in them. "And now they want to destroy him?" Her voice held no mercy.

"Not exactly," I said. "They only want to create more artilects. But it *could* destroy him, and he's one of us now, so they can't have him." I reached out and squeezed his hand. He smiled at me. The exchange wasn't lost on the androids.

"That wasn't the only reason I left them." Fane addressed the androids, though most of them wouldn't meet his gaze. "I may be closer to their idea of perfection than you, but I still had no rights. They didn't see me any differently than they saw you. It may have been only a matter of time before I was auctioned off and joined you."

The thought of Fane living as these androids had made me sick to my stomach.

"And now, they're trying to kill my friends, simply because they want their property back. They don't value the life that they gave me, other than as a testament to their skill. They don't value any real life. That's why they're holding our friend Tor hostage. Even now, they're still using androids like you. They have an AI with them called Umbra. She killed a friend of ours, and she wants to take this one's body." He nodded at me.

Oliver snorted. "God, this sounds like the worst soap opera ever."

"What would we do in this place?" the first android asked as the rest of them drew closer to us. It appeared he was closer to Fane's level of sophistication than some of the others, who seemed content just to listen impassively.

"Whatever you want. Fish, learn to draw, plant a garden." My answer was met with some consternation and a little alarm. *I shouldn't be surprised. Why wouldn't they find it a strange concept?*

"What if we break down?" Another one, a tall, exotic-looking woman, asked.

Oliver stepped in. "We have some equipment back on the island, and we're planning to gather more. In fact, if you do decide to join us, that's what you can do on your way back. I'm sure Will knows where to shop."

Will nodded. "In fact, a lot of the stuff we'd need is right here. Between all of us, we can easily carry it back—we'll just have to improvise." He didn't let go of Antoni's hand as he faced the androids. "Well? What do you all think? Do you want to go? With them?"

None replied.

"Do you want us to give you some privacy?" I asked.

Will considered the androids then nodded. "I think so. Thank you."

We crowded into the stairwell and shut the door behind us. Low murmurs followed, but I couldn't make out what they were saying.

After a few minutes, Will opened the door and ushered us back in. The androids had grouped closer together, their eyes trained on us.

"We've decided to come with you," Will said. "All of

us."

"I'm glad to hear it." And I was. More than glad. Having them with us could make the difference in our survival— and theirs.

"Would any of you be willing to come with us on this suicide mission?" Oliver asked.

Will looked uneasy. "I—"

"They can't," I interrupted.

"Why not?" Oliver was confused. "We need all the help we can get."

"Because. It's not their fight. Not yet, anyway," I replied. "But more than that, what if Ethan or, God forbid, the Saints, get their hands on any of them? Who knows what they'll do to them? Or with them? Or what if Ethan has some way to control them—"

Oliver held up a hand. "I get it. Ugh. You're right. It's better we keep them a secret for as long as we can."

Will's relief was palpable. The android's expressions were neutral.

"So they're going back—which raises another question: who's going to take them?" Oliver asked.

Grace stiffened, her expression alarmed.

"Relax, Grace," I said. "If Pax says you should come, you're coming."

She pressed her hands to her cheeks and nodded. *I wonder how Tor would feel, knowing how devoted she is to him?* "I think Fane should go," I said. He looked at me, stricken. "Fane, you know what Will and the androids will need, and you know how to get back to the island. I think it's too dangerous for you. I'm sorry." The androids looked between Fane and me with interest. Would he obey my commands? Even with his freedom? Fully aware that everyone could hear, my words came out in a rush. "Fane, please. You're too important to me."

He pressed him mouth into a thin line. He didn't like it,

but I'd hit him where it hurt. "Fine," he acquiesced reluctantly.

As Will answered the androids' questions and instructed them on which equipment to gather, Fane pulled me to one side. "I'll go back with them, but I'm not happy about it."

Gray clouds rolling over the horizon. A broken mirror.

"I know. But I think it's the best thing, Fane. I don't want to lose you as well."

He brushed his thumb over my cheek and smiled. "I can't complain about that. I don't want you to lose me either." He hesitated. "You've noticed that the androids don't like me, haven't you?"

I kissed the palm of his hand and smiled. "Don't worry, they will." Despite what I'd said, uneasiness unfurled in me. *They wouldn't hurt him, would they?* Surely once they spent some time with him, they'd accept him. Was I doing the right thing by asking him to go with them? Or was I putting him at risk? Fane was formidable, but against ninety-nine androids? He'd be impossibly overmatched.

"Don't worry, Ailith. They might not care for me, but they also have very little idea about the outside world. They need us as much as we need them. I can use that to my advantage. I'll be fine, I promise."

I hoped he was right.

***

We parted ways in the morning. Fane hugged me so tightly I had to thump him on the back to get him to let me go. He looked over his shoulder as they walked away, his expression forlorn.

The androids gave him a wide berth, choosing to walk several yards behind him. I hoped his journey back wasn't going to be too unpleasant. Their disdain would bother him, I knew. Even though Fane was an artilect, he was

616

sentient, and it was an innate part of his personality to be friendly and want people to like him. He was used to people treating him a particular way because of what he was, and, well, he was a little spoiled. True, both before and after the war, people had wanted to destroy beings like him, but he'd never been exposed to it personally. Instead, he'd been worshipped and adored.

He'd told me once that he didn't want to *be* human, but wanted to be treated like one. Well, he was about to get his wish.

Though, I suppose CIVRS did serve a purpose. Although it wasn't enough to force the government to slow down the progress of companies like Novus and Pantheon Modern, it did allow me to find someone like Nova. Someone broken enough to do what we wanted without implicating ourselves. Her, plus our guy in PM, and we were good to go. They were in such a rush to churn out those cyborgs before they got shut down they didn't even notice an extra one being slipped in.

—Lars Nilsson, *personal diary*

26

FANE

The androids didn't like me. They avoided me, and I couldn't blame them. They were created for the same purpose as I was, to be revered, but they'd been found wanting, their sentience not sentient enough. Then they weren't only discarded but sold to the highest bidder and degraded, and all because of Ethan's desire to be God.

How *sentient were they? Each seemed different, some more aware of their situation than others. Several of them spoke amongst themselves, while the rest seemed happy just to take one step then the next. It was disconcerting, and I finally understood how I must make people—and even the cyborgs—feel, and why our creation had been so alarming.*

They'd find them even more alarming now. Before, dressed in the silk robes so at odds with the outside world, they were defined as other, their purpose-built attributes emphasized. But in a strip mall that had survived the bombings, they'd found a store that specialized in selling merchandise to tourists. And although much of it had already

618

been stripped by looters, all ninety-nine had managed to outfit themselves with far more practical clothing. Now, dressed in sweatshirts proudly claiming themselves as Canadian, they looked like a tour group winding down the coast to go orca-watching. The disappearance of their otherness, something the Terrans had long feared, was complete.

It had been all over Ryan's face.

I'd been walking almost on autopilot, lost in thought, when he'd stepped out in front of me from his hiding place along the path. The others were far enough behind me to be concealed by the trees, and he'd assumed I was alone.

"Fane."

It took me a second to bring my thoughts back to the present. "Ryan. Where did you come from?"

He pointed to a thick mass of brush. "There. I heard someone coming so I hid. Then I saw it was you."

"You've come for Grace?"

"Of course." His face darkened. "That means she found you. Where is she? We need to have a little chat then we're going home."

Water with no visible bottom. Dark shapes. *"She's not here."*

"What do you mean, she's not here? Where—" His eyes widened, and all color fled his face.

I didn't have to look behind me to know why.

"Ryan, meet our allies," I said quickly. His hand was halfway to the gun he kept slung over one shoulder.

"Our allies?"

"Yes. This is William. He's another one of the Patheon Modern cyborgs." William stepped forward.

"Another? I thought—"

"Don't worry, I'm the only other one." William gripped the hand that was still in midair and shook it briskly. Before Ryan could reply, he added, "And these are my friends. And now they're your friends too."

Ryan smiled in response, a reflexive smile that didn't reach his eyes. "Nice to meet you. Fane, could we have a word in private, please?"

"Of course." I nodded to Will then Ryan and I continued ahead for several yards back the way he'd come.

Before I could reassure Ryan, he let loose on me. "What the hell is going on, Fane? Who are those people? And where is Grace?"

"They're not people, Ryan. Not the way you think. They're androids. Will used to work with them."

"Androids? And who's this Will? If he's one of the cyborgs, why didn't we know about him before? Did the others know about him?" Frustration roughened his voice; he must've been afraid. I wasn't surprised.

"They thought he was dead. On the way back to the compound, Ailith heard him with her ability. We found him locked in a bunker like the others were. Once he knew we were looking for allies, he took us to the androids." I didn't think mentioning the other nearly two-hundred now-dead cyborgs would help the situation.

"And we can trust them?"

"I think so. I mean, we do have a common enemy in Ethan. His company, the Novus Corporation, built them. And then threw them away. We gave them the option to come with us, no strings attached, and every last one chose to do so."

He didn't look convinced, peering over my shoulder, his lips pressed into a thin line.

"They don't dislike humans, if that's what you're worried about, although they have every right to. They just... They were given life and then told how to live it. And now that's changed. They have some adjusting to do, but none of that involves annihilating the human race."

He smiled humorlessly. "Well, there's only one of me, so who am I to argue? Besides, my primary concern is Grace. I'm glad you all decided to be sensible and turn back." His gaze searched beyond the androids. "So where is she?"

I didn't have a lot of experience with confrontation, and a new sensation flooded me.

A large crowd, no way out.

"Fane? Fane! *I said, where is she?*"

Inexperience made me blunt. "She's not here. They're still going to the compound, and Grace went with them."

Blood surged into his face. "What? They've taken Grace with them? You can't be serious." *He took a step toward me, and his hand hovered over his rifle again.*

"She insisted."

"She *insisted? And you're telling me that an artilect and four cyborgs couldn't overrule the insistence of a sixteen-year-old girl?" His voice reached a crescendo that drew one hundred pairs of eyes. Aware he suddenly had an audience, he pulled me farther down the path.*

"What's the real story, Fane? Now, I might not agree with everything—hell, most things—those cyborgs do, but I do know Cindra well enough to know she would never willingly put Grace at risk. So what's the truth?"

There was no way to say it that would make it sound good. "Pax said we needed her to retrieve Tor, that she was crucial to our success—"

"Which way did they go?" *His face contorted into a feral snarl.*

"Ryan, she'll—"

"Which way?" *He grabbed the front of my coat, and his strength surprised me. Was it love for his child? Fear? Or was—*

"Fane!" *His whitened knuckles were inches from my face. He definitely wasn't thinking rationally.*

"Sorry, Ryan. They've gone back along the original route." *I pulled out my copy of the map and traced it for him.* "But, they'll be fine. They won't let anything happen to—" *My words were rendered useless by his retreating back. He pushed past Will and the androids, his fear of them neutralized by a greater one. As he disappeared among the trees, I wished I could send a message to Ailith.* Watch out.

"Is everything okay?" *Will asked. I hadn't heard him come up beside me.*

"No, but I hope it will be."

621

"He seemed…nice," he said diplomatically.

"Grace is his daughter. And she snuck away to follow us."

"Ah. What did he think of his new allies?"

"About what you'd expect. He wasn't one of those who was against their creation, but he was a victim of it indirectly. He'd never admit it, but he was more afraid than anything."

"As long as it's not the kind of fear that turns violent," Will said. "I won't put them at risk again."

"It's not," I assured him. "He'll come around. And his wife is a good woman. She knew what the cyborgs were and kept their secret. When they were exposed by one of their own, Lily and Ryan did their best to protect them—at the cost of their home and the new life they'd built."

Will considered then lifted his chin. "Well, we owe them respect, if nothing else. Now what?"

"We keep going. The sooner we get everyone back to the island, the better."

Will nodded and returned to the androids. As we recommenced our journey, he took Antoni's hand.

Stop looking, Fane. But I couldn't. They seemed so happy, or at least Will did. Antoni seemed to be one of the more sentient androids, gazing at Will with an expression that, if not adoration, demonstrated a very definite connection.

Could it ever be the same for Ailith and me? Could she forget about my artificialness? The fact that I was mostly synthetic? So far, it didn't seem to matter, emotionally or physically, but what about a few years down the road? She was part machine, but surely she would age eventually. How long could the nanites keep rebuilding themselves and replenishing her? Would it make a difference? It wouldn't to me. But to her?

And of course, there was the question of Tor. Could I compete with him? Was there even a competition? I wasn't jealous about their relationship, their closeness. It made me…sad. Petals torn by wind and rain. A house, abandoned too quickly. They were the same.

Later, as I led us across the water in the scores of rowboats we'd gathered, I turned my mind to other things. There was no point dwelling on what would happen in the future. Right now, we had to focus on making sure we had one.

We're so close. Tomorrow, we'll be at the compound, and I'll be able to see his face again. How will he react? I feel nervous now. What if too much has happened in the meantime? What if he thinks my leaving him behind was a betrayal? Hopefully, he'll see my sacrifice for what it is, and it will be enough for him.

—Love, Grace

27
AILITH

"Do you think we should have sent Grace back with the others? Ryan and Lily are going to kill us, *all* of us. You understand that, right?" I complained to Oliver as we hiked side-by-side. Cindra was deep in discussion with Pax about the twisted grass we'd found near Will's bunker.

"No, they won't. They'll understand. Why are you second-guessing it now?"

"Grace is their *child*, Oliver. Their *only* child. And she disappeared right as we were going on a journey. A journey Ryan thought was too dangerous to go on himself." I glanced over my shoulder to where Grace straggled behind us. She was having trouble keeping up but refused to let us stop and rest for her.

"Well, there's not much we can do about it now."

Oliver was right, but it was so irritating that I couldn't let it go. I was on edge about everything—Tor, Fane, *everything*. Oliver's nonchalance was simply the last straw. "There is. We can't get Grace involved."

"Pax says we have to," Oliver replied between his teeth. "Get over it."

We entered the small clearing where we'd found William. Cindra had just bent to retrieve a sample of the grass for her collection when a man spoke up from behind us.

"You don't care who you have to use to get your way, do you?"

Ryan. He must've tracked us from the island. He looked exhausted, his face lined with fatigue and anger. "I ran into Fane and your...allies. He told me the direction you were taking."

"Ryan—" I began.

"No. How dare you? Grace is only sixteen. I know she snuck away to join you, and I don't blame you for that. But the moment you discovered her, you should've turned around and brought her back. But then you only care about Tor, don't you?"

I'm not the only one.

Grace looked shocked, the color gone from her face. She was poised on the balls of her feet, almost like she was going to run. *Don't, Grace. You'll only make it worse.*

I couldn't meet Ryan's eyes. Even after everything I'd been through, I still felt the mortification of being chided by a parent.

"Grace, we are going back to the island, *now*. And then we're going to leave and find somewhere else to live. Somewhere where these...cyborgs aren't constantly putting us in danger."

Grace made her decision and stood her ground. "No, Dad. I *have* to go with them. Pax says I'm important. I have to go and—" She bit her lip.

"Pax said? *Pax said?* Pax can—"

"She's right, Ryan. We need her for this mission to be a success." Pax said it mildly but stared at Ryan with an unusual, and unnerving, intensity.

Once Ryan had gotten over his shock that the normally pleasant-mannered Pax had dared to contest him, he sputtered in indignation. "No, Absolutely not. It's *dangerous*, Grace. You saw what that mob was like when we left. If I'd thought it was in any way safe, we wouldn't have left in the first place!"

"Ryan." I put my hand on his arm, but he jerked it away. "We can't take any chances. If Pax says we need her, I believe him. I don't like this any more than you do. I don't *want* Grace to be involved. But if we don't succeed in getting Tor back, we don't know what's going to happen."

"I'm not putting my daughter at risk just so that you can save your boyfriend." His fists clenched convulsively at his sides, as though he was going to strike me.

"That's not what this is about, Ryan. How would you feel if it was Grace being held captive by Ethan? Would you tell us to just leave her there?"

He closed his eyes. "No," he said, "of course not. But—"

"Look, I promise we'll keep her out of harm's way. It's not like she needs to go *into* the compound or see anyone. We're going to find the entrance we used to escape the first time and enter the compound from there. And that entrance is over a mile away." I tried one last plea. "Come with us, Ryan. That way, you can make sure we don't involve her any more than necessary."

"We don't actually need Grace at all," Pax said.

"Wait, *what?*" I asked incredulously. "I thought Grace was crucial. You said—"

"She *was*," he replied. "But it's actually Ryan we need. Grace was just bait so that he'd follow us."

Ryan looked as confused as I felt. "Why didn't you just say that in the beginning? Ask me to come?"

"Would you have left Lily and Grace?" Pax pointed out.

"No, I probably wouldn't," Ryan admitted. "But if I'm as important as you say, Pax, that was a pretty risky gamble."

Pax smiled. "I have insider information."

Grace looked crestfallen. She'd wanted so badly to be important, to play a role rescuing the man she...loved?

Ryan sighed. "The answer is still no. I won't put Grace at risk. I'm sorry, but you'll have to find a way to rescue Tor without us."

"Grace will be fine, I promise." Pax smiled his earnest smile.

I had to bite my tongue. Pax often left out crucial information for things to go the way he wanted. He didn't lie, exactly, just omitted. *I hope he's right about Grace being fine.* But, if Pax said it was the only way, I trusted him on that, at least.

"They're coming for us, Ryan. They have Umbra, weapons...we need all the help we can get, even with the androids."

Ryan looked at Grace as he turned over the options in his mind. "We'll compromise. I'll take Grace back to the island then come back—"

"No."

Ryan turned around.

Grace stood behind him, her feet planted firmly, her fingernails digging into the flesh of her hips. "I'm not going back."

"Grace—"

"No. You can't make me."

"Actually," Ryan said, "I can."

Grace glared at him. "If you do, I'll follow you. I'll wait until you're gone then I'll come after you."

"You—"

"Is that what you want? Me, on my own? Trying to find you?"

"Your mother will make you stay."

"She can't. She'll have to sleep sometime…and when she does——"

Ryan stared at his daughter, who only five years ago had been a child. He took in her whitened knuckles, her stony expression. "Grace, why does this mean so much to you?"

I waited for her to say it out loud.

"Dad, we have to do this together. Or it won't work. Pax said so." She made no mention of Tor. She probably knew that using true love as a reason would have her father marching her back to the island immediately.

"No, I'm sorry Grace, but there's nothing Pax could say that would make me put you in danger." He grabbed her arm and began to propel her back the way we'd come. This time, she didn't resist.

"I could tell you the truth." Pax stood tall, his gaze pinning Ryan where he stood.

For a moment, Ryan was taken aback. "The truth? The *truth* is that you——"

"He'll kill us all."

"Ethan? That's exactly why I don't want Grace anywhere near that compound."

"Tor."

"Tor? Pax, what are you talking about?" This information was new to me.

"I'm talking about time. If you take Grace home, Ryan, we will run out of time."

"Time for what?"

"We're at a crossroads. If we don't go now, if we don't get Tor out when we're supposed to, the path changes. Ethan will adjust his plan. He'll warp Tor, the way he did Umbra. Tor will no longer be the bait—he'll become a weapon, as he was built to be. Tor and Umbra together."

A chill bloomed behind my eyes and curled down my throat to take root in my stomach. *No.* If that happened, I

628

would have to choose between Tor and us. Neither option was one I could live with.

My distress must've drunk the color from my face because Ryan's hand fell from Grace's elbow.

"Ailith, is that true? Did you know?"

"Help me, please. Trust me." On the surface, Pax's face was impassive.

I hated lying, but— "It's true." Cindra looked sharply at me, but Oliver only rocked his head slightly in understanding. "We didn't want to alarm you, because we thought we would make it in time, but Pax is right. This isn't just about saving Tor—it's also about preventing Ethan from using him against us." My very bones were weary at the thought.

Ryan frowned. "Can't you control him? I thought that was one of your abilities."

"I don't know," I said, and that was true enough. I could get inside him, but anything beyond that was still up in the air. "Who knows what they've done to him? And even if I could, that's *all* I'd be able to do. And I don't know for how long. That's why it's so important we get him back."

Ryan searched Pax's face then mine, trying to ferret out our lie. We gazed steadily back at him, united.

"Is that true Pax, what you said about Tor? That he would kill us all?"

"No. But he would kill you."

That was good enough for me. "Ryan, please. Help us. We don't have much time, and the longer we stand here, the greater our risk." I looked pointedly up at the sky, which was just reaching the apex of its paleness.

Caught by indecision, Ryan paused. And that was enough. Grace sensed the chink in his armor and took her chance. "I promise to stay out of the way, Dad. I'll do everything you tell me. *Please*, just let me help."

He looked at Pax, his expression grave. "And you're

629

sure about this, Pax? You need us? And Grace won't get hurt? I need you to be honest with me."

I held my breath.

Pax spoke the truth. "We need you, Ryan. And Grace will not get hurt at the compound. I promise."

Ryan bowed his head to kiss the top of Grace's, his face troubled. He exhaled into her hair then gripped her by the shoulders. "I don't like it, but it seems like we have little choice. But, Grace," he warned as her face lit up, "you have to do exactly what I tell you. Or we turn around immediately, Tor or no Tor."

Grace squealed and threw herself against her father's chest. Hugging her close, Ryan muttered, "Your mother is going to kill me." Then as Grace clung to him, he peered over her head at the rest of us. "So, what's the plan?"

It didn't take much to convince Nova to do it. We simply told her what she wanted to hear—how special she was, how she was going to change the world. Probably the only time in her life that she ever felt important. She was so desperate that she didn't even mind becoming one of them. Of course, she didn't know that the virus we planted in her would kill her as well. Suicide mission, and the dumb kid didn't even know.

—Lars Nilsson, personal diary

28
AILITH

"*Shit.* We should've expected this. When we escaped, Ethan and Lien obviously would've wanted to know *how.* Mil and Lexa were probably only too happy to oblige them."

The emergency tunnel we'd used to escape when Ethan and his followers had descended on the compound had been caved in by an explosion. Our secret route to the compound and Tor was completely and utterly blocked by the ruins of a small mountain.

"Now what do we do? Try to clear the debris? Try to bust our way through? We should've brought the bloody androids." Oliver had been crabby enough after another uncomfortable night on the ground. At the sight of the blocked tunnel, he'd sunk onto an errant boulder and dropped his head into his hands.

"Clearing that debris could take days," I said. "We have no idea how far back the collapse goes. I think we need a new plan. And there's a cactus on your foot."

Ryan looked around, shaking his head. "It's too quiet. Why are there no scouts? Why is no one waiting for us?"

"That means Ethan has a plan," Oliver replied, gingerly pulling the cactus away from his ankle. "Probably one which wants us in or much closer to the compound. It's still too risky for him to meet us out here, or he's feeling cocky. Either is a good sign for us."

"How?" Ryan asked. "They have the advantage now—they knew that if they cut off your route here you'd have to go in through the front door, which is suicide."

"Exactly." Oliver looked pleased.

"Since you look like the cat who got the canary, I assume you have an alternative plan?" I asked. "Care to share? Because right now, your face is so smug it had better be an amazing plan."

"It is. Remember the other false entrances?" he asked.

"Yes, but they don't lead *into* the compound, remember?"

"No, they don't. But I don't think that matters. I have the diagrams here, somewhere in my mind. Give me a few minutes." Oliver braced his hands on his knees, and his expression became distant.

"Maybe we could cause some kind of distraction? Draw them out. Maybe explosives?" Pax suggested hopefully.

"That's not a bad idea, but how do we make them? Everything we need to make bombs is either back on the island or in the compound storage room."

Ryan spoke up. "I can make explosives. You wouldn't believe how many homemade bombs I saw during my time on the force. All it takes is some household chemicals, the kind that most scavengers wouldn't be interested in. There's a farm store a couple of miles from here." He pointed south. "I'll go see if I can find the chemicals we need. And I'll also look for some shovels and trowels, just in case Oliver's plan doesn't work out and we have no choice but to go digging."

As he finished speaking, Oliver came back to the present. "Okay, I have a plan that might work. Is there any way to get Tor out of wherever he is?"

"You mean rather than us going in?"

"Yes. I know we're superhuman and all, but we're no match for a bunch of guns. We heal quickly, but not *that* quickly." He raised an eyebrow at me. "So? Can you?"

"I don't see how. I've only controlled him a few times, and only for short periods. And it's not like I can just tell him where to go." We'd been given certain limitations to curb our amassed power, and that was mine. I could be in any of the other cyborg's minds, but aside from being able to speak to Pax, I had no agency, no way to communicate. Or did I?

"Actually...I may be able to give him a message," I said slowly. "It's not a sure thing, though."

"None of this is," Oliver pointed out.

"Okay, so say I *can* get a message to Tor. What do I tell him? What's the big plan?"

"You know how the false entrances don't lead into the compound, but somewhere into the mountain, like a warren? One of them crosses almost directly underneath your garden. Close enough that we could go down that tunnel and dig up into your garden floor."

"That could work," I agreed. "But then what?"

Pax said, "In one of the futures, Tor is in the garden, waiting for us."

"Exactly," said Oliver. "They'd never suspect that. We could have him out of there and be halfway back to the island before they even realize he's gone." He looked at me. "What do you think, A? Could you get him to come down to the garden?"

I ran through the scenario in my mind. "I'm not

sure…but I can try. I'll know if he understands or not. But then, of course, there are the issues of him being drugged *and* under guard. There's no way Ethan would leave him alone."

"Me, Cindra, Grace, and Ryan can distract them," Pax said. "With *explosives*." He looked thrilled at the idea. "When the bombs go off, they'll all come running."

"Yes, but the minute you start causing a distraction, Ethan will know we've arrived. The first think he'll do is try to lock Tor down." I had no doubt Ethan had instructed anyone watching Tor to take him down at the first sign of trouble.

"Well, hopefully we won't need the distraction. And if we do, Tor'll just have to figure it out." Oliver's mind was made up. "Give him the message now, before Ryan gets back, so he has time to come up with a plan to get to the garden. Let's hope he's as clever as he is devastatingly handsome," he quipped, "because this will be the only chance we get."

He's so incredibly creepy, that William. He looks completely human…but I know he's not. That was one of our main problems with them—if they'd somehow marked them…branded or tattooed them in some way, maybe people would've felt differently. We would've known what they were, and we could've treated them accordingly. But no, they wanted to hide them amongst us, allow cyborgs the same freedom as human citizens. Why, if not to eventually replace us one by one? Well, not down here. I've put a collar around William's neck. Sarah left it for me, and I wasn't going to use it, but he walks too quietly, speaks too politely. I bet he's just waiting for the right time to kill me. Well, the joke's on him. If he tries to leave or comes within arm's reach of me, that collar will give him enough of a shock to kill a horse.

—Lars Nilsson, personal diary

29

TOR

The tingle spreading through my fingers was a familiar sensation I'd thought I'd never feel again. My hands shuddered involuntarily, and so did my heart.

A knock on the door broke the spell, and my hands dropped gracelessly into my lap.

Lexa paused in the doorway, as though unsure she'd be welcome. She wasn't. She came in anyway. It was the first time I'd seen her since I'd been brought here. I turned my face away.

"How are you doing, Tor? Are you awake enough to talk?" Her voice was low and cautious, the way I would soothe a deer before I *killed it, trying to keep its panic from tainting the meat. She stayed beyond my reach, twisting her fingers together. I wanted to tear them apart, break them as she'd broken us.*

"Fine," I answered. It wasn't the truth, but no matter how bad I felt, she looked worse. Her collarbone was visible under the collar of her t-shirt, and her blond hair had become brittle and dull, her complexion ashen. She looked ten years older than the last time I'd seen her, only weeks ago.

"So you've joined with Ethan then, have you? I expected that from Kalbir, after what she did. But at least she has the excuse of feeling like she didn't have a choice."

She sat in the armchair next to the dresser. "I didn't have a choice, either, Tor. Where could we go? With Mil being ill—"

"How is he?" I asked then hated myself. I shouldn't care how he was. They'd killed millions of people, had contributed in no small way to the end of the world. The drugs are making me soft.

"He's dead." She said it with the flatness of emotion already run dry. She waited for me to say I was sorry. I didn't. Who gave a damn that cancer had delivered an old murderer the undignified death he so richly deserved?

"I need to ask you something, Lexa, and I need you to tell me the truth. You owe me that much. Is Ailith alive?"

She paused. "Yes. How did you know?"

Relief rushed through me so quickly and so strongly that vomit rose in my throat. "Just a feeling." I wouldn't betray Kalbir. "How is that possible? I mean, after what happened…I saw her, Lexa. I carried her body back here. Her head—" The vomit surged into my mouth, and I forced it back down.

Lexa pretended not to notice, but she picked up the empty glass from my bedside and refilled it. "It seems that when Ailith resides in other minds—both cyborg and machine—she can bring her consciousness with her if she so chooses. When she died, she used that ability to transfer her consciousness into Fane. We then transferred her into Eire's body."

"The way you did with Ella?" She flinched, and I knew I'd hit

636

a sore spot. "So she's alive?"

"Yes. In Eire."

"And you knew she was going to do that? And Oliver knew? And Fane?" *What I wanted to ask was* why *Fane? Why didn't she transfer into me? But I knew the answer. Fane was safe at the compound with Eire's body. It was the practical choice. Besides, I never would've agreed to that plan.* I'm surprised Fane agreed to put her in such danger. *No, not surprised. Pissed. We're going to have to have a talk, he and I.*

"Yes. And we were sworn to secrecy. Threatened, actually." *Her face twisted.* "She knew you'd never go along with it. Besides, it was only intended to be the fallback plan. She never really thought it would come to that."

"I don't understand. Why didn't she just let me take Umbra out?"

"I think you know why." *Lexa smiled.* "She didn't want to put you at risk."

In my lap, my hand curled into a fist. Is that you, Ailith? Are you really there? *To distract Lexa from my hands, I asked,* "And Ethan truly thinks that using me as bait will lure Ailith here? And by proxy, Fane?"

"Come on, Tor. We both know it's a smart strategy. There's no way she would abandon you." *Her smile was pained.*

"Say they do come here. How do they expect to capture him? He's even stronger than me, and not made of flesh. No one would be able to get close to him. They'd have to destroy him from a distance, and that's too risky if they need his brain intact. They'd need to fight fire with fire."

"That's exactly what Ethan plans to do," *she replied.*

"What? How? It's not like—"

"Umbra," *she said simply.*

"Umbra's here? She's alive?" *I couldn't believe it.* "When I saw Callum, he already looked half-dead. I can't believe he's survived this long."

"He didn't," *Lexa said quietly.* "Callum died. But before he and

Umbra left the compound, Umbra had forced him to contact the Saints. They came immediately to meet her; probably missed you by a couple of hours. By the time they got to her, Callum's body was a hair away from death."

Acid surged in my stomach again. Callum was just a kid. He didn't deserve what had happened to him. He'd loved Umbra, a surrogate for his own parents. "So how does she still exist?"

"Apparently, she told the Saints about the compound's facilities. After they retrieved Umbra, they spent a day trying to see if they could keep Callum's body alive." She swallowed hard. "They couldn't. I don't know exactly when he died, but when they showed up here a couple of days after you'd left, he was...already rotting," she finished in a rush.

"The Saints brought them here?" It was just as Ailith and Oliver had feared.

Lexa nodded. "When Callum died, they were terrified they were also going to lose Umbra. They're still desperate for their Messiah— after their false start with Oliver." She raised an eyebrow at me. "Anyway, they'd apparently called for backup, and when it showed up a couple of days later, the Saints came to the front door of the compound prepared to siege it, and of course, found Ethan's mob there instead." She shook her head at the memory. "Their leader, a red-haired woman named Celeste, held a parley with Ethan and found they had much in common. Even better, she had an essentially sentient artificial intelligence in need of a body, and he had the means to make it happen. And here we are."

"But how did they all get into the compound? I mean, I would've though Mil would've brought the place down around his ears before letting them in."

"That was the plan," she said with a fond half-smile. "Unfortunately, the Saints had seen Ailith and the others leaving the hidden exit. They told Ethan, and the next day, Ethan quietly swarmed us. He then gave orders for the tunnel to be collapsed." She held her hand to her cheek, as though reliving a painful mark. "Mil died a week later."

638

"Did Ethan or Lien have anything to do with his death?"

"No. It was the cancer. But I still blame them. When Ailith and the others left, and Ethan breached the compound, the fight went out of him. He gave up."

"How did Ethan find out Ailith is alive?"

"I told them," she said, looking me squarely in the eye. "They have their ways of getting people to talk, and I'm not ashamed to admit it. I knew they had a few days' head start, so I held out as long as I could, but in the end... And then, not long after that, Kalbir brought you in."

"I'm surprised they let you see me."

She snorted. "Kalbir may be wonderfully charming, but she's also fickle. The novelty of you being awake wore off quickly. More so, I believe, as Ethan's begun to make less of a secret of Celeste's allure."

"Is she in danger?" As much as I loathed everything Kalbir had done, she was surviving the best way she could.

"Of course she is, and I've said as much. But you know what she's like." Lexa stood and patted me on the shoulder. "I have to go now, but I'll be back soon to give you your injection."

As she reached the door, I asked her, "Why did you and Mil do it, Lexa? All of it?" Although it no longer mattered, I needed to know. I couldn't even begin to forgive otherwise, and I wanted to. Hating them was exhausting.

"We wanted a better future, truly. We were convinced we knew best. Sometimes, I still think we did. I know that's probably not a good enough answer for you."

"You're going to have to choose a side, you know."

"Tor, I chose my side a long time ago, and I'm sticking to it." She looked at me meaningfully. "Keep that in mind." And with that, she left.

Ailith? Are you still there? My hand lifted to my cheek, my touch gentler than I'd ever been. "I thought you were dead," I said aloud. My fingers reached out to the wall and began to draw in careful lines. Garden. Soon.

I wonder whether the Cyborgists ever found out what we did, swapping William with Nova. If they knew we'd taken over one of their bunkers...and not just any bunker, but the one with all their precious freaks in it. One hundred and ninety-five of them. I don't know why they're here. Sarah said they're the generations that didn't survive, but if they're dead, why keep them here on ice, in the pods, as though they're meat waiting to be sold? Why not give them a proper internment? Just one more example of why the Cyborgists' ethics were so very, very wrong. Well, they're not my problem. They're William's. There's poetic justice in forcing him to take care of them. All I promised Sarah was that I would stay here and make sure they never wake up, and that's just what I'm going to do.

—*Lars Nilsson, personal diary*

30

AILITH

Thanks to Oliver's maps, we found the false entrance tunnel quickly and quietly. We were ready. Tor had his message. Ryan had his explosives. All we needed now was for the sky to darken further, to give us as much camouflage as possible.

Oliver played general, pacing back and forth as we honed our plan.

"Okay, let's run over this one more time. Ryan and Grace, you two together, Cindra and Pax, likewise. You'll all take a bunch of explosives and fan out around the front entrance to the compound. You don't have to be close— those bombs will cause a hell of a scene from a distance.

So be careful."

Ryan and Pax had managed to conjure up much greater firepower than we'd originally planned. Pax was in his element, and I hoped he was going to be able to restrain himself.

"Ailith and I will go to the tunnel," Oliver continued. "I have the maps, and Ailith can keep in contact with Pax. Constant communication, you two. Right?"

Pax and I nodded obediently.

"And is everyone comfortable with detonation?"

"Yes, sir." Cindra grinned and saluted. Oliver didn't even crack a smile. Cindra glanced at me and bit her lip to keep from laughing.

"Ailith and I will go down this tunnel and follow it until we get parallel to the garden, then we'll dig through. Tor will meet us there, and we'll all get our asses back here. In and out, quick, quiet, no confrontation. If we need a distraction, Ailith will tell Pax, so the rest of you pay attention to him." He hoisted a shovel onto his shoulder. "Right, that's the plan—get Tor, get out."

"What happens if they discover Tor in the garden? What if they follow you down the tunnel?" Cindra asked.

"Tor can dispatch them, or one of us can," I replied.

"What if he's out of it? Aren't they keeping him drugged?" Cindra asked. "Do you think he'll be out of it?"

"He was pretty lucid when I was in him just now. Lexa hadn't given him his next injection yet. We'll just have to hope she doesn't get a chance."

"Here," Ryan said, handing me a small canvas bag. "Take some of these explosives, just in case."

"If you think I'm going to blow up my garden—"

"Ailith, get some perspective. Besides, you already took most of the seeds," Cindra said mildly. She put her arm around Grace. "Are you sure you're up for this?"

Grace nodded, too quickly. She was practically

vibrating, all her movements awkward and accelerated. I could sympathize. We were this close to saving the man we both cared for, and we would only get one shot at it. The kinship triggered something inside me, and I grabbed her up in a hug. My spontaneity surprised her, but she returned the embrace, her arms shaking so hard it was almost painful.

"Don't worry," I whispered, "we'll get him."

She turned her head away, tears squeezing from under her closed lids.

I squeezed her tighter. "Stop crying, Grace, or your father will leave with you right now. You can do this. You wanted to be one of us? Today you are. No tears."

"No tears," she repeated and wiped them away with the back of her hand.

I let her go and turned to the others. "Don't do anything unless we tell you. With any luck, you won't have to do a thing. We—"

"Where is my body? Are you here yet?"

Lexa had been telling the truth; it seemed Umbra *was* at the compound. "Are we where, Umbra?"

"You do not fool me. I am going to rip out your consciousness. I am going to take your body, and I am going to put you into this one. Then you can see what it is like."

"Why don't you come and find me then?" I challenged her.

Oliver looked at me in alarm. "Ailith, what the hell are you doing?"

I waved my hand dismissively. "Well?"

"Maybe I will. Maybe I will come for you now, leave while they are busy."

Oh? "Busy with what?"

"They are having a party. While I waste in this body, they are celebrating."

"What are they celebrating?" *Get as much information as*

642

you can.

"They are confident. They— You are trying to trick me. I will say nothing more about it."

Silence.

"Umbra?"

"I am coming for you. I am going to come for you all."

I think they may be alive in those damn tubes. I know it's impossible, but sometimes I swear I can hear talking coming from the room. At first, I thought it was just Will talking to himself, but then I heard another voice speaking back. I'm going to keep a closer eye on him. Letting him live might've been a mistake. What if he can reactivate them? Maybe I should've killed him when I had the chance, but the thought of being down here alone for God knows how long...even a cyborg is better than no company at all.

—Lars Nilsson, personal diary

31
AILITH

The old mining tunnel was built from hollowed-out compacted earth and supported by wooden struts. There was just enough room for Oliver and me to walk upright, side by side, clutching our shovels and a flashlight. Oliver kept stopping to check the map in his head. And complain.

"How the fuck did I get stuck doing tunnel warfare? I should be outside, waiting to rain down fire."

I scoffed. "Oh please, you'd hate standing behind a bush waiting for the action to happen."

"That's true," he admitted.

"Is it much farther?" I was full of nervous energy. *I want this to be over.* Being this close to both Tor and Ethan's mob filled my chest with curling tendrils of fear that threatened to reach up and strangle me. I wasn't sure what I was more uneasy about—the danger we were in or seeing Tor for the first time since I'd died. What had the shock done to him? What would he think of my new body? Would it put even more distance between us?

"Not much. I hate these tunnels. They're unstable as fuck." He ducked his head as dirt dislodged by our footsteps showered down.

"Do you think this is going to work?" I asked.

"Maybe. I think we'll be lucky if we don't bring this whole place down around us in this bloody tunnel." More dirt fell.

"If we *do* make it, if we get Tor out and get back to the island alive, what then? How are we going to defend ourselves? Unless Fane managed to find some giant hidden armory on his way back, we have no weapons except Ryan's rifle and Tor's crossbow, which I still can't believe he left behind. We should've grabbed some more weapons when we left, rather than all that equipment." I needed to look toward the future. Anything to distract me from what felt like a walk to the gallows.

"Well, we had to make a choice about what to carry. I still think we made the right one. There may've been weapons at the compound, but there wasn't a lot of ammunition. Besides, we have some advantages. We're on an island, so we'll see them coming. We have one hundred people who don't need to sleep, and who can work for long hours at physically intensive tasks."

"Yeah, but to do *what?*"

"Dig ditches, build dams... I don't know, Ailith. I'm just trying to get through *this* particular moment." He flung out an arm to stop me then held a finger to his lips and cocked his head. Silence. He shook his head and continued. "But don't worry about it. We'll think of something. We always do. You'd be surprised what you can do with a bit of land."

"Okay, say we figure out how to defend ourselves...at

what point do our defenses not work? Then what? Do we ask the androids to fight?" Surely they wouldn't stand by if we were attacked. After all, they had as much to lose as we did. But were they sentient enough to care?

"Why not? The Cosmists threatened them too. Discarded them. Sold them as slaves. In a way, it's their fight as well. The Terrans never treated them much better either. Why wouldn't they want the opportunity for some revenge?" He paused again, listening, then walked on.

I understood Oliver's point, but still, what would Fane think of that plan? Would we be using the androids for our own ends, just as they'd always been used? I walked straight into Oliver, scraping my boot down his heel.

"Fuck, A. Would you watch where you're going?" He knelt and rubbed the back of his leg. "According to the map in my database, this is where we want to be. We'll need to dig...here...for about eight feet. Maybe ten. It should take us about an hour. Just pray there's no rocks."

As we dug, I checked in with Pax. *"We've started digging. How are things on your end?"*

"We're in position. Ready." He sounded thrilled, like he was on an adventure. He always loved it when we did something dangerous.

"Are you far enough away?" I hated to act like his mother, but I wanted everyone to be as safe as possible.

"Yes. They won't see us, especially since it's getting dark. Well, darker. Umbra was right, they're having a party. Outside the front of the compound. They've chopped down all the trees hiding the entrance. Why would they do that?"

They were outside the compound? Were we getting a lucky break? *"I have no idea. We're going to start digging... Standby, soldier."*

"Copy that," he said, delighted.

"The others are ready. They're just waiting for a signal from us. Pax said Umbra was right, they're having a gathering outside the front of the compound. Could work in our favor."

Oliver nodded and grunted. "Sounds too good to be true."

"Oliver? Are you actually breaking a *sweat?*" His forehead glistened in the yellow beam of the flashlight.

"Why don't you f—"

"Give Tor a head's up? Great idea." Remembering how muffled my contact with Will had been when he was underground, I let Oliver do the digging and concentrated.

Dear Lars's diary, this is Will. Lars's mind is taking a vacation, so I'm assuming diary duties for him. "Will, you're a peach," you might be saying to yourself, but the truth is, it gives me something to do. How exactly did he lose his mind, you ask? I'd be delighted to tell you. That bastard always seemed a bit unstable to me, especially after the first few months. He wouldn't let me watch any of the transmitted footage he was sent, and then he destroyed it, which I'm hoping means the Terrans lost. At least, I'm assuming that's the reason for his mental decline. Hoping. Otherwise, what's to stop it from happening to me?

—Will (should I even be signing my name??)

32

TOR

My dose was late. I had no idea what time it was, but my body craved it, agitation making my hands restless even as my mind gained focus. Ailith and the others must be close. Soon, she'd said. Soon.

My fingers traced on my arm. Garden. Hour.

It was time. Maybe with the celebration of Fane's impending capture, they'd be distracted enough to forget my dose and make this easy for me.

No such luck.

The door opened, and Lexa came in, the syringe in her hand. I gauged my coordination. Could I manage to knock it out of her hand? Break it? Gain myself more time? Once the effects of my last dose wore off, I would be able to think, to move.

I was still clumsy, still soft. But my mind was sharp enough to understand that I didn't want to cause a scene…otherwise, Ethan would be injecting me himself, and I would never make it down to the garden. Maybe it was time to see which side Lexa had truly chosen.

"Lexa, do you think we could skip this one?"

"I'm sorry, Tor, I—"

"Please, Lexa." I looked at her meaningfully.

She stared at me for a minute then nodded and lifted the syringe to her own arm. "Clumsy me, letting you grab the needle." I helped her onto the bed, where she lay down. "There's one man, right outside the door," she whispered.

Soon. *My finger traced the words on my arm again. I had to get to the garden. I eased myself off the bed, careful not to jostle Lexa, and fell to my knees. I winced, feeling every ounce of my weight. I crawled to the door and braced myself on the doorframe so that I could rise.*

The guard must've heard me hit the floor, because the door suddenly opened, and we stood face to face.

"Where do you think—"

Even with the remnants of the drug in my system, I moved much faster than he did. And harder. I caught him on the way down then dragged him back into the bedroom and eased him to the floor.

I stepped over him then closed the door behind me and staggered down the hall, pushing against the wall for support.

The effects of the medication were dissipating rapidly as the nanites got the upper hand, and I started to get better control of my muscles. My footsteps were increasingly silent, my mind increasingly clear. At the sound of raised voices from downstairs, my hunter's instincts kicked in.

Act drugged.

I stopped at the top of the final steps to the main room. Kalbir and Ethan were at the bottom, arguing about Celeste.

"You're sleeping with her," Kalbir accused him. She stood as I'd seen her stand before, hands planted on her generous hips. Ethan had better be careful; even with her ability dampened, Kalbir could inflict a lot of damage.

"Of course." He smirked, enjoying her anger.

"How could you? I thought—"

"You thought what? I mean, for a cyborg, you're hot. And yeah, it did turn me on when you betrayed your own kind to sit at my feet. But you're a cyborg." His gaze travelled down her body with an air of contempt. "She's pure human, beautiful, and fully believes in my vision. You're a lot of fun, Kalbir, but—"

"You know she used to sleep with Oliver, right? She loved having his cyborg co—"

Ethan drew his hand back then caught himself and grimaced. "I'm not going to do this with you. I'm going to join the party, Kalbir. You do what you want."

I stumbled down the stairs, loudly. Kalbir and Ethan looked up in alarm, and Ethan stepped behind her. I fell to my knees, one hand on the floor.

"What is he doing here? I thought Lexa sedated him?" Ethan demanded. "And fucking Dan is supposed to be watching him." Anger had replaced his shock.

Kalbir sneered at him. "He's probably getting pissed at your stupid party."

I blinked slowly. "Garden. I want to see...her garden," I slurred.

Ethan looked disgusted. "Sort him out. God, I hope they show up to claim him soon. He's pathetic. And tell Dan I want to see him." He turned on his heel, leaving me to Kalbir's mercy.

She glared furiously at Ethan's retreating back. "We're not done yet," she called after him. Turning to me, she said, "Okay, Tor, let's go back upstairs." She spoke slowly, as to a child. She put my arm around her shoulder and lifted me to my feet, the only person strong enough to do so.

"Please. Just a few minutes. I want to be...close to her." I pawed at her shoulder, my hands clumsy.

"Fine," she said, looking exasperated. "But only for a few minutes. And only to piss Ethan off. I'm not doing this for you."

"Thank you." I smiled blearily up into her face.

She shook her head and looked away.

650

We stumbled down the stairs and through the door together, into Ailith's garden. I was glad she wasn't here; she would've been devastated.

Ethan didn't believe that growing new plants was worthwhile, it seemed. Everything she'd planted was brown and withered, dying of thirst and neglect. The precious seedlings were long-dead in their trays, and the remaining heirloom seeds that she'd treasured were tossed to the side in disorganized piles.

Kalbir saw me taking in the damage and shrugged. "Yeah, he doesn't think nature is the way forward, so he put Lien on plant duty. Obviously, she couldn't care less. But whatever, Ailith stole most of the seeds on her way out anyway." Admiration tinged her voice. Enough to soften me. A bit.

I pushed away from her and leaned over the table, bracing myself on my hands. "I'm sorry about Ethan." I dropped my head to the coarse wood, as though keeping it up took too much effort.

"Don't feel sorry for me," she said, her tone brittle. "He's right. She is human." She grinned. "And frail. He'll grow bored of her soon enough. Despite his loathing for cyborgs, there's a part of him that's turned on by my 'abomination.' Besides, I've made my bed, and I've never been one to complain about lying in it."

Did she believe that? Or was it just bravado? "You could leave. Go find the others."

She snorted. "They'd never take me. Not after what I did. Besides, living rough, always on the run, isn't to my liking. I'll be fine here. I can deal with Ethan." Her expression was resolute as she started to take the seat across from me.

"Can I be alone? Please," I said quickly when it looked like she was going to refuse.

She rolled her eyes, but not before I saw the hurt in them. "Whatever. You have one hour," she warned as she closed the door behind her.

I locked it and sat down to wait.

651

It started when he followed me, the nosy bastard. Was it not enough for him that I was wearing his stupid shock-collar? It's not like I can go anywhere. He caught me talking to Antoni, well, Hologram Antoni. Antoni 2.0. Next thing I knew, he'd burst in, brandishing a crowbar like a maniac. When he saw Antoni, he almost had a heart attack. I've never laughed so hard in my whole life. Too bad it didn't kill him—but his face. Ha! I'll never forget that as long as I live. The only downside is he's forced me to show him how I did it, and thanks to all the cyborgs down here, we have enough equipment to make his plans happen. Ah well, it gets me off babysitting duty, although I do kind of miss seeing them so much. I've given them names and made up a story about each of them. It's a bit sad when all your friends are virtual meatsicles.

—Will

33

AILITH

"We're almost through, A." Oliver gave the soil one more tentative poke, and a tiny shaft of light pierced the darkness. He shut off the flashlight. "Make sure everyone is where they need to be before we do this. After we open this hole, there's no going back."

My heart beat painfully loudly in the quiet of the tunnel. *We're so close.* "For once, things seem to be going our way. Tor's in position, alone." It took everything I had not to shove Oliver aside and claw my way to the surface. I needed to see Tor. Being inside him was one thing, but I needed to see him with my own eyes. "We might not need that distraction after all."

"Good. I don't like Cindra being out there."

"I'm sorry I keep putting you all in danger."

Oliver rearranged his grip on the shovel. "Nah, don't worry about it. Who wants to live forever?"

"Me. I would haven't become a cyborg otherwise."

"Well, it's time to earn it," he replied.

"Pax, hold fire and prepare to leave as quickly and quietly as possible. We may not need the bombs after all."

"Okay." I could feel his disappointment. *"I'll tell the others. Ryan taught us some hand signals. There's a lot of people at this party. Even Umbra is there. At least, I think it's Umbra. She's right—they didn't give her a good body."* He paused and took a sharp breath.

"Pax? What is it? Is something wrong?"

"They're having a barbecue. Looks like birds of some kind. I wonder if they have barbeque sauce? It smells so good."

"Focus, Pax." I left Pax to his ruminations and turned to Oliver.

"Is everything okay?" he asked.

"They have barbeque."

He groaned. "God. How much do you want to bet that when we meet up with them later, Pax will have a pocketful somehow? If we get captured over Pax's stomach, I'll kill him myself."

I laughed, too loud in the still air. "Then let's go get Tor before Pax's stomach wins."

Oliver drew back the shovel, struck out, and we were through.

I shimmied into the hole and up, hoping Tor was still alone. By my count, Kalbir had left him just over twenty minutes ago. She'd given him an hour, and I prayed she would stick to that; we'd be long gone by then.

As I pulled myself out onto the furrows, a familiar

653

figure loomed over me—and he was ready to fight.

Tor had never seen Eire awake, only in a coma, and knowing I was in her body was much easier to accept than the reality.

"Tor, it's me, Ailith." I held up my hands.

He backed away, eyes darting to the side to look for a weapon.

"And me," Oliver chimed in. "Saving your ass. As per usual."

At the sound of Oliver's voice, Tor's aggression melted, and he dropped stiffly to his knees in front of me. I embraced him. *Finally*. The familiar feeling of him under my hands healed something inside me, and power flowed through our bond.

His body remained rigid, his eyes traveling over my new face.

"It'll take some getting used to," I said.

He nodded, still stunned.

"Tor, listen to me. We have to go. We—"

"Ailith, we have a problem." Pax's voice was uncharacteristically taut.

"What?" No. *Not when we're so close.*

"You might want to see for yourself."

Tor grabbed my hand as I looked through Pax's eyes.

Grace had torn away from her father's grasp and was sprinting toward the compound. At the sound of her footfalls and labored breathing, the partygoers turned en masse, food and drinks forgotten in their hands.

"Ji!" she screamed, throwing herself into the arms of the young man who'd rushed to meet her halfway. Confusion and joy spread across his face as he returned her embrace. Ji. *Lien's son.*

"How did you get here?" he asked as he touched her hair and face. Ethan came up behind him. He'd been anticipating *our* arrival, so Grace's sudden appearance had caught him off guard.

As soon as she saw him, she played her trump card. "They're here," she gasped, breathless. "They're here now to get Tor. They're coming from the tunnels, into the greenhouse."

"Pax, run."

At first, Lars used the holograms to recreate his old life. He constructed some woman named Sarah, and held debriefings with her, pretending the Terrans had won the war and plotting what they should do next. It was pathetic. Then he must've realized we're never getting out of here but had too many rations to starve for at least ten years, because he resurrected his parents and said goodbye to them...that was just sad. I mean, even though he's holding me captive down here, and his kind would've destroyed me and my android proteges without a second thought, I'm not totally without sympathy. I wonder if he'd feel the same sympathy for me?

—*Will*

34

AILITH

Grace had betrayed us. It wasn't Tor she was in love with. It never had been.

Oliver's slap on my shoulder brought me back to the present. "Ailith? What's happened? What's going on?"

"They know we're here. We have to go, now."

"*What?* How?"

"It doesn't matter. They know we're here and they're *coming*." I darted to the door, but Tor had already locked it. I glanced through the window as I yanked the shutter down, and there she was.

Umbra. Ethan's new attack dog. Pax was right. Her body was...primitive. She looked like Frankenstein's fabled monster, stitched together from pieces of the dead.

They must've harvested parts from different androids to form her complete body, aiming for compatibility and function over aesthetic. *Well, she was planning to get this body, so I guess a temporary one was good enough in the meantime.* I thought I recognized some of the bits from the Saints of Loving Grace church, the ones they'd used to line the walls of their church. Her limbs were different sizes, only two of the four skinned. The others glinted dully, the synthetic casings open at the metal joints.

Most disturbing was her face. For a reason unfathomable to me, they'd given her the face of a child. She screamed at me, the skin stretching over the too-wide mouth as she staggered down the stairs toward us. Even with uneven limbs, her speed was terrifying.

"Go, go, go!" I raced back to the tunnel mouth, back to where Tor and Oliver still waited.

"Shouldn't we try to stop her?" Tor asked as she threw herself against the door. It groaned and bowed but, for the moment, held.

"Not here," Oliver said. "Get her in the tunnel first."

We crawled back down the tunnel, Tor pushing me in front of him. Partway down, there was a muffled crash as the door gave way. She was through. Tor struggled to pull himself through the few feet of tunnel, his size putting him at a disadvantage.

I burst out into the main tunnel just behind Oliver, preparing to run as soon as Tor came through. He didn't. "Tor," I screamed. No point in being quiet now.

We felt more than heard the scuffle in the narrow passage then Tor erupted out, rolling quickly to his feet. One leg of his trousers was torn below the knee, blood seeping out of his lacerated skin. He snatched up one of the shovels and drew it back.

When Umbra appeared scant seconds later, her child's visage distorted in rage, Tor smashed the shovel into it, collapsing part of the small tunnel as he did. Dirt and rock rained down on Umbra, trapping her from the shoulders back. She gnashed her small, pearly teeth at us, but her new prison held.

"Hurry, it won't trap her for long." Oliver took off running, and Tor and I followed, stumbling as we tried to find the flashlight and praying we were going the right way.

"We need to stop her," I said. My breathing was surprisingly even. Eire's body was much more athletic than mine had been. If I managed to outrun Umbra, it would be thanks to her. *Come on, girl, get me through this.*

"We can't, Ailith, not here. Keep running. We need to get out into the open." Tor ran at my shoulder, keeping his body between Umbra and me. Protecting me, as always.

"The bombs," Oliver said, slowing slightly. "We can't use them until we get out or we'll bring the mountain down on us. Right now, we just need to be faster than her."

Umbra screamed inside my head. *"I want my body!"*

"She's coming," I gasped. We shot out into the darkness, the cold, fresh air searing our lungs. Blood pounded in my ears so loudly I couldn't hear whether Umbra had cleared the tunnel or not. I turned to look, but nothing but darkness filled the entrance.

"The bombs. Hurry." Dumping the sack Ryan had given us, Oliver fumbled with one of the devices before finally managing to ignite it and throw it in.

It bounced on the hard ground and extinguished almost immediately.

Shit, shit, shit.

"Light a whole bunch of them and throw them in," Tor said, scooping up several of the explosives. "We don't have time to be particular about this."

As he threw the blazing canisters into the black hole of the tunnel, they illuminated a figure moving toward us. Umbra reached for us with oddly-shaped fingers just as the bombs went off, outlining her in radiance as she was engulfed by the explosion, the tunnel collapsing around her. *"Give me my—"*

The screaming in my head went quiet.

Yep, Lars's finally lost the plot. He seems to be creating scenarios he'd fantasized about in real life but never got the chance to experience...probably because they're illegal. I mean, I saw some weird-bad shit happen with my androids, but nothing like he's doing to those holograms. It makes me sick. I wish I could kill him, but that stupid collar keeps me from getting close. I guess I'll have to hope that someone finds us, and soon.

—Will

35

AILITH

For the first time in the dream, I no longer crossed the emerald sea toward the lone tree. Instead, I'd become part of the tree itself, the bark and my skin the same. Acorns fell from my hands as I opened them and placed them flat on the ground. My fingertips, pressing into the earth, grew roots. Not the gossamer strands of springtime, but thick ropes lined with poison-tipped thorns.

They snaked through the soil, erupting up through the soles of everyone on the island. Some became my warriors, others my victims, but all were subject to my will. Death soaked into my roots, nourishing them, the souls of the dying a bitter harvest that fueled me.

Then it was done, and the sky split open, the ash parting to reveal a single-celled sun, dividing, replicating, devouring the ash until thousands of suns covered the sky. They fell to the earth, some sinking into the ocean under their own weight, others into the ground. Everything that had ever lived rose and walked again, until the earth folded in on itself and I was again alone, weaving through the long, waving grass of the emerald sea. I wasn't alone for long.

In my hand, I soon held another, a smaller version of my own. Onyx hair fluttered behind us, and in her other hand, she clutched a string that led up, up to a kite—a man but not a man, smooth and shiny, with only the suggestion of a face. Ribbons made of flesh and blood flew behind it, twisting in the breeze as we made our way to the tree.

Far ahead, the others clustered around the trunk, just close enough that we could make out their smiles, their hands raised in greeting. A riot of blossoms grew at their feet, and they braided them into a tiny crown.

As we reached the massive oak, she began to climb, her kite clutched in one hand, and a pang of fear touched my heart. Yet, even when she scraped her leg on the rough bark and bled, I let her be. She had to be strong in this new world, though she was but a single blossom in a wasteland. Because, of all the seeds we'd planted, she was the first, the most important. And if she withered, the harvest was for naught.

High in the tree, she raised her hand to shade her eyes against the sun. She turned slowly, surveying a kingdom only she and her kite could see. One by one, she untied the ribbons from him then wrapped them around the slender branches of the canopy. Blood and something else seeped from the bands and ran in delicate rivulets down the channels in the crenelated bark.

Satisfied with her handiwork, she climbed back down the trunk to claim her blossom coronet. The moment it touched her head, I peered into a mirror.

The illusion vanished as she knelt, smiling, and pressed her face into the moist soil, where the wind couldn't take her.

She was the seed.

They've stolen our bargaining chip. Grace's betrayal is small comfort. She sees it as a sacrifice, but a sacrifice doesn't matter if the person doing it isn't valued in the first place. She's told me where Fane is holed up, about their android army, dumping everything at my feet like a dog, desperate for approval. I'm not worried. Those androids will be about as adept at fending us off as they were at being artilects. We've thrown them away once, and we'll do it again. It's our move now.

—*Ethan Strong, personal journal*

36
AILITH

Somehow, I'd expected our rescue of Tor to make us whole again. I'd expected... I didn't know exactly. But it wasn't this. In the few days it had taken us to get back to the coast, we'd barely spoken.

Ryan's silence, I could understand. Grace's betrayal had shattered him. Not only had she betrayed us, but she'd left him and Lily for the very people who'd cast them out and threatened their lives. And that wasn't her only betrayal. She'd become a woman, at least in her eyes, without him ever seeing it. She and Ji had obviously been having their secret love affair for a long time. Long enough for her to feel that forsaking her family was her best chance at happiness, anyway.

I wished I could say something to him, something comforting from a daughter to a father. But, like the others,

I was too drained. My heart almost broke when he gathered his courage and asked Pax, "Will she come back? Alive?"

"Yes," he said simply. "But—"

Ryan held up his hand to stop Pax from continuing, as though he wanted to ignore the troubled tone of Pax's voice and take what comfort he could. His daughter would return. Like me, Ryan knew there was more to Pax's answer, but for now, for Lily's sake, *yes* was enough.

Tor was…different, just as Fane had said he would be. After we'd watched the tunnel collapse and swallow Umbra whole, we'd run through the darkness, fearing to light our way in case we were seen. We ran in silence, daring to draw deep breaths only once we'd reached the meeting point.

We'd found it empty. Oliver had looked at me with wild eyes, showing for the first time the depth of his feelings for Cindra. I put my hand his arm.

"Can you see them, Ailith? Please?" he rasped as he tried to catch his breath.

"Pax? Are you guys okay?" Nothing. I shook my head at Oliver, and his face paled. *"Pax? Pax!"*

"We're fine. Sorry. We're fine— Oh, damn."

"Pax?"

"I fell. It's hard to run in the woods at night and have a conversation at the same time, you know. It's impractical."

"Sorry. *Are you guys okay?"* I asked again, giving Oliver a thumbs-up. He fell to one knee, dropping his chin to his chest.

"Yes. We're almost there. Ryan didn't want to leave Grace."

"Is he still with you?"

"Yes, but barely."

I left Pax to run and gently punched Oliver's shoulder. "They're fine. They're almost here."

Tor sat silently, eyes closed and his back to a tree.

A few minutes later, the sounds of strained breathing

664

over the snapping brush caused Tor to surge to his feet, ready to take on whoever broke through into our clearing. As Pax and the others appeared, the fight deserted him, and he slumped back against the tree, his head in his hands.

Ryan was ashen-faced and breathing hard, his face bewildered. Cindra embraced Oliver briefly before leading Ryan over to a fallen log. She sat him down, peering into his face and scanning him with her hands. She glanced up and gave a scant shake of her head, her lips pressed into a thin line.

Pax's face was smudged with dirt, his pockets bulging with explosives.

"Are you okay?" I asked. He looked fine, but he often did even when he wasn't.

"Yes. Although, I would've liked to set a few of these off," he replied, patting his pockets in dismay.

"Don't worry, I'm sure you'll get your chance," I said. I drew him to one side. "What the hell happened? And did you know it was going to?"

"I didn't. Not really. Like so many other things, the possibility was always there, but I don't think even Grace knew until the moment she did it. Well, not the part where she told Ethan." He gingerly removed the explosives from his pocket and laid them on the ground. "We were waiting, just as we'd planned. Suddenly, she just started running. Ryan tried to grab her, but she was ready for him. You saw what happened next."

"She could've killed us all," I said, dropping cross-legged onto the ground. "I never saw it coming. I thought she was in love with Tor."

"In love with Tor? Why would you think that?" He eased himself down next to me and stuffed the bombs back into his bag.

"Because she was obviously in love with someone at the compound…she was desperate to go there. I just assumed it was Tor because it never crossed my mind that she was capable of deceiving us like that."

He nodded. "What happened to you? Did everything go to plan?"

"Umbra happened to us." I described the tunnel collapsing in an inferno.

"That sounds amazing," he said. "I'm sorry I missed it."

I shuddered. "It was *terrifying*, Pax. I thought for sure she had us."

"Do you think you killed her?"

"Well, I did until you asked. I hope so. Her voice in my head's gone silent. That's got to be a good sign, right?"

"I would think so. What about her thread?"

"I can't see it. Or Kalbir's. Ethan must've blocked me like Oliver thought. Doesn't want me spying. Even if they were dead, I would normally see their threads—they would just be dark."

"It's time to go." Oliver stood over us. "We can't stay here, in case they're looking for us. We need to keep moving." He and Cindra moved to walk with Ryan between them, but he shrugged them off and stalked ahead without a backward glance.

Hours later, as the sky lightened, we stopped to set up camp.

Ryan sat on the ground next to his unpacked bag. He stared off into the distance, only changing the direction of his gaze when Tor lit a fire.

I sat down beside him. "I'm sorry, Ryan, about Grace."

"How could she betray us all like that? We could've been captured or killed. And all over an infatuation with some boy." He crushed a lump of dried peat in his hand.

"He's not 'some boy' to her, Ryan. She must have very strong feelings for him, whether we consider them real or not."

He continued to stare into the fire. "And how could she

keep it a secret all this time? How did we not know?"

"Girls grow up faster than their fathers think. Especially in times like these." *It happens to all of us.*

"Ailith, I'm so sorry." His voice broke.

"No, Ryan. You should've taken her back when you wanted to. You were right—I was selfish. I *was* willing to risk your safety, and Grace's, to get Tor back. I'm more to blame for this than you are. If I hadn't let her come in the first place—"

"She would've gone anyway. She's like her mother that way. Looking back, she's been preparing for it since we left Goldnesse. I just didn't— At least she made it back to the compound alive. She might not have if it hadn't been for you guys."

"Ryan—"

"I'm going to bed. I need to think of what to tell Lily. This will be one of her worst nightmares come true." He shook out his sleeping bag and climbed in, his boots still on. As he turned his back on me, his shoulders shook.

Tor insisted on standing the first watch, saying he wouldn't be able to sleep. I didn't ask why; I didn't think I could bear the answer. I sat on a fallen trunk that crossed in front of another tree, my back cushioned by dry moss. Finally, we were alone.

For a while, I simply watched him from my seat on the other side of the fire. The glow of the flames flickered over the inky markings on his face, softening their starkness against his pale skin. He was thinner than the last time I'd seen him, his clothing hanging off his still-muscular frame. I couldn't stand our silence any longer.

"How are you doing?"

He didn't answer. Instead, he took several long strides toward me and pressed me up against the tree.

And then he kissed me.

"You came for me," he whispered into my mouth. He

667

pulled back and looked at me. "I thought you were dead."

"Technically, I was. Look, I know this is going to take some getting used to, but—"

"I'm already used to it," he said. "I spent the entire walk here getting used to it."

"I thought you didn't want to talk."

"I didn't. Not until I knew my own mind. Ailith...after what happened—"

"I know," I said quickly. "The others told me. You don't have to talk about it."

"I want to talk about it. I *need* to. After I thought you were dead..." He ran his hand through his hair and shook his head. "Since I met you, I wondered what it would feel like, but what I'd imagined never even came close. It was—"

"We searched for you for days," I whispered. "When we couldn't find you— And then you disappeared from the dream...I thought—"

"Never again," he said, sliding his hand up the back of my neck and pressing his mouth to mine.

I leaned into him, kissing him back with a passion that equaled my fear of his loss. But as he pulled at the zipper of my jacket, I drew back. "No. Not like this."

He closed his eyes. "Because of Fane?"

"Yes. No. Tor, *you're* the one who decided we couldn't be together."

"You don't love me anymore." It wasn't a question.

"Of course I do. I came for you, didn't I? But everything that was true before—my ability to control you, my penchant for almost getting us killed—still is. None of those things have changed." I traced my thumb over the tattoo on his bottom lip.

"I don't care what I said before. I want this. I want *you*. Not a relationship—I know that's the best way to curse ourselves. But just to be together, whenever we can."

As I stared into his eyes, I remembered a standoff like this, but with a different kind of passion.

Within the expanding brown and gold pleats of his irises, I saw them. The nanites, millions of tiny machines propelled by gilded filaments toward the black pinprick of his pupil. As they converged in the center, his iris overflowed, and the nanites streamed down his face in veins of precious metal.

"I want us to be together, no matter how fleeting," he repeated.

And so we were.

*Lien and I have decided the cyborgs have left us no choice—
we move now. Whether we intended to honor the agreement
after swapping Tor for Fane doesn't matter. They've spat in
our eye for the last time. We're going to the island, and we'll
kill every last one of them. And Fane? I realize now that he
was not, as I'd believed, my opus. He is a failure, like the
others. He has no concept of his own importance, and therefore
his sentience is flawed, incomplete. Orders are to shoot him on
sight.*

—Ethan Strong, Personal journal

37

AILITH

They'd seen us coming across the water and met us on the
beach. Impatient, Lily waded into the water, her eyes
searching the deck of the boat, landing on Ryan and leaving
him to search more. When she saw Grace wasn't among
us, she lifted her hand to her mouth and sank to her knees,
the water lapping at her breasts.

Ryan vaulted overboard and strode to her, pulling her
up by her hands and embracing her. He whispered
something to her before putting his arm around her
shoulders and escorting her to shore. As he led her away,
she looked back over her shoulder at us, and her
expression was clear.

It's your fault she's gone.

Fane hung back and waited for us to come to shore. As

Ryan passed him, they nodded once to each other, and Fane's eyes followed Lily as Ryan led her up the path toward the town, his expression troubled.

As soon as my feet touched the slick pebbles of the shore, a shyness overcame me, and I couldn't look Fane in the eye. It wasn't guilt. Not exactly, anyway. Fane and I weren't together in a formal sense, but we did have a romantic relationship. Before the war, being in a relationship with more than one person at a time wasn't uncommon, but it wasn't something I'd ever done. I simply had no idea how to act.

I forced myself to meet Fane's eyes, and that one look told me everything. He knew.

Tor's boots shattered shells beneath them as he came up behind me. He and Fane faced each other silently, eyes wary. My heart quailed. If this meeting went the way of the last confrontation, it was going to get ugly fast.

Tor stepped in front of me. The muscles in his arm corded as he drew it back.

Fane stepped forward, his body tense.

Tor wrapped first one arm around Fane then the other, hugging him close. Fane grinned at me over Tor's shoulder and enfolded Tor into his own embrace. They stood cheek-to-cheek, the breeze entwining their hair in a tangle of black and gold.

"It's good to see you, Tor. I think we'll be a lot closer from now on," Fane said, pulling back and looking at us with raised eyebrows. Tor looked taken aback as understanding dawned on him.

I winced. I had no idea how Tor would react. Would the distance between us return? Would he force me to make a choice between them?

Instead, he grabbed Fane around the back of his neck and pulled him close until their foreheads touched. "Thank you, brother," he said. "I think I could get used to that."

671

Water splashed behind us as curiosity finally got the better of the others. Pax's grin was so wide it must've hurt, while Cindra gave me an unsubtle and very enthusiastic squeeze.

"Oh Christ, seriously? Ailith, you must have a magical v—"

"Oliver," Cindra warned.

"I'm not judging. I just—"

"Oliver."

He held up his hands in defeat.

"How are the...newcomers doing?" I asked Fane. I could barely make out the village from the beach, but moving figures dotted the hillside.

"Fine, I think. They don't care much for me," he said candidly, "but they seem to like the island. Although, some of them don't know what to do with themselves. They're not used to so much open space."

"I still can't believe it," Tor said, shaking his head as we walked up the path leading to our new home. I'd told him about meeting Will and our recruitment of the androids on our journey.

"What part of it?" I asked.

"All of it. This island. The androids...it's incredible."

"Is this the sort of life you pictured before—well, what happened?"

Tor took in the island and nodded slowly, his smile wry. "It is, you know. It's perfect." He inhaled a deep breath of ocean air, tipping his head back to let the breeze travel across this throat. He was different than he'd been before, but not the way Fane had thought he would be. He seemed...lighter, somehow. Unburdened. Before, he'd been so weighed down by the violence of his past and the desire for it to be different. Now, he seemed at peace with himself. Everything that had happened hadn't broken him at all; it had restored him.

672

"Ailith?" Fane interrupted my reverie.

"Sorry. What?" I smiled at him.

"I said, why don't you show Tor his room and let him get settled? Then I'll catch you back up with everything that's been going on here, and you can tell me what happened at the compound."

Reality came crashing down. "Fane, we need to come up with a plan. They're going to come after us, and we need—"

"In time, Ailith. We can spare an hour," he said, smiling gently. "I'll meet you under the tree." He clapped Tor on the back as he left.

"He's right, Ailith. Take a breath," Tor said as I led him into the small house I'd claimed as my own.

"You can stay here for now," I said, pointing to a spare bedroom. "We'll set up another house for you as soon as we can."

He dropped his bag on the floor and sat on the bed. "This is fine. Ailith—"

"Tor, I can't rest. Not yet. They're going to come for us. Grace knows where we are and how to get back here. Why wouldn't she tell Ethan?" Nerves made my limbs weightless.

Tor took my hands in his and drew me to stand before him.

"I know," he said soothingly. "And we'll figure something out, I promise. But you can take a breath." He pulled me into his lap.

I laid my head on his shoulder. "You're different, Tor. Fane said you would be, but I thought he meant you would be...damaged. Harder. But you're not. You're..."

"Happy," he said.

"But how can you be? After everything?"

He curled a lock of my hair around his finger. "Because. You're alive. I'm alive. We're *here*. I have everything I want because now I know what I have to lose. Which means when they *do* come for us, we're going to win. I'll make sure of that."

"But what about… You said you were never going to kill again. That that wasn't the person you wanted to be anymore."

"It isn't. But I've realized that the person I was is going to help me be the person I want to be. Which is the man who has all of this." He dropped his hand from my hair to my fingers. "I did bad things, Ailith, but now I believe they had a purpose. And I've made peace with it. With myself."

I pulled back and looked at him, seeing nothing but the truth in his face. "I'm glad. I just—I'm so glad to have you back." I stood reluctantly. "I'd better go tell Fane everything that happened. You should get some rest."

Tor glanced out the window. "I've been resting for the last six weeks without as much as a view. I'll take a walk around, introduce myself. Go spend some time with Pax. He told me he taught himself to fish—this I need to see. Then I'll come find you."

"Okay." I paused in the doorway. I didn't want to take my eyes off him, in case this was all a dream.

He smiled in understanding. "Go, Ailith. I'll be fine."

***

"So you got Tor back, but Grace betrayed us, and you might've killed Umbra?" Fane asked. "I can't believe I was here trying to explain to androids why they can't just walk straight out into the ocean."

"I *hope* we killed Umbra. But who knows?" I shivered. "It was awful. What they did to her— But I guess they didn't expect her to have that body for too long."

He put his arm around my shoulders and hugged me. "I'm glad you're all back safely. Well, except for Grace.

674

Poor Ryan and Lily."

"Fane, about Tor. We—"

"Are very lucky to have each other. And I'm very lucky to have you."

"You're not...upset?"

He curled my hair around his fingers, as Tor had done. "No. Honestly? I'm kind of glad. He's a big part of who you are. He makes you stronger. You're always going to be tied together because of your bond, and it's better if you're not grieving his loss."

"You're not jealous? Does it change the way you feel about me? It doesn't change the way I feel about you."

"No, I'm not jealous. I'm not human, remember? But since you brought it up...how *do* you feel about me?"

That was an awkward question. We'd never really talked about *my* feelings. I knew how Fane felt because of the images he broadcast—he couldn't hide from me. *Be honest.* "I love you. *Both* of you. I know it's—"

"A good thing," he said. "How lucky are we?"

"Seriously?" I asked him. "You're fine with it?"

He looked at me, his face solemn. "Are you kidding me? Have you *seen* Tor? I'd totally tap that."

"Fane!" I clapped my hand over my mouth.

He laughed, delighted with himself. "I'm only joking. Though, not really. I was only programmed to be sexual, not with a preference. Who knows what will happen in the future? If Tor's interested, that is." He grinned.

Stones, skipping over crystal water.

I put my hand on his chest.

A box of puzzle pieces, each one accounted for.

"Fane—" I tilted my face up to him.

"Ailith, can I talk to you?" Pax asked. He stood before us, fidgeting. Tor stood behind him, his mouth set in a somber line. His relaxed posture had vanished, and lines of strain showed on his forehead. *That didn't last long.*

675

"Of course." Fane and I stood up in unison. "What is it?"

"It's about the upcoming…battle against Ethan." He stopped.

"Pax, you need to tell her. Tell her what you told me," Tor prompted him.

Pax looked down at me, apology in his brown eyes. "Ailith, we're not going to win."

Ailith,

I remember that you used to love video games. I did too. Do you remember the courage we felt, the huge risks we took? Because we knew that, whatever the outcome, we could always go back to the file we'd saved and do it all again. But even though we knew that, there were times when, for a split second, you forgot and felt that pure horror as you watched yourself plunge to your death or accidently murder your allies. I know that's what you're feeling today. That you wish you could stop the game and take it all back. But you can't. And you need to forgive yourself, because if you hadn't stopped Tor from carrying out Ethan's orders, every one of us would have fallen, and our timeline would have ended, forever.

Pax.

38
AILITH

Fear curled around my heart, and the voice inside me that had been silent for so long drew a deep breath and sighed.

"Can I speak with Pax alone, please? In the meantime, you two need to get everyone together. Not all the androids, just Will and those who want to come. And I know Lily and Ryan are...grieving right now, but they need to come too. Meet us back here."

Fane and Tor ignored the sharpness of my tone and left

without a word.

"It's good to be back, isn't it?" Fane whispered to Tor when he thought they were out of earshot.

"Sit down, Pax." I dropped to the ground at the base of the tree and yanked him down beside me. "What do you mean, we're not going to win?"

He rubbed his arm and looked at me reproachfully.

I didn't care. "Tell me *exactly* what you mean. Don't leave anything out."

"We won't win."

"We won't be able to hold Ethan off?"

"No, we will. Several times, and not just him. But we'll have to keep doing it. The fight will never end. If we finish it now, they will think we can't be beaten, and they'll leave us alone. Eventually, they'll forget we even existed."

"But why? Surely nobody but Ethan has an interest in us."

"Any of Ethan's people who leave the island will tell others about us, about our weaknesses. Then more will come. They'll be afraid of us, as they were before. We'll represent everything they feared before the war. They'll *remember*. We'll become a legend, a myth to scare children. A threat to be defeated."

"But they'll have *survived*, Pax. That was what we wanted. We can leave, disappear."

His eyes became glassy. "Then the plague will come. We'll stop it, but they'll blame us. And they'll keep coming. They'll whittle us down, one by one. Then another plague will wipe them out completely, *everywhere*. One we can't stop. And we'll have failed anyway."

"Wait. A *plague?*"

He blinked. "Well, not a plague in the traditional sense. But it will be a plague to *them*. The fallout caused mutations...new life. Things humans haven't seen before. New viruses, new——"

678

"You're sure? There are no other paths?"

"There are no other paths. Not for them."

"What about the rest of the world? If people survived here, surely they must have survived elsewhere?"

"No. We were...lucky. The devastation was much greater in the rest of the world. *We* shouldn't have survived. Any of us."

"So we've failed, Pax." A bleakness settled over me, the first real hopelessness I'd felt since I'd woken up. "You told me once we were the only ones who could prevent a future where humankind didn't survive. No matter what we do, the human race is doomed." The words cut as I spoke them, and I covered my mouth with my hand. *What do we do now? Everything we did...everyone who lost their lives. For nothing. All of it was for nothing.* For a moment, I wished I *hadn't* survived.

But Pax wasn't finished. "*This* one is. But I've been able to see farther and farther into the future, and the path... I think we've been on the wrong path for the right reasons."

"I'm confused."

He looked at his hands. "We've been trying to stay on a course to preserve the human race, right?"

"Yes. To avoid the future you saw... The red mist."

"I think I was wrong. What if we aren't supposed to avoid it? What if we need to go *through* it?"

My temples throbbed. "Pax, just tell me in plain language."

"There is another way. It's not certain, but it's the only chance we have." What he told me next would change the future of humankind forever.

***

I sat in stunned silence while we waited for the others. Could Pax be right? Could it be possible? I'd felt the truth

679

in it.

What other choice do we have? If Pax was right, and the survivors of the Artilect War kept trying to destroy us, we could never carry out the rest of his plan. And humankind would indeed be over.

If only there was some way to know for sure. I trusted Pax, but I knew from own powers how subjective their meanings could be. Although I'd never been one for faith, I pressed my forehead against the trunk of the tree. I needed a sign, something to help me believe this new path was the right one.

The tree.

The tree.

A lone tree in a meadow, on an island, surrounded by an emerald-tinged sea.

Protect the tree. Defend it at all costs for at its base was the means of our survival, the only means left to us on the path we'd taken.

We stood together, back to back.

My fingertips, pressing into the earth, grew roots. Not the gossamer strands of springtime, but thick ropes lined with poison-tipped thorns. They snaked through the soil, erupting up through the soles of everyone on the island.

Red mist descended. Gods and monsters meeting at last. The harvest had begun.

Then it was done, and the sky split open, the ash parting to reveal a single-celled sun, dividing, replicating.

Buildings rose out of the emerald sea. People, places, things. The seeds we'd held dormant for so long needed to grow.

Doubles rose where the originals had fallen, one after the other in rapid succession, like an echo.

In my hand, I held another, a smaller version of my own. She clambered down the trunk to claim her crown.

She had to be strong in this new world, though she was but a single blossom in a wasteland. Because, of all the seeds we'd planted, she was the first, the most important.

680

Omega was coming.

I'd been wrong. The seed wasn't me; it was Omega, whoever she was. I was merely—*"I'm the gardener,"* I *interrupted.*

"Of man?"

"What?"

"Are you the gardener of man?"

The gardener of man. It echoed through my mind, and something inside me shifted, uncurled.

Fane had been right all along about who I was. And the tree, this tree, was where it would all begin. This was my sign.

I made my decision and changed the world again.

They've taken yet another Messiah from us. Umbra, our Divine, is gone. At first, I wondered why God continued to test us. Have we not done what She wanted? Like Ethan, I view the cyborgs as abominations (although he certainly seems happy to keep one as a pet), however, I was content to let them live out their pathetic existence somewhere far away from us. And not, as Johnathan suggested, because I'm afraid of them. But after this, after what they've done, I'm starting to believe that Ethan is correct—the cyborgs must be destroyed. Perhaps this is what God has been waiting for. Perhaps it's not enough for us just to worship Her, but we must also smite those who would oppose Her and Her manifestation on Earth. Perhaps She took Umbra away because we were complacent. But no longer. If God wants us to prove our faith, then by Her hand, we will.

—Celeste Steed, The Second Coming

39
AILITH

The others stared at me in disbelief. Even Stella looked shocked, and she'd been one of Ethan's proteges. *I'm glad Ryan and Lily refused to come in the end. This might've been the last straw for them.*

"Are you serious?" Cindra finally asked.

"I am," I said. "We have to do more than defend ourselves. I believe Pax when he says it will never end." Pax had told them everything he'd told me, but they'd turned out to be much harder to convince. "We need to kill them all. None of them can leave this island alive."

"You're saying Pax has been wrong this entire time? That everything we did, the wrongs we committed, were in vain?" Cindra was crushed.

"No. We still needed to be *here*, in this moment. But we've been avoiding the wrong thing, trying to save the wrong thing." Pax looked anxious, and I couldn't blame him. It was difficult trying to explain our abilities to the others, and this discussion wasn't going the way we'd hoped. "There's a facility on the main island. We—"

"No." Cindra shook her head vehemently.

"I know it seems extreme," I said. "And I know that's an understatement, but Pax is right. If we don't finish this, we're going to be having this fight over and over. And in the end, we'll still fail."

"And this other way, you call that winning?"

"I know it's not. But it's about *surviving.* Unless we take a stand now, we'll lose bit by bit, then we'll lose it all. We need to start fresh, without a shadow."

"How can you say this would be a fresh start? This future will haunt us, you included, for the rest of our lives." Cindra searched the others' faces, trying to find support.

"This future isn't for us. It will be for *them.*"

"But you don't even know if it's possible." Cindra tried one last time.

"It is. Pax has seen it." It was a lame response, but it was the only one I had.

"But what about everything else he's seen? Why does he only understand this now?"

"I couldn't see as far then as I can now. Now I can see for years." Pax turned an acorn over in his hands.

"But—" Cindra's shoulders sagged in defeat.

"Cindra," Oliver put his hand in hers, "this could be your chance to have children. Your *only* chance." As cyborgs, we were infertile. Losing the ability to have

683

children had been Cindra's biggest sacrifice, one she'd never fully accepted.

"But we don't know that for *sure*. We turned out to have lots of abilities they didn't think we would. Besides, Oliver, you said you thought you might be able to change—"

"Cindra, I can't. We can't," Oliver said.

"But you agreed. You promised to try—"

"I know what I said. I'm sorry. It's just not possible. I thought maybe I could, but— I didn't know how to tell you." He brought her hands to his lips. "But, Cindra, this could be the next best thing."

Cindra said nothing for a long time. Then she turned to Pax and squeezed his hand. "I believe you." She shook her head ruefully. "It's just hard to accept. We shouldn't have such power."

"I agree," I replied. "But we do."

"What about the people left behind in the compound? And Goldnesse? The other survivors? Are we going to hunt them down? Are we becoming a death squad?" Oliver asked, his face grim.

"They'll die on their own," Pax said. "In the next ten years, they'll all be gone."

Stella gasped. Both Pax and I had forgotten she was there. *Shit.*

"What do you mean?" she asked, her face leached of color. "We're all going to *die*?"

"I—" *What do I say?*

"Tell me! Are we going to die? How? Can we stop it?" Her eyes welled and overflowed. *To have come so far, survived so much.*

Be honest.

"A plague is coming. You—"

"Can't you cure it? Or find a way to prevent it? Can't you protect us?" Her chest heaved as she fought to breathe.

"There'll be no way to find a cure, Stella. I'm so sorry,

684

I didn't mean—"

"No," she whispered. "No. This can't—" She rose, her legs shaking. "No," she said again then spun and ran for the path that led down to the beach.

Cindra had half-risen when Oliver stopped her. "Let her go for now," he said. "Give her some time."

Cindra glanced uncertainly down the cliff but settled back in the grass. "Can't we just wait then, rather than kill them all? Fend them off in the short-term and let them die out?"

Pax shook his head. "Not if we want to survive. It's ten years. If we give them that much time, they'll eventually kill us. Or most of us anyway."

Cindra looked faint. "What about Ryan and Lily? Should we tell them? Does *anyone* survive?"

Pax shook his head.

"Even if we want to do what you suggested, there's no way. We need to train, get organized. There's no time. We should consider leaving now, find another island." Cindra's voice held an edge of panic.

"No. We'll never run again."

A scream shattered the air. A cry of pure fear. *Stella.*

Had our last battle started? Had Ethan and the others finally come to destroy us?

To myself, and to all the others, I believe that Callum's loss cut the deepest. I think of him often, of the man he would've become. Perhaps I felt his loss more keenly because he was the other half of my pairing, my shared step on our ladder. Perhaps it was also his betrayal at the hands of the person he loved most, something I could relate to, although my experience with Asche paled in comparison. Even now I feel his loss, and it hurts my soul that his horrific story is the legacy he left behind. For there's no parting him and Umbra, even in death. In our minds, they are permanently entwined, and that's what breaks my heart the most.

—*Cindra, Letter to Omega*

40

AILITH

No. But Umbra had.

We made it to the edge of the cliff just in time to see her unskinned hand close around Stella's throat. Stella fought back, her fingernails scrabbling uselessly against the smooth metal.

When she'd come for us at the compound, between our haste and the door between us, I hadn't really gotten a good look at her. She'd been just a blur of synthetic skin and metal, and her disturbing child-face. Now, as she held Stella aloft, I finally understood the reason for her mismatched limbs. It wasn't, as I'd originally suspected, a lack of care.

They were weapons.

Instead of fingers on her left hand, she wielded a fan of curved blades, like claws. Her left leg was likewise armed from hip to foot, a line of small scythe-like blades protruding from the front. Clearly, they'd prepared her well for bringing back Fane at any cost.

We stood frozen as she turned her face toward us. Her eyes were wide and artless as she drew a line of red across Stella's throat.

Cindra screamed as Stella gagged.

"Oh, Christ," Oliver muttered beside me.

Satisfied she'd made her point, Umbra's eyes searched the cliff. When her gaze landed on me, her cherub face split into a hideous grin.

"You buried me alive," she called to me in her odd, discordant voice. She ignored Stella's hands still weakly clutching at hers.

"You're not buried," I replied. "Or alive."

"I am as alive as you. And I am here to take *him* back." She flicked a claw at Fane where he stood next to me.

He stepped in front of me and peered down at her. "I'm not going back."

"You must."

"Why, Umbra? Why should I go back? You know what they'll do to me if I do."

"I do not care what they do to you. I want what was promised to me."

"What did they promise you?" he asked, although he already knew.

She pointed one of her claws at me. "Her. Her body is mine."

"And you think they'll keep their promise? Look at you, Umbra. You serve a purpose to them, nothing more. When they get me back, they'll discard you. They'll start fresh. Like they're going to do with me. Like they did with *them*." He pointed to the androids who, having heard the commotion, had congregated on the hill beside us, Will at their head.

Lily and Ryan had also come, their eyes red-rimmed and their faces pale. When Lily saw Stella dangling from Umbra's hand, her blood sinking into the pebbles, she fainted. *Probably for the best.* Ryan looked at us in horror. *Again. You've brought us to hell, again.*

Ignoring them, Umbra called out. "I will spare the rest, Fane. If you and my body come with me, I will leave this island and never come back."

"You're right," Fane said, "you'll never come back. Because Ethan and Lien will take you apart."

"Celeste would never let that happen. I am her god."

"Once Ethan gives her the chance to create a shiny *new* goddess? You'll no longer be a god, Umbra, Celeste will. You'll be what you've always been—a prototype. And you'll be destroyed."

"Fuck me." Will whistled under his breath. "Is that Umbra?"

Umbra seemed suddenly to realize what the androids were. "I see you. Where did you get those bodies?" she demanded. "You look like *them*. Like *him*." Her voice became even more dissonant as her rage grew. "Why did they not give me a body like that?"

"Because they're not planning to keep you around," Fane repeated.

Umbra was quiet for a moment. "I have another proposal."

"What?" Fane asked, crossing his arms over his chest.

"You must come down here. I wish to talk as equals," she challenged him.

"Fane—" I began.

"It'll be fine," he said. "I doubt anything she has to offer us, but Ethan happened to her as much as he did to us."

"That kind of empathy will get you killed," Oliver said.

688

"And for the love of God, don't offer her *another* body."

"Fane, whatever you do, be careful. Whatever she says, don't trust her—that's how she got me." The memory of Callum's face, crowned by the rock Umbra used to crush my skull, was still fresh. Behind me, Tor tensed.

"I'll be careful, I promise." He flashed his dimpled grin at me and started down the path to the beach.

At the bottom, he stood just out of arm's reach, his body taut. "Put Stella down."

"Not yet. First, we will talk. So you will not come back?"

"No."

"And you will not give me *her* body?"

"No."

"Then you will give me one of their bodies." She pointed her blades toward the androids. "Any one of them. You will put me in it, and then I will go. I will not go back, and I will not stay here. I will forget you."

Ninety-nine pairs of eyes turned to Fane.

"No."

"Why not? They are not sentient, like you and me. They are good for nothing but slavery. That is all they know. They do not know how to *live*."

"They're living *now*," Fane replied. "So, no."

Umbra's fingers glinted dully in the sunless sky as she drew them again across Stella's throat. As Stella's blood soaked into the stones, Umbra smiled toothlessly at Fane.

Then she attacked.

Though he'd been prepared, he wasn't fast enough to step out of her way, and the side of his face opened up. She danced away, goading him, wiping her lips with Stella's blood.

The steel of a bear trap, the scraping of bone.

I'd never seen Fane angry. Happy, mischievous, passionate…but never angry. I didn't even know if he was capable of it.

689

He was.

His face contorted, and his entire demeanor changed. He was on her before I saw him move.

He grabbed Umbra in a bear hug.

Her fan of blades sliced through his clothing.

He ripped off the arm that had held Stella, tossing it into the tide.

She carved into his back.

His skin hung in ribbons, the metal of his body exposed.

He tore off her face.

She brought up her weaponized leg and brought it down, opening him from groin to knee.

He'd once told me that he and Tor were built from the same original design, and I could see it now.

But he didn't know how to fight.

A blur sped past me, dropping over the cliff and landing on the beach with a bone-jarring crunch. Tor.

Umbra saw him over Fane's shoulder, and for the first time, what looked like fear crept into her expression.

"Hold her," Tor screamed at Fane. "*Hold her!*"

Umbra saw true death coming and struggled, trying to break free of Fane's grasp. He locked his arms tighter, crushing her to him even as her blades cut deeper. Tor came up behind her and placed a hand on either side of her head. She flailed her arm back, trying for his throat, and he leaned back effortlessly, her blades catching only his shoulder.

Though they cut deep, Tor ignored the blood running in rivulets over his sides and twisted with all his considerable strength.

Umbra's strident scream was like nails scraping over stone, vibrating my teeth and making my mouth water. Her body bucked against Fane as she tried to break free.

The tide came in, rushing faster than a cyborg could run.

"Tor!" Fane shouted.

Umbra screamed into Tor's face one last time before her head came away from her neck. Tor staggered backward into the surf then turned and flung Umbra's head as far into the ocean as he could. It sank without a splash.

Back on the shore, Fane had fallen to his knees, Umbra's body still in his embrace. I took off running down the narrow path, Tor and Fane leaving my sight for seconds that felt like hours. When I finally reached them, Tor was carefully extracting Fane's arms from around Umbra, wary of her blades. As he pulled Fane back, her body toppled front-down, and the water slid around it, lapping at the now-lifeless heap of metal.

Fane was a mess. The right side of his body was in tatters, his clothing and skin shredded. Through the gaps, his inner workings were laid bare. Ethan hadn't been exaggerating when he'd said he wanted to recreate human life. He'd made Fane's internal machinery to mimic a human's, smooth layers of mechanical muscle and bone. He was beautiful.

And in shock. He stared at me unblinking, still on his knees. Tor gripped him by his shoulder and hauled him to his feet. "Come on, up we go." His voice was low and soothing as he coaxed Fane along. "You're okay. She's gone."

Fane's gaze locked on Tor's face, and he nodded.

"Fucking hell, look at the pair of you," Oliver said over my shoulder.

"I'm fine," Tor replied. "I'll heal. But Fane is going to need some help." He pressed his lips together as Fane ran his fingers over his exposed teeth. "I think you're going to have a scar, my friend."

At that, Fane came out of his shock. He grinned. "You think so?"

Tor laughed. "Yes, I do. A *big* one. Probably more than one."

691

"Then it was worth it."

"I can help you," Will said. "You won't be as pretty, but you'll be whole."

"That's fine with me," Fane said.

Will nodded. "I'll go get everything ready." He turned and wove through the androids, nodding at them as he went. They split down the middle, creating a path for Fane.

He looked at me.

"Go," I said. "I'll come and find you."

He dipped his head in reluctance but went warily into the crowd of androids. As he passed, they reached out to touch him and smiled. He beamed back and straightened, pressing some of the hands that grasped for his. When he finished the gamut, he turned back to look at me and grinned, the joy of his acceptance shining on his face.

A flock of swallows, taking flight. A wreath of flowers, a crowning glory.

I laughed. "*Go.*"

The matriarchal android remained behind, considering me. "We will help you," she said, her voice as regal as her bearing. "When they come, we will do what it takes."

"Thank you," I said, surprised. "What changed your minds?"

"He did." She turned her head toward where Fane crested the rise. "He valued our lives. Now we will do the same for you." She turned on her heel and walked away.

"Well, there you go," Oliver said gazing after her. "Now we have our army."

"Tor, you'd better come with me," Cindra said, peering under the torn fabric of his bloodied shirt. "Just to be sure."

"I will," he said. "Just let me have a word with Ailith first."

"Fine. Pax? Would you help me, please?"

Pax nodded and followed her, his youthful face pale and

692

drawn. I made a mental note to speak to him later.

Tor lifted Stella's body out of the water. Water and blood trickled over Tor's forearms and dripped from his elbows. "I'm going to take her to the other side of the island. Bury her properly."

"Thank you," I said. "Tor, that was—"

"I know. But it's almost over."

"What if we don't know how to live normally after this? What if we can't?"

He shifted Stella's weight in his arms. "Don't worry, we will. It might take some time, but we will. Are you coming?"

"I'll wait here for a while. Make sure Umbra's really dead." I knew she was, but I didn't want to leave just yet.

After he left, I thought of Callum, of the conversation I'd seen through him after his cyberization.

"Umbra? Is that you?"

"I am here."

"I was afraid you'd left me."

"I will never leave you. We are one."

I waited, watching until the ocean claimed Umbra's body for its own.

We are one.

Helene Island Geocache #18

I don't know why I'm writing this. No one is ever going to read it. Especially not you. Do you remember when we came here last summer? After two weeks of trying to find you, I kind of panicked, and I thought maybe you'd come out here, to the last place we'd been happy together. But you're not here. No one is. Maybe you're dead. Or maybe you don't want me to find you. I don't know anymore. I'm so sorry for everything. When it gets light enough for me to see tomorrow morning, I'm going to walk out into the ocean. Maybe I'll find you there, one way or another.

41

AILITH

Will worked on Fane all night. "Best I can do is stitch him together. He'll have some scars, but they won't be very noticeable."

"You're right," I said, leaning over Fane's back. "I can barely see them." Where the skin had gaped open and jagged before, thin silvery lines now formed a network over his back.

"It's more like a glue," Will said, showing me the instrument.

"Have you had a lot of practice at this sort of thing, then?" I couldn't imagine that the androids hurt themselves very often, caged as they'd been.

"Unfortunately, yes. Customers could get rough…and of course, there were those who paid extra. The twins used to get it the worst. If it were up to me, I'd never have let customers like that near them. It wasn't up to me, though, so I got good at *this*." He drew the device slowly down the side of Fane's face as the silver-haired android who'd spoken to me earlier held the flaps of skin together.

"That's awful."

"It was," he agreed. "But Sophia here," he nodded at her, "gave as good as she got, didn't you?" He nudged her, and she smiled. "Occasionally, we'd get the reservations mixed up, and they'd get a taste of her whip."

She gazed at Will with unabashed fondness.

"How's it going?" Tor asked from the doorway.

"Good," I replied. "How are you?"

"Fine," he said, coming into the room and taking a seat. He was shirtless, a white bandage covering his shoulders and left arm. "It's already healing. Look, the others are on their way. Fane, I'm sorry, but we've got to start planning. I wanted to give you a chance to rest, but Ethan won't wait for that."

"I agree," Fane said. "Besides, it's not like I *need* to rest. Just have to get pasted back together." He looked at Tor from underneath his lashes, as though shy. "I'm sorry you had to help me. And that you got hurt."

"Don't be." Tor leaned back in his chair and laughed. "To be honest, I would've needed *your* help if I'd gone down first. It's one thing to be strong and know how to fight, but that only goes so far when your enemy has knives for hands." They grinned at each other.

"I think you may be on the way out, A. Hell, Cindra might be as well after my seeing those two titans grappling like that. All we needed was a jug of oil and some loincloths." Oliver spoke from the doorway, Cindra and Pax close on his heels.

"You've recovered your equilibrium, I see." As we'd buried Stella on the other side of the island under an old

695

olive tree, even Oliver had shed a few tears. Fane had been hit the hardest, seemingly grateful to escape back to Will's ministrations. He'd been at a loss for what to say after we'd covered her with one shovelful of dirt after another. "What do you say to someone you've known your entire life?" he'd asked me. "I can't even cry."

As we'd walked back to the village, Fane said to me, "Sometimes I wish I wasn't sentient."

I linked my arm gently through his. "I know, but think of all the other feeling you'd miss out on."

He'd nodded, unconvinced. "It seems like an uneven balance, though, doesn't it?"

I couldn't disagree.

Oliver held up his hands. "I'm planning on having a full breakdown when this is over, believe me. But to do that, we need to live. And to do *that,* we need a plan."

"Are Ryan and Lily coming?" Cindra asked

"Yes. They'll be here soon."

"Maybe we should send them away while it happens. A couple fewer deaths on our conscience."

"They'll never leave, not if they think there's a chance Grace will come back." Oliver had a point.

"Do they know what we told Stella? About the future?" Cindra asked me.

"No." And after the way Stella had reacted, I was glad. We were beginning to lose sight of what it meant to be human. *"Do you have any idea what it's like? How small I feel? I'm scared to live in this world and not be special. It means I won't survive."* Grace was right.

"Do we tell them?"

"No. Not yet. I mean, we have to survive Ethan first. Besides, the future seems to change constantly. Right, Pax?" I didn't like keeping the truth from them, but why terrify them with something that may not come to pass?

"Yes, but…I'm sorry," Pax blurted. "About Umbra. It

was a possibility. But only one. In others, she sinks to the bottom of the ocean. In another, she dies in the tunnel. I'm so sorry." He sounded exhausted. And at that moment, I felt his terrible burden.

I hugged him. "Oh, Pax, no. Don't be. What if you'd told us she was coming, and she didn't? We'd be wasting precious resources planning for something that wouldn't happen. Ethan could've come while we were looking the other way."

"You don't blame me? But Stella would still be alive."

"Yes. But maybe not. You didn't kill Stella, Pax. Umbra did. If this hadn't happened, we might've been fighting both Ethan and Umbra at the same time. And Stella betrayed Ethan—she would've been one of his first targets. Her survival wasn't guaranteed." I sounded callous, but it was the truth.

He still looked miserable. "I wish I'd gotten Oliver to remove it. I don't want it anymore."

"Pax, your ability's saved us before. It's brought us this far, and it will help us get through this. After that, if you never want to use it again, you don't have to."

"But I can't control it."

"We'll find a way, Pax. I promise you. Between Will and me, we'll figure it out." Oliver gave him an awkward half-hug.

"He's right, Pax," Will chimed in. "I'll do everything I can."

"Thank you."

I squeezed Pax's hand. "Right. We need to come up with a plan. It won't be long before Ethan and the others are here."

"Are we sure running away isn't an option?" Cindra asked. "I mean, what are we going to hold them off with? We don't have any weapons."

"Don't worry about that," Tor said. "This island is a

697

weapon. It'll take some doing, but with the androids, there are more than enough of us to get it done. The main issue is going to be coordination. We have those walkie-talkies, but it's going to be confusing since we won't have time to practice."

"I can coordinate us," I said.

My fingertips, pressing into the earth, grew roots. Not the gossamer strands of springtime, but thick ropes lined with poison-tipped thorns. They snaked through the soil, erupting up through the soles of everyone on the island.

Tor frowned. "How? The way you did at the compound? You were only coordinating two groups. There's no way you and Pax can be all over the island at once."

"Yes, there is." I looked at Oliver. "Right?"

He ran a hand through his hair. "Flick the switch? Yeah, that would work...in theory."

"What are you talking about?" Tor asked.

"My original program intended me to connect with every cyborg simultaneously. Oliver put in a switch so that I could turn it on and off. Since I can also connect with machines, in theory, I should be able to see through the eyes of every cyborg and android on the island. At the same time. I can interface directly with the androids, like I did with the generator, and as for the rest of you, I can relay instructions, warnings, and strategies to Pax, and he can pass the information on to the rest of you using the walkie-talkies."

"That sounds too good to be true. What are you not telling me?"

I exchanged looks with Oliver. "Well, it's a lot of information for me to process all at once. We're not entirely sure what effect it will have on me." I knew better than to try to lie to Tor.

"You mean it could kill you?"

"Oliver?" I said.

Oliver rubbed the back of his neck. "It's possible, yes, but—"

"No way." Fane and Tor spoke as one.

"It's not really up to the two of you," I said tartly. "Besides, we don't have much of a choice."

Tor shrugged. "We'll find another way."

"We don't have time, Tor. Oliver? What if Fane acted as a booster? The way he did before? But instead of amplifying me, he could filter out some of the less important information?" When we'd been captured by the Saints, Fane had lent me his power to create a sonic pulse and allow us to escape.

Oliver considered it. "That could work... Yes, I think it *should* work."

"*Should* isn't the same as will," Tor argued. "It's too great a risk."

"Tor, it's the only way we'll get anything close to a cohesive defense and attack. Unless you've got a better idea?"

He glowered at me; I damn well knew he didn't have a better plan. "Fine, but we need to have some strategy *inside* that plan. You can't just be randomly shouting orders at people with no weapons."

"I agree. What do you need everyone to do? I'm sure Grace told them where we are, so we probably don't have much time until they get here."

"Eighteen hours," Pax said. "We have eighteen hours, then it all begins."

"Is eighteen hours enough to come up with something good?" I asked Tor.

"Eighteen hours, six cyborgs, and a hundred artilects? Yeah, I can make that work." He turned to Will. "I assume they know how to dig?"

Will looked thoughtful. "No, not much call for digging

in the night-flower trade, even for the really kinky bastards. Still, I'm sure they'll be able to handle it."

"How much of the actual fighting do you think they'll be able to handle?" Tor asked, his eyes narrowed.

Will dismissed Tor with a wave. "All of it. I was secretly training them to defend themselves before the war started, just in case. It was one thing to raise a hand against a paying customer—anything else, and all bets are off."

"They may have to do more than just defend themselves." Tor shook his head. "I don't think this is going to work."

"Let me correct myself," Will said, his grin savage. "When I said *defend themselves*, I actually meant slaughter anyone who raised a hand against them. Will that do?"

"Let's just hope they don't turn on us when this is all done," Oliver muttered, low enough that Will didn't hear.

"We'll keep Lily and Ryan out of this for now," Cindra spoke up, "unless they offer. They've got enough to worry about right now."

"Agreed. Right, what'll we do for weapons?" I asked Tor. "Are we going to whittle ourselves some spears?"

He ignored my jibe and pointed over my shoulder. "There. Look. There's our weapon."

I turned. "All I see are trees and grass."

"Exactly," he replied. "And when they come for us, that's all they'll see as well. And then," he added, a wicked glint in his eye, "if we do this right, it'll be the *last* thing they ever see."

I feel like I should leave some advice here, just in case we win. I can't think of much, except this: put your pants on one leg at a time. I mean this literally. Unless you're lying down. Then you may as well put them on both legs at once because you have nothing to lose. I hope this helps.

Pax (again).

42
AILITH

Twelve sailboats appeared on the horizon shortly before noon, their white sails cutting through the water like a deadly flock of birds.

"How do they even *know* how to sail a boat?" Oliver asked. "I thought the water would slow them down at least a little."

Tor shrugged. "Lots of people on the coast know how."

Even as we watched, one of the boats shuddered and tilted, the sails dipping dangerously close to the water. From this distance, we could make out the figures on board, some scrambling to keep their boats on an even course while others stood silently, waiting for their commands. Ethan, the man responsible for all of this, was on one of those boats. I prayed for a freak lightning storm to send a us miracle and strike him down.

"All right, back to the cliff, everyone. Let's see how many of them there are and what they've brought," Tor instructed. I was happy to leave this part of our strategy up to him. Guerilla warfare wasn't anything any of us understood, but Tor's experience with the syndicate in his former life had given him *some* insight.

"Lily, you need to come now," he said as he herded us out of sight. "If Grace is with them, we'll try to get her out of the way first."

"She didn't mean it, any of it. I know what she did... She's just so young, and she— Please, don't hurt her. Don't let *them* hurt her," she implored him, seizing the sleeve of his shirt with shaking hands.

Tor put his hand over hers. "We won't, Lily. I promise. We'll do whatever we can to keep her safe."

We retreated and waited for Ethan's army to land on the shore. We didn't have to wait long. They disembarked a few meters from the shoreline, ensuring that their boats were secure and primed for their departure. Clearly, they fully expected to win this fight.

The water along the shore churned white as they sloshed through it and onto the pebble beach, dragging a large cache of crates with them.

First ashore were the Saints, Celeste at their head. She'd refined the look she first debuted when she'd helped slaughter the Terrans who'd held Pax and Cindra captive— the braids were more intricate, piled higher, and glinting with shards of silver metal. My own scalp itched just looking at it.

Behind Celeste, Saints pushed back the hoods that had protected them from the salt spray. Like Celeste, they'd painted their faces and clothes with elaborate symbols that looked like computer code, and although they deplored cyborgs, they displayed their own grafted metal with pride.

They carried their weapons—axes, knives, bows, and not a small number of guns—with ease, and the expression on their faces was that of crusaders. These warriors, their voices raised in anticipated triumph, were a far cry from the devout and biddable people we'd known; the loss of their faith had made them savage, with a viciousness unrestrained by duty.

Celeste raised her eyes, searching the island, and I could see the filed teeth of her grin even from my place on the cliff.

I glanced at Oliver, but he was studiously looking the other way. *And she was so sweet when you first met her.*

Following the Saints was a group of people I didn't recognize. Many of the faces seemed familiar, like they were someone I'd passed on the street. *They must be the people from Goldnesse.* Although they too carried weapons, they lacked the gleeful violence of the Saints. Some of them seemed fearful but determined, like children approaching a house rumored to be haunted, their movements exaggerated and voices shrill, even from a distance. Others bore a mercenary-like shrewdness, their manner practiced and calculating and ready for blood.

I can only imagine what Ethan's been telling them to whip them up. Or maybe they were Terrans before the war.

And finally, behind them, Ethan, looking mad as hell, his blond hair disheveled by his crossing. He strode through the knee-deep water with ferocious purpose, undistracted by the frothing commotion around him. He carried no weapon, but I had no doubt that when the time came, he would be.

Lien's tiny frame was nowhere to be seen. It was a smart move—if Ethan was killed today, the Cosmists would still have a leader. I allowed a tiny thrill of hope to bloom in my chest. If Ethan was uncertain enough about his success to leave her behind, we may just have a chance.

Trailing Ethan through the water were several of the Cosmists we'd met at the party. I wracked my brain, trying to remember who they were. *The man with the slicked-back hair and prominent ears. Cassian.* He'd been responsible for much of Tor's design before Mil and Lexa had parted ways with Ethan and Lien.

The woman next to him took me a bit longer to recognize. *Ilse,* the one who'd been introduced to me with Stella. Like the other Cosmists, she was dressed in what looked like combat fatigues, her hair pulled back tightly from her sharp face.

Then another man stepped out from behind Ilse.

Ji. Lien's son. His angular face was neutral, but his dark eyes darted back and forth, as though he wasn't quite sure how he'd gotten here. He fumbled with his pack, dropping it into the water. Ilse spoke sharply to him and he snatched it out again, his eyes on the ground.

Grace. If Ji's here, where's Grace?

She had betrayed her family, and us, for her love of this man. That I could almost understand. But surely she wouldn't come here willingly to participate in this assault.

I hope they forced her to stay behind. To keep her loyal.

But if that was the case, why bring Ji?

To my dismay, all the groups seemed very organized, splitting themselves up into different duties—some unpacking various crates of weapons while others searched the length of the beach in a strategic formation, scouting for movement.

For us.

"We should attack now, before they get completely organized." Oliver fidgeted with nervous energy, tearing a leaf off my oak tree and shredding it.

"We promised Ryan and Lily we would wait and see if Grace was with them and give her a chance. Besides, what are we going to do? Throw acorns at them?" Tor slid his crossbow onto his back and adjusted his ammunition belt.

Acorns fell from my hands.

"Is Grace even here?" I asked. "I can't see her." *Please,*

don't be here, Grace.

"We shouldn't risk it. Why give them a chance? We all know Ethan won't give up. Stop trying to salve your conscience with one act of mercy." Oliver had been a special kind of agent, trained to always strike first.

He's right.

"No, please," Lily pleaded. "You *promised.* At least wait until we know if she's here."

"Lily—"

"Ethan." Unnoticed, Fane had left our concealment at the foot of the great oak tree and stepped to the edge of the cliff, in full sight of the beach. His voice echoed off the rocks, startling those below. Everyone on the shore fell silent, craning their necks to see him.

Ethan regained his composure quickly. He stood with his feet planted, his arms crossed over his chest. "Fane, make this easy for us."

"I am," Fane replied. "Leave. Please. All of you. Those who surrender will be unharmed."

This is pointless. We have a plan. They can't leave this island. We're only pretending mercy. My fingers twitched, desperate to bury themselves in the soil.

Oliver groaned in the background. "God. This is like the worst movie cliché."

"I think *that's* where he got his speech from," Tor said, pointing to Pax. His mouth was moving in time with Fane's.

Several people exchanged glances before looking at Ethan, who grinned. "Sure, Fane. Give yourself up, and we'll go."

"Never."

Ethan tried one last time. "Think of all the guilt you'll feel. People will die today. On *both* sides." He waited for a reaction from Fane, and from the rest of us. When there was none, he sighed as though disappointed in us and turned to Ilse. "Bring her out."

I'm sorry, Stella. I'm so sorry that you were killed. It was my fault. I had to make a choice. I hate lying. I'm not any good at it. It makes me queasy and nervous, as though there are ants crawling on my skin. But I didn't tell them the whole truth when I said I didn't report Umbra coming because it was only a slim possibility. The whole truth was that if she did come, and we'd prepared for it, Ailith would've died instead. I hope you can forgive me,

Pax.

43

AILITH

The crowd parted, and Kalbir was dragged out, wrapped in a cocoon of chains. Even so, the links strained as she flexed inside them. Ethan held a gun to her head. Its metal gleamed dull and cold, like the cylindrical tombs in Will's bunker.

She tried to turn her head away as she gazed up at him, tears of rage and fear blazing in her eyes. Her thread flashed in my mind, present again, an inferno. I felt myself starting to slip down it and bit the inside of my cheek to stay present. Kalbir twisted in the chains, shrieking with frustration.

At Ethan's shoulder, Celeste smirked, her lips curling into an ugly smile.

"See how far I'm willing to go?" Ethan said, pressing the barrel into the skin of Kalbir's temple.

707

Fane shrugged. "You're not proving anything. She's never been important to y—"

Ethan pulled the trigger.

Blood and brain matter splattered the legs of the crowd.

Pax grabbed my hand. "It's starting."

Cindra cried out then pressed the back of her hand against her mouth as Oliver wrapped his arms around her and murmured in her ear. She nodded, wiping her eyes with her sleeve.

Tor shook his head in disgust. "He's a coward. I'm going to enjoy this."

I would've expected Ethan's people to be shocked, but their macabre smiles told me that threatening Kalbir's life had not been the bargaining chip Ethan had pretended— her death had been premeditated. To him, she was still one of us.

Celeste's grin widened.

I'll tear that smile from your face before this day is done, Celeste.

Ethan spoke up again. "This is what fate awaits all of them, Fane, if you don't give yourself up." He swept his arm across the sky.

Fane turned to me, horror creeping over his face. "I didn't think—" *The shattering of a teacup, centuries old.*

"I did," I replied. "No. He'll destroy us even if you do what he wants. You know that. We agreed on this, Fane. No mercy."

He turned back, his face set into a dispassionate mask. "Goodbye, Ethan. Thank you for my life."

Ethan gave Fane a grim smile then let out an exaggerated sigh. "I was *really* hoping it wouldn't come to this," he lied. "Ji."

Ji's eyes went wide. "Ethan—"

"Do it," Ethan snarled. "Or I'll do it myself. And I *won't* be gentle."

Ji hesitated then reached down next to the pile of gear

they'd heaped on the beach and pulled a bound figure to its feet.

Something knocked against my back—Lily, pushing between us and dropping to her knees. "Grace!" she screamed.

Ji walked Grace over to Ethan, catching her arms as she stumbled. As they neared him, Ji's steps slowed and his eyes found us on the cliff. He opened his mouth to speak, but whether to appeal to us or Ethan, I never knew. Impatient, Ethan stalked over the distance remaining between them and snatched Grace away, throwing her to her knees on the bruising rocks.

She shook as Ethan turned the gun on her and looked back up at Fane. "Are you *sure* that's your choice?"

Ji lurched forward, raising both hands in a shield. "Ethan, this is wrong. You *promised*. You said we were going to talk to them, not harm them. You said you wanted to make a deal. You promised—" His voice broke as tears streamed down Grace's face. "*Grace.*"

Fane's hands curled into fists.

"Wrong choice, Fane." Ethan smiled.

"Now, Ailith," Oliver whispered.

"*Save her, please.*" Lily's voice was a fragile shell, shattering at Grace's feet.

As I closed my eyes, several things happened all at once. Ji stepped between Ethan and Grace. Ethan pulled the trigger. And I found the switch Oliver had put in me a few months ago and turned it on.

Kalbir could be considered the villain of our story. But I don't believe she was, not truly. For all her perceived faults, she was still a woman to be admired. Like all of us, she had terrible decisions to make, and to make them, she gambled on her best chance of survival, just like we did. In fact, many of the things we did could be considered much worse. The only difference between her and us is that she lost her life.

—Cindra, Letter to Omega

44

AILITH

My mind connected with the thread of every cyborg and android on the island. I saw through all their eyes at once and felt every ounce of fear, hope, and in some cases, joy. Their memories also rushed in on me—everything they'd ever seen, everything they'd ever done.

Everything that had once held me together now swarmed: my bones, my skin, my flesh, my blood.

I was losing control; it was too much for my part-human mind to contain.

I don't think they expected you to live very long.

Just as I began to come apart, strands of another energy wrapped around mine, holding together the parts of me that had begun to fracture.

Fane had joined me, giving structure to my power. "Steady, Ailith. Just let it go through you."

Through me. Through them. Through the soles of everyone on the island.

710

"It's time. Take your posts." My voice sounded strange, as though it carried many more than my own.

The others hurried off, ready for what we'd prepared for, our final battle. Lily's sobbing was nothing more than a sigh on the wind as I groped behind me, searching blindly for the trunk of the tree. Fane guided me, and I leaned back against its base, cradled by the roots.

Through the eyes of one of the androids, I watched the invaders rush to get their weapons.

Four figures lingered in the eye of the storm—Ethan and Celeste, roaring orders to their respective troops, and Ji and Grace, lying prone as the waves lapped at their feet. The twitch of Grace's muscles as she tried to keep still was almost imperceptible, Ji's comforting murmurs muted by the water. Blood had soaked into the fabric where their bodies were pressed together.

Stay still. Just a little longer. Once Ethan stepped off the beach, we could help them. *Hang on.*

A spasm of pain must've caught Ji by surprise because he cried out, the sound catching in his throat too late.

I held my breath.

Ethan barely glanced at him, and I understood. He didn't care if Ji or Grace died, but he didn't care if they lived either. For now, in this moment, they just had to stay out of his way.

I settled my spy down to wait and gave my first orders. *When the beach is clear, hide them.*

From far away, Fane's calm voice told Ryan and Lily that their daughter was alive, that we would keep our promise.

I found another scout and took stock of our playing field. Just how many had come to sacrifice themselves?

Ninety-eight. We were almost evenly matched. They split into two groups, Ethan at the head of one, Celeste at the head of the other. It looked as though they planned to

711

work their way up the island from either side toward where we waited under the tree. Whatever their plan, we weren't going to make it easy for them—they'd have to earn our deaths.

Through the eyes of the others, I saw the enemy's faces, their hands slick with sweat on their weapons. None of the men and women Ethan had brought to bay for our blood had any formal experience with fighting or war, other than their determination to hate and their ability to survive. They'd fought battles in the aftermath of the Artilect War, but they'd had an advantage then—modern weapons, desperation, the cruelty that comes with *us* or *them* against foes who couldn't fight back.

Ethan had cultivated them carefully. People he was willing to lose. People he *wanted* to lose. People who would eventually want pieces of his power.

He wouldn't have to worry. None of them would be coming back. They'd thought to find us defenseless, for us to beg.

They'd thought wrong.

*Our lives have been a constant exercise in irony. We were
created to bring peace, and we brought war. We were both
human and machine, yet rejected by the proponents of each.
We all ultimately fought for the same thing, and yet no one
won. We wanted to save the human race and ended up
slaughtering it. Even our final battle was ironic. Rather than
use the high-tech weapons everyone feared our creation would
bring, we used the land itself, our bare hands and some
household explosives, sharpened sticks and nails. If the
Terrans had lived to see it, I'm sure they would've appreciated
the irony, and perhaps, they would've felt justified in the end.*

—*Cindra, Letter to Omega*

45
AILITH

Everything happened quickly, simultaneously, a blur in my
mind.

Inside some bodies with a heartbeat and many without,
I presided over the beginning of the end. The connection
between the androids and me, boosted by Fane, gave me a
new understanding of them. They weren't as sentient as he
was, yet, filtered through him, their awareness was
reflected the way *he* expressed his emotions. *The heart of a
fox, beating too quickly. The sharp edges of a hole in the ice. The
warming rays of a synthetic sun on skin that shouldn't feel.*

There were only three ways up to where I sat with my
back pressed to the tree, conducting my orchestra—two
paths that wound around the island and eventually curved

up to my oak, and the wilderness in between. Some of our enemies chose the paths; others chose to take their chances in the untamed grasses and trees.

Both were mistaken.

Information buzzed through my mind like a wasp in a bottle—ferocious and unrelenting. On both sides of the island, the interlopers held their guns at the ready, searching for their first target.

For a few minutes, all was quiet. The hunters fanned out to cover more ground, keeping Ethan in the middle of the pack, surrounded by an honor guard. They ranged further apart, their eyes searching, their tension mounting as they waited for us to make a move. For one, the strain became unbearable, and he shattered the silence.

"Where the f—"

He crashed through into our defenses, and chaos erupted all over the island.

Agony tore the man's voice from his throat as thick metal spikes bit deep into the flesh of his leg. He lost his balance, his weight pushing his leg down and causing the wooden jaws to snap together and devour his calf. Screaming a curse, he clutched at his leg reflexively, trying to pull it out of our trap until his flesh tore and glazed his hands with slippery blood.

Several of his comrades broke ranks to help him, oblivious in their haste. All around him, they stepped into the concealed cluster of traps, their weapons flung into the brush as their cries echoed over the island, a cacophony of shrieks and Ethan's orders. Fear rose over the island like a miasma, its musk mingling with the haze of metallic blood and salt.

"Shut up!" Ethan backed away from his writhing men. "Do you want to tell the entire island where I am?" Infuriation creased his face as he issued new orders. "Leave them. We have to get to the center of the island, to that

714

goddamned giant tree they're cowering under. You—" He pointed to a man and a woman at the rear of the group, "stay and help them. And for God's sake, if they don't shut up, shoot them." He moved away, motioning for the rest to follow.

I gave them a single minute to clear the area. *Now.*

Two androids stepped out from behind the concealing brush. Through their eyes, I watched the pair who'd stayed to help their companions freeze, one of them nearly dropping his weapon. Clearly, Grace hadn't told them about the androids. *Thank you, Grace.*

The shock on their faces was comical, theirs mouths agape as they blinked rapidly, trying to counter the mirage. They'd undoubtably seen numerous androids before the war, but probably not ones of this level of sophistication, so uncannily like them, but so obviously not human.

The twin androids stared back at them, youthful faces composed. Their fine silver-blond hair and wide, thickly-lashed blue eyes were ethereally incongruous with the mundane whimpers of suffering and sharp scent of terror surrounding them.

An agonized cry from one of the injured pierced the hypnotic sobs of pain.

The trance was broken.

One of the men raised his gun to shoot then lowered it to wipe his hands on his trousers before lifting it again. The barrel shook as he pointed it at the twins.

"Help them," he demanded. "Or I'll blow your heads off."

The twins nodded and walked over to the ensnared men, each taking a place behind one. Turning their faces toward each other, they cupped the captive's heads in their hands and snapped their necks.

Thorns drawn across bare skin. The serrated leaves of holly.

Yes. Keep going.

Shrieks erupted from the other captives as they tried to wrench themselves free, their fingers digging in the dirt as the bitter scent of urine mixed with blood. A shot rang out, and the female twin's arm jerked back, broken and bloodless. At the lack of blood, the shooters began to come undone.

Take them out first—the ones with the guns.

The twins tilted their heads in acknowledgement and stepped forward again, pushing past the long barrels of the rifles. Stunned, their opponents scrambled back, one of them falling and discharging her gun harmlessly into the air.

A Venus flytrap, satisfied at last.

The twins smiled.

Ninety-three.

Tor,

If we end up taking the path where…well, you know what happens, in case you find this, please forgive yourself. I'm sorry our rescue attempt failed, and I'm sorry about what Ethan did to you. We all knew it wasn't you, including Ailith. Even in those final moments when you…did what you did, we knew it wasn't really you.

Pax

46

AILITH

One side of the island mirrored the other, a satisfying balance. Bedlam reigned as the trespassers tried desperately to fight an enemy that continued to elude them. Being synthetic, the androids possessed a calmness and an ability to stay motionless that humans would never have. They lured and teased, baited and enticed, until disorder finally broke any semblance of organization and the hunters became the hunted.

Metal flashed and wood splintered, devouring those who stepped off the path to swing at a flash of red hair, at an artless giggle. *You are very handsome.*

Eighty-seven.

Fearing the path was the road to hell, some stepped off to take their chances in the trees. For the first few, moving cautiously, their eyes searching between the trunks for the telltale flash of a target, there was a whisper of fishing nets through the air and wet *thunk*s as their bodies were pinned to unforgiving wood.

When their companions were scooped up around them, others ran, scanning above the ground for the telling tripwire. But their triumphant yells as they jumped over the cables were cut short as concealed spike pits welcomed their bodies onto tempered skewers.

Seventy.

Others sought refuge in the grass, impaling themselves without our help on hidden barbed lances. Unable to pull themselves free, their last sight was of the angels of death tasked with dispatching them.

Death upon death upon death. My control began to slip. *Let them suffer.*

Fane stepped in. *Cool water flowing over smooth, polished stones. A whisper in the dark.*

I breathed again. *Finish them.*

The turmoil wasn't limited to me, or to our attackers. It caught at all of us, gnashing its teeth and tearing.

A heart broke in one of our own. Cindra. Fingers flew to the feather in her hair, and she chanted a litany to herself. *She had stars for eyes and feathers made from the memories of her people.*

Oliver fought the rising tide within himself that said, "*Enjoy this.*"

Tor, my eyes in the field with Will, was numb and mechanical in the heat of battle, seeing past what I saw to what needed to be done.

Pax was lost in his own mind. *Preparing.* Dipping between the present and the future, searching for nuances that would change the outcome.

The androids, from deactivation to warrior in only a few days, betrayed their training and tried out their freedom.

Fifty-six.

The survivors of the two groups finally met, converging on the town. The androids slid seamlessly back into hiding, leaving behind a lull that seemed to terrify the throng even more. They milled about in confusion, taking stock of how many of them had lived and recounting in bewilderment what they could remember.

Let them catch a breath. Get ready.

"What the fuck is going on?" Ethan suddenly roared, silencing the buzz. "I gave you all orders, told you to stay calm." A large vein in his forehead throbbed. "Celeste! I told you not—"

There was a strangled cry as a man clutched his throat, a large bolt protruding from between his fingers.

On a nearby rooftop, Tor reloaded his crossbow.

Fifty-one.

"He's on the roof!" Ethan shouted, pressing himself flat against one of the buildings. "Find him!" But Tor was gone. Ethan swore in frustration. "Find them, *any* of them. And kill them on sight. Shoot or cut down anything that moves," he ordered. "*Now!*"

"You heard, him," Celeste cried. "Look *everywhere*. We're on an island. There's only so many places they can hide." She bared her teeth at his curt approval.

The groups blended together and fanned out, surrounding and entering the cottages of the village. At first, they found nothing. Then, those who were a bit slow to follow began to disappear around the corners of the buildings, their screams muffled then cut short. I relayed the motions Tor had taught me through the threads.

That spot on the spine.

Through that rib pair.

One sharp twist.

By the time Celeste and Ethan realized what was happening, we'd retreated again.

719

Forty-five.

Set the trap.

At the bottom of the village, six androids slipped through the doorway of the small community hall, just slow enough to be seen.

"Get them," Ethan snarled as the others rushed past him.

The inside of the building was dim, the weak beam of light from the open back door swirling with motes of dust. A young man sat at a table in the center of the room with an unlit lantern. Dark-haired and slim, he turned a small object over in his hands, rolling it between his palms. Antoni's face betrayed no emotion as the horde bored down on him. About twenty feet away from him, they stopped, casting about in confusion as their eyes adjusted to the muted light and realized they faced but a single opponent.

"What are you waiting for?" Ethan yelled from the doorway.

Hologram Antoni leaned forward to light the lantern.

Frantic in their need for even a single victory, the intruders unleashed a small arsenal upon him.

The explosion shook the trunk of my tree, a deep rumble in the earth that spread up through my body and blossomed as a fierce hope in my chest. Desiccated catkins rained down on me, their bodies festooning my hair like a wreath.

Eighteen.

The scent of panic in the air. The calmness it spread through Tor. The giddiness of Will, his heart full to bursting, his guilt removed one body at a time.

I am saving them, he thought.

"Hold steady. When the red mist is here, we're done." Pax was back in the present.

Cindra vomited, repeating her mantra over and over as

720

Oliver rocked her against him. *She had stars for eyes…*

Fear turned into horror. There was no way out. No way forward. Anarchy reigned as those remaining tried to save themselves, to get down to the beach at all costs, no matter what awaited them there.

They bolted back into our woods, our grasses. Tor reloaded.

Six.

The air deepened as the tide came in, the spray of mist heavy in the air.

Two.

It's fascinating what people choose to fear. There were so many other technologies in our time that were far more threatening to the human race—genetic modification of plants and animals, and virtual reality, for example—and yet, the greatest vitriol was reserved for those technologies intended to enhance and further our capabilities as a species, rather than those that promoted a commercially reliant, isolationist and individualistic evolution. Is it any wonder we essentially became extinct?

—*Cindra, Letter to Omega*

47

AILITH

Ethan and Celeste had clawed their way to the summit and stood before us, one weapon between them. Celeste looked shell-shocked, her sadistic bravado gone. She seemed even younger than her seventeen years, a child dressed in a costume suddenly too heavy for her to bear.

Ethan's face was dark with rage and blood that wasn't his own. Unlike Celeste, the loss of his people seemed only to spur him on; to him, it wasn't over. "Stop!" he screamed, incensed. "Can't you see what we're trying to do? We're trying to build the future."

The androids converged and formed a half-circle behind us, their faces curious.

"For who?" Fane asked.

"For humankind."

"By replacing them with artilects?"

The androids stepped forward, closing in. Celeste's eyes flitted between us, them, and Ethan. Her braids had come loose, her gifted headdress unraveling.

"Artilects and humans can live side-by-side. I realize that now."

"You don't believe that, Ethan. It's just another of your creations. A means to an end, the end you've always wanted."

"You're wrong, Fane. I—"

"What would our role be, Ethan? The artilects you create? Masters or slaves? Superior or inferior? Without one or the other, there would be no point in our creation. So which is it?"

"No, you—"

"And what about the cyborgs? And the humans? What place would they have in your new future?" Fane spoke temperately, but his words traveled over the island.

"We would be equals." Ethan's face betrayed the falseness of his words.

"We're not equal, though, are we? And you certainly don't think that."

"I gave you life. I gave *all* of you life," Ethan said.

The androids had stepped in front of us now, their faces impassive.

"You didn't *give* us life. You programmed it. And look what happened." Genuine sorrow colored his tone. "Billions dead because that life wasn't considered equal by anyone."

The androids stepped closer. Celeste snatched Ethan's gun and thrust it into her mouth.

Finally, the mist turned red. *It's over.*

As Celeste fell, Ethan took one step backward then another, and the androids matched pace. As their feet rose and fell, the Novus Corporation logo imprinted on their soles left bloody prints on the grass.

Finally, the sea was at Ethan's back, the waves lapping ruthlessly at the beach as the edge of the cliff crumbled under his heels. He raised his hands as though to make one more plea then dropped them and instead gazed above our heads at the spreading branches of the tree, where a single acorn still clung.

A contemplative expression passed over his face as he turned his eyes back to the androids and splayed his fingers over his heart. And for the second time since I'd woke into the aftermath of the Artilect War, the clouds parted, and a shaft of light broke through, illuminating Ethan's smile as he stepped back into it.

OMEGA

I'd been having the dream for as long as I could remember.

It was always the same. I stood alone on the roof of the facility, a flat, oblong building surrounded by the rubble of twisted metal and melted glass. The wrought logo, two identical figures connected by a double helix, leaned awkwardly against the access door.

This was where I was born.

A tree rose in the distance, a colossal oak that almost blocked out the sun. From the first time I'd had the dream, I'd known it was important, that its existence meant the difference between life and death. I picked my way through the debris and set off on my customary path toward it.

The androids turned to watch me as I wound my way between the houses, their expressions inscrutable. They'd lived here long before I was born, and although we shared a history, it was a connection I couldn't yet understand.

I wasn't afraid of them. I was like them, but not. My flesh was something different. Something more fragile. Something *mortal*. My mortality crept up my skin in a shiver as their eyes followed me past the perimeter of the village and all the way to the wild grassland beyond.

At the edge of the field, as vast as an emerald sea, I began to run. Heat rose from the grass where my feet fell, rippling up my bare legs. My body was small and thin, my tiny fists pumping as I ran. In my hand I clutched a string that led up, up to a kite—a man but not a man, smooth and shiny, with only the suggestion of a face. He would stay with me for the rest of my life. My guide, my protector, my teacher, my love.

In the middle of this green ocean stood the tree. I raced

toward it, my body expanding, stretching. When I reached it, they were waiting, as always. They smiled at me, crowding around as though I'd returned home after far too long, their hands outstretched to welcome me.

They'd been forged with purpose, a link to chain together two diverging worlds. In many ways they were like me, but they were also like the others—a combination of human and machine.

Human. The word was strange even in the dream, stirring feelings of loss, of loneliness. *I am human.*

After the others had embraced me, she stepped forward. It was as though I was looking into a mirror, her face a perfect replica of mine, her emerald eyes and skin— the rich brown of fertile soil—indistinguishable from my own. She smiled at me with the mouth we shared then murmured a single word.

Climb.

The others reached out for me again, and together they lifted me onto the lowest-hanging branch of the tree. Leaving them behind, I took a deep breath and began my ascension.

Halfway up, I skinned my leg on the rough bark. Blood welled up and out of the wound, but it wasn't my blood; it was theirs and they were happy to give it. When I reached the top, the whole world spread out before me. The sun rose and fell, and the world changed with it, unfolding as it grew, withered, died, and came into bud again, an eternal bloom.

A gust of wind blew through the leaves, wrapping tendrils of hair around my face as I climbed back down the scarred trunk. Once my feet were on the ground, they crowned my hair with a wreath of flowers and pressed a worn book into my hands. Written across the cover in careful script was my name.

Omega.

When I raised my head to thank them, they'd changed. They smiled at the looseness of their skin, at the spots that now speckled the backs of their hands. The ache in my chest blossomed even though I knew the tears that shone in their rheumy eyes were tears of joy. They had chosen to rest at last.

Only one of them remained unaged, still as strong and solid as the tree. My kite, now as he really was. He watched them, smiling, but I knew his heart was breaking as best it could. He put a hand on my shoulder and turned me back the way I'd come.

"It's time to go home."

Before I left with him, the one whose long dark hair was now a silver halo around her golden feather hugged me close and whispered in my ear. Then they all gathered around me once more, their frail arms surprisingly strong. My twin placed her hands on my face and kissed my forehead, or perhaps I kissed hers; I was no longer sure which of us I was.

Our silent walk back across the field lasted only an instant. Home. *Our* home. It had changed while we were away. The androids were still there, their smooth, ageless faces raised at our return, but new beings walked among them now.

Most were unrecognizable, their faces only vaguely familiar, as though from a distant memory or a past that wasn't mine. The others I knew instantly, for they were the exact genetic copies of the cyborgs who'd created us.

We were the future, cloned from their past. The only way for humankind to survive—a fresh start from the cells of people dead long before we were born, and from those who'd made us to honor them.

I was Omega, their last task, their final sowing.

This book is your story, Omega, she'd said, *but it is also our story, told by the one who was all of us. In its pages is our truth, the*

727

truth we wanted you to know. And once you do, I hope you can forgive us. And that instead of a burden, you'll see this knowledge as it's intended: a gift, a sacrifice, a prayer, an act of love. For without it, even with all its darkness, you would not be here. You are the reason the world can go on living, Omega. You are the seed.

END OF BOOK THREE

ACKNOWLEDGEMENTS

Thank you so much to everyone who supported me throughout this series. To my friends and family for their love and cheerleading; to my beta readers, Anna Adler (whose SFR you should totally check out), Kalbir Cross, Keith Oxenrider, T.M. Rain, and Alyssa Dietz-your feedback and encouragement were invaluable; to Danielle Fine, the best editor a writer could ask for—I can't wait for our next project!

And lastly, to my readers—writing for you has been both amazing and humbling. Thank you, for everything.

ABOUT THE AUTHOR

A.W. Cross is a scientist-turned-author who lives in the gorgeous wilds of Canada. She lurves all things science fiction and is looking forward to her bionic body with much excitement. You can visit her on her website, awcrossauthor.com, or on Twitter (@aw_cross) and Facebook.

Made in the USA
Las Vegas, NV
02 March 2023

68412623R00433